STUDIES IN ROMANCE LANGUAGES: 11

John E. Keller, Editor

AMADIS OF GAUL

BOOKS III AND IV

A NOVEL OF CHIVALRY OF THE 14TH CENTURY
PRESUMABLY FIRST WRITTEN IN SPANISH

Revised and Reworked
by Garci Rodríguez de Montalvo
prior to 1505

Translated from the Putative Princeps
of Saragossa, 1508

BY

EDWIN B. PLACE AND HERBERT C. BEHM

THE UNIVERSITY PRESS OF KENTUCKY

Scholarly publisher for the Commonwealth,
serving Bellarmine University, Berea College, Centre
College of Kentucky, Eastern Kentucky University,
The Filson Historical Society, Georgetown College,
Kentucky Historical Society, Kentucky State University,
Morehead State University, Murray State University,
Northern Kentucky University, Transylvania University,
University of Kentucky, University of Louisville,
and Western Kentucky University.

Editorial and Sales Offices: The University Press of Kentucky
663 South Limestone Street, Lexington, Kentucky 40508-4008
www.kentuckypress.com

09 10 11 12 13   5 4 3 2 1

ISBN 978-0-8131-9232-1 (pbk: alk. paper)

This book is printed on acid-free recycled paper meeting
the requirements of the American National Standard
for Permanence in Paper for Printed Library Materials.

Manufactured in the United States of America.

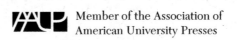

Member of the Association of
American University Presses

CONTENTS

FOREWORD

FOR BACKGROUND INFORMATION CONCERNING THE AMADIS *the reader is referred to the Preface of Volume I.*

Inasmuch as scholarly books seldom become "best-sellers," they frequently require a subsidy to assist in defraying publication costs. In the case of this Volume II of our translation it is a pleasure to express our gratitude for the substantial financial contributions made by Mr. Place's wife Marian, his eldest grandson, the Reverend Michael D. Place, and separately by all of his grandchildren acting as a group: Michael, Stephen, Christopher and wife Susan, William C., Kathi, Nancy, Robert, John, Scott and Ann. [1]

We thank also Marian Place for assistance in reading proof; and we owe a special debt of gratitude to Professor John E. Keller of the University of Kentucky, general editor of this Spanish series, for his unflagging support of the ambitious project of publishing this very lengthy work.

E. B. P.
H. C. B.

Berkeley, California, April 6, 1974.

---

1 *Listed according to age. Christopher and wife, Nancy and John have the surname Whicker; the others are Places.*

THE THIRD BOOK OF *AMADIS OF GAUL* BEGINS

In which are related some of the great disagreements and discords that there were in the house and court of King Lisuarte because of the bad advice that Gandandel gave the king in order to hurt Amadis and his relatives and friends; at the outset King Lisuarte ordered Angriote and his nephew to leave his court and all his dominions, and he sent a challenge to them, and they returned to him the confirmation of the challenge, as will be told subsequently.

The story relates that the sons of Gandandel and Brocadan having been killed by the hand of Angriote de Estravaus and that of his nephew Sarquiles, as you have heard, the twelve knights with great joy escorted Madasima to their tents. But King Lisuarte had removed himself from the window in order not to see them die, not for any good that he wished them, for now he considered them like their fathers as evil men, but on account of the honor that Amadis obtained from it, along with some discredit to his own court. Some days having passed before he found out that Angriote and his nephew were better from their wounds, so that they could ride horseback, he sent to tell them to leave his kingdom and not to travel any more through it; if not, he would give orders to enforce their banishment. Those knights complained greatly to Don Grumedan and to other knights of the court who were going there to see them and to do honor to them, especially Don Brian de Monjaste and Gavarte of the Fearful Valley, saying that since the king, forgetting the great services they had performed for him, thus treated and banished them, from then on he should not be surprised if they, having taken a contrary attitude, in the future became in large measure more irksome than in the past. And striking their tents, with all their company gathered together, they set out on the way to the Firm Island. And on the third day they found at a hermitage Gandeza. the niece of Brocadan and friend of Sarquiles, the woman who had him secluded where he heard and found out all the evil that her uncle Gandandel had plotted against Amadis, as is already related; who had fled out of the fear she had on account of it. And they took great pleasure with her, especially Sarquiles, who loved her dearly; and taking her with them, they continued on their way.

King Lisuarte, who in order not to see the good fortune of Angriote and his nephew had left the window, as has been said, went on into his palace hall very angry because things were being done which redounded to the honor and glory of Amadis and his friends. And there were Don Grumedan and the other knights who had just gone forth a short way with those who were going to the Firm Island, and they told him all that they had said to them and the complaint that they had of him, which made him much more angry and irritated. And he said:

"Although tolerance is a very precious quality and in the majority of affairs advantageous, sometimes it gives rise to greater mistakes, just as happens to me with these knights; for if as they withdrew from me, I had withdrawn from them, ceasing to show them good will and an attitude of esteem, they not only would not have dared to say what they have said to you, but would not even have dared to come to my court or enter my land. But as I did what reason obliged me to do, so God will consider it good in the end to give me the honor and them the payment for their madness, and I wish to have people go and challenge them for me and with them Amadis, by whom all are commanded, and there will be shown to what extent their pride suffices."

Arban, King of North Wales, who loved the king's service, said: "Sire, you ought to consider carefully this which you say before it is done, as much on account of the great worth of those knights who are so able, as because God has shown so clearly that justice is on their side; for if it were not so, although Angriote is a good knight, he would not have overcome as he did the two sons of Gandandel, who were deemed so valiant and courageous, nor would Sarquiles have overcome Adamas; by which it seems that the very righteous cause that they upheld gave and granted them that victory. And therefore, sire, I should consider it good that they be taken for your service, for it is not advantageous for any king to battle his own people when he is able to prevent it, because of all the harm that is done on both sides. And the people and property that are lost, the king himself loses without gaining any honor in conquering or overcoming his vassals. And many times from such disagreements great injuries are caused that inspire new thoughts in neighboring kings and great lords who under some constraint are in subjection, to try to emerge from it and to recover in the present much more than what they had lost in the past. And what is most to be avoided is causing vassals to lose the fear and respect for their lords, who by governing them with moderate prudence, holding them in subjection more by love than out of fear, are able to hold and command them as the good shepherd does his flock. But if the shepherd puts on them greater compulsion than they can bear, it often happens that they all jump and flee as the first one does, and by the time the error is recognized, it is difficult to correct. Therefore, sire, now is the time to remedy matters before more anger is enkindled, for Amadis is so humble in matters concerning you that with slight urging you would be able to win him back and with him all those who have left you on account of him."

The king said to him: "You speak well indeed, but I shall not give up what I have given to my daughter Leonoreta, and which they have demanded of me; nor is Amadis's power, although great, of any consequence compared to mine; and do not speak to me any more about this, but prepare arms and horses to serve me. And tomorrow Cendil of Ganota will leave for the Firm Island to challenge them."

"In the name of God," said they, "and may He do what He considers good, and we shall serve you."

Then they went to their quarters, and the king remained in his palace. As for Gandandel and Brocadan, you are apprised that when they saw their sons dead and that they themselves were losers in this world and the next, receiving what in our times many others like them do not receive — God protecting them, either so that by His mercy they reform or through His justice pay for everything together if they don't reform and hence have no redemption — they decided to go away to a small sparsely populated island owned by Gandandel. And taking their dead sons and their wives and household servants, they boarded two ships that they were holding in order to cross over to the Island of Mongaza in the event that Gromadaza the giantess had not surrendered the castles. And with many tears shed by them all and curses from those who watched them go, they left the port, and arrived where our story makes no further mention of them; but one can reasonably believe that those whom evil deeds accompany until old age, with them end their days unless the mercy of the very high Lord, more through His holy compassion than through their merits, comes to them in time for them to be redeemed.

Then King Lisuarte had all the great lords of his court and the knights of lesser degree assemble in his palace, and complaining to them about the offensive words that Amadis and his friends had spoken about him, he begged them to be concerned with it just as he was in matters that concerned them. They all told him that they would serve him as their lord in whatever he commanded them to do. Then he called Cendil of Ganota and said: "Mount at once and with a letter of accreditation go to the Firm Island and challenge for me Amadis and all those who seek to uphold the cause of Don Galvanes; and tell them to beware of me, for if I can, I shall destroy their bodies and possessions wherever I may find them, and that thus all those of my dominions will do."

Don Cendil, taking a voucher, armed and mounted, set out at once on his journey, as one who wanted to carry out the command of his lord. The king remained there a few days; then he departed for a town of his called Gracedonia, because it was very abundant in all things, at which Oriana and Mabilia were quite pleased on account of its being near Miraflores, and this was because the time was approaching for Oriana to give birth, and she thought that from there better than from any place else they would be able to deal with the matter.

And the twelve knights who were taking Madasima, traveled day by day without any pause until they came within two leagues of the Firm Island. There beside a river they found Amadis, who was waiting for them with close to two thousand three hundred knights very well armed and mounted, who received them with great pleasure, showing much esteem and respect for Madasima, and Amadis embracing Angriote many times, for through a messenger from his brother Don Florestan he already knew all that had happened to them in the combat. And while they were thus very joyously together, they saw descending by a road down a high hill, Don Cendil of Ganota, knight of King Lisuarte, the one who was coming to challenge them. As soon as he saw so many people so well armed, tears came to his eyes, he reflecting that they all had left the service of the king his lord, to whom he was a very loyal friend and servant, they being knights by whose adherence he had been highly honored and exalted. But drying his eyes, he put on the best countenance he could, and he had a good one, for he was a very handsome knight and very well spoken and vigorous; and he came up to the throng asking for Amadis, and they showed him where he was, in the company of the knights who had arrived from their journey. He went to them, and when they recognized him, they received him very well, and he greeted them with great courtesy and said to them: "Sirs, I come to Amadis and to all of you with a message from the king; and since I find you together, it will be well that you hear it."

Then they all came up to hear what he would say, and Cendil said to Amadis: "Sir, have this letter read."

And when it was read, he said to him: "This is for accreditation; now tell the message."

"Sir Amadis, the king my lord sends word that he is challenging you and as many as are of your lineage, and as many of you as are here, and those who are to strive to go to the Island of Mongaza; and he says to you that from now on endeavor to protect your lands and possessions and bodies, for he intends to destroy everything if he can; and he tells you to avoid going through his land, for he will order killed everyone he takes prisoner."

Don Cuadragante said: "Don Cendil, you have said what you were ordered to say, and thereby you have done right; since your lord threatens our bodies and possessions, these knights may say on their own account whatever they wish. But tell him from me that although he is king and lord of great lands, I love my poor body as much as he loves his rich one, and in nobility I am not his debtor, for I am as directly descended from kings as he is; and since I am to protect myself, let him and all his land watch out for me."

Amadis would have been pleased if the reply had been more conciliatory, and said to him:

"Sir Cuadragante, permit this knight to be answered by you and all those who are here; and since you have heard his embassy, you will agree that the reply be a joint one, as befits our honor. And you, Don Cendil of Ganota, may tell the king that it will be very difficult for him to do what he says. And go with us to the Firm Island and you shall test yourself in the arch of loyal lovers, because if you complete the test, you will be esteemed more highly by your sweetheart, and you will find her better disposed toward you."

"Since it pleases you," said Don Cendil, "I shall do so, but in the matter of love, I do not want to give out more concerning my affairs than what my heart knows."

Then they all went on to the Firm Island; but when Cendil saw the rock so towering and the strength so great, he was quite surprised, but he was more so after he went inside and saw the land so abundant; so that he recognized that nobody in the world could harm it. Amadis took him to his quarters and paid him great honor because Don Cendil was of very high rank.

Next day all those knights assembled and agreed to send a challenge to King Lisuarte, and decided that it should be by a knight who had come there with Dragonis and Palomir's forces, Sadamon by name, for these two brothers were sons of Grasugis, King of lower Germany, who was married to Saduva, sister of King Perion of Gaul; and so these, like all the others who were of high rank, sons of kings and dukes and counts, had brought there some troops in order to cross with Don Galvanes to the Island of Mongaza. And they gave to this Sadamon a letter of accreditation, signed with all their names, and they said to him: "Tell King Lisuarte, since he challenges and threatens us, to guard himself from us, for we shall do him all the harm we can; and let him know that when we have had time to prepare we shall cross to the Island of Mongaza; and that if he is a mighty lord, we are close to the time when his strength and ours will be known. And if he says anything to you, answer him as a knight that we—please God—shall vouch for everything provided it be not in the way of peace, because this never will be granted to him until Don Galvanes be reestablished on the Island of Mongaza."

Sadamon said he would carry it out fully, just as they commanded. Amadis spoke with his foster father, Don Gandales, and said to him: "It is important that you go to King Lisuarte on my behalf and tell him, without any fear you may have of him, that I hold his challenge and threats in very low esteem, less even than he thinks; and if I had known that he would be so ungrateful to me for all the services I have rendered him, I would not have subjected myself to such dangers in order to serve him; and that that pride and great rank of his with which he threatens me and my friends and relatives, the blood of my body has upheld for him; and that I trust in God, who knows all things, that this ingratitude will be corrected more through my strength than at his pleasure. And tell him that although I won the island of Mongaza, it will not be through my person that he lose it, nor will I cause trouble in any place that the queen may be, for the sake of her honor, for she is deserving, and tell her so if you see her; and since he wants some manifestation of my gratitude he will have it as long as I live, and in such a manner that the past manifestations that he has had he will not recall."

Agrajes said to him: "Don Gandales, try hard to see the queen, and kiss her hands for me, and tell her to order my sister Mabilia given to me; for since we have arrived at such a situation with the king, it is no longer necessary for her to be in his house."

Amadis was very sorry about what Agrajes had said, because through this princess he exercised all his effectiveness with his lady, and he did not wish to see her separated from her any more than if his own heart were separated from his flesh; but he did not dare contradict him in order not to reveal the secret of his love affair.

This having been done thus, the messengers went in company of Don Cendil of Ganota, and with great pleasure were housed at night in populated places. At the end of the ten days they arrived at the town where King Lisuarte was in his palace with a sufficiency of knights and other nobles. He received them pleasantly, although he already knew from a messenger of Cendil of Ganota that they were coming to challenge him. The messengers gave him the letter, and the king ordered them to tell all that was entrusted to them. Don Gandales said to him: "Sire, Sadamon will tell you what the high ranking men and knights who are on the Firm Island send to tell you, and afterwards I shall tell you what Amadis sends me for, because I come to you with a mandate and to the queen with a message from Agrajes, if it please you that I see her."

"I am quite pleased," said the king, "and it will be for her a pleasure to see you, who served her daughter Oriana very well all the while she dwelt in your land, for which I thank you."

"Many thanks," said Gandales, "and God knows how pleased I would be to be able to serve you, and how much I regret my present inability."

"Thus I consider it," said the king, "and may you not regret doing what you should, in fulfilling your obligations towards the one whom you reared, for otherwise it would count against you."

Then Sadamon told the king his mission just as it was already related, and finally challenged him and all his kingdom and all his men, as he was charged with doing. And when he told him not to expect to have peace with them if first he had not reestablished Don Galvanes and Madasima on the Island of Mongaza, the king said: "That agreement will be a long time in coming, if they expect that. So help me God, I shall never consider that I am king, if I do not break them of that great madness that they have."

"Sire," said Sadamon, "I have told you what I was commanded to say, and if I tell you anything from here on, it is not included in my mission. And replying to what you said, I tell you, sire, that he who would break the pride of those knights will have to be of great avail and of very great power, and it will be harder for you than anyone may think."

"That may well be true," said the king, "but now it will appear to what extent my might with that of my vassals, or their might, suffices."

Don Gandales told him on behalf of Amadis all that you have heard already, for nothing was left out, in the usual manner of one who was very well-spoken; and when he came to say that Amadis would not go to the Island of Mongaza since he had won it for him, nor to any place where the queen might be, in order not to annoy her, all of them considered it good and very loyal, and thus they spoke of it among themselves and the king thus considered it. Then he commanded the messengers to disarm and they would dine, for it was time. And thus it was done, for in the hall where he ate, he had them sit down at a table facing his, where his nephew Giontes and Don Guilan the Pensive and other distinguished knights ate, who on account of their valor went to extremes in paying them over and above all others honor, which caused their worth to be enhanced, and the others, if of less worth, to try to be their equals, so that they might be considered of equal rank by the king their lord. And if kings had such a style, they would cause their own subjects to be virtuous, courageous, loyal, fond of their service, and to esteem them much more than temporal wealth, while remembering those words of the famous Fabricius, consul of the Romans, spoken to the ambassador from the Samnites, whom he was going to conquer, concerning their bringing him great gifts of gold and silver, and other fine jewels, they having seen him eating on plates of earthenware, thinking thereby to placate him and turn him away from what the senate of Rome had ordered him to carry out against them. But he, exercising his exalted virtue, rejecting that which many in order to acquire, place their lives, their souls in great risk, said: "We Romans do not wish treasures, but to subdue and command those who own them."

Well, one cannot validate such words as these without knights of great prowess and worth, who serve their lords with very great love for the sake of the benefits and honors that they have received from them.

Then, being at that dinner, the king was very animated, telling all the knights who were there that they should prepare themselves as quickly as they could for the trip to the Island of Mongaza and that, if it were necessary, he in person would go with them. And after the tables were cleared, Grumedan took Gandales to the queen, who was willing to see him, at which Oriana and Mabilia were quite pleased, because they would obtain from him news of Amadis, which they very much wanted to know. And as he entered where she was, she received him very nicely and with great affection, and she had him sit before her beside Oriana; and she said to him: "Don Gandales, friend, do you know this maiden who is beside you, whom you have served well?"

"Lady," said he, "if I have done her some service, I consider myself fortunate; and so I shall consider myself each time that I can serve you, lady, or her; and thus I would do for the king if it were not against Amadis, reared by me, and my lord."

When the queen heard this from him, she told him that thus he should do.

"But while protecting his honor, you can, my good friend, counsel him and persuade him to make peace better than anyone else would be able to do, and I shall do so as much as I can with the king my lord."

"I shall gladly do that," said Gandales, "as much as I can and my advice may suffice; and in this may God do what He deems good."

The queen said to him: "Then let it be out of love for me, as you have said."

Gandales said to her: "Lady, I came with the message from Amadis to the king; and he commanded me to see you if I could, and to kiss your hands for him as one who regrets being separated from your service. And the same thing I say for Agrajes, who begs of you the favor of ordering his sister Mabilia given to him; for since he and Don Galvanes are not friendly with the king, she no longer has any reason to be in his house."

When Oriana heard this she was greatly grieved, for tears came to her eyes, and she could not restrain herself, not only because she had for her a heart-felt love, but also because without her she would not know what to do when she gave birth, for the time was already approaching. But Mabilia, who saw her thus, was very sorry for her, and said to her: "Ah, madam, what great wrong your father and mother would do me, if they were to separate me from you!"

"Do not weep," said Gandales, "for your situation is very well taken care of, for when you go from here, you will be taken to your aunt Queen Elisena of Gaul; for with the exception of this queen in whose presence we are, there is no other more honorable or better attended; and you will enjoy yourself with your cousin Melicia, who looks forward very much to seeing you."

"Don Gandales," said the queen, "I am very sorry about what Agrajes wishes, and I shall speak to the king about it; and if he takes my advice, this princess will not go from here, except married as befits a person of such high station."

"Then let it be at once," said he, "because I cannot stay any longer."

The queen sent word to call the king; and Oriana perceiving him coming, and that on his will alone her succor depended, went and knelt before him, saying to him: "Sire, you know how much honor I received at the court of the King of Scotland, and how at the time you sent for me, they gave me their daughter Mabilia, and in what a bad light I would be placed if I did not repay her for it; and furthermore she is the entire remedy for my infirmities and ills. Now Agrajes is sending for her, and if you take her away from me, you will inflict on me the greatest cruelty and injustice ever inflicted on anyone, without her first being rewarded for the honors that I received from her father."

Mabilia was kneeling with her and was clasping the king's hands, and weeping was imploring him not to permit her to be taken away; otherwise, in great despair, she would kill herself; and she embraced Oriana. The king, who was very discreet and understanding, said: "Do not think, daughter Mabilia, that because of the discord that exists between me and those of your lineage, I must forget how you have served me or that on that account I would cease to receive and favor all those of your blood who might wish to serve me, for because of some I would not hate the others, much less you to whom we owe so much. Until you have the reward for your merit, you shall not depart from my house."

She sought to kiss his hands, but the king was unwilling; and raising her up he had her and Oriana sit on a dais, and he sat between them. Don Gandales, who saw it all, said: "Ladies, since you have loved each other and have been together for so long, anyone would be unreasonable to separate you. And from you, Oriana, neither at my wish nor on my advice will Mabilia be parted from you, except in the manner that the king and you say; and I have told the king and the queen my mission, and the reply I shall give to Don Galvanes, your uncle, and Agrajes, your brother; and whether they be irked or pleased with it, they will consider good what the king does, and what you, madam, desire."

After this, he said to the king and queen: "Your Majesties, I wish to leave."

The king said to him: "Go with God, and tell Amadis that about this matter that he sent to tell me, namely, that he will not go to the Island of Mongaza since he caused me to have it, I well understand that he is doing it more to further his own interests than to augment my honor, and as I understand it, thus do I thank him for it, and from today on, may each one do what he understands."

And he left the chamber for the palace hall. The queen said: "Don Gandales, my friend, pay no heed to the angry words of the king or those of Amadis; but I still implore you to agree to bring about peace between them, for I shall do so; and give Amadis my regards and tell him that I am grateful for the courtesy of his sending to tell me that he would not cause annoyance anywhere I might be, and that I earnestly beseech him to honor it whenever he sees my command."

"Madam," said he, "I shall do everything in my power as you command."

And he bade her farewell. And she commended him to God that He might protect him and give him grace to restore friendship between the king and Amadis to its former basis. Oriana and Mabilia called him and Oriana said to him: "Don Gandales, my loyal friend, I am very sorry that I cannot reward you for what you have done for me, for time does not offer the opportunity nor do I have the wherewithal to repay properly your very great worthiness, but God will be pleased to have it done as I ought and wish to do it."

When Gandales heard this, he said: "Madam, since my services were small, I consider amply satisfying your great gratitude although there be no other reward; and lady, always command me in whatever I can serve you, since you know I am so devoted to your interests without heeding this enmity that now exists between Amadis and your father. And although he dislikes him, madam, don't you dislike him, for he has always served you ever since his youth when he was the Child of the Sea, and afterwards as a knight in all the encounters in which he has engaged in order to render you service; for in addition to the very important and distinguished services that he has done the king your father, from which he has received a poor reward, he freed you from the hands of that evil Arcalaus the Enchanter, from which you would not have been able to escape without very great dishonor. Therefore, madam, may it not appear that he is hated by all, since it is very well known that he does not deserve that; and for this reason, madam, my heart feels great sorrow at his receiving such a poor reward in payment for his great services."

Oriana, when she heard this, said with great humility: "Don Gandales, my good friend, in everything you speak the absolute truth, and I am greatly displeased with this enmity because according to the hearts of both, one expects nothing but great trouble and harm, the way the enmity continues to grow each day, if God through His mercy does not remedy it; but I trust in Him that He will halt this evil thing. And give Amadis my best regards, and tell him that I beg him very earnestly that, remembering the things that he experienced in this my father's house, he may temper those of the present and the future, taking the advice and mandate of my father, who appreciates and loves him very much."

Mabilia said to him: "Gandales, as a favor I ask you to give my regards to my cousin and lord Amadis and to my lord brother Agrajes, and to the virtuous lord Don Galvanes my uncle; and tell them not to worry about me or try to separate me from my lady Oriana, because it would be wasted effort, for I would rather lose my life than leave her, though it be their will. And give this letter to Amadis, and tell him he will find in it a complete account of my situation, and I believe he will receive great comfort from the letter."

Gandales, having heard this, bowed to them and left at once. And he, taking with him Sadamon, who had been with the king, they both armed themselves and started on their way. As they were leaving the town, they encountered a large well-armed contingent of the king's men, who were making a great display of preparing to go to the Island of Mongaza, which the king had ordered made in order that Gandales and Sadamon might see so many and such good troops, and might tell those who had sent them there, so as to instill fear in them. And they saw that among them were circulating as commanders, King Arban of North Wales, who was a courageous knight, and

Gasquilan the Arrogant, son of Madarque the fierce giant of the Sad Island and of a sister of Lancino, King of Suesa. This arrogant Gasquilan turned out to be vigorous and so valiant at arms that when his uncle Lancino died without heirs, everybody in the kingdom thought it good to take him for their king and lord. And when this Gasquilan heard of this war between King Lisuarte and Amadis, he left his kingdom, not only to be in the war but also in order to test himself in battle with Amadis, by order of a lady whom he loved very much; all of which in greater detail will be related completely in Book IV, wherein there will be a fuller account of this knight and the battle that he had with Amadis, son of King Perion of Gaul, and for this reason, no more will be told here in order to avoid prolixity.

Don Gandales and Sadamon, after they had observed those knights, went on their way, talking and giving their opinion on how good a contingent of men it was, but saying that they would be dealing with men who would not be frightened by them. And they kept traveling each day until they reached the Firm Island, where those who were waiting for them were greatly pleased with them. And when they were disarmed, they went into a beautiful garden where Amadis and all those gentlemen were disporting themselves. And they told them all that had happened to them with the king just as it had occurred, and about the troops that they saw who were about to go to the Island of Mongaza, and how they had those two captains, King Arban of North Wales and Gasquilan, King of Suesa, and the reason why the latter had come from such a distant land, for the principal reason was to fight Amadis and all of them, and that he was valiant and agile, and of very great renown among all those that knew him. Gavarte of the Fearful Valley said: "In order to cure that excessive desire and complaint that he has, here he will find very good and wise masters, Don Florestan and Don Cuadragante; and if they are busy, here am I who will present to him this body of mine, because it would not be right for him to have traveled such a long way in vain."

"Don Gavarte," said Amadis, "I tell you that if I were ailing, I would rather shun physic entirely and place all my trust in God, than to test your medicine or electuary."

Brian de Monjaste said: "Sir, thus you do not proceed with such great care as this one who is seeking us; and it will be well to help him so that he may be able to tell the masters in his land what he found here for such infirmities."

And after they had been talking and laughing for quite a long while with great pleasure, Amadis asked if there was anyone there who knew Gasquilan. Listoran of the White Tower said: "I know him very well, and I know a lot about him."

"Tell us about him," said Amadis.

Then he told them who his father and mother were, and how he had become king because of his great valor, and how he fought very fiercely, and how he had followed the profession of arms for eight years, and that he had done so well with them that his equal was not to be found in all his land or in those bordering it.

"But I tell you he has never encountered those whom he now comes to seek; and I found myself arrayed against him in a tourney that we had in Valtierra, and at the first encounter we fell with our horses to the ground; but the press was so great that we were not able to attack each other any more, and the match was won from the side on which I was through the fault of the knights who did not do what they should have done, and through the great valor of this Gasquilan, who was our mortal enemy; so that he carried off the honors for both sides, and he did not fall that day from his horse except that time that we met."

"Certainly," said Amadis, "you speak of a great man who is coming like a king of great prowess to make known his excellence."

"You speak the truth," said Don Cuadragante, "but meanwhile he made a mistake, for he should have come to us, for we are the lesser and he would have shown in that more vigor, since he could have done so without its affecting his honor."

"In that he did better," said Don Galvanes, "because although he came to those numerically strongest, it was to those who are weakest, for he would not have been able to test his strength if he had not had the best and strongest against him."

While they were speaking about this, the captains of the ships came and said: "Sirs, arm yourselves and prepare what you need and come on board the ships, for we have the wind very favorable for the voyage you want to make."

Then they all left the garden with great pleasure, and the press and the noise were so great not only of the troops but also of the apparatus of the fleet, that one could hardly hear; and very quickly they were armed and they loaded their horses on the ships, for all the other things that they needed were aboard, and very happily they put out to sea. And Amadis and Don Bruneo of Bonamar, who were going about among them in a boat, found together on one ship Don Florestan and Brian de Monjaste, and Don Cuadragante and Angriote de Estravaus, and they came on board with them. And Amadis embraced them as though a long time had passed since he had seen them, tears coming to his eyes from the very deep love that he had for them, and with the thought of how he would miss them; and he said: "My good sirs, I am glad to see you thus together."

Don Cuadragante said to him: "My lord, thus we shall go on sea and even on land, if perchance we are not separated; and thus we have arranged among us to maintain ourselves on this journey."

And they showed him a very wonderfully beautiful banner that they were bringing along on which were depicted twelve maidens with white flowers in their hands, not because they loved the maidens, but in remembrance of those twelve over whom this dispute began, who underwent such great danger in the prison of King Lisuarte; and to give more honor to Don Galvanes whom they were aiding, and to enable him to see with what love and affection they were undertaking that encounter; because affairs of friends taken on entirely voluntarily elicit complete gratitude; and if to the contrary, they elicit the opposite; and very rightly should the matter be thus viewed, for in proportion to the affection with which aid is given is the reward for the one who receives it. When Amadis saw the banner, he was very happy because they had showed it to him thus. And there he told them to be very careful to act wisely and not to rely more on their great strength than on prudence, because usually such matters as were not dealt with by them with tolerance and wisdom, although they might have had great strength, were lost causes; and for this reason lesser and weaker forces were frequently winners, achieving victory over more numerous and stronger fighting units; and that they should consider that each one of those who were going there was to be governor and captain of himself, because they were not to be governed by anyone else, but to rule and govern; for there was a great difference between the private battles that up to then they had waged and the general battles of large numbers of troops, because in such one's knowledge is revealed; for in the first mentioned, one's judgment had to concern itself only with what each one ought to do, and in the general battles, with one's own well-being and that of all the others whom the good are to rule; because just as most of the travail falls to them, so also do they achieve most of the honor and glory, and most of the discredit and dishonor when they are careless. He told them this and many other things, with which they were quite content. Then he bade them farewell, and taking with him in the boat Don Bruneo of Bonamar and Gandales, his foster father, he went through the whole fleet talking with all those knights until he went ashore and the fleet went forth behind the ship on which Don Galvanes and Madasima were traveling, which took the lead with such a fanfare of trumpets and Moorish pipes that it was a wonder to behold.

Just as you hear, this great fleet left that port of the Firm Island to go to the castle of the Boiling Lake, where the Island of Mongaza was, Amadis and Don Bruneo of Bonamar remaining on the Firm Island in order to cross into Gaul. Then that fleet proceeded over the sea with such good weather that after seven days they arrived one morning before dawn at the castle of the Boiling Lake, which was adjacent to the seaport. And then they all armed and prepared the small boats in order to land, and they placed walkways of planks and hurdles where the horses were to come off, and this they did very quietly so that Count Latine and Galdar of Rascuil, who were in the town with three hundred knights, might not hear them. But immediately they were heard by the watchmen, and they told those masters of theirs that there were armed forces about, but they did not know how many, for the night was very dark. And then the Count and Galdar dressed and went up to the castle, and they heard the bustle of the troops, and it seemed to them a large company, for with the dawn of day many ships were in sight; and Galdar said:

"Truly this is Don Galvanes with his companions and friends who are coming against us, and now may God not save me if out of my power they take the port as easily as they think."

And ordering all his troops to arm, and they themselves likewise, they came out of the town against them. And Galdar went to a port that was next to the town, and Count Latine to another near the castle at which Don Galvanes and Agrajes with all those who were helping were; in the lead of Galvanes' contingent went Gavarte of the Fearful Valley and Orlandin, and Osinan of Burgundy and Madancil of the Silver Bridge; and there went Count Latine with many soldiers both on foot and mounted. And Galdar with another large company came to the other harbor, to which Don Florestan and Cuadragante and Brian de Monjaste and Angriote and their other companions came. Then there began a cruel and dangerous battle between them with lances and arrows and stones, so that there were many wounded and killed; and those of the land defended the harbors until the hour of tierce. But Don Florestan, who was on a ship with Brian of Monjaste and Don Cuadragante and Angriote, where they had two companions with each of them and their horses, had Enil, that good knight of whom you have already heard in Book II, and Amorantes of Salvatria who was his cousin; and those with Brian were Coman and Nicoran, and those with Cuadragante, Landin and Orian the Valiant, and those with Angriote, his brother Gradovoy and Sarquiles, his nephew. And Florestan shouted loudly to lower the bridge and they would leave by it on their horses. Angriote said to him: "Why do you want to undertake such great folly? For even if we leave by the bridge, the water is so high before we reach the land that the horses will be swimming.

And so Don Cuadragante told him; but Brian de Monjaste was of the opinion of Don Florestan; and the bridge having been lowered, they both crossed over it. And coming to the end they made their horses jump into the water, which was so high that it touched their saddletrees. And to that place hastened many of their foes, who attacked them with great and deadly blows; and they defended themselves amid great peril, for no longer could they be of avail on account of their enemies being numerous. But then Don Cuadragante and Angriote arrived and joined them and so did those companions of theirs; but it was so steep a climb from the port and the troops so many who were defending it that they were unable to help. Palomir and Dragonis, who saw them in such danger, had the trumpets and Moorish pipes sound along with a great shouting of their troops, and ordered two galleys sent to land wherever God might direct them, and there went in each of them thirty knights very well armed, and the repulse was so great that all the galleys were shattered. There the noise was so loud and of so much outcry from both factions that it seemed as if everybody in the world was involved in the tumult. Dragonis and Palomir stayed in the water, which came up to their necks, and their knights with them clinging to the planks of the wrecked galleys and pushing each other ahead, going forward with great effort until the water came up to their waists. And although the forces on shore were numerous and well armed and were resisting with great courage, they could not prevent Don Florestan and his companions from landing, and then likewise Dragonis and Palomir with all of their men. When Galdar saw that his men were losing ground, not being able to stand up to their foes on account of their being now very powerful, with great courage and as best he could, he made them retreat in order that all of them might not be lost; for he was very badly wounded at the hands of Don Florestan and Brian de Monjaste, who knocked him from his horse; and he was so shaken up that he could hardly stay on another horse that his men had given him; and going toward the town he saw that Count Latine was coming with all his troops at top speed, and that Don Galvanes and Agrajes and their companions had already taken the harbor, as those on whose behalf the battle was being waged.

And now know you here that the Count had seized Dandasido, son of the old giant, and twenty other men of the town with him, holding them under suspicion that they must be enemies. They were in the castle in a prison that was in the highest tower, and with men who were guarding them; and as the battle continued between the knights, the jailers who held them came out on top of the tower to watch the battle. And when Dandasido saw that they were not guarding them, and that he had an opportunity to free himself, he said to those who were with him: "Help me and let us leave here."

"How will that be?" they asked.

"Let us break the padlock of this chain that holds everyone."

Then they put through the padlocks as quickly as they could some rope of hemp with which their hands and feet were tied at night, and with the great strength of Dandasido and of all the others they broke the lock, although it was quite heavy, and they all issued forth. And very quickly taking the swords of the jailers who were on top of the tower, as you have heard, they went there to them, for they were not paying attention to anything except the battle that was going on at the harbors; and they killed them all and shouted: "To arms, to arms for Madasima, our lady!"

When those of the town saw this, they took its strongest towers and killed all those that they were able to seize. When Count Latine perceived this, he entered by the gate out of which he had come and stopped at a house near it, and Galdar of Rascuil with him; so that they did not dare move forward, expecting death more than continued life. Those of the town were blocking off the streets between them and they were exerting themselves as much as they could with that great succor and were shouting to those outside to bring their lady Madasima there and to take possession of the town. Cuadragante and Angriote came up to a gate to find out the truth, and learning from Dandasido the true situation, they went to tell Don Galvanes. And they all mounted at once and brought Madasima, her beautiful face veiled, mounted on a white palfrey and wearing a cape of gold. And when they came close to the town, the gates were opened and one hundred of the most honorable men came out and kissed her hands, and she said to them: "Kiss the hands of my lord and husband Don Galvanes, for after God he freed me from death, and he has caused me to recover you who are my native-born subjects, and whom most unreasonably I had lost. And take him for your lord if you love me."

Then they all came up to Don Galvanes and kneeling on the ground with very humble words, they kissed his hands and he received them with good will and very affably, thanking them and praising them generously for the great loyalty and the good love that they had maintained for Madasima, their feudal ruler. And then they went into the town, where Dandasido came, who was very highly honored by Madasima and by all those gentlemen.

This having been done thus, Ymosil of Burgundy said: "It would be very good that all our enemies who are still in the town be killed."

Agrajes, who was moved to very great anger, said: "I have ordered the streets cleared and the order will be that all be dispatched without anyone's remaining alive."

"Sir," said Florestan, "do not permit anger and fury to have such mastery over you as to cause you to do a thing to which once it is done, you would prefer a speedy death."

"He talks sense to you," said Don Cuadragante; "it is sufficient that all be placed in the prison of Don Galvanes, your uncle, if it can be managed, because it is more advantageous for the victors to have the conquered alive than dead, considering the rotation of fickle and uncertain fortune; for just as it has shifted for them, it could shift in short order for those now prosperous."

It was agreed then that Angriote de Estravaus and Gavarte of the Fearful Valley should go and take care of the matter. They, on arriving at the place where Count Latine and Galdar of Rascuil were, found all their troops in very bad shape, and themselves badly wounded and greatly dejected because the affair had gone so badly against them; after a few talks held between them, they considered it good to entrust themselves to the will and discretion of Don Galvanes. Then this affair having been concluded, for the town and the castle were completely in the power of Madasima and of her protectors to the great pleasure of them all, the next day they received the news that King Arban of North Wales and Gasquilan, King of Suesa, with three thousand knights had arrived at the harbor of that island, and that they were all landing in great haste and were sending the fleet back to bring food to them. This placed them all in great agitation, knowing as they did the large number of opposing troops, and that their own men were in such bad condition. But, as men who feared shame, recalling what Amadis had told them: to do things in harmony, although the impulse of some was to go out and fight with them, their consensus was not to do so until all had their wounds cared for and their horses and arms in better condition.

So that one and all agreeing on this, the story will tell of Amadis and of Don Bruneo of Bonamar, who had remained on the Firm Island.

CHAPTER LXV

How Amadis asked his foster father Don Gandales for news of his experiences at court, and from there he and his companions left for Gaul; and concerning the things that happened to them as adventures on an island on which they landed, where they defended Don Galaor, the brother of Amadis, from danger of death, and King Cildadan from the giant Madarque.

After the fleet left the Firm Island for the Island of Mongaza, as you have heard, Amadis stayed on the Firm Island and Don Bruneo of Bonamar with him; and with the hurry of departure he had no opportunity to ascertain from his foster father, Don Gandales, the latter's experiences at the court of King Lisuarte. And calling him aside, strolling through a garden where he lodged, he sought to learn what had taken place. Don Gandales told him how he found the queen, and the affection with which she received his message and how much she esteemed him, and how she sent word to him begging for peace with the king. And furthermore he related what took place with Oriana and Mabilia, and what they replied to him; and he gave him the letter he brought from Mabilia, from which he found out how he had increased in family and was given to understand that Oriana was pregnant. Amadis heard it all with much pleasure, although with a great longing for his lady, for his heart found no rest or relief in anything; and thus he was alone in the tower of the garden in deep thought, with tears falling down his cheeks like a man distraught. But recovering his composure, he went to where Don Bruneo was walking about and gave orders to Gandalin to put his arms, and those of Don Bruneo, and the other necessary things aboard a ship, because come what might, he wanted to leave next day for Gaul. This was done at once; and morning having come, they put out to sea with favorable weather and then at times with the opposite; and in five days they found themselves beside an island that seemed to them very densely forested and apparently a fine land. Don Bruneo said: "Do you see, sir? What a fair land!"

"So it seems to me," said Amadis.

"Then let us stop here, sir," said Don Bruneo, "some two days, and it may be that on it we find some rare adventures."

"So let it be done," said Amadis.

Then they gave orders to the captain to bring the ship inshore, for they wanted to disembark to see that island, which seemed very beautiful to them, and also in order to find some adventures.

"God protect you from it," said the master of the ship.

"Why?" said Amadis.

"To guard you from death," said he, "or from very cruel imprisonment, for know you that this is the Sad Island, where that very fierce giant Madarque is lord, more cruel and harsh than any other that there is in the world. And I tell you that in fifteen years, no knight or matron or maiden ever disembarked on it who was not killed or imprisoned."

When they heard this they marvelled greatly, and with no little fear to undertake such an adventure; but as they were of such courage and since their true function was to rid the world of such evil customs, not fearing the danger to their lives more than the great shame that would accrue to them, should they abandon it, they told the ship's master in any event to bring the ship alongside the land, which was accomplished with great difficulty and almost by force. And taking their arms and mounted on their horses, bringing with them only Gandalin and Lasindo, Don Bruneo's squire, they went inland on the island, and they gave orders to their squires to help them as best they could if they were attacked by other men who were not knights. They said that they would do so. So they went on for a bit until they were on top of a mountain, and they saw near them a castle that seemed to them very strong and beautiful, and they went toward it to find out more about the giant. And coming near, they heard a horn being blown on the highest tower so raucously that it made all those valleys resound.

"Sir," said Don Bruneo, "according to what the skipper of the ship said, that horn is sounded when the giant goes forth to battle, and this is if his men cannot overcome or kill knights with whom they are fighting; and when he goes forth thus, he is so furious that he kills everybody he finds, and sometimes even his own men."

"Then let us go forward," said Amadis.

And it was not long before they heard a very great noise of many armed men, and of very heavy blows of lances and very keen, sharp swords; and taking up their arms they all went there. And they saw a very large body of men who had two knights and two squires who were on foot, surrounded, for they had killed their horses and they were seeking to kill them; but all four were defending themselves so bravely that it was a wonderful sight to see them. And Amadis saw Ardan, his dwarf, coming toward them; and when he saw the shield of Amadis, he recognized it at once, and shouted: "Oh, Sir Amadis, help your brother Don Galaor, for they are killing him, and his friend, King Cildadan!"

When they heard this, they went forward at the top speed of their horses, neck and neck, for Don Bruneo with all his strength would not yield any advantage in such an emergency to him or to any other. And going thus, they saw Madarque, the fierce giant, coming, who was the lord of the island, and he came on a big horse, and armed with plates of very strong steel and coat of mail of very thick mesh, and instead of a helmet a thick armored hood as clean and shining as a mirror; and in his hand a very strong javelin so heavy that any other knight or person who might exist could scarcely with great effort lift it, and a very large, heavy shield; and he came on shouting: "Get out of the way, you wretched weak people, for you cannot kill two knights, exhausted and as powerless as you are! Get out of the way and leave them to this javelin of mine that it may enjoy their blood!"

Oh, how God takes revenge on the unjust and is displeased with those who seek to follow pride; and this haughty arrogance, how quickly it is overthrown! And you, reader, observe how exemplified it was seen in that Nimrod who built the Tower of

Babel and others that I could tell about through the medium of the Scriptures, which I omit in order not to occasion prolixity.

Thus it happened to Madarque in this battle. And Amadis, who heard it all, was filled with great fear on seeing him so huge and so terrible; and commending himself to God's mercy, he said: "Now is the time to be helped by you, my good lady Oriana."

And he asked Don Bruneo to strike the other knights, for he wanted to resist the giant. And he grasped the lance under his arm and he spurred his horse against Madarque as hard as he could; and he struck him so hard on the chest that it caused him perforce to bend double over the haunches of the horse. And the giant, who seized the reins in his hand, struck so hard that he made the horse rear up on its hind legs; so that it fell on top of him and he broke a leg, and the horse had one shoulder dislocated, hence neither one of them could get up. Amadis, who saw him thus, grasped his sword and shouted, saying: "At them, brother Galaor, for I am Amadis, who will help you!"

And he went toward them, and saw that Don Bruneo had killed a nephew of the giant with a lance thrust through the neck, and with his sword was accomplishing rare deeds at which people marveled; and he delivered a blow on top of the helmet of another knight, whose helmet did not protect him from being cut clear to his skull, and he knocked him to the ground. Galaor jumped on his horse and did not leave the side of King Cildadan, but Gandalin came up and dismounted from his horse and gave it to the king, and he joined the two squires. When all four were mounted, you could have seen there the wonders they performed in overthrowing and killing as many as stopped before them; and the squires on their part inflicted great harm on the foot soldiers. So that in a short while the majority were dead or wounded, and the others fled to the castle fearful of the fierce blows they saw given to them. And the four knights went after them to kill them, until they reached the gate of the castle, which was closed, and they had no way of opening it until the giant came, for thus it was ordered and forbidden. And as for those who were fleeing, when those of them on horseback saw themselves without recourse, they dismounted, and all together they cast their swords down and went toward Amadis, who was coming forward; and kneeling before the feet of his horse, they begged him for mercy's sake not to kill them, and they seized the skirt of his coat of mail in order to escape from the others, who were coming at them. Amadis protected them from King Cildadan and Don Galaor, who because of the great harm they had received from them would gladly not have left any of them alive, and he took a guarantee from them that they would do what he commanded. Then they went where the giant was lying very dispossessed of his strength, for his horse lay on top of his broken leg, and it held him so beset that his soul was almost at the point of leaving his body. King Cildadan dismounted from his horse and ordered the squires to help him; and on their turning the horse over, the giant was more free of it, and he let him rest; for although on account of him, he and Don Galaor had reached the point of death, as you have heard, he did not have it in his heart to kill him, not because of him, who was an evil thing and arrogant, but because of his regard for his son Gasquilan, king of Suesa, who was a very good knight whom he loved. And so he begged Amadis not to harm him. Amadis agreed to it, and said to the giant, who was now more conscious: "Madarque, now you see your situation as it is; and if you wish to take my advice, I shall let you live, and if not, death is yours."

The giant said: "Good knight, since you leave death and life to me, I shall do your will in order to live, and I shall give you a guarantee of it."

Amadis said to him: "Then what I ask of you is that you become a Christian and that you and all of your men uphold this doctrine by building in this kingdom churches and monasteries, and that you set free all the prisoners you have and that from now on you do not keep this bad custom that you have had until now."

The giant, who had something else in his heart, said out of fear of death: "I shall do all as you command, for I see indeed, comparing my efforts and those of my men with yours that, except on account of my sins, I could not have been overcome for any other reason, especially by a single blow, as I was. And if you please, have me carried to the castle, and there you will rest; and what you command will be done."

"So let it be done," said Amadis.

Then he ordered his men to call those to whom he had given guarantees and they took the giant and carried him to the castle, where he entered, along with Amadis and his companions. And as soon as they were disarmed, Amadis and Don Galaor embraced each other many times, weeping from the pleasure they took in seeing each other; and they were all four very happy there until they were told on behalf of the giant, that their dinner was ready, as it was now time. Amadis said that they would not dine until all the prisoners had come there, in order that they might dine in their presence.

"That will be done at once," said the giant's men," for he has already ordered them freed."

Then they had them come in, and they were one hundred persons, among whom were thirty knights and more than forty matrons and maidens. All came with great humility to kiss the hands of Amadis, telling him to command them what to do. He said to them: "Friends, what will please me is that you go to Queen Brisena and tell her how the knight of the Firm Island sent you, and that I have found Don Galaor my brother; and kiss her hands for me."

They told him they would do everything he commanded, not only that but everything else in which they might serve him. Then they sat down to eat and were very well served with many viands. Amadis ordered them to give those prisoners their ships in which to travel, and thus it was done at once; and they all together set out on their way to where Queen Brisena was in order to carry out what was asked of them. Amadis and his companions, after they had dined, went into the chamber of the giant to see him, and they found caring for him a giantess, his sister, called Andandona, the most fierce and harsh woman that there was in the world. She had been born fifteen years before Madarque and had helped to rear him. Her hair was entirely white and so kinky that she could not comb it; she was so very ugly of countenance that she resembled nothing so much as a devil. She was excessively large and swift of foot. There was no horse, however wild it might be, nor any other beast, which she could not mount and tame. She shot with a bow and arrow so hard and so accurately that she killed many bears and lions and boar, and she went about clothed in their skins. Most of the time she dwelt in those forested regions in order to hunt wild animals. She was very hostile to the Christians and did them great harm, and she was much more so from then on, causing her brother Madarque to be more hostile until in the battle that King Lisuarte had with King Arabigo and the six other kings, King Perion killed him, as will be told later on.

After those knights were a while with the giant, and he had promised them to become a Christian, they went out to their own quarters where they lodged that night. And the next day, embarking in their ships, they went on their way to Gaul by an arm of the sea that on both sides was bordered by great groves of trees, in which that ugly giantess Andandona was waiting to cause them some distress. And when she saw them down below on the water, she descended the slope until she was immediately above them, on a cliff, and without being seen by them she chose the best dart she carried; and when she saw them so close, she brandished the dart, hurled it very powerfully and hit Don Bruneo with it on one leg, which it went through and struck the boat, where it was broken. And because of the great strength that she used and her evident intention to attack them, her feet slipped from the rock, and she landed in the water with such a mighty fall that it seemed as if a tower had fallen. And those who were watching her and saw her so terrible and dressed in black bearskins, really thought that she was some devil, and they began to cross themselves and commend themselves to God. And then they saw her emerge swimming so powerfully that it was a wonder, and they shot at her with bow and arrows; but she swam under water until she came out unhurt on the shore. And when she emerged on land, Amadis and King Cildadan each wounded her with an arrow through the shoulder; but as she came out she began to flee through the dense underbrush; so that King Cildadan who saw her thus with the arrows protruding, could not help laughing. And they came to the rescue of Don Bruneo, staunching his bleeding and laying him on his bed; but in a short while the giantess appeared on top of a hillock and began to shout: "If you think I am a devil, do not believe it; but I am Andandona, who will do you all the harm I can and I shall not stop on account of any hardship or tribulation that may befall me."

And she went running over those crags with such swiftness that there was nothing that could overtake her; at which all were astounded, for they really thought that she would die from her wounds. Then they learned all about her from two men prisoners

— whom Gandalin had put there into the galley in order to take them to Gaul, of which they were natives — whereat they were astonished; and if it had not been for Don Bruneo, who very insistently begged them to take him as quickly as possible to some place where he might have that wound cared for, they would have sought to return to the island and search it everywhere for that fiendish giantess and have her burned.

So they went, as you hear, until they left that course and entered the open sea, and talking of many things as men who sincerely esteemed one another without reservation. And Amadis told them how he was in disagreement with King Lisuarte, as were on his account all his friends and relatives who were in the court, and the reason for the disagreement. And he told them of the marriage of Don Galvanes and the very beautiful Madasima and how Don Galvanes had gone with that large fleet to the Island of Mongaza in order to have her win it, since it came to her by inheritance, telling them all the knights who went with him, and the great desire they had of helping her. When Don Galaor heard this, he was very sad about this news and felt heartsick, for he well understood the great misfortunes that could recur. And he was rendered greatly distressed, because although his brother Amadis whom he loved so deeply, and to whom he owed so much reverence, was on one side, he could not find it in his heart to refuse to serve King Lisuarte, with whom he lived, as will be told later on. Therefore, thinking about this and remembering how Amadis had departed from him from the Firm Island, he drew him to one end of the ship and said to him: "Sir brother, what grave, important thing could have happened to you, greater than the relationship and love between us, that you should thus conceal yourself from me as from a strange person?"

"Good brother," said Amadis, "since the cause of it had such a strength to break those strong bonds of that relationship and love that you speak of, you can well believe that it would be much more dangerous than death itself; and I beg you sincerely not to seek to know about it at this time."

Galaor, changing to a better attitude, for he was somewhat angered, seeing that it still was Amadis's desire to be secretive, dropped the subject, and they spoke about other things.

So they sailed for four days, at the end of which they put into port at a town in Gaul by the name of Mostrol; and at the time his father, King Perion, and the queen his mother were there, because it was a seaport opposite Great Britain, where they could better find out news of those sons of theirs; and when they saw the ship, they sent a messenger to find out who were the ones who were arriving. And when the messenger arrived, Amadis ordered that he be told to inform the king that King Cildadan was coming with Don Bruneo of Bonamar, for about himself or his brother he did not want them to find out anything at that time. When King Perion heard this, he was very happy, because King Cildadan would tell him news of Don Galaor, for Amadis had made known to him that both were in the house of Urganda. And he ordered all his retinue to mount, and he went forth to welcome them, for he loved Don Bruneo very much because he had been a few times at his court, and he knew that he held his sons in respect.

Amadis and Don Galaor mounted their horses, richly garbed, and went by another route to the palace of the queen; and when they came to her apartment they said to the doorkeeper: "Tell the queen that two knights of her lineage are here, who wish to speak to her."

The queen ordered them to enter; and when she saw them she recognized Amadis and Don Galaor because of the fact that they greatly resembled each other, and she had not seen him since the giant had snatched him away from her, and she cried out: "Oh, Lady Virgin Mary! And how does it happen that I see my sons before me!"

And her speech failing her, she fell on the dais as though insensible. And they knelt and kissed her hands very humbly; and the queen came down from the dais and took them in her arms and drew them to her and kissed them both many times without their being able to speak to each other, until their sister Melicia came in; when the queen released them that they might speak to her, for they were greatly surprised by her great beauty. Who would be able to describe the pleasure of that noble queen on seeing before her those knights, her so very handsome sons, considering the great anguish and grief which was always tormenting her, as she realized the dangers to which Amadis was exposed, being in suspense as to whether he would live or die, which would mean the same for her, and having lost Don Galaor so unpredictably when the giant carried him away, and seeing everything restored with such honor and fame? Certainly no one could tell about it adequately, if it were not she or someone else who had been in similar circumstances. Amadis said to the queen: "Madam, here we bring Don Bruneo of Bonamar, badly wounded; and ask you to honor him, as one of the finest knights in the world."

"My son," said she, "so it will be done, because you wish it, and because he has served us well; and whenever I can't see to his needs your sister Melicia will."

"Do so, lady sister," said Don Galaor; "Since you are a maiden, you and all the others who are should honor him highly as the one who serves and honors them more than any other knight. And the maiden whom he loves should consider herself very fortunate since without delay he was able to go under the enchanted arch of loyal lovers, which was a sure sign of his never having been unfaithful to her."

When Melicia heard this, her heart trembled, for she well knew that it was for her that that adventure was completed; and she answered as one who was very discreet and said: "Sir, I shall do in the matter the best I can, and God's will be done. This I shall do because you command it, and because I am told that he is a good knight and that he loves you very much."

The queen being with her sons just as you have heard, King Perion and King Cildadan arrived; and when Amadis and Galaor saw King Perion, they went to him, kneeling. Each one kissed his hand and he kissed them, the tears coming to his eyes from the pleasure that he felt. King Cildadan said to them: "Good friends, remember Don Bruneo."

Then, King Cildadan having already spoken to the queen and her daughter, they went together to Don Bruneo, whom knights brought from the galley in their arms by order of King Perion; and they placed him in a very luxurious bed in a chamber of the queen's apartment, one window of which looked out on a garden with many roses and other flowers. There went the queen and her daughter to see him, the queen expressing great regret over his wound, and he considering it a great favor on her part. And after she had been there a while, she said to him: "Don Bruneo, I shall see you as often as I can; and when something prevents me from doing so, Melicia will be with you and will care for your wound."

He kissed her hands for it, and the queen went away; and Melicia and the maidens who attended her remained there. And she seated herself in front of the bed where he could easily see her beautiful face, which rendered him so happy that if he could have had it so, he would not have wished to be well, because that view was healing and restoring another wound more cruel and more dangerous for his life. She undid the bandages about the wound and saw that it was large, but since it was open on both sides, she had hope of restoring him to health quickly; and she said to him: "Don Bruneo, I think that I shall heal this wound for you, but it is necessary that you in no wise disobey instructions, for if you did so, you could again be in great danger."

"Madam," said Don Bruneo, "may God never grant that I disobey your orders, for I am certain, if I were to do so, that no one could conceive of any remedy for me."

She understood the purport of this speech better than any of the maids who were there. Then she put a certain ointment on his leg, and on the wound, that took away almost all of the swelling and pain that he had, and she fed him with those very beautiful hands of hers, and she said to him: "Rest now, for when it is time, I shall see you."

And on leaving the room she met Lasindo, Don Bruneo's squire, who knew about how they loved each other; and Melicia said to him: "Lasindo, you who are better acquainted here, ask for whatever your master needs."

"Lady," said he, "may it please God to bring him to a time when he may requite this favor that you do him."

And coming closer to her, without being overheard, he said: "Lady, he who wishes to cure someone must have recourse to his most dangerous wound, from which the greatest distress comes to him. In heaven's name, have mercy on him, since he has so much need for it, not because of the pain that he is suffering from the wound, but from what he suffers and endures with so much pain on your account."

When Melicia heard this, she said to him: "Friend, for this which I see I shall provide a remedy if I can, for of the other I know nothing."

"Lady," said he, "you know that the mortal sorrows and pangs that he suffers because of you had such power as to place him before the images of Apolidon and Grimanesa."

"Lasindo," said she, "many times it happens that with the passage of time persons recover from such maladies as this one you say your master has had, without any other remedy being administered to them, and so it may have happened to your master; and therefore it is not necessary to seek a remedy for him from one who cannot give it."

And leaving him, she went to her mother. And although this reply was told by Lasindo to Don Bruneo, he was not disturbed, for he had believed her to hold the opposite to be true; instead, many times he blessed the giantess Andandona because she had wounded him, since with the wound he was enjoying that pleasure without which everything else in the world was to him great vexation and loneliness.

Just as you hear, King Cildadan and Amadis and Galaor were with King Perion of Gaul to the great delight and enjoyment of them all; and Don Brunco in the care of that lady whom he loved so much. And it happened that one day Galaor, taking aside the king his father, and King Cildadan and his brother Amadis, said to them: "I have believed, sirs, that even though I should try very hard, I would never find three others who would love me and wish for me honor to such a degree as you. And for this reason I want you to give me advice on that which next to one's soul, one ought to consider most important; and this is that you, sir and brother Amadis, put me with King Lisuarte, commanding me with great affection to be his liegeman. And now on seeing you in such a great estrangement from him, without my being dismissed from his house, I certainly find myself greatly distraught; because if I should adhere to your side, my honor would be greatly discredited; and if to him, for me it is deadly havoc to think of being your opponent. Therefore, good sirs, help me in this problem of mine, which is your very own, and seek my honor rather than the satisfaction of your own desires." King Perion said to him: "Son, you cannot do wrong in following your brother against a king so ungrateful and so intemperate; for if you have remained with him, it was by overlooking the wishes of Amadis; and with just cause you can bid him farewell, since as an enemy he seeks and endeavors to destroy your lineage, which has been of such great service to him."

Don Galaor said: "Sire, I trust in God and in your mercy, in which I place my honor, that never in the world will it be said that in a time of such rupture and when that king has such great need of my service, did I take leave of him, he not having dismissed me previously."

"Good brother," said Amadis, "although we are so obligated to obey the command of our father and lord, knowing his prudence to be such that what he may order will be much better than we would be able to carry out, trusting myself to his mercy, I say that at such a time as this you not be separated from, or dismissed by that king, unless it were with such a reason that it could be done without vituperation from anyone; for in regard to what concerns him and me, there cannot be any knights on his side so strong, no matter how strong they are, that the most high Lord is not more so, who knows the great services that I rendered him, and the bad reward that I had from the king without deserving it. And since He is the judge, I firmly believe that He will give to each one what he deserves."

Note double meaning: the one, refer the matter to God in whom is all the power; the other, since Amadis recognizes the great fondness that his brother has for the service of King Lisuarte, not to consider it important.

It having been decided by all that Galaor should go to King Lisuarte, King Cildadan then said to Amadis and Don Galaor: "Good friends, you know about my battle with King Lisuarte, which through your prowess was won; and you took away from me that great glory that I and my people would have achieved. And you also know, sirs, the agreements and constancy that I have promised, which are that he who was overcome should serve the other in a certain way; and since my bad luck was such that I was conquered by you, I must adhere to them, albeit unwillingly, as long as I live. And from the complaint and the sorrow that my heart has about this, it is always very dispirited; but as we subordinate everything to honor, and honor means negating one's own desires in order to pursue that to which one is duty bound, I am forced to come to the rescue of that king with the number of knights that I promised him as long as God wishes; and I wish to go with Don Galaor, for today after mass, a letter from the king reached me calling me to come to his aid as I must."

Whereupon they ended their conference by saying their farewells; and next day, having taken leave of the queen and her daughter Melicia, they embarked on a ship to cross over to Great Britain, where they put into port without any delay. And on landing they went directly to where they knew King Lisuarte was; he was very angry about what had happened to his troops on the Island of Mongaza, and about the great havoc that was wrought on them. And he decided not to wait for the many troops that he had ordered drafted, but instead to go with those knights who could be found most quickly. And three days before embarking on the ships, he told the queen to take Oriana his daughter and ladies and maidens-in-waiting, because he wanted to go hunting in the forest and enjoy himself with them. And she did so, for the next day they departed with great joy; and they camped in a meadow with trees that was within the forest. And there the king disported himself that day and obtained a large number of deer and other kinds of game, with which a great feast was made for all those who were there. And certainly, although he was there in the flesh, his heart and thoughts were centered more on the damage his troops had received on the island. And the feast and hunt now being over, he caused the things to be prepared that he needed for his voyage.

CHAPTER LXVI

HOW KING CILDADAN AND DON GALAOR ON THEIR WAY TO THE COURT OF KING LISUARTE MET A MATRON WHO WAS BRINGING A HANDSOME YOUTH ACCOMPANIED BY TWELVE KNIGHTS, AND THEY WERE ASKED BY THE MATRON TO BEG THE KING TO KNIGHT HIM, WHICH WAS DONE; AND AFTERWARD BY THE SAME KING HE WAS RECOGNIZED AS HIS SON.

As King Cildadan and Don Galaor were traveling on their way to where King Lisuarte was, they were told that he was preparing to cross to the Island of Mongaza; and for this reason they traveled on faster in order to arrive in time to cross with him. And it happened to them that they, having slept in a forest, at dawn heard a bell being rung for mass, and they went there to hear it. And on entering the hermitage they saw around the altar twelve very beautiful, richly painted shields, with fields of purple and castles of gold thereon, and in their midst was a white, very beautiful shield, trimmed with gold and precious stones. And as soon as they had said their prayers, they asked some squires who were there, whose those shields were; and they told them that they could in nowise tell, but that if they went to the house of King Lisuarte they would find out quickly. And at this juncture they saw coming through the yard the knights who were owners of the shields, each one hand in hand with a maiden; and behind them came the novice knight speaking with a matron, who was not very young; and he was of very good stature and so very handsome and gallant that hardly anyone would be found equally so. King Cildadan and Don Galaor marveled greatly to see a man of such unusual appearance and indeed thought that he came from a distant land, since in that land until then there was no memory of his having been seen. Thus they passed to the altar where they all heard mass. And after it was said, the matron asked them if they were from the court of King Lisuarte.

"Why do you ask?" said they.

"Because we wanted your company, if you please, for the king is in this forest near here with the Queen and many of their retinue in tents hunting and disporting themselves."

"Then what, please, do you desire of us?" said they.

"We want," said the matron, "as a courtesy that you ask the king and queen and their daughter Oriana to come here and dub this squire a knight, for he is such that he well deserves all the honor that may be done him."

"Lady," said they, "very gladly shall we do as you say; and we believe that the king will do so, as in all things he is courteous and discreet."

Then the matron and her maidens and they mounted at once and all together, and went to station themselves on a hillock that was near the road along which the king was to come. And it was not long before they saw him coming, and the queen and her retinue; and the king came in front, and he saw the maidens and the two armed knights; and thinking that they wanted to joust, he gave orders to Grumedan, who was riding with him along with twenty knights who were guarding him, to go to them and tell them not to seek to joust but to come to him. Don Grumedan went to them, and the king halted; and when King Cildadan and Don Galaor saw that he was halting they came down from the hill with the maidens and went toward him. And when they had gone a short distance, Don Galaor recognized Grumedan, and said to King Cildadan: "Sir, look, there comes one of the best men in the world."

"Who is he?" said the king.

"Don Grumedan," said Galaor, "the one who held the standard of King Lisuarte in the battle against you."

"That you can truly say," said the king, "for I was the one who seized the standard from him, and I never succeeded in taking it out of his hands until the staff broke; and I saw him perform so well at arms against me and my men that in nowise did I wish to break it."

After they took off their helmets so that they could recognize them, Don Grumedan, who was closer, recognized Don Galaor, and said in a loud voice, as was his wont: "Ah, my friend Don Galaor, be you as welcome as the angels of Paradise!"

And he went toward him as fast as he could, and as he came up, Galaor said to him: "My lord Don Grumedan, come and meet King Cildadan."

And he went to kiss his hands, and he received him very well; and he turned at once to Don Galaor, and they embraced many times as men who sincerely loved each other; and Don Grumedan said to them: "My lords, take your time, and I'll make known your arrival to the king."

And leaving them, he went up to the king and said to him: "Sire, I bring you news with which you will be happy, for there comes your vassal and friend Don Galaor, who has never failed you in time of need; and the other is King Cildadan."

"I am very glad," said the king, "of their arrival, for I well knew that if Galaor were in good health and unhampered, he would not fail to come to me, just as I would do in whatever might affect his honor."

At this juncture the knights came up, and the king received them very affectionately; and Don Galaor sought to kiss his hands, but he did not wish it; instead he embraced him in such a way that he really gave those who were watching to understand that he loved him sincerely. Then they told him what the matron and the maidens wanted, and how they had seen that novice who wanted to be a knight, and that he was very handsome and well formed. The king remained thoughtful for a bit, because he was not accustomed to knight anyone, except men of great valor, and he asked whose son he was. The matron said: "That you will not know now, but I swear to you by the faith I owe to God, that on both sides he is a descendant of legitimate kings."

The king said to Don Galaor: "What do you think should be done in this matter?"

"I think, sire, that you ought to do it and not make any excuse, for the novice is extremely graceful and handsome, and cannot fail to be a good knight."

"Since you think so," said the king, "let it be done."

And he gave orders to Don Grumedan to take King Cildadan and Don Galaor to the queen, and to tell her to come with them to that hermitage where he was going. They went there at once; and it is not necessary to tell you how they were received by the queen and by Oriana and all the others, for never were others received better or with more affection. And the queen having learned what the king commanded, they all went after him, until they arrived at the hermitage. And when they saw those shields, and the white one so beautiful and so fine among them, they marveled at it, but much more at the very handsome features of the novice; and they could not think who he might be, since until then they had never heard of him. The novice kissed the hands of the king with great humility, and the queen did not want to give him hers, nor did Oriana, he being a man of high rank. The king dubbed him knight, and said to him: "Take the sword from whomever you prefer."

"If it will please your grace," said he, "I shall take it from Oriana, and with this my wish will be satisfied, and my heart's desire will be fulfilled."

"Let it be done," said the king, "just as you say, since you are pleased."

And calling Oriana, he said: "My dear daughter, if you please, give the sword to this knight, who wishes to take it from your hand rather than from that of anyone else."

Oriana with great shyness, as a lady who considered him quite foreign, taking the sword, gave it to him, and thus his knighting was entirely completed. This having been done just as you have heard, the matron said to the king: "Sire, it is necessary that I leave at once with these maidens, for I am so ordered; and in this matter I cannot do otherwise, for were I free to do so, I should indeed like to stay here a few days. And Norandel, whom you have dubbed a knight, will remain in your service if you so order, and so will the other knights who came with him."

When the king heard this he was quite pleased, for he was quite taken with the novice knight; and he said to her: "Lady, God bless you."

She took leave of the queen and of the very beautiful Oriana, her daughter. And when she was about to take leave of the king she put in his hand a letter, without anyone's seeing her do so, and said to him in a very quietly whispered aside: "Read this letter without anyone's seeing it, and afterwards do what most pleases you."

With this she went away to her ship. And the king remained thinking about what she had told him, and he told the queen to take with her King Cildadan and Don Galaor, and go to the tents; and if he were late in returning from the hunt, that they should rest and dine. The queen did so. And when the king was by himself, he opened the letter.

Letter from the Princess Celinda to King Lisuarte.

Very exalted Lisuarte, King of Great Britain: I, the Princess Celinda, daughter of King Hegido, kiss your hands in greeting. You will indeed recall, my lord, when at the time that as a knight errant you were seeking great adventures, having finished many of them to your great honor, that chance and good fortune caused you to land in the kingdom of my father — who at the time had departed from this world — where you found me besieged in my castle, which was called Great Rosebush Castle, by Antifon the Fierce; who, on account of having his offer of marriage rejected by me for not being my equal in lineage, was trying to take from me all my land. With whom a battle of your person against his having been arranged, he trusting in his great valor, and you in my being a weak maiden, at great risk to your person you fought; and finally, he was overcome and killed; so that you by winning the glory of such a hard battle, put me at liberty and in all good fortune. Then, you, my lord, entering the castle, either because my beauty had brought it to pass or because fortune willed it, I becoming enamored of you, under that beautiful rosebush, having many roses and flowers over us, I, being deflowered by you, that youth was engendered, and according to his extreme good looks, that sin bore beautiful fruit and will be pardoned by the most powerful Lord. And this ring, which was given me by you with such great love and by me guarded, I send to you as an ever present witness with him. Honor him and love him, my good lord, dubbing him a knight, for he comes from kings on all sides. And taking from your side great courage and from my side the very abundant fire of love that I had for you, one ought to have great hope that it will be very well employed in him.

The letter having been read, immediately he recalled the time that he went as a knight errant through the kingdom of Denmark, when for his great deeds at arms that he accomplished, he was loved by the very beautiful Brisena, princess daughter of that king, and he had her for his wife as has already been related; and how he had found this Princess Celinda besieged and how he had experienced with her all that she had told him in the letter; and on seeing the ring, he was rendered more certain that it was true. And although the handsome appearance of the novice gave him great hope of his being an excellent knight, he resolved to conceal it until deeds gave testimony of his virtue. So he went hunting; and taking much game on that hunt, he returned highly pleased to the tents, where the queen was. And he went to the tent where he was told that King Cildadan and Don Galaor were, in order to honor them, and he was accompanied by the most honorable and nobly attired knights of his court; and before them all he began to praise highly their great deeds, just as they deserved, and on account of the great aid he was expecting from them in that war that he had with the best knights in the world. And with great pleasure he told them about the hunt that he had carried on and said that he would not give them anything from the hunt, laughing and joking in order to please them; and he ordered the game taken to Oriana, his daughter, and the other princesses, and sent word to tell them to share it with King Cildadan and Don Galaor; and he ate there with the knights with much enjoyment. And as soon as the tables were cleared, taking Don Galaor with him, he went under some trees; and putting his arm on his shoulder, he said to him: "My good friend, Don Galaor, how I love and esteem you, God knows, because always from your great courage and your counsel much good has come to me, and I feel great security in confiding in you, so much so that what I would not disclose to you, I would not tell my own heart. And leaving aside the most serious matters that will always be made known to you by me, I wish you to know about one matter that is on my mind at the present time."

Then he gave him the letter to read; and Don Galaor, on seeing that Norandel was his son, was very happy and said to him: "Sire, if you experienced hardship and danger in rescuing that princess, she has well repaid you with such a handsome son; for, so help me God, I believe that he will be so excellent that that concern that you now have to conceal him, will become much greater to reveal him. And if it pleases you, sire, I wish him for a companion all of this year so that some of the desire that I have to serve you may be employed on that person who is so close a blood relative."

"I thank you very much," said the king, "for what you say, because as nothing remains a secret, all the honor that accrues to this youth is mine. But how shall I give you for companion a youngster about whom we don't know yet what he will amount to, when I would consider myself very happy to be your companion. But since you are pleased, so let it be done."

Then they returned to the tent where King Cildadan and Norandel and many other knights of high rank were. And when all were quiet, Galaor stood up and said to the king: "Sire, you well know that the custom of your house and of the whole realm of London is that the first favor that any knight or maiden asks of the novice knight, must be granted by him straightway."

"That is true," said the king, "but why do you say so?"

"Because I am a knight," said Galaor, "and I ask Norandel to grant me a boon that I shall demand of him; and it is that my companionship with him be for a full year, during which we maintain mutual loyalty, and nothing separates us except death or imprisonment, which we cannot help."

When Norandel heard this, he marveled at what Galaor had said, and was very happy, because he already knew about his great fame and saw the signal honor that the king was doing him, out of so many good and valued knights, and knew that after his brother Amadis, there was no one else in the world to surpass him in prowess at arms, and he said: "My lord Don Galaor, according to your great excellence and merit, and the meagerness of mine, it really seems that this boon is requested more because of your great virtue than because I deserve it; but however that may be, I grant it to you, and I thank you for it as the one thing in the world, outside of the service of my lord the king, that could come to me to render me most happy."

King Cildadan, having noted the way matters were shaping up, said: "According to the age and good looks of you both, with abundant reason the boon could be asked and granted; and may God grant that it be for the best, and so it will be, as is done with things that are requested more because of reason than with desire."

The companionship between Don Galaor and Norandel having been agreed to, just as you have heard, King Lisuarte told them how he had determined to set out on the sea on the third day; because, according to the news that came to him from the Island of Mongaza, his departure was very necessary.

"In the name of God shall it be," said King Cildadan, "and we shall serve you in all that may be to your honor."

And Don Galaor said to him: "Sire, since you have completely the hearts of your men, fear only God."

"That is my opinion," said the king, "for although the strength of you all is great, your love and affection makes me much more secure."

That day they spent there with great enjoyment, and next day, having heard mass, they all mounted to return to the town. And the king told Don Galaor and Grumedan to go with the queen; and taking Don Galaor aside, he gave him permission to tell Oriana the secret of how Norandel was her brother and asked that she deem it confidential. With this he went to his hunters, and they to the queen, who was already mounted. And Don Galaor on coming up to Oriana, took her palfrey by the reins and entered into a conversation with her; much to her pleasure, as much on account of the great love the king her father had for him, as because it seemed to her that since he was the brother of her lover Amadis, his presence gave her great reassurance. Then while thus speaking of many things, they came to talk about Norandel, and Oriana said: "Do you know anything about this knight? For I saw you come in his company. In view of your great worth, this ought not to have been unless you know something about him, for all those who know you do not know any other person who is your equal except your brother Amadis."

"My lady," said Don Galaor, "my equality and courage are as far removed from Amadis's as earth is from heaven; and it would be very great madness for anyone to think of being his equal, because God made him unsurpassed in fortitude as well as in all the other good qualities that a knight ought to possess."

Oriana, when she heard this, began to think to herself as follows: "Ah, Oriana, what if some day comes when you find yourself without the love of such a man as Amadis and without such fame — as much at arms as for good looks."

And in order that her mood not be detected, she showed herself happy and joyful to have such a lover as no other woman could achieve.

"And in regard to what you say, lady, of the companionship that I have initiated with Norandel, I well believe according to his predisposition and the very honorable action that he took, that he will be an excellent knight. But another thing I found out about him, that will seem very strange, when it is known to everyone, caused me to do it."

"I believe it to be thus," said Oriana, "for you would not be moved, being the man you are, without good reason to take him as a companion; and if it can be told without any harm to your honor, I should be pleased to know it."

"The thing which you, my lady, would be pleased to know from me would have to be very precious indeed for me not to tell it to you," said he. "What I know of this, I shall tell you; but it is necessary that it not be known by any other person."

"You may be completely certain and assured," said she, "that thus it will be."

"Then know you, madam," said Galaor, "that Norandel is the son of your father."

And he told her how he had seen the letter from Princess Celinda and the ring, and all the latter had said to the king, Oriana's father.

"Galaor," said Oriana, "you make me very happy with what you have said and I am very grateful to you for it, because I could not have found it out from anyone else. Also you render me happy with the great honor that you have given to this knight with whom I have such close relationship; for certainly if he is disposed to be a good knight, in much greater measure he will be so with you; and if the contrary be true, your great excellence will cause him to be so."

"I am very grateful, madam, for the honor that you do me," said he, "although there may be in me the opposite; but be that as it may, it will always be put at your service and at that of the king, your father, and at that of your mother."

"So I consider it, Don Galaor," said she, "and may it please God through His mercy that they and I may be able to reward you for it."

Thus they reached the town, where Oriana remaining with her mother the queen, Galaor went to his lodging, taking with him Norandel his companion.

And next day, immediately after the king had heard mass, he ordered food taken to the ships, for the troops who were crossing with him were already on board with their arms and horses. And he, taking with him King Cildadan and Galaor and Norandel, having said farewell to the queen and his daughter and the ladies and maidens-in-waiting, all of whom were weeping, went to the port of Jafoque, where his fleet was. And once on board, he set out for the Island of Mongaza, where with favorable weather for the most part — though at times contrary — at the end of five days he had reached the port of that town from which the island took its name. And he found there at a very strong army camp King Arban of North Wales with the troops that you have already heard about, and he learned that they had had a great battle with the knights who held the town and that their own men had been routed from the field and all would have been lost if King Arban of North Wales had not taken advantage of some very precipitous cliffs where they were protected from their enemy; and how that very courageous Gasquilan, king of Suesa, was badly wounded by Don Florestan, and his men had carried him away by sea to where he might recover from his injuries; and also how they held Brian de Monjaste prisoner, who had plunged among his foes to attack King Arban of North Wales; and that after this fight they never more dared to leave those cliffs, where King Lisuarte found them; and that although the knights of the Island of Mongaza had attacked them many times, they never succeeded in harming them, because their position was so protected. All this having been ascertained by

King Lisuarte, he became greatly enraged at the knights of the island; and he ordered all the troops to leave the ships, with tents and other necessary things, and he set up camp in the countryside until he could find out about his foes.

Oriana was very pleased with the departure of the king her father, because the time was approaching when she had to give birth. And she called Mabilia and told her that according to the fainting spells and the way she was feeling, it could only mean that she was about to be brought to childbed; and commanding the other maidens to leave her, she went to her chamber, and with her Mabilia and the maid of Denmark, who beforehand had already provided all the things that they needed and that were useful for the delivery. Oriana was with labor pains until evening, and with them suffering somewhat from fatigue; but from then on they beset her much more frequently, so that she experienced very great distress and great anxiety, as one who until then knew nothing of such pangs. But the great fear that she had of being discovered in that dangerous situation in which she was, constrained her in such wise that she endured it without complaining; and at midnight the most high Lord, helpful to all, was pleased that she be delivered of a son, a very sprightly baby, leaving her free. He was then wrapped in very fine garments, and Oriana said they should bring him to her in her bed; and taking him in her arms, she kissed him many times. The maid of Denmark said to Mabilia: "Have you seen what this child has on its body?"

"No," said she, "for I am busy and have so much to do in helping it, and its mother to give birth to it, that I did not look otherwise."

"Well certainly," said the maiden, "it has something on its chest that other babies don't have."

Then they lit a candle and unwrapping the baby, they saw that it had under the right nipple some letters as white as snow, and under the left nipple, seven letters as red as live coals; but they were unable to read either set of letters, or what they said, because the white ones were of very obscure Latin, and the red ones in utterly incomprehensible Greek. And after they looked at this, they wrapped the baby up again, and put it beside the mother, and they decided it was to be taken at once to where it would be reared, as they had planned. And so it was done, for the maid of Denmark left the palace secretly and went around outside to the place where the window was that opened on the room, and her brother Durin with her, both on their palfreys. And Mabilia meanwhile had the child placed in a basket tied with a strip of cloth on top; and suspending the basket on a rope, she lowered it until it was placed in the hands of the maiden; who took it and went with it on the way to Miraflores, where as her own son it was to be brought up secretly. But in a little while, leaving the direct road they took a path that Durin knew that led through a very thick forest of trees, and this they did in order to go more secretly; and Durin went ahead and the maiden followed him. Thus they reached a spring that was in a plain unencumbered with trees. But immediately beyond there was a valley so dense and so forbidding that a person could scarcely enter it, because of the wildness and density of the wooded area, and there lions and other animals flourished. And at the head of this valley there was a little old hermitage in which dwelt Nasciano, a hermit, who was considered a very holy and devout man by all, and revered so highly that it was the opinion of the people of the vicinity that sometimes he was sustained by celestial food. And when he lacked food, he went looking for it through the land, without lions or any other animals harming him, although many of them he continually encountered as he was going about on his donkey; rather it seemed that they paid homage to him. And near this hermitage there was a cave among some rocks where a lioness was rearing her cubs; and often the good man visited and fed them when he had food, without fearing the lioness; instead she, when she saw him with them, drew aside from there until he had gone. With these cubs, after he had said his prayers, he was wont to spend his time, deriving enjoyment from seeing them romp about the cave.

And when the maid of Denmark and her brother came to that spring, she was very thirsty from the effort of the night and from the journey; and she said to her brother: "Let us dismount; and take this child, for I want to drink."

He took the child, wrapped as it was in expensive swaddling clothes, and put it on the trunk of a tree that was there; and as he was about to help his sister to alight, they heard some loud lion roars resound in the heavily wooded valley, so that those palfreys were so frightened that they began to flee at top speed without the maiden's being able to restrain her own mount; rather, she thought that it would kill her among the trees, and she kept calling on God to help her; and Durin came running after her intending to take her palfrey by the bridle rein and bring it to a halt. And he ran so fast that he went ahead of it and stopped it; and he found his sister so bruised and distraught that she could hardly speak; so he had her dismount and said: "Sister, stay here, and I shall go on this palfrey in search of mine."

"But go for the child," said she, "and bring it to me, lest something happen to it."

"I shall do so," said he, "and hold this palfrey by the reins, for I am afraid, if I took it, that I wouldn't be able to make it approach the spring."

And so he went on foot. But before that a strange occurrence took place; for that lioness that was rearing her offspring as you have heard, and had emitted a roar, was in the habit of coming each day to that spring to pick up the scent of the deer that were accustomed to drink at it. And when she arrived there, she walked all around sniffing from one side to the other; and while thus walking she heard the child crying, who was on the trunk of the tree, and she went for it, and took it by its clothing into her mouth between those very sharp teeth of hers, without touching its flesh, which was because it was God's will; and recognizing it to be food for her offspring, she went away with it; and it was already time for the sun to rise. But that Lord of the world, compassionate with those who seek mercy of Him, and with innocents who do not have the age or sense to ask for it, came to its aid in this way: that saintly Nasciano having sung mass at dawn of day, and going to the spring to refresh himself there, for the night had been very hot, saw that the lioness was carrying the child in her mouth; which was crying in a weak voice, as one just born that night; and he perceived that it was a baby, whence he was very disturbed concerning where she had gotten it; and immediately he raised his hand and made the sign of the cross, saying to the lioness: "Come, bad beast, and put down God's creature, for He did not create it for your sustenance."

And the lioness, her ears twitching as though fawning, came to him very meekly, and placed the infant at his feet, and immediately went away. Nasciano made over it the sign of the true cross, and afterwards took it in his arms and went with it to the hermitage. And passing near the cave where the lioness was rearing her offspring, he saw her suckling them, and he said to her: "I command you in God's name, in whose power are all things, that taking your teats away from your offspring, you suckle this child, and as you would them, you protect it from all harm."

The lioness came and lay down at his feet and the good man put the child to its teats, and putting some of the milk into its mouth, made it take the teat and suck; and from then on the lioness came very tamely to suckle it every time it was necessary. But the hermit sent at once a youthful servant of his who helped him at mass, and was his nephew, to go very quickly and to call his mother and father to come back immediately with him, but with no other companion, because he needed them badly. The boy went at once to a village where they dwelt, which was at the edge of the forest; but because the father was not there in the village, they were unable to come until ten days had passed, during which time the child was very well sustained by the milk of the lioness and that of a goat, and that of a sheep that had given birth to a lamb. These took care of the needs while the lioness went hunting for food for her offspring.

When Durin left his sister, as you have already heard, he went on foot as quickly as he could to the spring where he had left the child; and when he did not find it, he was quite frightened and looked everywhere, but found only the tracks of the lioness; hence he truly believed she had eaten it, and with very great distress and sadness he returned to his sister. And when he told her about it, she slapped her own face and set up a great wailing, cursing her luck and the hour at which she had been born, that under such circumstances she had lost all she held dear, for she did not know how to appear before her mistress. Durin comforted her weeping, but comfort was of no use, for her violent emotion and her sadness were so excessive that for more than two hours she was as if out of her senses. Durin said to her: "My good sister, what you are doing is of no benefit, and from it much harm might come to your mistress and her lover, for something of their affair might become known."

She saw that he was speaking the truth, and said to him: "Then what shall we do? For I haven't sense enough to know."

"It seems to me," said he, "that since my palfrey is lost, we ought to go to Miraflores, and stay there three or four days to give them to understand that some motive brought you there; and on returning to Oriana not to tell her a thing about this, except that the child is under good care, until she is well; and afterwards you will take counsel with Mabilia as to what should be done."

She said she considered that a good plan; and both mounting her palfrey, they went to Miraflores, and at the end of three days returned to Oriana; and the maiden with a cheerful mien told her how all was done as she had planned.

Then returning to the hermit who was rearing the child, know you that at the end of ten days there came to him his sister and her husband; and he told them how he had found that child under extraordinary circumstances, and that God loved it since thus He had sought to protect it; and he begged them to bring it up in their home until it knew how to talk, and to bring it to him to teach it. They said that they would do as he commanded.

"Then I want to baptize it," said the good man.

And so it was done; but when that matron unwrapped it at the fount, she saw the white letters and the red ones that it had, and showed them to the good man, who was greatly shocked thereby. And on reading them he saw that the white letters said in Latin: "Esplandian," and he thought that that must be his name, and so he gave it to him; but the red ones, although he strove diligently, he was unable to read, nor could he make out what they said. And immediately the baby was baptized with the name of Esplandian, by which he was known in many foreign lands for great events that happened because of him, just as will be related subsequently.

This having been done, the nurse carried him with great pleasure to her house, with the expectation that through him not only she but all her lineage would be protected, and with great diligence she brought him up as one who had her hope concentrated in him. And at the time that the hermit so ordered, they brought him to him, and he was very handsome and well reared, so that all who saw him greatly enjoyed looking at him.

CHAPTER LXVII

In which is related the cruel battle of King Lisuarte and his troops against Don Galvanes and his companions, and the liberality and greatness that the king displayed after the victory by giving the land to Don Galvanes and Madasima, they remaining as vassals while they dwelt in it.

As you have heard, King Lisuarte disembarked at the port of the Island of Mongaza, where he found Arban of North Wales and the troops who with him had taken refuge at an army camp located amid some crags — troops whom he ordered to go down at once to the plain and join the forces that he had brought. And he found out how Don Galvanes and his companions, who were at the Boiling Lake, had crossed the mountain range that they had between them, prepared to give them battle. And he moved at once with all his men against them, encouraging them as much as he could, as one who had fought with the best knights in the world; and he went until he came to within a league of them on the bank of a river, and there he stopped that night. And when the dawn of day appeared, they all heard mass and armed themselves, and the king made three divisions of them. Don Galaor had the first, of five hundred knights; and with him went his companion Norandel, and Don Guilan the Pensive and his cousin Ladasin, and Grimeo the Valiant, and Cendil of Ganota, and Nicoran of the Fearful Bridge, the very good jouster. And the second division he gave to King Cildadan with seven hundred knights; and there went with him Ganides of Ganota, and Acedis, the king's nephew, and Gradasonel Fallistre, and Brandoyvas, and Tasian and Filispinel, all of whom were knights of high rank; and in the middle of this division went Don Grumedan of Norway, and other knights who were going with King Arban of North Wales, who were charged with protecting the king without having anything to do with anything else. Thus they moved through the countryside, and appeared a very handsome and well armed body of soldiers, for so many Moorish trumpets and horns sounded that one could hardly hear; and they took up positions on a level field; and at the king's back went Baladan and Leonis with thirty knights.

The action of King Lisuarte and the troops that he brought, having been ascertained by Don Galvanes and the distinguished nobles who were with him, although there were for each one of them five men, and although the imprisonment of Don Brian de Monjaste and the departure of Agrajes to bring them food that they needed greatly handicapped them, they were not disheartened by this; rather with great vigor they gave encouragement to their men, who were but few for the battle, as those who were renowned for their noble feats at arms, as this story has related; and they agreed to make two divisions of themselves. The one was of one hundred and six knights and the other of one hundred and nine. In the first went Don Florestan and Don Cuadragante, and Angriote of Estravaus and his brother Grovedan and his nephew Sarquiles and his brother-in-law Gasinan, who was carrying the maidens' banner; and near the banner went Branfil and the good Gavarte of the Fearful Valley, and Olivas and Balays of Carsante, and Enil the good knight whom Beltenebros had placed in the battle of King Cildadan. In the other division went Don Galvanes, and with him the two brothers, Palomir and Dragonis, and Listoran of the Tower, and Dandales of Sadoca and Tantalis the Proud, and along with these divisions went some crossbowmen and archers. With this company, so unequal with respect to the large number of the king's troops, they went to enter the level field, where the others were waiting for them.

And Don Florestan and Don Cuadragante summoned Elian the Vigorous, who was one of the most spruce knights and who appeared better armed than the majority were; and they told him to go to King Lisuarte, he and two other knights with him who were his cousins, and to tell him that if he gave orders to remove the crossbowmen and archers from between the divisions of the knights, they would have one of the finest battles that he had ever seen. These three went at once to carry it out, having moved away from the battalions, appearing so fine that they were scrutinized intensively by everyone. And know you that this Elian the Vigorous was a nephew of Don Cuadragante, son of his sister, and of Count Liquedo, first cousin of King Perion of Gaul. And having reached the first division of Don Galaor they asked for a safe-conduct, for they were coming to the king with a message. Don Galaor gave them assurance and sent with them Cendil of Ganota, so that they would be safe from the others. And having come before the king, they said to him: "Sire, Don Florestan and Don Cuadragante and the other knights who are there to defend the land of Madasima, send us to tell you, if you please, to withdraw the crossbowmen and archers from between you and them, and you will see a fine battle."

"In the name of God," said the king, "remove yours and Cendil of Ganota will withdraw mine."

This was done at once, and those three knights went to their company, and Cendil went to Don Galaor to tell him with what request they had come to the king; and then the divisions moved, some knights against others so close that there was not between them the space of three bow shots. And Don Galaor recognized his brother Don Florestan by the face-guard of his helmet, and Don Cuadragante and Gavarte of the Fearful Valley, who were coming in front of their men. And he said to Norandel: "My good friend, see there where three knights are together, the best that could be found; that one with the red armor and white lions is Don Florestan, and the one with the blue armor and flowers of gold and purple lions is Angriote de Estravaus, and that one who has the blue field and flowers of silver is Don Cuadragante, and this one in front of everybody, with green armor is Gavarte of the Fearful Valley, the very fine knight who killed the serpent, whence he acquired this name. Now let us go attack them."

And then they moved forward, their lances lowered, and covered by their shields, and the three opposing knights came to receive them. But Norandel spurred his horse and turned to Gavarte of the Fearful Valley and attacked him so violently that he knocked him from his horse to the ground and the saddle on top of him; this was the first blow that he struck, which was considered by all a very noble beginning. And Don Galaor joined with Don Cuadragante, and they both attacked each other so fiercely that their horses and they fell to the ground; and Cendil came to grips with Elian the Vigorous, and although they broke their lances, and were wounded, they remained on their horses. At this time the divisions were joined and the noise of the shouts and of the blows was so loud that the Moorish trumpets and horns were not heard. Many knights were killed and wounded, and others knocked off their horses; great anger and fury arose in the hearts of those on both sides.

But the greatest melee was over defending Don Galaor and Don Cuadragante, who were fighting with great celerity at close quarters and striking each other with their swords in order to win, so that they frightened those who were watching them; and already there were from both sides more than one hundred knights dismounted with them in order to help them and give them their horses. But they were so close together and in such haste that they could not be separated; but during that hour what Norandel and Guilan the Pensive did for Don Galaor could not be related to you nor could what Don Florestan and Angriote did for Don Cuadragante; for as the attacking troops were more numerous than theirs, they charged at them; but they were so severely punished by their blows that they gave way and did not dare approach them. But finally so many men intervened between them that Don Galaor and Don Cuadragante had time to take their horses; and like angry lions they rushed into the fray, unhorsing and wounding those who were in their path, each one helping those on his side.

At that hour King Cildadan attacked with his division so fiercely that many knights were unhorsed on both sides; Don Galvanes came immediately to the rescue and entered the press so fiercely attacking his foes, that he gave them clearly to understand that the fight was his, and that battle had been joined for his cause; for he feared neither death nor danger, nor did he deem them of any consequence in comparison with injuring those whom he hated so much and who had come to disinherit him. And those of his division continued to hold steadfast; and since all were very courageous, picked knights, they wreaked much harm on their foes.

Don Florestan, who was very angry, considering Amadis his brother to be the leader in this dispute, although he was not there, and thinking that if it befitted those knights of his side out of their great valor to perform rare feats, it befitted him to accomplish much more, went about like a mad dog, seeking what major harm he could inflict. And he saw King Cildadan, who was fighting fiercely and was doing great harm to his foes, so much so that at that hour he was surpassing his men in fighting well. And he let himself go through the midst of the knights, for they were not able to hinder him with the many blows that they gave him; and he came up to Cildadan in such a rush and so eager to attack him that he could do nothing else but throw his strong arms about him, and the king his around him. And immediately they were aided by many knights who were guarding them. But their horses having swerved apart, they landed on the ground on foot, and grasping their swords they struck each other hard, deadly blows. But Enil the good knight and Angriote of Estravaus, who were protecting Don Florestan, performed so well that they gave him the horse; and when Don Florestan saw himself on horseback, he rushed into the melee performing marvels at arms, remembering what his brother Amadis would have been able to do, if he had been there.

And Norandel, who was wearing badly damaged armor through which blood was flowing in many places, and was using his sword up to the hilt with the many blows that he had struck with it, when he saw King Cildadan on foot, called to Don Galaor, and said: "Don Galaor, you see the situation your friend King Cildadan is in. Let us help him; if we don't he is dead."

"At once, my good friend," said Don Galaor, "may your great excellence appear, and let us give him a horse and stay with him."

Then they went among the troops, attacking and unhorsing as many as they overtook; and with a great effort they put him on a horse, because he was badly wounded from a sword cut that Dragonis had given him on the head, from which much blood was flowing down to his eyes. And at that hour the troops of King Lisuarte could not be of enough avail against the great strength of their foes to avoid being expelled in flight from the field without awaiting a blow, except for Don Galaor and a few other distinguished knights who kept on defending and withdrawing then until they arrived where King Lisuarte was. He, when he saw them coming thus vanquished, shouted: "Now, my good friends, may your excellence appear, and let us defend the honor of the kingdom of London."

And he spurred his horse, saying "Clarence, Clarence!" which was his surname, and charged at his enemies through the greatest crush; and he saw Don Galvanes, who was fighting fiercely, and he struck him so hard with his lance that it was broken to pieces, and he made him lose his foothold in the stirrups, and he embraced the neck of his horse and the king grasped his sword, and began to strike in all directions; so that there he showed a great deal of his courage and valor, and his men courageously held and kept on exerting themselves along with him. But all was in vain, for Don Florestan and Don Cuadragante and Angriote and Gavarte, who found themselves all together, performed such feats at arms that through their great efforts it seemed that their enemies would be overcome; so that everybody thought that from there onward they would not hold the field against them. King Lisuarte, who saw his troops thus withdrawn and badly off, was quite fearful of being vanquished; and he called Don Guilan the Pensive, who was badly wounded, and he came up to him, and also King Arban of North Wales and Grumedan of Norway, and he said to them: "I see our troops worsted, and I am fearful lest God, whom I have never served as I ought, not give me the honor of this battle. Now let us see to it that I can be said to be a king conquered or dead with honor, but not overcome alive with dishonor."

Then he spurred his horse and rushed among them without any fear for his death, And as he saw Don Cuadragante coming at him, he turned his horse toward him, and they struck each other with their swords on top of their helmets such mighty blows that they had to grasp the necks of their horses. But since the sword of the king was much better, he cut so deep that he made a wound in his head. But they were immediately helped, the king by Don Galaor and by Norandel and by those who were riding with him; and Don Cuadragante by Don Florestan and by Angriote de Estravaus. And the king, who saw the wonders that Don Florestan was performing, went up to him and with his sword struck such a blow on his horse's head that he knocked it down with him amid the knights. It was not long before he received the payment for it, for Florestan immediately came out from under his horse and went for the king, although many were protecting him, and he only reached the leg of his horse, and cutting through it completely knocked it with him to the ground. The king came out from under it so very agilely that Don Florestan was amazed; and he struck Don Florestan two blows with his very good sword, so that the armor did not keep it from cutting his flesh. But Florestan remembering how he had been the king's man, and the honors that he had received from him, refrained from striking him, covering himself with what little of the shield he had left; but the king, with the great fury he had, did not cease striking him as hard as he could. And not even on that account did Don Florestan seek to strike him, but seized him in his arms and would not let him mount or withdraw from him. There was a very great melee of both factions to help them, and the king called himself by name so that his men would recognize him; and at these shouts, Don Galaor came up, and reaching the king, said: "Sire, make use of this horse of mine."

And already Felispinel and Brandoyvas were with him on foot giving him their horses. And Galaor said to him: "Sire, make use of my horse."

But he, seeing to it that he not dismount, took Felispinel's horse, leaving Don Florestan badly wounded by that good sword of his, for he never delivered a blow that did not cut his armor and flesh, without the other's seeking to strike him, as has been said already. And Don Florestan was placed on a horse that Don Cuadragante brought him.

The king, gratuitously exposing his body to every danger, calling Don Galaor and Norandel and King Cildadan and the others who were following him, rushed into the greatest press of troops, attacking and wreaking havoc on all that he found in his path, so that he was credited at that time with the improvement of all those on his side. And Don Florestan and Cuadragante and Gavarte, and other distinguished knights, withstood the king and his men as much as they were able, performing wonders at arms; but as they were few and many of them battered and wounded, and their foes a great multitude of men who at the courage of the king had taken heart and charged so suddenly and so forcefully at them that, not only on account of their many wounds, but also because of the strength of the horses, they routed them from the field to the point of driving them to the foot of the ridge; where Don Florestan and Don Cuadragante and Angriote and Gavarte of the Fearful Valley, their arms broken to pieces, receiving many wounds, not only to help those on their side, but also to win back the lost field, their horses dead and they almost dead, remained recumbent on the field in the power of the king and his men; and together with them, likewise taken prisoners in an effort to rescue them, were Palomir and Elian the Haughty, and Branfil and Enil and Sarquiles, and Maratros of Lisanda, cousin of Don Florestan; and there were many dead and wounded on both sides. And Don Galvanes would have been lost many times if Dragonis had not rescued him with his troops. But finally he took him out of the press so badly wounded that he was too weak to stand up, so insensible was he; and he had him taken to the Boiling Lake; and he remained with that small company that had escaped by defending the ridge from the enemy.

Thus one can say with much fairness that because of the fortitude of the king and the great folly of Don Florestan in not wanting to strike or force him when he had him in his power, this battle was won as you hear; for one should compare that mighty Hector when he had the first battle with the Greeks at the time when they wanted to disembark in his great harbor of Troy, who having them almost overcome and fires set at many points in the fleet, where there was no longer resistance, there was by chance in that great melee his cousin Ajax Talamon, son of Ansiona his aunt; and Hector recognizing him and they embracing each other, at Ajax's request he withdrew the Trojans from the fight, taking from their hands that great victory and making them return to the city; which was the reason why, the Greeks having landed, their army camp having experienced so many deaths, so many fires, such great destruction, that very strong people, that very famous city outstanding in the world, was demolished and destroyed in such a way that never from the memory of man will it be dropped as long as the world endures; by which one is given to understand that in such encounters, pity and courtesy ought not to operate with friend or relative until victory is obtained and completed, because many times it happens in a way similar to that good luck and fortune that men have prepared by themselves: not knowing how to recognize it or use it as they should, they turn it to the aid of those who are considering it lost, and by taking it away from themselves, cause them to take it.

Then returning to the subject matter, when King Lisuarte saw that his enemies were off the field and taking refuge on the ridge, and that the sun was setting, he ordered that none of his men go ahead from then on, and placed his guards in order to be secure and because Dragonis, who with the troops had taken refuge in the mountain, had won the strongest passes of it. And he ordered his tents removed from where he had them before, and had them located on the bank of a stream that came down at the foot of the mountain. And he said that they should bring King Cildadan and Don Galaor; but he was told that they were immersed in grief over Don Florestan and Don Cuadragante, who were at the point of death. And as he had already dismounted, he asked for his horse, more to console them than with any desire to order help given those knights, because they were his foes; although he was moved somewhat to pity on remembering how Don Florestan in the battle that he had with King Cildadan placed his unprotected head in front of him and received on his shield that mighty blow of the valiant Gadancuriel so that it would not strike the king; and also how that same day he virtuously had stopped striking. And he went to where they were, and consoling them with affectionate words, by causing Florestan and Cuadragante to have medical attention, he left Galaor and Cildadan content. In this he was not so effective as to prevent Don Galaor from first swooning repeatedly over his brother, Don Florestan. But the king ordered them carried to a very good tent, and his physicians to care for them; and taking with him King Cildadan, he gave Don Galaor permission to spend the night with them there. And he took with him to the same tent the seven captive knights you have already heard about, where he had them cared for with the others. Thus as you hear, those wounded, unconscious knights and those who were prisoners were under the protection of Don Galaor where with the help of God chiefly, and of the physicians, who were very learned, before dawn of day came they had all recovered consciousness, the physicians certifying to Don Galaor that according to the state of their wounds, they would be turned over to him healthy and unimpaired.

Next day, Don Galaor being present, Norandel, his friend and Don Guilan the Pensive with him to keep him company in his great sadness on account of his brother and the others of his lineage, they heard the trumpets and horns sound in the king's tent, which was a signal for the troops to arm. And they bound their wounds very well so that they would not bleed, and arming themselves and mounting their horses, they went there at once, and found the king armed with fresh weapons, and on a rested horse, deciding with King Arban of North Wales and King Cildadan and Don Grumedan what he would do in the attack on the knights that were on the ridge. And the opinions were diverse, for some said that according to the bad state of their own troops, it was not right, until they were in better condition, to attack their enemies. And others said that since for the moment they were all fired with anger, they would be ineffective if they delayed further to engage in the affair, especially if at that time Agrajes should come, who had gone to Little Brittany for food and troops, because with him they would gather great strength. And Don Galaor, when questioned by the king as to what it seemed to him should be done, said: "Sire, if your troops are battered and weary, so too are your opponents; since they are few and we many, it would be better that they be attacked at once."

"So let it be done," said the king.

Then, his troops having been deployed, they attacked the ridge, Don Galaor leading the way, and Norandel his companion following him, and all the others behind them. And although Dragonis, with the troops which he had, defended for some time the passes and ascents of the ridge, so many crossbowmen and archers charged there, wounding many of them, that they made them perforce give way; and when the knights ascended to level ground, there was quite a perilous battle between them. But not being able finally to withstand the many troops, of necessity they had to withdraw to the town and castle. And immediately the king arrived, and ordering his tents and equipment brought, he laid siege to them and surrounded them; and he ordered his fleet to come and encircle the castle from the sea.

And because the relation of the events occurring then does not greatly concern this story, since it is about Amadis and he was not in this war, this account will stop here. Only let it be known that the king had them surrounded for thirteen months by land and by sea, for they were not afforded a rescue from any quarter, because Agrajes was ailing, and moreover did not have such equipment as to be able to damage the huge fleet of the king. And those inside lacking food, a pact was initiated between them that the king should set free all the prisoners, and that Don Galvanes should do the same with those that he held. And that the town and castle of the Boiling Lake be surrendered to the king, and that they should have a truce for two years. And although this was to the advantage of the king, in view of his great security he would not have been willing to agree if he had not had letters from the Count of Argamonte, his uncle, who had remained in the land, to the effect that all the kings of the islands were rising against him on seeing him engaged in that war, and that they were taking as chief and leader King Aravigo, lord of the islands of Landas, who was the most powerful among them; and that all this Arcalaus the Enchanter had plotted, for he in person had gone through all those islands inciting them to rebel and uniting them by assuring them that they would not encounter any resistance and that they would be able to divide among themselves that kingdom of Great Britain; hence Count Argamonte kept counseling the king to leave everything and return to his kingdom.

This news was the cause of bringing the king to the agreement that he of his own free will would not have desired, for he had wanted to take them all. So the agreement having been made, the king accompanied by many nobles went to the town, whose gates he found open, and from there to the castle. And Don Galvanes came out, and those knights who were with him, and Madasima with tears falling down her beautiful cheeks; and Don Galvanes came up to the king and gave him the keys and said: "Sire, do with this whatever be your will."

The king took them and gave them to Brandoyvas. Galaor approached him and said to him: "Sire, moderation and mercy, for it is needed; and if I have served you, remember it at this hour."

"Don Galaor," said the king, "if I were to consider the services that you have done me, a suitable reward would not be found, even if I were worth a thousand times more than I am; and what I shall do here will not be counted a part of what I owe you."

Then he said: "Don Galvanes, this which by force against my will you took from me, and by force I have won back again, I desire of my own free will, on account of your worth and the excellence of Madasima, and because of Don Galaor, who insistently begs me, that it be yours, it remaining under my sovereignty and you in my service; and those who be your descendants shall have it as theirs."

"Sire," said Don Galvanes, "since my ill fortune has not afforded me the opportunity to acquire it in the way that my heart desired, as one who has fulfilled his commitments without being in any way remiss, I receive it as a boon, under the condition that as long as I hold it I be your vassal; and if my heart should be otherwise inclined, that by turning it back to you, I be free to do whatever I desire."

Then the knights of the king who were there kissed his hands in token of fealty for what he had done, and Don Galvanes and Madasima as his vassals.

The war having been ended, King Lisuarte decided to return at once to his kingdom, and so he did; for after resting there for two weeks, during which time he, as well as the others who were wounded, were restored to health, taking with him Don Galvanes, and of the others those who wished to go with him, he embarked with his fleet. And sailing over the sea, he made port in his own land, where he found news of those seven kings who were coming against him. And although he considered it a serious matter, he did not let his own men know that; rather, he gave the impression that he deemed it unimportant. And leaving the sea, he went to where the queen was, by whom he was received with that true love which she had for him. And there, on verifying the news that those kings were coming, while not ceasing to disport and enjoy himself with the queen and his daughter, and with his knights, he prepared the things needed to resist that danger.

CHAPTER LXVIII

In which is related how, after Amadis and Don Bruneo remained in Gaul, Don Bruneo was very happy and Amadis sad; and how Don Bruneo decided to leave Amadis and to go in search of adventures. And Amadis and his father, King Perion, and Florestan decided to go and aid King Lisuarte.

When King Cildadan and Don Galaor left Gaul, Amadis and Don Bruneo of Bonamar remained there. But although they had a sincere affection for each other, they were very different in their lives, for Don Bruneo, being there where his lady Melicia was and talking with her, had no thought of anything else; but since Amadis was far away from his lady Oriana without any hope of being able to see her, everything at hand produced in him only great sadness and loneliness. And so it happened that one day while riding along the seashore with only Gandalin for company, he climbed to the summit of some crags to ascertain whether from there he would see any ships coming from Great Britain whereby he might obtain news of that land where his lady was. And after he had been there a short while, he saw a boat coming from the desired direction; and when it reached the harbor, he said to Gandalin: "Go and find out news from those who come there, and memorize it carefully, so that you may be able to tell it to me."

And he did this more in order to daydream of his lady, for which Gandalin was always a hindrance, than for any other reason. And when Gandalin left him he dismounted from his horse, and tying it to some tree branches, he seated himself up on a pinnacle in order the better to see Great Britain; and meanwhile, having all that so far removed and so without hope of recovery, bringing to mind the extreme delights and pleasures that he had had in the presence of his lady in that land where he did everything at her command, he was plunged into such deep sorrow that he never removed his gaze from that land, while shedding copious tears.

Gandalin went to the ship, and watching those who came in it, he saw among them Durin, brother of the maid of Denmark, and he went down quickly and called him aside; and they embraced each other fondly as men who had a deep regard for each other; and taking Durin with him, Gandalin brought him to Amadis. And on coming near where he was, they saw a diabolical figure of gigantic proportions that had its back to them, and was brandishing a javelin and hurled it at Amadis with great force; and it passed over his head, and that blow missed because of the loud shouts that Gandalin uttered. And Amadis, emerging from his daydream, saw that huge devil hurl another javelin; but he, by jumping aside, caused it to miss the mark. And grasping his sword, he went for it to strike it; but saw it go running so swiftly that nothing could overtake it. And it reached Amadis's horse, and on mounting it, cried out: "Ah, Amadis, my enemy! I am Andandona, the giantess of the Sad Island; if this time I did not succeed in what I desired, time will not be lacking in which to avenge myself."

Amadis, who wanted to go after her on Gandalin's horse, when he saw that it was a woman, stopped and said to Gandalin: "Mount this horse, and if you could cut off the head of that she-devil, it would be very good."

Gandalin, on mounting, went as fast as he could go after her; and Amadis, when he saw Durin, went and embraced him with great joy, for he fully believed he was bringing him news of his lady. And taking him to the rock where he had been before, he asked him about his arrival. Durin gave him a missive from Oriana which was a letter of accreditation, and Amadis said to him: "Tell me at once what word they sent by you."

He said to him: "Sir, your beloved is well, and sends you her best regards, and begs you not to worry, but to console yourself as she does until God brings other times. And she wants you to know that she has given birth to a son, which my sister and I took to Dalasta, the abbess of Miraflores, that she might rear it as the son of my sister,"—but he did not tell him how they lost it;—"and she entreats you, because of that great love that she has for you, not to leave this land until you have her command to do so."

Amadis was happy to hear from his lady and about the child, but that command that he remain there did not please him, for his honor would thereby be tarnished because of what people would say about him; but however that might be, he would not disregard her command.

And after being there a while ascertaining news from Durin, he saw Gandalin coming, who had gone after that she-devil, and he was leading Amadis's horse with Andandona's head tied to the breast strap by its long, gray hair, a sight which afforded Amadis and Durin great pleasure. And he asked him how he had killed her, and he said that while he was pursuing her, and she was endeavoring to dismount from the horse on which she was riding, in order to get into a boat that she had concealed under branches, in her haste she caused the horse to rear up, fall over backwards, and pinion her underneath, so that it crushed her.

"And I came up and ran over her, so that she fell outstretched on the ground, and then I cut off her head."

Amadis immediately mounted his horse, went off to the town, and ordered Andandona's head taken to Don Bruneo so that he might see it; and he said to Durin: "My friend, go to my lady and tell her that I kiss her hands for the letter that she sent me and for the message from her that you gave me, and that I beg her as a favor to have pity on my honor by not permitting me to dally here very long, for I must not disregard her command, because those who see me in such idleness, not knowing the cause of it, will attribute it to cowardice and timidity. And since a reputation for valor is achieved with great difficulty, and with slight forgetfulness and a brief interval of time may be damaged, if that great glory and fame (that up till now I have tried to win by remembering her and with her favor), I permitted to be greatly obscured, since all men naturally are more inclined with their evil tongues to injure what is good than to advocate, very quickly I would be in such discredit and dishonor that death itself would not be equal to it."

With this Durin returned to where he had come from.

And Don Bruneo of Bonamar — since he was now well improved from his body wound, and in that of the spirit even more cruelly wounded, as one who was seeing his lady Melicia frequently, which caused his heart to be set aflame with greater suffering on reflecting that his heart's desire could not be obtained without his making a great effort and incurring greater danger by performing such deeds that he be desired and loved for his great valor by a lady of such high degree — decided to withdraw from that great delight in order to pursue what he might achieve of what he most desired. And being ready to bear arms, when out hunting with Amadis, who had no other life but hunting, he said to him: "Sir, my age and the little honor that I have won constrain me to leave this very restful life and to proceed to another wherein with more praise and prestige I may be exalted. And if you are inclined to seek adventure, I shall wait for you; and if not, I ask your leave, for tomorrow I wish to be on my way."

Amadis, on hearing this, was tormented by great anguish, for he very ardently desired to fare forth, and was not able to do so because of the prohibition by his lady; and he said: "Don Bruneo, I should like to be in your company, because great honor could come to me from it; but the command of the king my father forbids my doing so, for he tells me that he needs me in order to take care of a few things in his kingdom; so for the present I cannot do anything but commend you to God's protection."

After they returned to the town that night, Don Bruneo talked with Melicia, and on being assured by her that if it were the wish of the king her father and that of the queen, she would be glad to marry him, he said good-bye to her. And so he took leave of the king and the queen, and assuring them of his deep gratitude for their kindness to him and pledging that he would always be at their service, he went to bed. And at dawn, after hearing mass, armed and mounted, being escorted on his way by the king and Amadis, he bade farewell to them with great humility and went on his journey to wherever fortune guided him; on which journey he performed many and rare feats at arms, which it would take too long to relate. But now no more will be told about him until the proper time.

Amadis remained in Gaul as you hear, where he dwelt thirteen months and a half, (during the period that the castle of the Boiling Lake was under siege by King Lisuarte,) going hunting for both small and big game, for he was more inclined to this than to anything else; and meanwhile his great fame and prowess became so beclouded and so scorned by all while praising the other knights who sought adventures at arms, that they heaped curses upon him, saying he had abandoned while in his prime what God had bestowed on him so surpassingly over all others. Especially was he censured by the matrons and maidens who came to him with grievous and outrageous wrongs for him to provide a remedy; and not finding it as they were accustomed to do, they went irately about, proclaiming the discredit of his honor. And although all or most of this came to his ears, whence he considered it his great misfortune, neither on that account nor because of anything else more cogent would he dare disregard or break the commandment of his lady. Thus he was, at this aforementioned time that you hear, defamed and reviled by all, hoping that his lady would command him, until King Lisuarte, learning through accurate reports that King Aravigo and the other six kings were already with all their troops on Leonida Island for the purpose of crossing over to Great Britain, and Arcalaus the Enchanter, who was goading them very zealously, assuring them that becoming masters of that kingdom was only a matter of going over to it, and many other things in order to induce them not to take any other measures, King Lisuarte — we repeat — readied as many troops as he could to resist them. And although he, with his stout heart and great prudence, indicated he had but little concern about that attack, the queen did not do so; instead with great anguish she affirmed to everyone the great loss the king had sustained in losing Amadis and his relatives; for if they were there, she would deem unimportant what that body of men could do.

But those knights who were routed on the Island of Mongaza, although they did not desire the welfare of the king, on seeing Don Galaor on his side, and Don Brian of Monjaste (who by order of King Ladasan of Spain was coming with two thousand knights whom he sent to aid Lisuarte — knights of whom Don Brian was to be the leader and was to serve the king), and

Don Galvanes, who was Lisuarte's vassal, agreed to be of assistance to him in that battle, from which great danger at arms was expected. And those who found themselves there were Don Cuadragante and Listoran of the White Tower and Ymosil of Burgundy, and Madancil of the Bridge of Silver, and others, companions of theirs who remained there out of regard for them. All worked zealously to prepare their arms and horses and what else was necessary, expecting that when those kings left that island, King Lisuarte would move out against them.

Mabilia spoke one day with Oriana, saying that it was careless at such a time not to consider what Amadis ought to do; for if by chance he went against her father, the danger for some of them could increase; for if her father's side were vanquished, in addition to the great harm that would come to her by losing the land that was to be hers, in accordance with his courage it was certain that the king would be killed; and similarly if the side on which Amadis was were overcome. Oriana, recognizing that she was speaking the truth, agreed to take the step of writing to Amadis not to go into that battle against her father, but that he could go anywhere else he liked, or stay in Gaul if he pleased. This letter of Oriana's was put in another from Mabilia and carried by a maid who had come to the court with gifts from Queen Elisena to Oriana and Mabilia; which maid having taken leave of them, on crossing over to Gaul, gave the letter to Amadis, who from the message, after having read it, was so happy that certainly he could not be more so, like a man who seemed to be emerging from darkness into the light. But he was placed in great concern by not being able to decide what he would do, for of his own volition he had no desire to be in battle on the side of King Lisuarte, and he could not go against him, because his lady forbade him; thus he was bewildered without knowing what to do. And then he went to the king his father with a more cheerful mien than he had had there until then, and while talking they both sat down in the shade of some elms near the seashore. And there they talked over things, and chiefly the news that they had heard from Great Britain concerning the uprising against King Lisuarte of those kings with such huge companies.

Then, while King Perion and Amadis were occupied as you hear, they saw coming a knight on a weary, exhausted horse, and his armor, which a squire was carrying, slashed in many places, so that its device did not show whose it was and the coat of mail rent and in bad condition, from which there was little protection. The knight was tall and appeared very well armed. They arose where they were and went to receive him to do him all honor as a knight who was seeking adventures. And being closer, Amadis recognized him, for he was his brother Don Florestan, and he said to the king: "Sire, there you see the best knight that I know with the exception of Don Galaor, and know you that Don Florestan is your son."

The king was very happy, for he had never seen him, and knew about his great fame, and walked faster than before; but Don Florestan, having arrived, dismounted and kneeling, sought to kiss the king's foot, but the king raised him up and gave him his hand, and kissed him on the mouth. Then they took him with them to the palace, and had him disarm and wash his face and hands, and Amadis had him put on some of his own clothes, very fine and well made, that had not been worn until then; and as he was large of body, well formed and handsome of countenance, his appearance was so prepossessing that there were few who looked as gallant as he. So they took him to the queen, and by her and by her daughter Melicia, he was welcomed with as much affection as either of his brothers would have been, for he was held in no less esteem in view of the great feats at arms which he had accomplished, which were known. And while they were speaking with him about some of them, he responded like a discreet and well-bred knight; and they asked him, since he came from Great Britain, about that matter of the kings of the islands and their forces. Don Florestan said to them: "That I know for certain; and believe me, lords and ladies, the strength of those kings is so great and they possess such unusually strong forces that I think that King Lisuarte will not be able to defend himself or his land — an inability which ought not to cause us much sorrow, in view of past events."

"Son Don Florestan," said the king, "I deem King Lisuarte, according to what I am told about him, to be possessed of such courage as well as the other good qualities which a king ought to have that he will emerge from this attack with the honor with which he has emerged from the others; and even though the opposite were true, it should not give us pleasure, because no king ought to be happy with the destruction of another king, unless he himself should destroy him for legitimate reasons that obliged him to do so."

Thus they remained for a while; then the king retired to his chamber, and Amadis and Don Florestan to theirs. And when they were alone, Florestan said: "Sir, I have come seeking you to tell you a thing I have heard everywhere that I have gone, for which my heart feels great sorrow; and may it not irk you to hear it."

"Brother," said Amadis, "I shall be pleased to hear everything said by you, and if it is such that it ought to be corrected, I shall do so with your counsel."

Don Florestan said: "Believe me, sir, everybody is speaking ill of you, discrediting your honor, thinking that unjustifiably you have ceased to bear arms and abandoned that for which you were born outstandingly good among all."

Amadis said to him laughing: "They are thinking of me what they should not, and from now on it will be done otherwise, and they will speak of it otherwise."

That day they spent with great happiness because of the arrival of that knight, whom many people came to see and to honor. Night having come, they retired to luxurious beds; and Amadis could not sleep, thinking about two things: the one, to do so much that year at arms that what they had said of him would be purged with the opposite; the other: what would he do in that battle that was expected? For according to its magnitude, he could not excuse himself for not being in it without great shame, since his lady prohibited his being against King Lisuarte and reason prohibited his going to his assistance, for the king had been ungrateful to him and had mistreated those of his lineage. But finally he decided to be in the battle in aid of King Lisuarte for two reasons: the one, because his troops were much fewer than the foes'; and the other because if the king were vanquished, the land that was to be his lady Oriana's would be lost.

The next morning Amadis took with him Florestan and went to the chamber of the king his father, and ordering everyone to leave, he said to him: "Sire, I did not sleep last night because I was thinking about this battle that is looming between those kings of the islands and King Lisuarte; for as this will be an outstanding event, all those who bear arms should be in such a great affair as it will be, on one side or on the other. And since I have been such a long time without exercising my person and thereby I have gained such ill fame as you, brother, are aware, finally because of my concern I have decided to participate in the battle, and on the side of King Lisuarte, not out of any love for him, but for two reasons that you shall now hear: the first, on account of his having fewer troops, for which reason all good men should lend aid; the second, because my thought is to die there, or do more than I would anywhere else I might be. And if I were on the opposite side from King Lisuarte, Galaor is on his side, and Don Cuadragante, and Brian de Monjaste, so that each one of these, according to his excellence, will have this same thought; and not being able to avoid meeting with me, you see that from this can result nothing but their death or mine. But my coming will be so concealed that I will not be recognized if I can help it."

The king said to him: "Son, I am fond of good men, and as I know this king of whom you speak to be one of them, my desire has always been prepared to honor him and help him as best I could; and if I am now withdrawn from it, it has been because of these differences which he has had with you and your friends. And since your intention is such, I also wish to be at his service and to see the things that will be done there. I regret that the business is so immediate that I shall not be able to bring the troops that I would like; but with those that I can raise, we shall go."

This having been heard by Don Florestan, he remained pensive for a while, and then said: "Sirs, on calling to mind the cruelty of that king and how he would have left us to die on the field if it had not been for Don Galaor, and the enmity he has for us without cause, there is no reason in the world why my heart should be disposed to aid him. But two things that occur to me at present cause my intention to be changed. The one is my love for you, sirs, whom I must serve and aid. And the other is that at the time that Don Galvanes made a compact with him, when the Island of Mongaza was turned over to him, we established a truce for two years; therefore, it is necessary that I serve him unwillingly. And I wish to go in your company, for my spirit would always be in great anguish if such a battle should take place without my being in it on one side or the other."

Amadis was very happy about how everything was being done according to his desire, and he said to the king: "Sire, you alone, and we who will serve you, should be accounted the equivalent of many soldiers. It only remains to plan how we may go secretly, and with distinctive and recognizable arms that may guide us so that we may be able to succor each other; for if you took more troops it would be impossible for our departure to be secret."

"Since that is your opinion," said the king, "let us go to my armory and take from it the most rare and distinctive arms that we find there."

Then, on leaving the chamber, they went into a yard where there were some trees; and while they were seated under them, they saw coming a maiden richly clad on a very beautiful palfrey, and three squires with her, and a pack horse with a pack on it. And she came up to the king after the squires helped her dismount, and she greeted them. And the king received her very well and said to her: "Maiden, do you seek the queen?"

"No," said she, "only you and those two knights, and I come on behalf of the lady of the Undiscovered Island, and I bring you here some gifts that she sends you; therefore order all the people to withdraw and I shall show them to you."

The king ordered them to retire. The maiden had her squires unfasten the pack that the palfrey was carrying, and she took out of it three shields, their fields of silver, with serpents in gold so artfully superimposed on it that they seemed alive, and their borders were of fine gold set with precious stones. And then she took out three knightly devices of the same design as the shields and three helmets, each different, one being white, another purple, and the third golden. The white one with one shield and its device she gave to King Perion, the purple one to Don Florestan, and the golden one with what went with it to Amadis. And she said to him: "Sir Amadis, my lady sends you these arms, and tells you to perform better with them than you have done since you entered this land."

Amadis was fearful that she would disclose the cause of it and said: "Damsel, tell your mistress that I esteem more highly that advice that she gives me than the arms, although they are rich and beautiful, and that I shall do with all my might as she commands."

The maiden said: "Sirs, my lady sends you these arms so that by means of them you may recognize and aid each other wherever it may be necessary."

"How did your lady find out," said the king, "that we would be in the battle, for even we do not know it?"

"I do not know," said the maiden, "except that she told me that at this hour I would find you together in this place, and that here I should give you the arms."

The king ordered that she be dined and received with high honor. The maiden, as soon as she had eaten, left at once for Great Britain, to which she had been ordered to go.

Amadis, when he saw such an equipment of arms, was in a hurry to depart, fearing that the battle would take place without his being in it, and this having been recognized by the king his father, the latter ordered that a ship be prepared secretly at once; in which with the pretext of going hunting, having boarded it at midnight one night, without any delay they crossed over to Great Britain, landing where they had previously found out that the seven kings had put into port. And they went into a forest amid thick underbrush, where their men set up a tent for them, and from there they sent a squire to find out what the seven kings were doing, in what location they were, and to strive to ascertain on what day the battle would take place. And likewise they sent a letter to the armed camp of King Lisuarte for Don Galaor, as though they were sending it to him from Gaul, and instructed this messenger to tell him verbally that all three of them were remaining in Gaul, and that they earnestly besought him to let them know about the condition of his health after he participated in the battle. This they did in order to remain more disguised.

The squire returned late next day, and told them that the troops of the kings were countless and that among them there were obvious foreigners who spoke diverse tongues, and that they had under siege a castle belonging to some maidens, and that although the castle was very strong, the maidens were suffering extreme hardship according to what he had heard; and that going through the army camp he had seen Arcalaus the Enchanter, who was talking with two kings and saying that it was important to have the battle at the end of six days, because rations would be hard to obtain for so many troops.

So they were very comfortable in that shelter, and with great enjoyment they were killing with bow and arrow the birds that came to drink at a spring that they had nearby, and even some deer; and on the fourth day, the other messenger arrived, and told them: "Sirs, I leave Don Galaor in good health and very courageous, so much so that all take heart from him. And when I told him your message and that all three of you were staying in Gaul together, the tears came to his eyes, and sighing, he said: 'Oh, Lord, if only it had been your pleasure that they should be together in this battle, on the side of the king as they used to be, I would have lost all fear!' And he told me that if he should come out of the battle alive, he would let you know at once about himself and about all that had happened."

"May God protect him," said they, "and now tell us about the troops of King Lisuarte."

"Sirs," said he, "he brings a very good company, with knights very distinguished and renowned, but compared to that of the enemy, it is said to be very small. And the king will be in sight of his enemies within these next two days in order to succor the maidens who are besieged."

And so it was, for King Lisuarte came with his troops and took a position on a hill a half league from the meadow where his enemies were, where they could see one another, but the troops of the seven kings were fully twice as many in number. There King Lisuarte remained that night preparing all his arms and horses in order to engage them in battle the next day. Now know you that the six kings and other noble lords paid homage that night to King Aravigo because they considered him their leader in that engagement and themselves to be guided by his command. And he swore to them not to take a larger share of that kingdom than any of the rest of them, that he wanted only honor for himself. And immediately they had all their troops cross a river that was between them and King Lisuarte; so that they took a position very near to him.

The next morning they all armed, and there stood before King Aravigo such a large number of troops so well armed that they considered their adversaries as nothing. And they said that since the king dared to engage them in battle, Great Britain was theirs. King Aravigo made nine divisions of the troops, each one of a thousand knights, but in his own he had fifteen hundred; and he gave them to the kings and other knights, and stationed them in close formation.

King Lisuarte ordered Don Grumedan and Don Galaor and Don Cuadragante and Angriote de Estravaus to distribute his troops and station them on the field in the formation in which they were to fight, for these men knew a great deal about all types of warfare. And then he came down the slope of the hill to station himself on the plain; and as it was at sunrise the sun was reflected on the armor, and those wearing it appeared so fine and so gallant that those enemies of theirs, who previously had held them in slight esteem, judged them differently. Those knights that I am telling you about made of the troops five divisions. And Don Brian de Monjaste had the first with one thousand knights from Spain who were his guard and whom his father had sent to King Lisuarte. And King Cildadan had the second with his own troops and with others that were given him. Don Galvanes and Agrajes, his nephew, had the third. Agrajes had come there out of love for him, and for his friends who were there, more than to serve the king. In the fourth went Giontes, nephew of the king, with plenty of good knights. King Lisuarte led the fourth, in which there were two thousand knights, and he requested and commanded Don Galaor and Don Cuadragante and Angriote de Estravaus, and Gavarte of the Fearful Valley and Grimon the Valiant to protect and look out for him. And for this reason he did not give them command of troops. Just as you hear, with this disposition they moved on the field very slowly against each other. But at this time there had already arrived on the plain King Perion and his sons Amadis and Florestan on their beautiful horses and with the arms of the serpent device, which flashed brightly in the sun; and they came straight ahead to place themselves between the two armies, brandishing their lances tipped with iron heads so spotless that they shone like stars; and the father was riding between his sons. They were the object of intense scrutiny by both armies, and gladly would each have had them on its side, but no one knew whom they intended to help, or recognized them. And they when they saw the division of Brian de Monjaste going to engage the enemy, spurred their horses and drew up near Brian's standard. And at once they turned against King Targadan, who was coming toward Brian. Don Brian was happy with their aid, but did not recognize them; and when they saw it was time, they all three went and attacked the division of that King Targadan so harshly that they aroused great fear in everyone. In that encounter King Perion struck that king so hard that he knocked him to the ground and a part of the iron lance head pierced his breast. Amadis struck Abdasian the Fierce, for he didn't lend him any arms, and the lance penetrated him on one side and came out the other, and he fell like a dead man. Don Florestan knocked Carduel down to the feet of his horse and the saddle on top of him. These three, as the most distinguished of that division, had come forward to engage in combat with those of the serpents. And immediately the latter grasped their swords, and passed through that first division, unhorsing as many as they found in front of them; and attacked the opposing second division. And when they saw themselves thus in the midst of both divisions, there you would have seen those great and marvelous deeds of theirs; for with the swords they fought so well that from neither side was there a man who approached them, and they had under their horses' hooves more than ten knights that they had overthrown. But finally, when their foes saw they were only three, at once they were raining mighty blows on them from all sides, so that there was really needed the help of Don Brian de Monjaste, who came up at once with his Spaniards, who were strong troops and well mounted. And they came in among them with such force unhorsing and slaying, and some of them dying themselves and falling to the ground, that those of the serpent device were rescued and their foes so defied that perforce those two divisions gave way until making contact with the third. And there was a very great melee and great danger to all, and many knights from both sides died. But what King Perion and his sons did, words are inadequate to describe. The disorder was so great that King Aravigo feared that his own troops, which had retreated, would cause the others to flee; and he shouted to Arcalaus to have all the divisions move up, and ordered that they break through in a sudden charge. And thus it was done, for all broke through together, and King Aravigo with them; but it was not long before the same was done by King Lisuarte. So the battalions were all mingled, and the blows were so many, and the shouting and uproar of the knights, that the earth trembled and the valleys kept resounding.

At this time King Perion, who was carrying on very bravely at the front, plunged so brashly among them that he might have lost his life; but immediately he was rescued by his sons, for many of those who were attacking him were killed by them, and the maidens from the tower shouted: "Bravo, knights, for the one with the white helmet fights the best!"

But during this supporting action the horse of Amadis was killed, and it fell with him in the thick of the fight, and those of his father and brother were badly wounded. And as they saw him on foot in such great danger, they dismounted and joined him. There many men charged to kill them, and others to help them; but they were in great danger, for if it had not been for the hard, cruel blows with which they attacked, so that their enemies dared not approach them, they would have been killed. And as King Lisuarte went charging up and down through the battalions with those six companions of his that you have already heard about, he saw those of the serpent device in such great danger, and said to Don Galaor and the others: "Now my good friends, show your prowess: let us rescue those who are helping us so well."

"Now, at them!" said Don Galaor.

Then they spurred their horses and went into the midst of that great press until they reached the standard of King Aravigo, who was shouting encouraging words to his own men. And King Lisuarte was charging so fiercely with that very good sword of his in his hand, and was striking so many and such deadly blows, that all were frightened on seeing him, and his protectors could scarcely keep up with him. And however much they attacked him, they could not resist strongly enough to keep him from reaching the standard and snatching it by force from the hands of the one who was holding it. And throwing it at the feet of the horses, he shouted: "Clarence, Clarence, I am King Lisuarte!" For this was his surname.

He accomplished so much and endured so long among his enemies that they killed his horse and it fell, from which fall he was quite shaken up, so that those who were protecting him could not lift him up on another horse. But immediately there arrived Angriote and Antimon the Valiant and Landin de Fajarque; and dismounting they put him on Angriote's horse, in spite of his enemies, with the help of those who were protecting him. And although he was badly wounded and shaken up, he did not leave there until Antimon and Landin de Fajarque mounted and brought Angriote another horse from those that the king had ordered circulated in the battle in order to be aided by them.

At the hour that this happened, the whole onus of the battle and the attack was on Don Galaor and Cuadragante, and there they demonstrated very well their great valor in withstanding and striking deadly blows; and know you that if it had not been for them, who with their mighty effort held the troops, King Lisuarte and those who were with him, when they were on foot, would have seen themselves in great danger; and the maidens of the tower were shouting that those two knights of the flowered device were getting the best of it. But not on that account could the troops of King Aravigo be prevented at that time from gaining the upper hand. And they were fast gaining ground; and the principal reason for it was that there entered fresh into the fray two knights of such great prowess at arms and so valiant that with them they believed they would overcome their enemies, because they thought that on the side of King Lisuarte there was no knight who could hold the field against them. One was named Brontaxar de Anfania and the other Argomades of the Deep Island. The latter bore green arms adorned with white doves, and Brontaxar, arms with enamel work of gold and crimson; and when they went into the battle they appeared so tall that their helmets and their shoulders towered above all the others, and as long as their lances lasted, not a knight remained in his saddle; and when they were broken, they grasped their great, massive swords. What shall I say to you? Such blows they delivered with them that already they were finding almost no one to attack, so severely were they dealing out punishment to everyone with them. And so they went forward, clearing the field of everyone, and the maidens of the tower were saying: "Knights, don't flee, for they are men, not devils."

But their men shouted, saying: "King Lisuarte is defeated."

When the king heard this, he began to encourage his own men, saying: "Here I shall remain either dead or victor, so that the sovereignty of Great Britain be not lost."

The large majority rallied to him, for it was very necessary. Amadis had taken now another very good, fresh horse, and was waiting for his father to mount; and when he heard those loud shouts saying that King Lisuarte was defeated, he said to Don Florestan, who was mounted: "What is this, or why do those contemptible people cry out?"

He said to him: "Don't you perceive those two strongest and most valiant knights ever seen, who lay low and destroy all whom they find before them, and have not even appeared in this battle until now, and with their strength they are succeeding in winning back the field for the troops on their side?"

Amadis turned his head, and saw Brontaxar de Anfania coming towards where he was, attacking and overthrowing knights with his sword; and sometimes he let it hang from a chain with which he had it fastened, and with his arms and hands was seizing the knights that he overtook so that none remained in the saddle and all moved away from him fleeing.

"Holy Mary, save us!" said Amadis. "What can this be?"

Then he took a sturdy lance that the squire who gave him the horse was holding, and remembering Oriana at that hour, and what great harm she would receive if her father should lose, he stood up in his saddle and said to Don Florestan: "Protect our father."

And this time Brontaxar came up closer and saw how Amadis was going straight toward him, and how he had the golden helmet; and because of the reports of the great things that he had been told about him before he himself entered the battle, he went forward with great fury, in a frenzy to meet him. And then he took a very thick lance, and said in a loud voice: "Now you will see a beautiful stroke if that man with the helmet of gold dares to await me."

And he spurred his horse, with his lance under his armpit, and went toward him; and Amadis, who was now in motion, likewise; and they struck each other with their lances on their shields, which were pierced at once and the lances broken; and they collided with each other with their horses' bodies so heavily that it seemed to each one that he had hit a hard rock. And Brontaxar was so dizzy that he could not hold himself on the horse, and he fell to the ground as if he were dead; and that great weight of his caused his whole body to come down on one foot, and he broke his ankle; and he bore a piece of the lance thrust through his shield, although it was strong. The horse of Amadis fell back a good four yards and was about to drop. And Amadis was so befuddled that he could not spur it or grasp his sword to defend himself from those who were attacking him. But King Perion who was already on horseback and saw the tall knight and the very hard clash that Amadis had had with him, was quite frightened and said: "Lord God, protect that knight. Now, son Florestan, let us aid him."

Then they came up so fiercely that it was wonderful to see them, and they plunged into the midst of all, attacking and unhorsing until they reached Amadis; and the king said to him: "What is this, knight? Take courage, take courage, for here am I."

Amadis recognized the voice of his father, although he was not completely conscious, and he grasped his sword and saw that many were attacking his father and his brother, and he began to strike right and left, although not with much force. And here they might have incurred great risk because the opposing troops were very courageous, and those of King Lisuarte had lost much ground and many were attacking to kill them, and very few in their defense. But at that time there hastened thither Agrajes and Don Galvanes and Brian de Monjaste, who were coming in great haste to encounter Brontaxar de Anfania, who was wreaking all the havoc you have already heard about; and they saw the three knights of the serpents in such danger. They came to their assistance as men whose hearts never failed them in any dangerous situation; and with their arrival many of the foe were killed and unhorsed, so that those with the arms of the serpent device were enabled to attack the enemy with less danger to themselves.

Amadis, who was now in full possession of his faculties, looked to the left and saw King Lisuarte accompanied by some knights who were awaiting King Aravigo, who was coming against him with a great force of troops, and Argomades in front of all, and two nephews of King Aravigo, valiant knights, and Aravigo himself shouting, encouraging his men, because he was hearing from the tower: "He of the gold helmet killed the tall devil."

Then he said: "Knights, let us help the king, for it is necessary."

Then they all went together and plunged into the crush of troops until arriving where King Lisuarte was; who when he saw the three knights of the serpent device near him, was so much encouraged, because he saw that he of the golden helmet had killed with one blow that very valiant Brontaxar de Anfania. And then he moved toward King Aravigo, who was coming close to him, and toward Argomades, who was coming with his sword in hand, brandishing it to strike King Lisuarte. He stopped in front of him of the gold helmet and his combat was ended by the first blow: he of the gold helmet, as soon as he saw the huge sword coming at him, raised his shield and received the blow, and his sword came down through the boss a good palm's length, and pierced the helmet to the depth of three fingers so that he narrowly missed killing him. And Amadis struck him on the left shoulder such a blow that he cut the coat of mail that was of thick mesh, and cut flesh and the bones down to the side in such a way that Argomades' arm with part of his shoulder was dangling from his body. This was the mightiest sword blow that was struck in the battle. Argomades began to flee like a paralyzed man who did not know what he was doing, and his horse returned him to where he had come from. And those in the tower were shouting: "He of the golden helmet frightens the doves."

And one of those nephews of King Aravigo, Ancidel by name, charged at Amadis and struck a blow with his sword on the face of his horse that cut it completely across, and the horse fell dead on the ground. Don Florestan when he saw this let himself go at him, as he was preening himself, and struck him on top of the helmet such a blow that he knocked him over on the neck of his horse; and Florestan seized him by the helmet so forcibly that on snatching it from his head he struck him down at Amadis's feet. And Don Florestan was wounded in the side by the point of Ancidel's sword.

At this hour King Lisuarte and King Aravigo were joined in battle, and their troops with each other, so that there was a hard and cruel battle between them, and they all had much to do to defend themselves from each other and to aid those who were falling dead and wounded.

Durin, Oriana's page, who had come there to bring news of the battle, was on one of the horses that King Lisuarte had ordered brought into the battle for rescuing the knights who needed them; and when he saw him of the gold helmet on the ground, he said to the other pages who were on horseback: "I wish to help that good knight with this horse, for I cannot render the king any better service."

And he plunged at once at great risk into the melee where the fewest troops were, and came up to him and said: "I do not know who you are, but on account of what I have seen, I bring you this horse."

He took it and mounted, and said to him in an undertone: "Ah, friend Durin, this is not the first service you have rendered me!"

Durin seized him by the arm, and said: "I shall not let you go until you tell me who you are."

And he bent down as low as he could, and said to him: "I am Amadis, and do not let anyone know it, except her whom you know."

And at once he went where he saw the greatest melee, performing rare and marvelous feats at arms just as he would have done if his lady had been present; for he considered that she was, since that one was there who would know very well how to tell her about it.

King Lisuarte, who was fighting with King Aravigo, struck him with his good sword three such blows that the latter didn't dare linger with him any longer; for as Lisuarte did not know that his adversary was the head and chief of his enemies, he did not use all his strength in striking him, and King Aravigo withdrew behind his men, cursing Arcalaus the Enchanter, who had caused him to come to that land by encouraging him to believe that he would win it.

Don Galaor exchanged blows with Sarmadan, a valiant knight; and since his arm was tired from the blows that he had given, and his sword was not cutting, he seized him in his very strong embrace, and pulling him from his saddle, knocked him to the ground, and he fell on his neck so that he was killed instantly.

And I say to you concerning Amadis, that remembering at that hour the wasted time when he was in Gaul, and how his honor was so vilified and derogated, and that that situation could only be repaired with the opposite, he performed such deeds that he no longer found anyone who dared face him; and there stood their ground with him his father and Don Florestan, and Agrajes and Don Galvanes, and Brian de Monjaste, and Norandel and Guilan the Pensive; and also King Lisuarte, who showed himself very valiant at that time. So they unhorsed so many of the foe, and so hemmed them in and frightened them, that not being able to stand it and having seen King Aravigo go fleeing wounded, abandoning the battle field, the enemy were put to flight, trying to seek refuge in the ships, and some in the hills which were nearby. But King Lisuarte and his men kept on attacking and killing them very cruelly, and those with the device of the serpent in front of all, for they did not leave them. And the majority took refuge in a ship with King Aravigo and in other ships that they were able to reach. But many died in the water and others were taken prisoners.

At this time when the battle was won, King Lisuarte turned back to the tents of his enemies, and there he lodged that night with great joy for the victory that God had given him. But the knights with the serpent device, when they saw that the field was abandoned, and that no defense remained, turned aside, all three of them, from the road along which they thought the king would return, and went under some trees where they found a spring. And there they dismounted and drank of the water, as did their horses; for they needed it very much in view of their great exertions of that day. And as they were about to mount in order to go away, they saw a squire coming on a hackney; and putting on their helmets so that they might not be recognized, they cautiously called out to him. The squire hesitated, thinking them to be of the enemies; but when he saw the device of the serpent, he came up to them without hesitation. And Amadis said to him: "Good squire, tell the king our message, if you please."

"Say whatever you please," said he, "for I shall tell it to him."

"Then say to him," said he, "that we knights of the arms with the serpent device, who were in his battle, beg him as a favor not to blame us for not seeing him, for it is necessary for us to travel very far from here to a foreign land, and to place ourselves at the mercy of one who we do not believe will have any mercy on us; and that we beg that the share of the booty that he would give to us, he order given to the maidens of the tower for the harm that was done them. And take to him this horse, that I accepted from a page of his in the battle, for we do not want from him any other reward except this which we mention."

The squire took the horse and left them, and went to the king in order to tell him the message. And they mounted, and traveled until they reached their shelter which they had in the forest; and after being disarmed and their faces and hands cleansed of blood and dust, and after attending to their wounds as best they could, they ate their supper, which they had very well cooked; and they lay down on their beds, in which very restfully they slept that night.

King Lisuarte, when he had returned to the tents of his enemies, the latter being already completely destroyed, asked about the three knights of the device of the serpents, but did not find anyone who could tell him anything except that they saw them going as fast as they could toward the forest. The king said to Don Galaor: "Perchance would that one with the golden helmet be your brother Amadis? For what he did could not have been vouchsafed to anyone except him."

"Believe, sire," said Galaor, "that it is not he, for not four days have passed since I had word from him that he was in Gaul with his father and with Don Florestan, his brother."

"Holy Mary!" said the king, "Who could it be?"

"I do not know," said Don Galaor, "but whoever it may be, may God give him good fortune, for with great effort and danger he won honor and glory above all others."

At this juncture, the squire arrived and told the king everything that they had commanded, and the king was greatly disturbed when he told him that they were going into such danger as you have already heard; but if Amadis said it jokingly, it turned out to be quite true, as will be related later. Therefore men should always give good predictions and forecasts in their affairs. And the horse that the squire brought fell dead before the king from the severe wounds that it had.

That night Galaor and Agrajes and many others of their friends lodged in the tent of Arcalaus, which was very luxurious and beautiful. On it they found depicted in silk and embroidery the battle that he had had with Amadis and how he had enchanted him, and other things that he had done. Next day the king at once divided the spoils among all of his men, and gave a large share to the maidens of the tower; and granting permission to leave to those who wished to go to their own lands, with the others he went to one of his towns called Gadampa, where the queen and his daughter were. The joy they took in each other's company it is needless to tell, for every woman, in view of what had happened, can imagine what it would be.

CHAPTER LXIX

HOW THE KNIGHTS OF THE SERPENT DEVICE EMBARKED FOR THEIR KINGDOM OF GAUL, AND FORTUNE CAST THEM WHERE THROUGH DECEIT THEY FELL, AT GREAT DANGER TO THEIR LIVES, INTO THE HANDS OF ARCALAUS THE ENCHANTER; AND HOW, ONCE FREED FROM THERE, THEY EMBARKED, RESUMING THEIR JOURNEY; AND DON GALAOR AND NORANDEL CAME BY THE SAME ROUTE SEEKING ADVENTURES, AND WHAT HAPPENED TO THEM.

For a few days King Perion and his sons rested in that forest; and when they saw the weather to be good and favorable, they put out to sea at once in their galley, expecting to be in Gaul shortly. But it turned out otherwise for them, for that wind was quickly changed and caused the sea to become rough, so that they necessarily had to turn back to Great Britain, not to the part where they were before, but to another more remote. And the ship arrived at the end of five days of storm at the foot of a mountain that bordered on the sea; and they had their horses and arms taken off in order to travel through that land until the sea calmed down and a more favorable wind came for them, and their men put fresh water, which they had lacked, on the ship. And after they had eaten, they armed themselves and mounted, and went inland in order to find out where they had landed. And they ordered those on the ship to wait for them, and they took three squires with them; but Gandalin had not gone there because he was very well known.

Just as you hear, they went up through a valley, at the head of which they found a plain, and they had not traversed it very far before they encountered beside a spring a maiden who was watering her palfrey. She was elegantly dressed, and over her dress wore a cloak of scarlet that was fastened with buckles and grummets of gold; and with her two squires and two maids, who were bringing along her falcons and dogs with which she was hunting. And when she saw them, she recognized them at once by the device of the serpents, and proceeded to demonstrate her great delight at the sight of them; and as she drew near she bowed to them with great humility, making signs that she was mute. They greeted her, and she seemed to them very beautiful and they felt pity that she should be mute. She came up to the one with the golden helmet and embraced him, and sought to kiss his hands; and after an interval of this, she invited them by signs to be her guests that night in her castle. But they did not understand her, and she made signs to her squires to explain it to them, and so they did. They, on seeing that good will and perceiving that it was already very late, went with her trustingly; and they had not gone far before they reached a beautiful castle. Considering the maiden to be very rich, since she was the mistress of the castle, on entering it, they encountered people who received them humbly, and other matrons and maidens, who all regarded the mute maiden as their mistress. Then they took their horses, and they conducted them up to a luxurious room that was probably twenty cubits above the ground floor. And having them disarm, they brought them rich robes to put on; and after they had talked to the mute damsel and with the other maidens, they brought a supper to them and they were very well served. And the maidens went away to their quarters; but it was not long before they returned with many candles, and well-tuned instruments in order to afford them pleasure; and when it was time to sleep, they left them and went away.

In that room there were three very fine beds, that the mute maiden had ordered made up, and they placed their arms beside each bed. They lay down and slept peacefully, as men who were weary and fatigued; and although their spirits were in repose, their lives were not, in view of the dangerous snare in which they were caught, which with good reason can be likened to what goes on in this world; for know you that that room was constructed very deceptively, for all of it was held up by a column of iron made like the worm of a wine-press and enclosed in another of wood that was in the center of the room; and the room could be lowered and raised from below by cranking an iron bar, for the room did not touch any wall. Therefore, when they awoke in the morning, they were some twenty cubits below where they had been when they went into it.

We can compare this beautiful mute maiden with the world in which we live; which, appearing beautiful to us, flattering us, delighting us without mouth or tongue, lures us with many delights and pleasures; which, while we follow it without mistrust, we embrace; and forgetting the anguish and tribulations that as an asylum are being prepared for us from such delights and pleasures; after we have pursued them and indulged in them, we lie down to sleep lulled by our dreams; and when we awake, already transferred from life to death — although more rightly one ought to say from death to life, it being everlasting — we find ourselves in an abyss so far removed from that great compassion of the very high Lord, that no redemption is left for us. And if these knights had it, it was because they were still in this life; in which no one, however evil and sinful he may be, ought to lose hope of pardon, provided that by giving up evil deeds he pursue those that are in accordance with the service of that Lord who can give pardon to him.

Then, returning to the three knights, when they were awake and did not see any sign of light, and perceived that the people of the castle were walking about overhead, they were greatly surprised, and arose from their beds; and searching gropingly for the door and the windows, they found them; but when they ran their hands over them, they came in contact with the wall of the castle, so that then they knew they were victims of deceit. While they were in great dismay on seeing themselves in such danger, there appeared at a window set high in the room a huge, brawny knight with a terrifying face, and in his beard and on his head more white hair than black. And he was clad in mourning, and on his right hand he wore a glove of white cloth that extended up to his elbow; and he said in a loud voice: "May you who lie in there be poorly lodged; for commensurate with the great distress you have caused me, you will find moderation and mercy, which will be very cruel and bitter deaths; and even with this I shall not be avenged; in view of what I received from you in the battle with the false King Lisuarte. Know you that I am Arcalaus the Enchanter; if you have never seen me, now know me, for never did anyone cause me distress that I didn't take vengeance upon him, with only one exception, and I still intend to have him where you are, and to cut off his hands for this hand of mine which he cut, if I do not die beforehand."

And the maiden who was beside him said: "Good uncle, that young man who is over there is the one who wore the golden helmet."

And she extended her hand toward Amadis. When they saw that that man was Arcalaus, they were in great fear of death, and they considered it strange to see the mute maiden, who had brought them there, speak. And know you that this maiden was named Dinarda, and she was the daughter of Ardan Canileo, and was very ingenious in evil deeds. And she had come to that land in order by some scheme to have Amadis killed, and for that reason she had pretended to be mute.

Arcalaus said to them: "Knights, I shall have your heads cut off in my presence, and shall have them sent to King Aravigo as a partial recompense for your disservice to him."

And he withdrew from the window and ordered it closed; and the room remained so dark that they could not see one another. King Perion said to them: "My good sons, this situation in which we are shows us the great changes of fortune. Who would have thought that once having escaped from such a battle, where so many of us knights underwent so many dangers with such fame, with so much glory, we should be deceived in such a manner by a weak maiden without tongue and without speech? Certainly, an astonishing thing it would seem to those who put their hope in worldly and perishable things without remembering how little they avail and in what low esteem they should be held. But to us who many times have tested it through experience, it ought not to appear strange or difficult, because, since our principal function is to seek adventures, both good and bad, it is therefore important to take them as they come, and employing our own resources in remedying them, to leave the rest of it, where these resources do not suffice, to that all-highest Lord in whom power is complete. Therefore, my sons, leaving aside the great sorrow that humanity brings to us, to you for me, and to me even more for you, let us leave to Him how He may be best served, to provide the remedy."

The sons, who had more regard for the piety of their father than for the peril or danger in which they were, when they perceived such great courage in him were very happy; and kneeling down, they kissed his hands, and he blessed them. Just as you hear, they spent that day without eating or drinking. And after Arcalaus had supped and a part of the night already had passed, he came to the window where they were with two lighted torches, and Dinarda and two old men with him, and he ordered it opened, and said: "You knights who lie there, I think you would eat if you had the wherewithal."

"Gladly," said Don Florestan, "if you ordered it to be given to us."

He said: "If I have any desire to give it, may God take it from me; but so that you be not entirely disconsolate, in lieu of the meal I am willing to tell you some news. Know you that just now, after dark, there came to the door of the castle two squires and a dwarf, who were asking for the knights of the arms of the serpent device. And I ordered them seized and cast in a dungeon that you have underneath you. From them I shall find out tomorrow who you are, or I shall have them dismembered."

Know you that what Arcalaus told them was really true, for those in the ship, on seeing that they were late, and that they had favorable weather for sailing, decided that Gandalin and the dwarf and Orfeo, the king's butler, should look for them; and these men they held in the dungeon as stated. The king and his sons were deeply grieved at this news, because it meant great danger. Amadis answered Arcalaus, saying: "I am very certain that after you find out who we are, you will not do us such harm as previously, for since you are a knight and have experienced many engagements, you will not consider bad what we did in helping our friends without any unworthy action, and as we would have done had we been on your side. And if there was some excellence in what we did, for this we should be esteemed more highly and be held in greater honor, which on the contrary we received in the battle; but treating us in such a way by holding us thus prisoners, you do not show courtesy."

"No matter who might engage in a dispute with you over that," said Arcalaus, "the honor that I shall pay you will be what I would pay Amadis of Gaul if I had him there; he is the one man in the world whom I like the least, and the one on whom I should most wish to avenge myself."

Dinarda said: "Uncle, even though you send the heads of these men to King Aravigo, meanwhile do not kill them with hunger; sustain their lives, so that with them they may endure greater punishment."

"Since it seems so to you, niece," said he, "I shall do so."

And then he said to them: "Knights, tell me truly which afflicts you more, hunger or thirst?"

"Since we must tell the truth," they said, "although eating first is more proper, thirst afflicts us very much."

"Then," said Arcalaus to a maiden, "niece, throw them a bacon pie so that they may not say I do not attend to their needs."

And he and all the others left there. That maiden beheld Amadis so elegant, and knowing about the great deeds that he had performed in the battle, she was greatly moved to pity for him and for the others; and immediately she put in a basket a jug of water and another of wine, and the meat pie; and suspending the basket by a cord, she lowered it to him, saying: "Take this and keep it secret for me, for if I can avail, you will not have a bad time."

Amadis thanked her very much for it, and she went away. With that they supped and lay down on their beds, and ordered their squires, who were there with them, to keep the arms in a place where they might find them; for if they were not dying of hunger, in some other way they would sell their lives dearly.

Gandalin and Orfeo and the dwarf were put in the dungeon that was under that overhead room where their masters were, and they found there a lady and two knights; one, who was her husband and already advanced in years, and the other their son, quite young, and they had been there one year. And while they were talking to each other, Gandalin told how, in coming in search of the three knights with the device of the serpent, they had been seized.

"Holy Mary!" said the knight. "Know you that those you speak of were very well received in this castle, and while they were asleep four men entered here and by cranking this iron lever that you see, they lowered with it this room overhead, so that they have been victims of great treachery."

Gandalin, who was very knowing, understood at once that his lord and the others were there, and the great danger of death in which they were; and he said: "Since that's the way it is, let us try to raise it; otherwise neither they nor we will ever get out of here. And believe that if they escape, we shall go free."

Then the knight and his son on one side and Gandalin and Orfeo on the other began to crank the lever, so that the room began at once to go up. And King Perion who was not sleeping peacefully, more because of worry about his sons than for himself, perceived it immediately and awoke them and said to them: "Do you see how the room is rising? I do not know why."

Amadis said: "Whatever the reason may be, there is a great difference between dying like knights and dying like thieves."

And then they leaped from their beds and had their squires arm them, and they waited for what might happen. But the room was raised, by a great effort on the part of those who were lifting it, as high as was necessary. And King Perion and his sons, who were at the door, saw light through the interstices of the door paneling and recognized that through there they had entered. And they all three laid hands on the door so forcibly that they forced it and came out at the castle wall where the watchmen were, with great impetuosity and ferocity marvelous to behold; and they began to kill and throw from the wall as many as they met, and to say: "Gaul, Gaul, for the castle is ours!"

Arcalaus, who heard it, was quite frightened; and thinking that it was treachery on the part of some of his men which had brought his enemies there, fled naked to a tower, and took up with him the portable ladder; and he had no fear concerning the prisoners, for he thought they were safely confined. And leaning out of a window he saw those with the arms of the serpent device going about the castle in great haste; and although he recognized them, he did not dare leave there or go down to them. But he shouted, telling his men to seize them, that there were only three of them. Some of his men who were lodged down below began to arm; but the three knights who had already cleared the wall of watchmen, came down to them at once, for they had heard them;

and in a short while they disposed of so many, either dead or wounded, that no one appeared to face them. Those who were in the dungeon and who heard what was happening, shouted for them to aid them. Amadis recognized the voice of his dwarf, for he and the matron were most frightened, and they went at once to take them out. And they contrived with great effort to break the eyebolts, and they opened the door, through which the prisoners came out. And on searching through low buildings that opened on the courtyard, the squires found their horses and their lords', and others belonging to Arcalaus, which they gave to the knight and his son, and a palfrey of Dinarda's for the matron; and they took them all out of the castle. And when they were mounted, the king ordered that fire be set to the houses that were inside, and the fire began to burn so fiercely that everything seemed one blaze; the flame that reached the tower was great. The dwarf said in a loud voice: "Sir Arcalaus, receive as patiently that smoke as I did when you hung me by the leg, at the time you were guilty of great treachery to Amadis."

The king derived much satisfaction from the way the dwarf insulted Arcalaus, and they all laughed heartily to see that that was the outcome of their effort. Then they went down the road that went from there to the ship, and on ascending a hill, they saw the great flames from the castle and heard the shouts of the peasants, who were enjoying it. So they traveled until they were on the high hill. Then dawn came and they saw down below their ship on the shore and went to it and embarked, disarming in order to rest.

The matron, when she saw the king disarmed, went and knelt before him, and he recognized her, and lifted her by the hand, embracing her with good will, for he esteemed her greatly. And the matron said to the king: "Sire, which of those men is Amadis?"

He said to her: "That one with the green acton."

Then she went to him, and kneeling, she sought to kiss his foot, but he raised her up and he was embarrassed by her action. The matron made herself known to him, saying she was the one who had cast him into the sea at the time he was born, in order to save the life of his mother, and that she asked his pardon for it. Amadis said to her: "Lady, now I know what I never before had ascertained, for even though I had learned from my foster father Gandales how he had found me in the sea, he did not know why it was; and I pardon you, for you did not wrong me, since what was done was in the service of that lady whom I must serve all my life."

The king greatly enjoyed talking about that time, and was laughing with them for quite a while; and so they went ahead over the sea, very happy about their adventures, until they arrived at the kingdom of Gaul.

Arcalaus, as you have already heard, was naked in the tower where he had sought refuge; and as the flames were reaching the door he could not come down at all. The smoke and the heat were so excessive that he could not protect or help himself, although he went into a vault; but there the smoke was so dense that it caused him great distress. Thus he remained for two days, for no one could enter the castle, so great was the fire; but on the third they came in without danger, and went up to the tower and found Arcalaus so unconscious that his soul was about to take flight. And by pouring some water into his mouth, they brought him to his senses, but with great effort. And they took him up in their arms in order to carry him to the town; and when he saw the castle burned and everything quite destroyed, he said sighing and with great sorrow in his heart:

"Alas, Amadis of Gaul, how much harm comes to me through you! If I can capture you, I shall wreak on you so many cruelties that my heart may be avenged of all the injuries I have received from you; and on account of you I swear and promise never to spare the life of any knight whom I capture, so that if you should fall into my hands, you may never escape from them, as just now you have done."

He stayed in the town four days in order to recover somewhat; and putting himself on a litter with seven knights to guard him, he departed for his castle of Monte Aldin, and the very beautiful Dinarda and another maiden, with him. That night they slept in the house of a friend of his, and the next day he was to arrive at his castle; and two thirds of the day being already over as he went his way, they saw going along the edge of a grove two knights who had been resting beside a spring that was there, and they were very splendidly armed, and on horseback they cut fine figures. When they saw the litter and the knights, they waited in order to find out what the trouble was. And while they waited, Dinarda came up to Arcalaus and said: "Good uncle, yonder you see two strange knights."

He raised his head, and when he saw them, he called his men, and said to them: "Take your arms and bring those knights to me, not telling them who I am; and if they resist bring me their heads."

And know you that the knights were Don Galaor and his companion Norandel. And the knights of Arcalaus told them, on approaching them, to lay down their arms and to come at the orders of the one who was coming in the litter.

"In God's name," said Galaor, "And who is he to so order, or what business is it of his whether we go armed or unarmed?"

"We do not know," said they, "but it is required that you do so, or we shall take off your heads."

"We are not yet at such a point," said Norandel, "that you can do so."

"Now you will see," said they.

Then they went and attacked each other, and from the first encounters two of them fell to the ground wounded or slain. But the others broke their lances on them, and did not move them from their saddles; and at once they grasped their swords and there occurred a harsh and cruel combat between them; but at the end, three of them being unhorsed and badly wounded, the two that remained did not dare await those deadly blows, and went away through the forest at the full speed of their horses. The two companions did not follow them; instead, they then went to find out who was traveling in the litter. And when they came up, the rest of the retinue that was with Arcalaus, broke into flight, with the exception of two men, both of them mounted on hackneys. Now Galaor and Norandel lifted the curtain, and said: "Sir knight, whom may God damn, is this the way you treat knights who are going along the highway with assurance? If you were armed, we would make you recognize that you are evil and false to God and to the world. And since you are ailing, we shall send you to Don Grumedan to judge and mete out the punishment that you deserve."

Arcalaus, when he heard this, was quite frightened, for he well knew that if Don Grumedan saw him, his death would be at hand. And as he was subtle in all matters, assuming a benevolent mien, he answered, saying: "Certainly, sirs, in your sending me to Don Grumedan, my cousin and lord, you do me a great favor, for he knows very well my good and bad qualities; but I consider myself unfortunate to be complaining unreasonably about myself, and my thought is only to serve all the knights errant. And I beg of you, sirs, that out of courtesy you listen to my misfortunes and afterwards do with me whatever your desire may be."

When they heard him say he was a cousin of Don Grumedan's, whom they loved so dearly, they regretted the discourteous words they had said to him, and they replied: "Now speak, for we shall gladly listen to you."

He said: "Know you, sirs, that I was riding armed one day through the forest of the Black Lake, in which I encountered a matron who complained to me of a wrong that was being done her; and I went with her and caused her rights to be sustained before Count Gundestra. And as I was returning to my castle, I had not gone far when I met that knight whom you killed yonder, whom may God damn, for he was a very depraved man, and two other knights whom he was bringing with him, and in order to obtain from me that castle, he attacked me. And I, when I saw this, leveled my lance and went for them, and did all I could defending myself; but I was overcome and taken prisoner. And he held me in a castle of his for one year; and if he did me any honor, it was to heal me of these wounds."

Then he showed them the scars, for he had many, because he, a valiant knight, already had given and received many.

"And since I was desperate, I agreed, in order to get out of his prison, to surrender the castle to him; but I was so weak that he could not bring me except on this litter. And I had intended to go at once to Don Grumedan, my cousin, and to King Lisuarte, my overlord, and demand the bringing to justice of that traitor who had robbed me — which, sirs, it seems to me, that without my asking for it, you have executed better than I had thought — and if there I did not find help, to seek Amadis of Gaul, or his brother, Don Galaor, and to beg them that, taking pity on me, they provide the remedy that they provide for all the others who receive injury. And the reason why those traitors attacked you was so that you might not find out from me, the one traveling in this litter, the reason for it that I have told you."

When they heard this, they were entirely convinced that he was speaking the truth; and begging his pardon for the discourteous words that they had said to him, they asked him his name. He said: "My name is Granfiles. I do not know whether you have heard of me."

"Yes, I have," said Don Galaor, "and I know that you greatly honor all knights errant, according to what your cousin has told me."

"Thank God," said he, "that already I am known for that by you. And since you know my name, I beg you earnestly as a courtesy, that you take off your helmets and tell me your names."

Galaor said to him: "Know you that this knight is Norandel, and he is the son of King Lisuarte, and I am Don Galaor, brother of Amadis."

And they took off their helmets.

"Thanks be to God," said Arcalaus, "that I was helped by such knights."

And carefully observing Don Galaor in order to recognize him, that he might do him harm if chance should put him in his power, he said: "I trust in God, sirs, that the time will yet come that fortune may place you in a position where the desire that I have concerning you may be satisfied; and I beg you to tell me what to do."

"Whatever be your desire," said they.

He said: "Then I wish to travel until I reach my castle."

"May God guide you," said they.

So he departed at once at an hour when it was already night, but there was a bright moon; and after he had disappeared over a slope, he left that road and took another more secluded one that he knew. The two knights decided that since their horses were tired and the night had come on, they would rest beside that spring.

"Since that is your opinion," said the squire of Don Galaor, "an even better lodging is being arranged for you than you think."

"How is that?" asked Norandel.

"Know you," said he, "that in that old building amid those brambles, two maidens who were traveling with the knight of the litter have hidden themselves."

Then they dismounted near the spring, and washed their faces and hands, and they went to where the maidens were, and entered through some narrow openings; and Don Galaor said in a loud voice: "Who is hidden here? Let me enter, and I'll make them come out."

Dinarda, when she heard this, was frightened and said: "Oh, sir knight, mercy, for I shall come out."

"Then do so," said he, "and I'll see who you are."

"Help me," said she, "for otherwise I shall not be able to come out."

Galaor approached and she held out her arms, which were visible in the moonlight; and he took her by the hands and removed her from where she was. And he was so greatly attracted by her, for he had never seen any other woman of more attractive appearance, and she was wearing a skirt of scarlet and a cape of white samite. Norandel brought the other maiden out, and they took them to the spring, where they supped with great pleasure on what their squires brought and what they found on a pack horse belonging to Arcalaus.

Dinarda was afraid that Galaor knew that she had put his father and brothers in the dungeon, and she wanted him to become enamored of her and to seek her love, which until then she had not given to anyone; and therefore she kept looking at him lovingly and expressed to her maid her praise for his very handsome appearance — all this with the thought that if he were to seduce her, afterwards it would not be that he would want to do her harm. But Galaor, who in accordance with his habits, in that affair had no other thought but how he could have her of her own free will as a mistress, was not long in reaching the understanding that she was quite willing; so that after supper, leaving Norandel with the maid, he went off chatting with Dinarda into the thicket of the forest. And he embraced her, and she threw her arms around his neck, showing him great affection, although she hated him — just as some women are accustomed to do, more through fear or greed than out of contentedness — whence it came about that that damsel who until then had been wooed by many, and in order to protect her chastity had cast them aside though she desired them as lovers, by that enemy of hers through the wish of her adverse fortune, though she considered it a boon, was changed by him from a maiden to a matron. Norandel, who stayed with the maid, urged her persistently to give him her love because he was much taken with her; but she said to him: "You can do your will by force, but it will not be of my free will unless my lady Dinarda commands it."

Norandel said: "Is this Dinarda Ardan Canileo's daughter, who is said to have come to this land to take counsel with Arcalaus the Enchanter on how to avenge the death of her father?"

"I do not know the reason for her coming," said she, "but she is the one you are talking about, and believe me that the knight who has obtained her love is fortunate because she is a woman more coveted and wooed by all men than any other; but until now no one has been able to possess her."

At this juncture, Galaor and Dinarda came to them, for they had greatly enjoyed themselves—I should say not both, for her sadness was greater than his pleasure. And Norandel took Don Galaor aside and said to him: "Don't you know who that maiden is?"

"No more than you," said he.

"Know you then that this is Dinarda, the daughter of Ardan Canileo, that one your cousin Mabilia told you had come to this land to accomplish by some trick the death of Amadis."

Don Galaor pondered a while and said: "Of her heart I know nothing, but from all appearances she shows that she loves me, and I would not do her harm for anything in the world, because of all the women I have ever seen she is the one who has made me happiest, and I do not want to put her aside for now. And since we are going to Gaul, I shall contrive through some amends that Amadis may make to her, how he may be forgiven by her."

While they were talking, Dinarda was with her maid, and she found out that she had not been willing to consent to Norandel's request and that she had revealed Dinarda's identity, for which the latter was very sorry; and she said: "Friend, on such occasions discretion in denying our desires is necessary, for otherwise we would be in great danger. I beg of you to do the will of that knight, and let us show them love until we see an opportunity to be rid of them."

She said that she would do so. Don Galaor and Norandel, after talking a while, returned to the maidens, and for part of the night were pleasurably and laughingly talking and dallying with them. Then, each one taking his own partner, they lay down on beds of grass that the squires had made, and there they slept and dallied all that night. Don Galaor then asked Dinarda the name of that evil knight who had sought to kill them, and he meant the one whom he had killed, and she understood that he meant the one on the litter, and she said to him: "How is it you did not find out when the litter came near that it was Arcalaus? The knights whom you routed were his."

"Is it true," said Don Galaor, "that that was Arcalaus?"

"Yes, very true," said she.

"Oh, Holy Mary," said he, "how subtly he escaped from death!"

When Dinarda heard that they had not killed him, she was the happiest woman in the world, but she did not reveal the fact; and she said: "There was a time today that I would have offered up my life for his; but now that I am loved by you and have your favor and regard, I should like him to die an ignoble death, because I know that he hates you with a passion; and what he wishes for you and for your relatives may it please God that it quickly devolve on him."

And embracing him, she showed him all the love she could. Just as you hear, that night afforded shelter; and day having come, they armed and took their mistresses and their squires, who were carrying their arms for them, and went on their way to Gaul to embark on the sea.

Arcalaus arrived at his castle at midnight, greatly frightened at what had happened to him. And he ordered that the gates be closed and that no person should enter without his order, and he had himself healed with the intention of being worse than before, and of committing crimes more evil than previously, as bad men do; for although God breathes into them, they do not wish or desire to be set free from those strong chains with which the devil has fettered them; rather with them they are carried down to the bottom of hell, as one must believe that this evil one was.

Don Galaor and Norandel and their mistresses traveled two days toward a harbor in order to cross over to Gaul; and on the third day they arrived at a castle, in which they decided to lodge. And finding the gate open they went inside without meeting anybody. But immediately there came out from the palace a knight who was the lord of the castle; and when he saw them inside, he frowned at his men because they had left the gate open; but showed a good countenance to the knights and received them very well. And he had them shown great courtesy, but against his will, because this knight's name was Ambades, and he was a cousin of Arcalaus the Enchanter and knew Dinarda, who was his niece, and elicited the information from her that they were conducting her against her will, she having been raped. And the mother of this Ambades wept with her secretly and would have liked to have them killed. But Dinarda said to her: "Let not such madness enter into you or my uncle."

Then she told them how they had routed the seven knights of Arcalaus, and all that they had done with him; and she said: "Madam, do them honor, for they are very vigorous knights, and tomorrow I and my maid will remain behind; and as they leave, let down the drawbridge, and thus we shall be out of danger."

This having been thus agreed upon with Ambades and his mother, they gave Don Galaor and Norandel and their squires their supper and good beds on which to sleep; and Ambades didn't sleep all night, so frightened was he at having such men in his castle. And when it was morning, he got up and armed, and went to his guests and said: "Sirs, I wish to accompany you and show you the road, for this function of mine is to go about armed in search of adventures."

"Host," said Don Galaor, "we thank you very much for it."

Then they armed themselves and had their mistresses mount on their palfreys, and they left the castle. But the host and the maidens remained behind; and when they and their squires were outside, they lowered the drawbridge, so that the deceit was effective. Ambades dismounted from his horse with great pleasure and went up to the battlements and saw the knights, who were waiting for the sight of someone in order to ask them for the maidens; and he said: "Go away, you wicked, false guests; may God confound you and give you as bad a night as you have given me; for the matrons whom you were intending to lay remain with me."

Don Galaor said to him: "Host, what is this you say? You will not be such a man that after having given us such great service and pleasure in this your house, at the end you exhibit such great treachery in taking our ladies from us by force."

"If it were thus," said he, "more pleasure would there be, because your anger would be greater; but I have taken them in accordance with their own free will, because they went with their enemies constrained by force."

"Then let them appear," said Galaor, "and we shall see if it is as you say."

"I shall do so," said he, "not to give you pleasure, but so that you may see how much you are detested by them."

Then Dinarda appeared on the wall, and Don Galaor said to her: "Dinarda, my lady, this knight says that you remain here willingly. I cannot believe it, because of the great love that exists between us."

Dinarda said: "If I showed you love, it was out of the excessive fear that I had; but you knowing me to be daughter of Ardan Canileo and you a brother of Amadis, how could it be that I would love you, especially when you are seeking to take me to Gaul into the power of my enemies? Go, Don Galaor, and if I did something for you, do not be grateful to me or remember me except as an enemy."

"Now remain," said Galaor, "with the bad luck that I hope God may give you, for from such a root as Arcalaus only such a sprout could come."

Norandel, who was very angry, said to his girl friend: "And you, what will you do?"

"The will of my lady," said she.

"May God confound her will," said he, "and that of this evil man who has thus deceived us."

"If I am evil," said Ambades, "still you two are not such that I would deem myself honored by vanquishing such men."

"If you are a knight, as you boast of being," said Norandel, "come out and fight with me, I on foot and you on horseback. And if you kill me, be assured that you will be removing a deadly enemy of Arcalaus; and if I defeat you, give us the maidens."

"How stupid you are!" said Ambades, "I despise you both. Well, what shall I do to you alone on foot, I being on horseback? And as to what you say about Arcalaus, my lord, for some twenty like you or like that other man, your companion, he wouldn't give a hang."

And taking a Turkish bow, he began to shoot arrows at them. They withdrew and returned to the road that they were traveling previously, talking about how the wickedness of Arcalaus extended to all those of his family; and laughing heartily together about Dinarda's reply and that of their host, and at Norandel's great anger, and how the host when out of danger, held him in low esteem. So they traveled for three days, lodging in towns and to their pleasure; and on the fourth day they reached a town that was a seaport called Alfiad, and they found two boats that were crossing to Gaul. And embarking on them, they soon made port where King Perion was, and also Amadis and Florestan. So it happened that Amadis, while in Gaul preparing to leave in search of adventures, in order to make amends and compensate for the very long time that he had remained there in such discredit to his honor — continuing each day to ride along the seashore while gazing at Great Britain, for there were his desires and all his well-being — on going for a ride one day with Don Florestan, saw the boats coming, and went there to find out the news. And on his reaching the shore, Don Galaor and Norandel were already coming ashore in a boat. Amadis recognized his brother and said: "Holy Mary! that is our brother, Don Galaor. May he be very welcome."

And he said to Don Florestan: "Do you recognize the other one who is coming with him?"

"Yes," said he, "that is Norandel, son of King Lisuarte, Don Galaor's boon companion. And know you that he is a very good knight, and showed himself to be such in the battle that we had with his father on the Island of Mongaza; but then he was not known as his son, nor was he until now, when the great battle with the seven kings occurred; at which time the king was pleased that it be revealed on account of the excellence as a knight that he possesses."

Amadis was very happy with him on account of his being a brother of his ladylove and because he knew that she loved him, as Durin had told him. At this juncture the knights reached the shore, and they disembarked where they encountered Amadis and Florestan on foot; who received them and embraced them repeatedly. And each of them having been given a palfrey, they went to King Perion, who was about to ride forth to receive them. And when they came up to him, they sought to kiss his hands, but the king did not give them to Norandel; instead, he embraced him and paid him great honor and took them to the queen, where they received no less. Amadis, as I have already said to you, had made arrangements to leave there four days later. And the day before his departure he spoke with the king and with his brothers, telling them that he had to leave them, and that the next day he would start out on his way. The king said to him: "My son, God knows the loneliness that I feel on account of it; but not on that account will I be putting obstacles in the way of your going to win honors and glory, as you always have done."

Don Galaor said: "Sir brother, if it were not for one quest in which Norandel and I are engaged and from which we cannot rightly withdraw, we would keep you company; but it is important that we carry it out, or that first a year and a day pass, as is the custom of Great Britain."

The king said to him: "Son, what quest is that? Can it be revealed?"

"Yes, sire," said he, "for we publicly promised it, and it is this: know you, sire, that in the battle that we had with the seven kings of the islands, there were on the side of King Lisuarte three knights with arms of the same device of serpents; but their helmets were different, for the one was white, another scarlet, and the third golden. These performed marvels at arms, to such an extent that all of us were amazed. Especially notable were those of the one who wore a golden helmet, for the prowess of this man I do not believe anyone could equal. Certainly it is believed that if it had not been for this knight, King Lisuarte would not have had the victory that he obtained. And when the battle was won, all three of them departed from the field so secretly that their identity could not be ascertained; and because of what is being said about them, we have promised to seek them and find out who they are."

The king said: "Here we have been told about those knights, and may God give you good news of them."

Thus they spent that day until night. And Amadis took his father and Don Florestan aside, and said to the former: "Sire, I wish to leave early tomorrow, and it seems to me that after my departure, Don Galaor should be told the truth about this quest in which he is engaged, because his effort would be in vain, for if not from us, he cannot ascertain the truth from anyone; and do show him the arms, for he will easily recognize them."

"You speak well," said the king, "and so it shall be done."

That night they were with the queen and her daughter and with many of her ladies and maidens-in-waiting, enjoying themselves very delightfully; but all felt they would greatly miss Amadis, and were regretting that he should want to go away they knew not where. Then having taken leave of all the ladies, they went to bed. And next day everyone heard mass, and came out to see Amadis off, who was going armed on horseback with Gandalin and the dwarf, without anyone else to keep him company. To Gandalin the queen gave enough money to last his lord for one year. Don Florestan begged him very earnestly to take him with him, but he was unable to comply with his request for two reasons: one, in order to be more free to think about his lady; and the other, if he participated only in the contests involving great danger in which he hoped to engage, by participating in them alone, he alone would achieve death or glory. And when they had traveled one league, Amadis bade them farewell, going on his way; and the king and his sons returned to the town, where he spoke aside with Don Galaor, his son, and with Norandel; and he said to them: "You are engaged in a quest for which you would not find a solution anywhere in the world except here, concerning which I give thanks to God, who has guided you here, for having saved you from great fruitless efforts. Now know you that the three knights of the arms device of the serpents, whom you are seeking, are myself and Amadis and Don Florestan. And I wore the white helmet, Don Florestan the scarlet, and Amadis the golden; and thus helmeted he performed the great, unparalleled deeds that you saw."

And he told them about the agreement they had made for that expedition and how Urganda had sent them the arms.

"And so that you may believe it completely and consider your adventure concluded, come with me."

And taking them to another room, which was the armory, he showed them the arms with the device of the serpents, pierced through in many places by mighty blows — arms which were very well recognized by them, because they had beheld them frequently in the battle, sometimes it having been their pleasure to come to their assistance, and at other times having great envy of what their owners were performing with them.

Don Galaor said: "Sire, God has been very good to us, as have you, in freeing us from this effort, because our intention was with all our might to look for the knights with these arms, and unless we came upon them in a situation where we could not disassociate ourselves from an offense to them without great shame, to fight with them to the death or die in the effort, and give everyone to understand, although there in general they did more than anyone else, specifically it would be judged otherwise."

"God has done it better," said the king, "through His mercy."

Norandel insistently asked him for those arms, but with much more circumspection they were conceded to him by the king. Then the latter related to them how they had been thrust into Arcalaus's prison, and by what adventure they had escaped from it. Tears came to the eyes of Galaor out of pity because of such great danger, and he told what had happened to him and Norandel with Arcalaus, and how calling himself Granfiles, he had escaped from them, and their whole experience with Dinarda, and how she stayed within the castle, and what had happened to them with Ambades. So they remained relaxing for two weeks; and having bade farewell to the king and queen, they embarked on a ship, taking with them those arms with the device of the serpents; and with good weather they crossed over to Great Britain. And having arrived at the town where King Lisuarte and his queen were, on disarming themselves in their quarters, they went to the palace to show them how they had finished their quest; and they took with them the arms with the device of the serpents in their cases. Galaor said to the king: "Sire, please have us given an audience with the queen."

"Yes," said he.

And they went at once to her apartments, and everyone with them to see what they were bringing. The queen was pleased with their arrival, and they kissed her hands. Galaor said: "Ladies and lords, you already know how Norandel and I set forth from here in quest of the three knights with the serpent device arms, who were in your battle and service; and God be praised, we have carried it out without effort, as Norandel will demonstrate. Then Norandel took in his hands the white helmet and said: "Sire, do you recognize this helmet?"

"Yes," said he, "for many times I saw it where I wished to see it."

"Well, King Perion, who esteems you greatly, wore this on his head."

And then he took the scarlet one and said: "You see here, this one which Don Florestan wore."

And taking out the golden one, he said: "You see, sire, this one worn by Amadis, who did in your service what no one else would have been able to do. Whether I speak the truth in that matter, or not, you are the best witness, for many times you found yourself among them, they enjoying fame and you, victory."

And he told them how King Perion and his sons had come secretly to the battle, and why they had gone away afterwards without being recognized; and how they had been thrown into Arcalaus's dungeon, and how they came out, burning the castle; and how he and Don Galaor had found Arcalaus in the litter; and how the latter had escaped by calling himself Granfiles, cousin of Don Grumedan, about which they laughed heartily with the latter, who was present there, and he with them, saying that he was very happy to have found such a kinship, of which he did not know. The king asked many questions about King Perion, and Norandel told him: "Do believe, sire, that in the whole world there is no king of a land of the size that he has who is his equal."

"Then nothing will be lost," said Don Grumedan, "through his sons."

The king fell silent in order not to praise Galaor in the latter's presence, nor any of the others, of whom he was very little enamored at that time; but he ordered the arms placed in the glass showcase of his palace, where others of famous men were displayed.

Don Galaor and Norandel talked with Oriana and with Mabilia, and gave them greetings and regards from Queen Elisena and her daughter; and they were received by them with great affection, as from ladies whom they loved very much. And they were very sad about what they told them concerning Amadis's unaccompanied sally to foreign lands of diverse languages to seek surpassingly dangerous adventures. Then they went to their lodgings and the king remained talking with his knights about many things.

CHAPTER LXX

WHICH RELATES CONCERNING ESPLANDIAN HOW HE WAS IN THE COMPANY OF NASCIANO, THE HERMIT; AND HOW AMADIS, HIS FATHER, WENT TO SEEK ADVENTURES WITH HIS NAME CHANGED TO KNIGHT OF THE GREEN SWORD; AND THE GREAT ADVENTURES HE HAD, TOGETHER WITH A RECITAL OF HIS VICTORIES.

When Esplandian was four years old, Nasciano, the hermit, sent word that he be brought to him; and he came well-bred for his age; and Nasciano beheld him so handsome that he was amazed; and blessing him, he drew him into an embrace, and the child embraced him as if he recognized him. Then he had the nurse return home, leaving a son of hers there, on whose milk she had nurtured Esplandian also; and both these youths went frolicking about the hermitage, at which the holy man was very happy, and he gave thanks to God for having been willing to protect such a youngster.

Then it so happened that Esplandian being tired of playing, flung himself down to sleep under a tree, and the lioness that you have already heard about, which came sometimes to the hermit, and he would give it something to eat when he had it, saw the child and went up to it, and circled it for a little while sniffing it, and then stretched out beside it. And the other child went crying to the good man, telling him that a huge dog was about to devour Esplandian. The good man came out and saw the lioness and went there; but she came up to him fawning on him, and he took the child in his arms, who was now awake. And when the child saw the lioness, he said: "Father, this is a beautiful dog; is it ours?"

"No," said the good man, "but it is God's, to whom all things belong."

"I should very much like it to be ours, father."

The hermit was pleased and said to him: "Son, do you wish to feed it?"

"Yes," said he.

Then he brought a leg of venison, which some crossbowmen had given him, and the child gave it to the lioness and went up to her and put his hand on her ears and her mouth. And know you that from then on the lioness always came each day, and watched over him while he was walking outside the hermitage. And when he was older, the hermit gave him a bow made to his measure and another to his foster brother, and they shot with them after having done their reading; and the lioness went with them; for if they wounded some deer, she was accustomed to bring it down, and sometimes some crossbowmen who were friends of the hermit would come there, and they would go hunting with Esplandian out of regard for the lioness, who would retrieve the game for them, and so Esplandian learned how to hunt. Thus his time was spent under the tutelage of that holy man.

And Amadis left Gaul, as we have already related, with the desire to perform such deeds at arms that those who had spoken in derogation of him and had discredited his honor on account of the long stay that by command of his lady he had made there would be given the lie. And with this thought he went into the land of Germany, where in a short while he became very well known; for many men and many women came to him with wrongs and injuries that had been done them, and he helped them obtain their rights, experiencing great confrontations and dangers to his person, fighting in many places with valiant knights, at times with one, at other times with two or three, just as the case might be. What shall I tell you? He did so much that through all of Germany he was known as the best knight that had ever entered that land; and he was known only by the name of the Knight of the Green Sword or the Knight of the Dwarf on account of the dwarf he brought with him. Since he made his sally, four years had gone by without his ever returning to Gaul or to the Firm Island or having news of his lady Oriana, of which the latter fact tormented him most, and he had such heartfelt grief that in comparison with it, all the other dangers and travail he considered pleasurable. And if he felt any consolation it was only from knowing for certain that his lady, being constant in remembering him, was suffering loneliness similar to his.

Then he traveled thus through that land all summer, and on the arrival of winter, fearing the cold, he decided to go to the kingdom of Bohemia and to spend the winter season with a very good king then reigning there — who was waging war against the Patin [the Fool], who was now emperor of Rome and whom Amadis hated very much on account of that episode involving Oriana his lady of which you have already heard — and this king's name was Tafinor, concerning whose great virtue and good deeds he had had reports; and he went on his way there at once. And it happened that on reaching a river, he saw on the other side many people going along, and they loosed a falcon at a heron, and it came and killed it on the side of the river where the Knight of the Green Sword was. And he dismounted, all armor clad as he was when traveling, and shouted to those on the other side to ask if he should feed it. They told him that he should. Then he fed it there what he saw was requisite, as one who had done so many times. The river was quite deep, and they could not cross there. And know you that King Tafinor of Bohemia was over there; and when he saw the knight and the dwarf with him, he asked whether any of those men recognized him. And there was no one who recognized him.

"Could it be," said the king, "perchance a knight who has been traveling through the land of Germany and has performed marvels at arms, of whom all are speaking as being a wonder, and they call him the Knight of the Green Sword, and the Knight of the Dwarf? I say so because of that dwarf that he is bringing along with him."

There was there a knight named Sadian, and he was the chief of those who were guarding the king; and he said: "That is certainly he, for he has a green sword girded on."

The king hurried to reach a ford of the river, because he of the Green Sword was coming already with the falcon in his hand. And as he came up to him, he said: "My good friend, be you very welcome to this land of mine."

"Are you the king?"

"Yes, I am," said he, "as long as it may please God."

Then Amadis came up with great reverence to kiss his hands; and he said: "Sire, pardon me, although I have not been remiss with you, for not recognizing you; I come to see and to serve you, for I have been told that you have a war with a certain man so powerful that you have indeed need of the service of your own knights and even of foreign ones. And although I be one of the latter, while I am with you, you can account me a native vassal of yours."

"Knight of the Green Sword, my friend, how grateful I am to you for your coming, and what you say to me, that heart of mine knows, and has thereby doubled its courage; and now let us retire to the town."

Thus the king went on talking with him, and by all he was praised for his good looks and for appearing better armed than any other that they had ever seen. When they arrived at the palace, the king gave orders that he be lodged there. And after he was disarmed in a luxurious chamber, he put on a splendid and becoming costume that the dwarf brought him; and he went where the king was, with a presence such as to accredit the great deeds attributed to him. And there he dined with the king, served as one would be at the table of such a good man. And the table having been cleared and everyone being quiet, the king said: "Knight of the Green Sword, my friend, your great renown and honorable bearing move me to ask help of you, although up to now I may not merit it, but God will be pleased that sometime you will be rewarded. Know you, my good friend, that I have a war against my wish with the most powerful man of the Christians, who is the Patin, emperor of Rome, who not only because of his great power but also out of his excessive conceit would like this kingdom, which God gave me independent, I to be subject and tributary to him. But I until now with the backing and strength of my vassals and friends have defended it vigorously against him, and I shall defend it as long as I live. But as it is hard and dangerous work for the few to defend themselves for a long time against the many, my heart is ever tormented in seeking a real remedy, for the present one is, besides God, only the excellence and strength of a few men against others; and because God has made you so supreme in the world in excellence and fortitude, I have great hope that your high courage, which as always strives for glory and honor, will desire to win it with these few. Therefore, good friend, help defend this realm, which will always be at your command."

The Knight of the Green Sword said to him: "Sire, I shall serve you; and may you judge my excellence according to what I accomplish."

Just as you hear, the Knight of the Green Sword remained in the house of King Tafinor of Bohemia, where great honor was done him, and in his company by order of the king, a son of his named Grasandor, and a count, the king's cousin, whose name was Galtines, so that he might be better accompanied and honored.

So it came about that one day the king was riding through the countryside with many nobles, and was talking with his son Grasandor and with the Knight of the Green Sword about the war, for the truce was coming to an end five days later; and while they were thus engaged in conversation, they saw coming along through the countryside twelve knights with their armor packed on palfreys, and with their squires carrying their helmets and shields and lances. The king recognized among them the shield of Don Garadan, who was a first cousin of the emperor Patin, and was the most highly esteemed knight of the entire dominion of Rome, and he was waging the war against this king of Bohemia; and the latter said to the Knight of the Green Sword, sighing: "Alas, how much trouble the one whose shield that is has occasioned me!"

And he pointed him out to him. And the shield had a field of scarlet and two golden eagles of a size commensurate with it. The Knight of the Green Sword said to him: "Sire, the more arrogance and audacity you receive from your enemy, the more trust you must have in the vengeance that God will give you. And, sire, since thus they are coming to your land trusting to your moderation, honor them and speak well to them, but don't agree to do anything unless it be to your own honor and advantage."

The king embraced him and said: "May it please God through his mercy that you be with me always, and that you do with what is mine whatever you like."

And they approached the knights, and Garadan and his companions went before the king, who received them with speech more friendly than was his heart, and bade them enter the town and paid them all honor. Don Garadan said: "I come with two proposals, of which first you shall be apprised, and concerning which you will need only the counsel of your own heart; and answer us at once, because we cannot wait, for the truce expires very soon."

Then he gave him a letter of accreditation that was from the emperor, in which he said that he was officially approving and sanctioning on his word of honor everything that Don Garadan might arrange with him.

"It seems to me," said the king, after having read the letter, "that he has no little faith in you. And now say what you were ordered to tell me."

"King," said Don Garadan, "although the emperor is of a higher lineage and seigniory than you, because he has to concern himself greatly with other matters, he wishes to terminate the war with you in one of two ways, whichever you prefer: the first one, if you wish to have a battle with Salustanquidio, his cousin, prince of Calabria, of a hundred against a hundred up to one thousand; and the second, of twelve knights against twelve, namely myself and these whom I am bringing along; for he will do so on condition that if you win, you and he will be quits forever; and that if you are vanquished, you remain his vassal, just as one discovers in the annals of Rome in times past that this kingdom was a dependency of the Roman empire. Now choose whichever you please; for if you refuse, the emperor serves notice on you that, leaving all other matters, he will come against you in person and will not leave here until he has destroyed you."

"Don Garadan," said the Knight of the Green Sword, "you have said enough arrogant things, not only on behalf of the emperor, but also on your own, for God often thwarts them with but little compassion, and the king will give you whatever reply that he pleases, but I wish to ask this: if he should take either of these battles, how would he be sure that what you say would be carried out with him?"

Don Garadan looked at him and marveled that he should reply without waiting for what the king would say; and he said to him: "Sir knight, I don't know who you are, but from your speech you seem from a foreign land, and I tell you that I deem you a man of little prudence in answering without the king's command; but if he considers good what you say, and agrees to what I ask of him, I shall explain what you are asking about."

"Don Garadan," said the king, "I ratify and authorize all that the Knight of the Green Sword has said."

When Garadan heard mentioned a man of such great deeds at arms, his heart was changed in two ways: one, he regretted that such a knight should be on the side of the king; and the other, he was pleased at fighting with him. And according to his secret feeling, he expected to overcome him or kill him, and win all that honor and glory that his adversary had achieved throughout Germany and the lands where they talked of no other knightly prowess save his; and he said: "Since the king now authorizes you to speak for him, tell me straightway whether he will choose one of these battles."

The Knight of the Green Sword said to him: "That the king will say in accordance with his preference, but I say to you that in whichever of them he may choose, I shall serve him, if he wants to put me in it, and so I shall fight in the war as long as I dwell in his house."

The king put his arm around his neck, and said: "My good friend, these words of yours have infused in me such great courage that I shall not hesitate to take either one of the courses of action offered to me, and I earnestly beg you to choose for me whichever you prefer."

"Certainly, sire, that I shall not do," said he; "rather, take counsel with your nobles concerning it and choose whichever be best; and command me as to whatever way I may serve you; for otherwise, the nobles would rightly be complaining of me, and saying that I was taking charge of what was beyond my capacity for discretion; but, sire, I still say that you ought to see the security that Don Garadan brings to make it a firm commitment."

When Don Garadan heard this, he said: "Although, sir knight, by your speeches you show yourself in favor of prolonging the war, I wish to show that for which you ask in order to forestall your delaying action."

The Knight of the Dwarf replied to him: "Do not be surprised at that, Don Garadan, because peace is a more delightful thing than engaging in perilous battles; but shame brings and occasions the opposite; and now you scorn me, for you do not know me; but as soon as the king gives you his reply, I trust in God that you will judge me otherwise."

Then Don Garadan, calling a squire who was carrying a coffer, took out of it a letter on which were thirty seals suspended on silken cords, and all were of silver except the one in the middle, which was of gold and was the emperor's, and the others were of the great lords of the empire; and he gave it to the king. And the latter withdrew with his nobles, and on reading it, found that what Garadan had said was true, and that indubitably he could choose either of the battles, and he asked them to advise him. Then as they talked about it, there were some who preferred the battle of one hundred versus one hundred, others that of the twelve against the twelve, saying that in a smaller number the king could better choose his knights. And others said it would be better to continue waging war as they had done until then, and not jeopardize their realm by depending on one battle. Therefore the votes were quite diverse. Then Count Galtines said: "Sire, defer to the opinion of the Knight of the Green Sword, who perchance has seen many events and has a great desire to serve you."

The king and all the rest agreed on this and had him called, for he and Grasandor were talking with Don Garadan and the Knight of the Green Sword was observing him carefully; and as he saw that he was so robust of body and that rightly he must possess great strength, it made him have some doubts about his battle; but on the other hand, he had seen him speak so many vain and arrogant words that they gave him hope that God would bring it about that his arrogance would do him in. And when he heard the command of the king, he went there, and the king said to him: "Knight of the Dwarf, my good friend, I beg you earnestly not to avoid giving us here your advice on what we have been talking about."

Then they told him about the different minds of which they were. Having heard it all, he said: "Sire, the determination of such a weighty affair is very serious, because the outcome is in the hands of God, and not in the judgment of men; but however that may be, speaking about what I would do, if it were my problem, I say, sire, that if I had a single castle and one hundred knights, and another man inimical to me having ten castles and one thousand knights should wish to take my castle from me, and if God should indicate a way whereby this might be settled by a battle between equal numbers of people I would consider that He was doing me a great favor; and on account of what I say, knights, do not fail to advise the king what may be most in his service, for in whatever way you decide, I must involve my person in it."

And he sought to leave, but the king took him by the border of his mantle and made him sit down beside him; and he said to him: "My good friend, we all agree with your opinion, and I wish the battle of twelve knights; and God, who knows the strength that is given me, will help me, just as he did King Perion of Gaul not long ago, when King Abies of Ireland gained entrance to his land in great strength, and he being about to lose it, everything was remedied by a battle that one single knight had with King Abies himself, who was at the time one of the most valiant and belligerent knights in the world, and the other so young that he was not yet eighteen years old; in which battle the King of Ireland died, and King Perion was completely reestablished in his kingdom. And a few days later by a marvelous coincidence he recognized him as his son. And until then he was called the Child of the Sea, and from there on his name was Amadis of Gaul, and he is the one who throughout the whole world is renowned as the most powerful and valiant knight extant. I do not know whether you know him."

"I have never seen him," said the Knight of the Green Sword, "but I dwelt for some time in those regions, and I often heard of this Amadis of Gaul, and I know two brothers of his who are not worse knights than he."

The king said to him: "Then having trust in God as that King Perion did, I agree to accept the battle of the twelve knights."

"In the name of God," said the Knight of the Green Sword, "that seems to me the best decision because, although the emperor may be greater than you, and may have more troops, so far as twelve knights are concerned, as good ones will be found at your court as at his. And if you can arrange with Garadan that the battle be with even fewer, I should consider it good, even if it came down to one against one; and if he should wish to participate, I will be the other, for I trust in God, in view of your very just cause and his excessive pride, that I shall afford you vengeance on him, and I shall end the war that you have with his lord."

The king gave him hearty thanks, and they went to where Garadan was complaining because they were delaying so long in answering him. And when they came up to him, the king said: "Don Garadan, I do not know whether it will be to your liking, but I have decided to accept the battle of the twelve knights, and let it be tomorrow without delay."

"So help me God," said Garadan, "you have answered as I wish, and I am very happy with such a reply."

He of the Green Sword said: "Many times men are happy at the outset, but in the end it turns out otherwise for them."

Garadan looked at him malevolently and said to him: "You, sir knight, seek to talk on every pact-making occasion. You indeed seem an outlander, since so outlandish and scant is your circumspection. And if I were to ascertain that you would be one of the twelve I would give you these gloves as my challenge."

He of the Green Sword took them, and said: "I certify to you that I shall be in the battle, and just as I herewith take these gloves from you, so in it I intend to take and carry away your head, for your great arrogance and your lack of restraint offer it to me."

When Garadan heard this, he was so furious that he became as if out of his mind; and he said in a loud voice: "Alas, how unlucky I am! Would that it were tomorrow and we were in the battle, so that all might see, Don Knight of the Dwarf, how your folly would be punished!"

He of the Green Sword said to him: "If you consider it a long interval from now until tomorrow, the day is still long enough for the one of us who may have good fortune to kill the other; and let us arm ourselves, if you wish, and let us begin the battle on condition that the one who remains alive may help his companions tomorrow."

Don Garadan said to him: "Certainly, sir knight, if you dare do as you have stated, I now pardon you for what you have said against me."

And he began to ask for his arms in great haste. The Knight of the Dwarf gave orders to Gandalin to bring his, and thus it was done. And Don Garadan's companions armed him, and the king and his son armed him of the Green Sword, and they withdrew outside, leaving him in the field where they were to fight. Don Garadan mounted a very beautiful, big horse and spurred it hard onto the field, and turning to his companions, said to them: "Have good expectation that once and for all, this king will remain subject to the emperor, and you with great honor without striking a blow. This I say to you because the entire hope of your opponents rests on this knight, whom, if he dares to meet me, I shall overcome immediately; and once this one is dead, they will not dare to come on the field tomorrow against me, or against you."

The Knight of the Green Sword said to him: "What are you doing, Garadan? Why are you so heedless that you let the day pass while you boast? For it will soon be apparent who's who, and boasting will be of no avail."

And spurring his horse, he went for him, and the other came at him, and they struck each other with their lances on their shields, which, although they were very strong, were pierced, with such mighty blows did they strike each other, and the lances were broken; but they collided with each other with shields and helmets with such ferocity that the horse of the Knight of the Green Sword fell back stunned, but it did not fall; and Garadan left his saddle and fell so hard on the ground that he was almost bereft of consciousness. And he of the Green Sword, who saw him writhing on the field in an effort to stand up but not able to do so, tried to go to him but his horse could not move, so tired was it; and he was wounded on the left arm by the lance, which had pierced his shield; so he dismounted at once, like a man who was quite enraged. And grasping his efficacious sword, he went at Garadan, who was quite shaken up, but more conscious, for he now had his sword in his hand brandishing it, and was well protected by his shield, but not so belligerent as before. And they went and struck each other so fiercely such deadly blows that those who saw it marveled greatly. But he of the Green Sword, since he caught him hurt from the fall, and was very angry, rained on him so many and such heavy blows that the other, not being able to stand it, retreated some distance away, and said: "Certainly, Knight of the Green Sword, now I know you better than before, and more than before I hate you; and although much of your prowess is manifest to me, not for this reason is mine enabled to determine which of us will be the victor. And if it seems to you that we should rest a while, let us do so; if not, come and fight."

He of the Green Sword said to him: "Certainly, Don Garadan, resting would be for me a much better course of action to take than fighting; but for you, in view of your great excellence and lofty prowess at arms, it would be the opposite, according to the words you have spoken today. And so that such a good man as you be not put to shame, I do not wish to leave the battle until it ends."

Don Garadan was very sorry, for he saw himself in very bad shape, and his armor and flesh cut in many places, from which much blood was flowing, and he was very much shaken from his fall. Then he remembered his arrogance, especially toward that one whom he had before him; but showing good courage, he strove to reach the end of his bad fortune by exerting himself to the limit, and at once they attacked each other as at first. But it was not long before the Knight of the Dwarf had him completely dominated so that all those who were there saw that even were he twice as good, it would avail him nothing in view of his weak effort. And as both were thus contending, Garadan fell senseless on the field, hurt by a mighty blow that the Knight of the Dwarf dealt him on top of his helmet — so mighty a blow that he could scarcely withdraw his sword; and he went immediately at him in a rush and removed Garadan's helmet and saw that that blow had split his head so wide open that his brains had been splattered about by it, at which he was greatly pleased on account of the distress of the emperor and the pleasure of the king whom he was desirous of serving. And cleaning his sword and putting it in the scabbard, he knelt and thanked God for that honor and favor that he had done him. The king, who saw him thus, dismounted from his palfrey and with two other knights stood beside the Knight of the Green Sword and saw his hands stained with blood, both his own and his foe's; and he said to him: "My good friend, how do you feel?"

"Very well," said he, "thanks be to God, for I shall still be with my companions in the battle tomorrow."

And then he had him mount a horse and they took him with very great honor to the town, where he was disarmed in his room and his wounds dressed. The Roman knights carried Garadan, thus slain, to their tents, and there grieved deeply over him, for they loved him dearly. And they considered themselves handicapped in the battle of the next day that they were awaiting, so much so that it made them reflect very seriously, believing that lacking him — and the Knight of the Green Sword remaining in opposition — they were in nowise up to waging it; and while discussing what they should do, they encountered two very grave problems: the first, what you hear, namely that that valiant companion of theirs was dead, and his enemy remained apparently able to fight; the other, that if they should give up the battle, the emperor would be dishonored and they would be risking death. But they were inclined not to engage in the battle, and to excuse themselves before the emperor by citing the arrogance of Garadan, and how against their will, he had undertaken the battle in which he had died. The majority were of this opinion and the others remained silent. There was among them a young knight of high rank, Arquisil by name, who was a direct descendant of the imperial line — so close a descendant that if the Patin were to die without a son, this man would inherit the entire kingdom; and for that reason he was disliked by the emperor, and the latter kept him away from his presence. When Arquisil saw the base agreement of his companions, and although up until then, being so young that he was not over twenty years of age, he had not dared to speak, he said to them: "Certainly, sirs, I am amazed at such good men as you falling into so great an error, for if anyone had advised you to do so, you would have been obliged to consider him as an enemy and not willingly accept such advice; for if you fear death, much greater is what your weakness and loss of royal favor is bringing upon you. What is it that you dread and fear? Is there a great difference between eleven and twelve? If you do so because of the death of Don Garadan, rather it ought to please you that a man so haughty, so unrestrained, is out of our company, because for his guilt the punishment would have come to us. Then if it is because of that knight whom you fear so much, I take the responsibility for him, for I promise you never to leave him until he is dead. Then with that man engaged for some length of time, reflect on the difference remaining between you and your foes. Therefore, sirs, do not give rise to such great fear in your hearts, since from your own proposals there will ensue for us a perpetually dishonorable death."

These words of this Arquisil had such great force that the intention of his companions was changed. And thanking him very much and praising his advice, they decided with great courage to undertake the battle.

The Knight of the Green Sword, after his wounds were dressed and he was fed, said to the king: "Sire, it will be well that you make known to the knights that they are to be in the battle tomorrow so that they may make arrangements and be here at dawn to hear mass in your chapel in order for us to go onto the field together."

"Thus it shall be done," said the king, "for my son Grasandor will be one, and the others will be such that with God's help and yours, we shall win the victory."

"May it not please God," said he, "that while I am able to bear arms, either you or your son bear them, since the others will be such that they would be able to exempt him and even me."

Grasandor said to him: "Sir Knight of the Green Sword, I shall not be exempt where your person is engaged, in this battle as well as in all others that might be waged in my presence; and if I were so worthy as to be granted a favor by such a knight as you, I would ask that you keep me in your company from now on; therefore in nowise shall I fail to be in this confrontation tomorrow, merely to learn something about your great exploits."

He of the Green Sword did him obeisance very respectfully for the honor that he was paying him, for he deserved it, and he said to him: "My lord, since such is your pleasure, so be it with God's help."

The king said to him: "My good friend, your arms are in such a state that they offer no protection, and I want to give you some which have never been worn, and which I believe will please you, and a horse such that although you have seen many others, you will find it to be unexcelled."

And at once he had it brought there bridled and saddled with very rich trappings. When he of the Green Sword saw it so beautiful and so well caparisoned, he sighed, thinking that if he were where he could send it to his loyal friend Angriote de Estravaus, he would do so, for by Angriote it would be put to good use. The arms were very fine and had a field of gold and scarlet lions, and the device likewise; but the sword was the best he had ever seen, with the exception of King Lisuarte's and his own; and after he had examined it, he gave it to Grasandor to use in the battle.

Next morning early they heard mass with the king and all armed themselves; and kissing his hands, they mounted their steeds, accompanied by many knights, and went to the field where the battle was to be. And they saw that the Romans had already come out armed and were mounting, their men blowing a lively air on many trumpets in order to give them courage, and Arquisil among them on a white horse and with green arms, saying to his companions: "Remember what we said, for I shall keep my promise."

Then they went against each other, and Arquisil saw the Knight of the Green Sword coming in front and he went at him, and they met with their lances, which were immediately broken. Arquisil left the saddle thrust back onto the haunches of his horse; but it so happened that he clutched the saddletree; and as he was vigorous and agile, he recovered his seat. He of the Green Sword passed on by him, and with a piece of the lance that he had left he struck the first man he encountered on his helmet and knocked it off his head and would have unhorsed him had not two knights struck him, one on his shield, the other on his leg, where on passing through the skirt of his coat of mail, the iron tip of the lance made a wound from which he felt considerable pain, and it made him more angry than he was before. And grasping his sword, he struck a knight, and the blow was glancing, and coming down on the horse's neck it sliced it completely, so that the animal went down to the ground and fell on its rider's leg, breaking it. Arquisil, who was already sitting erect in his saddle, quickly seized his sword, and went and struck the Knight of the Dwarf with all his might on top of his helmet, so that sparks flew from it and from the sword, causing him to bend his head somewhat. But he was not long in obtaining his reward, for Amadis struck him on his shoulder, and cut both his armor and his flesh, so that Arquisil thought that he had lost his arm. He of the Green Sword when he saw him thus, went on past him to attack the others, whom Grasandor and his men had in bad shape. But Arquisil followed him, and everywhere kept striking him, but not with as much force as at the beginning. He of the Green Sword turned toward him and struck him, but immediately went to attack the others, and was not desirous of attacking him because he esteemed him more highly than all those of his side, for he had seen him go ahead of his men in order to encounter him. But Arquisil was not heeding the blows administered to him; instead he plunged into their midst and attacked the Knight of the Green Sword as best he could. And at this time those of his side were already annihilated: some of them killed, others wounded, and the rest too exhausted to offer any defense. And as he of the Green Sword saw that Arquisil kept following him without fearing his blows, he said: "Is there no one who will defend me against this knight?"

Grasandor, who heard him, went with two other knights, and together they attacked him, and as they caught him weak and tired, they jerked him by force from his saddle and threw him on the ground, when at once they went at him to kill him. But the Knight of the Dwarf rescued him, and said: "Sirs, since I have received more harm from this man than from the rest, let me punish him."

Then they all withdrew, and he came up and said: "Knight, surrender if you don't seek to die at the hands of those who greatly wish your death."

Arquisil, who expected nothing short of death, was very happy and said: "Sir, since my fortune decrees that I not be able to do any more, I surrender to you, and I thank you for the life that you give me."

And he took his sword and gave it to him at once, guaranteeing him that he would do whatever he might command. He of the Green Sword dismounted and remained with him, and having him mount a horse that he ordered brought for him, and he mounting his own, they went to the king, who was waiting for them with great joy at seeing his dangerous war ended; and taking them with him, he went to his palace. There he in his own chamber lodged the Knight of the Green Sword, and the latter had his prisoner stay with him in order to do him high honor, because he deserved it, for he was a good knight of noble blood, as you have heard. But Arquisil said to him: "Sir Knight of the Green Sword, I beg you that out of courtesy — I remaining your prisoner to hasten to you whenever you call me and to be held in prison wherever it be so indicated to me by you — you give me permission to go and aid those surviving companions of mine and have the dead taken away."

The Knight of the Green Sword said: "I authorize you to do so; and remember the guarantee that you have given me."

And embracing him, he dismissed him, and Arquisil went to his companions, whom he found in such state as you can well understand. And immediately they arranged to bear away Garadan and the other dead men, and they started on their way. Therefore for the present no more will be told about this knight Arquisil until it be time to relate how high by his great worth he rose.

He of the Green Sword remained there with King Tafinor until he was healed of his wounds. And as he saw that the king's war was over, he thought that the worries and the mortal desires that his lady Oriana caused him, by which at that time he was greatly beset, he would better endure by traveling and in hardship than in that great luxury and ease in which he was living; so he spoke with the king, saying to him: "Sire, since your war is now ended, and the time has come when my luck does not permit me to be at ease, it is fitting that, denying my desire, I follow my fortune; hence I wish to leave tomorrow, and may God through His mercy bring me closer to the time when I may requite somewhat the honors and favors that I have received from you."

When the king heard this, he was disturbed and said: "Oh, Knight of the Green Sword, my true friend, take of my kingdom what you will, not only of its rule but also of its resources, but may I not see you depart from my company!"

"Sire," said he, "I have believed that by recognizing the desire I have to serve you, you would thus show me honor and favor;

but I have no longer the capacity, nor can I rest until my heart be where always my thought is."

The king, on seeing his firm desire, and considering him so self-assured and determined in his affairs that in nowise would he be deflected from his intention, said to him with a very sad countenance: "My loyal friend, since that is the way it is, two things I beg of you: one, that in case of need, should you be in any, you always remember me and this my kingdom; and the other, that tomorrow you hear mass with me, for I wish to speak with you then."

"Sire," said he, "this pledge that you give me I receive so that I may recall it if the occasion should present itself, and tomorrow armed and ready for travel, I shall be with you at mass."

That night the Knight of the Green Sword gave orders to Gandalin to prepare all that was needed, for he wanted to depart early the next morning, and Gandalin did so. That night he of the Green Sword could not sleep, because just as bodily travail had been suspended for him, so mental travail, on finding freer access for the great yearning and mortal desires for his lady which came over him, was fatiguing him all the more. And morning having come, after he had wept a great deal, he arose, and after arming himself, he mounted his horse — with Gandalin and the dwarf on their palfreys carrying what was necessary for the journey — and went to the king's chapel, where he found him awaiting him. Then, mass having been heard there, the king, after ordering all the others to go outside, leaving him alone with him, said: "My great friend, I ask you to grant me a boon, which will not be to the detriment of your journey or your honor."

"I consider it not to be detrimental," said he, "for you, sire, will ask strictly in accordance with your great virtue; and I grant the boon to you."

"Well, my good friend," said the king, "I ask you to tell me your name and whose son you are, and believe me that it will be kept a secret by me until it be divulged by you."

The Knight of the Green Sword stood a while without speaking, thinking about what he had promised; then he said: "Sire, would that your Grace be pleased to desist from this question, since it is not to your advantage."

"My good friend," said he, "do not hesitate to tell me, for it will be kept just as secret by me as by you."

He said to him: "Since such is your pleasure, although it be told not willingly, know you that I am that Amadis of Gaul, son of King Perion, of whom you spoke the other day during the arrangements for the battle."

The king said to him: "Ah, fortunate knight, of very noble lineage, blessed be the hour in which you were engendered, for so much high honor and benefit your father and mother and all your lineage have had through you, and subsequently those of us who are unrelated! And you have made me very happy by telling me, and I trust in God that it will be to your interest and advantage if I repay a portion of the great debt I owe you."

And although this king said that more out of good will than for any other need that he knew that knight to possess, it was fulfilled later on in two ways: one, that he caused to be set down in writing all the experiences at arms that he of the Green Sword had undergone in those lands; and the other, that he rendered very good assistance with his son and the troops of his kingdom in a great emergency in which Amadis found himself, as later on will be told in the Fourth Book.

After this, the Knight of the Green Sword mounted and took leave of the king, bidding him stay behind, though he wanted to ride forth to see him off. With Grasandor and Count Galtines and many other nobles riding forth with him, he set out on his way with the intention of going to the Islands of Romania and testing himself in the adventures that he might find in them; and when a half league from the town, those knights turned back commending him to God, and he continued on his way.

CHAPTER LXXI

HOW KING LISUARTE WENT OUT HUNTING WITH THE QUEEN AND THEIR DAUGHTERS, WELL ACCOMPANIED BY KNIGHTS; AND HE WENT TO THE HILLS IN WHICH THAT HOLY MAN NASCIANO HAD A MONASTERY, WHERE IN A RARE ADVENTURE HE ENCOUNTERED A GOOD-LOOKING YOUTH WHO WAS THE SON OF ORIANA AND AMADIS, AND THIS YOUTH WAS VERY WELL TREATED BY HIM WITHOUT HIS KNOWING WHO HE WAS.

In order to afford himself relaxation and pleasure to his knights, King Lisuarte decided to go hunting in the forest and to take with him the queen and their daughters, and all the ladies and maidens-in-waiting. And he commanded that tents be set up at the spring of the Seven Beech Trees, which was a delightful place. And know you that this was the forest in which the hermit Nasciano lived, and where he was rearing Esplandian, whom he had with him. Well, the king and the queen with their retinue having arrived there, while the queen remained at the tents, the king plunged with his hunters into the densest area of the forest, and as the land was protected, they secured a large bag of game. And it so happened that while the king was with his beaters, he saw a very tired deer coming; and intending to kill it, he went after it on horseback until it entered a valley. There a strange thing occurred, for he saw a youth of about five or six years of age, the most handsome he had ever seen, coming down the opposite slope conducting a lioness on a leash; and when the youth saw the deer he turned her loose against it, shouting for her to take it. The lioness went as fast as she could, and seizing it, threw it to the ground and began to drink its blood. And the youth came up very happy, as did immediately another boy a little older who was following him. When they reached the deer, they evinced great joy, and taking out their knives, they cut off the part the lioness was eating. The king remained among some bushes marveling at what he saw; but his horse became frightened at the lioness, so he was not able to approach them. And the handsome youth sounded a little horn that he was carrying suspended from his neck, whereupon two beagles came running, the one yellow and the other black, and the youth fleshed them on the deer. And when the lioness had eaten, they put her on the leash, and the older youth went away with her over the hills, and the other one behind him. But the king, who was now on foot and had tied his horse to a tree, sallied forth and called out to the handsome youth, who was bringing up the rear, to wait for him. The youth stopped, and when the king approached he beheld him so handsome that he was amazed; and he said to him: "Good youth, may God bless you and keep you in His service. Tell me where you have been reared and whose son you are."

And the youth replied, saying to him: "Sir, the holy man Nasciano, a hermit, has brought me up, and I consider him my father."

The king stood a long time, pondering how it was that a man so saintly and so old had a son so young and handsome, and finally he did not believe it. The youth sought to leave, but the king asked him in which direction the hermit's house was.

"Up this way," said he, "is the house in which we dwell."

And pointing out to him a little path not well trodden, he said to him: "That is the way you go to it, and good-by, for I want to go after that boy, who is taking the lioness to the spring where we have our game."

And he did so. The king returned to his horse, and mounting it, went along the path; and he had not gone far when he saw the hermitage located among some beech trees and very thick brambles. And on approaching it, he did not see anybody of whom to make inquiry; so he dismounted from his horse, and tying it beneath a portico, he went into the house and saw a man kneeling, praying from a book and dressed in monastic garb, his head quite hoary, and he himself said a prayer. The good man, having finished reading from his book, came to the king, who knelt before him, asking him to give him his blessing.

The good man gave it to him, asking him what he was seeking. The king said: "Good friend, I have found in these hills a very handsome youth hunting with a lioness, and he told me that you have reared him. And because he seemed to me very unusual in his good looks and bearing, and in leading that lioness, I come to ask you to tell me about him, for I promise you as a king that no harm will come from it to you or to him."

When the good man heard that, he observed him more closely than before and recognized him, for he had seen him at other times, and he knelt before him to kiss his hands. But the king lifted him up and embraced him and said to him: "My friend Nasciano, I come with a great desire to know the answer to what I ask you, and do not hesitate to tell me."

The good man took him out of the hermitage to the portico where his horse was, and seated on a bench, he said to him: "Sire, I certainly hold to be true what you tell me, that as a king you will protect this child, since God wishes to protect him. And since you would like so much to know about him, I tell you that through a very strange adventure I found him and reared him."

Then he told him how he had taken him from the mouth of the lioness wrapped in those fine swaddling clothes, and how he had nourished him on her milk and on that of a ewe until he acquired a real nurse, who was wife of a brother of his, whose name was Sargil.

"And this is the name of the other boy whom you saw with him."

And he said: "Certainly, sire, I believe that the child is of high rank, and I want you to know that he has the strangest thing that was ever seen, for when I baptized him, I found on the right side of his chest an obscure Latin inscription in white letters that read: 'Esplandian,' and so I gave him that name; and on the left side right over his heart he has seven more livid letters as red as a fine ruby, but I could not read them, for they are not in Latin, nor in our language."

The king said to him: "You tell me marvelous things, father, of which I have never heard, and I really think, since the lioness brought him as small as you say, that she could not have seized him except near here."

"I do not know about that," said the hermit, "nor let us concern ourselves to find out more about him than what pleases our Lord God."

"Well, I earnestly beg you," said the king, "to be tomorrow here in this forest at the Spring of the Seven Beeches to dine with me, and I shall bring there the queen and her daughters, and many others of our household. And bring Esplandian with the lioness just as I found him, and the other boy, your nephew, for I must be kind to him for the sake of his father Sargil, who was a good knight and served the king my brother well."

When the holy man Nasciano heard this, he said: "I shall do as you, sire, command, and may it please God through His mercy that it be in His service."

The king, mounting his horse, returned by the path along which he had come there, and he covered so much ground that he reached the tents two hours after noon. And he found there Don Galaor and Norandel and Guilan the Pensive, who were just then arriving with two very large deer that they had killed. With these knights he relaxed and laughed a great deal, but he did not tell them anything about his adventure. And when he asked that the tables be set for dinner, Don Grumedan came up to him and said: "Sire, the queen has not dined, and she asks you as a favor that before you eat, you speak with her, for it is important."

He got up at once and went thither, and the queen showed him a letter, sealed with a very beautiful emerald, and some cords of gold passed through it, and it had an encircling inscription that read: "This is the seal of Urganda the Unknown." And the queen said: "Know you, sire, that when I was coming along the road, there appeared there a maiden very richly dressed and mounted on a palfrey, and with her a dwarf on a beautiful roan horse; and although those who were riding ahead of me reached her first, she would not tell them who she was, nor would she tell Oriana and the princesses who were accompanying her. And when I came along, she approached me and said: 'Queen, take this letter and read it with the king today before you dine.' And departing from me at once with the dwarf following her, by spurring her palfrey she left me so far behind so quickly that I had no opportunity to ask her anything."

The king opened the letter and read it, and it read as follows: "To the most high and very honorable King Lisuarte: I, Urganda the Unknown, who do greatly esteem you, advise you for your own good, that at the time that the handsome youth reared by the three different kinds of nurses appears, you love and protect him well, for he will yet become a great joy to you, and will free you from the greatest danger that you have ever experienced. He is of noble lineage; and know you, oh king, that from the milk of his first nurse he will be so strong and so brave of heart that by his deeds at arms he will greatly overshadow all the valiant men of his time; and from the sustenance of his second nurse he will be mild, circumspect, humble, of very good will and more patient than any other man in the world. And from the rearing of his third nurse he will be to a high degree prudent, of great intelligence, a very orthodox Christian, and well-spoken. And in all his activities he will excel and be outstanding, and so highly esteemed and loved by good knights that no one of them will be his equal. And his great deeds at arms will be employed in the service of the most high God, he scorning what the knights of the present time pursue more for the sake of honor with mundane vainglory than with good conscience; and he will always keep himself on the right and his lady on the left; that is, his lady will not dominate him. And even more I say to you, good king: this youth will be the cause of bringing about an enduring peace in your lifetime between you and Amadis and his family, something not vouchsafed to anyone else."

The king, having finished reading the letter, made the sign of the Cross on seeing such words, saying: "The wisdom of this woman cannot be imagined or set down in writing," and he said to the queen: "know you that today I have found this same youth that Urganda mentions."

And he related under what circumstances he saw him with the lioness and how he went to the hermit and what he found out from him, and how the latter was to be with them the next day to dine and that he would bring that boy. The queen was very happy to hear it because she wanted to see the rare youth and to speak with that holy man about some things on her conscience. And the king on departing from her and telling her not to say anything about that, went to his tent to dine, where he found many knights waiting for him. And there he talked with them about the hunt which they had made and told them that next day no one should go hunting because he wanted to read to them a letter that Urganda the Unknown had sent him. And he ordered the beaters to take all the beasts that were there to a secluded valley, where they would be out of sight the whole day. He did this so that they would not be frightened by the lioness.

Just as you hear, they spent that day relaxing in that meadow that was covered with flowers and very fresh, green grass. The next day they all came to the tent of the king, and there they heard mass; and at once the king took them all with him and went to the queen's tent, which was set up near a spring in the meadow, which was very verdant for the season, for it was in the month of May, and that tent had its sidewalls raised so that all the ladies and princesses and other maidens-in-waiting of high rank appeared as if they were in their drawing-rooms. And there the knights of high standing came to speak to them. And all being assembled thus, the king ordered Urganda's letter, which you have already heard, to be read aloud, to which they listened in wonder as to the identity of that very fortunate youth. But Oriana, who had reflected on it more than the others, sighed for her son whom she had lost, thinking that perchance it might be he. The king said to them: "What do you think of this letter?"

"Certainly, sire," said Don Galaor, "I do not doubt that it will come about just as she says, for many other things foretold by Urganda have turned out to be so true; and although perchance many may be pleased with the arrival of this youth when God considers it good to show him to us, it should rightly please me more than all others, since it will be the cause of effecting the thing I most desire, which is to see my brother Amadis esteemed by you and in your service, with all his relatives likewise as they were previously."

The king said to him: "All is in the hand of God; He will do his will, and with that we shall be content."

Then while they were talking thus about these matters, as you hear, they saw the hermit coming, and his wards with him. Esplandian was coming in front, and Sargil his foster-brother behind him, and the latter was leading the lioness which was quite lean, on a leash. And behind them came two archers, the ones who had helped rear Esplandian in the wooded highlands; and they were bringing the stag that the king had seen killed, loaded on a beast of burden and on another two roe deer, and hares and rabbits that Esplandian and they had slain with their bows and arrows. And Esplandian was leading the two beagles on a leash, and behind them came the holy man Nasciano. And when those at the tents saw such a company, and the lioness so large and formidable, they stood up hastily and started to place themselves in front of the king. But he held out a scepter and made them stay in their places, saying: "He who has the power to lead the lioness will protect you from her."

Don Galaor said: "That may well be, but in my opinion we have weak defense in the huntsman who is leading her if she becomes angry, and this seems a sight to marvel at."

The boys and the archers waited for the good man to advance; and when he was already near at hand, the king said to his courtiers: "Friends, know you that this is the holy man Nasciano who dwells in these highlands. Let us go to him that he may give us his blessing."

Then they went and knelt before him, and the king said to him: "Fortunate servant of God, give us your blessing."

He raised his hand and said: "In His name receive it, as from a sinful man."

And then the king took him and went with him to the queen; but when the women saw the very fierce lioness who was rolling her eyes from side to side as she gazed at them and was holding her red tongue between her lips and showing her very strong, sharp teeth, they were quite frightened to see her. The queen and her daughter and all the ladies received Nasciano very well, and all were greatly amazed at how handsome the youth was. And he came before the queen with his game, and said: "Lady, we bring you here this game."

And the king himself came up to him and said: "Good youth, portion it out as you wish."

He said this to see what he would do about it. The youth said: "The game is yours, and you give it to whomever you wish."

"Still," said the king, "I want you to divide it up."

The youth became embarrassed, and a rosy blush suffused his face, which rendered him much more handsome; and he said: "Sire, you take the stag for yourself and companions."

And he went to the queen, who was talking with his foster father Nasciano; and kneeling he kissed her hands and gave her the roe deer. Then he looked to his right, and it seemed to him that next to the queen there was no one more worthy of being honored, according to her bearing, than Oriana, his mother, who did not recognize him. So he came up to her, knelt and said to her: "Lady, we do not hunt with our bows and arrows any other game except this."

Oriana said to him: "Fair youth, may God prosper you in your hunting and in all other things."

The king called him, and Galaor and Norandel, who were closer to him, took and embraced him many times, as if the kinship that they had with him attracted them to him. Then the king ordered them all to be silent, and he said to the good man: "Father, friend of God, now tell in the presence of everyone the story of this youth as you told it to me."

The good man there told them how, on leaving his hermitage, he had seen that a fierce lioness was carrying in its mouth that child, wrapped in swaddling clothes, for the sustenance of its offspring, and how by the grace of God she had placed it at his feet, and how she had given it some of her milk — not only she, but also a ewe with newborn lambs that he had, until he entrusted the baby to a nurse to rear. And he related to them all the things that had happened to the child in its rearing, for nothing was omitted, just as the book has related it. When Oriana and Mabilia and the maid of Denmark heard this, they looked at one another and their flesh trembled with pleasure knowing for certain that child to be the son of Amadis and Oriana, the one that the maid of Denmark had lost just as you have heard. But when the hermit came to tell of the white letters and the red ones that he had found on its chest, which he had all those ladies look at then and there, they absolutely believed their suspicion to be true, from which there was such great happiness in their hearts as to be indescribable. Especially happy was the very beautiful Oriana when she completely recognized that that was her son, whom she had considered lost.

The king asked the holy man very insistently for the youths so that he might have them reared. Nasciano perceiving that God destined them for that more than for the life he was affording them, although he would feel very lonely, yielded them up to him, but with great sorrow in his heart because he loved Esplandian very much. And when the king had them under his control, he gave Esplandian to the queen to serve in her presence; and a short time later she gave him to her daughter Oriana; who, as the one who had borne him, took great pleasure with him. Just as you hear, this child was under the care of his mother, she out of great fear having lost him during the flight with him as you have already heard, he having been snatched from the mouth of that very fierce lioness, then nourished on her milk.

These are wonders of that very powerful God, the protector of us all, which He performs when it is His will; and other sons of kings and of noble lords He causes to be reared wearing rich silks and very soft and delicate garments; and with so much love on the part of those who rear them, with such great regalement and care, without those who have them in charge sleeping or relaxing, then with a slight indisposition and a mild illness they have left this world. God being just in everything decrees that it happen thus, and so as a just thing it should be received by their fathers and mothers by thanking Him because He has sought to do His will, which can do no wrong, though we can.

The queen made confession, and Oriana likewise, to that holy man; to whom the latter had to reveal all of hers and Amadis's secret, and how that child was their son and by what accident she had lost it — which until then she had not mentioned to anyone in the world except to those who knew about it — begging him to remember him in his prayers. The good man was quite surprised at such love in a person of such high rank, who more than others was obliged to set a good example herself, and he rebuked her very severely, telling her to abstain from such great error, otherwise he would not absolve her and her soul would be placed in danger. But she told him weeping how, at the time that Amadis had freed her from Arcalaus the Enchanter, where first he had carnal knowledge of her, she had from him the kind of marital pledge one could and should obtain. The hermit was very happy about this, and it was the cause of much benefit for many people who were saved from cruel deaths that they were expecting, as the Fourth Book will relate at greater length. Then he absolved her and imposed the proper penance. And then he went to the king, and taking Esplandian with him, embracing him weeping, he said to him: "Child of God, by Him given to me to rear, may He protect and defend you and make you a good man in His holy service."

And kissing him, the hermit blessed him and surrendered him to the king; and having taken leave of him and the queen and all the others, bringing away with him the lioness and the archers, he returned to his hermitage, where our story will make ample mention of him later on. The king returned with his retinue to the town.

CHAPTER LXXII

CONCERNING HOW THE KNIGHT OF THE GREEN SWORD, AFTER DEPARTING FROM KING TAFINOR OF BOHEMIA FOR THE ISLANDS OF ROMANIA, SAW COMING A CROWD OF ATTENDANTS IN THE MIDST OF WHOM WAS GRASINDA; AND HOW A KNIGHT OF HERS NAMED BRADANSIDEL SOUGHT BY FORCE TO MAKE THE KNIGHT OF THE GREEN SWORD COME BEFORE HIS LADY GRASINDA; AND HOW HE OF THE GREEN SWORD FOUGHT AND VANQUISHED HIM.

We have already related to you how the Knight of the Green Sword, at the time he departed from King Tafinor of Bohemia, was desirous of visiting the islands of Romania, having heard that bellicose folk dwelt there; and so he did, not by the main route, but by traveling hither and yon righting and correcting many wrongs and injuries that were being done to weak persons, men as well as women, by arrogant knights; in which occupation he was wounded many times and at other times ailing, so that on occasion it was necessary for him, though against his will, to rest. But while he was in parts of Romania, he underwent there mortal dangers in combat with strong knights and fierce giants, over all of whom, though it was with great risk to his life, God willed to grant him victory, he winning so much glory, so much honor, that he was regarded by all as a marvel. But not on this account were these great encounters and efforts strong enough to remove from his heart those burning flames and mortal concerns and desires that came to him for his lady Oriana. And you can certainly believe that if it had not been for the counsel of Gandalin, who always gave him courage, he would not have had sufficient strength to keep his sad and afflicted heart from being dissolved in tears.

Then, traveling thus through those lands and living as you hear, journeying through all the regions that he could without surcease of body or mind, he arrived at a seaport town opposite Greece situated in a beautiful location and full of great towers and gardens as far as land's end, and it had the name of Sadiana. And because it was early in the day, he did not seek to enter it, but continued gazing at it, for it seemed beautiful to him, and he was pleased to behold the sea, which he had not seen since he had left Gaul, which had been more than two years before. And proceeding thus, he saw coming along the shore of the sea toward the town a large company of knights, ladies and maidens, and among them a lady dressed in very fine apparel over whom they held a beautiful canopy supported on four staffs to protect her from the sun. The Knight of the Green Sword, who did not derive pleasure from seeing people, but from traveling alone thinking about his lady, left the highway because he had no reason to meet them. And he had not withdrawn very far from them when he saw coming toward him a knight on a big horse and well armed, brandishing in his hand a lance, which he seemed to want to break. The knight was of excellent build, very burly and a good horseman, so that he appeared to possess great strength; and a maiden from the lady's entourage, richly dressed, was with him. And as the Knight of the Green Sword saw they were coming toward him, he stood still. The maiden came ahead and said: "Sir knight, that matron my lady who is yonder, gives orders to tell you to go at once to her at her request: this she tells you for your own good."

The Knight of the Dwarf, although the language of the maiden was German, understood her immediately very well, because he always had tried to learn the languages where he was traveling; and he replied to her: "Lady maiden, may God honor your lady and you. But tell me about that knight, what is it that he is seeking?"

"That has no relevancy for you," said she, "but do what I tell you."

"I shall not go with you under any condition if you do not tell me."

To this she replied saying: "Since that is the way it is, I shall do so, although not willingly. Know you, sir knight, that my lady saw you, and saw that dwarf who is with you, and because she has been told about a strange knight who is traveling thus through these lands performing wonders at arms, the like of which has never been seen, thinking that it is you, she wishes to honor you highly and reveal to you a secret that she has in her heart, which until now no one has learned from her. And since this knight understood her wish, he said he would have you come at her request even if you were unwilling to do so; which he can well accomplish, for he is more powerful at arms than anyone in these lands; and therefore I advise you that yielding to him, you come with me."

"Maiden," said he. "I am quite embarrassed not to accede to the request of your lady, but I wish you to see whether he will do what he has said."

"I am very sorry," said she, "for I am quite pleased with your speech and politeness."

Then she left him, and the Knight of the Green Sword continued on his way as before. When the other knight saw this, he said in a loud voice: "You, Sir Stubborn Knight, who would not go with the maiden, get off your horse at once and mount backward, taking the tail in your hand for a rein and with your shield upside down, and present yourself thus before that lady if you don't want to lose your head. Choose whichever you wish."

"Surely, knight," said he, "I do not have it now in my heart to choose either of these alternatives; rather I want them to be for you."

"Well now you will see," said he, "how I shall make you take one of them."

And he put the spurs to his horse with the expectation that at the first encounter he would hurl him from his saddle just as he had done to many others, because he was the best jouster that there was in those parts. The Knight of the Dwarf, who had already taken up his arms, went at him well protected by his shield, and that joust was decided by the first encounter, for their lances were shattered and the threat-making knight fell out of his saddle, and he of the Green Sword had his shield and coat of mail pierced, and the tip of the lance made a wound in his throat, from which he would suffer pain. And he passed by him, and removing the piece of the lance that was thrust through his shield, he turned toward Bradansidel, for that was the knight's name, and saw him stretched out on the field as though dead; and he said to Gandalin: "Dismount and take off the shield and the helmet from that knight, and see if he is dead."

And he did so; and the knight caught his breath and now stirred a bit, but not in such wise as to regain his senses. And he of the Green Sword put the point of his sword to the knight's face scratching it a little, and said: "You, knight who threatens and scorns those whom you do not know, have to lose your head or submit to the conditions that you specified."

He, with the fear of death, became somewhat more conscious and nodded his head. And he of the Green Sword said: "Won't you talk? I shall cut off your head."

Then the other said: "Alas, knight, for God's sake have mercy! for I shall carry out your command rather than die at a time when I would lose my soul, according to the state in which I now am."

"Well then, let it be done without more delay."

Bradansidel called his squires whom he had there; and at his command they put him on the horse backward, and they put the tail in his hand and hung the shield upside down from his neck, and thus they took him before the beautiful lady and through the center of the town, that all might see him and that he might be an example for those who out of great pride might wish to humble and scorn those they know not, and even God if they could reach Him, not thinking about the misfortunes that in this world and afterwards in the other are being prepared for them. And though the lady and her company and the people of the town greatly marveled at the misfortune which had overtaken that man whom they considered such a strong knight, as much and more did they extol and praise the fortitude of the one who had overcome him, affirming the truth of the great things that up to then they had heard concerning him.

Then this having been done as described, the Knight of the Green Sword saw the maiden who had called him, and who had seen the battle and heard all the words that they had exchanged previously; and going to her, he said:

"My lady maid, now I will go at the command of your lady, if you please."

"I am quite pleased," said she, "and so my lady Grasinda will be." For that was the lady's name.

So they went together; and when they arrived, he of the Green Sword beheld the lady so beautiful and so gay that since departing from his sister Melicia, he had not seen any other lady who was equally so. And likewise he seemed to her the most elegant and handsome knight, and of the most pleasing appearance when armed, of all those she had ever seen; and she said to him: "Sir, I have heard of many rare exploits at arms that you have performed since you entered this land. Now that I see you in person, I am quite sure they are to be believed. And also I have been told that you were at the court of King Tafinor of Bohemia, and of the honor and benefit that accrued to him through you; and I have been informed that you are called the Knight of the Green Sword or of the Dwarf. Because with you I see it all verified, thus I shall call you. But I entreat you earnestly for your own sake, for I see you wounded, that you be my guest in this town of mine, and you shall have your wounds treated; for such facilities for this you will not find elsewhere in the whole region."

He said to her: "My lady, after seeing the good will of your request, if there were anything in which I might risk danger and travail in order to serve you, I would do so — all the more since treatment of my wounds is what I so greatly need."

The lady, taking him with her, departed for the town. And an old knight who was leading her horse by the bridle rein, held out his hand and gave the rein to the Knight of the Green Sword; and he himself went on to the town to arrange for the knight's lodging, for he was the lady's majordomo. The Knight of the Dwarf conducted the lady, chatting with her on several topics; and if previously she had esteemed him highly for his great fame, even more highly did she now esteem him on observing his great discretion and elegant speech; and likewise he was impressed by her, for she was very beautiful, and very witty in all that she said. As they entered the town, all the people came to their doors and windows to see their lady, for she was very much loved by all, as was the knight, whom they held in high regard for his great deeds, and he seemed to them the most handsome and gallant person that they had ever seen; moreover they were thinking that he had accomplished no better exploit at arms than to have overcome Bradansidel, because he was feared by everyone.

So they reached the lady's palace, and there she had him quartered in a very luxurious chamber, furnished as befitted the house of such a noble lady, and she had him disarmed and his hands and face cleansed of the dust of travel, and he was given a rose-red cloak to put on. When Grasinda saw him thus, she was amazed at how handsome he was, for she hadn't thought that a male human being could be so good-looking, and she had a specialist of hers in wound healing, the best and most learned to be found in all those parts, come there at once to care for his wounds. This man examined his throat and said to him: "Knight, you are wounded in a dangerous place, and it is necessary to rest; if you didn't, you would find yourself in great trouble."

"Doctor," said he, "I beg of you, by the faith that you owe to God and to your lady who is here, that as soon as I am able to ride horseback, you tell me so; because it is important that I have no rest or repose until God through His mercy brings me to that region of my heart's desire."

And on saying this, his concern became so augmented that he could not prevent the tears from coming to his eyes, at which he was very greatly embarrassed; and wiping them away quickly, he assumed a cheerful mien. The physician treated the wound and fed him what was necessary; and Grasinda said to him: "Sir, rest and sleep, and we shall go dine; then at the proper time we shall see you; and tell your squire to ask uninhibitedly for everything you may need."

Whereupon she took her leave. And he, when in his bed thinking very intently of his lady Oriana — for in her all his joy, all his happiness were mingled with torments and with passions that were continually battling with each other — already tired fell asleep.

Concerning Grasinda I tell you that after she had dined, she retired to her chamber, and recumbent on her bed, she began to think about how handsome the Knight of the Green Sword was and about the great things that she had been told concerning him. And although she was so beautiful and rich, and of such high rank as to be the niece of King Tafinor of Bohemia and had been married to a knight of high degree who had lived only one year and without issue, she decided to have the Knight of the Green Sword for a husband, although she regarded him as only a knight errant. And on considering how she might make her intention known to him, she remembered that she had seen him weeping, and she thought that would only be out of love for some woman with whom he was enamored, but could not have. This made her pause until she could find out more about him. And when she ascertained that he was awake, taking with her her ladies and maidens-in-waiting she went to his room to pay her respects to him and for the sake of the great pleasure and delight that she experienced in seeing him and talking with him. And no less did he have; but his thought was far removed from what she was thinking. Thus that lady was keeping him company, affording him all the pleasure that could be given him. But one day, not being able to endure any longer, on taking Gandalin aside, she said to him: "Good squire, so help you God and give you good fortune, tell me one thing if you know it, which I wish to ask you, and I promise you that it will never be revealed by me. And it is this: whether you are aware of any woman with whom your lord is greatly and steadfastly in love."

"Lady," said Gandalin. "This dwarf and I have lived with him only a short time, for because of the great things that we learned about him, we agreed to serve him; and he told us not to ask about his name or his affairs; otherwise we should leave at once and good luck to us. And since we have been with him, we have seen so much of his prowess and valor that he has greatly astonished us, for he is one whom, my lady, you can unhesitatingly believe to be the best knight there is in the world; and of his affairs, I know nothing more."

The lady held her head bowed, and her gaze lowered, for she was absorbed in thought. Gandalin, who saw her thus, believed that she was in love with his lord; hence he wanted to deflect her from what she could in nowise achieve; so he said: "Lady, I see him frequently weeping, and with such anguish of heart that I wonder how he can keep on living. And this, in view of his great courage that belittles everything ferocious and fearful, I believe comes upon him only because of some overflowing, steadfast love that he has for some woman, because this is the kind of ailment for whose remedy neither courage nor discretion suffices."

"So help me God!" said she, "I believe what you tell me, and I am very grateful to you. Go to him, and may God give him relief in his distress."

And she went along to her attendants, disposed not to strive henceforth for what she had been planning, for on account of seeing him so calm in word and deed she believed he would not change his mind.

Just as you hear, the Knight of the Green Sword was in the house of that great lady, the beautiful and rich Grasinda, being healed of his wounds — a house where he received as much honor, and as much pleasure as if, instead of the poor knight errant that he seemed, it had been made known to her that he was the son of such a noble king, as his father, King Perion of Gaul, was. And when he saw himself in such a state of health as to be able to bear arms, he gave orders to Gandalin to make ready the things needed for travel. The latter told him that everything was prepared. And at this juncture, as they were talking, Grasinda entered, and with her four maidens of hers; and he, approaching her and taking her by the hand as she seated herself on a dais which was draped with a silken cloth embroidered in gold, said to her: "My lady, I am ready to go on my way, and the honor that I have received from you causes me great concern as to how I shall be able to requite it. Therefore, my lady, if in any way my service can procure you any pleasure, it will be done quite willingly."

She replied: "Certainly, Sir Knight of the Green Sword, I believe implicitly what you say; and when I ask satisfaction for the pleasure and service that you have found here, if there was any, then without any hesitation or embarrassment there will be revealed to you what no one until now has ascertained from me. But I very greatly entreat you to tell me to what region your desire is most inclined to go."

"To Greece," said he, "if God should so direct, in order to see the life of the Greeks and their emperor, of whom I have heard good reports."

"Then I wish," said she, "to be of assistance for that voyage, and this will consist in my giving you a very good ship provided with sailors who will be assigned to you, and with food to suffice for a year; and I shall give you the physician who healed you, whose name is Elisabad, for another such man of his profession would be hard to find anywhere — all this on condition that if you are free to do so, you be back in this town with me within a year."

The knight was very happy about that help, for he had great need of it and had been greatly worried about where he might obtain it; so he said to her: "My lady, if I didn't requite you for these favors that you do me, I would consider myself the most unfortunate knight in the world; and such would I deem myself if I learned that you, through shyness or embarrassment, were failing to ask it."

"My dear sir," said she, "when God brings you back from this voyage, I shall ask of you what my heart has desired for a long time and which will promote your honor, although some danger is risked."

"So be it," said he, "and I trust in your great circumspection that you will not ask of me anything other than what I ought rightly to grant."

"Then you will relax here," said Grasinda, "these next five days, while the things needed for the journey are being prepared."

He agreed to do so, although he had wished to leave there the next day. In the space of time specified the ship was provided with all necessary supplies. And the Knight of the Green Sword with the physician Elisabad, in whom he, next to God, had great confidence for the maintenance of his health, boarded it. And having said farewell to that beautiful lady, and the sails having been unfurled, using the oars they undertook their voyage, not directly to Constantinople, where the emperor was, but to the islands of Romania, which they had not yet traversed, and to others under the rule of Greece, through which the Knight of the Green Sword went quite opportunely, performing great deeds at arms fighting with foreigners, some impelling him to chastise their arrogance with great reason; and combatting others who because of his great fame had come to pit their strength against his. Therefore he experienced many encounters and dangers and had many wounds, which, once he had achieved victory and honor, were considered glorifying by everyone, and of them he was healed by that great physician whom he brought with him.

Then while he was engaged in this great and constantly shifting voyage, sailing to many islands, one after another, the sailors, resenting it on account of great fatigue, complained to the captain. And when he told the Knight of the Dwarf, it was agreed that although it was the latter's desire to finish seeing all those lands, since the tired sailors resented it, they should turn the ship directly toward Constantinople; so that from that round trip, if God did not disturb it, he would return at the end of a year's time just as he had promised Grasinda. With this agreement, to the joy of all the men of the ship, they made the voyage to Constantinople with a good and favorable wind.

In the second Book we told you that the Patin, being a knight without any state — only hoping to have one after the death of Sidon his brother who was emperor, on account of the latter's not having a son to inherit the empire — on hearing of the great fame of the knights who at that time were in Great Britain in the service of King Lisuarte, decided to come and test himself with them. And although at the time he was very much in love with Queen Sardamira of Sardinia, and to serve her undertook that journey, on arriving at King Lisuarte's court — where he was received with great honor in accordance with his noble lineage — and seeing the very beautiful Oriana, Lisuarte's daughter, who had no equal in beauty in the world, he became so enamored of her that forgetting his old love in his pursuit of that new one, he asked her father for her in marriage. And although the reply was such as to arouse some just hope, the desire of the king was very far removed from such a union. But Patin, considering that he had obtained what he desired, wishing to demonstrate his strength, thinking that thereby he would be loved more by that lady, went through those lands to look for knights errant in order to fight with them. And his ill-luck, that guided him thus, was to appear in the forest where at that time Amadis, despairing of his lady, was weeping very bitterly. And there, after each had said his say, the Patin in praise of love, and Amadis complaining of it, they had their battle in which the Patin fell to the ground from their jousting; and afterwards, on recovering his horse, by a single blow of the sword he was so badly wounded on the head that he came many times to the point of death; for which reason, leaving undecided his marriage to Oriana, he returned to Rome; where a short time later, the emperor his brother having died, he was chosen emperor. And not forgetting that passion which Oriana had aroused in his heart, believing that with the higher rank in which he was placed he would win her more easily, he decided to ask King Lisuarte again for her hand in marriage; a task which he entrusted to a cousin of his named Salustanquidio, prince of Calabria, a knight famous at arms, and along with him to Brondajel of Roca, his chief steward, and to the archbishop of Talancia; and with them were to go as many as three hundred men, and the beautiful Queen Sardamira with many ladies and maidens-in-waiting to escort Oriana when they brought her back with them. They, seeing that to be the wish of the emperor, began to prepare the things needed for the journey, which will be described in more detail later on.

CHAPTER LXXIII

HOW THE NOBLE KNIGHT OF THE GREEN SWORD AFTER LEAVING GRASINDA TO GO TO CONSTANTINOPLE WAS SO CONSTRAINED BY ILL FORTUNE WHILE AT SEA AS TO BE CARRIED TO THE ISLAND OF THE DEVIL, WHERE HE FOUND A FIERCE BEAST CALLED THE ENDRIAGO, AND FINALLY ACHIEVED VICTORY OVER IT.

The Knight of the Green Sword was sailing over the sea with his company on his way to Constantinople, as you have heard, with a very good wind, when it suddenly changed to the opposite, as often happens, and the sea became so rough, so violently so, that neither the strength of the ship, which was great, nor the knowledge of the sailors was able to cope with it sufficiently to keep it from being frequently in danger of being sunk. The rain was so heavy, the wind so powerful and the sky so dark, that the sailors greatly despaired of their lives being saved by any means, just as the physician Elisabad and all the others might have done, if it had not been for the great mercy of the most high Lord. Many times, both by day and by night the ship was so filled with water that they were not able to relax, nor eat or sleep, without their experiencing fright, for there was no peace aboard except what fortune was pleased to let them have.

Thus they traveled for a week, not knowing or guessing to what part of the sea they were going, without the storm's abating a jot for one moment; at the end of which time with the great force of the winds, one night before dawn the ship was grounded so violently that they were not able to dislodge it by any means whatever. This gave as great comfort to everyone as if they had been brought back from death to life. But morning having come, the sailors on recognizing the place where they were, namely, the island that is called Devil's Isle, which a fierce beast had depopulated entirely, the anguish and the sorrow of their hearts were doubled, for they deemed their danger much greater than that which they had expected at sea. And beating their faces with their hands, weeping copiously, they came to the Knight of the Green Sword, without saying a word to him. He, greatly surprised that their joy was thus changed to such great sadness and not knowing the cause of it, was quite nonplussed, and asked them what sudden brief circumstance had changed so quickly their pleasure to great weeping.

"Oh, knight!" said they, "our tribulation is so great that our strength is not sufficient to relate it, but let that physician Elisabad tell about it because he well knows for what reason this Devil's Isle has its name."

The physician, who was no less disturbed than they, encouraged by the Knight of the Dwarf, but with his flesh trembling and his speech troubled, told the knight with great seriousness and fear what he wanted to know, speaking thus: "Sir Knight of the Dwarf, know you that of this island on which we have landed, a giant named Bandaguido was lord, who with his great ferocity and harshness made most of the other giants living nearby his vassals. He was married to a gentle giantess of good family; and for all the molestation and cruelty that the husband with his wickedness perpetrated on the Christians by killing and destroying them, she out of pity made amends every time she could. By this matron Bandaguido had a daughter whom, after she was a grown-up maiden, nature had so adorned and enhanced in beauty that throughout a large part of the world one could not find another woman of her rank and lineage to equal her. But since great beauty is soon combined with vainglory, and vainglory with sin, this maiden, on seeing herself so attractive and graceful, and so elegant and worthy of being loved by everybody, and perceiving that no one, because of the ferocity of her father, had dared importune her, as a last resort took to loving her father with a gross and very disloyal love; so that many times, when the mother had risen from bed beside her husband, the daughter on coming there, would embrace and kiss him showing him much love, while joking and laughing with him. The father, at first received that with the love that is due a daughter from her father; but its very long continuance, her great overwhelming beauty and the very slight conscience and virtue of the father caused that evil, ugly desire of hers to be effective. From which we ought to draw the moral lesson that no man in this life should have such confidence in himself as to cease to avoid and elude improper conversation and familiarity, not only of sisters and other women relatives, but also of his own daughters; because from this evil passion, if it comes at the height of his natural ardor, seldom are judgment, conscience, and fear sufficient to impose on him a check adequate for withdrawing. From this very ugly sin and very great error there resulted immediately another and greater one, as often happens to those who, forgetful of God's pity and doing the Devil's will, seek with one great evil deed to remedy another, not recognizing that the true medicine for sin is genuine repentance and penance, which cause a man to be pardoned by that noble Lord who on account of similar errors placed himself after many torments on the Cross, where He died as a true man and was resurrected as the true God. For this wretched father, being fired with love for his daughter and she likewise for him, in order that they might enjoy their evil desire more uninhibitedly plotted to kill that noble matron, who was his wife and her mother, the giant having been informed by his false idols, whom he worshiped, that if he married his daughter, there would be engendered in her the fiercest and strongest thing to be found in the whole world. And putting their plan into execution, that wretched daughter whom her mother loved more than herself, on walking through a garden talking with the mother, under the pretense of seeing something unusual in a well brought her to look at it, then gave her a push, casting her into its depths so that in a short while she was drowned. The daughter made an outcry, saying that her mother had fallen into the well. All the men hastened there including the giant, who was a party to the deception; and when the men saw that the lady, who was greatly beloved by all of them, was dead, they wept bitterly. But the giant said to them: 'Do not grieve, for the gods have desired this; and I shall take a wife in whom will be engendered an individual such that through him we shall all be feared and shall dominate those who wish us ill.' Everybody fell silent out of fear of the giant, and did not dare take any action. And then that day, publicly before everyone, he took as his wife his daughter Bandaguida, in whom on that unfortunate night, by order of the devils in whom she and her father and husband believed, was engendered an animal in the form that you shall now hear. It had its body and face covered with hair, and all over its body it had overlapping horny scales so resistant that no weapon could pierce them, and its legs and feet were very big and strong. And on its shoulders it had wings so large that they covered it down to the feet, and they were not feathered, but with a gleaming, hairy, leatherlike hide as black as pitch, so impenetrable that no weapons could hurt it. With those wings it covered itself as a man does with a shield. And from under them there extended very strong arms just like a lion's paws, all covered with horny scales smaller than those of its torso; and each of its hands had the shape of an eagle's with the claws of its five fingers so strong and so large that nowhere could there be anything strong enough, once within its grasp, to escape from being crushed immediately. It had two teeth in each one of its jaws so strong and so long that they protruded from its mouth a cubit's length; and its eyes were big and round, very red like live coals, so that from a long distance, when it was dark, they were visible and all the people fled from it. It jumped and ran so nimbly that there was no deer that could outrun it; it seldom ate and drank, and during certain periods not at all, for it did not suffer thereby. Its entire enjoyment was killing men and other living creatures; and when it found lions and bear that defended themselves somewhat, it became very angry and emitted through its nostrils a vapor so frightful as to seem a fiery flame; and it would make a raucous outcry terrible to hear, so that all living things fled from its approach as from that of death. It stank so that there was nothing it did not infect; it was so frightful when it rattled its scales together and ground its teeth and made its wings clatter, that it seemed to be making the earth tremble. Such is this beast called the Endriago" — said the physician Elisabad — "and even more I tell you: the great force of the sin of the giant and his daughter caused the Devil to enter into it, so that it increased mightily in strength and harshness."

The Knight of the Green Sword was greatly amazed by what the physician told him concerning that devil called the Endriago, born of man and woman; and the other people were quite frightened; but the knight said to him: "Master, then how could a thing so terrible be born of woman?"

"I will tell you," said the master, "according to what is set forth in a book that the emperor of Constantinople has, whose island this was, and he lost it because his resources were not great enough to kill this devil. Know you," said the master physician, "that when she felt herself pregnant, Bandaguida told the giant about it; and he was very pleased, because he saw to be true what his gods had told him, and so he believed that the rest of it would be. And he said that three or four nurses were needed for what she would bear, since it was to be the strongest thing in the world. Then as that evil creature grew larger in the womb of its mother, since it was the creation and work of the devil, it made her fall sick many times, and the color of her face and eyes became yellow like the color of poison; but she considered it all good, believing that according to what the gods had said, her son would be the strongest and fiercest ever seen, and that if it were such, she would seek some way to kill its father, and would marry the son, for this is the greatest danger for evil people: to become so corrupt and to take such delight in sin that although the grace of the most high Lord breathes on them, not only do they fail to feel it and recognize it, but also they abhor and reject it as an irksome thing foreign to them, being in thought and deed ever intent on extending their evil acts because they are subjugated and conquered by them. Well then, her time having come, she gave birth to a son, and not under much stress, because evil things always until the end appear agreeable. When the nurses who were provided to care for it saw an infant so unlike any other, they were quite frightened; but being very much afraid of the giant they remained silent and wrapped it in the clothes they had for it; and one of them, venturing more than the others, gave it her teat, and it took it, and sucked so forcibly that it made her cry out loudly. And when they took it away from her, she fell dead from the large amount of poison that had penetrated her. This was at once reported to the giant, and on seeing that son of his, he marveled at such a grotesque creature; and he decided to ask the gods why they had given him such a son. He went to the temple where he kept them, and they were three, one having the figure of man, the second that of a lion, and the third, that of a griffon. And after making his sacrifices, he asked them why they had given him such a son. The idol who was in the shape of a man said to him: 'It is fitting that it be such, because just as its deeds will be rare and marvelous, so it is proper that it be so, especially for destroying the Christians, who are trying to destroy us; and for this reason I gave it some resemblance to me by making it in accord with men's free will, which all beasts lack.' The second idol said: 'Well, I sought to endow it with great ferocity and fortitude such as we lions have.' The other one said: 'I gave it wings and claws, and agility over and above that of all animals there will ever be on earth.' The giant, having heard this, said to them: 'How shall I rear it, since the nurse was killed as soon as she suckled it?' They told him: 'Have the other two nurses suckle it, and these also will die; but let the one who remains nourish it with milk from your herds for one year, and by that time it will be as tall and as handsome as we are, who have been the cause of its being engendered. And take note that we forbid you or your wife or any other person to see it during this entire year, except that woman whom we told you to have take care of it.' The giant ordered that it be done just as his idols had told him; and in this way that evil beast was reared just as you hear. At the end of a year when the giant found out from the nurse that it had grown very large, and they heard it utter frightful raucous cries, he decided with his daughter, whom he had as wife, to go and see it; and immediately they came into the room where it was, and they saw it running and jumping about. And when the Endriago saw his mother he came toward them, and leaping up thrust his claws in her face and split her nose open and destroyed her eyes. And before she could escape from its hands, she was dead. When the giant saw that, he grasped his sword to kill it, but gave himself such a blow on one leg that he cut it entirely off, so that he fell to the ground and very shortly was dead. The Endriago leaped over him; and going out of the room, leaving all the people of the castle infected, it went away to the mountains. And not much time passed before the island was depopulated because of the people the monster slew and because those who could obtain boats and ships fled by sea; and thus depopulated it has remained for the past forty years. This is what I know about this evil, devilish beast," said the physician.

"Master, you have told me extraordinary things, and God our Lord is very patient with those who fail in their obligations to him; but finally if they do not reform, He gives them punishment as great as has been their wickedness. And now I beg you, master, to say mass tomorrow, because I wish to see this island, and if He directs me, to return it to His holy service."

That night they spent in great fright not only concerning the sea, which was very rough, but also because of the fear they had of the Endriago, thinking that it might come at them from a castle near there that it held, where it often dwelt. And dawn having come, the master physician said mass and the Knight of the Green Sword heard it with great humility, beseeching God to help him in that danger in which he intended to put himself for His service, and if it were His will that his death should come about there, praying that He through His pity, have mercy on his soul. And then he armed himself and had his horse brought on land, and Gandalin with his; and he said to those of the ship: "Friends, I intend to enter that castle, and if I find the Endriago there, to fight with it; and if I do not find it, I shall examine the castle to see whether it is in such condition that you may be lodged there until the sea becomes calm. And I shall search for this beast through these forest areas; and if I escape from it, I shall return to you, but if not, do what you consider best."

When they heard this they were very much more frightened than they had been before, because even out there on the sea all their courage was not enough for them to endure their fear of the Endriago, and they considered it a greater peril and danger than the great wildness of the sea, and greater than the courage of that knight might forestall by going of his own free will to look for it in order to fight with it. And certainly all the other great things that they had heard about him and had seen that he had done at arms rated as nothing in comparison with this. And master Elisabad, though he was a man of learning and a cleric, was greatly astounded, and was constrained to remind him that since such things were not within the nature of man, they were to be avoided in order not to commit the unforgivable sin of suicide. But the Knight of the Green Sword answered that if he were to keep in mind that obstacle of which he spoke, he would be prevented from leaving his land in quest of dangerous adventures; and though some had been surmounted by him, were it known that he abandoned this one, all of them by themselves would count for nothing; therefore it was important for him to kill that evil, grotesque beast or to die, as those men were formerly obliged to do, who, leaving their own country, were wont to go to a foreign one in order to win glory and honor. Then he looked at Gandalin; who, while the knight was talking with the physician and with those of the ship, in order to help him had armed himself with the arms that he found there; and when he saw him on his horse, weeping profusely, he said to him: "Who has put you up to such a thing? Disarm yourself, for if you are doing it to serve me and help me, you already know that it is not to be by your losing your life, but by staying alive so that you can relate the manner of my death there where exists the principal reason and reminder on account of which I receive it."

And forcibly making him disarm, he went away with him to the castle, and on entering it they found it deserted, except for birds; and they saw that there were good buildings inside, although there were some in ruins; that the main gates were very strong, and there were heavy padlocks with which to lock them; all of which greatly pleased him. And he ordered Gandalin to go summon all those of the ship and to tell them of the good facilities they had in the castle; and he did so. All disembarked immediately, although with great fear of the Endriago, but the storm at sea was continuing, so they entered the castle, and the Knight of the Green Sword said to them: "My good friends, I intend to go and search through this island for the Endriago, and if it goes well with me, Gandalin will sound this horn, and then you may believe that the Endriago is dead and I alive; and if it goes ill with me, it will not be necessary to make any signal to you. And in the meantime close these gates and bring some provisions from the ship, so that you may remain here until the weather is more propitious for sailing."

Then the Knight of the Green Sword left all of them weeping. But the demonstrations of weeping and bitterness that Ardian his dwarf made were indescribable, for he tore his hair and slapped his face, and beat his head against the wall, calling himself wretched because his bad fortune had brought him to serve such a man, for a thousand times he had been about to die watching the extraordinary things that he had seen him undertake, and lastly this one which the emperor of Constantinople with all his great seigniory had not dared or was not able to correct. And when he saw that his lord already was going through the countryside, he went up a stairway of stone to the top of the wall almost swooning because of his deep grief for his lord. And master Elisabad ordered an altar set up with the holy relics that he had brought along in order to say mass; and he had everybody take lighted tapers; and kneeling they prayed God to protect that knight who for His service and to preserve their lives was deliberately exposing himself to death.

The Knight of the Green Sword was going along, just as you hear, with that courage and bearing that his brave heart vouchsafed him, and Gandalin behind him weeping bitterly, believing that the days of his lord would come to an end with the end of that day. The knight turned to him, and said to him laughing: "My good brother, don't have such faint hope in the mercy of God, or in the sight of my lady Oriana, as to be in such despair, for I have before me not only my delightful memory of her, but her in the flesh; and my eyes behold her, and she is telling me to protect her from this evil beast. Then what do you think, my true friend, that I ought to do? Don't you know that on her life or death my own depends? Will you counsel me to permit her to be killed, and that I die before your eyes? May it not please God that you should think so. And if you do not see her, I do, for she is before me. Then if only my memory of her has caused me to undergo to my great honor the things that you know about, how much more ought her very own presence to avail."

And on saying this his courage waxed so great that he yearned to find the Endriago. And on entering a wild mountain valley with many hollowed out rocks, he said: "Shout, Gandalin, because thereby it may be that the Endriago will hasten to us; and I beg of you that if I die here, you try to take to my lady Oriana that which is entirely hers, namely, my heart. And tell her that I am sending it to her in order not to give an accounting before God of why I was carrying with me what did not belong to me."

When Gandalin heard this, he not only shouted, but tearing his hair and weeping, he uttered loud cries out of his desire for his own death before seeing that of his lord whom he loved so much. And it was not long before they saw the Endriago coming out from among the rocks much fiercer and stronger than it ever had been, the cause of which was that as the devils saw that this knight was relying more on his mistress Oriana than on God, they had an opportunity to enter into it more powerfully and to render it more furious. And they were saying: "If we save him from this man, there is no other in the world so daring or so strong as to venture to attack such a creature."

The Endriago was approaching so enraged spewing from its mouth fumes mingled with jets of fire, and gnashing its teeth, frothing greatly at the mouth and causing its horny scales and its wings to make such a clatter that it was frightful to behold. And the Knight of the Green Sword was frightened, especially on hearing the hissing and horrible raucous cries that it made; and although it might be described in words, that would be nothing in comparison with seeing it. And when the Endriago saw him, it began to make great leaps and outcries, as one for whom a long time had passed without its having seen any man; and then it came at them. When the Knight of the Green Sword's horse and that of Gandalin saw it, they began to run away, so frightened that their riders could scarcely hold them, and emitting very loud snorts. And when he of the Green Sword saw that it was not possible to approach it on horseback, he dismounted very quickly, and said to Gandalin: "Brother, withdraw to one side with that horse so that we not lose both horses; and witness the fortune that God may be willing to grant me against this very frightful devil; and beg Him out of pity to direct me as to how I may remove it from here so that this land may be restored to His service; and if I have to die here, pray that He have mercy on my soul. And in the other matter do as I have told you."

Gandalin could not answer him, for he was weeping so loudly because he saw his lord's death so certain, unless God miraculously should save him. The Knight of the Green Sword took his lance and covered himself with his shield. As a man who already had accepted death, he lost all his fear; and with all his strength, and on foot just as he was, he went at the Endriago.

The devil, when he saw him, came at him at once, and spewed fire from his mouth with a smoke so black that they could hardly see each other. And he of the Green Sword rushed forward through the smoke, and coming up close to it, through very good luck, struck it with the lance in the eye, so that he crushed it. And the Endriago grasped the lance in its claws, receiving it in its mouth and grinding it to pieces with the iron head and a little of the shaft thrust through its tongue and gills, for it had charged so hard that it had impaled itself on it. And it gave a leap in order to seize him, but with the handicap of the crushed eye it could not; being inhibited also because the knight protected himself with great strength and keenness of heart, as one who saw himself at death's door. And he grasped his very good sword and attacked the monster, which appeared groggy, not only because of its crushed eye but also because of the great amount of blood flowing from its mouth. And because of its loud snorting and panting most of the blood was going down its throat and almost choking it; and it could not close its mouth or bite with it. And he came up to it from the side and struck it such a heavy blow on its scales that it seemed to him that he had merely struck a hard rock, for he cut nothing. As the Endriago saw him so close, it thought to seize him in its claws, but it only reached his shield and jerked it away from him with such force that it caused him to fall on his hands. And while the devil tore it to pieces with his very strong claws, the Knight of the Green Sword had the opportunity to get up; and when he saw himself without a shield, and that his sword was not cutting anything, he well realized that his action counted for nothing unless God should enable him to destroy the other eye, for it availed him nothing to try to strike it anywhere else. And like a furious lion, with all fear laid aside, he went toward the Endriago, which was very faint and weak, both from the quantity of blood it was losing and from the crushed eye. And as things which have taken place in the service of the Devil fail and perish, and our Lord, already angered that the Devil had had such power and had done such harm to those who, although sinners, believed in His holy Catholic faith, sought to give strength and special grace — for without it no one would be able to undergo or dare hope to await such great danger — to this knight so that he might put an end, in defiance of all natural laws, to that thing which had put an end to many, among whom were those unfortunates, his father and mother; and intending to strike it in the other eye with his sword, God sought to guide him so that he thrust it through one of the nostrils of its nose, for it had very wide ones. And with the tremendous force that he expended and that which the Endriago was bringing to bear, the sword pierced through to its brain. But the Endriago, when it saw him so close, embraced him with his very strong and sharp claws and tore all the armor from his back and the flesh and bones as far as his vital organs. And as the monster was suffocated by the large amount of blood that it was imbibing and on account of the sword thrust that had penetrated to its brain — and especially the sentence that had been given it by God and which could not be revoked — being unable to sustain itself any longer, it opened its arms and fell senseless to one side as if dead. The knight, when he saw it thus, drew his sword and thrust it through its mouth as far as he could so many times that he finished killing it. But I want you to know that before dawn broke, the Devil came out of its mouth, and went through the air with a very great thunderclap, so that those who were in the castle heard it as clearly as if it had been beside them. Thereby they were quite frightened, recognizing that the knight was already in battle. And although they were locked up in such a stronghold and with such crossbars and padlocks, they were not very sure of their lives. And if the sea had not been still very wild, they would not have dared to delay in going out to it. But they turned to God with many prayers to deliver them from that danger and to protect that knight who for His service was undertaking such an extraordinary exploit.

Then, since the Endriago was killed, the knight withdrew, and on going toward Gandalin, who was already coming toward him, he could not hold himself upright and fell in a faint beside a stream of water that flowed nearby. Gandalin, when he arrived and saw his very frightful wounds, thought he was dead, and letting himself fall from his horse, began to shout loudly while tearing his hair. Then the knight came to his senses somewhat and said to him: "Ah, my good brother and true friend! Already you see that I am dying. I beg you in the name of the rearing I had from your father and mother and the great love that I have always had for you, that you be as good to me after my death as you have been during my lifetime, and when I am dead that you take my heart and carry it to my lady Oriana. And tell her that since it always was hers and she has had it in her possession since that first day that I saw her, and as long as it was enclosed in this troubled body, and never for a moment was it displeased to serve her, to keep it with her in remembrance of the one whose it was, although as another's property he held it, because from this memory wherever my soul may be, the latter will receive rest and peace."

And he could not speak any longer. Gandalin, when he saw him thus, did not try to answer. Instead, he mounted his horse very quickly, and climbing up on a hillock, sounded the horn as loudly as he could as a signal that the Endriago was dead. Ardian the dwarf, who was in the tower, heard it, and shouted to master Elisabad to hasten to his lord, that the Endriago was dead; and he, since he was prepared, mounted with all the equipment that was needed, and went as quickly as he could in the direction that the dwarf indicated to him. And he had not gone far when he saw Gandalin on top of the hill; the latter when he saw the physician, came running to him, and said: "Alas, sir, for God's and mercy's sake succor my lord, for it is very necessary, and the Endriago is dead!"

The physician, when he heard this, was quite pleased with that good news that Gandalin was announcing, not knowing how badly the knight was injured; and he hastened as fast as he could with Gandalin guiding him, until they came to where the Knight of the Green Sword was. And they found him quite irrational and out of his head, uttering very loud groans. The physician went to him and said: "What is this, sir knight? Where has your great courage gone at the hour and time that you have greatest need of it? Do not fear dying, for here is your good friend and loyal servant master Elisabad, who will help you."

When the Knight of the Green Sword heard master Elisabad, although he was completely bereft of his senses, he recognized him and opened his eyes, and tried to raise his head, but could not; so he lifted up his arms as if he were seeking to embrace him. Master Elisabad then took off his cloak and spread it on the ground; and he and Gandalin having lifted him and placed him on it, they disarmed him as gently as they could. When the physician saw the wounds, although he was one of the best in the world of that profession, and had seen many deep wounds, he was quite frightened and was despairing of his life; but as one who loved him and considered him the best knight in the world, he intended to exert all his effort to save him. And on examining the wounds he saw that the whole injury was in the flesh and in the bones, and that it had not touched the vital organs. He then cherished greater hope of healing him, and he set his bones and ribs, sewed up his flesh, applying such medication and bandaging his whole body all around so well that he stopped the bleeding and the air that was escaping through his wounds. And then there came to the knight greater consciousness and strength, so that he was able to talk; and opening his eyes, he said: "Oh, Lord God all powerful, who through thy great compassion didst will to come into the world and take human form within the Virgin Mary; and in order to open the gates of Paradise that were kept closed, thou didst will to suffer many injuries, and finally death at the hands of that corrupt and wretched folk! As one of the greatest of sinners, I beg of you, Lord, to have mercy on my soul, for my body is condemned to earth."

And he fell silent and said no more. The physician said to him: "Sir knight, I am quite pleased to see you so discerning, because from That One whom you ask for mercy will come to you the true medicine, and after Him from me as His servant; for I shall wager my life on yours, and with His help I shall heal you. And do not be fearful of dying this time; just be heartened enough to expect to live instead of expecting to die."

Then he took a sponge medicated against the poison, and put it to his nose in such wise that it greatly stimulated him. Gandalin kissed the hands of the physician, kneeling before him, begging him to have pity on his lord. The physician ordered him to mount and go quickly to the castle, and bring some men so that they might transfer the knight on a litter before night fell. Gandalin did so; and the men having come, made a litter as best they could out of wood from that forest. And putting the Knight of the Green Sword on it, they bore him on their shoulders to the castle; and the best chamber that there was there having been prepared with fine bed-linen that Grasinda had ordered placed on board the ship, they put him to bed so nearly unconscious that he did not feel it; and he remained all night in this state, for he never spoke, groaning piteously as one who was badly wounded, and trying to speak, but not being able to do so.

The physician ordered his own bed to be made there, and remained with him to comfort him, applying to him such medication as was calculated to draw out that very bad poison that he had absorbed from the Endriago, so that by dawn such very efficacious remedies he had applied to him that he put him into a very restful sleep. And then he ordered all to withdraw so as not to awaken him, because he knew that that sleep was very good for him. And his sleep having come to an end after a long interval, he began to shout with great urgency, saying: "Gandalin, Gandalin, protect yourself from this very cruel, evil devil so that it not kill you!"

The physician, who heard him, went to him laughing more light-heartedly than he really felt, for he still feared for the knight's life; and said: "If you had protected yourself as he has, your fame would not be so widespread through the world."

He raised his head and saw the physician and said to him: "Master, where are we?"

He came up to him and took him by the hands, and saw that he was still delirious; so he ordered food brought to him, and he fed him what he perceived was needed to give him strength. And the knight ate like a man out of his senses. The physician remained with him administering to him such restoratives as one would administer who in that profession was talented to the highest degree to be found anywhere; and before the hour of vespers he was again completely conscious, so that he recognized everybody and was talking to them. And the physician never left him, caring for him and applying to him so many remedies needed for that illness that not only with them but principally by the will of God, who desired it, he saw clearly from the appearance of his wounds that he would be able to bring him back to health; and at once he said so to all those who were there, who were very happy, thanking that sovereign God because He had freed them from the storm of the sea and from the danger of that devil. But greater than the joy of all others was that of Gandalin his loyal squire and that of the dwarf as the ones who had for him a heartfelt love, for they returned from death to life. And then they all gathered around the bed of the Knight of the Green Sword with great pleasure, comforting him, telling him to disregard the illness he had, in view of the honor and good fortune that God had given him, for so far in feats at arms and of courage He had never permitted any man on earth to be his equal. And they insistently begged Gandalin to try to tell them the whole affair just as it had happened, since he had seen it with his own eyes, so that they might be able to give an account of such great knightly prowess. And he told them he would gladly do so on condition that the physician administer to him an oath on the holy Gospels, so that they might believe his account and with truth put it in writing, in order that a thing so outstanding and so mighty an exploit might not be forgotten by people. Master Elisabad administered the oath in order to be more certain concerning such a great deed. And Gandalin told it all completely just as the story has related it. And when they heard it, they were astounded at it as a story of the greatest deed of which they had ever heard. And although none of them had ever seen the Endriago, because its body had fallen among some bushes, on account of succoring the knight they had not been able to heed anything else.

Then they all said that they would like to go and see the Endriago. And the physician told them to go and he gave them many medications to combat the poison. When they beheld a thing so fearful and so unlike all the other living creatures that they had seen up to that time, they were much more amazed than before and were not able to believe that there had been in the world a heart so bold as to dare attack such great deviltry. And although they knew for certain that the Knight of the Green Sword had killed it, it seemed to them only that they had dreamed it. After they had looked at it for quite a while, they returned to the castle, meanwhile discussing how that Knight of the Green Sword had been able to accomplish such a great deed. What shall I say to you? Know you that they remained there more than three weeks before the Knight of the Green Sword showed sufficient improvement for them to dare lift him up from the bed where he was. But since his return to health was permitted by God and the great diligence of that physician Elisabad was improving it, he became meanwhile so much improved that he would have been able to set out over the sea without any danger. And when the master saw him in such a good state of health, he spoke with him one day and said to him: "My lord, now through the goodness of God, who has willed it — since no one else would have been sufficiently powerful — you have reached such a point that I dare with His help and your good effort to allow you to fare forth on the sea, to go wherever you please. And because we lack some very necessary things, not only what relates to your health but also to the sustenance of the other people, it is necessary that provision be made for remedying the situation, because the longer we stay here, the more we shall be lacking."

The Knight of the Green Sword said to him: "My dear sir and true friend, I give many thanks and acknowledgments to God because thus He has willed to protect me from such danger, more out of His Holy pity than because of my merit; and nothing can be compared with His great power, because all is permitted and directed by His will, and to Him one must attribute all the good things that occur in this world. And aside from what is His, you, sir, I have to thank for my life, for I certainly believe that today no one else born into this world would have been competent to minister to me as you have. And although God has shown me such great mercy, fortune is very adverse to me, for the reward for such a great benefit as I have received from you I cannot satisfy except as a poor knight who possesses nothing but a horse, and armor rent asunder just as you see."

The physician said to him: "Sir, I need no satisfaction other than the glory that I possesss, which is to have preserved from death, after God, the best knight ever to bear arms; and this I dare to say in your presence because of what you have accomplished in mine. And the reward that I expect from you is much greater than what any king or noble lord would be able to give me, for it is the assistance that many troubled men and women who will have need of your help will find in you, for you will aid them; and it will be for me a greater reward than any other to have been the cause, after God, of restoring them."

The Knight of the Green Sword was embarrassed to hear himself praised, and said: "My lord, leaving this matter about which we are speaking, I wish you to know upon what my will is most determined. I had wanted to traverse all the islands of Romania, but because of what you said to me about the fatigue of the sailors I changed my intention and we turned back with Constantinople as our destination, a project which the very unfortunate weather, as you have seen, prevented us from carrying out. But since the weather is now favorable I still have a desire to revert to it and see that great emperor, so that, if God brings me back to where my heart yearns to be, I may be able to describe some rare things that seldom can be seen except under such circumstances. Master Elisabad, in the name of the regard that you have for me, I beg you not to be annoyed because of this, for some day you will be rewarded by me; and from Constantinople we may return, if it please Almighty God, to the rendezvous within the deadline which that very noble lady Grasinda set for me; because it is necessary to keep it, as you well know, in order that if I can, in accordance with my desire I be enabled to requite some of the great favors that I have undeservedly received from her."

CHAPTER LXXIV

HOW THE KNIGHT OF THE GREEN SWORD WROTE TO THE EMPEROR OF CONSTANTINOPLE, WHOSE ISLAND THAT WAS, CONCERNING HOW HE HAD KILLED THAT WILD BEAST, AND HIS NEED OF SUPPLIES. THESE THE EMPEROR PROVIDED VERY PROMPTLY, AND HE REPAID THE KNIGHT WITH GREAT HONOR AND HIGH REGARD FOR THE HONOR AND SERVICE THAT HE HAD DONE HIM IN FREEING FOR HIM THAT ISLAND WHICH FOR SUCH A LONG TIME HE HAD CONSIDERED LOST.

"Since this is your wish, sir," said Master Elisabad, "you must write to the emperor about what has happened to you; and there will be brought from there some things that we lack for the journey."

"Master," said he, "I have never seen him, nor do I know him, and therefore I refer it all to you to do whatever seems best to you, and in this matter you will be doing me a very great favor."

Master Elisabad in order to please him wrote at once a letter informing the emperor of everything that had happened to the foreign knight, called the Knight of the Green Sword, since he departed from Grasinda, Elisabad's suzerain; and how having accomplished many great deeds at arms in the islands of Romania — deeds which no other knight could have done — he was pursuing his way from where he had been; and how the great storm at sea had cast him upon the Island of the Devil, where the Endriago was; and how that Knight of the Green Sword out of his own desire, and against the wishes of them all had sought out the Endriago and in combat had killed it. And he wrote to him in detail how the battle had occurred and the wounds with which the Knight of the Green Sword had emerged, so that there was nothing of which he did not inform him; adding that since that island was now free of that devil and was under his sovereignty, he should give orders that steps be taken to repopulate it; and that the Knight of the Green Sword was petitioning him as a favor to order the island named the Island of Holy Mary.

This letter, written as you have heard, he gave to a squire, a relative of his whom he had there with him, and he ordered the squire to go in that ship, taking along the sailors that were needed, and give the letter to the emperor, and to bring back from there the provisions that they lacked. The squire immediately put out to sea with his company, for now the weather was very favorable, and on the third day the ship reached port. Then leaving it, he went to the palace of the emperor; whom he found with many nobles, as befitted such a noble lord; and kneeling he said to him: "Your servant, Master Elisabad, does obeisance to you and sends you this letter, from which you will receive very great pleasure."

The emperor took it, and on reading it, was greatly astonished at its contents, and he said in a loud voice so that everybody heard him: "Knights, some news has come to me so extraordinary that its like has never been heard."

Then there came up to him Gastiles, his nephew, son of his sister the Duchess of Gajaste, who was a good young knight; and Count Saluder, brother of Grasinda, the lady who had bestowed such great honor on the Knight of the Green Sword; and many others with them. The emperor said to them: "Know you that he of the Green Sword, whose great deeds at arms accomplished in the islands of Romania have been reported to us, of his own free will has fought with the Endriago and has killed it. And if at such a deed as this everyone did not marvel, what could come about that would inspire awe?"

And he showed them Elisabad's letter, ordering the messenger to tell them verbally how it had occurred; the latter told it in full as if it had all taken place in his presence. Then Gastiles said: "Certainly, sire, this thing is very miraculous, for I have never heard of any mortal man's fighting with the Devil, with the possible exception of those saints with their spiritual arms, because such as they indeed could have done so with the aid of their saintliness. And since such a man as this has come into our land with a great desire to serve you, it would be wrong not to do him great honor."

"Nephew," said he, "you speak well; and you and Count Saluder prepare some ships and bring him to me, for we should regard him as something never before seen. And take with you master painters to paint and bring back to me an exact likeness of the Endriago, because I shall order a representation cast in metal which will include the knight who fought with him and be of their respective size and appearance. And I shall have these figures placed in the very same place where the battle took place, and on a large copper plaque I shall cause a description of the battle to be inscribed, together with the name of the knight. And I shall order a monastery established there in which friars may live in order to restore that island to the service of God; for the people of that land were very much harmed with the evil apparition of that devil."

All were very happy about what the emperor said, and more than anyone else were Gastiles and the marquis because the emperor was ordering them to go on such a journey, where they would be able to see the Endriago and the man who had slain him. And after readying the ships, they set out on the sea and crossed over to the Island of Holy Mary, for thus the emperor ordered it to be called henceforth. And when the Knight of the Green Sword learned of their coming, he commanded that his quarters be adorned with the best and richest materials that Grasinda had ordered placed on his ship; and he was already so improved in health that sometimes he would walk about in his room. And they came to the castle richly clothed and accompanied by noble gentry, and the Knight of the Green Sword came for some distance out of his room to receive them. There they talked together very courteously, and he had them sit down on the daises that he had ordered constructed for them. As he had already ascertained from Master Elisabad that the marquis was a brother of Elisabad's liege lady Grasinda, on that occasion he gave him many thanks for what his sister had done for him — that is to say, the honors and favors that he had received from her, and how after God she had saved his life by giving him that physician who had successfully treated him and rescued him from death. The Greeks who had come there kept scrutinizing the Knight of the Green Sword; and although on account of his weakness his appearance had greatly suffered, they said they had never seen a knight so handsome and well-spoken. Gastiles, who was greatly enjoying himself, said to him: "Good sir, my uncle the emperor wishes to see you, and through us he begs you to go to him so that he may order that honor shown to you which he is under obligation to render because of your service to him in winning back this island that he had deemed lost, which is honor you deserve."

"My lord," said the Knight of the Dwarf, "I shall do what the emperor commands, for my desire is to see him and to serve him to the degree that a poor foreign knight, such as I am, can."

"Then, let us view the Endriago," said Gastiles, "and the masters that the emperor sent will see it in order to sketch it very accurately in accordance with its form and appearance."

The physician said to him: "Sir, it is necessary that you go well equipped against the poison; if not, you might greatly endanger your lives."

Gastiles replied: "Good friend, that is your responsibility."

"And I shall assume it," said he.

Then he gave them some small boxes of medication to apply to their nostrils while they were looking at the monster. Immediately they mounted, and Gandalin went with them in order to direct them to it, and on the way was engaged in relating to them what had happened to his lord and himself in those places they were traversing, how that battle had come about, and how at his shouts, while he was tearing his hair on seeing his lord so close to death, that devil had emerged, and the good fortune that came to them, and all that had happened to them, just as you have heard. At this moment they reached the stream where his lord had fallen in a faint, and from there he conducted them through the thicket near the rocks, and they found the Endriago dead, which caused them great fear, so much so that they did not think that either in this world or in hell was there another beast so grotesque and fearful. And if until then they had esteemed highly what that knight had done, on seeing that devil they esteemed him still more; for although they knew the Endriago to be dead, they did not dare scrutinize it or approach it. And Gastiles said that such courage as to dare to attack that beast ought to be disregarded, for it was so great that it ought not to be attributed to any mortal man, but to God, for to Him, and none other, it was owing. The masters scrutinized and measured it completely in order to copy it just as it was, and so they did, because they were wonderfully excellent in that craft.

Then they returned to the castle, and found that the Knight of the Dwarf was waiting for them in order to dine; and they were served there, allowing for the place where they were, to their great pleasure and joy. Thus they all took their ease at the castle for three days while viewing that land, which was very beautiful, and the garden and the well into which the wretched daughter had pushed her mother. Then, on the fourth day they all put out to sea, and in a short while they made port at Constantinople, landing below the palace of the emperor. The people came to their windows to gaze at the Knight of the Green Sword, for they were quite desirous of seeing him. And the emperor gave orders to bring them some steeds to ride. At that time the Knight of the Green Sword, already much more improved in health and appearance, was clad in very handsome, luxurious garments that the King of Bohemia had had him accept when he took leave of him. Suspended from his neck was that rare and precious green sword that he had won by virtue of the abundant love he had for his lady; and on seeing it and recalling the time when he won it and the delightful life he was then leading in Miraflores with that lady whom he loved so much and who was so far away, he shed many tears as anguishing as they were delightful, after the manner of those who are subject to, and tormented by, such passion and joy.

Then, after debarking and mounting those fine, richly caparisoned palfreys which had been brought to them, they went their way to the emperor, who was already coming to meet them well accompanied by grandees sumptuously attired. And all the others stood aside as the Knight of the Green Sword came up and sought to dismount in order to kiss his hands. But the emperor, when he saw this, did not permit him to do so; instead he went up to him and threw his arms around him, showing very great regard for him, for such was his feeling; and he said: "By heaven, Knight of the Green Sword, my good friend, although God has made me of such high estate and I am a descendant of those who have held this very great sovereignty, you deserve honor more than I do, for you have won it through your own great courage by undergoing such terrible dangers, which no one else has undergone; whereas I have the honor that came to me while I was asleep and without my deserving it."

The Knight of the Dwarf said to him: "Sire, one can satisfy measurable things but not this, for God through his great power has caused me to be so greatly praised; and therefore, sire, it will remain for my person to serve Him until death in whatever things He may command me to do."

While they were speaking thus, the emperor returned with him to his palace; and he of the Green Sword kept observing that great city and the rare and marvelous things that he saw in it, and the many people who came out to see him. He humbly and earnestly gave thanks to God because He had guided him to such a place as this, where he was receiving such honor from the greatest man of the Christians, and all that he had seen in other places seemed to him nothing in comparison with that. But he was even more amazed when he entered the great palace, for there it seemed to him that all the wealth of the world was brought together. In it was an apartment where the emperor was wont to lodge the noble lords who came to him, and this was the most beautiful and delightful one to be found anywhere in the world, not only for its luxurious rooms but for its fountains and very exotic trees; and there he gave orders for the Knight of the Green Sword to stay, and also Master Elisabad to care for his health, and Gastiles and Marquis Saluder to keep him company. Then leaving him to rest, he went away with his nobles to his own quarters. All the people of the city who had seen the Knight of the Green Sword spoke highly of his very good looks and much more of that great courage of his, which was superior to that of any other knight. If he had been greatly surprised to see such a city as that one and such a large number of people, much more were they astonished at the mere sight of him; hence by all he was praised and honored more than any king, grandee or other knight who had come there from abroad.

The emperor said to his wife the empress: "Madam, the Knight of the Green Sword, the one about whose many famous deeds we have heard, is here; and not only because of his great valor but also on account of the service he has rendered us in winning back for us that island which was in the power of that evil parricide for such a long time — in short, since he has performed such an exploit as this, it is right to do him great honor. Therefore order your apartment to be very well adorned in such wise and manner that wherever he may go, he be enabled to praise it with justice and to speak of it as I used to speak to you about other palaces that I have seen in a few places. And I wish your ladies and maidens-in-waiting to be attired and adorned in a manner befitting persons who serve such a noble lady as you."

And in consideration of all that he was saying, she replied: "In the name of God, all will be done as you command."

Next morning the Knight of the Green Sword arose and donned luxurious and handsome garments, such as he was wont to wear, and he and the marquis and Gastiles and Master Elisabad all went together to attend mass with the emperor in his chapel, where he was waiting for them; and then they went to see the empress. But before they reached her, they encountered many ladies and maidens-in-waiting lavishly arrayed in sumptuous costumes, who after greeting them decorously, made room for them to pass. The apartment was so luxurious and so well decorated that with the exception of the opulent forbidden chamber of the Firm Island, the Knight of the Green Sword had never seen another such; and his eyes became weary looking at so many beautiful women and the other fine sights that he was seeing. And on coming into the presence of the empress, who was on her dais, he knelt before her with great humility, saying: "Madam, I give great thanks to God for bringing me where I might behold your highness and your superiority over all other ladies in the world, and your house occupied and adorned by so many ladies and maidens-in-waiting of such high rank; and I am very grateful to you, madam, for having been willing to see me. May it please God through His mercy to bring me to a time when I may be able to requite Him somewhat for these great favors. And if I, madam, do not succeed in expressing properly those things that my will and my tongue would like to say, since this language is foreign to me, I ask you to pardon me, for I learned it only a short time ago from Master Elisabad."

The empress took him by the hands and told him not to remain kneeling, and had him seat himself near her; and she remained talking with him a long while about those subjects that such a noble lady might properly discuss with a foreign knight with whom she was not well acquainted. He responded with such prudent consideration and grace that the empress, who was very discerning, and was observing him closely, said to herself that his courage could not be so great as to exceed his courtesy and discretion. At this time the emperor was seated in his chair, talking and laughing with the ladies and maidens-in-waiting as one who because he did them many favors and arranged fine marriages for them was dearly beloved by them all. And he said to them in a loud voice so that all the ladies heard him: "Honorable ladies and maidens, you behold here the Knight of the Green Sword, your loyal servant. Honor him and love him, for thus does he all of you in the world; for by exposing himself to very great risks in order to have you obtain justice, many times he has been at the point of death, according to what I have heard about him from those who are familiar with his great deeds."

The duchess, mother of Gastiles, said: "Sire, may God honor and love him and reward him for the help he gives us."

The emperor had two princesses stand up, who were daughters of King Garandel, at that time king of Hungary; and he said to them: "Go for my daughter Leonorina, and let no one except you two escort her."

They obeyed; and in a short while they came back escorting her arm in arm. And although she came very well arrayed, it all seemed as nothing compared with the naturalness of her great beauty: for there was not a man in the world who saw her who did not marvel and rejoice to behold her. She was a girl not yet nine years old; and coming up to where her mother, the empress, was, she kissed her hand with a humble curtsy and sat down on the dais below where she was. The Knight of the Green Sword gazed at her with delight, marveling greatly at her beauty, for she seemed to him more beautiful than any girls he had seen in the regions through which he had traveled. And he recalled then the very beautiful Oriana, his lady, whom he loved more than himself, and the time when he began to love her, for she was probably of that same age, and how the love that he had devoted to her then had grown and never decreased; and he remembered the good times with their many great delights that he had had with her, and the adverse times with their many cares and heartfelt sorrows that he had endured because of her, and about how he was not expecting to see her for a long time; so that in this reverie he remained for quite a while. He was so stirred by these memories that tears came to his eyes as if he were out of his senses; so that all saw him weeping, for because of his great excellence, they all were focusing their attention on him. But he, coming to his senses and being greatly embarrassed, wiped his eyes and assumed a cheerful mien. However the emperor, who was closest to him and had seen him in such tears, paid close attention in order to perceive anything that might have caused it. But not seeing any more signs of emotion in him, he was very desirous of finding out why a knight so strong, so discreet, had shown such great weakness in his presence and that of the empress and so many other people, that even on the part of a woman would have been deemed bad in such a place if she had been as animated as the knight had been with him. But he really thought that he would not have wept had there not been some great mystery involved. Gastiles, who was beside him, said: "How can it be that such a man as this should weep in this fashion in such a place?"

"I would not ask him about it," said the emperor, "but I think that he was constrained by love to do so."

"Well sire, if you wish to find out why, there is no one who would know except Master Elisabad, whom he greatly trusts and who speaks with him often in private."

Then he ordered Elisabad summoned and had him sit down beside him; and commanding that everyone else withdraw, he said to him: "Master, I want you to tell me a fact if you know it; and I promise you as emperor that no harm will come thereby to you or anyone else."

The master said to him: "Sire, I have such confidence that your virtuous Highness will do so and always favor me, even if I do not deserve it, that if I know the fact in question, I shall tell it to you very willingly."

"Why did the Knight of the Green Sword weep just now?" said the emperor. "Tell me, for on seeing it I am startled; and if he has any need of my help, I shall provide it for him so fully that he will be well satisfied."

When the physician heard this, he said: "Sire, I would be unable to say, because he is the one man in the world who best conceals what he wishes not to be known, because he is the most discreet knight you have ever beheld. But I often see him crying and grieving so bitterly that he seems to have lost his senses, and he sighs with very great yearning, as if his heart were breaking. And certainly, sire, in my opinion it is the great power of love that torments him as he longs for the woman he loves; for if it were any other kind of suffering, I am sure that it would be disclosed to me before being revealed to anyone else."

"Certainly," said the emperor, "I concur in what you say; and if he loves some woman, would to God that she might turn out to be in my dominions, for I would give him so much wealth and rank that there would be no king or prince who would not be pleased to give me his daughter as a wife for him. And I would take this action very gladly in order to keep him with me as a vassal; for regardless of how much I might do for him, his service to me, in view of his great valor, would be superior. And I greatly entreat you, master, to encourage him to stay with me, for all that he may demand will be granted him." And he remained in thought for a bit, for he fell silent, and then he said, "Master, go to the empress and tell her privately to beg the knight to stay with me; and do you so advise him out of regard for me, and in the meantime I shall arrange something that has come to mind."

The physician went to the empress and to the Knight of the Dwarf; and the emperor called the beautiful Leonorina his daughter and the two princesses who were in attendance upon her, and spoke with them for a long while very earnestly, but nothing of what he said to them was overheard by anyone. And he having now finished his conversation, Leonorina kissed his hands and went with the princesses to her room, and he remained talking with his nobles. The empress spoke with the Knight of the Green Sword in favor of his staying with the emperor, and the master urged him and counseled him to do so. And although that would be the best and most honorific opportunity that could come to him during the life of King Perion his father, he could not find it in his heart to accept it, for he encountered no rest or repose except in thinking about being back in that land where his greatly beloved lady Oriana was; so that neither pleading nor advice was able to influence him or cause him to renounce that desire that he had. And the empress indicated by signs to the emperor that the knight was not yielding to her entreaties. The emperor arose and going to them said: "Knight of the Green Sword, would it be in any way possible for you to remain with me? To this end there is nothing to be asked that I would not grant, were it in my power to do so."

"Sire," said he, "so great is your virtue and eminence that I would not dare, nor would I know how, to ask for such a boon as it would grant me, but there is not in me strength enough for my heart to permit it. And sire, do not blame me for not complying with your mandate; for if I were to do so, death would not leave me in your service for very long."

The emperor truly believed that his emotion was caused only by a great excess of love, and everyone else thought so. Then at this juncture that beautiful Leonorina entered the palace with her radiant mien, which annulled all the beauty of other women, and the two princesses with her. And she wore on her head a very fine coronet and another even finer she carried in her hand, and she went directly to the Knight of the Green Sword and said to him: "Sir Knight of the Green Sword, I have never reached a time when I ask any boon except from my father, but now I wish to ask one of you. Tell me what you will do?"

And he knelt before her, and said: "My good lady, who would be of so little understanding as to fail to carry out your command if he were able to fulfill it? And I would be very foolish not to do your will; and now, my lady, demand what you please, for unto death it will be fulfilled."

"You make me very happy," said she, "and I thank you very much, and I wish to ask of you three boons."

And taking the beautiful coronet from her head, she said: "Let this be one: that you give this coronet to the most beautiful maiden you know, and greeting her on my behalf, you tell her to send me her command by letter or messenger, and that I send her this coronet, for such are the gifts that we have in this land, although I do not know her."

And then she took the other coronet, in which there set were many pearls and precious stones of great value, especially three that would illuminate a room completely, however dark it might be; and giving the coronet to the knight, she said: "Give this to the most beautiful matron you know. And tell her that I am sending it to her in order to make her acquaintance, and that I greatly entreat her to make herself known to me by her command; this is the other boon. And before I ask the third one of you, I wish to know what you will do with the coronets."

"What I shall do," said the knight, "will be to grant at once the first boon and free myself of it."

Then he took the first coronet, and placing it on her head, said: "I place this crown on the head of the most beautiful maiden that I now know; and if there be anyone to contradict, by force of arms I shall make him recognize it."

All were quite pleased with what he did, and Leonorina no less, although she was embarrassed to see herself praised; and they said that with justice he had granted the boon. And the empress said to him: "Certainly, Knight of the Green Sword, I would prefer for myself those men whom you might conquer by armed might to those ladies whom my daughter might overcome with her beauty."

He was embarrassed to hear himself praised by such a noble lady; and without making any reply, he turned to Leonorina, and said: "My lady, do you wish to ask of me the other boon?"

"Yes," said she, "and I beg you to tell me the reason why you wept, and who the lady is who has such great dominance over you and over your heart."

The knight changed color and lost his previous good countenance, so that all recognized that he was disturbed by that demand; and he said: "Lady, please desist from this demand and make another that may be more to your advantage."

And she said: "This is what I demand, and I wish nothing more."

He bowed his head and was hesitating for a bit so that his having to tell seemed to everyone to be very difficult for him. And it was not long before he lifted his head with a happy mien and gazed at Leonorina, who was in front of him; and he said: "My lady, since I cannot otherwise free myself from my promise, I say that when you first entered here and I looked at you, I bethought myself of the age and the period at which you now are, and there came into my heart the remembrance of such a period when already it was so good and delightful that since I had already experienced it, it made me weep as you have seen."

And she said: "Well, tell me now who the lady is by whom your heart is commanded."

"Your great courtesy," said he, "that has never been remiss to anyone is against me. This constitutes my great misfortune; and since I cannot help it, I must speak contrary to my pleasure. Know you, lady, that the one whom I love the most is the same one to whom you are sending the crown, who in my opinion is the most beautiful matron of any I have ever seen, and even, I believe, of any that there are in the world. And by Heaven, madam, do not seek to learn more from me, for I am freed of my promise."

"You are free," said the emperor, "but in such wise that we don't know any more than before."

"Well it seems to me," said he, "that I have told more than ever before issued from my mouth, and this has been caused by the desire that I have to serve this beautiful lady."

"So help me God," said the emperor, "you must be very guarded and secretive in your love affair since you attach such importance to its having been revealed. And since my daughter was the cause of it, it is necessary that she ask your pardon."

"This mistake," said he, "many others have made, and never did they find out so much about me; so that although about them I might have complained, what has to do with your very beautiful daughter I consider a favor, because she, being so noble and so outstanding in the world, has sought so carefully to learn about the affairs of a knight errant such as I. But you, sire, I shall not pardon so easily, for according to the long and secret conversation you had with her previously, it is quite evident that she did it more because of your desire than hers."

The emperor laughed exceedingly, and said: "In everything God has made you accomplished. Know you that it is just as you say; therefore I wish to set straight what pertains to her and to me."

He of the Green Sword knelt to kiss his hands, but he was unwilling, and the knight said: "Sire, I receive these amends in order to take advantage of them when perchance you are more unconcerned about it."

"That cannot be," said the emperor, "for my memory of you will never falter, nor those amends be lacking whenever you desire them."

These words were exchanged between that emperor and the Knight of the Green Sword almost facetiously; but there came a time when the effect of them resulted in a great deed, as will be related in the fourth Book of this story.

The beautiful Leonorina said: "Sir Knight of the Green Sword, although you have no complaint against me, I am not on that account free of all blame for importuning you so insistently against your will; and as amends for it I wish you to have this ring."

He said: "Madam, you will give the hand that wears it to me to kiss as your servant, for the ring cannot be worn on any other hand without its complaining of me."

"Still," said she, "I wish it to be yours, so that it may remind you of that concealed snare that I set for you, and how with such great subtlety you escaped from it."

Then she took off the ring and threw it onto the dais in front of the knight, saying: "Another such remains with me in this coronet which I do not know whether you gave me rightly."

"Those beautiful eyes and wonderful hair are great and good witnesses, along with everything else that through His special grace God has given you."

And taking the ring, he saw that it was the most beautiful and rarest that he had ever beheld, nor in the world was there any other precious stone like the one set in it except the one that remained in the coronet. And while the Knight of the Green Sword was thus scrutinizing it, the emperor said: "I want you to know where this stone came from. You see already that the half of it is the finest and most resplendent ruby that has ever been seen, and the other half is a white ruby, which perchance you have never seen, for it is much more beautiful and more valuable than the red one; and the ring with an emerald such that one like it would be hard to find anywhere. Now know you that Apolidon, who is so famous throughout the world, was my grandfather; I do not know whether you have heard so."

"I know that very well," said he of the Green Sword, "because, being a long time in Great Britain, I saw the Island called Firm, where there are great marvels that he left, and that island, according to what the people remember, he won in a way greatly to his honor; for while carrying off the daughter of the emperor of Rome, he landed on that island amid a great storm, and according to its custom, he was forced to fight with a giant who at the time ruled over it; whom by slaying very courageously, he remained as lord of the island, where he dwelt a long while with his mistress Grimanesa. And according to records he left behind there, more than a hundred years went by during which no knight excelling him in prowess at arms put into port there. I have already been there, and I tell you, sire, that you appear to be of that lineage according to your appearance and that of their effigies that he left under the arch of loyal lovers, which appear truly alive."

"You make me very happy," said the emperor, "by reminding me of facts concerning that man, who in his own time had no equal in excellence; and I beg you to tell me the name of the knight who by demonstrating more valor and strength than he, won the Firm Island."

The knight said: "His name was Amadis of Gaul, son of King Perion, whose so very many extraordinarily great exploits are bruited about everywhere, the one who was found on the sea as a newborn babe, enclosed in a chest. And under the name of Child of the Sea, he killed in single combat the mighty King Abies of Ireland, and then was recognized by his father and mother."

"Now I am happier than before, because, according to the astounding reports concerning him, I do not deem it a discredit that he has excelled my grandfather in excellence, since he surpasses all those now living. And if I thought that he, being the son of such a king and such a noble lord, would venture so far from his own land, I would certainly think you were he; but what I am saying makes me doubt it; and moreover, if you were he, you would not be so rude as to fail to tell me so."

He of the Green Sword was greatly disconcerted by this speech, but he still sought to conceal his identity; and not answering this at all, he said: "If it may please your Majesty, tell me how the stone was divided."

"I will tell you that," said he, "gladly. Well, Felipanos, who at the time was King of Judea, sent to Apolidon, my grandfather, about whom I'm telling you, when he was ruler of this empire, twelve very fine coronets of great value; and although large pearls and precious stones came in all of them, in that one that you gave to my daughter there was this stone that was entirely whole. Then Apolidon, on seeing that this crown was the most beautiful on account of the stone, gave it to Grimanesa, my grandmother; and she, in order that Apolidon might have his share of it, ordered a master craftsman to divide it and make that ring with half of it; and after she gave it to Apolidon, the other half remained in that coronet just as you see; so that ring was divided because of love and because of it was given away. Hence I believe that my daughter gave it to you out of good love, and it will be possible that out of another, greater love it will be given away by you."

Thus it came about later just as the emperor said, and finally it was returned to the hand of that lady from whom it had come by that man who, during three years which elapsed without his seeing her, performed many feats at arms and endured many great cares and sufferings out of love for her, as is related in a continuation of this story which is called *Las Sergas de Esplandián*, which means *The Exploits of Esplandian.*

Just as you hear, the Knight of the Green Sword relaxed for six days at the court of the emperor, being so honored by him, and by the empress, and by that beautiful Leonorina, that he could not have been more so. And remembering that he had promised Grasinda to be with her within a year, and that the deadline was approaching, he spoke with the emperor, telling him that he had to leave there. And then he asked him as a favor to command him to serve him wherever he might be; saying that he would not be in any place with so much honor or pleasure or need, that he would not leave it all to serve him; and that if he should become aware of his having need of him for his service, he would not wait for his command, but without it would be constrained to hasten to him from wherever he was.

The emperor said to him: "My good friend, this very sudden departure you will not be taking without my displeasure, if it can be avoided without your breaking your word."

"Sire," said he, "it cannot be avoided without my honor and veracity incurring great discredit, as Master Elisabad knows, for I have to be at a place where I have promised to appear within a specified time."

"Well, since that is the way it is," said he, "I beg you to enjoy yourself here for three days."

He said he would do so, since that was his command. At this time he was in the presence of beautiful Leonorina, and taking him by the cloak, she said to him: "My good friend, since at the request of my father you are remaining three days longer, I wish that at my request you remain two more, and during these days that you be my guest and that of my maidens where they and I dwell, because we wish to speak with you without anyone's disturbing you, unless it would be the two knights who would be most pleasing to you as companions at meals and during the night. And this boon I ask you to grant willingly; if not, I shall have these maidens of mine seize you, and there won't be anything for me to thank you for."

Then more than twenty very beautiful and splendidly garbed maidens surrounded him; and Leonorina, laughing heartily with much enjoyment said: "Let him be until we see what he will say."

He was very happy with what that beautiful little lady was doing, considering it the greatest honor that had been done him there; and he said to her: "Blessed and beautiful lady, who would make bold to refuse to do your will, if he had the expectation, should he not do it, of such harsh confinement? And I agree to what you command, both to this and to everything else that may be of service to you and to your father and mother. And may it please God out of His mercy, my good lady, that the honors and favors that I receive from you and from them may come to me at a time when they may be requited and repaid in service by me and by my family."

This was carried out very completely, not by this Knight of the Green Sword but by that son of his, Esplandian, who gave aid to this emperor at a time and period when he had great need of it, just as Urganda the Unknown had prophesied in the fourth

Book, in a prophecy which will be told later in due time. The maidens said to him: "You have made a good decision; otherwise you would not have been able to escape from a greater danger than was that of the Endriago."

"That's what I think, ladies," said he, "for greater harm could come by angering angels than the Devil, which the Endriago was."

The emperor and the empress and all the nobles who were there took great pleasure in these verbal exchanges; and the witty replies that the Knight of the Green Sword gave to all that was said to him seemed to them very fine; therefore this even more than his great courage caused them to believe him to be a man of high rank, because courage and valor often thrive in persons of low fortune and coarse mind, and seldom do modest courtesy and a polished upbringing, because this is committed to those who come from pure, noble blood. I do not affirm that all attain it, but I do say that as a thing to which they are so constrained and obligated they ought to attain it, just as this Knight of the Green Sword did; for by encircling the bravery of his strong heart with a border of great tolerance and a pleasant manner with others, he prevented pride and anger from finding an opportunity whereby they could harm his great integrity.

Hence the Knight of the Green Sword remained there for three days with the emperor, having Gastiles, the latter's nephew, and the Marquis Saluder take him about that city and show him the rare things that were in it, since it was the capital and most important place of all Christendom; and staying afterwards in the palace — most of the time in the chamber of the empress talking with her and with other great ladies by whom she was attended and accompanied. And then he moved to the apartment of the beautiful Leonorina, where he met many daughters of kings and dukes and counts and other noblemen, in whose company he lived more honored and more graciously than anywhere save in the presence of Oriana, his lady; they asking him very earnestly to tell them about the marvels of the Firm Island, since he had been on it — especially about the Arch of Faithful Lovers and the Forbidden Chamber, and who and how many had been able to see the beautiful images of Apolidon and Grimanesa — likewise asking him to tell them about the manners of the ladies and maidens of King Lisuarte's court, and the names of the most beautiful. He answered everything for them very discreetly and humbly with what he knew about it as one who so many times had seen and frequented that court, just as the story has related.

And thus it happened that while gazing at the great and abundant beauty of that princess and her maidens, he began to think about his lady Oriana, reflecting that if she were there, all the beauty in the world would be united. And he recalled how remote and far away from him she was without his having hope of being able to see her, and he became so dismayed that he was almost out of his senses; so that those ladies knew that nothing of what they were saying to him was being heard by him. And thus he remained for a long interval, until Queen Menoresa, who was suzerain of the great island called Gabasta and was after Leonorina the most beautiful woman of all Greece, took him by the hand and by drawing him to her made him emerge from that profound absorption; from which he came forth groaning and sighing like a man who felt great sorrow. But as soon as he was conscious, he became very much embarrassed, for he well knew that he would be called to account by all of them; and he said: "Ladies, do not consider it strange or extraordinary that he who sees your great beauty and grace that God has bestowed on you should be reminded of some good fortune, if he had seen it previously and with great honor had experienced delights, and undeservedly had lost it in such wise that I do not know when I can recover it through any zeal or effort that I might be able to muster."

He said this to them with that sadness which his tormented heart transmitted to his countenance; so that those maidens were moved to great pity for him. But he, with considerable effort restraining the tears that came from his heart to his eyes, strove to restore to himself and to those damsels their lost cheerfulness. In these and other like activities, the Knight of the Green Sword spent there the time promised. And now as he was about to take leave of them, those ladies were presenting him gifts of great value. But he would accept only six swords that Queen Menoresa gave him, which were some of the handsomest and most finely ornamented ones to be found anywhere. And she said that she was giving them to him only in order that when he gave them away to his friends, he might be reminded of her and of those ladies who had such affection for him. The beautiful Leonorina said to him: "Sir Knight of the Dwarf, I beg you as a courtesy that if it be possible you come back soon to see and stay with my father, who greatly esteems you. And I know that you will afford him and all the noblemen of his court great pleasure and us ladies much more, because we shall be under your protection and defense if anyone should disturb us. And if this cannot be, I, along with all these ladies, beg you to send us a knight of your lineage, whom you may deem fit to serve us wherever he be needed by us, and with whom we may speak in remembrance of you and thus dispel some of the loneliness in which your departure leaves us; for indeed we believe, judging from your own qualities, that you have relatives who can substitute for you without occasioning you much embarrassment."

"Madam," said he, "that can be said very truthfully, for there are in my family such knights that compared with their excellence mine would be considered as nothing at all; and among them there is one whom I trust that if out of God's mercy he can come to serve you, those great honors and favors that I have received from your father and from you without my deserving them, he will repay with such services that, wherever I may be, I may believe myself to be already relieved of this very great debt."

He said this with reference to his brother Galaor, for he was thinking of having him come there where there would be so much honor for him, and where also his very great excellence would be esteemed to the proper degree. But this was not carried out as the Knight of the Green Sword had thought; rather instead of his brother Don Galaor, there came there another knight of his line at such a juncture and time that he made that beautiful lady suffer so many anxieties and such worry as would be hard to describe; because he underwent both by sea and by land such rare and dangerous adventures, that no other in his time, nor for long afterwards, was known to be his equal, as will be recounted in a sequel proceeding from these Books, entitled *The Exploits of Esplandian*, as has already been told you.

Then, with that lady Leonorina very earnestly begging him to come back or send them that knight about whom he was talking, and he promising her to do so, and she giving him permission to depart, all the ladies went up to the palace windows, which they did not leave until they lost sight of him as he went sailing away over the sea in his galley.

You have previously been told how the Patin sent Salustanquidio, his cousin, with a great retinue of knights, and Queen Sardamira with many ladies and maidens-in-waiting, to King Lisuarte to ask for the hand of his daughter Oriana in marriage. Now know you that these messengers, wherever they went, gave letters from the emperor to the princes and grandees whom they met on their way, in which he begged them to honor and serve the empress Oriana, daughter of King Lisuarte, whom he already considered his wife. Although they by their words showed a willingness to do so, among themselves they prayed God that such a good lady, daughter of such a king, might not come to a man so scorned and hated by all the people who knew him and very rightly so, because his rudeness and arrogance were so excessive that to no one, no matter how great he might be, of those of his empire and of the other realms that he was able to bring under his sway, did he do honor; rather, he scorned and vilified them, as if thereby he believed his status to be rendered more enhanced and secure.

Oh such a mad thought for any prince to entertain: that when he is justifiably hated by his own people, he could be beloved of God! Then if he is hated by God, what can he hope for in this world and in the next? Certainly, nothing else but to be dishonored and destroyed in both, and to have his soul forever in Hell.

So those emissaries reached a port opposite Great Britain called Zamando, and there they waited until they found boats in which to cross; and meanwhile they sent word to King Lisuarte that they were coming to him with a message from the emperor, their lord, with which he would be quite pleased.

CHAPTER LXXV

HOW THE KNIGHT OF THE GREEN SWORD LEFT CONSTANTINOPLE IN ORDER TO CARRY OUT THE PROMISE MADE BY HIM TO THE VERY BEAUTIFUL GRASINDA; AND HOW, BEING DETERMINED TO SET OUT WITH THIS LADY TO GREAT BRITAIN IN ORDER TO CARRY OUT HER COMMAND, IT HAPPENED WHILE HE WAS OUT HUNTING THAT HE FOUND DON BRUNEO DE BONAMAR BADLY WOUNDED. AND ALSO HEREIN IS RELATED THE ADVENTURE WHEREBY ANGRIOTE DE ESTRAVAUS ENCOUNTERED THEM, AND TOGETHER THEY ALL CAME TO THE HOUSE OF BEAUTIFUL GRASINDA.

The Knight of the Green Sword having set out from the port of Constantinople, the weather became good and favorable for his voyage, which was undertaken with the thought that he might [ultimately] be going to that land where his lady Oriana was. This caused him to be very happy, although at that time he had been more worried and tormented on her account than he had ever been before, because he had sojourned three years in Germany and two in Romania and in Greece, and meanwhile not only had he failed to receive any message from her, but also had had no news concerning her. Well, things turned out so favorably for him that in three weeks he made port at that town where Grasinda was. And when she learned this, she was very happy, for she already knew that he had killed the Endriago and knew about the mighty giants which on the islands of Romania he had overcome and slain. And she donned her finest garb, as the rich and noble lady that she was, in order to receive him; and she gave orders to bring horses for him and for Master Elisabad on which to ride away from the ship. And he of the Green Sword dressed himself in rich apparel, and he on a beautiful horse and the physician on a palfrey went to the town, where his rare and famous exploits already having become known to everyone, he was regarded and honored as a wonder by them all, as likewise was the master, who had important family connections and was very influential there. Grasinda came out with all her ladies and maidens-in-waiting to receive him in the courtyard. And he, on dismounting, made a low bow to her and she to him, as persons who had an honest affection for each other. Grasinda said to him: "Sir Knight of the Green Sword, in everything God has made you punctilious, for after you experienced so many dangers, so many rare adventures, your good fortune, which has willed it thus, has brought you to carry out and redeem the pledge that you left with me, because five days from today the year's time limit promised by you expires, and may it please Him to dispose your heart to fulfill as completely the other boon that is still to be asked."

"Madam," said he, "never shall I, God willing, be remiss in what is promised by me, especially to such an excellent lady as you are, who has been so good to me; for if I put my life at your service, one ought not to thank me, since because of your giving me the physician Elisabad I am still alive."

"May the service be well employed," said she, "since it is so greatly appreciated. And now come and dine, for I cannot willingly ask you to do anything — no matter how much — without your great energy causing you to do more."

Then they conducted him to the patio with the beautiful trees, where once he had been healed of the wound, as has been told you. And there he was served, and Master Elisabad likewise, in the way they would be in the house of a lady who had such affection for them; and in a chamber that was adjacent to that courtyard the Knight of the Green Sword lodged that night. Before he went to sleep he talked a very long while with Gandalin, telling how happy at heart he would be to be going to where his lady love was, if the boon promised that lady Grasinda did not prevent it. Gandalin said to him: "Sir, take happiness when it comes, and leave the rest to God our Lord, for it may be that the boon promised the lady will help to augment your pleasure."

So he slept that night somewhat more peacefully; and in the morning he arose and went to Grasinda's chapel to hear mass with her, she being attended by her ladies and maidens-in-waiting. After it was over, she commanded everyone to retire, and taking him by the hand, there on a stone bench she sat down with him, and addressing him she said: "Knight of the Green Sword, you should be informed that a year before you came here, all the matrons who were extremely beautiful over and above all others were together at a wedding for which invitations had been issued by the Duke of Vaselia, at which wedding my escort was my brother the Marquis Saluder, whom you know. And all the ladies being together, and I with them, there entered there all the nobles who had come to those festivities; and my brother the marquis, I know not whether out of affection or folly, said in a loud voice, so that all heard it, that my beauty was so great that I excelled all the matrons who were there, and that if anyone should deny it, he by force of arms would make him admit it. And I do not know whether on account of his valor or because it seemed to the others just as it did to him, suffice it to say that because no one responded to his challenge, I remained adjudged the most beautiful of all the beautiful matrons of Romania — which is large, as you know — so that therefore my heart is ever quite proud and happy. And it would be much more so and at a much higher level if through you I might obtain what my heart so greatly desires; and I would not spare personal effort, nor the expense for attendants, however great that may be."

"My lady," said he, "demand whatever will give you most pleasure, and may it be something that I can carry out, because it definitely will be put into execution at once."

"My lord," said she, "then what I ask you as a favor is since I know for certain that there are at the court of King Lisuarte of Great Britain, the most beautiful women in the whole world, that you take me there, and that by force of arms if it cannot be otherwise, you cause me to win that great distinction for beauty over all the maidens who may be there — which here in these parts I won over the matrons, as I have already told you — by declaring that in Lisuarte's court there are no maidens so beautiful as is a matron that you are escorting. And if anyone should deny it, that you make him recognize it by force of arms. I shall wear a fine coronet that you shall wager on my behalf; and likewise have the knight who fights with you wager another, so that the victor may carry off both in token of having the most beautiful woman on his side. And if God causes us to leave there with honor, you shall take me from there to the island called Firm, where they tell me there is an enchanted chamber which no woman, either matron or maiden, can enter except the one who surpasses in beauty the very beautiful Grimanesa, who in her time had no peer. And this is the boon that I ask of you."

When this was heard by the Knight of the Green Sword, he was completely unmanned, and said with a very sad countenance: "Alas, lady, you have slain me! And if you have done me great favors you have transformed them for me into greater harm."

And he was so stricken as to be at his wits' end. He was thinking that if with such a purpose he were to go to the court of King Lisuarte, he would be ruined with his lady Oriana, for he feared her more than death; and he well knew that in the court there were very good knights who would undertake the enterprise on her behalf, since they would have justice and reason on their side so completely; and that in view of the very great difference between Oriana's beauty and that of all other women in the world, he could not emerge from the said quest that he would be undertaking except dishonored or dead. And on the other hand he thought that if he failed to keep his word to that lady, from whom without her knowing his identity he had received so many honors and favors, it would be a very great degradation of his fame and honor; so that he was in the greatest danger that he had experienced since he had left Gaul. And he cursed himself and his ill fortune, and the hour he was born and his having come to those lands of Romania. But immediately he suddenly bethought himself of a great remedy: he remembered that Oriana was not a maiden and that he who would enter into combat on her behalf would be doing so mistakenly; therefore when afterwards he would be able to see her, he would make her understand the reason why that was taking place. And this remedy having been found, he abandoned his great worry, which had tormented him greatly by placing him in the greatest possible predicament — one in which he never had expected to find himself — and at once he became again very happy and of good countenance, as if nothing had hapened on his account; and he said to Grasinda: "My good lady, I ask your pardon for the annoyance I have caused you, for I am willing to carry out all that you ask of me, if it be the will of God. And if I hesitated somewhat, it was not of my own will, but because of my heart's desire which I cannot resist, for it was directing its journey to another region; and that was the cause of the words that I spoke, it being what in all respects has me subjugated. But the great honors that I have received from you have such cogency that overcoming my secret desire, they leave me free so that without any delay I am enabled to carry out what is so greatly to your liking."

Grasinda said to him: "Certainly, my good sir, I believe quite implicitly what you tell me. But I say to you that I was very greatly disturbed when I saw you thus."

And extending her very beautiful arms and placing them on his shoulders, she pardoned him for what had occurred, saying: "My lord, I long to see the day when your great prowess at arms will enable me to wear on my head that coronet which will be won through you from the most beautiful maidens of Great Britain, I returning to my land with that great distinction with which I, out of all the matrons of Romania, departed from it."

And he said to her: "My lady, she who is to go on such a journey must not cease to worry, for you are to pass through very strange lands and among people of diverse languages, where great hardship and danger are presented; and if I had not promised the boon, and if my advice had been asked, it would have been that a person of such high honor and station as you are ought not to risk such danger in order to win that without which she can get along very well and with great distinction, being possessed of so much beauty and loveliness."

"My lord," said she, "I am more pleased with the good effort that you have mustered for the journey than with the advice that you would give me; for since I have such a helper as you, without any misgivings I expect to satisfy my desire, which has been striving for so long to attain satisfaction. And these strange lands and people that you mention can very easily be avoided, since by sea better than by land our journey can be made, as I am informed by many who know about it."

"My lady," said he, "I am to protect and serve you; command whatever best satisfies your desire, for that will be carried out by me."

"I thank you very much," said she, "and do believe that I shall bring the kind of adornment and retinue that such a leader as you deserves."

"In God's name," said he, "may it all be."

Thus their conversation ended for the time being. After the Knight of the Green Sword had been there two days, he had a desire to go hunting, being a man who, when he had no cause to take up arms, was accustomed to pass the time in other pursuits. And taking with him some knights who were there, and beaters skilled in their task, he went to a very dense forest two leagues from the town, where there were many deer. And they set him up with two very beautiful dogs in a line of beaters between the thickly wooded mountain and a forest that was not very far from it, where the game was accustomed to appear most frequently. It was not long before he killed two very large deer, and the beaters killed another; and it being now nearly night, the huntsmen sounded the horn. But the Knight of the Green Sword, as he was about to go to them, saw a marvelously beautiful deer coming out of a thicket; and when he set the dogs on it, the deer, on seeing itself hard pressed, plunged into a large lake, thinking to seek refuge there; but the dogs went in, for they were very eager for the game, and they took it; and the Knight of the Green Sword on coming up, killed it. Gandalin — who was with him, for in his companionship he took great delight and had talked with him a great deal on that expedition about how he was intending to go quickly to the land where his lady was, taking great comfort in talking about it (as one who had not seen her for a long time, as you have heard) — dismounted very quickly and fleshed the dogs, who were very good, being a person who had demonstrated that skill many times.

This having taken time, it was already nightfall, so that they could scarcely see. And putting the deer very quickly into a thicket and scattering over it some green boughs, they mounted their horses. On account of the great density of the thickets they quickly lost their sense of direction as to which way they should go. They did not know what to do; and without knowing where they were going, they traveled a while through the wooded hilly area, thinking to encounter some road or some member of their company; but not finding any, by chance they happened upon a spring. And there their horses drank, and already without hope of obtaining any other shelter, they dismounted. Taking off the saddles and bridles, they let the horses graze on the green grass that was nearby. But he of the Green Sword, bidding Gandalin to watch over them, went toward some large trees that were near there, so that by being alone he might better think about his affairs and his lady. And on coming close to the trees he saw a dead white horse, gashed by mighty blows; and he heard among the trees a very pitiful groaning, but could not see from whom it came, for the night was dark and the trees had a very thick growth. And seating himself under a tree, he remained listening in an attempt to learn who that could be; and it was not long before he heard him say with great anguish and pain: "Alas, miserable hapless wretch, Bruneo de Bonamar, now it is fitting that your earthly desires, by which you have always been so tormented, should come to an end and die with you! Now you will not see that noble friend of yours, Amadis of Gaul, on account of whom you have endured such anxiety and travail throughout foreign lands, — Amadis, who was so esteemed and loved by you above all others in the world; for without him and without relative or friend to grieve over you, you must pass from this life to cruel death, which is already drawing near!"

And afterwards he said: "Oh my lady Melicia, flower and paragon more than all other women in the world, never more will you be seen or served by your loyal vassal Bruneo de Bonamar, the one who neither in word nor deed has ever ceased to love you more than himself! My lady, you lose what you can never recover, for certainly, my lady, there will never be another who will love you as faithfully as I. You were the one by whom I was sustained and made happy because of my delectable memories of you, whence came to me knightly courage and ardor, without my being able to requite this by serving you; and now that I was doing so by undertaking to find this brother whom you love so much, from whose quest I never would have departed without finding him, nor have dared to appear before you, my bad luck, not affording me any opportunity to render you this service, has brought me to the point of death, which I always have feared would come to me on your account."

And then he said: "Ah, my good friend Angriote de Estravaus! Where are you now, for so long we remained firm in this quest? And to think that at the end of my days I cannot have aid or succor! Cruel was my fortune to me when last night it willed that the two of us be separated; harsh and painful was that parting, for now as long as the world endures we shall never more see each other; but may God receive my soul, and may He protect your great loyalty as it deserves."

Then ceasing to speak, he groaned and sighed very pitifully. The Knight of the Green Sword, who had heard it all, was weeping very bitterly; and when he saw him quieted down, he went to him and said: "Oh, my lord and good friend Don Bruneo de Bonamar! Do not grieve, and have hope in that very merciful God, for He has willed at such a time for you to be found in order to help you with what you really need, which will be medication for the illness on account of which you suffer pain. And do believe, my lord Don Bruneo, that if one can be remedied and restored to health through the knowledge of mortal man, you shall be with the help of our Lord God."

Don Bruneo thought because he saw him weeping so bitterly that it was his squire Lasindo, whom he had sent to look for some priest to hear his confession; and he said: "My friend Lasindo, you are very late, for my death is approaching. Now I beg of you that as soon as you take me from here, you go directly to Gaul and pay my respects to the princess, and give her this part of a sleeve from my shirt on which seven letters are written with a stick dipped in my blood, for my strength was not sufficient for more. And I trust that out of her great courtesy that pity which she did not have for me by sustaining my life, on seeing the letters with some feeling of grief, she will have for my death, considering that I have received it in her service while seeking with so much danger and travail that brother whom she loves so much."

The Knight of the Green Sword said to him: "My friend Don Bruneo, I am not Lasindo, but the one on account of whom you have received so much harm. I am your friend Amadis of Gaul, who regrets your perilous situation as much as you do.

Do not fear, for God will help you, and I shall with a physician such that with His help he will restore you to health as long as your soul be not departed from your flesh."

Don Bruneo, although he was very befuddled and weak from the great amount of blood that he had lost, recognized him by his speech, and holding out his arms to him, took and embraced him, the tears falling down his cheeks in great abundance. But he of the Green Sword likewise weeping and holding him embraced, shouted to Gandalin to come to him quickly; and when he arrived he said to him: "Alas, Gandalin! You see here my lord and faithful friend Don Bruneo, who on account of searching for me has undergone great hardship and now is at the point of death. Help me disarm him."

Then they both took him and very gently they disarmed him and laid him on a tabard of Gandalin's and they covered him with another belonging to the Knight of the Green Sword. And Amadis ordered Gandalin to climb up on some knoll as quickly as he could and wait until morning; and then to go to the physician Elisabad in town, and tell him on his behalf that in the name of the great trust that he had in him to come at once to him bringing everything needed to heal a knight who was badly wounded, and to believe that this knight was one of the best friends he had; and to beg Grasinda as a favor to order brought there, in order to carry him to the town, such equipment as befitted a knight of such noble lineage and of such great prowess at arms as he was. And while he of the Green Sword remained there with Don Bruneo, holding his head on his knees and comforting him, Gandalin went at once with that message; and going up on a high hill of the forest, day having come, he saw the town immediately; and spurring his horse, he went toward it. And so with that haste that he made, he entered the town without answering anything to those who questioned him, in order not to stop, and everybody thought some accident had happened to his lord. And he arrived at the house of the physician Elisabad, who, after hearing the message from the Knight of the Green Sword and remarking Gandalin's great haste, believed the matter was very serious, took everything that was necessary for such an emergency and mounting his palfrey awaited the guidance of Gandalin, who was relating to Grasinda what had happened to his lord and what he was asking her as a favor. And leaving her, they took the road to the mountainous region, whence in a short space of time they arrived at the place where the knights were. And when the physician Elisabad saw that the Knight of the Green Sword, his faithful friend, was holding the head of the other knight on his lap and was weeping profusely, he really thought that he loved him dearly; and he came up laughing and said: "My lords, do not fear, for God will quickly provide counsel whereby you will be happy."

With this, he went up to Don Bruneo and examined his wounds, and found them swollen and inflamed with the cold of the night. But he put on them such medication that his pain was relieved immediately, so that sleep came to him, which was a great benefit and relief to him. And when he of the Green Sword saw that, and that the physician considered Don Bruneo in very little danger, he was very happy, and embracing him, said: "Ah, Master Elisabad, my good lord and my friend, how lucky for me has been your companionship, from which so much good and so much benefit has resulted! I ask God for mercy's sake that at some time I may be able to reward you for it, for although now you see me as a poor knight, it may be that before much time passes, you will judge me otherwise."

"So help me God, Knight of the Green Sword," said he, "I find it more satisfying and agreeable to serve and to help you than you would by giving me a reward; for I am quite certain that I shall never lack your generous gratitude; and about this matter let us not speak any more, but go eat dinner, for it is time."

And so they did, for Grasinda had ordered it brought to them very well prepared, as one who besides being such a noble lady, took great pains to please the Knight of the Green Sword at every opportunity. After they had eaten, they were talking about how beautiful those beech trees were that they saw there, and how in their opinion they were the tallest trees that they had ever seen anywhere.

And while they were looking at them, they saw a man on horseback coming, and he was carrying two heads of knights hanging from his horse's breast band, and in his hands a battle axe all red with blood. And when he saw that group of people by the trees, he stopped and was of a mind to go away. But the Knight of the Green Sword and Gandalin recognized him, for he was Lasindo, Don Bruneo's squire; and fearing that if he came up to them, in all innocence he would reveal their identity, he of the Green Sword said: "All of you remain quiet, and I shall see who that man is who is fearful of us, and for what reason he is carrying those heads in that manner."

Then mounting a horse and with a lance, he went toward him, and told Gandalin to follow him.

"And if that man does not await me, you will pursue him."

The squire, when he saw that they were coming toward him, kept retreating into the forest out of the fear that he had, and he of the Green Sword kept following him. But on reaching a valley, where the others could not hear or see them, he began to call out to him, saying: "Wait for me, Lasindo; do not fear me."

When he heard this, he turned his head and recognized that it was Amadis; and with great pleasure came to him and kissed his hand saying to him: "Alas, sir! You do not know the misfortunes and bad news about my lord Bruneo, who has participated in so many dangerous exploits while looking for you through foreign lands."

And he began to grieve sorely, saying: "Sir, these two knights told Angriote that they left Don Bruneo dead here in this forest, whereupon he cut off their heads and told me to put them beside him if Don Bruneo was dead, and if alive, to present them to him on his behalf."

"Oh, God!" said the Knight of the Green Sword. "What is this you are telling me? For I found Don Bruneo, but not in such a state of health as to be able to tell me anything. And now stop a moment, and Gandalin with you as if he had caught up with you and told you the news about your lord; and when you are in my presence, call me the Knight of the Green Sword."

"Already concerning this," said Lasindo, "I had been warned that I was to do so."

"And yonder you will tell us the news you know."

And immediately he returned to his company and told how Gandalin had gone after the squire; and in a little while they saw them both coming. And when Lasindo came up and saw the Knight of the Green Sword, he dismounted quickly and went and knelt before him, and said: "Blessed be God who brought you to this place, in order that you might be the restorer of the life of my lord Don Bruneo whom you love so dearly."

And Amadis raised him up by the hand and said: "My friend Lasindo, be you welcome, and you will find your lord in good condition. But now tell us why you bring those human heads with you."

"Sir," said he, "put me before Don Bruneo and there I shall tell you, for I have been ordered thus to do so."

Then they went to him where he was in a tent that Grasinda had ordered brought there with the other things. And Lasindo knelt before him and said: "My lord, you see here the heads of the knights who did you such great wrong, and your loyal friend Angriote de Estravaus sends them to you. When he ascertained the treachery they had perpetrated on you, he fought them both and killed them. And he will be here with you in a short while, for he has stopped at a convent which is at the edge of this forest to have a wound treated that he has in the leg; and when the bleeding is arrested, he will come at once."

"God help him!" said Don Bruneo, "and how will he contrive to come here?"

"He told me to come to the highest trees of this forest, where I would find you dead, for he thought so because of what one of these traitors told him before he killed him; and his mourning for you beggars description."

"Oh, God," said the Knight of the Green Sword, "protect him from harm and from danger. Tell me," he said to Lasindo, "shall you be able to guide me to that monastery?"

"I shall," said he.

Then he told Master Elisabad to have Don Bruneo carried on a litter to the town. And arming himself with Don Bruneo's arms, he mounted his horse and plunged into the forest, and with him Lasindo, who was carrying his shield and helmet and lance. And on arriving where the night before he had left the deer under the tree, they saw Angriote coming on his horse, his head bowed because he was mourning, whereat he of the Green Sword was greatly pleased. And immediately he saw coming behind Angriote four knights very well armed who were calling out to him in loud voices: "Wait, Sir false knight; you must lose your head in exchange for those that you cut off from those men who were worth much more than you."

Angriote turned his horse toward them, grasped his shield and prepared to defend himself against them without seeing him of the Green Sword; who had already taken up arms, and going as fast as his horse could carry him, overtook Angriote before the others arrived, and said: "Good friend, do not fear, for God will be on your side."

Angriote thought, according to his arms, that he was Don Bruneo, so that he was happy beyond comparison. But the knight of the Green Sword attacked the first one who came in front of the others. He was Bradansidel, the man with whom he had already jousted and forced to grasp the horse's tail in his hand while riding backwards, as you have already heard; and he was one of the most valiant at arms to be found in all that region. And he of the Green Sword struck him above his shield on the chest under his helmet flap so hard that he hurled him from the saddle to the ground unable to move hand or foot. And the three attacked Angriote and he them as one who was very valiant. But he of the Green Sword grasped his sword and rushed in with such fury among them dealing them such mighty blows that from a slash that he dealt one of them on top of the shoulder his armor was not able to prevent his being cut to the flesh and bone, so that he fell at the feet of Angriote, who marveled exceedingly at such strokes, for he could not believe that there was such prowess in Don Bruneo, because the knight had already overthrown another man. The remaining one saw him of the Green Sword coming at him, and not daring to await him, began to flee as fast as his horse could run. He of the Green Sword went after him to attack him, and the other out of his great fear missed the ford of a river and fell into deep water; so that, though his horse reached shore, the knight because of the weight of his arms was drowned. Then, giving his shield and helmet to Lasindo, the Knight of the Green Sword returned to Angriote, who was amazed at his great valor, thinking that he was Don Bruneo, as I already have told you. But on coming up close he recognized that it was Amadis, and he went to him with arms outstretched, thanking God for having enabled him to find him. And he of the Green Sword likewise went and embraced him, with tears of good will coming to the eyes of both, for they loved each other dearly. And he of the Green Sword said to him: "Now there becomes apparent, my lord, that faithful and true love you have for me in seeking me for such a long time through lands fraught with so many dangers."

"My lord, I cannot do so much, nor strive so hard to honor and serve you as not to be all the more under obligation to you, since you enabled me to possess that lady without whom I would not have been able to sustain life; and let us drop this matter, since the debt is so great that it can hardly be repaid. But tell me whether you know the unfortunate news about your great friend Don Bruneo de Bonamar."

"I already know the reports," said he of the Green Sword, "and they are auspicious, since God out of His mercy willed that I should find him at such a time."

Then he told him how he had found him, and how he left him in the care of the best physician that there was in the world, with the assurance that he would live. Angriote raised his hands to heaven thanking God for having thus restored him. Then they prepared to leave, and on passing by the knights that they had overcome, they found one of them alive. He of the Green Sword stopped, and leaning down, said to him: "Evil knight whom may God damn, tell me why, thus predisposed, you wish to kill knights errant. Tell it at once; if not, I shall cut off your head; and tell whether you were implicated in the misfortunes of the knight who bore these arms that I have."

"That he cannot deny," said Angriote, "for I left him with Don Bruneo and with two others in his company, and afterwards I found the two boasting that they had killed Don Bruneo; whom, by telling him that an attempt was being made to burn a sister of theirs, they were bringing along to help them; so that all of them must have been involved in the treachery, because Don Bruneo went with them under a pledge of safe-conduct in order to rescue the maiden so that she might not suffer, and I went away with an old knight who that night had lodged us, in order to force the return to him of a son of his who was being held prisoner at some tents down here on a river bank; and it turned out so well for me that I forced his return to him and I put into his own prison the one who had him imprisoned; and in this manner we parted from each other. Now let this man tell why they were guilty of such great treachery toward Bruneo."

He of the Green Sword said to Lasindo: "Dismount and cut off his head, for he is a traitor."

The knight was quite frightened and said: "Sir, for God's sake, have mercy, for I shall tell you the truth about what happened. Know you, sir knight, that we found out that these two knights were looking for the Knight of the Green Sword, for whom we have a mortal hatred; and on learning that they were his friends, we decided to kill them. Then thinking we could not accomplish it by taking them on together, we used those stories that this knight has related. And while going on our way on the pretext of setting the maiden free, talking, with our heads and hands disarmed, we arrived at that spring of the Tall Beeches; there, while the knight was watering his horse, we took up our lances, and I, who was next to him, snatched his sword from the scabbard; and before he could defend himself, we knocked him off his horse and gave him so many wounds that we left him for dead, as I think he will be."

He of the Green Sword said to him: "Why do you so hate me, as to commit such treachery?"

"What!" said he, "Are you the Knight of the Green Sword?"

"Yes, I am," said he, "and here you see that I am carrying it."

"Well, now I shall tell you what you ask. You will certainly recall how a year ago you passed through this land and that knight who lies dead there fought with you" — and he pointed to Bradansidel — "and he was the most vigorous and the strongest knight in this whole land, and the battle was in the presence of beautiful Grasinda. And Bradansidel with great arrogance imposed the condition that the one defeated was to observe, which was that while riding backwards on his horse, his shield upside down and the tail of the horse in his hand as rein, he should pass before that beautiful lady through the center of her town; which Bradansidel as the one defeated had to carry out to his great dishonor and discredit. And for this dishonor that you inflicted on him, he hated you implacably, as did all of us who are his relatives and friends; hence we fell into that error that you have seen. Now order me killed or let me live, for I have told you what you wanted to know."

"I shall not kill you," said he of the Green Sword, "because wicked men while living die many times and pay for what their evil deeds deserve, for in view of your vices that will be carried out just as I say."

And in order to carry the deer he ordered Lasindo to take a horse from among those that were running loose; then unbridling the remaining horses and running them through the forest, they went toward the town, where they expected to find Don Bruneo; and they brought along in front of them the deer on the horse.

The Knight of the Green Sword was moved to ask Angriote for news about Great Britain; hence the latter told him what he knew, although it had been a year and a half since he and Don Bruneo had left there on their expedition. Among other things, Angriote said to him: "Know you, my lord, that in the house of King Lisuarte there is a youth, the rarest and handsomest ever seen, concerning whom Urganda the Unknown has made known by her letter to the king and queen the great things in which if he lives he is to excel."

And he related how the hermit had brought him up, after snatching him from the mouth of a lioness, and the way King Lisuarte found him, and he told of the white and red letters that he had on his chest, and of how the king was rearing him very honorably because of what Urganda had said; and he said that in addition to the youth's being so handsome and graceful, he was also very well-mannered in all respects.

"God protect him!" said the Knight of the Green Sword. "You describe to me a very rare youth. Now tell me, about how old is he?"

"He may be about twelve years old," said Angriote, "and he and Ambor de Gadel, my son, serve Oriana, who shows them much favor, so good is their service — to such a degree, that in that house of the king there are no others so honored nor so admired as they. But they are very different in appearance, for one is the most handsome to be found anywhere and much the better mannered, whereas Ambor seems to me very lazy."

"Oh, Angriote," said the Knight of the Green Sword, "do not pass judgment on your son at a time when he is too young to succeed in being at all self-disciplined. And I tell you, my good friend, that if he were a little older and Oriana should wish to give him up, I would take him with me, and I would make Gandalin a knight, for he has served me and taken care of me for such a long time."

"So help me God," said Angriote, "he deserves that very well indeed, and I believe that knighthood will be very properly conferred on him, since he is one of the best squires in the world. And if he were a knight and my son were to come in to serve you in his place, then I would lose the suspicion that I have, and I would become very hopeful that from accompanying you he would emerge such a man that he would do great honor to his lineage. And now let us drop the matter until the proper time, for God will decide it." And then he said to him: "Know you, sir, that Don Bruneo and I have traveled through all the regions of these islands of Romania, where we learned of the great feats that you have accomplished at arms, not only against very arrogant knights, but also against powerful and evil giants; for all the people who know about this are still amazed at having seen how one man alone could withstand such confrontations and dangers. And there we found out about the death of the fearful and mighty Endriago, whence you have caused us to wonder greatly how you dared to attack the Devil himself, for we were told that Endriago was his embodiment and that devils engendered it and brought it up, although it was the son of that giant and his daughter. I beg you, my lord, to tell me how you dealt with it so that I may hear about the most rare and terrifying thing that has come about through the effort of mortal man."

And the Knight of the Green Sword said to him: "Of the matter that you ask about, Gandalin and the physician who healed Don Bruneo are better witnesses than I, and they will tell you about it."

While talking just as you hear, they reached the town, where they were received by Grasinda, Angriote having been already warned that Amadis was not to be called by any name other than Knight of the Green Sword; and they met a number of armed knights, who by order of Grasinda were about to go look for them. And taking the latter with her, she brought them to the chamber of the Knight of the Green Sword, where Don Bruneo de Bonamar had been put to bed. When they went in and found him in good condition, who could tell you of the pleasure they experienced as all three beheld themselves together? And likewise that very beautiful lady was pleased, considering herself very highly honored by being in her house under the protection of such distinguished knights — a house in which they had found the shelter and aid that with difficulty they would have been able to encounter anywhere else. Then Angriote was given medical attention for his leg wound, which was much inflamed on account of travel and the effort he had put forth in the battle with the knights. And on another bed close to Don Bruneo's he was placed; and when these wounded men had eaten what the physician ordered, the others came out in order to let them rest. And the Knight of the Green Sword was fed in another room, and there he kept telling Grasinda about the prowess and great valor of those very faithful friends of his. After he had eaten, she went away to her ladies and maidens-in-waiting, and he of the Green Sword to his companions, for he loved them dearly; and he found them awake and talking. He ordered his bed placed next to theirs, and there they relaxed with much enjoyment, talking about many things they had experienced. The Knight of the Green Sword told them about the boon he had promised the lady and what she was asking of him, and how she was preparing to go by sea to Great Britain, which pleased Don Bruneo and Angriote very much because already, having found what they were seeking, they were desirous of returning to that land.

So he of the Green Sword, and Don Bruneo de Bonamar and Angriote de Estravaus were staying, just as the story relates, in the house of that beautiful lady Grasinda with much regalement and pleasure. And when they were in condition to set out by sea without endangering their health, the fleet of ships was already prepared, being equipped with food for a year, and with seamen and fighting men to the extent needed. And one Sunday morning in the month of May they embarked in the ships, and with favorable weather began to sail on their way to Great Britain.

CHAPTER LXXVI

CONCERNING HOW QUEEN SARDAMIRA WITH THE OTHER EMISSARIES WHOM THE EMPEROR OF ROME WAS SENDING TO BRING ORIANA, DAUGHTER OF KING LISUARTE, TO HIM, ARRIVED IN GREAT BRITAIN; WHAT HAPPENED TO THEM IN A FOREST, TO WHICH THEY HAD REPAIRED TO TAKE RECREATION, WITH A KNIGHT ERRANT WHOM THE EMISSARIES HAD INSULTED; AND THE PAYMENT THAT HE GAVE THEM FOR THE RUDE THINGS THEY HAD SAID TO HIM.

The emissaries of the emperor Patin on arriving in Lombardy obtained ships and crossed to Great Britain; and they put into port at Fenusa, where King Lisuarte was, by whom they were received with great honor; and he ordered good lodgings, with all the other things that they needed, to be given to them in great abundance. At this time many nobles were with the king, who was awaiting others for whom he had sent in order to take counsel with them concerning what he should do about the marriage of his daughter Oriana; hence he set a time limit of one month for giving the emissaries his answer, thus arousing great hope in them that it would be such as to render them happy. And he decided that Queen Sardamira — whom the emperor had sent there with twenty ladies and maidens in order to provide company for Oriana and to serve her on the return voyage across the sea — should go to Miraflores, where Oriana was, and expound to her the greatness of Rome and the high station that she would occupy through that marriage by having at her command so many kings and princes and numerous other noble lords. King Lisuarte was doing this because he knew that his daughter was greatly opposed to that marriage, and so that this queen, who was very clever, might incline her to it. But at that time Oriana was so troubled and with such great anguish that she was at her wits' end and unable to talk, because she thought that her father would hand her over to the Romans against her will, whence death would ensue for her and her lover Amadis.

So Queen Sardamira left for Miraflores, and Don Grumedan with her by command of the king in order to wait on her; and to protect her went knights of Rome, and of Sardinia, where she was queen. Thus it happened that while they were on a riverbank — which was verdant and adorned with beautiful flowers — waiting for the heat of the day to pass, her knights, who were boastful at arms, put their shields outside their tents, and they were five; whereupon Don Grumedan said to them: "Lords, have your shields put inside the tents, unless you wish to uphold the custom of the land, which is that any knight who places his shield or lance outside of his tent or house or hut where he is lodged, must engage in a joust with any knights who may demand it of him."

"We well understand that custom, and for that reason we are putting them outside," said they; "may God ordain that before we go from here, a joust be demanded by someone."

"In the name of God," said Don Grumedan, "since a few knights are accustomed to pass along here, and if they come, let us see how you fight."

And they being there, just as you hear, it was not long before there came that esteemed and valiant Don Florestan, who had traversed many lands looking for his brother Amadis, but had never found out anything about him; and he was going along greatly afflicted and very sad. And because he had learned that people from Rome and from other regions who had crossed the sea had come to the court of King Lisuarte, he came there to ascertain from them some news about his brother. When he saw the tents near the road along which he was going, he went thither to find out who was there; and coming up to the tent of Queen Sardamira, he saw her seated on a dais. She was one of the beautiful women of the world, and the tent had the flaps raised, so that all her ladies and maidens-in-waiting were in view. And in order better to observe the queen, who seemed to him so attractive and so elegant, thus mounted on horseback he went up between the ropes of the tent to see her better, and remained there for a time gazing at her. And while he was doing so, a maiden approached him saying: "Sir knight, you are not very polite to be on horseback so near such a good queen and the other ladies of noble rank who are there; it would be better to look at those shields yonder, which challenge you, as do their owners."

"Certainly, very good lady," said Don Florestan, "you speak quite truly; but perforce my eyes, out of their desire to see the very beautiful queen, caused me to fall into such a great error; and begging pardon of the good lady and of all of you other ladies, I shall make whatever amends may be decreed by her."

"You speak well," said the maiden, "but it is necessary that the amends be made before the pardon."

"Good maiden," said Florestan, "to that I shall attend at once if it can be done by me, provided that it be not demanded of me that I desist from doing what I must do against those shields; or else do order them placed inside the tent."

"Sir knight," said she, "do not believe that the shields were placed there so thoughtlessly; for before they are taken away, they will have triumphed by the great effort of their owners over all the others who pass by here desiring to defend themselves against them, in order to take their shields back to Rome with the names of the knights their owners inscribed on their bosses as evidence of the superiority that the Romans have over the knights of other lands. And if you want to protect yourself from incurring shame, return to where you came from, and your shield and name will not be carried where with public announcement your honor will be discredited."

"Maiden," said he, "if it please God, I shall protect myself from these shames that you tell me about; and I don't trust so much in your esteem for me as to rely on any of these counsels of yours; rather I intend to carry these shields to Firm Island."

Then he said to the queen: "Madam, may you be commended to God, and may He, who made you so beautiful, give you much joy and pleasure."

And he moved toward the shields; and Don Grumedan, who had heard clearly all that had been exchanged in conversation with the maiden, esteemed him highly, and even more so when he heard him speak of the Firm Island, for at once he thought that he was probably of the lineage of that very powerful Amadis, and he well believed that he would do what he had told the maiden concerning carrying the shields to the Firm Island; hence he was quite pleased with the opportunity to see how the Roman knights were at arms. Though he did not recognize Don Florestan, the latter seemed to him very marvelously well armed and a very fine rider, and so he was; and he considered him very courageous in undertaking such a great project; hence he had for him every good wish, and this to an even greater extent if he had known he was Don Florestan, whom he greatly esteemed and honored. And as for Don Florestan, who saw himself before him, and knew that there was not in the entire court a knight who had such an understanding of affairs at arms as he did, his courage and ardor grew in him so that he did not feel a jot of cowardice. So he went up to the shields and put the tip of his lance against the first and second, and the third and fourth and fifth; doing this because in this sequence they were to go to their jousts, one after the other according as the shields were touched. This done, he withdrew a bowshot's distance into the field, hung his shield on his neck, took a good thick lance and seating himself erectly in the saddle, remained waiting. And Don Florestan always had with him, whenever he could, two or three squires in order to be better served and so that they might carry for him lances and battle axes, which he knew very well how to use, for in many lands there would not be found any other knight who jousted as well as he. And since the Romans were likewise waiting, for wearing their armor they were in a tent, they rushed to mount quickly and go to him. But Don Florestan said to them: "What is the meaning of this, sirs? Do you want to come all together against one? You are violating the custom of this land."

Gradamor, a Roman knight, by whom the others were commanded, asked Don Grumedan to tell them how they should proceed, since he knew how better than anyone else. Don Grumedan said to him: "Just as the shields were touched one after the other, so in that order the knights are to go to their jousts. And if you believe me, do not go recklessly, for according to the appearance of that knight, he will not want any shame for himself."

"Don Grumedan," said Gradamor, "the Romans are not like you people who speak highly of yourselves before the fact is established; and as for us, even what we do accomplish we allow to be forgotten. And therefore there are no men who are our equals, and may it please God that our battle with that knight be over this proposition, even if my companions should not lend a hand in it."

Don Grumedan said to him: "Sir, may you experience now with that knight whatever pleases God; and if he emerges safe and sound from these jousts, I shall bring it about that over this proposition that you set forth, he fight with you. And if perchance there be such an impediment that he cannot do it, I shall take upon myself the battle in God's name. And go now to your joust, and if you come out of it successfully we shall remain in the presence of this noble queen, so that we not be able to withdraw."

Gradamor laughed as it were in scorn and said: "Now would that we might have that battle of which you speak as close at hand as the joust with that foolish knight who dares await us."

And he said to the knight of the first shield that was touched: "Go now and carry on in such wise as to exempt us from the scant prestige that would be won by overcoming that knight."

"Now be at ease," said the knight, "for I shall deal with him for you entirely according to your wish; and deal with the shield and with his name as you are commanded by the emperor to do. The horse, which seems to be a good one, shall be mine."

Then on horseback he crossed the river and went forward adjusting his weapons against Don Florestan; who, when he perceived him coming thus and saw that he had crossed the water, spurred his horse and went at him, and the Roman likewise. They collided with horses and shields in such wise that they missed their mark with their lances; and the Roman, who was the poorer horseman, went to the ground without delay. His fall was so heavy that he had his right arm broken, and he was badly stunned, so that to those who were watching it appeared that he was dead, for so he seemed to them. And Don Florestan ordered one of his squires to dismount and to take his shield and put it in a tree, and likewise he had him take the horse. And he returned to the place where he was before, giving indications that he was blaming himself because he had missed in the encounter; and he placed the tip of his lance on the ground while waiting. Then he saw another knight coming toward him, and he went for him as fast as his horse could carry him, but that time he did not make a mistake with his blows; rather, he struck so hard on the shield that he pierced it with so mighty a thrust that he hurled him from the horse, and the saddle on top of him on the ground, with the lance having been thrust through the shield and through the flesh, so that it penetrated to the other side. And Don Florestan passed by him very jauntily riding well, and then he turned toward him and said to him: "Sir Roman knight, the saddle that you took with you is yours, and the horse mine; and if you should wish to tell about these efforts in Rome, I grant you permission to do so."

And he was saying this in a loud voice so that the queen and her ladies and maidens-in-waiting heard it plainly. I tell you that Don Grumedan was extremely happy when he perceived what the knight from Great Britain was saying and doing to the one from Rome; and he said to Gradamor: "Sir, if you and your companions do not show yourselves to be better, there is no reason to tear down the walls of Rome to enter when you arrive there."

Gradamor said to him: "You consider very important what has happened; well, if my companions should finish their jousts, I shall make you say something else, and not with such conceit as you now have."

"We are close to seeing it," said Don Grumedan, "for the way it seems to me, that knight of the Firm Island defends his wearing apparel well; and I trust completely in him to render unnecessary the battle that I have scheduled with you."

Gradamor began to laugh without relish, and said: "When the accomplished fact comes to my knowledge, I shall grant you all that you say."

"In the name of God," said Don Grumedan, "and I shall have my horse and my arms ready in order to carry out what I have said, for according to your opinion, that knight will last but a short time on the field; although I believe that his thought is very different from yours."

And it caused the queen much sorrow to hear the foolish remarks of Gradamor and the other Romans. But Don Florestan had the shield and the horse taken from the knight who was on the ground as though dead and lacking any feeling; and when they extracted from him the lance fragment, the knight cried out in a pitiful voice, demanding confession.

Don Florestan, taking a lance, returned to the same place where he had been before. And it was not long before he saw another knight coming on a big beautiful horse, but not with as much vigor as the first knight; and he rode as hard as he could against Don Florestan, but the encounter was oblique, so that the lance missed its mark and the shock was deflected. And Don Florestan struck him on the helmet and, breaking its straps, knocked it off his head and sent it rolling over the field; and he made him clutch the horse's neck, but without his falling. Then Don Florestan raised his lance on high and came toward him very angry; and the knight who saw him coming thus, raised his shield; and Don Florestan struck such a blow on it that he jammed it into his face, so that stunned he dropped the reins from his hand. And when he saw him so befuddled, Don Florestan dropped his lance and jerked the shield so hard that he pulled it off his neck; and he struck him on top of the head two such heavy blows that he caused him to fall from his horse so bereft of his senses that all he did was to roll over and over on the field. And Florestan ordered that the horse be taken and that he be given his lance, and he went to the Roman, and said to him: "From now on, if you are able, you can go to Rome to shed tears over the knights of Great Britain."

And settling himself in his saddle, he went toward the fourth knight, whom he saw coming against him. But the latter's joust was ended at the first encounter, for Don Florestan met him with such force that he and his horse fell to the ground and the knight had his leg broken near his foot; and when the horse got up, the knight remained on the ground without being able to rise. Don Florestan had the shield and the horse taken as the others had been.

Then he took a very good lance from his squires and saw that Gradamor was coming at him with some very beautiful, fresh arms, and on a blossom-colored horse, big and handsome; and he was brandishing his lance as if he wanted to break it. Don Florestan was very furious with this man because he had threatened him. And Gradamor said in a loud voice: "Don Grumedan, do not fail to arm yourself, for before you are on your horse, I shall bring it to pass that this knight who is waiting for me will have need of you to aid him."

"Now we shall see," said Don Grumedan, "but on account of your boasting, I do not want to put myself in that struggle until I see how you come out."

Gradamor, who had already crossed the water, saw Don Florestan coming at him as fast as his horse could run and very well protected by his shield; and he lowered his lance in order to attack him, riding against him at full speed. Both the knights were strong and valiant; as they met with their lances, Gradamor pierced his shield, putting through it a good palm's-length of the staff of the lance, and there it broke. And Don Florestan pierced his shield right through to his left side, shattering the armor plate with the force of his blow, which was great, and hurling him out of the saddle into a depression that was there full of mud and water; then he passed by him, and ordered his squire to take his horse. And Don Grumedan, who saw this, said to the queen: "Madam, it seems to be that now I shall be able to relax a bit, while Gradamor wipes off his arms and looks for another knight to fight."

The queen said: "Cursed be their follies and arrogance, which cause everyone to be enraged against them, and then they experience ignominy."

Gradamor lay thrashing around a while in the mud and water; and when he emerged, he was greatly distressed by what had happened to him. And he took his helmet off and with his hand he wiped away the water and mud that he had in his eyes and on his face, shaking it off as best he could; then he laced the helmet on his head. And Don Florestan, who saw him thus, went up to him and said to him: "Sir knight threatener, I tell you that if you do not use the sword better than the lance, neither my shield nor my name will be taken to Rome by you."

Gradamor said to him: "I am sorry about the test with lances, but I bear this sword only to avenge myself, and at once I shall have you see whether you dare uphold the custom of this land."

And Don Florestan, who understood it much better than he, said to him: "And what custom is this that you speak of?"

"That you give me my horse," said he, "or that you dismount from yours and on foot we test ourselves at sword play; and the game will be regular, and let the one who plays most poorly remain without receiving any courtesy or mercy."

Don Florestan said to him: "I well believe that you would not maintain this custom if you were the victor; but I intend to dismount from my horse because it is not right that a Roman knight as handsome as you are should mount a horse only to be knocked off by someone else."

Then he dismounted, gave his horse to his squires and grasped his sword. Then covering himself very well with his shield, he went quickly toward him with great fury, and they attacked each other very fiercely with their swords, so that the battle was quite savage and it seemed to all very dangerous because of the anger that there was between them. But it was not long before Don Florestan, who was more vigorous and stronger in skill at arms, seeing that the queen and her women were watching him — as was Don Grumedan, who much better than they knew about such activities — exerted all his strength, giving him such great and mighty blows that Gradamor, although he was very valiant, could not stand it and kept retreating from the field and withdrawing toward the tent of the queen, trusting that Don Florestan out of respect for her would forego pursuit. But Don Florestan stopped in front of him, and made him return immediately to where he had come from; and he wearied him so greatly that Gradamor fell outstretched to the ground, bereft of all his strength. His sword dropped from his hand, and Don Florestan took his shield and gave it to his squires; then he seized him by his helmet and jerked it off so forcibly from his head that he dragged him for a bit over the field, and he threw the helmet into the mud hole that you have already heard about. Then he returned to him, and seizing him by one leg, sought to throw him in along with his helmet; and Gradamor began to cry out for him in Heaven's name to have pity. And the queen, who saw him, said: "That wretch bartered poorly when he stipulated that the victor should not show any courtesy to, or have any mercy on the vanquished."

And Don Florestan said to Gradamor: "A stipulation that such an honorable knight as you made, it is not right to break, and I shall hold you to it very fully, as you will now see."

He, when he heard this, said: "Alas, wretch that I am, for I am as good as dead!"

"That is so," said Don Florestan, "unless you carry out my command in two matters."

"Tell me what they are," said he, "for I shall take care of them."

"One is," said Don Florestan, "that in your own handwriting and with your blood and that of your companions, you write your name and theirs on the bosses of the shields; and when this is done, I shall tell you the other thing that I wish you to do."

And while saying this he held over him his sword, which he was brandishing, and underneath it Gradamor was trembling with great fear. And he had a scribe of his called, and ordered him to take the ink out of his inkwell, fill it with Gradamor's blood and write his name on the shield, since he was not able to do so, and all the names of his companions on the other shields, and to do it quickly so that he not lose his head. This was immediately done thus, whereupon Don Florestan cleaned his sword and put it in the scabbard, and mounted his horse; and he mounted it with such agility that it seemed he had not labored at anything that day. He gave his shield to the squire, but in order that Grumedan might not recognize him he did not take off his helmet. The horse he was on was big and beautiful, and of a rare color, and the knight was of a size and stature so impressive that few would be found of such attractive appearance as he was when armed. And he took in his hand a lance with a fine, handsome pennon and he confronted Gradamor, who had already risen to his feet; and brandishing the lance, he said to him: "Your life depends solely on Don Grumedan's asking me on your behalf that I not kill you in his presence."

He began to shout, calling on Don Grumedan for God's sake to help him, since on him depended his life or his death. Then Don Grumedan came on foot just as he was, and said: "Surely, Gradamor, if mercy or pity are not available to you, this is with great justice, because out of your arrogance that is the way you asked for it from this gentleman; but I beg him to let you live, because I shall be very grateful and much obliged to him for it."

"That I shall gladly do," said Don Florestan, "for you, and everything else that may be to your honor and pleasure."

And then he said: "You, Sir Roman Knight, from today on whenever you please, you will be able to tell at the judicial hearing in Rome, if you go there, of the very arrogant statements and great threats that you have made against the knights of Great Britain, and how you resisted them, and the great glory and honor that you won from them in the very short period of one day; and tell it thus to your emperor and to the potentates so that they may have pleasure from it. And I shall make known on Firm Island how the knights of Rome are so liberal and generous that they give freely their horses and arms to those whom they do not know. But as regards this gift that you have made me I do not have to thank you for it, and for it I am grateful to God, who wished to give it to me against your will."

As for Gradamor, who was so battered and close to death, when he heard these words, they were for him more devastating than his wounds. And Don Florestan said to him: "Sir knight, you shall carry back to Rome all the arrogance that you brought from there, since they love and value it; for the knights of this land will have none of it, and they only recognize what you abhor, which is courtesy and good will. And if you, my lord, are as enamored as you are valiant at arms, and wish that I take you to Firm Island, you may test the enchanted arch of faithful lovers who go there with the fidelity of their lady loves. And with this glory and honor that you bring from Great Britain your own lady love will esteem you much more; and if she is of good understanding, she will not exchange you for anyone else."

I say to you about Don Grumedan that he was delighted to hear those words, and laughed heartily to see the haughtiness of the Romans humbled. But Gradamor did not do so; rather he heard the words with great heartbreak, and said to Don Grumedan: "Good sir, for God's sake, order me to be taken to the tents, for I am in dire straits."

"That is quite apparent from your appearance and that of your arms," said he, "and it is your own fault."

Then he had the squires pick him up to carry him away. And Don Grumedan said to Don Florestan: "Sir, if you please, tell me your name, for such a fine man as you should not conceal it."

And he said to him: "My lord Don Grumedan, I beg you not to be vexed that I not tell you, for in view of the discourtesy that

I exhibited to that very beautiful queen, in nowise would I want her to learn it, for I feel very guilty; although she and her maidens are more so, for their great beauty was the occasion for my doing wrong, since they deprived me of my understanding. And I beg you, my lord Don Grumedan, to arrange with them that by taking from me whatever amends I may be able to make, they pardon me; and that you send me their reply to the round hermitage that is near here, for there I shall lodge today."

Don Grumedan said to him: "I shall do what you wish to the full extent of my ability, and with the message that I obtain I shall send to you my squire, and if to my liking, the message that he will bring to you will be good, just as you deserve."

The Knight from the Firm Island said to him: "I beg you, my lord Don Grumedan, that if you know any news about Amadis, you tell me."

And as for Don Grumedan, who loved very much the one he was asking about, tears came to his eyes out of his longing for him, and he said: "So help me God, good knight, since the time he departed from Gaul, from the house of his father King Perion, I have had no news whatever of him; and I would be very happy to hear some and to impart it to you and to all his friends."

"I well believe that," said Don Florestan, "in view of your good will and the great loyalty that dwells in you, sir; for if all men were such, disloyalty and lack of restraint would not find a dwelling place anywhere in which to lodge, and would perforce be expelled from the world. And God be with you, for I am going to the hermitage that I told you about, to wait for your squire."

"God be with you," said Don Grumedan.

And he went away to the tents, and Don Florestan to where his squires were. And he ordered that the horses he had won be taken to the tents, and that the blossom-colored horse be given on his behalf to Don Grumedan because it seemed to him a good one, and that the other four be given to the maiden who had talked with him, to do with them whatever she wished, and to tell her that Don Florestan sent them. Don Grumedan was very happy with the horse on account of its having belonged to the Romans and much more on learning that that man was Don Florestan, whom he greatly loved and esteemed. And the squires gave the other horses to the maiden, saying to her: "Lady Maiden, that knight whom you rebuffed today with your words in praise of your Romans sends you these horses to give to whomsoever you please, and asks that you take them as a token of verification of the words that he spoke."

"I thank him very much for them," said she, "and he certainly won them with great prowess and high excellence; but it would have pleased me more than to receive these four if he had left here only his own horse."

"That may well be," said one of the squires, "but whoever is to win his horse will need better knights than these who were seeking it of him."

The maiden said: "Do not wonder that I wish the honor of these more than his, for with him I am not acquainted nor do I know who he is. But however that may be, he has sent me a fine gift, and I regret having said to such a good man anything that might anger him; hence I shall make it up to him in whatever way he may command."

Thereupon they returned to their lord who was awaiting them, and they told him what had occurred, at which he was pleased. After commanding his squires to take the shields of the Romans, he went to the round hermitage to await Don Grumedan's message and because that was on the direct road to Firm Island; for he had no desire to enter the court of King Lisuarte and he would like to speak to Don Gandales, who had the Island in charge, in order to ask him whether he knew any news concerning his brother, and to place there the shields that he was bringing.

But I tell you that Don Grumedan went at once before Queen Sardamira and very humbly told her what Don Florestan had charged him to say, and he told her Don Florestan's name. The queen listened very attentively and said: "Could this possibly be Don Florestan, son of King Perion and of the Countess of Selandia?"

"He is the same one you mention, madam; and do believe that he is one of the most courageous and courteous knights in the world."

"I do not know how things have gone for him hereabouts," said she, "but I tell you, Don Grumedan, that the sons of the

Marquis of Ancona speak in rare terms of him, of his great prowess at arms and his high accomplishments, and of how intelligent and prudent he is; and this is to be given credence because these men were his companions in the great wars in which he participated in Rome, where he dwelt for three years when he was a young knight. But they did not dare to mention his excellence in the presence of the emperor, who does not like him, nor does he wish to hear him praised."

"Do you know," said Don Grumedan, "why the emperor does not like him?"

"Yes," said the queen, "because of his brother Amadis, against whom the emperor holds a deep-seated grudge because Amadis overcame the perils of Firm Island that the emperor was going to conquer, and went there before him; and for this reason he hates him very much for having taken away from him the honor and the prestige that he would have obtained by winning that Island."

Don Grumedan smiled at this and said: "Certainly, my lady, his complaint is unreasonable; instead I understand that for this alone he ought to have esteemed him, since he prevented him from obtaining there the greatest dishonor that perchance had ever befallen him, for there were many other knights of great excellence at arms who attempted it, and only that one, whom God made supremely great over all those in the world in strength and in all the other qualities that a good knight should have, succeeded in winning the Island. And do believe, my lady, that another adventure was the cause of the emperor's hating him."

The queen said: "By the faith that you owe to God, Don Grumedan, tell me about it."

"Lady," said he, "I shall tell it to you, and do not become angry about it."

And laughing she said to him: "Whatever it may be, I wish to know about it."

"In God's name," said he.

Then he told her all that had happened to the emperor with Amadis in the forest on the night when he was boasting about love and Amadis was lamenting, and all the words that passed between them, and how the battle went, just as you have already heard in the Second Book. The queen derived great satisfaction from hearing about it; and made him tell it to her three times, saying: "So help me God, Don Grumedan, according to what you tell me, that knight really made it plain that one can serve love when content with it, and do the opposite when love has been contrary to him. But in my opinion, that was small cause for occasioning hatred between the emperor and Amadis."

CHAPTER LXXVII

HOW QUEEN SARDAMIRA SENT HER MESSAGE TO DON FLORESTAN, BEGGING HIM, SINCE HE HAD OVERCOME THE KNIGHTS, INJURING THEM SERIOUSLY, TO BE WILLING TO BE HER PROTECTOR AS FAR AS THE CASTLE OF MIRAFLORES, WHERE SHE WAS GOING TO TALK WITH ORIANA; AND HOW THEY GOT ALONG THERE.

While Queen Sardamira and Don Grumedan were talking thus concerning this matter about which you have heard, she listened happily to what he had to say because that journey that the emperor had made under the name of the Patin had been because of his love of her, for he had loved her dearly; and while intending to win her, he had come to Great Britain to test himself with the good knights who were there. Concerning what had happened to him with Amadis, he had said nothing to her; hence inwardly she was highly amused at his having concealed it from her. Don Grumedan said to her: "Lady, give me whatever message you please for me to transmit to Don Florestan."

She reflected for a bit; then she said: "Don Grumedan, you see my knights so disabled that they cannot protect either me or themselves, and it is necessary that they stay behind for their own well-being; therefore I should like, since the knights of this land are what they are, for Don Florestan to be my escort along with you."

He said: "I say to you, my lady, that Don Florestan is so courteous that there is nothing that a matron or maiden might ask of him that he would not do, especially for you, who are such a great lady and to whom he is to make amends for the mistake he made."

"I am quite pleased," said she, "with what you say to me; and now give me someone to guide that maiden, and I shall send my message to him."

He gave her four squires, and the queen sent with a letter of accreditation the maiden who had acquired the horses, and told her privately what to say. Mounting her palfrey and accompained by the squires, the maiden made her trip in great haste; so that on reaching the round hermitage she found Don Florestan, who was talking with the hermit, and she had herself dismounted from the palfrey. And as she was not veiled, Don Florestan recognized her at once and received her very well. She said to him: "Sir, there was a time today when I did not think I would be looking for you, because my thought was that the affair between you and our knights would turn out differently."

"Good lady," said he, "they were to blame, for they demanded of me what I could not excuse without being disgraced. But just tell me whether the queen your lady will lodge tonight there where I left her."

The maiden said to him: "My lord, the queen sends greetings to you; and take this letter that I bring from her."

He looked at it and said: "Lady, tell me the message entrusted to you, and I shall do its bidding."

"It is not unreasonable," said she, "that you do so, rather it involves your good knightly honor and courtesy; and I say to you that she ordered me to tell you that the knights who were protecting her you left so disabled that she cannot make use of them; and since this inconvenience came to her from you, she wishes you to be her protector until you bring her to Miraflores, where she goes to see Oriana."

"I thank your lady very much for what she sends word to me to do, and I consider it a great honor and favor to serve her. Now let us leave here at an hour that will enable us to be at her tent by dawn."

"In the name of God," said the lady, "and now I tell you that you are well known to Don Grumedan, for he told the queen that such a reply as you are giving would be elicited from you."

The maiden was greatly pleased by the fair speech and great courtesy of Don Florestan, and by the fact that he was handsome and charming. In all respects he seemed to her a man of high rank, as indeed he was. Then they supped there together and remained talking about many things for most of the evening. And when it was time to go to sleep, arrangements were made for the maiden to be housed in the hermitage, and Don Florestan remained with the squires under the trees, where he slept that night very peacefully after the day's exertion. But when it was time, the squires woke him, and arming himself, he took with him the maiden and the rest of the company, and went along the way to the tents, which they reached in the early morning. The maiden went to the queen and Don Florestan to the tent of Don Grumedan, who was already up and was talking with his knights, being about to hear mass. When he saw Don Florestan he was extremely happy; and they embraced each other with great pleasure, going at once to the tent of the queen. Don Grumedan said to him: "Sir, this queen wishes you to escort her; it is good that you do so, for she is a very noble lady. And it seems to me she does not barter badly in gaining you and losing her knights."

He said this to him laughing.

"So help me God," said Don Florestan, "I should like very much to be able to serve her in any way pleasing to her, especially since I am going in company with you, for it has been a long time since I saw you."

"Sir, how pleased I am to see you," said he, "God knows. And tell me, what did you do with the shields that you took from here?"

"I sent them last night by one of my squires to your friend Don Gandales on Firm Island so that he may put them in a place where they may be seen by all who come there and so that those from Rome may know of it, if they wish to come in quest of them."

"If they do that," said Don Grumedan, "Firm Island will be well provided with their shields and arms."

While thus chatting, they arrived in the presence of the queen who already knew about their coming. Don Florestan went before her and sought to kiss her hands, but she did not wish it, placing her hand on the sleeve of his coat of mail as a sign of sincere welcome and saying to him: "Don Florestan, I am greatly pleased with your arrival and the effort that you are willing to put forth in my service. Since you have thus made amends for the harm you did to my knights, it is right that you be pardoned for it."

"My good lady," said he, "I regret no effort or toil in serving you; rather I should regret it if I had left you vexed; and in this matter I receive honor and great favor; in whatever else there may be, I beg you, madam, to command me as your knight and servant, and with complete devotion your commands will be carried out by me."

The queen asked Don Grumedan if he was ready for the journey. Having heard what she was saying, he said: "Lady, when you please, you can go, and these wounded knights I shall have taken to a town that is near here, where they will be given medical attention for their wounds until they are healed; because in view of their wounds, they could not go with us until they are well."

"So let it be done," said she.

Then they brought to the queen a palfrey as white as snow, and it came saddled with a saddle all trimmed with gold, wondrously well wrought, and likewise the bridle; and she dressed in very fine apparel, wearing around her neck strands of pearls and precious stones of great value, which enhanced her beauty exceedingly. Immediately her lavishly adorned matrons and maidens mounted their horses; and with Don Florestan taking the queen's horse by the rein, they started out on the journey to Miraflores.

I am telling you that Oriana already knew about their coming, which greatly distressed her, for there was nothing in the world that was more irksome to her than to hear the emperor of Rome discussed; and she knew for certain that this queen was not coming for any other purpose. But she was quite pleased with the coming of Don Florestan, when she found out he was accompanying the queen, because she wished to ask him for news of Amadis and to complain to him about the king her father. But although her agitation was great, she thought it well to order the house embellished with beautiful and luxurious daises in order to receive them, and she dressed herself in the best garb she had, and so did Mabilia and her other maidens.

And when Queen Sardamira entered the palace where Oriana was, Don Florestan and Grumedan were escorting her. When

Oriana saw her coming, she was very well impressed by her; and she thought that if her errand were not such as it was, she would take great pleasure in being with her. When the queen drew near, she bowed before Oriana and sought to kiss her hands, but she drew them back and said to her that she was a queen and a lady; whereas she, Oriana, was a poor maiden on whom her sins were seeking to wreak harm. Then Mabilia and the other damsels greeted her, showing very great pleasure for the sake of affording it to the queen. But that Oriana did not exhibit, for she had never had any since the Romans had been at her father's court. But I tell you that with Don Florestan and Don Grumedan she took great delight, for her heart found some repose with them. They all sat down on a dais, and Oriana had Don Florestan and Don Grumedan sat facing her; and after she had chatted a while with the queen, she turned to Don Florestan and said to him: "Good friend, it has been a long time since I last saw you, and I regret it, as I am very fond of you, as are all those who know you. And great is the loss that you and Amadis and your friends cause in being out of Great Britain, in view of the great wrongs and injuries in it that you used to set right. And cursed be those who were the cause of alienating you from my father, for if you were together here right now, as was your wont, a certain ill-starred woman who now awaits her misfortune in being disinherited and brought to the point of death, could have had hope of some remedy. And if you had been here, you would have argued in her behalf and you would have defended her just as you always have, for you never left unprotected those in trouble who needed you. But such has been the ill-fortune of this woman I mention that everything fails her but death."

And when she said this, she wept bitterly, and this for two reasons: first, because if her father should hand her over to the Romans, she expected to throw herself into the sea; and second, because of her longing for Amadis, of whom Don Florestan, whom she had before her and who greatly resembled him, reminded her. And Don Florestan, who was very understanding, readily recognized that she was speaking of herself, and said: "My good lady, God succors great distress with His pity, and do have hope in Him, my lady, for He will give you counsel concerning your problems. And regarding what you say about Amadis my lord brother, whom I so greatly desire to see, just as in some places his help is lacking, so in others those who need it, find it; and do believe, my good lady, that he is in good health and uninhibited in strength, and is going through foreign lands performing miracles at arms and helping those who receive wrongs, as the one whom God made the most excellent in this world, surpassing all others whom He has caused to be born in it."

Queen Sardamira, who was near them and heard all the conversation, said: "Ah, may God protect Amadis from falling into the hands of the emperor, who mortally hates him; and I should regret the emperor's anger on account of Amadis's being so highly esteemed, and on your account, Don Florestan, for he is your brother."

"Madam," said he, "many others esteem him and desire his well-being and honor."

"I say to you," said the queen, "that according to what I have learned, there is no man whom the emperor hates as much as he does him, unless it be a knight who dwelt for a time at the court of King Tafinor of Bohemia, at a period when the emperor's men were warring against the king; and that knight about whom I'm telling you killed in combat Don Garadan, who was the best knight there was among all the relatives of the emperor and in all the dominion of Rome, unless it be Salustanquidio, this very honorable prince who has come to your father with a mandate from the emperor concerning your marriage. And that knight about whom I am telling you, the day after he killed Don Garadan, through his great prowess at arms vanquished eleven other knights of the emperor, who were among the best that there were in Rome. And by these two battles about which I am telling you, that knight freed the King of Bohemia from the war that he was having with the emperor, from which war he had not expected any relief except by losing his whole kingdom; so that on an auspicious day such a noble knight entered his court to remedy his troubles."

Then Queen Sardamira told them in great detail the reason for the battles and how the war was concluded so greatly to the honor and advantage of King Tafinor, just as this Book has recounted to you. And after she had ceased speaking, Don Florestan said: "My good lady, do you know the name of that knight who participated to his honor in all those events?"

"Yes," said she, "for he is called the Knight of the Green Sword or the Knight of the Dwarf, and to each of those names he answers when called; though everyone holds the belief that he is concealing his real name. But because they say he bears a large sword ornamented in green and is accompanied by a dwarf, he is called by these names, and even though he takes another squire with him, the dwarf is never separated from him."

When Don Florestan heard this, he was very happy, and truly believed that it was probably Amadis, his brother; in view of the description of him he was hearing. And Oriana and Mabilia thought so too. Don Florestan, after some reflection decided that as soon as King Lisuarte's convocation of nobles was over he would go in search of him. And Oriana, who was dying to speak with Mabilia, said to the queen: "Good lady, you have come from afar, and need to relax. It will be well for you to rest in the good quarters you have."

"So be it," said she, "since you, madam, so order it."

Then they all went together to the queen's living quarters, which were very delightful, not only with their trees and fountains but also with very luxurious apartments. And leaving her there with her matrons and maidens-in-waiting and with Don Grumedan, who was seeing to their service, Oriana returned to her own chamber; and taking Mabilia and the maid of Denmark aside, she told them that she truly believed that that knight of whom Queen Sardamira had spoken was probably Amadis. And they said that they likewise thought so; and Mabilia added: "Madam, now a dream is explained that I had last night, which is that it seemed to me that we were placed in a room completely closed and we heard outside a very loud noise, so that we were frightened; and your knight was breaking down the door and asking for you in a loud voice. I pointed you out, for you were lying on a dais; then taking you by the hand, he led us all out of there and put us in a marvelously high tower, and said, 'You stay in this tower and do not fear anyone.' And at this moment I awoke. For this reason, madam, I am greatly heartened, for Amadis will come to your rescue."

When Oriana heard this, she was very happy and embraced her, weeping, for the tears were streaming down her very beautiful cheeks; and she said to her: "Oh, Mabilia, my good lady and true friend, how well you come to my rescue with your courage and good words! And may God decree out of His mercy that your dream turn out just as you say; but if this be not His will, that He bring it to pass that after Amadis comes, we both die and neither of us remains alive."

"Stop this," said Mabilia, "for God, who made him so fortunate in matters involving others will not forsake him in his own affairs. And speak with Don Florestan, showing him great affection, and beg him that he and his friends strive as hard as they can to prevent your being carried away from this land, and that he tell Don Galaor so on your behalf and his own."

But I say to you that Don Galaor, without being told was already involved in this concern, because of counseling the king about it the way he did, and we shall tell you how it came about. Know you that King Lisuarte had gone hunting, and with him Don Galaor; and after they had hunted, the king on going through a valley, drew rein on his palfrey and after all the others had gone on ahead, he called Don Galaor and said to him: "My good friend and loyal servant, never on any matter have I asked of you advice from which I did not derive benefit. Already you know about the great power and high standing of the emperor of Rome, who has sent to ask for my daughter as his empress. And I know of two aspects of this that are greatly to my advantage: first, if I marry my daughter so honorably, she becomes mistress of such a mighty power, and I have that emperor to help me every time that it be necessary; and second, that my daughter Leonoreta will be mistress of, and heiress to, the throne of Great Britain. And of this I intend to speak with my nobles, for whom I have sent, in order to see what they will advise me concerning this marriage. And in the meantime, if you please, tell me here where we have privacy, what you think of this; for since you are quite familiar with it, I consider that you will counsel me in the matter in every way that will greatly redound to my honor."

Don Galaor, when he heard this, remained in thought for a bit; then he said: "Sire, I am not of such great mentality, nor have I had enough experience with things of this kind to know how to cope with a matter of such great importance as this is. And therefore, sire, may I be excused from it, if you please, because those nobles of whom you speak, with whom it is to be discussed, will tell you much better what may be to your honor and in your service, because they will determine it much better than I."

"Don Galaor," said the king, "I still want you to tell me your opinion; otherwise I would experience the greatest distress imaginable, especially since until today I have never received from you anything but much pleasure and help."

"God forbid that I offend you," said Don Galaor; "since you are still pleased to test my stupidity, I will do so. And I say that as for your stating that you will marry your daughter very honorably and with great dominion, this seems to me much the opposite, because she being your hereditary successor to this realm after you die, you could not do her greater harm than by taking it from her and putting her under the domination of a foreigner over whom she will have neither command nor power. And in the event that she achieve the objective of such ladies, which is offspring, and these in due course she sees married, then she will be placed under greater subjection and in more poverty than before, on seeing another empress giving orders. As for your statement that you would be helped by the emperor, surely, sire, in view of your own great worth and that of your knights and friends who are so effective, whereby you have improved your dominions and enhanced your great fame throughout the world, rather it would discredit you to think and believe that that man would afford you relief in case of necessity; for in view of the arrogant ways that everyone says he has, for you it would turn out to be quite the opposite, because on account of him you would always be having affronts and very fruitless expenses. And what would be worse than this is that it would be adjudged a service that you were rendering him, and in such a role you would be perpetually recorded in his books and chronicles. Therefore, sire, this which you deem a great honor, I consider the greatest dishonor that could come to you. And as for what you say about bequeathing the British crown to your daughter Leonoreta, this is a much greater error, for thus it happens that from one mistake there come many unless good discretion stands in the way. To take away, sire, this dominion from a daughter so outstanding in the world, when it comes to her rightfully, and to give it to one who ought not to have it, may it never please God that I should give such advice; and I do not mean merely with reference to your daughter, but from the poorest woman in the world I should be averse to her own possessions being taken away. This I have said on account of the fidelity that I owe to God and to you, and to my soul and your daughter, for because I am your vassal, I consider her my lady suzerain. And please God, I am going away tomorrow, bound for Gaul; for the king my father, I know not for what reason, has summoned me. And if you please, I shall leave a written statement in my own handwriting, which you may show to all your nobles, embodying what I have said to you; and if there be a knight who says the opposite because of deeming it better, I shall fight him and make him recognize that all that I have said is the truth."

The king, when he heard this from him, was displeased with his reasoning, although he did not reveal the fact; and he said to him: "Don Galaor, my friend, since you wish to go, leave me the written statement."

But he was not asking for it in order to show it, unless it became very necessary.

Just as you have heard, King Lisuarte went along with Don Galaor until they came to his palace; and that night they took their ease with great pleasure and with everyone talking about this marriage — but the king more than anyone, for he was very desirous of it. And next morning Don Galaor gave to him the written statement, bade him and the nobles farewell, and left for Gaul. And know you that the purpose of Don Galaor in this action was to hinder that marriage because he did not feel it to be to the advantage of the king, and also because he suspected an affair between Amadis and Oriana, daughter of King Lisuarte, although no one had told him about it, and he wished to go away to where he could no longer talk about the marriage, knowing already the king to be entirely determined to carry it out. And Oriana knew nothing of this, and therefore she begged Don Florestan, as you have heard, to speak on her behalf to Don Galaor.

So just as you hear they spent that day at Miraflores, Queen Sardamira being greatly astounded by the great beauty of Oriana, for she could not have believed that any mortal would be so beautiful, although Oriana was very much less so than she was wont to be, on account of the great anguish and the tribulation of her heart, which were very deep-seated emotions, for she feared that marriage with the emperor and had no news of her beloved Amadis of Gaul. For the time being the queen did not seek to speak to her about the matter of the emperor, but on other matters involving news and pleasure. But the next day when she did speak to her about it, she had such a response from Oriana, although it was decorous and courteous, that never again did she dare talk with her about it.

Then Oriana, knowing that Don Florestan wanted to leave, took him with her and brought him under some trees that were there, where there was a very fine dais; and having him seat himself opposite her, she told him openly her whole wish and the great pressure that her father was putting on her by seeking to disinherit her and send her to foreign lands, asking Florestan to feel sorry for her since she expected only death; and telling him that not only to him whom she loved so much and in whom she had such great hope and trust, but also to all the grandees of that kingdom and to all the knights errant, she intended to complain, that they might have commiseration and great pity for her and beg her father to change his mind.

"And, my good lord and friend Don Florestan," said she, "do thus beseech him to this end and counsel him to do so, making him understand the great sin which he is committing because of this very great cruelty and wrong that he seeks to perpetrate on me."

Don Florestan said to her: "My good lady, without any doubt you can well believe that I must serve you, in all that I be commanded by you, with as much willingness and humility as I would serve my lord King Perion my father. But this which you tell me to beg of your father, I cannot in any wise do because I am not his vassal, nor will he take me into his counsel knowing that I hate him for the harm that he has done me and my family. And if he has had some service from me, there is no reason for him to be grateful to me for it, because I did it by command of my brother and lord Amadis, whom I could not, nor ought not contradict. Amadis, not for the king your father's sake but because if this land were lost, you would lose it, arranged to be in that battle of the seven kings and to bring with him King Perion and me, as you already know. Because he considers you one of the best princesses in the world, if now he were to find out about this outrage and wrong that is being done you so greatly against your will, do believe, my lady, that with all his forces and friends he would set about remedying it; and I do not mean merely for you who are such a noble lady, would he do it, but for the poorest woman in all the world. And do you, my good lady, have genuine hope, for there will still be time to be able to help you if it pleases God, for I shall not stop until I am on the Firm Island, where the knight Agrajes is, who very greatly wishes to serve you on account of that rearing that his father and mother gave you, and because of the great love that you have for his sister Mabilia. And there we shall take counsel on what can be done."

"Do you know for certain," said Oriana, "that Agrajes is there?"

"I know it," said he, "for Don Grumedan told me so, and he found it out through a squire of his whom he sent to him."

"Thank God!" said she, "May He guide him; and please greet him warmly for me. Tell him that in him I have that genuine hope that I rightly must have. And if in the meantime you should learn any news of your brother Amadis, let me know so that I may tell his cousin Mabilia, who is yearning to see him and may God contrive that you and Agrajes come to some good understanding about my situation."

Don Florestan, kissing the hands of Oriana, bade her farewell; and taking with him Don Grumedan, he went to Queen Sardamira, and said to her: "Madam, I wish to set forth, and wherever I may go I am your knight and servant; as such I beg you to consider me and to command me in whatever I may be of service to you."

The queen said to him: "She who would not wish for service and honor from a man of such great valor as you, Don Florestan, are, would be very much lacking in understanding, and if it be God's will, into such an error I shall not fall; rather I receive your kind courtesy and give you heart-felt thanks, and always I shall remember to ask of you whatever you may be able to do for me."

Don Florestan, who was observing her closely, said: "May God, who made you so beautiful, requite you for that reply to me, since for the present I cannot except with words and good will."

And with this he took leave of her, and of Mabilia and all the other ladies who were there. And begging Don Grumedan that if he should ascertain any news of Amadis, he let him know at the Firm Island, he went to his lodging, armed himself and mounted his horse, and with his squires started out on the direct road to the Firm Island, where he wanted to go with the intention of speaking with Agrajes and planning how with the aid of his friends, Oriana might be rescued, if her father gave her to the Romans.

CHAPTER LXXVIII

HOW THE KNIGHT OF THE GREEN SWORD, WHO AFTERWARDS WAS CALLED THE GREEK KNIGHT, AND DON BRUNEO DE BONAMAR AND ANGRIOTE DE ESTRAVAUS TOGETHER CAME BY SEA ACCOMPANYING THAT VERY BEAUTIFUL GRASINDA, TO THE COURT OF KING LISUARTE, WHO WAS RESOLVED TO SEND HIS DAUGHTER ORIANA TO THE EMPEROR OF ROME TO BE THE LATTER'S WIFE; AND CONCERNING THE THINGS THAT OCCURRED WHEN HE OF THE GREEN SWORD ANNOUNCED HIS QUEST.

With Grasinda there went sailing over the sea the Knight of the Green Sword, Don Bruneo de Bonamar and Angriote de Estravaus, at times with favorable weather and at other times with the opposite, according as God ordained it, until they reached the ocean which is aligned with the coast of Spain. And when the Knight of the Green Sword saw himself so close to Great Britain, he sincerely thanked God for it because, having survived all the many dangers and storms he had experienced on the sea, He had brought him to where he could see that land where his lady was; so very great joy filled his heart. Then with great delight he had all the ships draw close together, and he begged all the men who were in them not to call him by any name other than the Greek Knight, and he ordered them to strive to reach Great Britain. Then he sat down with Grasinda on her dais; and said to her: "Beautiful lady, now the time desired by you is drawing near, at which time, if it pleases God, what your heart so greatly has desired and still does will be carried out. And with certainty believe, madam, that on account of toilsome fatigue or danger to my person, I shall not fail to repay you somewhat for the favors that you have done me."

"Greek Knight, my friend," said she, "I have faith that God will so ordain it, for if His will had been otherwise, He would not have given me such a knight as you as protector; and I thank you very much for what you say to me, since on being so close to such an encounter my heart seems to double its ardor."

The Greek Knight commanded Gandalin to bring the six swords that Queen Menoresa had given him in Constantinople. Gandalin brought them and placed them before him. And he gave two of them to Don Bruneo and Angriote, who were amazed to see the richness of their ornamentation. Then the Greek Knight took another for himself, ordering Gandalin to put it with his arms, and meanwhile to stow away his green one where it would not be seen. He did this so that in the court of King Lisuarte, where he was going and where he wished to conceal his identity, it might not be revealed by the green sword. And while they were thus engaged in this matter, just as you hear, it being between nones and vespers, Grasinda, who was quite seasick, arranged with the Greek Knight and with Don Bruneo and Angriote for her to be taken on deck so that by the sight of land, she might experience some relief. And all four being there talking about whatever pleased them most, as they continued on their way, at the hour that the sun was about to set they saw a ship that was becalmed on the sea, and the Greek Knight gave orders to the sailors to go straight toward it. On coming within earshot of it, the Greek Knight told Angriote to ask those on the ship for news. And Angriote hailed them very courteously and said: "Whose is this ship and who goes in it?"

They when they heard this question said to him: "The ship is from the Firm Island and two knights are traveling in it who will tell you whatever you please."

When the Greek Knight heard them mention the Firm Island his heart was made happy, as were his companions', because they wanted to hear them speak concerning what they wished to know. And Angriote said: "Friends, I beg you as a courtesy that you tell those knights to come here, and we shall ask them for news that we were desirous of having; and if you please, tell us who they are."

"That we shall not do, but we shall tell them your request."

And having been summoned, the two knights stationed themselves there beside their men. Then Angriote said: "Sirs, we should like to learn from you in what place King Lisuarte is, if perchance you know."

"All that we know," said they, "will be told you. But beforehand, we should like to know one thing on account of which in order to acquire definite information about it, we have suffered great travail and expect to suffer even more before we ascertain it."

"Say what you please," said Angriote, "for if I know the answer, you shall know it."

They said: "Friend, what we want is to find out news of a knight named Amadis of Gaul, the one whom all his friends, by traversing foreign lands, are suffering and dying to find."

When the Greek Knight heard this, tears came to his eyes very quickly out of the great pleasure that his heart felt when he saw how loyal all his relatives and friends were; but he remained silent. And Angriote said to them: "Now tell me who you are, and I shall tell you whatever I know about that."

One of them said: "Know you that my name is Dragonis and this companion of mine is Enil, and we intend to traverse the Mediterranean from one end to the other and to search its ports in order to find out news of this man about whom we are asking."

"Sirs," said Angriote, "may God give you good news of him. And in these ships come people from many regions. I shall ask whether they know something about the matter, and I shall gladly tell you."

He made this statement by order of the Greek Knight; then he said to them: "Now I beg you to tell me where King Lisuarte is, and what news you know of him and of Queen Brisena his wife, and of their court."

"I shall tell you that," said Dragonis; "know you that he is in one of his towns that is called Tagades, which is a large seaport opposite Normandy; and he has convoked his assembly of noblemen, at which are all his nobles, in order to take counsel with them as to whether he will give his daughter Oriana to the emperor of Rome, who is asking for her as his wife. Also at his court are many Romans in order to escort her, among whom the leader is Salustanquidio, prince of Calabria, and many others whom he commands, who are knights of high degree. And they have with them a queen, Sardamira by name, to accompany Oriana, whom the emperor is already calling empress of Rome."

When the Greek Knight heard this his heart trembled and for a time he was in utter dismay. But when Dragonis came to tell of Oriana's grief and tears and of how she had sent a complaint to all the grandees of Great Britain, his heart became at ease and he regained courage, thinking that since it grieved her, the Romans would not be so many or so strong as to prevent him from rescuing her either by land or by sea; and that deed he would perform for the most lowly maiden in the world, not to mention her, on account of whom, were he to lose hope of having her, he would not be able to live for a single moment. And he gave many thanks to God because he had arrived in that land at a time when he could repay his lady in some degree for the great favors she had done him, and because by rescuing her, he would have her as he desired without its being her fault. And with this he became as happy and cheerful as if he had the rescue already carried out and concluded. Then in an undertone he told Angriote to ask Dragonis where he had found out that news. And on being asked by him, Dragonis replied: "Four days ago there arrived at the Firm Island, from which we departed, Don Cuadragante and his nephew Landin, and Gavarte of the Fearful Island and Madancian of the Bridge of Silver, and Helian the Lighthearted. These five came to take counsel with Don Florestan and Agrajes, who are there, concerning their opinion as to how they should enter upon the search for Amadis, the one we are seeking. Don Cuadragante wanted to send to the court of King Lisuarte in order to learn from those foreign people who are there some news of that very courageous Amadis, but Don Florestan told them not to do so, that he had come from there and they did not know any news; and his squires have told of a fight which Don Florestan had with the Romans, whence his great prowess will be praised as long as the world endures."

When Angriote heard this, he said: "Sir knight, tell us what man that is, and what deeds he performed that are praised so highly."

"He is," said Dragonis, "a son of King Perion of Gaul, and in his great excellence he much resembles his brothers."

And he told them all that had happened to the Roman knights in the presence of Queen Sardamira, and how he had brought their shields to the Firm Island, and the names of the owners of the inscriptions written with their blood.

"And this Don Florestan related there the news that we are telling you, and how the knights of Queen Sardamira were so disabled that at her request Don Florestan escorted her until he left her at Miraflores, where she was going to see Oriana, the daughter of King Lisuarte."

The Greek Knight and his companions were very happy about that good fortune of Don Florestan. And when the Greek Knight heard Miraflores mentioned, his heart leaped, for he could not calm it as he recalled the delightful time he spent there with that lady who was its mistress; and leaving Grasinda and the other knights, he drew Gandalin aside and said to him: "My true friend, you have already heard the news about Oriana, for if it should come to pass thus, she and I would suffer death. I beg you to be very careful about what I shall command you, which is this: that you and Ardian the dwarf take leave of me and of Grasinda, saying that you wish to go with those of the ship in search of Amadis. And tell my cousin Dragonis and Enil the news about me, bidding them to return immediately to the Firm Island. And when you arrive there you will tell Don Cuadragante and Agrajes that I earnestly entreat them not to leave there, that I shall be with them within two weeks and that they detain with them all those knights our friends who are there, sending for more if they know of any. And tell Don Florestan and your father Don Gandales to have all the ships that are there supplied with food and arms, because I must go with them to a place to which I am committed to go, about which they will be informed by me when I see them. In this matter exercise great care, for you already know what is at stake in it for me."

Then he called the dwarf and said to him: "Ardian, go with Gandalin and do whatever he commands."

Gandalin, who was eager to carry out the order of his lord, went to Grasinda and said to her: "Madam, we intend to leave the Greek Knight in order to enter upon the quest with those knights who go searching for Amadis in that ship; and may God reward you for the favors that we have received from you, madam."

And in like manner they took leave of the Greek Knight and of Don Bruneo and Angriote, and commending them to God they went on board the ship. Angriote said to Dragonis and Enil: "Lords, here are a squire and a dwarf who are joining the quest that you are pursuing."

But when they saw that it was Gandalin and the dwarf they were very happy. And when they learned from them the definitive news, they departed from the fleet with their galley and set out for the Firm Island.

The Greek Knight and Grasinda with her retinue continued sailing over the sea toward Tagades, where King Lisuarte was. King Lisuarte was there, in that town of his, and there were assembled with him many grandees and other nobles of his kingdom, whom he had convoked in order to take counsel with them concerning what he should do about the marriage of Oriana his daughter, for whom the emperor of Rome in order to wed her, by means of emissaries was asking very insistently of him. And all the nobles were telling him not to accede to this, for it was a thing in which he would be erring greatly against God by depriving his daughter of that dominion which she was to inherit and by putting her in the power of a foreigner of lewd and very inconstant character — so inconstant that just as for the present he was very desirous of that marriage, so in a short space of time he would take some other notion into his head; for it is very certain that this is the way of men. But the king, being irked by this aforementioned advice, remained ever firm in his resolve, God permitting it, concerning that Amadis who had made secure his kingdom and his life so many times by rendering him such outstanding services, by elevating him to the greatest fame, to the greatest height that any king of his time had attained, while obtaining undeservedly such poor thanks for it that the king's grandeur and great honor would be discredited and humbled, as will be told in the fourth Book. But even this King Lisuarte, not in order to turn away from his purpose but with the result that his stubbornness and severity be more clearly manifest to all, deemed it well that Count Argamonte, his uncle, who was very old and suffering from gout, be summoned to the same council. The count purposely was certainly unwilling to leave home, for he, since he recognized the wrong desire that the king had in that matter, would be contradicting him completely; but when he saw the king's mandate, he went there at once. When he reached the palace gate, the king came out to receive him, and taking him by the hand went with him to his dais and had him sit beside him, saying to him: "Good uncle, I had you summoned, and these nobles whom you see here, in order to obtain advice about what I ought to do concerning this marriage of my daughter with the emperor of Rome, and I earnestly beg you to tell me your opinion, and that they do likewise."

"My lord," said he, "it seems to me a very difficult thing to advise on this matter as you command, because here there are two things to consider: one is the wish to follow your will, and the other is the wish to contradict it; for if we contradict it, you will take offense as most kings do, because with their great power they want to content and satisfy their own opinions while not being chided or opposed by those whom they can command. If we agree with the other alternative, you put us all in a fine situation with God and His justice, and in great disloyalty and treachery to the world if by us it be agreed that your daughter, being the heiress to this realm after your death, should lose it; because she has that same right to it — and even a stronger one — as you had to receive it from the king your brother. Then consider well, sire, that you would have felt just the same at the time that your brother died, if, shutting you out from what by right you ought to have, it had been given to someone else to whom it did not belong. And if perchance it is your intention that by making Oriana an empress and Leonoreta mistress of this kingdom of yours, you leave them both as very great and very honored ladies, and if you regard everything in the light of reason, it may turn out to the contrary; for since you are not rightfully able to disturb or upset the order of your ancestors, who were lords of this realm, by taking away or by increasing, the emperor by having Oriana your daughter for his wife, will obtain for himself the right to inherit it through her. And as he is powerful, if you were deceased, with little effort he would be able to take possession of it, so that both ladies being disinherited, this land so honored and distinguished in the world, would become subject to the emperors of Rome, without Oriana's having any more command over it than might be granted to her by the emperor, so that instead of her being a suzerain you would leave her a dependent. And for this reason, my lord, if God wishes, I shall excuse myself from giving advice to one who much better than I knows what he ought to do."

"Uncle," said the king, "I well understand what you are saying to me; but it would have pleased me more if you and they had spoken favorably to me of what I have said and promised to the Romans, since in nowise can I withdraw from it."

"On that account do not stop," said the count, "for everything depends on how it is to be done and guaranteed; and there by maintaining your dignity and word of honor decorously, you can deflect or promote according to what is best for you."

"You speak well," said the king, "and for now let no more be said."

Thus that convocation of nobles was brought to an end and they went to their abodes.

And the sailors who were coming in the ships of beautiful Grasinda — in which were the Greek Knight, Don Bruneo de Bonamar and Angriote de Estravaus, who were sailing over the sea as you have already heard — espied one morning the mountain that had the name Tagades, from which was named the town where King Lisuarte was, which was at the foot of the mountain; and they went to where their lady was talking with the Greek Knight and with his companions, and they said to them: "Lady and lords, give us a reward for good news, for if this wind does not change, within one hour you will be putting into port at the harbor of Tagades, to which you wish to go."

Grasinda was very happy, and the Greek Knight likewise, and they all went to the ship's rail, gazing with great joy at that land they had wanted so much to see; and Grasinda gave many thanks to God for having thus guided her, and with great humility she implored Him to direct her affairs and to have her leave there with the honor that she desired. But as for the Greek Knight I tell you that his eyes took great delight in seeing that land where his lady was, from whom he had been so far away for such a long time. And he could not keep the tears from coming, and he turned his face away from Grasinda so that she might not see them; wiping them away as secretly as he could. And putting on a fair countenance, he turned to her, saying: "My lady, have hope that you will go from this land with the honor that you desire, for I am very reassured on seeing your great beauty, which makes me certain of having right and justice on my side; and since God is the judge, it will be His will that the honor be yours."

Grasinda, who had been fearful, as one who had now arrived at the crucial moment, was much encouraged, and said to him: "Greek Knight, my lord, I have much more confidence in your good fortune and good luck than in the beauty that you mention; and if you keep that in mind, it will cause your good reputation to be enhanced as in all the other great undertakings that you have with such good fortune carried out, and it will render me the happiest woman alive."

"Let us leave it to God"; said he, "and let us talk about what must be done."

Then they called Grinfesa, an unmarried daughter of the majordomo, who was good, intelligent, and somewhat familiar with the French language, which King Lisuarte understood; and they gave her a letter in Latin that they had written previously, to give to King Lisuarte and Queen Brisena; commanding her not to speak or answer except in the French language as long as she was among them, and after receiving the replies to return to the ships. The maiden, taking the letter, went to the chamber of her lady and dressed herself in very costly and beautiful garments; and as she was in the bloom of youth and quite beautiful, her appearance was such that she made a fine impression on those who beheld her. Her father the majordomo ordered splendidly caparisoned palfreys and war horses taken off the ship, and the sailors launched a small boat in which they took the maiden and two of her brothers — both good knights — and two squires bearing the arms, and landed them quickly opposite the town. The Greek Knight ordered Lasindo, Don Bruneo's squire, landed in another boat and told him to go by another route to the town and ask for news of his lord, saying that he had been ailing in his own land at the time that Don Bruneo set out on the search for Amadis; and with this pretext he bade him make a great effort to find out what assurance of safe-conduct was being given to his maiden, and in any case to return to him in the morning, for he would have people waiting for him with a boat. Lasindo left him and went to carry out his order.

And as for the maiden, I tell you that when she entered the town everyone beheld her with pleasure, and they said that she came wondrously well attired and accompanied by those two knights. And she kept inquiring where the king's palace was. Thus it happened that the handsome youth Esplandian and Ambor de Gadel, son of Angriote, who by order of the queen were there to serve her as long as the foreigners remained, were both coming out to hunt with goshawks, and they encountered the maiden. As they saw that she was asking for the palace of the king, Esplandian gave his falcon to Sargil and went to her, for he saw that she was wearing foreign garb; and he said to her in the French language: "My good lady, I shall guide you, if you please, and I shall point out the king to you if you do not know him."

The maiden regarded him intently and was greatly impressed by his good looks and charm, so much so that in her opinion she had never seen in her life a man or woman so handsome; and she said: "Gentle youth, whom God made as well favored as handsome, I thank you very much for what you say to me, and thank God that I find myself with such a good escort."

Then her brother gave the rein to the youth, and taking it, he went with them until they arrived at the palace. At this time the king was in the courtyard under a finely wrought portico, and with him many nobles and all those men from Rome. He had just then promised them his daughter Oriana to take to the emperor, and they had just accepted her as their lady. The maiden, having already dismounted from her palfrey, entered the gate escorted by Esplandian, and her brothers with her; and as she came up to the king she knelt and sought to kiss his hands, but he did not yield them, because he was not accustomed to doing so except when conferring a signal favor on some maiden. Then giving him the letter, she said to him: "Sire, it is necessary that the queen and all her maidens hear it read; and if perchance the maidens are annoyed by hearing its contents let them try to have some good knight represent them, as has my lady, by whose order I come here."

The king ordered King Arban of North Wales and his uncle, Count Argamon, to go for the queen and to bring with her all the princesses and maidens that were in the palace. This was carried out, so that the queen came with such a retinue of ladies, both beautiful and richly adorned, as would be hard to find in all the world; and she seated herself near the king with the princesses and all the other ladies around her. The maiden message-bearer went and kissed the hands of the queen, saying to her: "Lady, if my quest appears strange to you, do not wonder, since for such things God made your court the finest of all those in the world, and the king's and your own great excellence are the cause of this. And since here is to be found the remedy that elsewhere is lacking, hear this letter and grant what is requested of you in it, and there will come to your court a beautiful matron and the valiant Greek Knight who attends her."

The king ordered it read, and it was as follows: "To the very noble and honorable Lisuarte, King of Great Britain: I, Grasinda, beauty queen of all the matrons of Romania, give orders that homage be done you; and I make known to you, my lord, that I have come to your land under the protection of the Greek Knight. The purpose of my coming is that, just as I was adjudged the most beautiful matron of all those of Romania, so pursuant to that distinction, which rendered my heart so happy, I want to be declared more beautiful than any of the maidens at your court, in order that with the victory in both categories I may be able to remain in that state of enjoyment that I so greatly desire. If there be a knight who on behalf of any one of your maidens may wish to dispute this, let him make ready for two things: first, to do battle with the Greek Knight; and the other, to display on the field a rich coronet, like the one I wear, in order that the victor may be able to give them both to the lady for whom he is fighting as a token of his having won that victory. And very noble king, if this for which I come you are pleased to permit to take place, order me and all my attendants, and the Greek Knight, to be given assurance of safe-conduct; if not, only from those who wish to do battle with him. And if the knight who fights on behalf of the maidens be conquered, let a second knight come forth, and likewise a third, for the Greek Knight out of his great excellence will hold the field against all comers."

The letter having been read, the king said: "So help me God, I believe that the matron is very beautiful, and the knight esteems himself no little at arms; but however that may be, they have initiated a great fantasy which without injury they could have avoided. However, people's desires are diverse, and on them they set their hearts and do not fear the risks that can come to them. And you, maiden, may retire, and I shall give orders that the assurance of safe-conduct be proclaimed publicly just as your lady requests, so that she will be able to come whenever she likes; and if she finds no one to dispute her claim, she will have satisfied her desire."

"My lord," said she, "you respond just as we expected, for from your court no one can rightly go away with any complaint. And because the Greek Knight brings with him two companions who will request jousts, it is necessary that they have the same assurance of safe-conduct."

"So be it," said the king.

"In the name of God," said the maiden. "Then tomorrow you will see them in your court. And you, my lady," said she to the queen, "give orders to your maidens to be where they may see how their honor is advanced or lessened by their champions, for my lady will do so; and God be with you."

Then she took leave of them and went away to the ships, where she was received with great pleasure. After she told them how she had delivered her message, they at once ordered their arms and horses taken off the ships, and they had a very luxurious tent and two small tents set up on the seashore; but that night only the majordomo with some servants came on land to guard it.

And now know you that at the time that the maiden messenger from Grasinda left King Lisuarte and the queen with the message that you have already heard, Salustanquidio, cousin of the emperor of Rome, who was present, stood up, and a good one hundred Roman knights with him; and he said to the king in a loud voice, so that all heard him: "My lord, I and these nobles of Rome who are here before you wish to ask a boon of you that will be to your advantage and to our honor."

"I am quite pleased to grant whatever boon you may ask," said the king, "especially the kind you mention."

"Then permit us," said Salustanquidio, "to undertake the quest on behalf of the maidens, for we shall give much better returns for it than the knights of this land of yours, because we and the Greeks know one another well, and the latter fear us merely on account of the name 'Romans' more than they will on account of the actual accomplishments of those from here."

Don Grumedan, who was there, stood up, and went before the king and said: "Sire, although it may be a great honor to princes for daring quests by foreigners to be made at their courts, and however much they may augment their honor and royal status, very quickly these daring quests might turn out to be dishonor and discredit if they are not received and regulated with good discretion. And this I say, sire, because of this Greek Knight who has just come on such a quest; and if his great arrogance should bring it about that those who in your court might seek to contradict him be vanquished by him, although the danger and harm would be theirs, the publicity and discredit would be yours. Therefore, sire, it seems to me that it would be well, before anything is decided by you, that you wait for Don Galaor and Norandel, your son, who according to what I have learned, will be here within five days; and by that time Don Guilan the Pensive will be improved and will be able to take up arms. And these will undertake the enterprise in such fashion that your honor and theirs be protected."

"That cannot be," said the king. "Already I have granted them the boon; and they are such that they will provide a favorable outcome, even for a greater action than this one."

"It can well be," said Don Grumedan, "but I shall bring it about that the maidens whom this concerns not authorize it."

"Desist from that," said the king, "for all that I do for the maidens of my household is done and completed; including this which is demanded of me."

Salustanquidio went and kissed the hands of the king and said to Don Grumedan: "I shall finish this battle to my honor and that of the maidens; and since you, Don Grumedan, esteem so highly those knights that you mention and yourself as well, thinking that they would conclude it better than we, if I emerge from the battle in such condition as to be able to bear arms, I shall take two companions and I shall fight with those knights you mention and with you; and if I am not able to fight, I shall supply another in my place who easily will be able to excuse me from doing so."

"In the name of God," said Don Grumedan, "I accept this battle for myself and for those who may wish to enter with me."

And taking a ring from his finger, he held it out to the king, saying to him: "Sire, you see here my gage on my own behalf and on that of those who may enter the battle with me. And since this was demanded by them, you cannot justly refuse it if they do not concede their own defeat."

Salustanquidio said: "The seas will be dry before a Roman goes back on his word, except to his honor. And if your old age has done away with your brains, your body will pay for it, should you put it into the battle."

"Certainly," said Don Grumedan, "I am not so young as not to be full of days; and what you think will be for me a disability, I consider a major help, for during my life I have witnessed many things, among which the fact that arrogance never has had a good outcome; and thus I expect it to happen in your case, since according to your boasting you are the very epitome of it."

King Arban of North Wales stood up to answer the Romans as did a good thirty knights who were seeking to participate in the battle along with him, and more than one hundred others. But the king, who knew him well, extended his scepter and ordered them not to speak on that subject, and he gave the same order to Don Grumedan. Count Argamon said to the king: "Sire, command one and all to go to their quarters, for it is to your discredit for such speeches to be made in your presence."

The king did so; and the count said to him: "What do you think, sire, of the folly of these Romans, who thus belittle those of your court while not showing any respect for you? Then what will they do, when they are in their own land, or how will your daughter be treated? For they tell me, sire, that you have already promised her to them. I do not know what deceit this betokens: that as a man so discreet and who has had such good fortune through God's will and your own good sense, instead of giving thanks to Him for it, you wish to try His patience and vex Him. Look out, for very quickly He could bring it about that fortune turn its wheel; and when He is thus angered by those on whom He has conferred many favors, not with merely one lash, but with many very cruel ones He chastises them. And if the things of this world are transitory and perishable, their glory and fame lasts no longer than while they are visible; nor is each one judged except as he is seen at present, for all that good fortune you have and that lofty elevation at which you now are would be consigned to oblivion, sunken underground, if fortune were hostile to you; and if some recollection of it be had, it would be only to discredit you in the present by blaming you for the past. Remember, sire, the very great mistake that you made without justification in separating from your court such an honorable body of knights as were Amadis of Gaul and his brothers and those others of his family, and many other knights who left you on their account whereby formerly you had been so honored and feared by everyone. And having now scarcely recovered from that mistake, do you seek to initiate another which is worse? Well, this comes to you only because of your large amount of arrogance; for if it were not so, you would have feared God and taken counsel with those who will serve you loyally. I, sire, herewith acquit myself of that fidelity and vassalage that I owe you, and I desire to go away to my lands; for if it be God's will, I shall not see the weeping and bitterness in which your daughter Oriana will indulge at the time that you hand her over, for I have been told that you are ordering her to come from Miraflores."

"Uncle," said the king, "speak no more of this matter, for it is done, and it cannot be undone. And I beg you to stay for three days in order to see how these combats will come out that are scheduled, and to be judge of them along with whatever other knights you wish. This do because owing to the time that you dwelt in Greece you understand the Greek language better than any other man in my land."

Argamon said to him: "Since it so pleases you, I shall do so; but when the battles are over, I shall not tarry any longer, for I would not be able to stand it."

The conversation being over, the count went to his lodging, and the king remained in his palace.

Lasindo, Don Bruneo's squire, who by order of the Greek Knight had come there, well ascertained all that had happened in the king's presence after the maiden had left there. And he went at once to the ships and related how the Romans had asked the king for permission to participate in the combats and the latter had granted it to them, the words that Don Grumedan had exchanged with Salustanquidio, and how they had set the time for their combat, and all the other things taking place there about which you have already heard. And furthermore, he told how the king had sent for his daughter Oriana in order to hand her over to the Romans as soon as the battles had taken place. When the Greek Knight heard that the Romans were to engage in the combats and fight on behalf of the maidens, he was very happy; because what he had dreaded most about that confrontation was the thought that his brother Don Galaor might take on that battle on behalf of the maidens, for this he would consider more serious than any other challenge that might come to him, because Don Galaor was the knight who had put him in more dire straits than any other knight with whom he had fought, giants not excepted, as the first Book of this story relates. For he firmly believed that if Galaor had been at the court, as the most highly esteemed at arms of all those who were there, he would have taken up this challenge; from which only one of two things could have resulted; either the death of Amadis or his killing his brother Don Galaor, who would have suffered death rather than anything that would reflect discredit upon him. And therefore he was happy to learn that Galaor was not at court; and besides this, that he would not be fighting any of his friends who were at the court. And he said to Grasinda: "Lady, in the morning let us hear mass in that tent; and prepare yourself very elegantly, and bring well adorned whatever maidens you like; and we shall go and conclude this affair in which we are engaged, for I trust in God that you will obtain that honor so much desired by you and for which you have come to this land."

Whereupon Grasinda withdrew to her stateroom, and the Greek Knight and his companions to their own ship.

CHAPTER LXXIX

HOW THE GREEK KNIGHT AND HIS COMPANIONS TOOK GRASINDA FROM THE SEA AND ESCORTED HER WITH HER RETINUE TO THE LISTS, WHERE HER KNIGHT WAS TO DEFEND HER CAUSE BY FULFILLING HER QUEST.

They landed Grasinda with four maidens, and went to hear mass at the tent; and from there all three knights rode forth armed on their war horses, and Grasinda on her richly caparisoned palfrey so elegantly decked out in cloth of gold and silks, with precious stones and pearls so valuable that the greatest empress in the world could not have worn more of them; because she, always anticipating that day which she had now reached, long beforehand had prepared to have for it the most beautiful and finest things that she could come by as the noble lady that she was; for not having husband or children or family, and being abundantly provided with great lands and income, she did not think of spending the latter on anything except what you hear; and her maidens likewise were dressed in exquisite garb. And since Grasinda was naturally beautiful, those artificial enhancements increased her beauty so greatly that all those who looked at her considered it a wonder, and her appearance gave great courage to the man who was to fight on her behalf. She wore on her head only the coronet that she had won as a token of being the most beautiful of all the matrons of Romania, as you have already heard. The Greek Knight led her horse by the rein, and was clad in armor that Grasinda had ordered made for him, and his coat of mail was as white as moonlight, his heraldic device was of the same designs and colors as Grasinda was wearing, and it was fastened together with cords woven in gold;

also on the helmet and the shield were painted the same insignia that the visor of his helmet bore. And Don Bruneo wore green armor, and on his shield there was depicted a maiden and before her an armed knight, both portrayed in curlicues of gold and scarlet; and the knight seemed to be begging a favor from her. And Angriote de Estravaus was riding a sturdy, agile horse, and bore arms of vair in silver and gold. He led by the rein the horse of the maiden of whom you have already heard, who had gone to the king with the message. And Don Bruneo was escorting another maiden, her sister. All the knights wore their helmets laced, and the majordomo and his sons were with them. With such a company they arrived at the lists at the edge of the town where the combats were usually held. In the center of the lists there was a pillar of marble as high as a man's stature, and those who came there in quest of jousts and combats were accustomed to put on it a shield or helmet, or a bouquet of flowers or a glove, as a gage. The Greek Knight and his companions having arrived there, they saw the king at one end of the field, and at the other end the Romans, and among them Salustanquidio with black armor bearing a device of gold and silver serpents. He was so tall that he seemed a giant, and he was mounted on an extraordinarily big horse. The queen was at her windows and the princesses beside her, as was Olinda the beautiful, who among her lavish adornments wore on her beautiful hair a splendid coronet.

When the Greek Knight arrived on the field, he saw the queen and the princesses and other matrons and maidens of high rank; and as he did not perceive his lady Oriana, whom he was wont to see among them, his heart trembled with longing for her. And when he saw Salustanquidio standing so strong and fierce in appearance, he turned his face toward Grasinda and saw her already somewhat dismayed, so he said to her: "My lady, do not be frightened on seeing a man so huge of body, for God will be for you, and I shall cause you to win what will give pleasure to your heart."

"May it thus please Him through His compassion," said she.

Then he took from her the splendid coronet that she had on her head, and went slowly forward on his horse and placed it on top of the marble pillar; then he returned at once to where his squires were, who were holding for him three very strong lances with ornate pennants of various colors. Taking the one that seemed to him the best, he hung his shield from his neck and went to where the king was, and having bowed to him, said in the Greek language: "God save you, king. I am a foreign knight who has come from the kingdom of Greece with the intention of testing myself with your knights who are very good; and not independently, but because of the desire of the lady who in this matter can command me. And now, since my luck decrees it, it seems to me that the duel will be between me and the Romans. Give orders to them to place on the pillar the maidens' coronet in accordance with what my maiden stipulated with you."

Then he brandished his lance vigorously and spurred his horse forward as hard as he could, and placed himself at one end of the field. The king did not understand what he said to him, for he did not know the Greek language; but he said to Argamon, who was beside him: "It seems to me, uncle, that according to his appearance that knight will not want the discredit for himself."

"Certainly, sire," said the count, "although you have suffered some embarrassment because of these people from Rome being at your court, I would be very glad to have some of their arrogance suppressed."

"I do not know what will happen," said the king, "but I believe that a beautiful joust is in the making."

The knights and the other people of the king's household, who saw what the Greek Knight had done, marveled and were saying that they had never seen so elegant and handsome an armed knight except Amadis. Salustanquidio, who was near and saw how all the people had their eyes on the Greek Knight and were praising him, said very angrily: "What is this, people of Great Britain? Why do you marvel on seeing a crazy Greek knight who only knows how to prance about the field? It really seems that you do not know them as we do, for they fear the name 'Roman' as they do fire. What a sign of your not having seen or experienced great deeds at arms when you marvel at such a petty one as this will be. Well, now you will see how that man, who armed and on horseback seems so handsome to you, will look when he lies cold and dishonored on the ground."

Then he went to the vicinity of where the queen was and said to Olinda: "My lady, give me that coronet of yours, for you are the one whom I love and esteem above all other ladies; give it to me, my lady, and do not fear, for I shall return it at once together with that one which is on the pillar, and with it you will enter Rome, for the king and the queen will be glad to have me take you with Oriana, and make you my lady and mistress of my land."

Olinda, who heard this, had no liking for his crazy talk, and her heart and flesh trembled, and her face turned red, but she did not give him the coronet. Salustanquidio, who saw her thus, said: "Do not be afraid, my lady, to give me the coronet, for I shall bring it about that with your winning this honor, that crazy matron, who has sought to stake it on the strength of that Greek coward, will go from here without it."

But in spite of all this, Olinda would not give it to him at all, until the queen removed it from her head and sent it to him. And taking it in his hand he went and placed it on the pillar beside the other one. Then in great haste he asked for his arms, and three Roman knights quickly gave them to him; and he took his shield and hung it from his neck, put the helmet on his head, and taking a lance thicker than any other, with a long, sharp tip, he settled himself on his horse. And when he saw himself so huge and so well armed, and saw that everybody was looking at him, his courage and arrogance increased, and he said to the king: "Now I want your knights to see the difference between them and the Romans, for I shall overcome that Greek; and if he said that after conquering me he would fight with two, I shall fight with the two best that he brings; then if they lack the courage, let the third come on."

Don Grumedan, who was boiling with anger on hearing that and on seeing the patience of the king, said to him: "Salustanquidio, you have forgotten the battle that you are to have with me if you escape from this one, and you demand another!"

"That is easy to carry out," said Salustanquidio.

And the Greek Knight said in a loud voice: "Misshapen evil beast, what are you talking about? Why do you let the day go by? Pay attention to what you are to do."

When he heard this, he turned his horse toward him, and they moved toward each other with their horses on the run, their lances lowered and they themselves protected by their shields.

Their horses were nimble and swift, and the knights strong and angry; so they both collided in the middle of the lists and neither missed his blow. And the Greek Knight struck him below the boss of the shield, piercing it, and the lance hit some strong metal plates and could not pass through them. But he had thrust at him so hard that he hurled him out of his saddle, so that everybody was amazed; and he passed by him looking very gallant bearing Salustanquidio's lance thrust through his shield and through the sleeve of his coat of mail, so that everybody thought he was wounded, but it was not so. And pulling the lance from his shield he flourished it aloft and went to where Salustanquidio was, and saw that he was not stirring and was lying as if dead. And it was no wonder, for he was big and heavy and had fallen from his horse, which was tall, and his armor heavy and the field very hard; so that everything together was the cause of bringing him as close to death as he was. And above all he had broken his left arm on which he had fallen, near the hand, and most of his ribs were dislocated. The Greek Knight still mounted, who had thought that Salustanquidio was more vigorous, stopped and bent over him, placing the tip of his lance on his face, for his helmet had fallen from his head with the force of the fall; and he said to him: "Knight, do not be so ill-disposed as not to confer the maidens' coronet on that beautiful matron, for she deserves it."

Salustanquidio did not answer, and leaving him there, the Greek Knight went to the king, and said in his own language: "Good king, that knight, although now he is without arrogance, is not willing to grant the coronet to that lady who is waiting for it, nor is he disposed to defend it or make answer. Grant it to her in judgment, as is right; otherwise I shall cut off his head and the coronet will be conferred."

Then he returned to where the knight was, and the king asked what he had said. And the count his uncle made him understand it, and said to him: "Yours is the blame, if you let that knight die in your presence. Since he cannot defend himself, by right you can render judgment concerning the coronets in favor of the Greek Knight."

"Sire," said Don Grumedan, "let the knight do what he wishes, for in the Romans there are more tricks than in a fox; because if Salustanquidio lives, he will say that he would still be capable of continuing the battle, if you had not been so hard pressed regarding a judgment."

Everybody was laughing at what Don Grumedan said, and they were breaking the Romans' hearts. And the king, who saw the Green Knight dismount from his horse and be about to cut off Salustanquidio's head, said to Argamon: "Uncle, hasten and tell him to forbear killing him, and to take the coronets, for I grant them to him, and let him bestow them where he should."

Argamon went toward him, shouting to him to hear the king's command. The Greek Knight drew back and shouldered his sword. At this moment the count came up and said to him: "Knight, the king begs you for his sake to forbear killing that knight, and he commands you to take the coronets."

"I am pleased," said he, "and know you that if I fought with some vassal of the king, I would not kill him if what I had begun I could finish in any other way. But as for the Romans, kill them and dishonor them as the evil men they are in imitation of the deceitful ways of that arrogant emperor, their lord, from whom all of them learn to be arrogant, and in the end cowards."

The count returned to the king and told him what the knight had said. And the knight mounted his horse and taking both coronets from the pillar carried them to Grasinda. And he placed on her head the maidens' coronet, and gave the other to one of her damsels to keep safe.

The Greek Knight said to Grasinda: "My lady, your affair is in the state that you have desired, and I through the mercy of God quit of the boon that I promised you. Go you, if you please, to the tents and take your ease, and I shall wait to see whether the Romans with this grief that they have had will come out on the field."

"My lord," said she, "I shall in nowise leave you, for I can have no greater rest or enjoyment in anything than in seeing your great deeds of chivalry."

"Do," said he, "what you wish."

Then he spurred his horse and found it strong and rested, for it had exerted little effort that day; and he hung his shield from his neck and took up a lance with a very beautiful pennant. And he summoned the maiden who had come there with Grasinda's message, and he said to her: "Friend, go to the king and tell him that he already knows that he agreed that if I remained after the first battle, I would maintain the field against any two knights who together might oppose me. And now it behooves me to comply with that piece of folly and I beg him as a favor that he not command any of his own knights to fight with me, because they are such that they would not win any honor with me in overcoming me; but that he let me fight with the Romans, who have begun their battles, and he will see whether I, being a Greek, will fear them."

The damsel went to the king, and in the French language told him what the Greek Knight had ordered her to say to him.

"Madam," said the king, "I am displeased that no one from my court or my realm is fighting with him. He has carried on today to his honor and I esteem him highly; and if he were pleased to remain with me, I would make it worth his while. I forbid that those of my court and demesne be permitted to fight him, for I have other matters to attend to; but let those of Rome, who are on their own, do as they please."

The king said this because he had much to do in connection with the departure of his daughter Oriana, and because he did not have in his court at that time any of his highly esteemed knights, who in order not to behold the cruelty and injustice that he was inflicting on his daughter, had departed from there. There were in the court only Guilan the Pensive, who was ailing, and Cendil de Ganota, who had had his legs pierced by an arrow with which Brondajel de Roca, a Roman, had wounded him in a forest that the king was scouring in an effort to shoot a deer.

The reply that the king gave her having been heard by the maiden, she said to him: "Sire, many thanks for the kindness and favor that you show the Greek knight, and be assured that if he had wished to remain in Greece with the emperor, all that he might have asked would have been granted him; but his only desire is to travel freely through the world helping matrons and maidens who receive wrongs, and many others who rightly ask him for aid. And in these matters which are constantly coming to his notice, he has done so much that it will not be slow in coming to your attention, whence by you, and by the others who do not know him, he will be more highly considered and appreciated."

"So help you God, maiden, tell me to whom that knight probably owes allegiance."

"Certainly, sire, I do not know; but if his mighty heart is subjugated by anything, I believe it is probably only by some lady with whom he is desperately in love, and that he is placed under her sway. Now God be with you, for I am returning to the Greek Knight with this reply; and whoever seeks him, yonder on this field he will find him until noon."

The reply having been heard, the Greek Knight proceeded slowly to where Grasinda was, giving to one of the sons of the majordomo his shield and to the other his lance, and in order not to be recognized he did not remove his helmet. He told the one who had received the shield from him to go and place it on top of the pillar, and to say that the Greek Knight had ordered it so placed as a challenge to the Roman knights in order to abide by what he had promised. And he took Grasinda's horse by the rein and remained talking with her.

There was among the Romans a knight, Maganil by name, who next to Salustanquidio was considered to have the greatest prowess at arms, and they really thought that two knights of that land would not hold the field against him; and he had brought two brothers with him, likewise good knights. So when the shield was placed on the pillar, the Romans looked to this Maganil as if they expected from him honor and vengeance. But he said to them: "Friends, do not look at me, for I cannot do anything about that matter, because I have promised Prince Salustanquidio, if he should emerge from his battle in such condition that he could not fight, that I will assume the responsibility for the battle with Don Grumedan, and my brothers with me. And if he does not dare fight with us, and his companions don't dare either, since because of him I was to undertake it, then for you I shall take vengeance on the knight."

And while they were talking thus, there came two knights of their company, Romans, well armed with splendid armor and on beautiful horses. The one was called Gradamor and the other, Lasanor, and they were brothers, nephews of Brondajel de Roca, being sons of his sister, who was belligerent and haughty, as likewise were the husband and the sons; for which reason and on account of their being nephews of Brondajel, who was chief majordomo of the emperor, they were very much feared by their own men. And these men having arrived on the field, just as you hear, without speaking or bowing to the king they went up to the pillar and one of them took the shield of the Greek Knight and struck with it such a blow on the pillar that he broke the shield into pieces, and he said in a loud voice: "Damn anybody who permits a Greek shield to be placed before Romans as a challenge to them."

The Greek Knight, when he saw his shield shattered, was so furious that his heart was burning with anger. And leaving Grasinda, he went and took up the lance that his squire was holding for him; not looking for a shield, although Angriote told him to take his; and he charged at the knights of Rome and they at him. And the one who had broken his shield he struck with his lance so hard that he hurled him from the saddle and in the fall his helmet was knocked from his head so that he remained stunned without being able to rise, and everybody thought he was dead. And there the Greek Knight had lost his lance, so he put hand to sword and turned to Lasanor, who was dealing him mighty blows, and he struck Lasanor on top of the shoulder and cut through his armor and his flesh to the bone, causing the lance to fall from his hand; and the Greek Knight gave him another blow on top of the helmet so that Lasanor on losing his stirrups was forced to embrace his horse's neck. And as he saw him thus, he quickly transferred his sword to his left hand and seizing the shield from him, jerked it from his neck, so that the knight fell to the ground, but got up at once out of fear of death. And he saw his brother on foot with sword in hand, and he went to join him. The Greek Knight, fearing that he would kill his horse, dismounted from it, taking on his arm the shield he had seized, and with drawn sword went toward them and attacked them so violently that the brothers could not endure it or hold the field; so that those who were watching him were amazed to see him so valiant as to hold them in low esteem. Thus he made the Romans acknowledge his prowess and their own weakness. He then struck Lasanor a blow on the left leg in such wise he was unable to remain standing and begged him for mercy; but he pretended not to understand him, kicking him in the chest and knocking him flat on the ground. Then he turned to the other one, who had broken the shield, but the latter did not dare wait, for he very much feared death, which was approaching; and he went to where the king was, in a loud voice imploring him as a favor not to allow him to kill him. But the Greek Knight, who was following him, stopped in front of him, and by dint of the mighty blows that he dealt him, made him return to the pillar. When he came up to it he circled around it to protect himself from the blows. The Greek Knight, who was very angry, was trying to strike him, and at times was striking the pillar, which was of very hard stone, causing sparks of fire to flash from it and from the sword. And when he saw him too tired to move, he took him in his arms and squeezed him so hard that he deprived him of all his strength; after which he let him fall to the ground. Then he took the shield and struck him with it such a blow on the head that the shield was broken to pieces and the Roman appeared to be dead. And he put the tip of his sword at his face and pushed it a little, and Gradamor trembled, hiding his face out of great fear; and putting his arms over his head in dread of the sword, he began to exclaim: "Ah, good Greek, sir! Do not kill me, and command me what to do."

But the Greek Knight indicated that he did not understand him; and as he perceived him to be conscious he took him by the hand and striking him on the head with the flat of his sword forced him unwillingly to stand, and made signs to him to climb up on the pillar. But he was so weak that he was not able to do so, so the Greek Knight helped him; and while he was thus standing at ease, he pushed him so hard that he made him fall outstretched. And as he was big and heavy, and had fallen from an erect position, he remained so crushed that he did not stir; and the Greek placed the fragments of the shield on his chest, and going to Lasanor, took him by the leg and dragged him to his brother's side. And everybody thought that he intended to behead them; and Don Grumedan, who was watching him with pleasure, said: "It seems to me that the Greek has well avenged his shield."

The youth Esplandian, who was watching the combat, thinking that the Greek Knight intended to kill the two knights whom he had overcome, and being sorry for them, spurred his palfrey, calling to Ambor his companion, and went to where the knights were. The Greek Knight who saw him coming thus, waited for him to see what he wanted; and as he came closer, he seemed to him the most handsome youth of any he had ever seen in his life. Esplandian came up to him and said: "Sir, since these knights are in such a state that they cannot defend themselves and your prowess is well known, free them as a favor to me, since to you all the honor accrues."

He gave him to understand that he did not comprehend him. And Esplandian began to call in a loud voice to Count Argamon to come over there, because the Greek Knight did not understand his language. The count came at once, and the Greek asked him what the youth wanted. He replied: "He asks you for those knights, begging that you give them to him."

"I should like to kill them," said he, "but I hand them over to him."

And he said to the count: "Sir, who is this very handsome youth, and whose son is he?"

The count said to him: "Certainly, knight, I shall not tell you that, for I do not know it, nor does anyone who is in this land."

And he related the manner of his rearing. "I have already heard of this youth in Romania, and I think he is called Esplandian. And I was told that he had some letters on his chest."

"It is true," said the count, "and indeed you may see them if you wish."

"I shall be very grateful to you for it, and to him for showing them to me, for it is a strange thing to hear and even more so to see."

The count asked Esplandian to show them to him. And he came up closer and he was wearing a jerkin and French hood embroidered with lions of gold and a narrow, close-fitting belt, and his gold tunic and hood were fastened with gold buttons. Unbuttoning some of the buttons he showed the Greek Knight the letters, at which the latter was amazed, considering it the strangest thing he had ever heard of. And the white letters said "Esplandian," but the red ones he could not decipher, although they were well delineated and formed. He said to Esplandian: "Fair youth, God bless you."

Then he took leave of the count and mounted his horse, which his squire was holding there for him; and going to where Grasinda was, he said to her: "My lady, you have been bored awaiting [the outcome of] my mad actions, but put the blame on the arrogance of the Romans who have caused them."

"So help me God," said she, "on the contrary, your good fortune makes me very happy."

Then they moved on from there toward the ships, and Grasinda with great exultation and joy in her heart, and the Greek Knight with no less in having thus disposed of the Romans, for which he gave many thanks to God. Then having arrived at the ships, and having the tents put aboard, they set out at once on their way to the Firm Island.

But I tell you concerning Angriote de Estravaus and Don Bruneo that they remained on a galley by command of the Greek Knight in order secretly to help Don Grumedan in the combat that he had scheduled with the Romans, the Greek Knight having begged them that after undergoing that confrontation in whatever manner might please God, they try to find out some news concerning Oriana and proceed at once to the Firm Island.

The good youth Esplandian was profusely thanked by the Roman knights for what he had done in freeing them from the death to which they were so close.

CHAPTER LXXX

HOW KING LISUARTE SENT FOR ORIANA IN ORDER TO HAND HER OVER TO THE ROMANS, AND CONCERNING WHAT HAPPENED TO HIM WITH A KNIGHT FROM THE FIRM ISLAND, AND THE BATTLE THAT TOOK PLACE BETWEEN DON GRUMEDAN AND THE COMPANIONS OF THE GREEK KNIGHT AGAINST THE THREE ROMAN CHALLENGERS; AND HOW, AFTER THE ROMANS WERE DEFEATED, THE COMPANIONS OF THE GREEK KNIGHT WENT TO THE FIRM ISLAND, AND WHAT THEY DID THERE.

You have heard that Oriana was at Miraflores, and with her Queen Sardamira, who by order of King Lisuarte went to see her in order to tell her about the greatness of Rome and the vastly increased dominion in prospect for her through that marriage to the emperor. Now know you that the king, her father, having already promised her to the Romans, decided to send for her in order to arrange for her transportation. And he commanded Giontes, his nephew, to take with him two other knights and some servants and to bring her, and not to permit any knight to speak with her. Giontes took Ganjel de Sadoca and Lasanor, with others as servants, and went to where Oriana was; then taking her in a litter — for otherwise she could not come, as she was faint from much weeping — and her maidens, and Queen Sardamira with her own retinue, they left Miraflores and were advancing along the road to Tagades, where the king was.

And on the second day there happened what you shall now hear. For near the highway, under some trees, beside a spring was a knight on a brown horse. He was very well armed; and over his coat of mail he wore a green armorial device that was secured at both ends with green cords in gold buttonholes, so that he seemed to them extremely handsome. And he took a shield and slung it from his neck, and took a lance with a green pennant and brandished it a little; then he said to his squire: "Go and tell those protectors of Oriana that I beg them to give me an opportunity to speak with her, that it will not be to their harm or to hers; and that if they do so, I shall be grateful to them for it; and if not, it will grieve me, but it will be necessary to attempt what I can."

The squire went up to them and told them the message; and when he said to them that he would use force in order to speak with her, they laughed and said to him: "Tell your lord that we shall not let him see her, and that when he tests his strength, he will have accomplished nothing."

But Oriana, who heard him, said: "What matters it to you if the knight should speak to me? Perhaps he brings me some pleasing news."

"Lady," said Giontes, "the king your father commanded us not to permit anyone to come up to you or speak with you."

The squire went away with this reply, and Giontes made preparations for the combat. And when the knight in green heard her, he went at him at once, and they struck each other mighty blows on their shields, so that their lances were shattered; but Giontes's horse from the great force of the collision had one leg dislocated, so that it fell with its master, and on account of its pinning one of his feet underneath along with the stirrup in which he had it, he could not rise. The knight in green passed by him, riding in fine style, and returned at once, saying: "Knight, I beg you to let me speak with Oriana."

He said to him: "Because of my protection you will no longer be deprived of it, although my horse has the blame."

Then Ganjel de Sadoca shouted to him to protect himself and not lay hands on the knight, for he would die for it.

"Would that I had you in such a state," said he.

And he went against him as fast as his horse could carry him with another lance that his squire gave him, and he missed the encounter; and Ganjel de Sadoca struck him on the shield, whereby he broke his lance, but he did him no other harm. And the knight returned to him, for he saw him with sword in hand, and he struck him so hard that the lance went to pieces, and Ganjel went out of his saddle and had a hard fall. Then Lasanor came up; but the knight, who was very skillful in that profession, protected himself so well that he caused him to miss his lance thrust so that Lasanor lost the lance from his hand, and they collided so violently that their shields were broken and Lasanor had the arm broken with which he was holding it; and he of the green arms, who had returned to him with sword in hand, saw that he was in a state of shock, so did not seek to attack him; but he unbridled Lasanor's horse and hit it on the head with the flat of his sword, causing it to go fleeing over the field with its master. And when he saw it go thus, he could not help laughing.

Then he took a letter that he was carrying and went to the litter where Oriana was. And she, who thus saw him overcome those three knights so well at arms, thought that he was Amadis, and her heart trembled. But the knight came up to her with great humility and held out the letter saying: "Lady, Agrajes and Don Florestan have sent you this letter, in which you will find news that will give you pleasure. And God be with you, madam, for I am returning to those who sent me to you; for I know for certain that they will have need of me, although I be of slight valor."

"You seem to me the opposite," said Oriana, "according to what I have seen; and I beg you to tell me your name, for such great effort you have put forth in order to give me pleasure."

"Madam," said he, "I am Gavarte of the Fearful Valley, who am much grieved by what the king your father is doing to you. But I trust in God that it will be very difficult to bring it to a conclusion; instead, so many of your subjects and others will die that it will be known everywhere."

"Oh, Don Gavarte, my good friend, may it please God through His mercy to bring me to a time when this great loyalty of yours to me may be rewarded!"

"Madam," said he, "my desire has always been to serve you in everything as my legitimate suzerain, and in this matter much more, since I know the great injustice that is being done you; and I shall come to your aid with all those who seek to serve their suzerain."

"My friend," said she, "I beg you earnestly thus to set it forth wherever you may be."

"I shall do so," said he, "since I can in good faith."

Then he took leave of her. And Oriana went to Mabilia, who was with Queen Sardamira, and the queen said to her: "It seems to me, my lady, that we have been on a par as regards our escorts. I do not know whether their weakness has brought it about, or the misfortune attendant upon this journey, that here where yours have been defeated and maltreated, mine likewise should have been."

They all laughed heartily at what the queen said, but the knights were so ashamed and abashed that they did not dare appear in their presence. Oriana remained there for a time, while the knights were caring for themselves, for the horse that carried Lasanor could not bring him back for a long while. She withdrew with Mabilia, and they read the letter, in which they discovered that Agrajes and Don Florestan and Don Gandales were informing her that Gandalin and Ardian the dwarf were already on the Firm Island, that Amadis would be with them within a week; and that by them he had sent word to have a large fleet made ready — for it was needed in order to go to a very well-known place — that they had the fleet thus readied; and that she was to take pleasure and have hope that God would be on her side. They were happy beyond compare with that news, as persons who through it were hoping to live, because they considered themselves dead if that marriage should take place. And Mabilia comforted Oriana and begged her to eat, but she up to that time on account of her great sadness would not and could not eat, nor now out of great joy.

So they went along their way until they reached the town where the king was; but first he and the Romans came out to meet them, along with many other people. When Oriana saw them, she began to weep copiously and had herself helped down from the litter and all her maidens with her; who when they saw her weeping so piteously, wept, tore their hair, and kissed her hands and clothing as if they had her dead before them, so that they produced great sorrow in everyone. The king, who saw them thus, was greatly disturbed and said to King Arban of North Wales: "Go to Oriana and tell her that I feel the greatest distress in the world at what she is doing, and that I am sending word to order her to get back into her litter and her maidens likewise, and putting on a better countenance to go to her mother; for I shall tell her news at which she will be happy."

King Arban told her so, just as he was ordered to do, but Oriana answered: "Oh, King of North Wales, my good cousin! since my great lack of fortune has been so cruel to me, you and those who have undergone many perils in order to help sad and troubled maidens, can you not help me with arms? At least help me with your words; advise the king my father not to do me so much ill, and not to wish to tempt God, so that his good fortune that until now He has given him, He may not change to the contrary; and strive, cousin, to have him come to me here, and to have Count Argamon and Don Grumedan come with him, for by no means shall I depart from here until this is done."

King Arban in this whole affair did nothing but weep bitterly, and not being able to reply to her, returned to the king and told him Oriana's message; but to him it became a serious matter to meet her publicly in that confrontation because the more her grief and anguish became known to everybody, the more his own guilt was augmented. Count Argamon on seeing him hesitate, begged him insistently to do so, and so forcefully did he urge him that Don Grumedan having come, the king with those three went to his daughter. And when she saw him, she went toward him on her knees as she was, and her maidens with her; but the king dismounted at once and raising her by the hand, embraced her. And she said to him: "My father, my lord, have pity on this daughter who inopportunely was engendered by you, and hear me in the presence of these nobles."

"Daughter," said the king, "say what you please, for with the fatherly love that I owe you, I shall hear you."

She let herself fall to the ground to kiss his feet. And he drew aside, and lifted her up. She said: "My lord, your wish is to send me to the emperor of Rome and separate me from you, from the queen my mother and from this land of which God made me a native. And because of this departure, I hope only for death, either that it come to me, or that I give it to myself; therefore in nowise can one comply with your desire, from which there results for you a great sin in two ways: the one, for me to be disobedient to your command, and the other to die because of you. And so that all of this may be avoided and God be served by you, I wish to enter a convent and live there, leaving you free to dispose of your kingdom and realm at your will; and I shall renounce all the rights that God gave me to it to Leonoreta my sister, or to someone else, according to your desire. And sire, you will be better served by the one who marries her than by the Romans, who on account of me, when they have me there, will become immediately your enemies; so that by this means that you think to win them, in the selfsame way you not only lose them, but as I have said, you make them your mortal enemies, who will never think of anything except how they will come into possession of this land."

"My daughter," said the king, "I well understand what you are saying to me, and I shall give you the reply in your mother's presence. Get back into your litter and go to her."

Then those gentlemen placed her in the litter and carried her to the queen, her mother; and Oriana having come to her, the latter received her with much affection, but weeping, for that marriage was being made much against her will.

But neither she nor all the grandees of the realm nor the other lesser nobles were able to deflect the king from his purpose. And this brought it about that Fortune, already angered and weary from having elevated him so high and placed him in such prosperity — because of which much more than was his wont he was becoming subject to wrath and arrogance — should seek, more for the sake of restoring his soul than his honor, to change it for him to the opposite, as in the Fourth Book of this great story will be related to you, for there it will be set forth in greater detail.

But the queen with the great pity that she had was consoling her daughter; and the daughter with many tears, kneeling with great humility, was begging her for mercy, saying that since she was outstanding in the world for seeking help for those in tribulation, who more than, or as much as, she, could be found engaged in this and other matters involving great compassion? To those who saw them, the mother and daughter were in an embrace, blending with the great delights of the past the anguish and great sorrow that many times come to people without anyone's being able to escape them however great or prudent he may be.

Count Argamon, King Arban of North Wales and Don Grumedan took the king aside under some trees, and the count said to him: "Sire, I was maintaining the deliberate intention of not speaking to you any more on this matter because, your great discretion being so extreme among all men through your knowing best what is good and the opposite, I might properly and honestly be excused. But since I am of your blood and am your vassal, I am not happy or satisfied with what has been said, because I see, sire, that just as sane men many times do what is right, so when they err just once, their error is greater than that of any madman, for making bold because of their knowledge and not taking advice, with love, hatred, cupidity or pride blinding them, they fall so low that they can rise only with great difficulty. Beware, sire, for you are committing great cruelty and a great sin, and very quickly you could receive such a lashing from the Lord on high that your great brilliance and fame might be greatly obscured. Accept advice this time, considering how many prudent men, casting aside their own counsel, suppressing their own desires have followed your advice and complied with your wishes; because if trouble comes to you from so doing, you can blame them more than yourself, for this is the great help and relief of those who err."

"Good uncle," said the king, "I well remember all that you have said to me before, but I cannot do anything more than carry out what I have promised these men."

"Then, sire," said the count, "I ask of you permission to leave for my own estate."

"God be with you," said the king.

Thus they abandoned that conversation, and the king went off to dine. And the tables having been cleared, he ordered Brondajel de Roca called, and said to him: "My friend, now you see how much against the will of my daughter and all my vassals, who greatly love her, this marriage is being made. But recognizing that I am giving her to so honorable a man and placing her among you, I shall not withdraw from what I have promised you. Therefore prepare the ships, for within three days I shall hand over Oriana to you with all her matrons and maidens of honor. And take the precaution, in order that no disaster may occur, that she not leave her stateroom."

Brondajel said to him: "All will be done, sire, as you command; and although now it is becoming hard for the empress, my mistress, to leave her own land where she knows everyone, when she sees the grandeur of Rome and its great dominion, and how kings and princes will bow before her to serve her, it will not be long before her will is very contentedly satisfied; and shortly such reports will be written to you, sire."

The king embraced him laughing and said to him: "So help me God, Brondajel, my friend, I think that you Romans are such that you will know quite well how to bring it about that she be restored to happiness."

And Salustanquidio, who already had risen from his bed, begged him as a favor to command Olinda to go with his daughter and promised him that when he should be a king, as the emperor had promised him on his arrival with Oriana, he would take her for his wife. The king was pleased with this, and highly praised her to him at great length, saying that in view of her discretion and modesty and great beauty, she very well deserved to be queen and mistress of a great land. Just as you hear, they spent that evening, and next day they loaded on the ships all that they were to carry. And Maganil and his brothers appeared before the king, and very haughtily said to Don Grumedan: "Now you see how the day of your shame is approaching, for tomorrow the time limit expires for the battle to take place which you stupidly sought. Do not think that the departure or anything else will prevent it, for it is necessary, unless you acknowledge yourself vanquished and as a man of much more age than brains or prudence you pay for the nonsense that you uttered."

Don Grumedan, who was almost out of his mind on hearing that, rose to answer. But the king, who knew him to be very sensitive in matters of honor, had misgivings about him and said: "Don Grumedan, I beg you as a favor not to speak about this matter. And prepare yourself for the battle, since you better than anyone else know that such trials of disputes consist more in deeds than in words."

"Sire," said he, "out of respect for you I shall do what you command, and tomorrow I shall be on the field with my companions. And on it there will be demonstrated the excellence or shortcomings of each one of us."

The Romans went to their lodgings. And the king called Don Grumedan aside and said to him: "Whom do you have to help you against these knights? They seem to me strong and valiant."

"Sire," said he, "I have on my side God, and this body and courage and hands that He gave me; and if Don Galaor comes tomorrow before the hour of tierce, I shall have him, for I am certain that he will uphold my cause, and I would not worry then about a third knight. And if he does not come, I shall fight with them, one by one if it can be done by rights."

"Don't you see," said the king, "that the battle was sought as of three against three? And thus you agreed to it, and they will not want to change it, because thus in the hands of Salustanquidio they have it set up and sworn to. And Don Grumedan," said the king, "so help me God, I have very great sorrow in my heart because I see you lacking such companions as you need in such an encounter; and I have great misgivings as to how this affair of yours will turn out."

"Sire, do not fear," said he; "in a small space of time God renders great mercy and assistance to anyone He pleases, and I have gone against arrogance with restraint and good will; and that fact, which conforms to God's will, will help me. And if Don Galaor does not come, nor any other of the good knights of your court, I shall put in with myself the two that I deem best from among these knights of mine."

"That is nothing," said the king, "for you have the fight with strong men skilled in such a calling; and such companions do not suffice for you. But, my friend Don Grumedan, I shall give you better counsel. I wish secretly to place my own person with you in this battle, for many times you have risked yours in my service; and, my loyal friend, I would be very ungrateful if at such a time I did not stake my life and my honor on your behalf in payment for the many times that you have put your life at the point and on the verge of death in order to serve me."

During all this the king held him embraced, with tears falling from his eyes. Don Grumedan kissed his hands and said to him: "May it not please God that such a loyal king as you are should fall into such an error for the sake of one who will be always concerned with enhancing your fame and honor; and although, sire, I may consider this as one of the most outstanding favors that I have ever received from you, and my services cannot suffice to repay you for it, it will not be accepted by me because you are a king and judge who must sit in judgment on foreigners with as much justice as on your own people."

Fortunate are the vassals to whom God gives such kings, who considering more important the love that they owe to them than the services that the latter render, oblivious to their own lives and grandeur, wish to expose their bodies to death for them as did this king on behalf of a poor knight, although he himself was very rich and abounding in virtues.

"Well, since that is the way it is," said the king, "I cannot do anything else except pray God to help you."

Don Grumedan went to his abode and gave orders to two knights of his to make preparations to be with him in the combat the next day. But I say to you that although he was very courageous and strong, and skilled in arms, he was brokenhearted, because those whom he was putting into the battle with him were not such as he needed in such a great emergency; for he was of such high and strong courage that he would rather suffer death than do or say anything that might bring shame upon him. But he did not show this; rather, quite the opposite. That night he spent in St. Mary's chapel, and in the morning they heard mass with great devotion, and with Don Grumedan praying God to let him conclude that combat to his honor, and if it were to be His wish that there his life come to an end, to have mercy on his soul.

And then with great courage he demanded his arms; and after he had donned his strong and very white coat of mail, he put on a device exhibiting his colors, for it was scarlet with white swans. And he had not yet finished arming himself when there entered through the door the beautiful maiden who previously had come with a message from Grasinda and the Greek Knight. And with her came two maidens and two squires; and she carried in her hand a very beautiful and richly ornamented sword. She asked for Don Grumedan, and they pointed him out to her at once. She said to him in the French language: "Sir Don Grumedan, the Greek Knight, who has great affection for you on account of the reports that he has had of you since he came to this land and because he has learned about a battle that you have scheduled with the Romans, leaves you two very good knights whom you have seen as his escort. And he sends word to you not to seek any others for this battle and on his word of honor to accept them without any fear; and he sends you this beautiful sword which already has been proven to be very good, as you have seen, by the mighty blows that he delivered with it on the pillar of stone when the knight went fleeing from him."

Don Grumedan was very happy when he heard this, considering the straits in which he was situated, and that in company with such a man as the Greek Knight only those of great worth could go.

"Maiden, may good fortune attend the good Greek Knight who is so courteous to one he does not know; and his great circumspection causes this. May it please God that for me may come a time when I may be able to repay him for it."

"Sir," said she, "you would appreciate him greatly if you knew him, and thus you will these companions of his as soon as you have tested them. And now mount your horse, for at the entrance to the field where you are to fight, they are waiting for you."

Don Grumedan unsheathed the sword and saw how very clean it was and that there did not appear on it any sign of the blows that it had struck on the pillar; and making the sign of the cross over it, he girded it on and left his own behind. And mounting the horse that Don Florestan had given him when he won it from the Romans, as you have already heard, appearing thus mounted a handsome and valiant old man, he went to the knights who were awaiting him; and all three greeted one another very serenely, but Don Grumedan was unable to recognize either one of the others. Thus they entered the field so well appointed that those who loved Don Grumedan took great pleasure. The king, who had already come, was astounded that those knights, without any reason and not knowing Don Grumedan, should want to risk such great danger; and when he saw the maiden, he ordered her summoned. She came before him, and he said to her: "Maiden, for what reason have these two knights of your company wished to participate in such a dangerous fight, not knowing the one for whom they do so?"

"Sire," said she, "the good as well as the bad are known by their reputations; and the Greek Knight, on hearing about Don Grumedan's great skill and the combat that he had scheduled;

and knowing that at this time, very few of your good knights are here, saw fit to leave these two companions of his to help him; for they are of such great excellence and prowess at arms that before noon has passed, the great arrogance of the Romans will be crushed even more, and the honor of your men well sustained. And he did not want Don Grumedan to know about it until he found them on the field, as you, sire, have seen."

The king was very happy with such aid, for he had been brokenhearted, out of fear that some misfortune might happen to Don Grumedan through his own failure to help him in that combat; and he was very grateful to the Greek Knight, although he did not show it to the degree that he felt it.

The three knights, with Don Grumedan between the other two, placed themselves at one end of the lists and awaited their foes. And immediately there entered on the field King Arban of North Wales and the Count of Clare on their side to judge them, and on the side of the Romans were Salustanquidio and Brondajel de Roca, all by order of the king. Very shortly the Romans who were to fight arrived, mounted on beautiful horses and wearing fine new armor; and as they were tall and sturdy, it seemed very likely that they must have great strength and valor. They brought with them bagpipes and trumpets and other instruments that made a great clamor, and were accompanied by all the knights from Rome. Thus they came before the king, and they said to him: "Sire, we want to take the heads of those Greek knights to Rome, and may it not irk you for us to do so with Don Grumedan's, for we should be sorry to distress you; or else order him to retract what he has said, and to concede the Romans to be the best knights to be found in any land."

The king did not respond to what they were saying, but said: "Go and fight your battle, and let those who win the heads of the others do with them whatever they think best."

They entered the field, and Salustanquidio and Brondajel took their places on one side of the lists, and King Arban and the Count of Clare placed Don Grumedan and his companions on the other. Then the queen came with her matrons and maidens-in-waiting to the windows to see the combat; and she ordered Don Guilan the Pensive, who was weak from his illness, to come there, and Don Cendil de Ganota, who had not yet fully recovered from his wound; and she said to Don Guilan: "My friend, how do you think this affair in which my father Don Grumedan is involved will come out" — for the queen always used to call him father because he had reared her — "for I see those devils so big and so valiant that they greatly frighten me?"

"My lady," said he, "all deeds at arms are in God's hands, and depend on the justification that men take on their own behalf being in accordance with Him, for they are not dependent on great valor. And lady, since I know Don Grumedan to be a very wise knight, God-fearing and a defender of justice, and the Romans to be so intemperate, so arrogant, motivated only by caprice, I say that if I were where Grumedan is with those two companions, I would not fear those three Romans, even though a fourth were to join them."

The queen was greatly comforted and encouraged by what Don Guilan said to her and she earnestly besought God to help her foster father and deliver him with honor from that danger. The knights who were on the field spurred their horses toward each other, going forward at full speed; and as they were very skillful at arms and in their saddles, they collided very violently with their shields, for none missed in the encounter, so that their lances were broken. Then there happened what had never been seen by anyone in any battle at the king's court, out of all those fought by so many against so many: all three Romans were hurled from their saddles onto the field, and Don Grumedan and his companions went on by in fine style without being unhorsed by them. Then they turned their horses at once toward them, and saw how they were trying to rise and join each other. Don Bruneo had a wound, not serious, in his left side from the lance of the one with whom he had jousted. Very great was the distress that the Romans felt from that jousting, and great the pleasure of the other people, who hated them and loved Don Grumedan. The knight in green said to Don Grumedan: "Since you have shown them that you know how to joust, it is not right for us to attack them on horseback, when they are on foot."

Don Grumedan and the other knight said that he was right. So they dismounted, giving their horses to someone to hold; and all three of them went together toward the Romans, who were no longer as gallant in appearance as before; and he of the green arms said: "Sir knights of Rome, you have left your horses; this must be only because you hold us in slight esteem, since although we may not be so renowned as you, we did not want you to take this honor from us, and for that reason we dismounted from ours."

The Romans, who previously had been very reckless, were frightened on seeing themselves so quickly unhorsed, made no reply and held their swords in their hands and their shields before them. At once the knights attacked each other very fiercely and delivered many hard, telling blows, until all who were watching them marveled; and in a short while their valor and fury were evidenced on their armor, for in many places it was rent open and blood was issuing forth, and likewise their helmets and shields were badly damaged. But Don Grumedan, who because of the great hatred and fury that possessed him, was hastening ahead of his companions, on account of receiving more blows was badly wounded. And his companions, who were those whom you know, and who feared shame more than death, on seeing that the Romans were defending themselves, displayed their strength and began to belabor them with mighty blows from which up to then they had abstained; so that the Romans were frightened, thinking that their strength was doubling. And they were so beset and driven back that they no longer thought about anything except defending themselves, and they were retreating so dazed that they were not up to making a united stand. But the others, who had them beaten, did not let them ease up or rest, for at that time those enemies of theirs were doing wonders just as if during the whole day they had not previously struck a blow. Maganil, who was the best of the brothers, the most valiant, and the one who during the whole day had given much evidence of the fact — on seeing his shield broken to bits and his helmet cut and dented in many places, and that he had no protection from his coat of mail — went as fast as he could toward the queen's window, while he of the vair colored arms, who was following him, gave him no respite. Then Maganil cried out: "Lady, have mercy for God's sake; don't let me be killed, for I grant to be true all that Don Grumedan said."

"Damn you," said he of the vair, "for that is well-known."

And taking him by the helmet he pulled it off his head and feigned that he intended to decapitate him. And the queen, who saw it, withdrew from the window. Don Guilan, who was there at the queen's windows, as you have heard, said to him: "Sir Knight from Greece, do not be covetous to take to your land a head so arrogant as that. Let him, if you please, return to Rome, where his qualities are appraised, and there they will be detested."

"I shall do so," said he, "because he asked for pity from her ladyship the queen and because you wish it, although I do not know you. I leave him to you; order his wounds cared for, because he is cured of folly."

And on returning to his companions he saw that Don Grumedan had one of the Romans on his back on the ground, and he had his knees on his chest, meanwhile dealing him heavy blows on the face with his sword hilt, and the Roman was yelling: "Alas, Sir Don Grumedan! don't kill me, for I acknowledge to be true all that you said in praise of the knights of Great Britain, and what I said to be a lie."

The knight of the vair colored arms, who was quite pleased with Don Grumedan's situation, called the judges to witness what the knight was saying and how he of the green arms had chased the other one from the field, for the latter had already fled from him. But Salustanquidio and Brondajel were so sad and so crushed on seeing that very (for them) degrading victory that without saying a word to the king they left the field and went to their lodgings, giving orders to bring to them those knights who had made retraction, since their luck had gone so greatly against them. Don Grumedan, on seeing that there remained nothing more to do, with permission of the judges mounted along with his companions, and they went to pay their respects to the king. And he of the green arms said: "Sire, God be with you, for we are going to the Greek Knight in whose company we are very honored and fortunate."

"May God direct you," said the king, "for well have you and he demonstrated to us that you are highly skilled at arms."

So they took leave of him. And the maiden who had come there with them, came up to the king and said: "My lord, hear me in private, if you please, before I go away."

The king made everybody leave, and said to her: "Now say whatever you wish."

"Sire," said she, "you have been until now the most highly esteemed king among Christians, and you always have enhanced your reputation, and one of your good qualities is that you have always kept in mind the concerns of maidens, by doing them favors and helping them in accordance with law, being very cruel to those who were doing them wrong. And now that great hope they had in you having been lost, they all consider themselves abandoned by you, in view of what you are doing to your daughter Oriana, by desiring her so without cause or reason to be disinherited of what God made her heiress. They are greatly terrified and frightened at that noble nature of yours being in this respect so reversed, for they will have very little trust in its remedies when so against God, against your daughter and all your subjects you exhibit such cruelty, when more than anyone else you are obligated not as a king, who must protect the rights of everyone, but as a father; for even if by everyone she were forsaken, by you, she ought to be received and comforted with great love. And not only is it a bad example to the world, but to God her lament, her tears will cry out. Take heed, sire, and bring the end of your days into conformity with their beginning, since more glory and fame have they given to you than to anyone else living today. And, my lord, God be with you, for I am going to those knights who are awaiting me."

"Good-by," said the king, "for so help me God, I consider you a good woman and of good understanding."

She joined her protectors, and escorting her, they went to the ship, for the weather was becoming favorable for their journey. Then they immediately left the port; and as they knew that King Lisuarte was to hand over his daughter Oriana to the Romans, and on what day it was to be, they were eager to proceed so that the Greek Knight might learn of it; thus in two days and two nights they caught up with him, because he was waiting for them. They were received very properly and with great pleasure for thus having concluded those adventures so greatly to their honor. The maiden told them how the battle had gone and what had been done in aid of Don Grumedan and the very great need he had had through lack of companions, and the pleasure that he took with her and the thanks that he sent the Greek Knight for such help; she told it all, for nothing was left out.

Grasinda said to her: "Did you find out what the king is ordering done with his daughter?"

"Yes, madam," said the maiden, "Four days after you left there they are to embark her to be carried away in the custody of the Romans. But the spectacle, madam, of the tears that she and her maidens and all those of the kingdom are shedding no one can adequately describe."

Tears came to the eyes of Grasinda and she prayed God that, showing His infinite mercy in the case of this great injustice, He send Oriana some relief. But the Greek Knight was very happy about that news because he already had it in his heart to seize her, and he was longing to come to grips with the Romans; and once this was done, he would take delight with his lady to the relief of his sad heart — a relief attainable in no other way; for of the opposition of King Lisuarte and that of the emperor he did not entertain a very high opinion because he fully intended to give them plenty to do. And what afforded him most happiness was to think that this would be done without any blame's being attached to his lady.

So thus talking and idling just as you hear, they reached one day at the hour of tierce the great port of the Firm Island. And those of the island, who already knew the time of their arrival through Gandalin, saw the ships when they were still a great distance away and recognized from their appearance that Amadis was coming. The joy of everyone was very great, for they loved him very much, and they hastened with great speed to the shore, and with them all the nobles of his lineage and from among his friends who were expecting him. And when Grasinda reached the port and saw so many people and the joy that everywhere they were manifesting, she greatly marveled, and even more when she heard many say: "Welcome to our lord who has been away from us for so long." And she said to the Greek Knight: "Sir, why do these people show you such great reverence and honor, saying 'Welcome to our lord'?"

He said to her: "Lady, I ask pardon of you for concealing my identity from you for such a long time, but I could do no less without great risk to my self-respect; and so I have done throughout all the foreign lands that I have traversed, for no one has been able to find out my name. And now I want you to know that I am the lord of this island, and I am that Amadis of Gaul of whom you probably have heard now and then; and those knights that you see there are relatives and friends, and the other people are my vassals. And it would be difficult to find elsewhere the same number of knights who would equal them in great valor."

"Though I, sir," said Grasinda, "am pleased to know your name, likewise my heart is sad for not having rendered you the homage that a man so noble and of such lineage deserved; and for having treated you as a poor knight errant I consider myself as very unfortunate. If anything consoles me it is only that the honor that in my land was done you, if any of it was pleasing to you, can be attributed only to your worth as an individual, without conceding any portion of it to your high estate and royal lineage, or to these knights whom you praise so highly to me."

Amadis said to her: "Madam, let this matter not be discussed further, for the honors and favors that I have received from you have been so many and so great and at a time that neither by me nor by those whom you see there, who are worth more than I, could they be repaid."

Then they reached the port, where everyone was awaiting them; and there was Don Gandales with twenty palfreys on which the women were to go up to the castle. But for Grasinda they disembarked a very beautiful palfrey with trappings studded with gold and silver, and she was dressed in wondrously fine apparel. And from the boat from which she and Amadis were issuing a very strong gangplank on which they might disembark was run to the sandy beach. On shore there awaited them Agrajes and Don Cuadragante and Don Florestan and Gavarte of the Fearful Valley, and the good Don Dragonis, and Orlandin and Ganjel de Sadoca, and Argamon the Valiant, and Sardonan, brother of Angriote de Estravaus, and their nephews Pinores and Sarquiles, Madansil of the Silver Bridge, and many other nobles who were seeking adventure — altogether more than thirty knights. And Enil, that wise, good knight, was already on the boat talking with Amadis, and Ardian the dwarf and Gandalin were with Grasinda's maidens. Then Amadis took Grasinda by the arm and brought her from the boat to the shore, where with great circumspection and courtesy she was received by all those lords, and he gave her into the keeping of Agrajes and Florestan, who placed her on the palfrey. All were very much pleased with her great beauty and fine dress. So they brought her, just as you hear, and her matrons and maidens likewise, to the Island, where they lodged her in the beautiful apartments where Amadis and his brothers had dwelt when the island was won. There in order to do her more honor, most of those knights dined with her, for Don Gandales had provided very fittingly for the occasion, with Ardian the dwarf, who was beside himself with pleasure, serving as butler, saying many things to make them laugh. But Amadis amid all this merrymaking never let Master Elisabad leave him; instead, he took him by the hand and introducing him to everybody, told them that God and he had enabled him to keep alive, and at table he had him sit between him and Don Gavarte of the Fearful Valley. But all these pleasures and the sight of those knights, whom Amadis loved so much, could not keep his heart from being in great suspense as he reflected that the Romans might be able to cross the sea with Oriana before he encountered them; and he could not calm down or be at ease by concerning himself with any other matter because in comparison with her, whom he loved so much, everything else produced in him great longing.

So all having dined with great enjoyment, and the tables being cleared, Amadis begged them not to leave their seats, for he wanted to speak to them, and they acceded to his request. Then Amadis, when he saw that those knights who were at table were quietly awaiting what he might say to them, spoke to them in this wise: "My noble lords, since you saw me last I have traversed many foreign lands, and many great adventures have been experienced by me which it would take too long to recount; but the ones which gave me most concern and entailed for me the greatest danger involved the rescue of matrons and maidens from many wrongs and injuries being done them, because just as they were born with weak hearts to obey and their strongest weapons are tears and sighs, so those of strong courage urgently ought among other matters to take up their own arms to help them and to defend them against those who with scant virtue mistreat and dishonor them, just as the Greeks and the Romans did in ancient times by crossing the seas, laying waste the lands, winning battles, killing kings and casting them out of their realms, merely to obtain satisfaction for the rapes and injuries committed against women; whence so much fame and glory has remained for them in their histories, and will last as long as the world endures. So what occurs in our own times, who knows better than you, my good lords? For you are witnesses who can testify that many outrages and perils on this account occur each day. I am not making to you a very lengthy speech setting before you authentic examples from antiquity with intent through them to rally your hearts, for they are in themselves so strong that if their excess strength could be divulged throughout the world, no coward would remain in it. But because you remember past good deeds, with greater concern and with greater desire present good deeds are striven for and undertaken. So coming to the point, I have found out since I came to this land about the great wrong and offense that King Lisuarte seeks to do his daughter Oriana, for though she is the legitimate successor to his realm, excluding her from it in violation of all law, he is sending her to the emperor of Rome for his wife, and according to what I am told, much against the wish of all of Lisuarte's subjects, and moreover, against her own wishes; for she, uttering great laments and great complaints to God and to the world, very compellingly is protesting. So if it is true that this King Lisuarte without fear of God or of the people, is perpetrating such cruelty, I say to you that we were born here below at a bad time if it be not remedied by us; because were we to allow it to go on, the dangers and travail that up to now we have braved to win honor and glory have slipped by and have been forgotten. Now let each one of you, if you please, state his opinion, for I already have made mine manifest to you."

Then Agrajes, by request of all those knights, made answer and said: "Although your presence, my lord and good cousin, has doubled our strength, and the things that previously we greatly feared, with it now seem frivolous and insubstantial, we, with little hope of your coming, having found out about what King Lisuarte seeks to do, had resolved to go to the aid and relief of the situation, not allowing such great constraint to take place; preferring that either they or we be transmitted from life to death. And since we are all in agreement in our desire, let us be so in the deed, and as speedily as that glory that we desire can be obtained without its being lost through our negligence."

Agrajes's reply having been heard by those knights, all of them unanimously considering it good, said that the rescue of Oriana should be accomplished without delay; for if it was true that they were wont to risk their lives for many trivial things, with greater will they should do so in this very outstanding matter, which would yield them perpetual fame in this world.

When Grasinda beheld their unanimity, embracing Amadis, she said: "Oh, Amadis, my lord! Now your great valor is clearly apparent and that of your friends and relatives, in carrying out the greatest rescue operation that knights ever accomplished; for not only for this good lady, but also for all the matrons and maidens of the world it is being done; because the good and courageous knights of other lands, following your example in this matter, with greater concern and boldness will intervene in what they ought rightly to do for ladies; and the intemperate and those devoid of virtue out of fear of being so harshly constrained will refrain from committing wrongs and offenses against them. And, my lord, go forth with God's blessing, and may He guide and direct you. I shall wait for you here until I see the outcome, and afterwards I shall do whatever you ask."

Amadis thanked her very much, and left her under the protection of Ysanjo, the governor of the Island, so that he might serve her and show her all the delightful things that were on that island, and do great honor to her great friend, Master Elisabad. But the master said to him: "Good sir, if I can serve you in my way, it is only in such causes as these on which you are setting forth, for from bearing arms, in conformity with my obligation as a priest you will have exempted me, so that I shall not remain behind under any circumstances; rather, if you please, sir, I wish to be of assistance to you with this skill that God gave me; for I well know, according to the great folly of the Romans and your own persistence, that you will be well served and aided by me."

Amadis embraced him saying: "Ah, master, my true friend! may it please God out of His mercy that what you have done and are doing for me may be repaid to you by me. And since you are pleased to go, let us embark at once with God's help."

When the fleet was equipped with all that was necessary for the voyage and the crew was on board, shortly after dark, with Amadis giving orders that all other journeys be deflected so that no information of themselves be ascertained, they all went on board the ships, and without making any sounds or noise they began to sail toward that area which the Romans would traverse (according to the route that it would be proper for them to take), in order that they might intercept them.

CHAPTER LXXXI

How KING LISUARTE DELIVERED UP HIS DAUGHTER VERY MUCH AGAINST HER WILL, AND CONCERNING THE RESCUE OF THE VERY BEAUTIFUL ORIANA THAT AMADIS WITH ALL THE OTHER KNIGHTS OF THE FIRM ISLAND EFFECTED; AND HOW THEY TOOK HER TO THE FIRM ISLAND.

As King Lisuarte was determined to hand over his daughter Oriana to the Romans, with so firm an intention to do so that nothing of what you have heard could shake it, the appointed time promised by him having arrived, he spoke with her, trying in many ways to induce her to accept voluntarily that journey that was so agreeable to him; but in no way could he lessen her lamenting and grief; therefore very angrily he left her and went to the queen, telling her to quiet their daughter, since what he had done was to little avail, and he could not avoid what he had promised. The queen, who had spoken with him many times about the matter in an effort to find some impediment, but always had found him adamant in his intention, without further parley sought only to carry out his orders, although her heart felt a surfeit of anguish; and she commanded all the princesses and other maidens who were to go with Oriana, to board the boats at once. She left with Oriana only Mabilia, Olinda and the maid of Denmark; and she ordered all the clothes and fine adornments that she was giving her daughter to be taken to the ships. But Oriana, when she saw her mother and her sister, went to them manifesting very great sorrow, and seizing her mother by the hand began to kiss it; and the queen said to her: "Good daughter, I beg you now to be content with this which the king orders you to do, for I trust in the mercy of God that it will be for your good and that He will not wish to abandon you and me."

Oriana said to her: "Madam, I believe that this separation of you and me will be forever because my death is very near at hand."

And saying this she fell in a faint and the queen likewise, so that they were quite unconscious. But the king, who immediately intervened there, had Oriana picked up just as she was and carried to the ships, and with her Olinda; who, kneeling with many tears, was begging him as a favor to let her go to her father's court, and not to order her to go to Rome. But he was so angry that he would not listen, and had her borne away behind Oriana and commanded Mabilia and the maid of Denmark to go likewise at once. Then all the women having been put aboard with the Romans, just as you hear, King Lisuarte mounted and went to the port where the fleet was, and there he comforted his daughter with paternal kindliness, but not in such a way as to give her hope that his purpose was changed. And as he saw that this was ineffective in relieving her distress, he felt a degree of pity, so that tears came to his eyes; and leaving her, he spoke with Salustanquidio, and with Brondajel de Roca and the Archbishop of Talancia, enjoining them to protect her and serve her, for there he was handing her over as he had promised. And he returned to his palace, leaving on the ships such weeping and distress on the part of the ladies and maidens-in-waiting when they saw him go, as to defy all description.

Salustanquidio and Brondajel de Roca, after King Lisuarte had left them, now having Oriana and all of her maidens in their power aboard the ships, decided to put her in a room that was very lavishly decorated for her; and she having been placed in it and with her Mabilia, for they knew the latter to be the maiden whom she loved most in the world, they locked the door with strong padlocks. And they left on the ship Queen Sardamira with her retinue and many others of Oriana's ladies and maidens-in-waiting. Salustanquidio, who was yearning to win Olinda's love, had her taken to his ship together with another group of maidens, not without their lamenting loudly on seeing themselves separated from Oriana their lady; who on hearing in the room where she was what they were doing, and how they came to the door of the room clutching at it and calling on her to help them, repeatedly swooned in Mabilia's arms.

Then everything having been thus arranged, the Romans set sail and went their way well pleased to have brought to a conclusion what the emperor their lord so greatly desired. And they had a very large imperial banner hoisted to the top of the mast of the ship in which Oriana was traveling, and had all the other ships doing guard duty in circular fashion around it. And as they were thus proceeding very proudly and happily they glanced to their left and saw Amadis's fleet, which was greatly outstripping them by coming between them and the land from which they were endeavoring to depart; and that was the situation because Agrajes and Don Cuadragante and Dragonis and Listoran of the White Tower had arranged among themselves that before Amadis arrived, they would engage the Romans in battle and endeavor to rescue Oriana, and for that reason they were placing themselves between the Roman fleet and the land.

But Don Florestan and the good Don Gavarte of the Fearful Valley, and Orlandin and Imosil of Burgundy likewise had planned with their friends and vassals to be the first at the rescue, and they were going at top speed between the Roman fleet and Agrajes's ships. And Amadis with his ships well supplied with people, including not only his friends, but also those natives of the Firm Island, was coming at greater speed in order that he might be the first to effect the rescue. Concerning the Romans I tell you that when they saw the fleet from a distance, they thought that it was probably non-belligerents traversing the sea; but on seeing that they were divided into three groups and that two of them were cutting them off on the landward side, and the other was following them, they were quite frightened, and immediately there was a great hubbub among them, with voices crying out: "To arms, to arms, for a foreign force is coming."

And then they armed themselves very quickly and they placed the crossbowmen, for they were bringing along very good ones, at their proper stations, as they did the other forces. And Brondajel de Roca with many good knights of the emperor's household, was on the ship where Oriana was, and where they had placed the banner of the emperor that you have already heard about. At this time the battle was joined; and Agrajes and Don Cuadragante engaged Salustanquidio's ship, where they were carrying beautiful Oriana, and they began to attack each other very fiercely. Don Florestan and Gavarte of the Fearful Valley, who went into the middle of the fleet, were attacking the ships on which were traveling the Duke of Ancona and the Archbishop of Talancia, who had a considerable force of their vassals, very well armed and strong, so that the fighting was intense between them. And Amadis caused his ship to be sent against the one which carried the banner of the emperor, and gave orders to his men to stand by; and putting his hand on the shoulder of Angriote, spoke thus: "Sir Angriote, my good friend, remember the great loyalty that you have always had and do maintain for your friends; try to afford me vigorous aid in this affair. And if God wills that I finish it well, here all my honor and all of my good fortune will reach their zenith; and do not remain apart from me any more than you can help."

He said to him: "My lord, I can do no more than lose my life on your behalf and in aid of you so that your honor be protected; and may God be for you."

Immediately the ships came together. Great on the part of both sides was the attack with arrows and stones and lances, for it seemed it was raining, so thickly were they being discharged and hurled. And Amadis along with his men was concerned only with bringing his ship into contact with that of the foe; but they were not able to do so, for the enemy, although there were many more of them, did not dare to draw near, in view of how fiercely they were being attacked; and they were defending themselves with great iron hooks and many other arms of various kinds. Then Tantiles of Sobradisa, Queen Briolanja's majordomo, who was in the forecastle, when he saw that the will of Amadis could have no effect, ordered a very thick, heavy anchor brought, which was fastened to a very strong chain; and from the forecastle they hurled it onto the enemies' ship, and he and many others who were helping him pulled on it so hard that by main strength they brought the ships together in such fashion that they could in nowise be separated unless the chain broke. When Amadis saw this, he went forward, with great effort forcing a passage through the crowd of people who were huddled very closely together; and following in his wake came Angriote and Don Bruneo; and when he reached those in front, he put one foot on the gunwale of his ship and jumped to the other vessel, an action which none of his foes could prevent or hinder. And as the leap was great and he was proceeding with great fury, he fell to his knees and there they struck him many blows; but he got up much against the will of those who were attacking him so heavily and drew his good, gleaming sword. Then he saw that Angriote and Don Bruneo had come on board with him and were attacking the enemy with very strong, hard blows, and shouting: "Gaul, Gaul, for here is Amadis," for this he had asked them to say if they succeeded in boarding the ship.

Mabilia, who was locked in the room with Oriana, on hearing the noise and the voices and then that name, took Oriana by the arms, more dead than alive, and said to her: "Have courage, lady, for you are being rescued by that fortunate knight, your vassal and faithful friend."

And Oriana arose asking what could be the matter, for she was so faint from weeping that she heard nothing, and was almost sightless.

And after Amadis had gotten to his feet and grasped his sword, and had seen the marvelous deeds that Angriote and Don Bruneo were performing, and how the others from his ship quickly joined forces with them, he went with his sword in hand toward Brondajel de Roca, whom he found confronting him, and gave him on top of his helmet such a mighty blow that he struck him down prone; and if his helmet had not been so resistant he would have split his head in two. And he did not go forward because he perceived that his enemies were subdued and were asking for mercy. And when he saw the very fine armor that Brondajel was wearing, he was certain that he was the one whom the others were protecting; and taking off his helmet he struck him on the face with his sword hilt, asking him where Oriana was. And Brondajel pointed out the room with the padlocks, saying that he would find her there. Amadis went there quickly and called Angriote and Don Bruneo; and with the great strength that together they exerted, they broke down the door and went inside, where they saw Oriana and Mabilia. And Amadis went and knelt before Oriana to kiss her hands, but she embraced him and took him by the sleeve of his coat of mail, which was completely stained with the blood of his enemies.

"Oh, Amadis!" said she, "beacon light for all women in distress, now your great excellence is evinced by your having rescued me and these princesses, who have been plunged into such great sorrow and tribulation. Throughout all the lands of the world praise for you will be known and exalted."

Mabilia knelt before him and took him by the skirt of his coat of mail, for since he had his gaze fixed on his lady, he had not seen her; but when he perceived her, he raised her up, and embracing her with much love, said to her: "My lady cousin, I have greatly missed you."

And he sought to leave them in order to see what was to be done, but Oriana took him by the hand and said: "In God's name, sir, do not forsake me."

"My lady," said he, "do not fear, for on board this ship are Angriote de Estravaus and Don Bruneo and Gandales with thirty knights who will protect you; and I shall go to help our men, who are having a very great battle."

Then Amadis went out of the room; and he saw Landin de Fajarque, who had fought those who were in the forecastle, and they had surrendered to him; and Amadis ordered, since they were giving themselves up as prisoners, that none be killed. And then he went on board a very beautiful galley in which were Enil and Gandalin with some forty knights from the Firm Island; and he gave orders to guide it toward that area where he had heard the battle cry of Agrajes, who was fighting with those of Salustanquidio's big ship. And when he arrived, he saw that they had already boarded it; and he came alongside with his galley in order to board the ship, and the one who helped him was Don Cuadragante, who was already on board. And the press and noise were very great, for Agrajes and those of his company were going about attacking and killing very cruelly. But after they saw Amadis, the Romans jumped overboard, some into their lifeboats and others into the water. Some of them died and others reached the other ships not yet surrendered. But Amadis still pressed forward through the crowd of people asking for Agrajes his cousin. When he found him he saw that he had Salustanquidio at his feet, for he had given him a severe wound on the arm, and the latter was begging him for mercy. But Agrajes, who previously had found out how he loved Olinda, did not cease to strike him and bring him to the point of death, as one whom he greatly hated. And Don Cuadragante was telling him not to kill him, for he would have in him a valuable prisoner. But Amadis said to him laughing:

"Sir Don Cuadragante, let Agrajes carry out his desire, for if we take him away from him, as many of us as he finds are dead men, for he will not leave a single man alive."

At this speech the head of Salustanquidio was cut off, the ship entirely delivered, and the banners of Agrajes and of Don Cuadragante placed on top of the forecastle and the quarterdeck house, both very well guarded by many good, very vigorous knights. This done, Agrajes went at once to the room where they told him that Olinda, his lady, was, who was asking for him.

Amadis and Don Cuadragante, and Landin and Listoran of the White Tower, all together went to see how it was going for Florestan and those who were protecting him; and at once they boarded the galley that Amadis had brought there, and immediately they met another of Don Florestan's galleys on which was a knight, his maternal relative, whose name was Ysanes, who said to them: "Lords, Don Florestan and Gavarte of the Fearful Valley report to you that they have killed or imprisoned all the men of those ships, and they hold the Duke of Ancona and the Archbishop of Talancia."

Amadis, who took great pleasure from this, sent to tell them to join their galley with the one that he had taken, on which Oriana was, for there they would hold a council on what to do. Then they gazed in all directions and saw that the fleet of the Romans was destroyed, that none of them had been able to escape, although they had attempted it in a few lifeboats; but they were overtaken and seized, so that there remained no one who could carry the tidings [to Rome]. And they went directly to Oriana's ship and on it Brondajel de Roca was a prisoner. After coming on board they removed the armor from their heads and hands and washed off the blood and sweat; and Amadis asked for Don Florestan, for he did not see him there. Landin de Fajarque said to him: "He is with Queen Sardamira in her stateroom, for she was loudly calling for him, saying that he should be summoned quickly, for he would be her protector; and she is at the feet of Oriana begging her to have mercy, and not to allow her to be killed or dishonored."

Amadis went there and asked for Queen Sardamira, and Mabilia identified her to him as being the one in her embrace, and Don Florestan was holding her hand. Amadis went before her very humbly and sought to kiss her hands, but she withdrew them; and he said to her: "Good lady, do not fear anything, for, by having Don Florestan, whom we all respect and follow, at your service and command, you have everything as you wish, not to mention our desire, which is to serve and honor all women, each according to her merit. And since you, good lady, are among them all very distinguished and outstanding, thus it is eminently right that much attention be given to rendering you content."

The queen said to Don Florestan: "Tell me, good lord, who is this very courteous knight who is such a friend of yours?"

"Lady," said he, "he is Amadis, my lord and brother, with whom we are all here for this rescue of Oriana".

When she heard this, with great pleasure she stood up before him and said: "Good Sir Amadis, if I did not receive you as I should, do not blame me, for my not being acquainted with you was the cause. And I give many thanks to God that in this very great tribulation, He has made me a beneficiary of your courtesy and placed me under the protection and guardianship of Don Florestan."

Amadis took her by the hand, led her to Oriana's dais and there had her seat herself; and he sat down with Mabilia, his cousin, for he very much desired to speak to her. But in all this Queen Sardamira, although she knew the fleet of the Romans to be defeated and destroyed, and many of the men killed and others prisoners, there had not yet come to her notice the death of Prince Salustanquidio, whom she with good and faithful affection loved very much and considered the noblest and greatest of all those under the suzerainty of Rome; nor did she find out about his death until quite a bit later. While they were all seated just as you hear, Oriana said to Queen Sardamira: "Your Majesty, until now I have been vexed by the words that you said to me at the outset, because they were spoken about a matter that I considered so repugnant; but recognizing how you have abstained from them, and your prudence and courtesy in everything else involving you, I tell you that I shall always love you and shall honor you with all my heart, because what irked me you were forced to do without being able to do anything else, and what gave me happiness flowed and proceeded from your noble nature and inherent virtue."

"Lady," said she, "since such is your understanding, it will be unnecessary for me to make any more excuses for it."

While they were talking about this, Agrajes arrived with Olinda and the maidens who had been segregated with her. When Oriana saw her, she rose to meet her and embraced her as if much time had passed since she had last seen her, and she kissed her hands. And turning to Agrajes, she embraced him with great affection; and thus she received all the knights who came with him; and she said to Gavarte of the Fearful Valley: "My friend Gavarte, you have acquitted yourself well of the promise that you gave me, and how much I thank you for it, and the desire I have to reward you, the Lord of the world knows."

"Lady," said he, "I have done what I should as your vassal. And you, madam, as my rightful suzerain, when the time comes, do remember me, for always I shall be at your service."

At this time there were gathered together there all the most honorable knights of that company, who withdrew to one end of the ship to speak about what course of action they would take. And Oriana called Amadis to one side of the dais, and said to him in a whisper: "My true friend, I beg and command you, in the name of that true love that you have for me, that now more than ever the secret of our love affair be maintained; and do not speak to me when we are alone but in the presence of everyone; and what you are pleased to tell me confidentially, convey it by speaking with Mabilia. And endeavor to take us from here to the Firm Island, because if I am in a safe place God will resolve my problems, for He knows that I am in the right."

"Madam," said Amadis, "I live only in the hope of serving you, for if this hope were to fail me, life itself would be wanting; and as you command, it shall be done. And about going to the Island, it will be well that by Mabilia you send word to that effect to these knights, so that it may seem to proceed more from your desire and will than from mine."

"That is the way I shall do it," said she, "and to me it seems a good idea. Now go," said she, "to those knights."

Amadis did so, and they talked about what should be done from then on; but as they were many, their opinions were diverse, for to some it seemed that they ought to take Oriana to the Firm Island, others to Gaul, and still others to Scotland, Agrajes's home land, so that they were not coming to any agreement. At this juncture, Princess Mabilia arrived with four maidens. Everybody welcomed her very cordially, and they seated her in their midst. And she said to them: "Lords, Oriana begs you, out of your kindness and the affection that you have shown for her by this rescue, that you take her to the Firm Island; for there she wishes to remain until she is on amicable terms with her father and mother; and she begs you, lords, that to such a good beginning you add a good ending by considering her great misfortune and the coercion applied to her, and that you do for her what you are accustomed to do for other maidens who are not of such high degree."

"My good lady," said Don Cuadragante, "the good and very courageous Amadis and all we knights who have participated in her rescue are desirous of serving her until death, not only personally but also through our relatives and friends, for they can do much and they will be many; and all of us will be together in her defense against her father and against the emperor of Rome, if they do not achieve reason and justice concerning her. And tell her that if God wishes, it will be done without fail just as I have said, and that she keep that firmly in mind, for if God helps us it will not fail because of us. And if with deliberation and courage this service has been rendered her, that in the same manner with another greater effort and a greater accord she will be aided by us until her safety and our honor are assured."

All those knights approved what Don Cuadragante replied, and with much courage they voted that they would never abandon this undertaking until Oriana was restored to freedom and sovereignty, being assured and certain of having them if she should outlive her father and mother. Princess Mabilia took leave of them and went to Oriana; and the reply and assurances that she brought back from her mission having been ascertained by

Oriana, the latter was greatly comforted, believing that the permission of the just Judge would guide matters in such a way that the outcome would be what she desired. With this agreement those knights went to their ships to give orders concerning the disposition of booty and of the prisoners, who were numerous. They left with Oriana all her maidens and Queen Sardamira with hers, and Don Bruneo de Bonamar and Landin de Fajarque and Don Gordan, brother of Angriote de Estravaus, and Sarquiles their nephew and Orlandin, son of the Count of Urlanda, and Enil, who was wounded by three wounds, which he was concealing as a man who was courageous and inured to great exertion. To these knights was entrusted the protection of Oriana and of those ladies of high degree who were with her, and they were enjoined not to leave the ladies until they were landed on the Firm Island, to which they had agreed to take them.

HERE ENDS THE THIRD BOOK OF THE NOBLE AND VIRTUOUS KNIGHT AMADIS OF GAUL

NOTES

Chapter LXV

At the conclusion of the discussion which took place concerning whether Galaor should support Amadis in the latter's quarrel with King Lisuarte, or should fulfill his feudal obligation to the king, a short gloss addressed to the reader is rather clumsily inserted. Whether this gloss is to be attributed to Montalvo, or was interpolated earlier by some copyist of the primitive Book III, is not clear.

Chapter LXVI

The rapport between the hermit Nasciano and the birds and beasts of the forest in which he dwelt is strongly reminiscent of the traditional accounts of St. Francis of Assisi (1182-1226), founder of the Franciscan order.

Chapter LXIX

The nudity of the fleeing Arcalaus, when he was aroused from slumber by the escape of King Perion and his sons from their confinement, is to be explained by the fact that the mediaeval man was accustomed to sleep in the nude. (See Léon Gautier, *La Chevalerie* [Paris, 1885], p. 535.)

Chapter LXX

The mention of *Romania,* made at the end of this chapter, is probably a vague reference to the old Byzantine empire. (Cf. C. Du Cange, *Glossarium mediae et infimae latinitatis* [Niort, France, 1883-7, in 10 vols.], art. *Romania.*)

THE FOURTH BOOK OF AMADIS OF GAUL

HERE BEGINS THE FOURTH BOOK of the noble and virtuous Amadis of Gaul, son of King Perion and Queen Elisena, which deals with his exploits and the great feats at arms accomplished by him and other knights of his lineage.

MONTALVO'S PREFACE

JUST AS THE LENGTH AND ANTIQUITY of the past have left many great events for us to remember, so it is equally credible that an infinite number of others have remained hidden without any memory of them remaining. And on this account I think that famous witty sage, Giovanni Boccaccio, made no mention in his *De casibus virorum illustrium* of anything noteworthy happening in the earliest period, the one extending from the first ancestor down to Nimrod; nor of anything in the period from Nimrod to King Latinus of Latium, thereby skipping over very long stretches of time, during which one very justifiably must believe that great happenings occurred; but all memory of them having been lost, Boccaccio was unable to present any account of what took place.

And for the same reason very extraordinary things and many great edifices are to be found throughout the world without its being known who their original founders and builders were. And not only of those very ancient times, but even of our own we could cite similar cases.

Then of course we shall not deem strange after so many years the appearance of this book, which was found hidden away in that very ancient sepulcher mentioned in the Preface to Book I, first of the three Books of *Amadis;* and in which mention is made of that Catholic and virtuous prince Esplandian, son of Amadis, to whom these two adjectives have been very aptly applied, as the most esteemed formal designations, and by such he sought to be entitled, rejecting all others — which, although they may appear loftier, are more in keeping with what is temporal than with what is divine; for when life comes to an end, they end likewise, just like thick high-extending smoke; which, when the flame from which it proceeds is extinguished, is dissolved and obliterated without any vestige or trace of it remaining —; considering that he who is a Catholic would be God's friend, would be thankful to be His lieutenant, His viceroy in those great empires and suzerainties, thankful to fear and serve Him, thankful to treat his great estate not as his very own, but lent to him, hoping to give a very strict accounting to his Lord; recalling sad death, fearful Hell, and glorious Paradise whereby he would escape from damnation and reach what is firm and safe, which would cause his soul to attain to endless delight. Then while he existed he would be humane, gracious, liberal in his generosity — but guided by reason rather than by impulse —, compassionate, possessed of the diplomacy by reason of which princes and grandees are beloved and willingly served by their subjects and vassals with prayers and petitions to Almighty God as well as by exposing themselves to death in battle. And besides this, even though they set great store by their estates, these subjects, unpressured and without grief, would deliver them to their overlords wherever they would be well used in virtuous, Catholic enterprises. Then shall we dare to say that the desire of this prince was effected and he realized it as much in deed as in thought? Yes, indeed, if any credence of the kind that be not feigned it ought to yield concerning what is written of him about these exploits of his; because, according to what appears in them, as long as he remained youthful he always feared God, persevering in complete virginity, in a saintly life, in augmenting his holy faith, avoiding the use of his great strength and the ardor of his brave heart against those of his own religion, many times staking everything, even at the risk of death, against the infidel enemies of the Redeemer of the world. And after he had reached his elder years and had attained such high estate as to be emperor of Constantinople, King of Great Britain and Gaul, then continuing to tread the path of virtue, he was most humane, most liberal, best known to his subjects, conferring boons upon them, bringing them together, honoring them as friends, admonishing them concerning their mistakes with compassion and with a tender heart devoid of any haughty or vengeful harshness, desiring that justice be done with reason rather than with wrath; and many other good ways he had which it would take too long to enumerate and which afford evidence why justly and with reason he could be described by those two excellent adjectives "Catholic" and "virtuous," whereby the Lord of the world permitted that in addition to what his soul was able to achieve in glory at his life's end, so much time having already elapsed with the recollection of his great deeds remaining so hidden and concealed as has been said already, it should be made known to everyone, not because he needed it, but in order that it be an example to those who more truly than he possess very great states and seigniories, who will wish to read his history in order that, with their haughtiness, wrath and rage put aside which render them enemies of the One of whom they ought to be friends and servants, they may turn and direct these emotions against those infidel enemies of our holy Catholic faith, since their travail and their expenditures, and finally death, if it should overtake them, would be all in all very well employed because thereby perpetual blessed life is won.

CHAPTER LXXXII

Concerning the great lamentation that Queen Sardamira made over the death of Prince Salustanquidio.

At the end and termination of the Third Book of this great story you were told how King Lisuarte, against the wish of all his subjects, of both high and low degree, and of many others who desired to be of service to him, handed over to the Romans his daughter Oriana in order to marry her to the Patin, Emperor of Rome; and how Prince Salustanquidio was taken at sea and killed by Amadis and his companions, who had been together on the Firm Island, and by them were taken prisoner Brondajel de Roca, chief majordomo of the Emperor, and the Duke of Ancona and the Archbishop of Talancia; and many of their men killed or captured, and the whole fleet in which they were transporting Oriana destroyed. And now we shall tell you what happened as a result of this.

Know you that this great battle having been won, Amadis with other knights of his party, leaving on their ship Oriana and Queen Sardamira and all of the other matrons and maidens who were with her, and certain knights to protect them, boarded another ship and went to order security measures taken with the fleet of the Romans and with the spoils, which were very great, and with the prisoners, who besides being many, were for the most part of great substance, for such it was fitting to send on such a mission. And on coming to the ship in which Prince Salustanquidio lay dead, they heard great outcries and lamentations. And the cause of it as ascertained was that his companions, both knights and others who had gathered around him, were engaged in the most tremendous mourning in the world, extolling his achievements and greatness; so that Agrajes's men who had the ship in their possession were unable to remove or dislodge them from there. Amadis ordered them transferred to another ship in order to stop their lamenting, and he ordered the body of Salustanquidio placed in a coffin in order to have him given the interment that befitted such a lord, although he was an enemy, since he had died like a man in the service of his master. And this was the reason that they had pity for him as well as for the others who remained alive, giving express orders that life be given to them; which to virtuous knights ought to happen so that wrath and rage having been put aside, reason by remaining free may inform judgment in order that it may pursue virtue.

The noise of this weeping was so great that the report reached the ship where Oriana was, to the effect that those people were mourning for that prince, so that it was ascertained by Queen Sardamira. Although until then she had known, and with her own eyes had seen the whole fleet of his side destroyed, and many killed and taken prisoner, she had not been apprised of the death of that knight. And when she heard it, out of her great sorrow she was beside herself, and forgetting the fear and great foreboding that she had had up to then, desiring death more than life, wringing her hands very passionately and in great perturbation, she fell to the floor, saying these words: "Oh, generous prince, of very high lineage, leading light and model for the whole Roman Empire! What grief and sorrow your death will be for many men and women who have loved and served you, and were expecting from you great benefits and favors! Oh, what sad news it will be for them when they learn of your unfortunate and disastrous end! Oh, great emperor of Rome, what anguish and sorrow you will have on learning of the death of this prince, your cousin, whom you loved so greatly and regarded as a strong pillar or shield of your empire; and of the destruction of your fleet, with the very inglorious deaths of your noble knights! And above all, to have taken from you by force of arms with such great dishonor to you, the thing that you loved and desired most in the world! You may well say that if the fortune of a knight errant who followed adventure, and from such a petty status elevated you so high as to place you on such a pinnacle as is the imperial throne, sceptre and crown, with a hard blow it has sought to degrade your honor to the point of placing it in the abyss of hell, center of the earth; that from such a blow can ensue for you only one of two extremes: either to hide it by remaining the most dishonored prince in the world; or to avenge it by placing your person and great estate in much anguish and weariness of spirit, and at the end having from it all a very doubtful outcome; for certainly in what I have seen since my disastrous fortune brought me to Great Britain, there is not in the world an emperor or king of such high estate that these knights and those of their lineage, who are many and powerful, will not wage war and battle against him; and I consider them to be the flower of all the chivalry of the world, although from them so much evil and sorrow has come to me. And now my afflicted heart weeps more for the living and for the misfortune that one may expect in the future from this mishap than for the dead, who have already paid their debt."

Oriana, who saw her thus, had great pity for her, because she considered her very sensible and well meaning; except for the first time that she spoke to her about the Emperor's suit, which rendered her very angry, and she begged her not to talk to her about it any more. She always found her to be very courteous and a person of great discretion in never again angering her, preferably saying to her things that would give her pleasure. And she called Mabilia and said to her: "My friend, try to stop the Queen's weeping and comfort her as you know how to do; and do not heed anything she may say or do, because, as you see, she is almost out of her mind, having much reason to complain. But what I am obliged to do is what the victor must do to the vanquished when he has him in his power."

Mabilia, who was very kindly, went to the Queen, and kneeling, while taking her by the hand, said to her: "Noble Queen and lady, it is not fitting that a person of such high degree as you should be thus overcome and subjugated by fortune; for although all of us women are by nature weak in physique and courage, there is much benefit to be derived from the old stories about those women who stout-heartedly sought to repay their debt to their ancestors by displaying in adversity the nobility of lineage and blood from which they are descended. And although now you suffer from this great blow from your adverse fortune, remember that that self-same Fortune highly honored and elevated you, but not that you might be able to enjoy it any longer than her fickle will might permit and that you have lost it more through her fault than yours, because it always has pleased her, and still does, to turn things upside down and to try such games as these. And therefore you must consider that you are in the power of this noble princess, who with the great love and good will that she has for you, has compassion for your grief, remembering to provide you with that companionship and show you that courtesy that your virtue and royal estate command."

The Queen said to her: "Oh, most noble and gracious princess! Although the discretion of your words has such virtue that they could comfort every grief, however great it might be, my fortune is ill-starred to such a degree that my weak, tormented spirit cannot endure it. And if some hope for this great despair comes to mind, it is none other than to see myself, as you say, in the power of this very high and noble lady, who out of her great goodness will not permit my standing and reputation to be discredited, because this is the greatest treasure that every woman ought to guard most carefully and fear to lose."

Then Princess Mabilia with great promises assured her that Oriana would order carried out exactly what she desired. And lifting her up by the hands, she had her sit down on a dais, where many of those ladies who were there came to keep her company.

CHAPTER LXXXIII

HOW AT THE ASSENT AND COMMAND OF PRINCESS ORIANA, THOSE KNIGHTS BROUGHT HER TO THE FIRM ISLAND.

After Amadis and those knights departed from Salustanquidio's ship and saw that the entire fleet of the Romans was in the possession of his own men without any opposition, they all gathered together on Don Florestan's ship and reached the agreement that, since Oriana's wish and their own inclination was to go to the Firm Island, it would be well to carry this out. And they ordered all the prisoners put in one ship, with Gavarte of the Fearful Valley, and Landin, nephew of Don Cuadragante, together with a lot of the other knights to guard and hold them securely. And in another ship they ordered the booty, which was very great, to be placed, with Don Gandales, foster father of Amadis, and Sadamon, who were two very prudent and faithful knights, to guard it. And to all the other ships they assigned men-at-arms and sailors to pilot them, and each one of them remained in his own ship, just as he had departed from the Firm Island.

These preparations having been made, they requested Don Bruneo de Bonamar and Angriote de Estravaus to inform Oriana, and to bring back to them her wishes concerning what she would command, so that thus they might be carried out. These two knights went into her stateroom, knelt before her and said to her: "Good lady, all of the knights who are here gathered to aid you, in order to continue in your service inform you that the entire fleet is made ready and is prepared to move from here. They wish to know your wish, because they will carry it out with complete devotion."

Oriana said to them: "My great friends, if for this love that you all show for me and what you have involved yourselves in for my sake, I should never have the opportunity to reward you, from now on I would despair of my life. But I have faith in our Lord that out of His mercy He will be willing that just as I have it in mind, I may be enabled to carry it out. And tell those noble knights that the decision that was taken in this matter, which is to go to the Firm Island, should be put into effect; and after having arrived there, counsel shall be taken on what ought to be done; for I have hope in God, who is the just judge and knows all things, that this situation which now seems in such open rupture, He will guide and convert into great honor and pleasure; because as concerns just and true causes, as this is, even though at the beginning they appear harsh and arduous, as apparently now, from the outcome one must expect only good fruit; and from things that are the opposite, that which falsehood and disloyalty are wont to produce."

With this reply these two knights returned. And it having been made known to those who were awaiting it, they ordered the trumpets sounded, with which the fleet was very well equipped; and with much joy, and amid great shouting on the part of the lowliest, they set sail from there. All those great lords and knights set forth very happy and in high spirits, and firm in their determination not to part from one another nor from that princess until they had achieved the end and good outcome of what they had begun. And as all were of noble blood and of great feats at arms, their vigor and courage increased because they knew the great justice that they had on their side, and saw themselves in disagreement with two such eminent princes, whence they expected only to gain much honor, no matter whether favorable or adverse things should happen to them, and that they would perform in this undertaking, if it should end in rupture, great deeds for which they would be forever praised, and in the world a perpetual memory of them would remain. And as they were setting out all armor-clad, with very fine arms, and they were many, even to those who had no knowledge of their prowess, they would have appeared a company belonging to a great emperor; and certainly they did so appear, for it would be hard to find at the court of any prince, however great he might be, so many knights of such lineage and valor gathered together.

Therefore, what can one say here, except that you, King Lisuarte, ought to have reflected how, when you were a prince without an inheritance, chance had put you over such a great realm and such suzerainties, giving you brains, vigor, virtue, moderation, and precious generosity, more completely than to any of the mortal men of your time; and by putting on the diadem or precious crown, to become overlord of such an aggregation of knights as to be respected and held in great esteem in all parts of the world? And it is not known whether through the same chance's being transformed into mischance or by your own poor understanding you have lost it, receiving such great reverses in the high esteem in which you had been held and in your honored fame, that the satisfying of this situation is in the hand of God to give to you or to take away; but, upon my word of honor, rather do I understand that it is in order that you live with your mischance wounded and brought low from that height at which you were placed, which you will regret all the more to the same degree that you had prosperous times without any reverses to distress you greatly. And if you complain of such as this, complain of yourself, for you sought to lend an ear to men of little virtue and less probity, believing what you heard from them rather than what you with your own eyes saw; and together with this, without any pity or conscience you gave such latitude to your free will that not heeding the many warnings by many people, nor the sorrowful weeping of your daughter, you sought to place her in exile and in complete affliction, God having adorned her with so much beauty, with so much nobility and virtue, over and above all those women of her time. And if her honor to some degree can be impugned, in view of her excellence and her sound thinking, and the outcome that resulted from it all, one should attribute it to the consent of God, who wished it and it was His will, rather than to any other error or sin, so that, if Fortune by turning its wheel is unfavorable to you, you released that wheel from its fastenings.

Resuming then our narrative: just as you hear, the fleet was sailing over the sea, and in seven days they arrived at daybreak at the port of the Firm Island, where, in joyous celebration, there were fired many shots from lombards. When those on the island saw so many ships arriving there, they marvelled, and armed, they all hastened to the marina; but as soon as they arrived they recognized the ships as those of their lord Amadis, by the pennants and devices that they carried on their main topsails, which were the same as they had borne on leaving there. And at once launching their small craft, men went out, and Don Gandales with them in order to arrange for lodging as well as for the purpose of making a bridge of small craft from land to the ships to enable Oriana and those lords to disembark.

CHAPTER LXXXIV

How princess grasinda, on learning of the victory that amadis had achieved, accompanied by many knights and ladies, adorned herself in order to go to receive oriana.

From these whom I mention to you, the very beautiful Grasinda, who had remained there, ascertained the arrival and everything that took place; and at once with great diligence made ready to receive Oriana, whom on account of the good publicity given to her everywhere she was more eager to see than she was anyone else in the world. And so, as a lady of high degree and very rich, she wanted to show herself; for at once she donned a skirt and jacket overlaid with rare skill with a scattering of golden roses; these being set off and encircled with pearls and precious stones of great value, a costume which up until then she had not worn or shown to anyone, because she was keeping it to wear when she tested herself in the Forbidden Chamber as she later did. And on her beautiful hair it was her will to place only the coronet, a very fine one, which with her beauty and the excellence of the Greek Knight she had won from all the maidens who at that time were at the court of King Lisuarte, with great acclaim for them both. And she mounted a white palfrey equipped with saddle and bridle and the other trimmings all covered with gold enameled with designs wrought with great skill, for she was keeping this so that if Fortune should permit her to accomplish that venture of the Forbidden Chamber, she might return by way of King Lisuarte's court with these fine, imposing adornments, and make herself known to Queen Brisena and to Oriana, her daughter, and to the other princesses and ladies and maidens, and return to her native land with great glory. But this she had, and it was very far from being accomplished as she planned, because although she was very well adorned and beautiful in the opinion of many, and much more so in her own, she fell far short of equalling the very beautiful Queen Briolanja, who had already tried that adventure without being able to succeed in it.

Well, with this imposing finery that you hear that this lady Grasinda was wearing, she started on her way, and with her, her matrons and maidens splendidly dressed, and ten knights of hers on foot, who led her palfrey by the reins, without anyone else approaching her. And thus she went to the seacoast, where with haste the bridge had just been finished, of which you have already heard, as far as the ship on which Oriana was arriving; and having arrived there, she stood at the entrance to the bridge, awaiting Oriana's sally, who was already prepared to land, all those knights having gone to her ship in order to accompany her. And dressed more in keeping with her ill-fortune and the modesty befitting her, than to the enhancement of her beauty, she saw this lady and asked Don Bruneo if that was the one who had come to the court of the king, her father, and had won the coronet from the maidens. Don Bruneo told her that it was she, and to honor and welcome her, for she was one of the good ladies of her rank in the world. And he told her a great deal about her and of the great honors that Amadis and Angriote and he had received from her. Oriana said to him: "It is quite right that you and your friends should greatly honor her and esteem her, and I shall do so."

Then Don Cuadragante and Agrajes locked arms with her, and Don Florestan and Angriote with Queen Sardamira, and Amadis alone with Mabilia, and Don Bruneo and Dragonis with Olinda, and other knights with the other princesses and matrons; and all the knights were wearing armor and laughing very animatedly in order to encourage and afford them pleasure. As Oriana approached land, Grasinda dismounted from the palfrey and knelt at the end of the bridge, and took her by her hands in order to kiss them; but Oriana withdrew her hands, and did not wish to give them to her; instead she embraced her with great affection, as a woman accustomed to being very humble and gracious toward those with whom she ought to be. Grasinda, as she saw her so close and beheld her great beauty, was greatly astounded, although it had been highly praised to her. According to the difference she found on seeing her, she would not have been able to believe that any mortal person could attain such great beauty; and kneeling just as she was, for Oriana had never been able to make her rise, she said to Oriana: "Now, my good lady, very rightly must I thank our Lord and render Him service for the great favor He did me in your not being at the court of the king your father at the time that I came there; because surely, although to guard and protect me I brought the best knight in the world, in view of the fact that my claim was by reason of beauty, I declare that he could have seen himself in great danger if at arms God aids the right, as they say, and I would have been thwarted in winning the honor that I won, which in view of the great superiority and advantage that your beauty has over mine, I would not have esteemed very highly, even if the knight who had fought for you had been very weak, for my claim would not have attained the goal that it did."

Then she looked toward Amadis and said to him: "Sir, if from what I have said you take offense, pardon me, because my eyes never have seen the like of what they have before them."

Amadis, who was very happy because his lady was being praised thus, said: "My lady, I would be very wrong to consider bad what you have said to this noble lady, for if I should complain of it, it would be against the greatest truth that one could ever utter."

Oriana, who was somewhat embarrassed to hear herself thus praised, and more so with the thought of the ill fortune she had at the time than of being so esteemed for her beauty, answered: "My lady, I do not wish to respond to what you have said of me, because if I were to contradict it, I would offend a person of such good understanding, and if I should affirm it, it would be a great embarrassment and affront for me. I only want you to know that such as I am, I shall be very happy to enhance your honor as much as I can as a poor, disinherited maiden."

Then she asked Agrajes to escort Grasinda and place her beside Olinda and accompany her, and she remained with Don Cuadragante, and he did so likewise. And all having left the bridge, they placed Oriana on a palfrey, the most richly caparisoned ever seen, which her mother, Queen Brisena, had given her for when she should enter Rome; and Queen Sardamira on another, and likewise all the other ladies, and Grasinda on her own. And however much Oriana insisted, she could not prevent or deter all those lords and knights from accompanying her on foot, from which she suffered much embarrassment; but they thought that all the honor and service they did her would redound to their own enhancement.

Just as you hear, they entered the island through the castle, and brought those ladies with Oriana to the tower with the garden, where Don Gandales had had lodging made ready for them. The tower was the outstanding feature of the entire island, for although in many parts of it there were luxurious houses of elaborate design where Apolidon had left the enchantments, concerning which a more extensive account is given in Book II, his principal residence, where he stayed longest, was that tower. And for this reason he constructed in it so many things of such opulence that the greatest emperor in the world would not have dared or have undertaken to build another like it. There were in it nine apartments arranged three to a floor, some being above others, each one distinctive in style; and although some of them had been built through the ingenuity of men who knew a great deal, everything else was, by Apolidon's art and great knowledge, wrought so wonderfully that no one in the world would be capable of knowing how to estimate, and much less, to understand, its great subtlety. And because it would be an immense task to tell about it all in detail, it will only be said that this tower was located in the middle of a garden that was surrounded by a high wall of very handsome masonry, and with respect to its trees and plants of every variety, and its fountains of very fresh water, the most beautiful ever seen. There were many trees that bore fruit the whole year, others that had beautiful flowers. This garden had on the inside fastened to the wall elaborate arcades shut off with gilded gratings, from which that greenery was visible; and along them one could walk all the way around without being able to go out except through some gates. The floor was paved with stones, some crystal white, others red and transparent like rubies, and still others of diverse appearance, which Apolidon had ordered brought from some islands that are located in that part of the Orient where precious stones are produced, and in those islands are found much gold and other things that appear here in other lands, and which are created by the great heat of the sun, which there beats down continually; but the islands are not populated except by wild beasts, so that until the period of this great sage Apolidon — who out of his genius made contrivances whereby his men, without fear of losing their lives, were enabled to reach them, from which the neighboring peoples profited — no one previously had gone to them; so that from that time on the world was stocked with many things of a kind that until then had never been seen, and from there Apolidon obtained great wealth.

On the four sides of this tower there came from a high mountain range four springs that encircled it, brought in metal pipes, and the water from them gushed so high out of some gilded basins of copper and from the mouths of animals that from the first floor windows they could indeed take the water, which was collected in some round stone receptacles which were set in the pillars themselves. From these four fountains the whole garden was irrigated.

Well, in this tower about which you are hearing were lodged Princess Oriana and those ladies of whom you have heard, each one in the lodging she merited and as Princess Mabilia had ordered them allotted. Here they were served by matrons and maidens, with everything, and abundantly, that Amadis had ordered given them. And no knight entered the garden or where they dwelt, for such an arrangement was pleasing to Oriana, and so she sent to request all of those lords to approve it, inasmuch as she wanted to be as if cloistered until some basis of agreement and peace was established with the king her father. All of them considered it very virtuous on her part, and they praised her good motive, and sent word to tell her that in that, just as in everything else that might be to her service, they would do nothing but carry out her wishes.

Amadis, although his anguished heart found no stability or remedy anywhere, except when he was in the presence of his lady, because being with her was his whole objective for repose, and without it, great anguish and mortal desires tormented him continually, as you have heard many times in this great story; seeking more her contentment and fearing a hundred thousand times more the loss of her honor than his own death, more than anyone displayed satisfaction and pleasure at what that lady considered good and decorous, taking as a remedy for his sufferings and cares the fact that he now had her in his power in a place where he did not fear the rest of the world, and where rather than lose her, he would lose his life, whereupon those great flames that continually burned his sad heart would cease and become cold.

All those lords and knights and those of lower rank were lodged appropriately in those places on the island that were most in keeping with their rank and quality, where in great abundance they were given the things necessary for good and pleasant living; for although Amadis had always gone about as a poor knight, he found on that island great treasures acquired out of the income from it, and many other jewels of great value that the queen his mother and other great ladies had given him; which, on account of his not having any need of them, had been sent there. And besides this, all the inhabitants and dwellers on the island, who were quite rich and reserved, were very happy to provide him with large provisions of bread and meat and wines, and the other things that they were able to give him. So just as you hear, Princess Oriana was brought to the Firm Island with those ladies and lodged there, as were all the knights engaged in her service and aid.

CHAPTER LXXXV

How amadis had those lords assemble, and the speech that he made to them, and what they agreed to do in the matter.

Amadis, however much he might show great courage, since he had it, thought a great deal about the outcome that might result from this great affair, as the one on whom all responsibility fell, although there were there many princes and noble lords and knights of high degree; and he already had his life condemned to death if he didn't succeed in that great undertaking which was threatening and imperilling his honor. And when all were sleeping he was awake thinking about the remedy that must be applied; and with this preoccupation, with the approval and on the advice of Don Cuadragante and that of his cousin Agrajes, he had all those lords summoned to assemble at Don Cuadragante's quarters in a great hall therein, which was one of the finest in the whole island. And all having come there, for no one was missing, Amadis stood up, holding by the hand Master Elisabad, to whom he always paid much honor, and spoke to them in this wise: "Noble princes and knights, I have had you assemble here in order to remind you that through all parts of the world where your fame extends, the great lineages and estates from which you come are known, and that each one of you in your own lands could live with many luxuries and pleasures, having many servants, with other great facilities that one is accustomed to obtain and possess for the recreation of a life of enjoyment and ease while accumulating wealth. But you, having considered that there is as great a difference between the pursuit of arms and that of pleasures and the acquisition of worldly goods as there is between the judgment of men and that of ignorant beasts, have renounced that for which many men become lost souls; wishing to pass up large fortunes in order to bequeath laudable fame by pursuing this military occupation of arms, for since the beginning of the world down to our own time no good fortune of worldly men could, or can, equal its conquest and glory; whereby up to now you have gathered neither profit nor dominions, but rather, the engagement of your bodies, covered with wounds, in great and dangerous undertakings, until arriving a thousand times at the point and threshold of death, while hoping for and desiring glory and fame more than any other gain that might come from it; in reward for which, if you wish to know, prosperous and favorable Fortune has been willing to place in your hands such a great victory as at the present time you have. And I do not say this to you with reference to the vanquishment of the Romans, which, in accordance with the difference between your strength and theirs, ought not to be rated very highly, but on account of this very noble and excellent princess's having been rescued and aided by you in order that she might not receive the greatest injury and wrong that any person of such high station has received for a long time; because of which besides having increased greatly in your fame, you have performed a great service to God, making use of that for which you were born, which is to help the persecuted by putting a stop to the injuries and outrages that are done them. And what one should esteem most and should give us the greatest contentment is to have displeased and angered two such high and mighty princes as the Emperor of Rome and King Lisuarte; with whom, if they are unwilling to become just and reasonable, it will be in order for us to have great combats and wars. Well, henceforth, noble lords, what can be expected? Certainly, nothing except that we, as men who uphold reason and truth to the shame and discredit of those who reject and scorn it, shall win very great victories, which will resound throughout the whole world. And if from the high station of our foes something may be feared, well, we are not so lacking in the support of many other great lords, both relatives and friends, that we cannot easily fill these fields with knights and foot soldiers in such great numbers that no adversaries, however many they may be, can see after one day's battle the Firm Island; therefore, good lords, on this matter, let each one speak his opinion — not about what he wishes, for much better than I, you know and love virtue and know what you are in duty bound to do — but about what one ought to do in order to support this cause and carry it forward with that courage and prudence of yours."

With much good will that graceful, forceful talk which was made by Amadis was heard by all those lords; who, considering that they had among them so many who would know how to answer very well in accordance with their great discretion and courage, for a while were all silent, bidding one another to speak. Then Don Cuadragante said: "My lords, if you consider it good, since you all remain silent, I shall speak what my judgment enables me to know and respond."

Agrajes said to him: "Sir Don Cuadragante, we all beg you to do so, because in view of your being the man you are and the great deeds undertaken by you and with such great honor accomplished, it is more fitting for you to reply than for any of us to do so."

Don Cuadragante thanked him for the honor he was accorded and said to Amadis: "Noble knight, your great discretion and good moderation have satisfied our wishes so completely, and you have said what should be done in such wise that to have to reply to it all would be a matter of great prolixity and annoyance to anyone listening. I shall say only what ought to be remedied at the present time, which is that since your will in the past has been not to pursue passion or hatred but only to serve God and adhere to your oath as knights, which is to suppress violence, especially that done to matrons and maidens who have neither strength nor assistance except from God and you, this be made manifest by your messengers to King Lisuarte and he be requested by you to recognize his past error and deal justly and reasonably with this princess, his daughter, by relaxing the great coercion that he is applying to her, giving such guarantees that with good reason and the certainty that our honor will not be discredited we may be able and obligated to restore her to him; and that of what pertains to us concerning him not to make any mention, because once this present crisis is resolved, if resolving it is possible, I trust so much in your virtue and great courage that even he will sue us for peace, and he will consider himself quite satisfied if it is granted by you. And while our emissaries are on their journey, inasmuch as we do not know how things will turn out, let anyone who may wish to seek us out, find us, not as knights errant, but as princes and noble lords; and it would be well that our friends and relatives, who are many, by us be notified, so that when it is time for them to be called they may be able to come in time for their effort to have the effect that it should."

CHAPTER LXXXVI

HOW ALL THE KNIGHTS WERE VERY CONTENT WITH ALL THAT DON CUADRAGANTE PROPOSED.

Those knights were very content with Don Cuadragante's reply, because in their opinion there remained nothing more to say. And it was immediately agreed that Amadis should inform King Perion, his father, asking for all help and favor, from him and from all his knights as well as from any others who were his friends and vassals, when he should be called upon; likewise that he should send word to all the others who he knew would be able and willing to lend support, for there were many for whom with great danger to his person he had done great things on behalf of their honor and to their benefit; and that Agrajes should send an emissary or should go to the King of Scotland, his father, with a similar message; and that Don Bruneo should send word to the Marquis, his father, by Branfil, his brother, that the former make ready with great diligence as many fighting men as he could, and that they should not leave there until they had his order; and that all the other knights who were there on the Firm Island and who had estates and friends should do likewise.

Don Cuadragante said that he would send Landin, his nephew, to the Queen of Ireland, and that he believed that if King Cildadan, her husband, supported King Lisuarte with the number of men at arms that he was obligated to send, she would afford to all those of her kingdom who might wish it, an opportunity to come and serve, and that of those as well as of his own vassals and other friends of his a good force would arrive.

This having been decided thus, they asked Agrajes and Don Florestan to inform Princess Oriana, so that concerning everything she might order what would be most helpful to her. And all thus united, they left the meeting in high spirits, especially those who were of lower rank, who to some degree had been considering this business as very perilous, fearing the outcome of it more than they revealed; and as they now had seen the great care and foresight exhibited by the grandees, and that by reason of it great assistance was expected, their courage mounted and they lost all fear.

And on arriving at the castle gate, which commanded a view of the whole island, they saw coming up the hill an armed knight on horseback and five squires with him, who carried his arms and other personal effects. All stood still until they found out who he might be; and as they saw him closer at hand, they recognized that he was Don Brian de Monjaste, whence very great pleasure ensued for them, because he was loved by all and deemed a good knight. And certainly he was, for aside from his being of such an exalted station, as son of Ladasan, King of Spain, he, in his own right, was of high repute for prudence and courage everywhere he was known; and in addition to this he was a knight who more than anyone else in the world loved his friends, and was always joking and having fun when with them as one who was very discreet and well-bred. And so they loved him and took great pleasure with him. And all together they came down the hill on foot just as they were; and he, when he saw them, was greatly surprised and could not imagine what adventure had brought them together, although he had been told something after he landed. And he dismounted and went toward them with outstretched arms and said: "I want to embrace you all together, since I consider you all as one."

Then those who were coming in front arrived, and behind them Amadis. And when Don Brian saw him, whether he was greatly pleased thereby, it is unnecessary to state; because, besides the close kinship that he had with him, in that they were sons of brother and sister (for the mother of this Don Brian, wife of the King of Spain, was the sister of King Perion), he was the knight whom he loved most in the whole world. And he said to him, laughing: "Are you here? Well, I was coming in search of you, for even if we completely lacked adventures we would have plenty to do looking for you, the way you hide."

Amadis embraced him and said: "Say what you will, you have arrived in a place where I shall quickly exact amends for it. And these lords command you to mount your horse and get on this island, where a dungeon is being readied for the likes of you."

Then all the others came up to embrace him; and although against his will, they made him mount his horse, and they went with him on foot up the hill until they arrived at Amadis's quarters, where he dismounted, and his cousins Agrajes and Don Florestan disarmed him and ordered a scarlet robe brought for him to wear. And when his armor was removed, and he saw about him so many and such noble knights with whose excellence and prowess he was familiar, he said to them: "A company of so many excellent knights could not have been brought together here except for some very important secret business and reason. Tell me what it is, my lords, for I want very much to know, because I heard something of it after I came to this land."

All begged Agrajes to give the account of it, as the one who had been present at everything that had transpired. And so that in it and in what was still to come Don Brian might have a great desire to further and favor it, he told him everything just as our story has related it, blaming King Lisuarte and praising and approving very earnestly what those knights had done and were about to do in the future. When Brian de Monjaste heard this, he deemed it excessive, as a person of great discretion who considers the outcome rather than the beginning. And if it had been about to be done, without his knowing the secret of Amadis's love affair, it might have been possible for his advice to be negative, or at least that the action should be toned down by going through other more legitimate channels without its reaching such extremes as it had at present; for according to the knowledge he had of King Lisuarte's being so sensitive and protective regarding his honor, the offense having become so great, he indeed thought that an equally great vengeance would be sought. But seeing that the affair had reached such a state that more aid than advice was required, especially since Amadis was at the head of it, very earnestly he approved what had been done, speaking highly of the great propriety with which they had proceeded in dealing with Oriana, and promising them to safeguard her person with as many of his father's fighting men as he could obtain. He told them that he wanted to see Princess Oriana so that she might ascertain from him how wholeheartedly he would serve her. Amadis said to him: "Sir cousin, you have just come from the road and these lords have not dined; do rest and dine while word is being sent to them of your arrival, and in the afternoon the call on Oriana can be better made."

Don Brian approved of this; and therefore those lords, having taken leave of him, went to their lodging. And afternoon having come, Agrajes and Don Florestan, who were chosen by them to speak with Oriana, as stated, took Don Brian with them, and all three went, elegantly attired, to where Oriana was, and they found her waiting for them in Queen Sardamira's apartment, accompanied by all those ladies that you have heard about and of whom the story has given you an account. Then having arrived there, Don Brian went to Oriana and knelt to kiss her hands, but she drew him to her and would not yield them to him; instead she embraced him and received him with the great courtesy characteristic of a lady in whom was to be found all the nobility in the world. And she said to him: "My lord Don Brian, be you very welcome, for although, in view of your nobility and integrity, at any time you would deserve to be well received, at this present time you should have a much better reception. And because I believe that those noble knights, who are friends of yours, have related to you everything that has happened referring to them, it will not be necessary for me to say anything, or remind you either of what you ought to do; because in view of the way you have used advice and made it familiar, your discretion is better qualified to give it than to seek it."

Don Brian said to her: "My lady, the reason for my coming has been that it has been a long time since I left the battle that the king your father had with the seven kings of the islands, and since I went to my father in Spain; while I was involved in a dispute that he was having with the Africans, I learned that my cousin and lord Amadis had gone to foreign lands, where no news of him was being ascertained; and as he is the flower and model of my whole family, and the one whom I most hold in high esteem and love, his absence produced so much grief in my heart that I strove for some settlement to be made in order to set forth in quest of him. And reflecting that in this island of his rather than anywhere else I would be able to find some news of my cousin, I came here whither my good fortune and luck have guided me, not only to find him, but to come at a time that the desire that I always have had to serve you may be evinced by action. And as you, my lady, have said, I already know what has happened, and am even somewhat preoccupied with what may result from it, in view of the harsh nature of your father the king. In whatever manner it may come and chance direct it and be able to involve me personally, I offer myself and prepare with utmost willingness to provide a remedy."

Oriana gave him many thanks.

CHAPTER LXXXVII

How all the knights had a great desire to serve and honor Princess Oriana.

It is quite right that it be known and not remain forgotten for what reason these knights and many others who will be mentioned later desired to serve this lady with so much love and good will, exposing themselves in the greatest degree, as they were, to confrontations with such high-ranking princes. Could it be perchance on account of the favors that they had received from her, or because they knew about the secret and circumstances of her love affair with Amadis and on that account were favorably disposed toward it? Certainly I say that neither thing caused their wills to be impelled to do so, because although she was of such high estate, time had not given her an opportunity to be able to do a favor to anyone; since she did not possess anything more than a poor maiden would. Then with regard to what has to do with her love affair with Amadis, already this great story, if you have read it, gives you testimony of how secret it was. Since it is probably for some reason, do you know what it was? Because this princess was always the most gentle, well-bred and courteous — especially with serene humility — to be found in her time, remembering to honor and treat each one well, according to his merit; for this is a snare and a net in which the grandees who do so catch many of those who have little obligation to serve them, as we see every day; for without any other self-interest, they are praised by them orally, out of their good will much beloved, obligated to serve them, as these lords were doing for that noble princess.

Well, what shall be said here of the grandees who exhibit great scorn and excessive presumption to those to whom they ought not to exhibit it? I shall tell you: seeking to involve themselves with lower-class people in harsh retorts, with enraged gestures, depreciative of their courtesies and favors, they are held in less esteem, less respected, verbally abused with the desire that some reverse come to them to do them an ill turn and anger them. Oh what a great mistake! And what little understanding: for lack of a favor so small as giving a gracious reply, a friendly glance, that costs so little, to lose being loved, esteemed and served by those to whom they have never granted a boon or rendered help! Do you want to know what often happens to these disdainful scorners? I will tell you: like those who squander and waste their own wealth, having no regard for place or time, giving it where they should not, they are considered, instead of generous and liberal, as stupid and foolish; so those, likewise, by failing to honor those whose honoring would be deemed a virtue, by humbling and subjugating themselves to others who are their superiors or perchance their equals, which is considered service with slight effort rather than a virtue.

Well, returning to the subject at hand, the conversation of Brian de Monjaste having been finished, and reverence paid to Queen Sardamira and those princesses along with Grasinda, Agrajes and Don Florestan came to Oriana, and with great respect told her everything that those knights had commissioned them to tell; having considered it a good decision, she transmitted to them and left them the responsibility for what ought to be done, since the doing and purpose of it pertained more to knights than to maidens; sending word to beg them earnestly always to remember, in compliance with their honor, to seek and solicit peace with the king her father concerning what related to her and her reputation. This done, Oriana, leaving Don Florestan and Brian de Monjaste with Queen Sardamira and those ladies, took Agrajes by the hand, and went to seat herself with him at one side of the room. And she spoke to him thus: "My good lord and veritable brother Agrajes, although the confidence and hope that I have in your cousin Amadis and in those noble knights is very great, for they most carefully and with great diligence with due regard for their honor will support completely what relates to me, I have much more confidence in you, since it is a fact that I was reared for a long time at the court of the king your father, where from him as well as from the queen your mother I received many honors and had many good times; and especially by their having given to me Princess Mabilia, your sister; of whom I can well say that if God our Lord was the first to give me life, so, after Him, this lady has given it to me many times; for if it had not been for her great prudence and comfort, in view of my sufferings and above all, my adverse fortune, which since the Romans came to my father's court has harassed me, without her help it would have been impossible for me to endure life. And so on this account as well as for many other reasons that I could mention, for which if God would only give me an opportunity to pay in full, I am so obligated; and believing that just as I have it on my mind, you recognize that when the time comes, I would carry it out just as I have said, it affords me a reason why the secrets of my suffering heart be told you rather than anyone else; and so I shall do, for what will be concealed from everyone to you alone will be made manifest. And for the present I only urge you as earnestly as I can that, laying aside the anger and vexation that you may have with respect to my father, complete peace and harmony be established by you and on your advice between him and your cousin Amadis; because, in view of his great courage, and the enmity for so long a time so obdurate, my only fear is that any argument put forth out of sincere affection will not be able to satisfy him; and if by you, my veritable brother and friend, some remedy can be applied in this matter, not only will many people be kept and protected from suffering brutal deaths, but also my honor and reputation, which perchance is in disrepute in many places, will be cleared with that assistance that befits its uprightness."

This having been heard by Agrajes, with much courtesy and humility he answered thus: "With much justice one can and ought to agree with all that you, madam, have said, for according to what I have learned from the king my father and from my mother, their desire is to be able to help as much as possible to increase your honor and high standing as presently will be demonstrated; for as regards my sister and me it will not be necessary to declare it, because our actions afford evidence of very wholeheartedly seeking and desiring to serve you. And coming to what you ask of me, I tell you the truth is, madam, that more than anyone else I am at outs with the king your father; for, just as I am a witness of the great and outstanding services that Amadis my cousin and all of us of his lineage have rendered him, as is well-known to everyone, so I am of his great ingratitude and poor return for service received; for by us no favor was ever asked of him, except the island of Mongaza for my uncle Don Galvanes, which was won to the greatest honor of his court, and by the one who won it at the greatest danger to his life, just as you, my good lady, have seen with your own eyes; and to think that all of us did not suffice, nor the excellence and great worthiness of my uncle, to enable his obtaining such a small thing by remaining his vassal and under his suzerainty; instead, rejecting us, casting aside our supplication with as much discourtesy as if, instead of being — as we were — men in his service, we had become enemies to him. And for this reason I cannot deny that insofar as I was concerned I was taking great pleasure in helping to put him in such straits and need, that repenting of what he had done he would give everyone to understand the great loss that he sustained in us, realizing the honor that our services were rendering him. But just as man by denying and suppressing his own will gains more merit in the sight of God by doing it in His service, so I, madam, complying with yours am willing to deny and suppress my anger, in order that in this matter, which is so serious to me, I may be able to recognize other things which my anger has me so obligated to serve it; but this will be with much moderation, because as I am among these lords regarded as a chief enhancer of your honor, it would be a major cause of contributing weakness to many of them if they perceived it in me."

"So I ask it, my good friend," said Oriana; "for well I know, in view of the seriousness of what has happened and the one with whom this great dispute is, that it is necessary not only to render strong aid but with much care to render strong the very weak. And because much better than I would know how to plead for it, you know what is proper and at what time it can be advantageous or harmful to you, I leave it to you with that true affection that exists between us."

Thus they finished their conversation and returned to where those ladies and knights were. Agrajes could not take his eyes away from his lady Olinda, as the woman who was much loved by him with great ardor, which one must believe to be true, since on account of it she was worthy to pass under the enchanted arch of loyal lovers, as the second Book of this story has related; but as he was of noble blood and upbringing, for such are obligated without much coercion, rejecting passion and ardor, to serve virtue; and knowing the chaste life that Oriana was pleased to lead, he was determined to suppress his own desire, even though he might feel greatly annoyed in so doing, until he saw how the initiated negotiations came out.

So they kept on talking for a while about many things, and those knights, as very courageous men, were encouraging their adherence by dispelling the fear that women are accustomed to have in situations so unusual for them as the one in which they were. Then having taken leave of the ladies, and given the reply of Oriana to those who had sent them to her, they began with great diligence to put into effect what they had agreed upon, and to dispatch the emissaries who were going to King Lisuarte, a mission which was unanimously assigned to Don Cuadragante and Don Brian de Monjaste, for they were such as to be suitable for such an embassy.

CHAPTER LXXXVIII

How amadis spoke with grasinda, and what she replied.

Amadis went to the lodging of Grasinda, whom he loved and esteemed very much, not only for herself but also for the numerous honors that he had received, and which he did not think had been repaid, although he had done for her what our story has related, considering that there are very great differences between those who perform feats of prowess because of their courage while not having much acquaintance with those who benefit from them, and those who, after they have so benefited, requite and repay them; because the first is out of a generous heart, and the second, although it may involve good acquaintanceship and gratitude, nevertheless is a recognized debt that is being repaid. And seated with her on a dais, he spoke to her thus: "My lady, if the service and pleasure that your virtue deserves are not being rendered you by me as I desire and would wish, may I be pardoned, because what you see going on is to be blamed for it; and in order that your noble nature might so adjudge it, leaving this aside I have decided to speak to you and to ask that as a favor you tell me the goal of your desire and will — because it has been a long time since you left your land, and I do not know whether from that fact your heart receives any distress — in order that as soon as your command is known, it may be carried out."

Grasinda said to him: "My lord, if I had not held the belief that from your companionship and friendship the greatest honor had accrued to me that could come to me from anything, and that all the service and entertainment provided for you in my house — if there was any that afforded you contentment — had been repaid and requited, it would be discernible by the person of poorest knowledge in the world. And because this is very certain and known to all, I wish, my lord, that my whole desire, exactly as I have it, be made manifest to you. I see that although here are gathered so many princes and knights of great valor for the rescue of this princess, you, my good lord, are the one to whom all look and defer, so that on your brains and courage depend all the hope and good fortune that they expect; and in view of your great courage and nature, you cannot avoid taking complete charge of everything, because it devolves on no one else as justly or as rightfully as on you; whence it will be necessary that your friends and defenders come to your aid and try to support your honor and high estate. And because chiefly out of my desire I consider myself one of them, I wish that my desire may so appear in its execution; and I have decided that Master Elisabad should go to my land, and very carefully have all of my vassals and friends provided and fitted out with a great fleet against the time when it may be necessary for them to come, sir, and serve you according to your commands. And meanwhile I shall remain in the company and service of this lady, along with the others that she has with her, and I shall not part from her, nor from you, until the conclusion of this business tells me what I should do."

When Amadis heard this from her he embraced her laughing and said: "I believe that if all the rest of the virtue and nobility that there is in the world were lost, in you, my good lady, it could be recovered; and since it pleases you thus, so let it be done. It is necessary that in your service and at my request, Master Elisabad, although it may work a hardship on him thereby, go to the Emperor of Constantinople with a message from me to the effect that in view of the gracious offer that was given to me by the emperor, and the dissatisfaction, of which many told me when I went to those regions, that he has with the Emperor of Rome, and knowing that the dispute is chiefly with him, I am sure that displaying his usual great virtue, he will give orders that I be aided just as if I had done him great service."

Grasinda said that she considered it a good decision and that in view of the great affection that the master had for him, her order for what might be serving her was unnecessary, and that such a journey with a message from such a person the latter would consider honor and relief rather than toil. Amadis said to her: "My lady, since your desire is to remain with Oriana, it will be right that just as the other princesses and great ladies, like you, are with her and in her apartment, you be there also and from her receive that honor and courtesy that your great virtue deserves."

And then he gave orders to summon his foster father Don Gandales, and he asked him to go to Oriana and tell her the great desire that that lady had to serve her, and how she was putting it into execution, and to beg Oriana on his behalf to take her with her and to render her that same honor that she was rendering those ladies of highest degree in her company; which was done thus, for Oriana received her with that affection and good will with which she was accustomed to welcome and receive such persons, but not so much for the present service as for the past that she had rendered Amadis in giving him such equipment in order that he might go to Greece; and especially in giving him Master Elisabad, who, after God, as the story has related in the third book, gave life to him and to her, for she would not have been able to live one day after his death, and this was when he healed him of the deep wounds that he acquired when he killed the Endriago.

This having been done thus, after Grasinda gave all the credentials necessary to Master Elisabad in order that he might carry out what is set forth above, and begged and commanded him that knowing what Amadis wanted him to do for him, he execute it in the way a thing of such great importance ought to be executed, the master replied to her that on account of any failure to expose his person to every peril and hardship, he would not fail to carry out what he was commanded to do. Amadis thanked him very heartily for it and at once resolved to write a letter to the Emperor, which read thus:

Letter from Amadis to the Emperor of Constantinople.

Very exalted Emperor: I, that Knight of the Green Sword, who is known by his own name as Amadis of Gaul, am writing to convey to Your Majesty my respects and to recall to Your Majesty's memory that offer that more because of his great virtue and nobility than on account of my services, he was pleased to make to me; and because now has come the time in which I need chiefly Your Majesty, and all my friends and defenders who may wish to pursue justice and reason, as Master Elisabad will tell Your Majesty in more detail, I beg that credence be given him and that his mission have that effect of help that I with my person and all those who are to protect and follow would place at your service.

The letter having been finished and the detailed accreditation given to the master, as will be evident later, taking leave of Amadis and of his lady Grasinda, he put out to sea to make his journey, which had such a perfect outcome as will be told in due time.

CHAPTER LXXXIX

HOW AMADIS SENT ANOTHER MESSAGE TO QUEEN BRIOLANJA.

The story says that after Amadis had sent Master Elisabad on his way and housed Grasinda with Princess Oriana, he gave orders to summon Tantiles, the majordomo of the beautiful Queen Briolanja, and said to him: "My good friend, I was wishing that you would take the trouble and care on my behalf that I would take in matters that concerned you, and that is, that considering the point at which my honor is, and how much it can be enhanced with good precaution and preparation, and how it could be discredited by the contrary, you go to your lady, and as one who has seen the whole situation, tell her what is fitting, striving hard to have her order all her soldiery and friends to be prepared for an emergency. And tell her that she knows already that what relates to me is her concern, since if I lose, it is a loss to her service."

Tantiles answered thus: "Sir, just as you command I shall do at once; and you can indeed be certain that nothing could come about in which the queen my lady could take so much pleasure as in the coming of a time when you may recognize the great love and good will that she has to carry out all that you might wish to command involving her and her whole kingdom. And with regard to this, do not worry, for I shall come when it is necessary with that equipment and those requisites that a great lady such as this one should send to the man who, after God, gave her whole kingdom to her."

Amadis thanked him heartily for this, and gave him a letter of accreditation that was sufficient for him as a person who governed his whole state. He then set out over the sea in a ship that had come there, and did what will be told later. This having been done, Amadis withdrew with Gandalin, and said to him: "My friend Gandalin, you see whether I have need of friends and relatives in this emergent situation in which I have put myself without being able to avoid it; and although I feel great distress at seeing you sent far away from me, reason obliges me to do so. Already you see how it is agreed upon by all these knights that all of our friends be solicited and forewarned so that they can come in time to uphold our honor. And although I am very hopeful that many persons for whom I have done much, as you know, will want to repay the debt to me which they owe, much more hope do I have that King Perion, my father, rightly or wrongly, will support what concerns me. And because you, better than anyone else and most uninhibitedly will tell him that this concerns me so much, and how by wish and intent of everyone, although here there are so many famous knights of high lineage, to me alone do they look as their leader, it will be well that you leave at once to go to him, and that you tell him what you have seen and know to be relevant to the emergent need in which you leave me. And besides the other things, you will tell him how I do not fear any armed force from anywhere in the world, in view of this force of ours, but that it would be unduly hard on him if I, who am his son and the eldest, should not be able to respond to these two princes, were they to come against me, in the same form and manner that they call me to account. And because I understand that you are thoroughly familiar with everything, it will not be necessary for me to tell you more except that before you leave, go and speak with my cousin Mabilia to see whether she has some message for her aunt and Melicia, my sister; and you will see how my lady Oriana is, because although she is reticent with other people, to you alone she will disclose her desires and wishes. And this having been done, you will leave at once with this written letter of accreditation that I give you.

You will say to the king, my lord, that His Highness already knows that since God willed that I be knighted by his hand, my thought has never been to assume any status other than that of knight errant, and as best I could to right the wrongs and injustices done to the many who receive them, especially matrons and maidens, who ahead of all others should be succored. And for this reason, I have subjected my person to many trials and dangers, without expecting any other recompense for it than serving God and winning glory and fame from the people; and with this wish, when I left his kingdom, I endeavored to travel through foreign lands looking for those who needed my help and defense, seeing what I had not seen before, where I experienced many adventures, as you can certainly tell him if he wishes to find out about it; and that after a long time, on coming to this island I learned that King Lisuarte, not paying any attention to the fear of God, nor to the advice of his subjects, nor to others who, though not his subjects, were solicitous of his honor and desired to serve him; rather with complete cruelty and great discredit to his fame, sought to disinherit Princess Oriana, his daughter, who after he passes away is to be mistress of his dominions, in order to give the inheritance to another, younger daughter, who had no right to have it come to her, by giving Oriana to the Roman emperor as his wife. And since this princess complained to all those who saw her and to the others through her messengers, with much weeping and manifestations of anguish on her part, so that they might take pity on her and not consent to her being disinherited so very unjustly, that just Judge, the Emperor of all things, heard her, and through His willingness and permission many princes and great knights were assembled on this island in order to help her, where I found them when I came, and from them I learned of this very great act of violence that was taking place; and with their assent and counsel it was decided that, since in cases of this kind more than in any others, knights have the obligation to intervene, in this particular case, which was so flagrant, a remedy should be applied, so that what until now with much danger and with great effort on our part we had won, must not be lost in one single case, for reason did not dictate it; because, in view of the magnitude of the case, failure to intervene would be attributed more to cowardice and scant courage than to any other cause. And so it came about that the fleet of the Romans having been destroyed and many persons slain and the rest taken prisoner, this princess, with all her matrons and maidens, was seized by us and rescued. Moreover we have decided to send Don Cuadragante of Ireland and my cousin Brian de Monjaste to King Lisuarte to persuade him on our behalf to be willing to be reasonable; and that if it be the case that he is not willing to be so, but on the contrary, wishes to be harsh, there will be need of my father's assistance primarily — and afterwards that of all those who are our friends — an assistance which I beg him to have ready with as many troops as can be obtained, for when they are called for. And pay my respects to my lady the queen, and ask her to order my sister Melicia sent here so that she may keep Oriana company, and so that her nobility and great beauty be to many as well known by sight, as they are by reputation."

This done, he said to him: "Prepare to go in whatever one of those ships that you find best equipped, and take along someone to guide you, and speak with my cousin Mabilia before you leave, as I said."

Gandalin told him that he would do so.

Agrajes spoke with Gandales, foster father of Amadis, telling him to leave for Scotland and go to the king, his father, and with the latter the task of writing could indeed be avoided, because Gandales was so faithful to him and had been for so long, and was so trustworthy in all matters, that he was considered now more as a relative and counsellor than as a vassal; therefore it is to be believed that this knight with complete dedication and diligence would accomplish the purpose of this trip so vital to his former ward Amadis, who was the thing that he loved most in the world; and how he did it will be told later.

CHAPTER XC

HOW DON CUADRAGANTE TALKED WITH HIS NEPHEW LANDIN, AND TOLD HIM TO GO TO IRELAND AND SPEAK WITH THE QUEEN, THE FORMER'S NIECE, SO THAT SHE MIGHT AFFORD AN OPPORTUNITY TO SOME OF HER VASSALS TO COME AND SERVE HIM.

Don Cuadragante spoke with Landin, his nephew, who was a very good knight, and he said to him: "Beloved nephew, it is necessary that as speedily as possible you leave here and reach Ireland, and speak with the queen, my niece, without King Cildadan's knowing anything about it; because, in view of what he has sworn and has promised King Lisuarte, it would not be right that he be told anything about this. And tell her the situation in which I am placed, and that although here there are many knights of high degree, from me because of who I am and of the lineage from which I come, much is expected and counted on, as you, nephew, see. And tell her Majesty that I earnestly beg her to afford to those of her vassals who want to come and serve me an opportunity to do so; and that she believe that the revolt is here so great that from such situations it often results that states and seigniories are overthrown, so that vassals are left as lords and lords as vassals; and for this reason may she not hesitate to order this which I beg of her, and thus with those of the latter category whom you may be able to recruit, as well as those from among my vassals and friends, make ready a fleet — the largest possible — and with it you will stand ready for when you see my summons."

Landin responded to him that with the help of God he would employ such care that he would be satisfied, and that much of Don Cuadragante's valor and greatness would be made manifest.

With this he bade him farewell, and in one of those ships that they took from the Romans he put out to sea, and what he achieved from this journey will be told later.

Don Bruneo of Bonamar spoke with Lasindo, his squire, directing him to leave at once and go to his father the Marquis and Branfil, his brother, with his letter, and that he should speak very earnestly with his brother, and on his behalf beg him that without involving himself in any other matter he should endeavor to gather together as many fighting men as he could, and ships for them, and that he not leave there until he saw his order. And furthermore, he said to him: "Lasindo, my good friend, although you see here so many knights of high repute, you must really believe that most of this action belongs to Amadis; therefore whether I have reason to help him, laying aside the great affection that he has for me, which greatly obligates me to give him help, you already know, for he is a brother of my lady Melicia and he is the one whom she loves and esteems more than anyone else in her family. Well, if he were my enemy I would have no recourse but to be obedient to his will and mandate because this would be in obedience to her service and will; then the opposite being true, in that he is the man whom I love most in the world, with even more dedication and volition I must prepare to support his honor and status, especially in this matter, in which no one is more involved than I, or more concerned. All of this, my good friend, leaving aside the matter of my lady, you can discuss with my father and with my brother, because it will constrain them to fulfill what very rightly ought to be fulfilled as an obligation to my honor; although as far as Branfil, my brother, is concerned, I am sure that he would rather be here and have participated in what has happened than win a great dominion, because by temperament and desire he is more inclined to win knightly glory and fame than to other things of the kind that other men who look to worldly pleasures more than to virtue desire."

Lasindo said to him: "Sir, as far as I am concerned, it is not necessary to tell me more than what I know is necessary. I trust in God that from there we shall bring you equipment such that your lady may be very well served and your status much more greatly honored."

Whereupon he left in another ship, and what he did the story will relate when it is time; for this Lasindo was a very good squire and of great lineage, and he was going forth with complete dedication and good will; and he so carried out his mission that much to his own honor in the negotiation he greatly increased the aid to Amadis.

CHAPTER XCI

How amadis sent a message to the king of bohemia.

As for Amadis, as the one who had such a great responsibility on his shoulders, especially with reference to his lady, his thoughts were ever intent on providing what was needed; hence he resolved to send Isanjo, a very honorable knight of very great discretion, whom he found to be governor on the Firm Island at the time that he won it, an office which had come down to him from his ancestors, as the second Book of this story relates in greater detail. And withdrawing with him, he said: "My good lord and noble friend, knowing your virtue and good sense, and the desire you always have had ever since you knew me to protect my honor, and that which I have to reward you for it when the opportunity should arise, I have decided to involve you in a little toil, because in view of the one to whom I am sending you, only a messenger such as you is requisite; and this task is that you are to go at once to King Tafinor of Bohemia with a letter of mine, plus the letter of acceditation that will be sent to you — whereby in full detail you will inform him about this situation that is shaping up, and how much trust and hope I have in his favor. And I trust in God that from your embassy great benefit will accrue to us because he is a very noble king, and with great love and affection he put himself at my disposal at the time that I left his court."

Isanjo responded and said: "Sir, for much more than what may constitute serving you my will is ready, for I consider this journey an honor rather than as hardship or toil. And insofar as I am concerned, you can be sure, my lord, that in this matter as in everything else that may be an enhancement of your status,

I must involve myself even to the point of death. And therefore, lord, it is only necessary that the requisite documents be prepared, for my departure will be whenever you consider it good."

Amadis thanked him for it with great affection, recognizing from the willingness with which he answered him that good will should not be less appreciated than good deeds, because the latter derive from the former, which is their foundation. Then with this agreement Amadis wrote a letter to the king, which read as follows: "Noble King Tafinor of Bohemia, if at the time that I was at your court as a knight errant, I rendered you any service, I consider myself very well repaid for it, in view of the honors and benefits that I have received not only from you but from all your people. And if I now send a message to presume upon your kindness by asking for help in my need, it is while having in mind only your noble desires and great virtue which in that short time that I was at your court, I saw ready to pursue every just cause consistent with complete virtue and good conscience; and as for this knight who on my behalf will set forth in greater detail the situation which is developing, I ask for him, after sending word that credence be given him, that his mission have that effect which one sent to me on your behalf would have."

The letter having been finished and the credential dictated, Isanjo had a ship made ready, and departed at once as he was ordered; and one can very well say that his journey was well worth while in view of the troops that this good king sent to Amadis, as will be told later.

CHAPTER XCII

About how Gandalin talked with Mabilia and with Oriana, and what they directed him to tell Amadis.

The story relates that these messengers having left, as you have heard, Gandalin was in great distress because of his eagerness to go where his lord had commanded him, because he had ordered him not to leave until he had seen Amadis's cousin Mabilia. He went at once to Oriana's apartments, where no man could enter without her special command, and they were in that tower that you have already heard about, which was guarded and kept safe only by matrons and maidens. And on reaching the garden gate he told them to tell Mabilia that Gandalin was there, that he was leaving for Gaul and that he wanted to see her before departing. This having been made known to Mabilia, she told Oriana, and when she heard it she was quite pleased, and gave orders that he enter. And when he arrived where Oriana was, he knelt before her and kissed her hands. And then he went to Mabilia to tell her what his lord had commanded him. Mabilia said to Oriana so audibly that everybody heard it: "Lady, Gandalin is leaving for Gaul. See whether you have any messages for him to transmit to the queen and to my cousin Melicia."

Oriana told her that she was pleased to send word by him, and she came to where they were, apart from all the others, and said to him: "Alas, friend Gandalin! What do you think of my ill fortune? For the thing that I most desired in the world was to be in a place where I could never have your lord out of my sight; and to think that my luck should have placed me in his power under circumstances of such a nature, that I dare not see him without his honor and mine being greatly discredited! You may well believe that my wretched heart thereby suffers such great agitation that if you experienced it, you would have great pity for me. And in order that he may become aware of this, not only for his consolation but also in order to absolve me from blame, you will tell him to devise a way whereby he and all those knights may come to see me; and he will seek a means by which I may be able to talk with him in the presence of everyone without anyone's hearing what is going on. And this will be with your departure as a pretext."

Gandalin said to her: "Oh, lady! How right you are to keep in mind the remedy that this knight needs, for on this trip that we took I have had such a hard time in order to keep him alive! If I were able to tell it, much greater sorrow and anguish would your heart suffer than what it actually does; for it is certain, my lady, that the great exploits at arms that in those foreign lands he achieved and took part in, which were so great and so many as not only to be impossible for anyone else to imagine, let alone perform, did not put his life in one one-thousandth as much jeopardy as his memory of you and his being away from you placed him. And because speaking about this is quite futile since it is unending, there only remains to be said to you, lady, to have pity on him and comfort him; since according to what I have seen and truly believe, your life rests on his."

Oriana said to him: "My good friend, you may say that with great truth; for without him I would not be able or willing to live, for life to me would be much more painful and grievous than death. And let us not speak any more of this; but go at once to him and tell him my message."

"Thus it will be done and carried out, my lady."

With this he took leave of them and went to his lord. But before he did so Oriana commanded him in the presence of those ladies who were there not to leave until she had him given a letter for Queen Elisena and another for her daughter Melicia; and he said that he would obey, and he begged her to send him promptly on his way, because all the other messengers had already gone, and only he remained.

So he took his leave and went to Amadis, and told him everything that Oriana had said to him, and his reply, and how she sent a message to order him and all those lords to go and see her under some pretext, because she wished to speak to him. Amadis, when he heard this, remained for a while in thought, and then said to him: "Do you know how that can best be done? Speak with my cousin Agrajes and tell him that while you were speaking with Mabilia to ascertain whether she had some message to send to Gaul, she told you that it seemed to her that it would be well for him to contrive some way with all these lords who are here as to how they might go to see and encourage Oriana, because in view of the seriousness of the situation in which she was — so unusual for her — her seeing them and their encouragement were necessary for her, and besides whatever you may see that it will be necessary to tell her, and by this means what she commands will be done much better."

And then he said to him: "Tell me, how did my lady appear to you? Is she sad at seeing herself in this situation?"

Gandalin said to him: "Already, sir, you know her great good sense, and how in her can appear only the virtue of her noble heart; but certainly it seems to me that her appearance indicates sadness rather than happiness."

Amadis lifted his hands heavenward and said: "Oh, very powerful Lord! May it please you to give me an opportunity to be able to afford a remedy befitting the honor and service of this lady, and may my death or my life ensue as Fortune may direct."

Gandalin said to him: "Lord, do not be dismayed; for just as in other things, God has always done more for you and has furthered your honor more than that of any other knight, so in this which you have undertaken so rightly and justly He will do so."

So Gandalin left Amadis, and went to Agrajes and told him all that his lord commanded and what he saw was most befitting. Agrajes said to him: "My friend Gandalin, it is quite right that it be done just as my sister orders, and it will be carried out at once; for if until now it has not been done, the only reason is the knowledge of these knights that Oriana is disposed to live the most chaste life she can; and it will be well that we go and tell Amadis, my cousin."

And taking him with him, he went to Amadis's quarters and told him what Mabilia his sister had communicated to him, by

Gandalin. He answered, as if he had known nothing, that he would defer to her opinion. Then Agrajes talked with those knights and took measures so that without their knowing that Oriana wanted it, they should go to see and comfort her; he telling them that under such circumstances even the most courageous had need of consolation; which to a greater degree should be given to weak womankind. Everybody considered it a good idea and they were quite pleased with it, and they decided to see her the next afternoon. And so they did; for dressed in very elegant uniforms, and on their well-caparisoned palfreys, and with their swords all adorned with gold plating, they arrived at the apartment where Oriana was; and as all were young and handsome, they presented such a fine appearance that it was wondrous to behold. And Agrajes had already sent word to Oriana that he wished to see her, and she sent for Queen Sardamira and for Grasinda, and for all the princesses and matrons and maidens of high degree who were with her, so that they all might be assembled with her to receive them.

CHAPTER XCIII

How Amadis and Agrajes and all those knights of high rank who were with him went to see and comfort Oriana and those ladies who were with her, and concerning the things that happened.

Those knights, on arriving where Oriana was, all greeted her with great reverence and respect. And afterwards all the other ladies. And she received them with very good will as a lady who was of very noble quality and upbringing. Amadis told Don Cuadragante and Brian de Monjaste to go to Oriana, and he went to Mabilia, and Agrajes to where Olinda was with other ladies, who were matrons, and Don Florestan to Queen Sardamira, and Don Bruneo and Angriote to Grasinda, whom they greatly loved and esteemed, and the other knights to other matrons and maidens, each one to the lady he liked best and from whom he hoped to receive most honor and favor. Thus they were all talking with great enjoyment about matters most agreeable to them.

Then Mabilia took her cousin Amadis by the hand and went to one side of the room with him and said to him, so that all heard it: "Sir, have Gandalin summoned so that in your presence I may tell him what to say to the queen, my aunt, and to Melicia, my cousin, and for that you commission him, since with your message he is going to King Perion in Gaul."

Oriana, when she heard this, said: "Then I also wish him to take my messages to the queen and to her daughter along with yours."

Amadis had Gandalin summoned, who was in the garden with the others who were to travel, for he well knew that they were to call him. And as soon as he had come he went to the part of the room where Amadis and Mabilia were, and they talked with him a long while. And Mabilia said to Oriana: "Lady, I have concluded my business with Gandalin; see whether you have any word to send by him."

Oriana turned to Queen Sardamira and said to her: "Madam, entertain Don Cuadragante while I go send a message by that squire."

And taking Don Brian de Monjaste by the hand, she went where Mabilia was. And as she reached her, Don Brian de Monjaste said to her, as a man who was very gracious and courteous in everything befitting a knight: "Since I am chosen to be an emissary to your father, I do not wish to be present at a mission dispatched by maidens, for I fear, in view of how artful you ladies are and the wit that you display concerning everything that you desire, that you will involve me in more courtesy than befits what these knights have bidden me to say."

Oriana said to him, laughing very charmingly: "My Lord Don Brian, on that account I brought you here with me, in order that on seeing ours, you may temper somewhat your anger at my father; but I am afraid that your heart is not so subjugated by, or so fond of, the ways of women as to enable them in any wise to deflect or hinder your purpose."

That very beautiful princess said this to him in jest with such wonderful grace because Don Brian, although he was a young man and very handsome, was more given over to arms and palace matters involving knights than to achieving the amorous conquest or the captivation of any woman; although in matters in which women needed his defense and help he was wont to expose his person to every affront and danger in order to enable them to obtain their rights; and he loved them all, and he was very much loved by them all, but he loved no one woman in particular. Don Brian said to her: "My lady, just on that account I wish to betake myself away from you and your flattery, in order not to lose in a short time what I have won during a long period."

And so with everybody laughing, he left Oriana, and returned to where Grasinda was, whom he very much desired to know on account of what he had been told about her.

When Amadis saw himself before his lady, whom he loved so deeply, and whom he had not seen for such a long time, for he did not count seeing her at sea because it had been amid such great confusion and with so many people about, as the third Book has related, his whole flesh and his heart trembled with pleasure on beholding her great beauty, and in his opinion she was more animated than he had expected to find her; and he was so beside himself that he could not say or speak a word, so that Oriana, who did not take her eyes off him, recognized it at once, and went up to him, and took him by the hands under his mantle and squeezed them as a token of great love, just as if she had embraced him. And she said to him: "My true friend above all others, although my fortune has brought me the thing that I desired most in the world, which is to be in your possession, where my eyes as well as my heart might never be separated from you, my great misfortune has willed that it be in such wise that now more than ever it behooves me to avoid contacts with you, in order that this case, so outstanding and so publicized as it will be throughout the world, may be made known to all with that fame that is owed the eminence of my station and the virtue which this eminence obliges me to maintain; and that it may appear that you, my beloved friend, more for the sake of pursuing that nobility for which you always have striven in succoring the distressed and needy who lack help, always upholding right and justice; than that for any other reason you entered upon such a great and outstanding undertaking as this appears at present; because if the principal motive of our love affair were made public, both by those on your side and by your opponents, our love would be judged in diverse ways. And for this reason it is necessary that what with much anxiety and great effort up to now we have concealed, henceforth with those same efforts and even though they might be greater, we maintain. And let us consider our being free as a remedy, taking at any time we prefer what can best satisfy that for which our desires yearn; but let this be for when no other remedy can be found; and so let us endure until it pleases God to bring it to that end that we desire."

Amadis said to her: "Alas, lady, in Heaven's name, let no accounting or excuse be made to me for what concerns my serving you; for I was born into this world only to be yours and to serve you as long as I have this soul in my body; for in me there is no other desire or other good fortune foretold except to carry out whatever your wish may be. And what I, madam, beg as a reward for my deadly suffering and desires is only that there never be absent from your memory the concern to command me in whatever I may be of service to you; for this will be a large share of the remedy and relief that befits my impassioned heart."

And when Amadis was saying this, Oriana was watching him, and she saw the tears fall from his eyes, so that they were wetting his whole face; and she said to him: "My good friend, I agree with what you say; and it is not new for me to believe that in everything you would do my will, so how I would like to embrace and satisfy yours, that Lord knows from whom nothing is hidden; but it is necessary, as I have said, that for the present restraint be exercised. And in the meantime while He is remedying it, if you desire my love with that insistence with which you have always wanted it, I beg of you that the anxieties and fatigues of your heart be put aside by you; for there can no longer be much delay before in one way or another our secret becomes known, and with peace or with war we are united in the way that we have desired for such a long time. And because we have talked a long while, I wish to return to those knights so that they may not have any suspicion. And you, sir, dry those tears from your eyes as secretly as possible, and stay with Mabilia, for she will tell you some things that you, my lord, do not know — nor until now have I had the opportunity to tell you them — with which your heart will experience much pleasure and happiness."

Then she ordered Don Cuadragante and Don Brian de Monjaste summoned, and with them she returned to where she had been previously. Amadis remained with Mabilia, and there she told him all about Esplandian, how he was his and Oriana's son and all the things that had happened at his birth as well as during his rearing, and how the maid of Denmark and Durin, her brother, while carrying him to be reared at Miraflores, lost him, and the lioness seized him, and the rearing that the hermit gave him. She related it all to him in great detail, leaving out nothing, just as the third Book of this great story narrates it. When Amadis heard this, he was very happy over it, for he could not have been more so; and after that great thrill of joy that his heart felt was over, he said to her: "My lady and good cousin, know you that when I was with this very noble matron Grasinda at the time when those knights Angriote de Estravaus and Don Bruneo arrived there by chance, Angriote told me about Esplandian; but he was not able to tell me whose son he was; and then I remembered the letter that you sent to me on this island by my foster father Gandales, in which you informed me that I had increased in family, and I thought, in view of the time that you wrote me, which was the time Angriote mentioned to me, and since it was not known from where or whose son that youth was, that it could be my and Oriana's son; but this was conjecture, and not with any other assurance. But now that I know it for certain, do believe, lady and beloved cousin, that I am happier about it than if I had been made lord of half the world. And this I do not say on account of the youth's being to such an extent so extraordinary, but because he is the son of such a mother; for just as God distinguished her and set her apart in beauty, as well as in all the other fine qualities that a good lady ought to have, from all other women born into this world, so He willed that the things that proceed from her both of sweetness and of bitterness be superlative and set apart from others; for I, as one who tests and senses it through experience, can very well say so. Oh lady cousin, if only I were able to tell you the anguish and great affliction that my wretched heart has undergone during this time that you have not seen me! For without doubt you can believe that in comparison with them, all the dangers and affronts that I experienced in those foreign lands, must be deemed only the fear and fright that one has in dreams, or that which happens in fact and in truth! And God being willing to have pity on me, sought to bring me to the time when I might save her from a great affront and myself from the most grievous death that ever a knight died; whence already my heart, which nowhere up to this hour was finding rest or repose, is secure because the outcome of this business can be only to win her completely to the satisfaction of her desires and mine, or lose my life, whereby all temporal things come to an end for me. And since my good fortune has wished to aid and bring relief to my anxieties, it is quite right that all of us be engaged in remedying hers, for as a person who has never seen herself in such straits, nor realized what is befalling her, she will not, as I see it, be exempt from very great anxieties; and you, my lady, who in times past have been the greatest protector of her life, at this time counsel her and give her courage, setting forth to her that neither in the sight of God nor that of her father is she responsible for what has happened nor can she rightly be blamed by any person in the world. Then if she fears the great power of her father together with that of the Emperor of Rome, you may, my lady, tell her how so many of us and of such competence are in her service that if I did not fear her anger, I would seek them out in their own realms; and this she may very well be able to see as soon as Don Cuadragante and Don Brian de Monjaste come back from this trip that they are taking to see her father, from which we shall ascertain whether he wishes peace or we have war. And meanwhile, keep me advised concerning what she enjoys most and is most helpful to her, so that it may be carried out according to her wishes."

Mabilia said to him: "My lord, if I tried to tell you what I have endured since you left this land, in order to comfort and relieve her anguish and sorrows, especially after the Romans came to her father's court, I would never be through. And therefore, and because you understand completely the great love she has for you, I shall cease talking to you about it. And what you, my lord, command, I continue to carry out, although she has become so much more discreet that not only in matters familiar to her because of her upbringing — conditioned by the nature and weakness of women — but also of all the other things that to us women are very new and strange, she is cognizant and perceptive with that spirit and courage necessary to her royal rank; and if it is not so with what pertains to you, for that renders her beside herself, in everything else she has what it takes to console the whole world. And of the things in which she will take pleasure, you will be kept informed by me."

With this they concluded their conversation, and returned to where Oriana was. Gandalin bade them farewell, and went and put out to sea in order to go to Gaul. We shall tell about him in due course. After these knights had remained quite a while with Princess Oriana and those ladies who were with her talking about many very pleasant subjects, and giving them great encouragement as a group, they took leave of them and returned to their own quarters, where very pleasurably and happily they were dwelling, having in great abundance everything they needed, and seeing all the marvels of that island — the like of which could not have been seen in any other part of the world — designed and set up by that great sage Apolidon, who had left them there while he was its lord.

But now the story will cease to speak of them in order to tell about King Lisuarte, who knew nothing of all this.

CHAPTER XCIV

How the news of this annihilation of the Romans and the rescue of Oriana reached King Lisuarte, and what he did about it.

On the day that he handed his daughter over to the Romans, King Lisuarte accompanied her for a short distance out of town, and with much paternal commiseration offering her consolation to some extent, and at other times with excessive passion dashing her hopes that his resolve could be altered in any way; but the two approaches afforded scant comfort and help, and her sobs and laments were so great that there was not a man in the world that she would not have moved to pity for her. And although the king her father had been in that affair very harsh and very cruel, he could not deny that paternal love that he owed to his very exhausted daughter, and involuntarily the tears came to his eyes; and without saying any more to her, he turned away much sadder than his face revealed; and first he spoke with Salustanquidio and with Brondajel de Roca, insistently charging them to take good care of her. And he returned to his palace, where he found great weeping by men as well as women on account of Oriana's departure, for which the very peremptory order that was given by him to them did not suffice as a remedy, because this princess was more cherished and more beloved by everyone than was any other person in Great Britain.

The king glanced about the palace and did not see any knight he was wont to see, except Brandoyvas, who told him that the queen was in her chamber weeping with great sorrow. He went to her, and did not find in her apartment any of the ladies and princesses and other maidens by whom she was usually very well attended. And as he saw everything so deserted and changed from what it usually was with respect to knights as well as women, and those who were there with such great sadness, he had such great concern that his heart was shrouded in darkest gloom, so that for a while he did not speak. And he entered the room where the queen was, and when she saw him enter, senseless she fell in a faint on a dais. The king lifted her up and embraced her, holding her in his arms until she revived, and as he saw her now in better condition and more composed, he said to her: "Lady, it does not befit your prudence and virtue to show such weakness on account of any adversity, much less for this situation in which so much honor and advantage is received; and if you wish to hold my love and favor, let it cease so that this be the last of it, for your daughter is not going so bereft that she cannot be deemed the greatest princess that there ever was in her family."

The queen could not make any reply to him, but just as she was, she let herself fall face downward on a bed, sighing out of the great anguish of her heart.

The king left her and returned to his palace, where he found no one with whom to talk except King Arban of North Wales and Don Grumedan, who showed in their gestures and faces the sadness that they had in their hearts; and although the king was very discreet and patient, and knew how to conceal everything better than anyone else, he could not control himself so well as not to reveal clearly in his gestures and speech the grief that he had in secret. And immediately he thought that it would be a good idea to betake himself away to the forest with his huntsmen until time had a chance to heal what for the present had no good remedy. And he gave orders to King Arban to have tents brought to the forest and all the equipment needed for the chase, because he wanted to go hunting the next morning without delay. And thus it was done; for that night he did not seek to sleep in the queen's chamber so as not to occasion more suffering for her than she had endured already. And next day after hearing mass, he went on his hunt, on which, since he found himself alone, his sadness and meditation rendered him much more disturbed, so that nowhere did he find rest; for as this man was a king so noble, so gracious, desirous of possessing the best knights that he could have, as already he had had them, and with them had come to him all the honors and good fortune and luck commensurate with his desires, and now in such a short space of time to see everything changed and so much to the contrary of that to which he was accustomed and which his nature desired, his discretion and strong heart did not have enough strength to prevent his being subjected many times to great anguish. But as often happens, when Fortune begins to order her changes, she is not content with the anger that men feel of their own volition, but she with great cruelty desiring to augment and increase it, pursuant to her habit, which is not to be consistent in anything, there where this king was, sought to demonstrate it; so that forgetting that sorrow, which in her opinion he had acquired for such slight cause and so willingly, he might suffer from another harsher blow of which he was unaware; for some of the Romans who had fled from the Firm Island having come, and knowing that the king was there, they went to him and told him all that had happened to them — just as the story has related it, for nothing was omitted — as men who had been present at all of it.

When the king heard this, although his grief was very great, since it was for a happening to which he was so unaccustomed and which concerned him so much, with a good countenance, not showing any sorrow, after the manner of kings, he said to them: "Friends, I am very sorry about the death of Salustanquidio and your loss, for with regard to what concerns me, I am accustomed to receiving affronts and giving them to others. And do not depart from my court, for I shall order that you be given help concerning everything that you need."

They kissed his hands and asked him as a boon to remember the other men, their companions, and those lords who were taken prisoner with them. He said to them: "Friends, I wish you to have no fear, for the situation will be remedied as befits your lord's honor and my own."

And he ordered them to go to the town, where the queen was, and that they should say nothing about that matter until he came; and they did as he bade them. The king went hunting for three days, filled with an anxiety that you can understand; and then he returned to where the queen was, and in the opinion of everybody with a happy countenance, although at heart he felt as he should feel in such a situation. And after dismounting he went to the queen's chamber. And as she was one of the noble and wise women of the world, in order not to incite him to more outbursts of anger, seeing that thereby her desire was furthered but little, she pretended to him that her grief was greatly alleviated. So the king on his arrival gave orders for everyone to leave the room, and sitting down with her on her dais, he said to her: "In matters of little importance that come by chance, people have some right and freedom to display anger and melancholy, because just as they arise from a trivial cause, so with a small remedy they can be easily obviated. But in those very grave situations that are quite distressing, especially in matters of honor, it is quite the contrary, because for situations of this kind the gravity will be slight and will so appear, and the harsh measures and vengeance very great. And, to be specific, you, queen, have greatly missed your daughter, as is the way of mothers, and in this matter you have displayed much sorrow, just as over such marriages many other people are wont to do. But I am on record as saying that in a short time it would have been forgotten; but what ensues from this is such that without excessive anger being evinced, with great diligence and courage amends for the situation are to be sought. Know you then that the Romans who carried away your daughter, with all their fleet have been crushingly defeated and taken prisoner, and many of them killed along with their prince Salustanquidio, and she with all her ladies and maidens in waiting taken by Amadis and the knights who are on the Firm Island, where they hold her very victoriously and with great pleasure; so that it may well be said that such a stupendous thing as this has never before happened within the memory of man. And therefore it is necessary that you with great discretion, as a woman, and I with great courage as a king and knight, apply the remedy that rather by action than by superfluous regrets befits your decorum and my honor."

This having been heard by the queen, she remained silent a while without making any reply. And as she was one of the matrons who, more than anyone else in the world, loved her husband, she thought to herself that in a matter such as this, and with such men, it was more necessary to impose harmony than to enkindle discord; and she said: "Sire, although you take deeply to heart what has happened and what you know concerning your daughter, if you judge it by harking back to that time when you were a knight errant, you will think, in view of the lamentations and grief of Oriana and all her maidens, and the great length of time that they persisted in it, whence cause was given for its being widely publicized, that since it was a subject of conversation for everyone, although it wasn't a very great act of violence, one should not be surprised that those knights, as men who have no other life style except to succor matrons and maidens when they receive some wrong and injury, should have dared to do what they have done. And although, sire, she was your daughter, you already have handed her over to those who on behalf of the Emperor came for her; and the violence or injury concerns him more than you, and now at the outset it ought to be taken with the kind of moderation whereby you may not seem to be the object of this affront, for if it is done otherwise, it will be hard to conceal the fact."

The king said to her: "Now, lady, remember, as I have said, what befits your own decorum, for in what concerns me, with the help of God the amends will be taken that He requires for the eminence of your status and mine."

Thereupon he left her and went away to his palace. And he ordered King Arban of North Wales summoned and Don Grumedan, and Guilan the Pensive, who was already recovering from his illness. And withdrawing with them, he told them the whole business about his daughter, and about his interview with the queen, because these three were the knights, out of all those of his kingdom, in whom he had most trust. And he begged and commanded them to think earnestly about it and to tell him their opinions, so that he might take measures most befitting his honor, and that for the moment, without more deliberation, he did not wish them to make any reply to him.

Thus the king remained deliberating for several days concerning what he ought to do. The queen remained greatly concerned and distressed on seeing the intransigency of the king her husband and his maintenance of it against those who she knew would rather lose their lives than one jot of their honor, which likewise she expected of the king. So that no affronts that might have come to him, however great they were, as this story has told you, did she consider as amounting to anything in comparison with this one.

Then while she was in her chamber mentally reviewing many endless schemes for achieving a remedy for such a rupture, a maiden entered who told her that Durin, the brother of the maid of Denmark, had arrived there from the Firm Island, and that he wished to speak with her. The queen gave orders for him to enter, and he knelt and kissed her hands, and gave her a letter from Oriana, her daughter, for it appeared that when Oriana saw the determination of the knights of the Firm Island, which was to send Don Cuadragante and Brian de Monjaste to the king her father with the message that you have already heard, she decided that it would be well, in order to facilitate their mission, that before they had arrived at the court of the king her father, to write and send a letter to the queen her mother by this Durin; and so she did. Then when the queen received the letter, tears came to her eyes out of longing for her daughter, and because she could not recover her unless God through His mercy should help, without great danger and affront to the king her lord. And so she remained silent for a while, for she could not say anything to Durin, and before she questioned him further, she opened the letter to read it, and it read as follows:

CHAPTER XCV

CONCERNING THE LETTER THAT PRINCESS ORIANA SENT TO QUEEN BRISENA, HER MOTHER, FROM THE FIRM ISLAND, WHERE SHE WAS.

"Most mighty Queen Brisena, my lady mother, I, sad and unfortunate Oriana, your daughter, with great humility, beg to kiss your feet and hands. My good lady, you already know how my adverse fortune, wishing to be more adverse and inimical to me than to any other woman there ever was or ever will be, without my deserving it brought it about that I was banished from your presence and dominion with such great cruelty by the king, my lord and father, and with so much pain and anguish for my sad heart that I myself wonder how it can maintain life for a single day. For my great ill fortune not content with what happened first, on seeing how I was disposed to fulfill in cruel death the obedience that rightly or otherwise I owe to the king, my father, rather than disobey his command, has sought to give me a remedy much more cruel for me than the suffering and sad life that in the first instance I expected to have; because if I died, it would be merely the death of a sad maiden, for whom in view of her great misfortune, death would be much more befitting and pleasant than life. But from what is now expected, if, after God, you, lady, taking pity on me, do not achieve a remedy, not only I but also many other people who have no guilt, with very cruel and harsh deaths will end their lives. And the cause of it is that, either by permission of God, who knows the great injustice and injury that is being done me, or because my ill fortune, as I have said, has willed it, the knights who were on the Firm Island destroyed the fleet of the Romans with wholesale death and imprisonment for those who sought to defend themselves. I was taken with all my matrons and maidens and carried to that same island, where they hold me, and I am treated with as much reverence and decorum as if I were in your royal court. And because they are sending to the king, my lord and father, certain knights with peace as an objective if some way for it were proposed in what relates to me, I decided that before they arrived there to write this letter, by means of which and on account of the many tears that with it were shed, and without it, are being shed, I beg your great nobility and virtue to ask the king my father to have pity and compassion for me, by having higher regard for the service of God than for the perishable glory and honor of this world, and that he not seek to put in jeopardy the high estate in which, with great favor until now, fickle Fortune has placed him here; for he, better than anyone else, knows the great violence and injustice that, without my deserving it, has been done me."

Having finished reading the letter, the queen gave orders to Durin not to leave without her reply, because it was necessary to speak first with the king. And he said that he would do just as she commanded, and he told her that all the princesses and ladies and maidens who were with their lady sent their respectful regards to her. The queen sent to request the king to come alone to her chamber because she wanted to speak with him; and he did so. And when they were alone in the room, the queen knelt before him weeping, and said to him: "Lord, read this letter that your daughter Oriana has sent to me, and have pity on her and on me."

The king raised her by the hands, and took the letter and read it, and in order to give her some satisfaction said to her: "Queen, since Oriana writes here that those knights are being sent to me, it may possibly be a mission such that with it the dishonor received may receive amends; and if it be not so, consider that it is better that my honor be upheld with some danger than that my reputation be discredited without it."

And begging her earnestly that, leaving everything to God, in whose hand and according to whose will it was, she cease to agonize, he left her forthwith and returned to his palace. The queen ordered Durin summoned and said to him: "Friend Durin, go and tell my daughter that until those knights come, as she writes in her letter, and the mission that they bring be known, there is nothing that I can reply to her, nor is the king her father able to make up his mind; and that once they have arrived, if a way to harmony can be found, I shall strive for it with all my might. And give her my love, and the same to all her ladies and maidens, and tell her that it is now time for her to show of what stuff she is made, the most important element in her reputation, for without this, she would have nothing valuable or estimable left; and the other element by enduring the anguish and sorrows as a person of such high degree; for just as God gives estates and great dominions to people, so their anguish and cares are very different in degree from those of persons who are of lowest social status; and that I entrust her to God, that He may protect her and bring her back with great honor into my keeping."

Durin kissed her hands and started out on his return trip; of which no more will be said, because from this journey he brought back no word of agreement, nor did Oriana as a result of the reply of the queen, her mother, remain hopeful of what she desired.

The story relates that when King Lisuarte one day was in his palace about to dine with his nobles, a squire entered the door and gave the king a letter, which was one of accreditation; and the king took it, and on reading it said to him: "Friend, what do you want and whose man are you?"

"Sire," said he, "I am from Don Cuadragante of Ireland, for I come to you with his message."

"Then say what you wish," said the king, "for I shall listen to you gladly."

The squire said: "Sire, Don Cuadragante and Brian de Monjaste have arrived in your kingdom from the Firm Island with a message from Amadis of Gaul and the princes and knights who are with him. And before they entered your court they wished you to know about it; because, if they can come before you under a safe conduct, they will state to you their mission; and if not, they will proclaim it broadcast through the land and return to where they came from. Therefore, sire, give me your reply as to what your pleasure will be, so that they not tarry."

This having been heard by the king, he remained for a while without saying anything, which every great lord ought to do in order to afford himself an opportunity for reflection. And considering that from enemy missions there always results more advantage than disadvantage, because if what they bring is helpful, great lords accept it; and if to the contrary, they derive important information. And also because to refuse to hear one's opponents shows scant tolerance, he said to the squire: "Friend, tell those knights that with complete security while they are in my kingdom, they can come to my court, and that I will listen to all that they wish to say to me."

With this the messenger returned. The king's reply now having been ascertained, Don Cuadragante and Brian de Monjaste left the ship, clad in very splendid armor, and on the third day they reached the town when the king had just finished dining. And as they went through the streets, all observed them closely, for they were well known; and people said to one another: "Cursed be the traitors who with their false meddling caused our lord, the king, to lose such knights and many others of great valor!"

But others, who knew more about how it had all happened, attributed all the blame to the king, who chose to subordinate his prudence to envious scandalmongers. Thus they went through the town until they arrived at the palace; and having entered the courtyard, they dismounted from their horses and entered where the king was, and they greeted him very courteously, and he received them with good will. And Don Cuadragante said to him: "It is fitting that great princes hear with all passion renounced and put aside the messengers who come to them because if the mission that they bring to them satisfies them they ought to be very glad to have received it graciously; and if to the contrary, they ought to apply the remedy with strong wills and stout hearts rather than with peevish responses. And it is required of messengers to say with decorum what is entrusted to them, without fear of any danger that may come to them from so doing. Our coming to you, King Lisuarte, is by order and request of Amadis of Gaul and many other great knights who are on the Firm Island, who make known to you that while traveling through foreign lands seeking dangerous adventures, taking the just ones upon themselves and punishing the unjust, just as the greatness of their virtue and strong hearts require, they learned from many people how you, more for the sake of following your own whim rather than reason and justice, not heeding the great admonishments of the grandees of your realm or the many tears of humbler folk, or remembering in good conscience what is owed to God, sought to disinherit your daughter Oriana, successor to your realm after your life is over, in favor of your younger daughter; and Oriana amid much weeping and very disconsolate grief, without any pity you handed over to the Romans, giving her as wife to the Emperor of Rome against all right and without consent, not only without hers but that of all your subjects. And as such matters as these stand out in the sight of God, and He is the one to remedy them, He has been willing to permit, this matter having become known to us, that we should apply the remedy to a situation in which such great wrong was being done to His service. And so our action was taken, not with the wish or intention to do harm, but to do away with great unjust violence, from which intention we could not desist without great shame, for the Romans who were carrying her off having been overcome, she was taken by us and carried, with the great respect and reverence that befitted her nobility and high estate, to the Firm Island, where we have left her accompanied by many noble ladies and great knights. And because our purpose was only to serve God and uphold the right, those lords and great knights decided to request of you that in what relates to that noble princess, you be willing to provide some way whereby, stopping the great injury and well-recognized violence, she may be reinstated in your affection with the firmness that is necessary to truth and good conscience. And if perchance you, king, feel some resentment at us, let it await the proper time, for it would not be right to associate what is true concerning that princess with what is doubtful with regard to us."

The king, after Don Cuadragante had finished his speech, replied in this wise: "Knights, because excessive words and harsh replies do not entail virtue, or make weak hearts strong, my reply will be brief and with more patience than your quest deserves. You have carried out what, in your judgment, is most satisfying to your honor, with more excessive arrogance than extraordinary force, because it ought not to be accounted great glory to waylay and conquer those who are traveling unsuspectingly in complete security, not bearing in mind that since I am God's lieutenant, to

Him and to no one else, am I obliged to give an accounting of what is done by me. And after the satisfaction for this is exacted, one will be able to speak about the action that is requested by you; and because everything else will be fruitless, any argument is unnecessary."

Don Brian de Monjaste said to him: "Nor for us is anything else necessary except that, since now we know your will and the accounting that we owe to God for what has taken place, both the parties to the dispute put into execution what most befits their honor."

And having been dismissed by the king, they mounted their horses and rode away from the palace; and Don Grumedan with them, whom the king ordered to guard them until they left the town. When Don Grumedan saw himself with them away from the presence of the king, he said to them: "My good lords, I regret very much what I see, for I, knowing the great prudence of the king and the nobility of Amadis and of all of you, and the many friends that you have here, had great hope that this irksome matter would have some good outcome; and it seems to me that since quite the contrary is true, now more than ever I see it endangered, until our Lord be pleased to impose that harmony that is needed. Therefore I earnestly beg you to tell me how Amadis fares at such a time on the Firm Island, for it has been a long while since any news of him has been had, although many of his friends have searched for him with great zeal through foreign lands."

Don Brian de Monjaste said to him: "My lord Don Grumedan, about what you say of the king and of us, since you deem him so wise, it will not be necessary to give you a very long commentary, except that the great violence that the king did his daughter is well known, as is the reason why we were obliged to take her; and certainly, leaving aside his anger and ours, we would have been pleased if some compromise had been arrived at in what concerns Princess Oriana and him. But since he is still pleased to proceed against us with great severity, more so than with a just cause, he will see that extricating himself from the situation will be harder for him than his initial involvement appears to him to be. And as for what, my good lord, you ask concerning Amadis, you shall learn that until he went forth from this court, calling himself the Greek Knight — and took with him that matron on account of whom the Romans were defeated and the maidens' coronet won — none of us had ever learned any news about him."

"Holy Mary, save us!" said Don Grumedan. "What are you telling me? Is it true that the Greek Knight who came here was Amadis?"

"It is true beyond any doubt," said Don Brian.

"Now I tell you," said Don Grumedan, "that I consider myself a man of poor discernment, for I really should have thought that a knight who performed such rare deeds at arms against all the others must have been none other than he. Now I ask you, the two knights whom he left here to help me in the battle that I had scheduled with the Romans, who were they?"

Don Brian said to him, laughing: "Your friends Angriote de Estravaus and Don Bruneo de Bonamar."

"Thank God," said he, "for if I had recognized them I would not have been so fearful concerning my combat as I was; and now I know that I won in it very little glory, since with such helpers I would not have rated very highly the defeat of twice their number."

"So help me God!" said Don Cuadragante, "I believe that if it had been judged by your courage, you alone would have been enough for them."

"Sir," said Don Grumedan, "whatever I may be, I have a great deal of esteem and good will for you all, if only it should please God to give some good ending for this matter about which you come."

Thus they continued to talk until they left the town and for a bit beyond. And when Don Grumedan was about to bid them farewell, they saw coming from hunting the handsome youth Esplandian and Ambor, son of Angriote de Estravaus, with him; and Esplandian was carrying a hawk, and was riding a very beautiful and richly caparisoned palfrey that Queen Brisena had given him. And he was wearing fine garb, for on account of his very unusual good looks as well as because of what Urganda the Unknown had written about him to King Lisuarte, as the third Book of this story relates in greater detail, the king and the queen ordered him to be completely provided with whatever he needed.

And when he came up to where they were, he greeted them, and they him. And Brian de Monjaste asked Don Grumedan who that very handsome youth was, and he said to him: "My lord, he is called Esplandian, and was reared under extraordinary circumstances, and very great things concerning his future Urganda predicted to the king in a letter."

"So help me God," said Don Cuadragante. "There on the Firm Island we have heard much about this youth; and it will be well for you to call him, and we shall listen to what he says."

Then Don Grumedan called him, for he had already passed by, and said: "Good youth, turn back, and you shall send regards to the Greek Knight, who treated you so courteously in giving you the Romans that he was about to kill."

Then Esplandian returned and said: "My lord, I would be very happy to know where I could send them to that very noble knight, as you request and he deserves."

"These knights are going to where he is," said Don Grumedan.

"He tells you the truth," said Don Cuadragante; "for we shall bear your message to the one who used to call himself the Greek Knight, and who now is called Amadis."

"What, sirs! Is this the Amadis of whose great deeds of chivalry everyone speaks so highly and who is so outstanding among all?"

"Yes, certainly," said Don Cuadragante, "this is he."

"I tell you truly," said Esplandian, "one ought to value highly his great valor, since so famous is he among so many good knights. And the envy people have of him does not embolden many to become his equal; since no less ought he to be praised for his great circumspection and courtesy; for although I caught him in great fury and anger, he did not fail because of this to do me great honor, for he gave me those knights whom he had overcome, from whom he had received great provocation, for which I am very grateful to him. And may it please God to bring me to a time that with as much honor as he did me, I may repay him for it to that same extent."

Those knights were very happy with what they heard him say, and they considered his very handsome looks quite unusual, as well as what Don Grumedan had told them about him, and especially, the grace and discretion with which he spoke with them. And Don Brian de Monjaste said to him: "Good youth, may God make you a good man just as he has made you handsome."

"Many thanks," said he, "for what you say to me; but if He has some blessing in store for me, I should like it now in order to serve the king, my lord, who has so great a need of the service of his subjects. And, sirs, God be with you; for it has been quite a while since I left the town."

And Don Grumedan took leave of them, and went with him, and the other two went and boarded their ship to return to the Firm Island. But now the story ceases to speak of them, and returns to King Lisuarte.

CHAPTER XCVI

About how King Lisuarte asked King Arban of North Wales and Guilan the Pensive for advice, and what they replied to him.

After those knights left King Lisuarte he gave orders to summon King Arban of North Wales, and Don Grumedan and Guilan the Pensive, and he said to them: "Friends, you already know the situation in which I am placed by these knights from the Firm Island, and the great discredit that I have received from them; and certainly, if I did not obtain satisfaction in such a way that that great pride that they have might be broken, I would not consider myself a king, nor would I think that anyone else would consider me as such. And in order to give that accounting of myself that prudent men should give, which is to conduct their affairs with much counseling and deliberation, I wish, as I had said to you, that you tell me your opinion, so that concerning the matter I may decide what best serves my interest."

King Arban, who was a good knight and very prudent, and who was a great supporter of the king's honor, said to him: "Lord, these knights and I have reflected and discussed a great deal, as you have commanded us to do, in order to give you the best advice that our judgment may achieve; and we find that, since it is your will not to come to any agreement with those knights, one should seek with great diligence and much discretion the preparation by which they may be brought to book and their madness restrained; for we, sire, on the one hand, see that the knights who are on the Firm Island are many and very powerful at arms, as you know, because already, through the goodness of God, all of them were in your service for a long time. And besides their own strength and valor, we are assured that they have sent to many places for great assistance, which we believe they will find, because they are of noble lineage, being sons and brothers of kings and of other great men, and by their own efforts they have won many other friends. And so when forces from many places come, a great host is quickly assembled. And on the other hand, sire, we see your house and court greatly stripped of knights, more than at any time that we remember, and the greatness of your estate has led to involving you in many enmities which now will reveal their ill-will towards you, for many infamies of this kind are wont to be revealed by emergencies that in prosperity are suspended and silenced. And for these reasons as well as for many others that could be mentioned, it would be well that your servants and friends be called upon and that it be ascertained of what value they are to you; and especially the Emperor of Rome, whom this concerns more than you, as the queen has said to you. And once the strength available to you has been determined, sire, you can be accordingly harsh, or take the course it affords you."

The king considered himself well advised and said that was the way he wished to do it. And he ordered Don Guilan to assume the responsibility of being his messenger to the emperor, for such a mission befitted such a knight as he. He answered: "Sire, in this and much more my will stands ready to serve you. And may it please God through His mercy that just as I desire, it may be carried out to the enhancement of your honor and high estate; and may its dispatch be quick, for your order will be executed at once."

The king said to him: "With you, only a message of accreditation will be necessary, and it is this: that you tell the emperor that he of his own free will sent to me Salustanquidio and Brondajel of Roca, his chief majordomo, along with a sufficiency of other knights, to ask for my daughter Oriana's hand in marriage; that in order to satisfy him and to acquire him as a relative, against the wishes of all of my subjects, who considered her their future liege lady in the event of my death, I arranged to send her to him; although with great pity on my part, and much grief and anguish on her mother's at seeing her taken away from us into lands so foreign; and that she having been received by your men along with her ladies and maidens, and they having sailed on the sea beyond the limits of my kingdom, Amadis of Gaul with other knights his friends sallied forth with another fleet from the Firm Island, and that all the emperor's forces having been annihilated and Salustanquidio killed, my daughter was taken by them along with all those men who remained alive, and carried away to the same island, where they hold her, and that they have sent their messengers to me, by whom they offer me some agreements; but that I, recognizing that this affair concerns him more than me, have not wanted to come to any agreement with them until I inform him concerning what has happened; and that he be advised that what I would be most satisfied with, is that there where they hold her they be besieged by us in such fashion that we give the whole world to understand that we as great princes have punished them as thieves and pirates for this very great insult that concerns us so greatly. And beyond this, tell him whatever you think best in this matter; and if he is in agreement, tell him to take action at once, because injuries always grow when the amends that should be made for them are delayed."

Don Guilan said to him: "Sire, all will be done as you command, and may it please God that my journey have the effect embodied in my desire to serve you."

And taking a letter certifying to his credibility, he departed and put out to sea; and what he accomplished the story will tell later.

This done, the king ordered Brandoyvas summoned and commanded him to go to Don Galvanes in the Island of Mongaza so that the latter might come to him at once with all the forces of the island; and he commanded Brandoyvas to go from there to King Cildadan in Ireland and tell him likewise, and to contrive that he come with the largest war-waging force that he could assemble to wherever he ascertained King Lisuarte to be. And likewise he commanded Filispinel to go to Gasquilan, King of Suesa, and tell him the situation in which he was; and that since he was such a famous knight and took such delight in striving to accomplish heroic feats, now he had the opportunity to demonstrate the strength and daring of his heart. And thus he sent word to many others of his friends, allies and servants, and to his entire realm to be prepared for action by the time that these messengers returned. And he gave orders to look everywhere for many horses and arms in order to put as many troops on horseback as he could.

But now we shall drop this subject, for nothing more will be said about it until the proper time, in order to tell what Arcalaus the Enchanter did. The story relates that when Arcalaus the Enchanter was in his castle, hoping always to perform some evil deed, according to his custom and that of evil men, there came to him the sensational news of the discord and open rupture that existed between King Lisuarte and Amadis; and whether from it he took pleasure, it is needless to say, for these were the two men whom he hated most in the world, and never from his thoughts and concern did he exclude reflection on how he might be the cause of their destruction. And he thought that in such a situation as this he might be able to bring it about that he could do them harm, for he could not find it in his heart to aid either one of them. And as in all misdeeds he was very subtle, he decided to try to assemble another, third army, not only of the enemies of King Lisuarte, but also of Amadis's, and to place them in a location such that if the adversaries had a battle, very easily those on his side would be able to overcome and destroy those who survived. And with this resolve and desire he mounted his horse, taking with him the servants he needed, and went his way, both by land and by sea, to King Arabigo, who had emerged so battered from the battle that he and the other six kings his companions had with King Lisuarte, as the third Book of this story relates, because of the great harm and disgrace that he had received from Amadis and his relatives. And when Arcalaus arrived, he said to him: "Oh, King Arabigo! if you have that courage and strength that is requisite for the greatness of your royal estate, and that discretion which you must have to govern it, that contrary Fortune which in times past was so unfriendly to you, with much repentance for it wishes to make such amends that with a double victory, the great discrediting of your honor may be expunged, a victory for which, if you are wise, you will recognize that the means is in your hands. You, King, shall know that while I was in my castle greatly preoccupied in pondering your defeat and in seeking a way whereby it might be offset — because from the enhancement of your royal estate there accrues to me, as your servant, a very great benefit — I learned through a very reliable report that your great enemies and mine, King Lisuarte and Amadis of Gaul, are arrayed against each other in complete and extreme rupture, and for a reason of such nature that no remedy or solution is expected nor can there be any, except great battling and strife culminating in the utter defeat of one of them, and perchance of both. And if you are willing to take my advice, it is certain that not only will it be a reparation for the defeat that you had in the past because of me, but also your estate will be enhanced by many more seigniories, and afterwards by all those of us who wish to serve you."

King Arabigo, when he heard this, and saw Arcalaus arriving from such distant lands and in such haste, said: "Friend Arcalaus, the great length of your journey and the fatigue of your person impel me to consider your coming important and to believe all that you may say to me; and I wish that what you are saying be explained to me in detail because never on account of adverse times will my wish cease to be attentive to what befits my high rank."

Then Arcalaus said to him: "You shall know, King, that the Emperor of Rome, being desirous of taking a wife, sent word to King Lisuarte that he should give him his daughter Oriana; and the king on beholding his high rank, although this princess is his rightful heiress to Great Britain, was disposed to give her to him, and handed her over to a first cousin of that same emperor, called Salustanquidio, a very powerful prince. And as he was transporting her by sea with a great company of Romans, Amadis of Gaul with many knights who are his friends intercepted them. And this prince having been killed and his entire fleet destroyed, and many others of those whom they found in it taken prisoner or killed, Oriana was abducted, and taken in charge and carried to the Firm Island, where they hold her. The discredit that comes from this to King Lisuarte and to the emperor you can already recognize. And I want you to know that this Amadis of whom I speak is one of the knights wearing the serpent device who opposed you and the other six kings who were with you in the great battle that you had with King Lisuarte. And this man was the one who wore the golden helmet; and that by virtue of his great prowess and courage, victory was snatched from your hands. So that on account of what I am telling you about, King Lisuarte on the one hand and Amadis on the other are summoning as many troops as they can; whence rightly it can and should be adduced that the emperor himself, in order to avenge the great grief of his heart and the derogation of his honor, will come in person; so thereby you can judge if there is a battle, what harm from it can befall them. And if you wish to call your companies, I shall give you as a helper Barsinan, lord of Sansuenia, son of the other Barsinan whom King Lisuarte caused to be executed in London; and I shall give you moreover the whole great group of relatives of the good knight Dardan the Haughty, whom Amadis slew at Windsor, which will be a great company of very good knights. And likewise I shall have the King of the Deep Island come, who with you escaped from the battle. And with all this armed force we shall be able to put ourselves in such a location, to which I shall be the guide, that a battle between them having taken place, you will have both the victors and the vanquished at your mercy without any danger to your own troops. Then, what can result from this except that, besides your winning such a great victory, all Great Britain will be under your rule, and your royal estate placed at a higher pinnacle than that of any emperor in the world? Now, consider, mighty king, whether for such small effort and danger you wish to lose such great glory and dominion."

When King Arabigo heard this, he was very happy and said to him: "My friend Arcalaus, this is a great affair that you have told me about, and however unwilling I am to tempt Fortune further, it would be great madness to forego things that very reasonably bid fair to yield great honor and profit; because if they come out as one expects, and reason itself guides them, men receive that fruit that their effort deserves. And if it comes out for them to the contrary, they do that to which out of virtue they are obligated, by giving the accounting of their honor that ought to be given, not considering their past misfortunes so important that they fail to attempt their remedy when the opportunity presents itself, without those past misfortunes keeping them overwhelmed, downcast, and dishonored all the days of their lives. And since that is the way it is, do not worry about what my responsibility will be concerning my troops and friends; for the rest of it make provision with that dedication and diligence that you see necessary for such an action."

Arcalaus, having obtained the king's promise, left for Sansuenia, and spoke with Barsinan, reminding him of the death of his father and that of his brother Gandalod, the one whom Don Guilan the Pensive had overcome and brought as a prisoner to King Lisuarte, who ordered him flung down from a tower, at the foot of which his father had been burned to death. And furthermore he told him how at that time he had had plans made for his father to be King of Great Britain, that he had been holding King Lisuarte and his daughter prisoners, and how by that traitorous Amadis he had been completely thwarted; that now he had the opportunity not only to take vengeance at will upon his enemies, but also that great realm that his father had failed to obtain he now had the opportunity to acquire; and that he should take courage, for without it, great things can seldom be achieved, and that if Fortune had been so adverse to his father, repenting of it, she would be willing to requite him for injury received. And furthermore he told him that King Arabigo was making ready with all his resources because he saw the enterprise so certain of victory that it could in no wise fail, and he told him about all the other assistance of which he had assurance for this affair, and many other things as a man who always had carried on such activities and had become a past master of evil deeds.

As Barsinan was a very haughty young man, and in wickedness resembled his father, with but slight pressure and effort he induced him to comply with everything he sought; and very belligerently and with excessive conceit Barsinan replied that with complete dedication and willingness he would take part in this expedition, taking with him most of the fighting men from within his realm and all those from without who might wish to follow him. Arcalaus, when he heard these statements, was happy at the way he was encountering support for the fulfillment of his desires; and he told him that everything should be made ready immediately in expectation of his summons, for it was quite necessary to attend to this matter with diligence.

And from there he went very speedily and with a joyful heart to the king of Deep Island, and had a very long talk with him. And so much did he tell him and such arguments did he present to him that the same as he had the others, he caused him to be persuaded to make ready all his troops very methodically, as a man who was under such necessity to do so.

This having been done, he returned to his own land and spoke with the relatives of Dardan the Haughty, inasmuch as he believed that great advantage would come from such talking to everyone; and as secretly as he could he made compacts with them, telling them of the great preparations he had under way. So he awaited the proper time to carry out the plan about which you have heard.

But now the story speaks no more of him until it is time, and it returns to the narration of what happened to Don Cuadragante and Don Brian de Monjaste after they left the court of King Lisuarte.

CHAPTER XCVII

How don Cuadragante and Brian de Monjaste with ill fortune lost their way at sea; and how by chance they encountered Queen Briolanja, and what happened to them while in her company.

Don Cuadragante and Don Brian de Monjaste after they left Don Grumedan, as the story has related, went their way until they reached the port where they had their ship, which they boarded to go to the Firm Island with the reply that they were bringing from King Lisuarte. And all that day the sea was very tranquil with a fair wind for their voyage; but night having come, the sea began to swell so unfortunately and so violently that they thought they would be completely wrecked and drowned. And the storm was so great that the sailors lost their bearings, until then maintained, amid such confusion that the ship was proceeding out of control over the sea; and thus quite fearful they traveled all night, for in such a situation neither arms nor stout hearts suffice. And when the dawn of day appeared, and the sailors were able to get their bearings better, they found that they were very near the kingdom of Sobradisa, where the very beautiful Queen Briolanja was the sovereign. And at that hour the sea began to be becalmed, and as they were endeavoring to resume their proper course, although they would be turning back for a very great distance, they saw coming on their left an extraordinarily large ship. And as their own vessel was very swift, so that it could not receive any harm from the other, even if it were that of an enemy, they decided to wait for it; and as they came closer and viewed it more at will, it seemed to them the most beautiful they had ever seen, in size as well as in luxurious equipment, for the sails and ropes were all of silk, and it was decorated, all that was visible of it, with very costly hangings. And at its rail they saw very splendidly attired knights and maidens chatting. Don Cuadragante and Brian de Monjaste were greatly amazed to see it, and could not imagine what might be on board. And at once they ordered one of their squires to go in a small boat and find out whose large ship that was, and who was aboard it. The squire did so, and on asking those knights to be kind enough to tell him, they answered that Queen Briolanja was on board, that she was going to the Firm Island.

"Thank God," said the squire, "with such good news, those who sent me here will be greatly pleased."

"Good squire," said the maidens, "tell us, if you please, who are these men you mention?"

"Ladies," said he, "they are two knights who are pursuing the same course as you, and the hazards of navigation have brought them hither; where, in view of what they are encountering, it will be a great respite for their travail. And because they will reveal their identity to you as soon as I return, it is not necessary to ascertain anything from me."

With what you hear he returned and said to them: "Sirs, you should be greatly pleased with the news that I bring, and the recent storm and the roundabout course should be deemed well worthwhile, since you have such company for going to your destination. Be advised that on the ship is Queen Briolanja, who is going to the Firm Island."

Those two knights were greatly overjoyed at what the squire told them, and immediately gave orders to steer their own craft to the ship. And when they were nearer, the maidens recognized them, for once before they had seen them at the court of King Lisuarte, when the queen, their lady, was there for some time; and they went very happily to tell their lady that two knights, good friends of Amadis, were there and that one was Don Cuadragante and the other Don Brian de Monjaste. The queen, when she heard this was very happy, and with the matrons she had with her came out of her stateroom in order to receive them; for Tantiles, her majordomo, had told her how he had left them on the Firm Island as they were departing to go to King

Lisuarte. And when she came out, they were already on board the ship, and they went to kiss her hands, but she did not wish it; instead she put an arm around each one and thus with great pleasure held them briefly in her embrace; and as soon as they arose, she embraced them again and said to them: "My good lords and friends, I am very thankful to God because I have encountered you, for nothing could have happened to me at this time to afford me more pleasure, unless it were to see Amadis of Gaul, the man whom so rightly and logically I should esteem, as you know."

"My good lady," said Don Cuadragante, "it would be a great injustice were it not as you say; and for the pleasure that you have with us, may God thank you, and we shall serve you in whatever you command."

"Many thanks," said she. "Now tell me how it is that you have come close to this land."

They told her how they had left the Firm Island with a message from those lords who were there for King Lisuarte, and all that they had experienced with him, and how they remained in complete rupture without any agreement, for nothing was omitted; and that when they sought to return, the great storm of the previous night had thrown them off course to that place where they considered their fatigue and travail well worthwhile since on that course they were being enabled to serve and protect her until they escorted her to her destination. The queen said to them: "Indeed I have not been very secure, nor have I been without great fear of the storm you mention, for I certainly never thought that we would be able to weather it; but as this ship of mine is very heavy and large, and its anchors and ropes very stout, it pleased the will of God that ill-fortune was never able to break or dislodge them. And in this matter of King Lisuarte that you mention to me, I learned from my majordomo Tantiles that you were going to him on this mission, and indeed I said to myself that since this man is so strong a king whom Fortune has favored and exalted so completely in all respects, deeming very serious what happened to Oriana, he will seek to test and prove his might rather than arrange for any peace treaty. And for this reason I agreed to call together my whole kingdom and all my friends who are outside of it; and with much insistence to beg and command them to be ready and equipped for war against the time they see my letter. And I am leaving everyone with great good will to serve me, and my majordomo with them to direct and bring them. And meanwhile I thought that it would be well for me to go to the Firm Island to be with Princess Oriana and experience with her whatever danger God may have in store for her. This is the reason why you find me here, and I am very happy that we shall be going together."

"My lady," said Don Brian de Monjaste, "from such a lady and one so beautiful as you, one expects only complete virtue and nobility, just as you exemplify."

The queen asked them to have their ship come alongside hers and requested that they travel with her; and so it was done, for they were lodged in a very elegant stateroom, and they regularly ate with her at her table, while conversing on topics they preferred.

So just as I am telling, they went their way over the sea toward the Firm Island. Now at this juncture be advised that at the time that Abiseos, uncle of this queen, was killed together with his two sons — in revenge for his having slain his brother the king, Briolanja's father, whose kingdom he had seized — by Amadis and Agrajes, as the first Book of this story relates in more detail, there remained another younger son of his, whom a knight, who was his faithful subject, was rearing. This youth was now a very robust and strong knight in view of his showing in the great confrontations in which he had been involved. And as until then he had been very young, he thought only — nor did discretion afford him opportunity to do otherwise — of having recourse to arms, rather than of striving for what was worthwhile. And as he was now of age he had some of his father's vassals who had fled, who reminded him of the death of his father and his brothers; and alleging that that kingdom of Sobradisa by right was his, and that that queen was keeping it from him by force; and that if he was as courageous for the correction of a matter so incumbent upon him to correct as for other things, with but little effort he would be able to recoup that great loss and be a great lord, by returning now to the kingdom, or desiring such advantage as honorably, being the son of a king, he might be able to utilize. So this knight, whose name was Trion, since he was desirous of ruling, kept thinking about these things that those vassals of his father were telling him, and awaiting a suitable opportunity for the realization of his desire. And as he now learned about this very great discord that existed between King Lisuarte and Amadis, he thought that Amadis would have so much to do in that situation that he would have no memory of the other. And that even if he did recall it, in view of his embroilment with such grandees, his forces would not suffice for wholesale rescue operations; for this knight was the major obstacle that he was encountering, since he knew of the departure of Queen Briolanja and how poorly escorted she was, for in her whole ship she carried less than twenty men at arms, none of them very effective.

Immediately he sallied forth from a castle left to him by his father Abiseos, the only possession of which Abiseos was lord when he killed the king, his brother, and he went to a house of his friends; and not telling them the occasion for it, he gathered some fifty men well armed and some crossbowmen and archers. And equipping two ships, he put out to sea, his intention being to seize the queen and to profit greatly thereby, and if he saw an opportunity, to take the whole kingdom from her. And knowing the course she was taking, one afternoon he came into view ahead of her without any suspicion concerning him having been conceived; and as from afar those on the ship saw those two vessels, they spoke about it to the queen, and Don Cuadragante and Brian de Monjaste came out at once to the ship's rail; and these men who were present saw that they were coming directly toward them, and they armed themselves and they gave heed only to maintaining their course, and so the others, who were approaching, came so near that they could easily hear each other, whatever they might be saying.

Then Trion said in a loud voice: "Knights who travel in that ship, tell Queen Briolanja that Trion her cousin is here, who wishes to speak to her, and that he orders her men not to defend themselves; otherwise, not one of them will escape being killed."

When the queen heard this, she became very fearful and terrified, and said: "Sirs, this is the greatest enemy that I have; and since now he ventures to do this, it is not without great incitement and a heavy force."

Don Cuadragante said to her: "My good lady, do not be afraid, for please God very quickly he will be punished for his madness."

Then he ordered a man to tell him that if he was willing to enter alone the queen's presence she would gladly receive him. And he said: "Since that is the way it is, I will see her, in spite of her and of all of you."

Then he ordered a knight, a ward of his father's, with the one vessel to attack the ship on the other side and to try to board it, and he did so. When Don Brian de Monjaste saw them withdraw, he told Don Cuadragante to take what he pleased of their forces and guard one side, and that he with the remainder would defend the other, and so they did; for Don Cuadragante remained at the side where Trion wanted to fight, and Brian de Monjaste at that of the other knight. Don Cuadragante ordered his men to stay in front and he remained as concealed as he could behind them; and he told them that if Trion should try to come on board, not to stop him.

The affair being at this point, the ship was attacked from both sides very strongly, because those who were fighting were quite convinced that she had no defense or danger for them; for they knew nothing about the two knights from the Firm Island. And when they arrived, Trion, out of his great arrogance and his desire to finish his project, on arriving leaped unsuspectingly onto the ship, and the queen's forces began to retreat in accordance with their orders. Don Cuadragante, when he saw him on board, advanced through the midst of his men; and since he was very large of body, as the story has told you in Book II, when Trion saw him, he well recognized that he was not of those whom he knew about; but on that account he did not lose courage; instead he went at him with great daring, and they gave each other such mighty blows on top of their helmets that sparks flew from them and from the swords. But as Don Cuadragante was of greater strength and was striking him at will, Trion was so overwhelmed by the blows that his sword fell from his hand, and he went to his knees on the deck, and Don Cuadragante looked around and saw that his adversaries were boarding the ship as fast as they could, and he said to his men: "Take this knight."

Then he went over to the others, and he gave the first one that he found in front of him such a heavy blow on top of the head that he was too far gone for medical help. The others when they saw their lord taken prisoner and that knight killed, and the strong blows that Don Cuadragante was giving to one and all, tried as hard as they could to return to their ship. And with the pressure that Don Cuadragante and his men were putting on them, some saved themselves, and others died in the water; so that in a short time they were all overcome and ejected from their vessel, which Don Cuadragante's forces now held as their own. Then he glanced at the other side where Brian was fighting and saw that he was aboard the other vessel with his foes, and that he was wreaking great havoc on them; and he dispatched some of the men he had that they might go and help him, and he remained with the others awaiting his enemies, should they wish to attack. And with this help that reached Brian and with those men he had, very quickly they were all overcome; because that knight, their captain, was killed there and they saw that Trion's ship was withdrawing as conquered. Then those who were alive were asking for mercy; and Don Brian gave orders that none was to be killed, since they were not resisting. And so it came about that they took them prisoners and seized the vessel.

Queen Briolanja during all of the confusion remained within her stateroom with all her ladies and maidens, all of them praying to God on bended knees to protect them from that danger, and to protect those knights who were helping and defending her. While they were thus engaged, one of her men came and said: "Lady, come outside and you will see that Trion is taken prisoner and all his company battered and disrupted, for these knights from the Firm Island have performed great wonders at arms, which no one else would have been able to do."

When the queen heard this, she was as happy as you can well imagine; and she raised her hands and said: "Almighty Lord God, bless you that at such a time and by such good fortune you brought to me these knights, for from Amadis and his friends only good luck can come to me."

And having left her room, she saw that her men were holding Trion prisoner and that Don Cuadragante was on guard lest the foes approach to fight; and she saw that Don Brian de Monjaste's men were in possession of the vessel that he had won. And she came up to Don Cuadragante and said to him: "My lord, I give great thanks to God and to you for what you have done for me, for I was indeed in great danger with regard to my person and my kingdom."

He said to her: "My good lady, you see your enemy here; give orders that punishment be meted out to him."

Trion, when he heard this, was not sure of his life; and knelt before the queen and said: "Lady, I ask you for mercy that I may not die; keep in mind your great self-restraint and that I am of your blood; and if I have vexed you at any time, I shall be able to compensate by serving you."

As the queen was very noble, she took pity on him and said: "Trion, not for what you deserve, but more on account of what pertains to me, I assure you of your life until with these knights I look into the matter further. And I order that he be put into his room under guard."

At this juncture, Don Brian de Monjaste came to the queen and she went and embraced him; and she said to him: "My good lord, how are you?"

He said to her: "Lady, very well and very happy to have had such good fortune as to be able to be of some service to you. I have a wound, but thank God, it is not dangerous."

Then he showed his shield, and they saw that an arrow had penetrated it and part of the arm on which he was holding it. The queen with her own beautiful hands removed it as gently as she could, and she helped him to disarm, and his wound was given treatment as many other times his more serious wounds had been treated; for his squires, as well as those of all other knights errant, always went well supplied with the things that were urgently needed for wounds. All were very happy about that good fortune that had come about for them; and when they sought to go after Trion's vessel, they saw that it was far away, and they gave up their attempt. And they hoisted their sails and went their way straight to the Firm Island without any obstacle arising for them.

It happened then that at the hour that they reached the port, Amadis and most of the lords were disporting themselves by riding their palfreys about over a fertile plain that lay at the foot of the slope leading up to the castle, as they were frequently accustomed to do. And when they saw those ships arriving in the harbor, they went down there to find out whose they were; and on reaching the sea, they found the squires of Don Cuadragante and those of Don Brian de Monjaste, who were coming ashore in a small boat and were going to notify them of their arrival and that of Queen Briolanja, so that they might come out to meet them. And when they saw Amadis and those knights, they told them the message of their lords, with which they were very happy; and everyone reached the shore as did the others from the ship; they greeted each other with much laughter and great joy. And Don Brian de Monjaste said to them: "What do you think about our coming back here richer than when we left? You have not done so; all you have done is to stay locked up like wastrels."

Everybody began to laugh and they told him that, since he came so proud, to show them the profit he had made. Then they lowered a rather large boat, and the queen and both of them got into it in addition to other men who rowed them to shore. And all those knights dismounted from their palfreys and went to kiss the queen's hands, but she did not want to yield them; instead she embraced them very affectionately. Amadis came up to her and sought to kiss her hands; but when she saw him she enfolded him in her very beautiful arms and held him so for a while, for she would not let him go, and the tears came into her eyes and rolled down her very beautiful cheeks out of the pleasure that she experienced in seeing him; because since the battle that King Lisuarte had had with King Cildadan, when she saw him at Fenusa, that town where the king was, she had not seen him. And although now she was no longer thinking of marrying him, and entertained no hope of it, he was the knight that she loved most in the world, and for whom she would rather put herself and her realm in danger than do him any injury. And when she released him she could not speak, so moved was she by great joy.

Amadis said to her: "Lady, I give many thanks to God, who has brought me to where I could see you, for I have greatly desired to do so, and now more than at any other time, because at the sight of you these knights will be afforded great joy, and much more you will afford your good friend Princess Oriana, for I believe that no person could have come to her who would give her as much happiness as you, my good lady."

She responded, saying: "My good lord, on that account I left my kingdom, principally to see you, which was the thing I most desired in the world to do; and God knows the anxiety that until now I have had in spending so long a time without being able to ascertain any news of you, although I have tried hard. And now when my majordomo told me of your arrival and gave me your letter, at once I decided, leaving everything for which you asked in readiness, to come to you and to this lady you mention, because now is the time that her friends and servants should demonstrate the desire and love that they have for her. But if it had not been for God and these knights, who by great luck joined me, I could have experienced great danger to my person on this voyage; which they as the ones who saved the situation by their great efforts, will tell about; and let it be for when there is more time."

After the queen came ashore, all her ladies and maidens and knights followed, and the beasts that they had on board were brought off, and for the queen a palfrey, very well caparisoned, as befitted such a lady. And all mounted and went on to the castle where Oriana was; who, when she learned of their arrival, manifested such pleasure as was wondrous to behold; and she requested Mabilia and Grasinda and the other princesses to go out to the entrance to the garden to receive her, and she remained with Queen Sardamira in the tower. When Queen Sardamira saw the pleasure that all were evincing at the news that was brought to them, she said to Oriana: "My lady, who is this woman who is coming, who has given so much pleasure to everyone?"

Oriana said to her: "She is a queen, the most beautiful one, not only in appearance but also by reputation, that I know of in the world, as now you will see for yourself."

When Queen Briolanja reached the garden gate and saw so many well attired ladies, she was quite astonished, and she experienced the greatest delight in the world at having come there. And turning to those knights, she said to them: "My good lords, God be with you, for those ladies free me from wanting your company any longer."

And laughing very engagingly, she had herself helped to dismount and joined them, and at once the gate was closed. They all came to her and greeted her with much courtesy. And Grasinda marvelled greatly at her beauty and consummate grace. And if she had not seen Oriana, for the latter had no equal, she certainly would have believed that there was no woman in the world so good looking as she. Then they took her to the tower where Oriana was, and when they saw one another they went toward each other with outstretched arms and embraced very lovingly. Oriana took her by the hand and brought her to Queen Sardamira, and said to her: "My lady queen, speak to Queen Sardamira and do her great honor, for she well deserves it."

And she did so, for with great courtesy they greeted each other, each one of them respecting the royal prerogatives of the other; and taking Oriana between them, they seated themselves on her dais with all the other ladies surrounding them. Oriana said to Queen Briolanja: "My good lady, it is very courteous of you to come to see me from such a distant land, and I thank you for it very much, because such a journey could only have been made out of superabundant love."

"My lady," said the queen, "with great ignorance and a great deficiency in politeness I should be charged if at this period in which you are, I did not make known to the whole world the good wishes I have for your honor and for the improvement of your situation; especially since this is the main responsibility of Amadis of Gaul, whom I esteem and to whom I owe so much, as you, my lady, know. And when I ascertained from Tantiles that he was here, I immediately ordered my whole kingdom made ready to come for whatever he may command; and it seemed to me that meanwhile I ought to make this journey in order to bear you company or see him, whom I greatly desired to see more than any other person in this world, and to be, my lady, with you until your problem is settled, and may it please our Lord that it be according to your desires."

"So may it please Him," said Oriana, "out of His holy pity; and I have hope that Don Cuadragante and Don Brian de

Monjaste will be bringing back some agreement made with my father."

Briolanja, who knew the fact that they were not bringing any, did not wish to tell her so. So they remained conversing for a long while about matters that afforded them most pleasure. And when it was the supper hour, the maid of Denmark said to Oriana: "Remember, lady, that the queen has been traveling and will wish to sup and rest, and it is already time for you to go to your apartment; and take her with you, since she is your guest."

Oriana asked her if all was in readiness. She said that it was. Then Oriana took Queen Briolanja by the hand and took leave of Queen Sardamira and Grasinda, who went to their apartments, and she went with her to her chamber, showing her great affection. And as soon as they arrived there, Briolanja asked who that very well dressed, beautiful matron was who was beside Queen Sardamira. Mabilia told her that her name was Grasinda and that she was very noble and very rich, and she told her the reason why she had come to the court of King Lisuarte, and the great honor that there Amadis had caused her to win, and the honor that she had done him when she was unaware of his identity. And she related in great detail all that Grasinda had experienced with Amadis, for whom she had such great affection, when he was calling himself the Knight of the Green Sword, and how he was on the verge of death when he killed the Endriago, and a physician whom this matron had given him, the best physician that could be found far and wide, restored him to health; all this she told her with nothing left out.

When the queen heard this, she said: "Wretched woman that I am, why did I not know of it before, for she came up to speak to me, and I passed her by very rudely. But amends will be made; for even if her merit had not deserved it, only for having done so much honor with such benefit, I am greatly obligated to honor her and afford her pleasure all the days of my life; because, after God, I have no other help for my troubles, nor for the contentment of my heart except this knight; and after supper have her summoned because I wish her to make my acquaintance."

Oriana said: "Queen, my friend, you are not the only one who ought to honor her for this reason, for here you see me who, if it had not been for that knight you have mentioned, would be today the most distracted and hapless woman ever born, because having been rejected as heiress to the realm of which God had made me suzerain, I would be in a foreign land with such loneliness that there would have been nothing left for me but death. And as you probably have ascertained, this noble knight, helper and benefactor of the persecuted, without his being motivated by anything except his splendid virtue, has involved himself in what you are witnessing in order that my rights may be protected."

"My lady and friend," said the queen, "let us not talk about Amadis, because he was born only for such things; for just as God distinguished him and set him apart from everyone else in the world for his great strength, likewise did He will that he be so in all the other good qualities and virtues."

Then seated at the table they were served many and diverse viands, as befitted such distinguished princesses, and they talked of many things that were to their liking. And after they had dined, they told the maid of Denmark to go for Grasinda and tell her that the queen wished to speak with her. The maiden did so, and Grasinda came with her at once; and when she entered where they were, Queen Briolanja went and embraced her, and said to her: "My good friend, pardon me, for I did not know who you were when I came here; for if I had known, I would have received you with greater love and affection, because your virtue deserves it; and for the great honor and good help that Amadis received from you, we his friends are greatly obligated to thank you for it, and on my own behalf I say to you that never shall I be in a position to repay you for it that I do not do so, because even if I give it out of my own resources, I give you what is his; for all that I have is his, and as his I consider it."

"My good lady," said Grasinda, "if in any way I did honor to this knight whom you mention, I am as well satisfied and happy about it as ever was any person concerning some one to whom he had afforded pleasure; and for what you say to me, I give greater thanks to your own virtue than to any debt that he may be owing me, for would that it might please God to afford me an opportunity to be of service to him for the excessive repayment he has made me for what he received from me."

Then Mabilia said to her: "My good lady, tell us if you please how you became acquainted with Amadis and for what reason he met with such a good welcome from you, since you did not recognize or know his name."

She told them everything, just as the third Book of this story relates it in more detail. And they laughed a great deal about Brandasidel, the one whom he forced to ride horseback mounted backward, with the tail in his hand. And she told them how she had entertained him in her house for some days, badly wounded, and how before he came to that land she had heard of the very great and rare exploits at arms that he had performed throughout all the islands of Romania and of Germany, where all those who knew about them were astonished at how such very dangerous deeds had been accomplished by a single knight, and of the wrongs and great injuries that he had righted for many matrons and maidens and other persons who had had need of his aid and succor; and how she had recognized him by the dwarf and by the green sword that he carried, distinguishing marks which had provided him with names. And likewise she described to them the whole battle that he had with Don Garadan, and the one he waged subsequently with the other eleven knights, and how on account of overcoming them, he saved the King of Bohemia from a very cruel war with the Emperor of Rome; and many other things she related to them that she had found out about him in those regions, which would take too long to recount; and then she said to them: "On account of these things that I heard about him, and because of what I saw of him in person, I wish you to know, ladies, what happened to me personally. I was so pleased with him and with his great deeds, and as I was for that land quite a great lady and highborn and he was going about in the guise of a poor knight, without my having had any more information concerning him than what I have stated, I considered it a good idea to take him in marriage; and I had thought that if I had him, no queen in the whole world would be my equal. And as I saw him so reserved, and so very pensive and distraught, and knowing the fortitude of his heart, I suspected that that depression came over him only because of some woman whom he loved. And to render myself more certain of it, I spoke with Gandalin, who seemed to me a very sensible squire, and I asked him about it; and he, recognizing what I was aiming at, on the one hand denied it, and on the other hand gave me to understand that his grief probably was not on account of anything except some woman whom he loved; and I saw indeed that he had told me that in order that I might rid myself of that thought and not proceed further, since it would be fruitless. I was very grateful to him for it, and from that time on I have refrained from thinking any more about it."

Briolanja, when she heard this, glanced laughingly at Oriana, and said to her: "My lady, it seems to me that this knight, through more regions than I thought, goes about disseminating this ailment; and remember what I had said to you on this subject in the castle of Miraflores."

"I well remember it," said Oriana.

This was that Queen Briolanja on going to see Oriana at this castle of Miraflores, as the second Book relates, told her that almost the same thing had happened to her with Amadis.

So about that as of other matters they remained talking until it was bedtime; and Grasinda took leave of them and returned to her own chamber, and they remained in theirs. And for Queen Briolanja they set up in Oriana's room a bed beside hers, because she and Mabilia slept together; and there they lay down to sleep, where that night they lay in repose.

CHAPTER XCVIII

CONCERNING THE MESSAGE THAT DON QUADRAGANTE AND BRIAN DE MONJASTE BROUGHT FROM KING LISUARTE, AND WHAT ALL THE KNIGHTS AND LORDS WHO WERE THERE DECIDED ABOUT IT.

The next morning all those noble lords and knights gathered to hear mass and the message that Don Quadragante and Don Brian de Monjaste were bearing from King Lisuarte. And the mass having been heard, all being together there, Don Cuadragante said to them: "Good lords, our message and his reply were so brief that we cannot tell you anything but that you ought to thank God because with much justice and reason, and while winning great glory and fame, you can test the courage of your noble hearts, for King Lisuarte does not wish any measure other than severity."

Whereupon he told them all that had transpired with him, and how they knew for certain that he was sending for aid to the Emperor of Rome and to other friends of his. Agrajes, in whom none of this occasioned regret, although by the mandate and request of Oriana, until then he had become quite moderate, said: "For certain, good lords, I have believed that, according to the state in which this affair rests, it would be very much more difficult to seek security for this princess and for the repute of our honor than aid for this war; and up until now because she begged and implored me very insistently that insofar as I could I cool your anger and my own, I have avoided talking as much as my heart desired. But now that the termination of her hope is known, which was to imagine that measures could be taken for dealing with the king her father, and they are not to be found, I am free from what I had promised her more for the sake of serving her than of my own volition; and I say, my lords, that insofar as my desire and wish are concerned, I am much happier about what you bring back than if King Lisuarte had agreed to what you asked him on our behalf, because it might have been that, under the pretext of peace and harmony, he might have entered into cunning contracts with us whereby we could have been victims of some deception, because King Lisuarte and the emperor, as powerful men, with little trouble could very quickly have gathered together their forces, which we would not have been able to do, inasmuch as our forces have to come from many regions and very distant lands. And although the danger to our persons, because of our being in this very strong fortress, would have been forestalled and rendered nil, while affording us some advantage, the danger to our honor would not have been offset. And for this reason, lords, I consider a declared war better than parleys and a simulated peace, since through the latter, as I have said, more harm could come to us than to them."

They all said that he spoke the truth, and that immediately one ought to take precautions regarding the coming of troops, and to wage battle against them within their own land. Amadis, who was very mistrustful and very fearful lest harmony by some means could be brought about and he would have to hand over his lady; even if her honor and that of all of them were completely assured and protected, for the desire of his tortured heart would remain in such dire straits out of grief and sadness by reason of his putting her where he would not be able to see her, that it would now be impossible to endure life; when he heard what the messengers were reporting and what his cousin Agrajes said, even if it had made him lord of the whole world it would not have pleased him so much, because no affront or war or travail did he consider as anything in comparison with keeping his lady as he had her; and he said: "Sir cousin, your actions have always been those of a knight, and thus all those who know you deem them; and we who are your blood relatives ought greatly to thank God for having cast among us a knight who in affronts is so careful of his honor, and in matters of advice fosters it with such discretion. And since you, as well as these lords, have decided on the better course, it will be useless for me to do anything but follow whatever your wish and theirs may be."

Angriote de Estravaus, who was a wise and very valiant knight, and who loved Amadis very faithfully, well recognized that although he did not come forward to speak and was deferring to the will of everyone else, he was well pleased by the rupture; and Angriote attributed this more to his great valor's not being satisfied except by such dangerous confrontations as that was, than to anything else that he knew about him; and he said: "Lords, you should all be pleased with what your messengers have brought back and with what Agrajes has said, because that is what is certain and sure. But aside from what the former and the latter have set forth, I say, sirs, that war is for us much more honorable than peace; and because there are so many things that could be said in favor of this, that saying them would cause you much annoyance, I wish only to remind you that ever since you have been knights, your ambition always has been to seek what was dangerous and of major risk in order that your courage, separately from that of other men, might be inured to it and win that glory desired by many and achieved by very few. Then if this by reason of great insistence and distress of mind is achieved, when at any time in the past have you attained it so completely as at present? For certainly, although in furthering this ambition of yours you may have succored many matrons and maidens, one does not recall that so lofty an ambition of this kind has ever been attained by you or by your forebears, nor even in the future will it be attained until much time has elapsed. And since Fortune has satisfied our desire so completely, bringing it about that, just as our souls in the next world are immortal, our fame may be likewise in this one in which we live, let care be taken that what she offers for us to win, be not lost through our fault and negligence."

Having approved all that these knights had said, and putting into execution their opinion, they decided to send messages at once summoning all the forces on their side, and thereupon they left to dine. And for the moment the story ceases to speak of them and returns to the messengers that they had sent, as has been mentioned and the story has related.

CHAPTER XCIX

How the physician Elisabad arrived in Grasinda's land and from there went to the Emperor of Constantinople with Amadis's message, and what he obtained from him.

The story says that Master Elisabad traveled far over the sea until he came to the land of Grasinda, his lady. And there he ordered all the leading grandees of the seigniory summoned, and he showed them the credentials and command that he bore from her, and asked them very insistently to carry out her order at once. And they with great good will replied to him that all of them were ready to put it into execution far better than if she were present. And at once they gave orders that troops of cavalry and crossbowmen and archers and other men of war be recruited, and that many ships should be made ready, and other new ones built. And when the physician saw the good preparation, he left the care of it to a knight, his nephew, a young man named Libeo; and begging him to proceed in the matter with much care, he put out to sea and went to the Emperor of Constantinople. And when he arrived, he went to the palace, and was told that the emperor was conferring with his nobles. The physician entered the room and came up to kiss his hands, kneeling to the floor; and the emperor received him graciously, because he knew him of old and considered him a good man. The physician gave him the letter from Amadis, and as the emperor read it, he was greatly astonished that the Knight of the Green Sword was Amadis, whose acquaintance he had for a long time been desirous of making on account of the extraordinary things that many of those who had seen him had told the emperor concerning him;

and he said to him: "Master, I am quite vexed at you if you knew the name of this knight and did not tell me; because I am ashamed that a man of such high estate and lineage and so famous throughout the whole world should have come to my court and not have received in it the honor that he deserved except only as a knight errant."

The physician said to him: "Sire, I swear by the holy orders I have taken that until he ceased to call himself the Greek Knight and made himself known to my lady Grasinda, and to us all, I never knew that he was Amadis."

"What!" said the emperor. "He called himself the Greek Knight after he was here?"

The physician said: "Then, sire, has not the news reached your court of what he accomplished while calling himself the Greek Knight?"

"Certainly," said the emperor, "I have never heard about it until now."

"Then you will hear great things," said he, "if it please your Grace that they be told."

"I greatly approve of your telling them," said the emperor.

Then the physician related to him how after they had left there, they arrived where his lady Grasinda was, and how on account of the boon that the Knight of the Green Sword had promised her, he escorted her over the sea to Great Britain; and for what reason and how before he arrived there, he ordered that he be called nothing but the Greek Knight; and the battles that he had in the court of King Lisuarte with Salustanquidio and the two other Roman knights who had entered the fight against him on behalf of the maidens, and how he overcame them so easily; and he related the highly insulting remarks that the Romans were making before they entered the battle, and how they told King Lisuarte that he should assign to them that difficult action against the Greek Knight, for after learning that he had to fight with them, he would not dare to await them, because the Greeks feared the Romans like fire. He told him everything, not omitting anything, as one who had witnessed it all. All who were there were greatly astounded at such knightly excellence and very happy about how he had broken the great pride of the Romans to their very great dishonor. The emperor spoke at length in high praise of him and then said: "Master, now tell me your accreditation, for I shall hear you."

The physician told him all about the matter of King Lisuarte and his daughter, and why she was taken at sea by Amadis and those knights, and the things that the natives of the kingdom had undergone with the king, and of how Oriana had sent everywhere messages of complaint of that great injustice that the king her father had done her with such cruelty by disinheriting her without reason from a kingdom so great and so honored, of which God had made her the heiress; and how not heeding his conscience or exercising any pity, desiring that another younger daughter inherit his realm, he handed her over to the Romans to the accompaniment of great lamenting and sorrow not only by her but by all who saw her; and how at these complaints and great lamentations of that princess there banded together many knights errant of distinguished lineage and of very high exploits at arms, of whom he gave in full the names of the majority; and how they had found Amadis, who had not known anything about this, there on the Firm Island. And there he with them had taken counsel on how this princess might be rescued, and how such a great outrage as that should not take place before their eyes; for if it was true that they were obligated to remedy the outrages perpetrated against matrons and maidens, and for them they had endured up to that time many hardships and dangers, they were obligated even more by that very notorious outrage so obvious to the whole world, and that if they did not aid that lady, not only would they lose the memory of the help and protection that they had given to others, but also they would remain dishonored forever, and it would not be fitting for them to appear where men of integrity were. And he told him how the fleet put out to sea and the great fight they had with the Romans, and how finally the latter were overcome, and Salustanquidio, the emperor's cousin, killed, and Brondajel de Roca and the Duke of Ancona and the Archbishop of Talancia taken prisoner, and the others prisoners or slain; and how they brought that princess with all her ladies and maidens, and also Queen Sardamira, to the Firm Island; and from there they had sent messengers to King Lisuarte requesting and begging him that, ceasing to wreak such great cruelty and injustice upon his daughter, he be willing to return her to her kingdom without any reprisals; and that under such security measures as in such a situation were proper in the view of other kings, they would send her to him at once with all the spoils and prisoners they had taken. And that what he, Elisabad, on behalf of Amadis was asking of him, the Emperor of Constantinople, was that if it should turn out that King Lisuarte should not be willing to make a just settlement — still persisting in his evil intention and not disposed to withdraw from it, and the Emperor of Rome helping him against them with a great aggregation of troops — for his Grace as one of the chief representatives of God on earth having been left to maintain justice, all the more so since the very great outrage being done this very virtuous princess was so notorious, it would be a very good reason to help her; and beyond this, giving some aid to that noble knight Amadis in order to harass those who might not wish justice would help prevent such great violence and wrong as was being done in that affair; and besides his serving God in the matter and doing what he should, Amadis and all of his family and friends would be obligated to serve him all the days of their lives.

When the emperor had heard all of this, he saw indeed that the situation was grave and one involving great action, not only because of its character, but also because he knew the great excellence of King Lisuarte, and how highly the latter had always regarded his own honor and fame; and also because he was acquainted with the arrogance of the Emperor of Rome, who was more accustomed to pursue his desires than to follow prudence or reason. And he indeed believed that this could not be cured except by a mighty onslaught, and it gave him grave concern; but on considering the great justice that those knights had on their side and how Amadis had come from such a distant land to see him, and he had given him his word, although it had been lightly given and not said in the sense that Amadis took it, he endeavored to consider his own greatness, remembering some arrogant acts that the Emperor of Rome had committed against him in times past; and he answered Master Elisabad, and said to him: "Master, you have told me of great events, and coming from such a good man as you are, what you say can and should be believed; and since mighty Amadis has need of my help, I shall extend it to him so fully that that promise he extracted from me, although it might seem to some degree lightly given, he may find to be very true and completely fulfilled, as the word of such a highly placed man as I am, and given to such an honorable knight as he is; because never have I made an offer in any matter that in the end I did not make good."

And all those who were there were quite pleased with what the emperor replied, and especially Gastiles, his nephew, the one who, as you have already heard, went with Amadis when he called himself the Knight of the Green Sword, at the time he slew the Endriago. And he immediately knelt before the emperor, his uncle, and said: "Sire, if it may please your Grace and my services should merit it, do me this signal favor: that I be sent in aid of that noble and virtuous knight, who has honored so highly the crown of your empire."

The emperor, when he heard this, said to him: "Good nephew, I grant it to you, and I am pleased that it be so, and from now on I command you and Marquis Saluder to take charge of outfitting a fleet that is such and as excellent as the greatness of my estate requires; because otherwise honor could not accrue to me thereby. And if it is necessary, you and he shall go in it and you will be able to give battle to the Emperor of Rome, as is fitting."

Gastiles kissed his hands and considered it a very great favor on his part. And just as he commanded, so did he and the Marquis carry out his order. When Master Elisabad saw this, you can well imagine the pleasure that he felt. And he said to the emperor: "Sire, for what you have said to me I kiss your hands on behalf of that Knight; and for my being the one who carries back such a message, I kiss your feet; and because for the present I have much left to do, may you be so kind as to give me permission to leave. And if the Emperor of Rome musters his troops for action, for he is a very impetuous man in such matters, and — I repeat — if he does muster them, likewise as a consequence may you order yours summoned so that they may reach at the same time those who expect them."

The emperor said to him: "Master, go you with God, and leave that to me, for if there be an emergency, there you will see who I am and how highly I value Amadis."

So the physician took leave of the emperor and returned to the land of his lady Grasinda.

CHAPTER C

How gandalin arrived in gaul and told king perion what his lord had directed him to say; and the reply that he received.

Know you that Gandalin arrived in Gaul, where with much pleasure he was received on account of the good news that he brought concerning Amadis, of whom they had not had any news for a long time. And immediately he took the king aside and told him all that his lord had directed him to say, just as you have heard. And as this was a king so courageous that he feared no danger, no matter how great it might be, especially if it related to that son who was a shining mirror in all the world, and whom he loved so deeply, he said: "Gandalin, what you tell me on behalf of your lord will be done at once; and if you see him before I do, tell him that I would not consider him a knight if he had allowed that outrage to take place, because to great hearts is vouchsafed such enterprises. And I tell you that if King Lisuarte is not willing to listen to reason, it will be to his own detriment. And bear in mind that I ask you not to say anything about this to my son Galaor, whom I have here very ill, so much so, that many times I have considered him more dead than alive, and even now he is in great danger; nor to his companion Norandel, who has come here to see him, for I shall tell him about it."

Gandalin said to him: "Sire, it shall be done as you command, and I am quite pleased to be warned about him, for I had not given thought to it and might have erred."

"Then go and see him," said the king, "and tell him news of his brother, and be careful that he not perceive at all what you come for."

Gandalin went to the room where Galaor was in such a weak condition and so ill that he was astonished to see him. And when he came in, he knelt to kiss his hands, and Galaor gazed at him and recognized that it was Gandalin, and the tears came to his eyes because of his pleasure, and he said: "My friend Gandalin, be you indeed welcome. What do you tell me of my lord and brother Amadis?"

Gandalin said to him: "Sir, he is healthy and well on the Firm Island, and with a great desire to see you; and he does not know, sir, of your illness, nor did I know about it until my lord the king told me about it, for I came here with Amadis's mandate to inform him and the queen about his arrival there. And when he finds out about the state of your health, he will be very sorry about it, since it concerns the one whom he loves and esteems more highly than anyone else of his lineage."

Norandel, who was there, embraced him and asked him about Amadis, and how he was; and he told him what he had told Don Galaor, and he related to them some of the things that had happened to them on the islands of Romania and in those foreign lands. Norandel said to Don Galaor: "Sir, it is right that with such news as this you take courage and throw off your illness, because we are going to see that knight; for so help me God, he is such that even though it were for nothing except to see him, all those who are worth anything ought to deem of small concern the exertions of their journey, even if it were very long."

While thus they were chatting and Galaor was questioning Gandalin about many things, the king entered, and took Norandel by the hand; and while the others were talking of other things, he took him out of the room. And when they were where Don Galaor could not hear them, the king said to him: "My good friend, it is important for you to go at once to your father the king, because, according to what I have found out, he will need you, and all his vassals. And do not bother with other quests, because I know for certain that he will be very well served by your coming. And of this do not say anything to your friend Don Galaor, because it would cause him to be greatly disturbed, from which much harm might come to him, because of his weakened state."

Norandel said to him: "My lord, from such a good man as you are one ought to take advice without further questioning of its motive, because I am sure that it will be just as you say; and I shall take leave tonight of Don Galaor, and tomorrow I shall put out to sea, for I have my ship there awaiting me every day."

The king did this in order that Norandel might discharge his obligation to his father, and also that he might not perceive that he was giving orders to prepare his troops and summon his friends.

So that day they were more cheerful concerning Don Galaor because he was happy with the news of his brother. Gandalin told the queen what Amadis begged her to do, and she told him that all would be done in accordance with his message.

"But, Gandalin, my friend," said the queen, "I am very much disturbed at this news, because I understand that my son will be in great anxiety and afterwards in great danger to his person."

"Lady," said Gandalin, "do not fear, for he will have so many troops that neither King Lisuarte nor the Emperor of Rome will dare attack him."

"So may it please God," said the queen.

Night having come, Norandel said to Don Galaor: "My lord, I am resolved to go away, because I see that your illness is a long one, and in order not to take advantage of it, it will probably be better that I devote myself to other matters, because as you know, I have been a knight only a short while, and have not won as much honor as I would need in order to be considered among good knights as a man of some valor, and what I learned about your illness deflected me from a journey on which I had started when I left the court of my father the king, and now I must go to another region, where my presence is needed, and God knows the pain that I feel in my heart at not being able to continue in your company. But, God willing, in this intervening time while I accomplish what I cannot avoid doing, you will have improved in health, and I shall have the obligation to come to you, and we shall go together in quest of a few adventures."

Don Galaor, when he heard this, sighed with great anguish and said to him: "The sorrow that I, my good friend, feel in not being able to go with you, I do not know how to express; but since thus it pleases God, one cannot do anything else. And His will must be done just as He wishes. And may you go commended to God, and in the event that you see the king your father and lord, kiss his hands for me, and tell him I remain in his service, although more dead than alive, as you, sir, perceive."

Norandel went away to his room, and was very sad on account of the illness of Don Galaor, his faithful friend. And next morning early he heard mass with King Perion, and took leave of the queen and her daughter and of all the ladies and maidens-in-waiting; and the queen commended him to God, as did her daughter and all the other ladies and maidens, as women who loved him deeply; and so he embarked at once on the sea. And here the account merely states that without incident and with good weather he reached Great Britain and went on to where the king his father was, and was by him as well as by everyone else well received, as the good knight that he was.

CHAPTER CI

HOW LASINDO, SQUIRE OF DON BRUNEO DE BONAMAR, CAME WITH THE REQUEST OF HIS LORD TO THE MARQUIS AND TO BRANFIL, AND WHAT HE ARRANGED WITH THEM.

Lasindo, squire of Don Bruneo of Bonamar, arrived where the Marquis was, and when he told the request of his lord to him and to Branfil, the latter was so distressed at not having participated with those knights in what had taken place and at not having been a participant in taking possession of Oriana, that he wanted to kill himself. And he knelt before his father and very humbly begged him as a boon to order put into execution what his brother had sent word to ask. The Marquis, since he was a good knight and knew about the great friendship that his sons had with Amadis and with all of his lineage, from which great honor and esteem was accruing to them, said to him: "Son, do not be distressed; for I shall carry it out so completely and I shall send you, if necessary, with such a good company, that it will not be the poorest one there."

Branfil kissed his hands; and immediately orders were given to prepare the fleet and the crews for it, for this Marquis was a very great lord and very wealthy, and had in his realm many good knights and many other well armed men of war.

CHAPTER CII

HOW ISANJO CAME WITH THE MESSAGE OF AMADIS TO THE GOOD KING OF BOHEMIA, AND THE GREAT REASSURANCE THAT HE RECEIVED FROM HIM.

Isanjo, the knight from the Firm Island, arrived in the kingdom of Bohemia and gave the letter from Amadis and the letter of accreditation to King Tafinor. No man would be able to describe how pleased the king was when he saw him; and he said: "Knight, may you be welcome, and I am very grateful to God for this message that you bring to me; and from what will be done, you will be able to see with what good will it is received and whether your journey is well employed."

And calling his son Grasandor, he said to him: "Son Grasandor, whether I am obliged to take cognizance of the great assistance and benefits that the Knight of the Green Sword rendered me while he was in my kingdom, you well know; for besides my having been protected by him and the honor of my royal crown enhanced, he freed me from the most cruel and dangerous war that ever a king had, both on account of my having it with a man so powerful as the Emperor of Rome, and because he was inherently so haughty and unreasonable, whence the only outcome to be expected was that you and I would be ruined and destroyed, and perchance finally slain. And that noble knight whom God brought to my court for my well-being restored everything to my honor and that of my kingdom, as you have seen. And so, as a witness of it, I ask you to see this letter that he sends to me, and what this knight has told me on his behalf; and with all diligence to make preparations so that that great benefit that we received from that knight may be requited by us. And know you that this knight's name is Amadis of Gaul, the one whose very famous exploits are recounted throughout the world. And in order not to be recognized he called himself the Knight of the Green Sword."

Grasandor took the letter and listened to what Isanjo told him, and answered his father, saying: "Oh, my lord, what very great relief my heart receives from the fact that that noble knight should need the favor and help of your royal estate, and on seeing the recognition and gratitude that you have, sire, for the past things done by him! For my will to be satisfied there remains that your Grace be pleased, while Count Galtines remains behind to bring the troops if necessary, to grant me permission, along with twenty knights, to go at once to the Firm Island; because although in this dispute some way out may be vouchsafed, it will be a great honor for me to be in the company of such chivalry as is assembled there."

The king said to him: "Son, I would have deemed it good if you had waited to see the outcome of this, and you might have brought that equipment that it befitted my honor and yours to take; but since you are pleased with this, let what you ask be done, and choose whatever knights you please, and I shall order that a ship in which you may travel be made ready at once. And may it please God to give you a good journey so greatly to the honor of that noble knight that with our whole estate we may repay to him the debt that he singlehandedly left us."

This was done at once. And this Grasandor, prince and heir of this King Talinor of Bohemia, took with him the twenty knights most to his liking and put out to sea, and went his way bound for the Firm Island.

CHAPTER CIII

How Landin, nephew of Don Cuadragante, arrived in Ireland and what he obtained from the queen.

Landin, nephew of Don Cuadragante, arrived in Ireland with the message from his lord and secretly talked with the queen and told her his lord's request. And when she heard about such great and dangerous strife, although she knew that her father, King Abies of Ireland, had been killed by the hand of Amadis, as the first Book of this story relates, and she always had for him in her heart that harshness and enmity that in such a case one is accustomed to have, she reflected that it would be much better to help and remedy the present injuries than those past ones, which were almost forgotten. And she spoke with a few men whom she trusted, and with them she found a way whereby without the knowledge of the king her husband, Don Cuadragante, her uncle, was greatly helped, she having in mind that by augmenting Amadis's forces King Lisuarte would be destroyed and her husband, King Cildadan, along with his kingdom would be free from being bound and in vassalage to him.

Therefore, just as we have told you, all these troops were forthcoming with that good will and desire victors are required to have. But now the story ceases to speak of them in order to relate what the messengers of King Lisuarte did.

CHAPTER CIV

How don Guilan the Pensive arrived in Rome with the message of King Lisuarte, his lord, and concerning what he did on his mission to the Emperor Patin.

Don Guilan the Pensive traveled so far on his day-by-day journeying that twenty days after he left Great Britain he was in Rome with the Emperor Patin, whom he found with many people and great preparations for receiving Oriana, whom he expected each day, because Salustanquidio, his cousin, and Bronjadel de Roca had written him that they already had matters settled and that in complete security they would soon be with him, and he was greatly astonished at how late they were. And Don Guilan, wearing armor just as he did on the journey, except on his hands and head, entered the palace and went to where the emperor was, and knelt and kissed his hands, and gave the letter to him that he was carrying. And the emperor recognized him without difficulty, for frequently he had seen him at King Lisuarte's court at the time that he was there, when he returned very badly wounded from the blow that Amadis had struck him at night in the forest, as the second Book of this story relates; and he said to him: "Don Guilan, be you very welcome; I understand that you come with Oriana, your lady; tell me where she is, and my men who are bringing her."

"Sir," said he, "Oriana and your men remain in a place not proper for you or them."

"How is that?" said the emperor.

He said to him: "Sire, read that letter, and whenever you please, I shall tell you why I come, for there is much more to it than you can imagine."

The emperor read the letter, and saw that it was accredited; and as in all things he was very unpredictable and unrestrained, without considering any other procedure he said to him: "Tell me now the contents of this accredited letter in the presence of all these who are here, for I would not be able to restrain myself longer."

Don Guilan said to him: "Sire, since it pleases you, so be it. King Lisuarte, my lord, informs you that Salustanquidio and Bronjadel de Roca, and many other knights with them, arrived in his kingdom, and on your behalf asked of him his daughter Oriana to be your wife; and he, knowing your excellence and greatness, although this princess was his rightful heiress and what he and the queen his wife loved most in the world, in order to take you as a son and to win your esteem, against the will of all those of his kingdom, he gave her up to them together with that retinue and those adornments that befitted the greatness of your state and his own; and that they having set out over the sea, when outside the boundaries of Great Britain, Amadis of Gaul accompanied by many other knights sallied forth with another fleet, and your men having been put to rout, and many killed, including Prince Salustanquidio; and Brondajel de Roca and the Archbishop of Talancia and the Duke of Ancona taken prisoner, and many others with them, Oriana was seized, with all her ladies and maidens and Queen Sardamira; and all the prisoners and spoils were carried away to the Firm Island where they are holding her; and that from there they have sent messengers with a few proposals for negotiation, but that he has not been willing to entertain them until you, sire, whom this act so greatly concerns, know of it and see how you feel about it, notifying him that if it appears to you as it does to him that they ought to be punished, it be shortly, so that a long interval may not render the injury greater."

When the emperor heard this, he was quite astounded, and said with great sadness of heart: "Oh, wretched Emperor of Rome, if you do not punish this, it does not befit you to live a single hour in this world!"

And he turned and said: "Is it certain that Oriana is seized and my cousin dead?"

"Certain, without any doubt," said Don Guilan, "for everything has occurred just as I have told you."

"Then, knight, go back now," said the emperor, "and tell the king, your lord, that for this injury and revenge for it, I take the responsibility, and that he concern himself only with watching what I shall do; for if I seek to be his relative, it is not in order to cause him travail or anxiety, but to avenge him on anyone who harasses him."

"Sire," said Don Guilan, "you respond like the great lord that you are and as a knight of great courage; but I am aware that you are contending with men of such caliber that the resources there as well as those from here will be needed. And the king, my lord, until now has obtained complete satisfaction from all those who have offended him, and so he will from now on. And since I find in you, sire, such good security, I shall leave; and give orders to put into execution what is suitable, and very quickly, with such equipment as is needed to take vengeance without the contrary action's being received."

Whereupon Don Guilan took leave of the emperor, and not very content, for since this was a very noble knight and very prudent and brave, and he had seen that emperor speaking with such little authority and so heedlessly, he carried great concern in his heart to see the king, his lord, in the company of a man so impetuous, from which, unless by very good luck, nothing could come to him except complete discredit and dishonor. And so he made the return trip, lamenting frequently the great loss that the king, his lord, through his own serious fault, had sustained in losing Amadis and all his relatives, and many others of worth, who on account of him used to be in the king's service, and now they were such great enemies of his. Then with great effort he reached Great Britain, and was well received by the king and by all those of his court. And he spoke immediately with the king and told him all that he had observed in the emperor, and how he was preparing to come in great haste; and moreover he said to him: "May it be God's will, sire, that from your relationship with this man honor may come to you; for, so help me God, with very slight contentment do I come from where he holds sway, and I cannot believe that troops with such a leader will accomplish anything good."

The king said to him: "Don Guilan, I am very happy to see you come back safely in good health, and since I have you and others like you who will serve me, we shall need only the troops of the emperor; for even though he does not command or lead them, you knights suffice to govern him and me; and since he accepts it thus, it is necessary that he find us here so well safeguarded that on seeing it he will not rate his own strength so highly as he now does."

Thus was the king making ready very diligently everything necessary; for well he knew that his opponents were not failing to summon all the troops they could obtain, because he had learned that the Emperor of Constantinople and the King of Bohemia and King Perion and many others were summoning their forces in order to send them to the Firm Island; and he was of the opinion, in view of the excellence of Amadis and of all those knights who were with him, that when they saw themselves with those very great forces, they could not refrain from seeking him inside his kingdom. And for this reason he was not ceasing to look for help from everywhere, since he saw that it would be needed; and also he learned that King Arabigo and Barsinan, lord of Sansuenia, and many others with them, were preparing a great fleet, and he could not imagine what their destination was. At this juncture, Brandoyvas arrived, and told him that King Cildadan was preparing to carry out his mandate, and that Don Galvanes was imploring him not to order him to be against Amadis and Agrajes, his nephew; and that if he was not happy about this, he would leave to him free and unrestricted the Island of Mongaza, as he had agreed at the time that he received it from him that while he held it, he should be his vassal, and when he did not wish to be so, that by leaving the island to him he would be free. The king, as he was very sensible, although his need was great, saw clearly that Don Galvanes was right, and he sent word to tell him to remain, that even if in that military expedition he did not serve him, a time would come there when he could make amends for it.

Then a few days later Filispinel came back from King Gasquilan of Suesa, and told the king that he had received him very well, and very willingly would come to his aid, and to fight Amadis, in order to fulfill what he so greatly desired.

The king on learning the great resources that he had, decided not to delay, and ordered his nephew Giontes summoned, and said to him: "Nephew, it is necessary that you go at once as quickly as can be to the Patin, Emperor of Rome, and tell him that I am satisfied with what Don Guilan told me on his behalf, and that I am going to my town of Windsor, because it is near the harbor where he is to disembark, and that there I shall bring together all my companies; and I will be encamped in the field awaiting his arrival, that I entreat him earnestly that it be as quickly as he is able; because, in view of his great strength and mine, if immediately at the outset we surpass our opponents in troops, they will lack much of the help from those who would be coming tardily; and you, nephew, do not leave him until you come in his company, for your arrival will give him a greater desire and concern to come himself."

Giontes said to him: "Sire, what you command will not fail to be carried out by me."

The king left then for Windsor, and gave orders to summon all his troops. And Giontes put out to sea in a ship equipped and made ready with what was needed in the way of sailors as well as provisions for such a voyage to Rome.

CHAPTER CV

How GRASANDOR, SON OF THE KING OF BOHEMIA, MET GIONTES AND WHAT HAPPENED BETWEEN THEM.

We have told you that Grasandor left the court of his father, the King of Bohemia, in a ship with twenty knights in order to go to the Firm Island. While sailing over the sea, guided by chance, one night he happened upon Giontes, nephew of King Lisuarte, who with his message was going to Rome to the emperor, as you have already heard. And as they saw themselves close to each other, Grasandor gave orders to his sailors to steer toward that ship in order to seize it. And Giontes, as he was carrying only the company needed to sail the ship, and a few other servants, and was traveling on a business that was so important for the king his lord, thought only to avoid all confrontations and complete his journey as he had been ordered to do. But he was not able to withdraw sufficiently to keep from being captured and brought armed just as he was before Grasandor, and he asked him who he was. And he told him he was a knight of King Lisuarte who was going with the latter's message to the Emperor of Rome, and that if he out of courtesy would order him to be set free that he might continue his journey, he would thank him very much for it, since he had no motive or reason to detain him.

Grasandor said to him: "Knight, although I expect very quickly to be arrayed in aid of Amadis of Gaul against that king that you mention, and therefore not to be obliged to treat well any of his men, I am willing to grant you complete clemency and let you go, provided that you tell me your name and the message that you are taking to the Emperor."

Giontes said to him: "If by not telling you my name and for what I am going, I gained more honor and the king were better served, it would be futile for you to ask me, for it would be in vain. But because my mission is public, and in telling it, as well as who I am, I comply better with my obligation, I shall do as you ask. Know you that my name is Giontes, and I am a nephew of King Lisuarte's and the message that I bear is to bring the emperor with all his forces as quickly as I can in order that he join the king, my uncle, and go against those who captured Princess Oriana at sea, as I believe you have learned, because such an important event can not avoid being made public in many regions. Now I have told you what you want to know, let me go, if you please, on my way."

Grasandor said to him: "You have spoken like a knight. I set you free to go wherever you wish, and come back quickly with the one you mention, for you will find ready those for whom you are looking."

So Giontes went his way, and Grasandor gave orders to one of those knights who were going with him, that in a small boat that they had on board, he return to his father and tell him that news, and that since the affair was at such a stage, he asked him as a favor to notify him when the emperor and his troops were starting out to go to King Lisuarte, and that without any other notice being sent to him to dispatch all his troops to the Firm Island with Count Galtines, because if his reinforcements were the first, they would be much more highly appreciated. And thus it was done, for this King of Bohemia, when he learned this news, at once ordered his fleet to leave with many troops well armed, as one who was imbued with great affection and love with regard to augmenting the honor and advantage of Amadis.

Grasandor followed a straight course over the sea, and without any delay reached the harbor of the Firm Island; and when some of those on the island saw them, they told Amadis and he gave orders to go and find out who was arriving on the ship, and so they did. And when he was told that it was Grasandor, son of the King of Bohemia, he was greatly pleased, and mounting a horse he went to the lodging of Don Cuadragante; and they took Agrajes with them, and went to welcome him. And when they arrived at the harbor, Grasandor and his knights had already disembarked and were all on horseback; and when he saw Amadis coming toward him, he went ahead of his men and advanced to embrace him, and Amadis likewise, saying to him: "My lord Grasandor, be you very welcome, and I am greatly pleased to see you."

"My good lord," said he, "may it please God out of His mercy that you may always be pleased with me, and that your pleasure may be as augmented as mine is in knowing that the king my father and I can repay some of that great debt in which you left us; and it will be well for you to know some news that I discovered during the journey I have just made, and that you apply in time the proper remedy."

Then he related to them all that he had ascertained from Giontes, just as you have heard that he received it, and how from there he sent word to his father in order that after the latter learned that the troops of the emperor were moving, he, without receiving any further call, might send at once all his troops; concerning which he should have no doubt but that they would come before those of the enemy, and that from then on he should not worry about the call.

Don Cuadragante said to him: "If all of our friends help us with such good will as this lord, we shall have little fear from this attack."

So they went to the castle, and Amadis took Grasandor to his own quarters and had his men lodged and gave orders to provide them with everything they needed; and he sent word to all those lords to come and see that very honorable prince who had come to them; and so they did, for at once they all came to Amadis's quarters, expensively clad in fighting garb, as was always their habit in places where they were off duty. And when Grasandor saw them, and saw so many knights whose fame was so bruited about through all parts of the world, he was astonished and considered himself highly honored to be in the company of such men. All came up with great courtesy to embrace him and he, them, and they showed him great esteem. Amadis said to them: "Good lords, it will be well for you to know what this knight has told us concerning what he found out about King Lisuarte."

Then he related everything to them as you have already heard it, and everyone said that it would be well that other messengers be dispatched to call together the troops that were in readiness. And so it was done. And because this writing would be very long and tedious if there were told in detail the things that occurred on these journeys, we shall only tell you that when these messengers arrived at their destinations, the troops were called together by their lords, and having put out to sea they all traveled to the Firm Island, each ship with those who will be mentioned here: King Perion brought three thousand knights from among his vassals and friends. King Tafinor of Bohemia sent fifteen hundred knights with Count Galtines. Tantiles, majordomo of Queen Briolanja, brought twelve hundred knights. Branfil, brother of Don Bruneo, brought six hundred knights. Landin, nephew of Don Cuadragante, brought from Ireland six hundred knights. King Ladasan sent from Spain two thousand knights to his son Don Brian de Monjaste. Don Gandales brought from King Languines of Scotland, father of Agrajes, fifteen hundred knights. The troops of the Emperor of Constantinople that Gastiles, his nephew, brought, numbered eight thousand knights. All these troops that the story lists, arrived at the Firm Island. And the first one who came there was King Perion of Gaul, because of his having made haste, and because his land was closer than any of the others; and whether he was cordially welcomed by his sons and by all those lords, it is not necessary to say, and likewise the great pleasure that he had with them; and by him it was decided that all the troops of the Firm Island were to go forth with their tents and gear to a plain that was below the slope leading up to the castle — a very level and very beautiful plain surrounded by many groves and in which there were many fountains, and so it was done, for from then on all were encamped in the field; and as additional troops arrived, they were immediately billeted there. And as soon as all were assembled, who would be able to describe to you what knights, horses, and arms were there? Certainly you can believe that within the memory of man there were never such well chosen and so many troops as these at any time brought together in aid of any prince.

Oriana, whom this rupture grieved deeply, did nothing but weep and curse her ill-fortune, since it had brought her to the point that such a great loss of troops — unless God remedied the situation — would occur because of her. But those ladies who were with her comforted her with much love and compassion, saying that neither she nor those who were in her service were at fault in any of this, in the sight of God or that of the world; and although she was unwilling, they had her climb up to the highest point in the tower, from where the entire meadow and all the troops were visible. And when she saw all that field covered with troops, and so much armor gleaming, and so many tents, she could only think that the whole world was there assembled; and while all the ladies were gazing, for they were not paying heed to anything else, Mabilia went up to Oriana and said to her very quietly: "How does it seem to you, lady? Is there anyone else in the world who has such a servitor and lover as you have?"

Oriana said: "Oh, my lady and true friend! What shall I do? For my heart can in nowise endure what I see; for from this only great misfortune can come to me, because on one side is this man of whom you speak, who is the light of my eyes and the consolation of my sad heart, without whom it would be impossible for me to be able to live; and on the other is my father from whom, although I have found him very cruel, I cannot withhold that true love that as his daughter I owe him. Then, wretched woman that I am, what shall I do? For no matter which one of these men is destroyed, I shall always be all the days of my life the saddest and most unfortunate woman that ever was."

And wringing her hands, she began to weep. Mabilia took them in her clasp and said to her: "Lady, for God's sake I beg you to lay aside this anguish and have hope in Him, who many times to show His great power brings on such frightening things that offer very little hope for their being remedied; and subsequently with well considered counsel He brings them to an end in a way contrary to what men expect. And thus, lady, it can happen in this case, if it so pleases Him. And even assuming that the rupture be permitted by Him, you must consider that violent action as great as the one that was perpetrated against you cannot be remedied without another greater one. Then thank God that it is not your responsibility, as these lords have told you."

Oriana, who was very sensible, well understood that she was speaking the truth, and was somewhat comforted. Then they remained viewing the scene for a long while, and afterwards they withdrew to their apartment.

King Perion, after he saw all the troops billeted, took with him Grasandor, son of the King of Bohemia, and Agrajes, and said that he wanted to see Oriana; and so he went with them to the castle, and ordered Amadis and Don Florestan to remain with the troops. Oriana, when she learned of the coming of the king, was quite pleased because she had not seen him since he at her request had knighted Amadis of Gaul when he was called the Child of the Sea, at the time he was at the court of King Languines of Scotland, father of Agrajes, just as the first Book of this story relates; and she assembled with her all those ladies to welcome him. Then the king and those knights having arrived at her apartment, they entered Oriana's presence, and the king greeted her with great courtesy, and she greeted him very humbly, and afterwards he greeted Queen Briolanja and Queen Sardamira and all the other princesses and ladies. And Mabilia came to him and knelt seeking to kiss his hands, but he withdrew them and embraced her with great love, and said to her: "My good niece, from the queen, your aunt, and from your cousin Melicia I bring many messages and best regards to you as one whom they love and esteem, and Gandalin will bring to you a communication from them, for he remained behind in order to accompany Melicia, who will be here with you shortly, and will keep this lady company, for she so well deserves it."

Mabilia said to him: "May God thank them on my behalf for what, sire, you tell me, and I shall requite them for it in whatever way I can; and I am very happy about the coming of my cousin, and so this princess will be because for a long time she has desired to see her on account of the fine things that she has heard about her."

The king turned to Oriana and said to her: "My good lady, the same reason that has caused me to be regretful and deeply moved concerning your trials constrains me to find a remedy for them — which I greatly desire to do — and therefore I have come here, where may our Lord be pleased to give me an opportunity whereby service to you and your honor may be enhanced as both you and I, my good lady, desire. And I am very much surprised that the king, your father, so sensible and so punctilious in all the good ways of life that a king ought to possess, in this affair, which so greatly concerns his honor and reputation, has behaved so cruelly and pusillanimously; and since in the first instance he had been so mistaken, he ought to have made amends in the second; for these knights tell me that they besought him with great courtesy, and he would not listen to them. If in his own defense he has any excuse, it is only that great mistakes have this malady: people don't know how to turn their backs on them in order to return to a good understanding; instead, by being inflexible in their obstinacy they think that with more mistakes and greater insults they can remedy the original errors. Since the benefit and honor that from this affair is being prepared for him, only God knows, for He is the all-knowing Judge of the great injustice that he does you, so that in this very notorious affair He will show very strikingly His power. And you, my lady, in Him have great hope that He will help you and restore to you that high standing that your rights and great virtue deserve."

Oriana, as she was very intelligent and understood everything better than any other woman, gazed fixedly at the king, and he seemed to her so fine not only in his person but also in his speech, that she had never seen anyone else who to her seemed so to such an extent. And well she recognized that that man deserved to be the father of such sons, and with much justice was praised and his fame widespread throughout the world as one of the best knights that there were in it; and she was so comforted on seeing him, that if the love that she had for her own father, who was keeping her in very severe anguish and worry, had not been so great, she would not have cared had the whole world been against her, as long as she had on her side such a leader and the troops that he expected to command; and she said to him: "My lord, what thanks for what you have said to me can a poor wretched, disinherited maiden such as I am give to you? Certainly only those thanks that you have been given by all those women whom up to now with great danger to yourself you have succored, which are to serve God in return and win that great fame and distinction that you have won among peoples. One thing I ask be done for me in addition to the great benefits that I am receiving from you, my good lord, and that is that in everything in which agreement may be reached, it be achieved with the king my father; because not only our Lord will be served by avoiding the deaths of so many troops, but I would consider myself the most fortunate woman in the world if the rupture could be ended."

The king said to her: "Matters have reached such a state that it would be very difficult for agreement of the two parties to be reached; but often it happens that at the height of a rupture harmony is achieved, which could not be found with great effort up till then, and thus in this matter it may happen. And if such an agreement is found, you may be certain, my good lady, that not only in the service of God but also in yours, with complete devotion, it will be approved very willingly by me, as one who desires greatly to serve you."

Oriana thanked him with deep humility, as one in whom complete virtue reigned more than in any other woman.

While King Perion was talking with Oriana, Agrajes and Grasandor were conversing with Queen Briolanja, Queen Sardamira, and Olinda and other ladies. And when Grasandor saw Oriana and those other ladies so more extremely beautiful and gracious than all those he had ever seen or heard, he was so astonished that he did not know what to say, and he could only believe that God with His own hand had fashioned them. And although no other lady could equal Oriana and Queen Briolanja and Olinda in beauty, unless it were Melicia, who was about to arrive, he liked so well the charm and grace and elegance of Princess Mabilia, and her modesty, that from that hour on he agreed in his heart not to serve or love any other woman except her. And thus was his heart made a prisoner, for the longer he gazed at her the more affection she aroused in him, as at times and in such acts usually happens.

Then, while he was so well-nigh distraught, as a young knight who had never before left his father's kingdom, he asked Agrajes if he would be willing out of courtesy to tell him the names of those ladies who were there with Oriana. Agrajes told him who they were and the eminence of their rank; and as Mabilia was still with King Perion and Oriana, he asked him about her also. And Agrajes told him that she was his sister, and that he believed there was not a woman in the world of a better disposition or more beloved by all who knew her. Grasandor kept silent for he said nothing, and in his heart he was sure that Agrajes was speaking the truth; and so he was, for all who knew this Princess Mabilia loved her for the great humility and grace she possessed.

While they were having such enjoyment in order to afford it to Oriana, who was not able to be cheerful, Queen Briolanja said to Agrajes: "My good lord and great friend, I must speak with Don Cuadragante and Brian de Monjaste in your presence on a certain matter, and I beg you to have them come before you leave."

Agrajes said to her: "Lady, that will be done at once."

And he directed one of his men to call them, and they came. And the queen drew them aside with Agrajes, and said to them: "My lords, you already know about the danger in which I saw myself, from which, after God, your prowess delivered me; and how you put Trion, that cousin of mine, whom I hold a prisoner, in my custody. And while pondering what I shall do with him, on the one hand I see him to be the son of Abiseos, my uncle, who killed my father so wrongly and treasonably, and that the seed of such a wicked man ought to perish, in order that, if it is sown elsewhere, such treason might not spring up from it; and on the other hand because the close kinship that I have with him constrains me, and that often it happens that sons are very different from their parents, and that the assault that this one made was the act of a youth motivated by a few evil advisers, as I have learned, I am unable to make up my mind what to do. And therefore I have had you summoned, so that, as persons whose great discretion in this matter and in everything has insight as to what one should do, you may tell me your opinion."

Don Brian de Monjaste said to her: "My good lady, your good sense has so well encompassed what might be said about this matter, that there remains nothing to advise, except to remind you that one of the reasons why princes and grandees are praised and their estate and persons secure, is clemency, because with this they follow the teaching of that One whose ministers they are; to whom, when people do what they should, everything else ought to be left. And it would be well, in order to clarify your hesitation in determining which one of the two courses of action that you, my lady, have mentioned, you should follow, that you order him to come here and for the most part by speaking with him, one could to some extent form a judgment concerning what, in his absence, could neither be seen nor finally divined."

They all considered this a good idea, and thus it was done, for the queen asked King Perion to tarry a while until she reached a decision with those knights about a matter of great importance to her. Trion having arrived, he appeared before the queen with great humility, and with such a bearing that he made quite clear the great lineage from which he had sprung. The queen said to him: "Trion, I have reason to pardon you or to order vengeance exacted for the transgression that you committed against me. You know that, since what your father did to mine is also well known to you. But no matter what events have taken place, recognizing that the closest relative that I have in this world is you, I am moved, not only to have pity for your youth, if there is in you the acquaintanceship with reason that you ought to have, but to hold you in that rank and honor that I would if instead of the enemy that you have been to me, you had been my friend and adherent. Now in the presence of these knights I want you to tell me how you feel about it, and may your statement be so frank that whether good or the opposite, there issue fearlessly from your mouth the truth that a man of such high station ought to speak."

Trion, who was expecting some other worse news, said: "Lady, in what relates to my father I do not know how to answer, because the tender age at which I was excuses me; in regard to my own actions, it is true that, by my own desire and will, as well as by that of many others who counseled me, I had sought to put you in such straits, and so free myself that I would be able to attain the rank that the greatness of my lineage demands. But, since Fortune, both in the first instance involving my father and brothers and in this second one has chosen to be so adverse to me, there remains for me no defense except by recognizing you to be the true heiress to that kingdom that was left by our grandparents; and that I attain with many services the great compassion and mercy that you show me, and by your will what by force my heart was desirous of attaining."

"Then if you, Trion," said the queen, "do so and are a loyal vassal to me, I shall be to you not merely a cousin but a true sister, and from me you will obtain those favors with which your honor may be satisfied and your rank content."

Then Trion knelt and kissed her hands. And from then on, this Trion was to this queen so loyal in all things that he governed the entire kingdom exactly as she commanded; from which grandees ought to learn to be inclined to clemency and compassion in many instances requiring them to exercise it with everyone, and especially with their relatives, giving thanks to God that, they being of the same blood and ancestry, He made them lords over them, and the latter their vassals; and although sometimes these err, to tolerate the vexation of it in view of the great domination they exercise over them.

The queen said to him: "Then letting bygones be bygones, and setting you free, I wish that, taking charge of governing and commanding these troops of mine, you do whatever be Amadis's will."

Those knights praised highly what this very beautiful and generous queen did, and from then on this knight was by them much sought after and honored, as will be told later in more detail, and by all the others acquainted with his excellence and great courage.

King Perion took leave of Oriana and of those ladies, and with those knights he returned to the encampment. And Queen Briolanja highly recommended to Agrajes that he introduce Trion, her cousin, to Amadis, and tell him all that had happened with him, and thus it was done; for he told him everything in detail.

Then King Perion having arrived at the encampment, he found that at that time Balais de Carsante was arriving there with twenty knights of his lineage, who were very good and very well armed and equipped, to serve and aid Amadis. And I want you to know that this knight was one of those whom Amadis had released along with many others from the cruel dungeon of Arcalaus the Enchanter, and the one who had cut off the head of the maiden who brought Amadis and his brother Don Galaor together in order that they might slay each other. And certainly if it had not been for him, one of them, or both, would have had to die, as the first Book of this story relates. Balais told the king and those knights that King Lisuarte was encamped near Windsor, and that, according to what he had been told, the king might have as many as six thousand mounted men and other troops on foot, and that the Emperor of Rome had arrived at the port with a great fleet, and all the troops were disembarking and establishing their encampment near King Lisuarte's; and that furthermore, Gasquilan, King of Suesa, had come, and that he brought eight hundred knights, good fighting men; and King Cildadan had already come there with two hundred knights, and that he thought that for two weeks they would not move from there, because the troops were arriving very worn out from their voyages. This information this Balais de Carsante was enabled to ascertain thoroughly because a very good castle that he had was within King Lisuarte's realm, being located at a place where without much effort he could obtain news concerning the troops.

So they spent that day at ease in the field, preparing all their weapons, armor, and horses for the battle, although their armor was all newly made, fine and resplendent, as will be described later on.

Next day very early Master Elisabad arrived at the harbor with Grasinda's troops, in whose fleet came five hundred knights and archers. And when Amadis found out about it, he took Angriote and Don Bruneo and went to welcome him with that good will and love that reason made obligatory. And they had all the troops disembark and they lodged in the encampment with the others, and Libeo, the master's nephew, with them as their captain. And they took the master between them and with great pleasure brought him to King Perion; and Amadis told him who he was, and what he had done for him, as the third Book of this story relates, when the Endriago was slain, and how there could not have come to them at such a time anyone else who would have helped them so much. The king received him well and with good grace and said to him: "My good friend, let the argument remain until after the battle, if we should come out alive, as to whom my son Amadis should be most grateful: to me, who after God, created him from nothing; or to you, who returned him alive from death."

The master kissed his hands and quite pleased said to him: "Sire, let it be as you direct; for until further investigation is made I do not want to yield to you any advantage as to whom he is most obligated."

All derived great pleasure from what the king said and the reply of Master Elisabad. And he said at once to the king: "My lord, I bring you two pieces of news that you need to know; and they are: that the Emperor of Rome has already left with his fleet, in which according to what I have been assured by persons whom I sent there, he carries ten thousand mounted men; and furthermore there came to me a message from Gastiles, nephew of the Emperor of Constantinople, that he was already at sea with eight thousand horses which his uncle was sending in aid of Amadis, and that in his opinion, three days hence he would arrive in port."

All those who heard it were very happy and very much encouraged with such reports, especially the troops of lowest rank. So just as you hear, King Perion was with all that company, looking after the arriving troops and making ready the things needed for the battle.

CHAPTER CVI

How the emperor of Rome arrived in Great Britain with his fleet and what he and King Lisuarte did.

The story says that Giontes, nephew of King Lisuarte, after he left Grasandor, as you have heard, went directly to Rome, and not only because of his haste but also on account of the emperor's, very quickly the great fleet was armed and equipped with those ten thousand knights about whom we have already told you; and at once the emperor put out to sea, and without encountering any obstacle on the way he arrived in Great Britain at that port of the town of Windsor, where he knew King Lisuarte was. And when the latter learned of it, he mounted, along with many nobles and those two kings, Cildadan and Gasquilan, and went to welcome him. And when he arrived, the majority of the troops had already disembarked, and the emperor with them. And when they saw one another they went to embrace each other, and they greeted each other with much pleasure. The emperor said to him: "If you have received any discredit or vexation because of me, I am here, so that your honor will be satisfied with a double victory; and since I alone was the cause of it, I should like for you to give me the opportunity to take vengeance with my own men alone, so that it may be for everybody a lesson and an admonishment that no one should dare to anger such a great man as I am."

The king said to him: "My good friend and lord, you and your troops arrive seasick as a result of your long voyage; order them to disembark and set up camp, and they will be refreshed from the ordeal they have suffered. And meanwhile we shall have word concerning our enemies; and once it is known, you will be able to take the position and counsel that you prefer."

The emperor wanted the departure to be immediate; but the king, who knew better than he what was needed and with whom they were in contention, restrained him until the proper time; for he well perceived that his whole cause depended on that battle. So they were in that camp for a good week, marshalling the troops that each day came to the king.

Then it so happened that while the emperor and the king and many other knights were riding one day through those meadows and fields surrounding the camp, they saw an armed knight on horseback coming and a squire with him who was carrying his armor; and if someone were to ask me who it was, I would tell him that it was Enil, the good knight, nephew of Don Gandales. And when he reached the camp, he asked if Arquisil, a relative of the Emperor Patin was there, and he was told that he was, and that he was riding with the emperor. When he heard this, he was very glad, and went to where he saw men riding, for he was sure that Arquisil would be there; and when he came up to them he found that the emperor and those kings were conversing in a field near a riverbank about matters pertaining to the battle. And Enil found out that Arquisil was with them, and he went toward them and greeted them very humbly, and they told him he was very welcome, and asked what he wanted. Enil, when he heard this, said: "Sirs, I come from the Firm Island with a message from that noble knight, my lord Amadis of Gaul, son of King Perion, for a knight called Arquisil."

When Arquisil heard that he was asking for him, he said: "Knight, I am the one you seek; say whatever you wish, for it will be heard."

Enil said to him: "Arquisil, Amadis of Gaul informs you that when he was calling himself the Knight of the Green Sword, while he was at the court of King Tafinor of Bohemia, there arrived there a knight named Don Garadan with eleven other knights accompanying him, of whom you were one; and that he had a battle with the said Don Garadan, in which the latter was overcome and killed, as you saw; and that immediately next day he had one with you and with your companions — he and eleven other knights — as had been agreed upon; and that you and they being overcome, he took you prisoner, from which situation at your request, he set you free; and that you promised as a loyal knight, that any time that you were called upon, you would again submit to him. And now through me he calls upon you to fulfill what a man of such high rank and such a noble knight as you are, ought to fulfill."

Arquisil said: "Certainly, knight, in all that you have said, you have spoken the truth; for it happened just as you say. There remains only the question of whether that knight who called himself the Knight of the Green Sword is really Amadis of Gaul."

Some of those knights who were there told him that he could believe without doubt that he was. Then Arquisil said to the emperor: "You have heard, sire, what this knight asks of me, from which I cannot be excused without fulfilling what I am obligated to do, because you may believe that he saved my life and prevented from killing me those who had a great desire to do so. And therefore, sire, I beg you not to be irked at my departure; for if under such circumstances I were to forego it, it would not be right that a man so powerful and of such high lineage as you should consider me his relative or keep me in his company."

The emperor, as he was very violent and usually gave more heed to the satisfaction of his feelings or preferences than to the integrity of his high rank, said: "You, knight, who have come on behalf of Amadis, tell him that he ought to be sated with occasioning me the annoyances that petty men are wont to occasion great ones, for otherwise he is set well apart from them, and that the time will come when he will find out who I am and what I can do, and that he shall not escape anywhere, not even in that cave of thieves in which he is taking refuge, from paying sevenfold, to my full satisfaction for what he has done to me. And you, Arquisil, carry out what is asked of you, for it will not be long before I put into your hands this person of whom you are a prisoner, so that you may do with him whatever you please."

Enil, when he heard this, was furious, and with all fear suppressed, he said: "I well believe, sire, that Amadis knows you, for he has already seen you another time, more as a knight errant than as a mighty lord, and likewise you have seen him when you did not leave his presence so easily. Well, in the present situation, just as you come in another guise, so he is coming to look for you. Let him who knows what is past form his own judgment, and let God judge the future, for that is granted only to Him."

When King Lisuarte saw that, he was afraid that that knight might receive some injury by command of the emperor, from which he would feel great sorrow, and this he had deduced from all that he had heard him say, because it was quite foreign to his nature to be anything as king but reasonable in speech and severe in action. And before the emperor said anything, he took him by the hand and said to him: "Let us go to our tents, for it is time to sup, and may this knight enjoy the liberty that messengers are wont and entitled to have."

Thus the emperor went away as angry as if his vexation had been with someone of as high rank as he. Arquisil took Enil to his tent, and paid him high honor; and then armed himself, and mounting his horse went with him.

Then here the story does not tell a thing about what happened to him, except that they arrived at the Firm Island in peace and harmony; and when they were near the encampment, and Arquisil saw so many troops, for now those of the Emperor of Constantinople had arrived, he was greatly astonished to see them; and he fell silent, for he said nothing; instead he pretended not to be looking. And Enil took him to the tent of Amadis, where not only by him but by many other noble knights he was very well received.

So Arquisil was there four days during which Amadis took him about with him and showed him all the troops and the distinguished knights, and he told him their names, which were very well known through all parts of the world for the prowess and great feats of arms of those who bore them. He marveled greatly on seeing such knighthood, especially that of those very famous knights; for he indeed believed that if the emperor were to meet with some reverse it would be only through these men, for concerning the other troops he had little fear, nor would he have paid any heed to the matter if they had not had such leaders, for the strength of the latter would suffice to strengthen all those on their side. And he saw clearly that the emperor his lord had need of great resources to do battle with them, and he considered himself unlucky to be a prisoner at such a time; for if he had been very far away, on hearing of an affair so outstanding and great as that was, he would have come in order to be in it. Then, since he was present and yet not able to participate, he considered himself the most unlucky man in the world; and he became so immersed in meditation that without feeling or desiring it, the tears fell down his cheeks. And in this state of great anguish he decided to test Amadis's virtue and nobility. Thus it came about that while the valiant Amadis and many other great lords and brave knights were in King Perion's tent, and Arquisil with them because he had not yet been told where he was to be held prisoner, he stood up where he was and said to the king: "Sire, may it please your Grace to hear me with Amadis of Gaul in the presence of these knights."

The king told him he would gladly hear all that he might care to say. Then Arquisil related there all that had happened to him in the battle that Don Garadan and he and his other companions had had with Amadis and the knights of the King of Bohemia, and how they had been overcome and battered, and Don Garadan slain and how Amadis with great courtesy had freed him from the hands of those who had the great desire and intent to kill him, and how at his request and petition Amadis had set him free and allowed him to go so that he could give some help to his badly wounded companions, leaving him as a pledge his faith and promise as his prisoner to hasten to him whenever summoned, as in more detail the third Book of this story relates, and that now he had been summoned by Amadis, and had come, as they saw, to keep his word and be at the place appointed according to his order; but that if Amadis, using with him that liberality that out of his great courtesy and virtue he was accustomed to exercise with all those in need of his favor and aid, were to give him permission to serve as he ought his lord the emperor in that battle which was expected to be waged as an event so outstanding in the world, he promised as a good and faithful knight that in his presence and that of all others there, if he remained alive, to complete his term as prisoner. Amadis, who at the time was on his feet with him in order to honor him, responded: "Arquisil, my noble lord, if I were to pay heed to the arrogance and the rude speech of the emperor your lord, I would treat everything connected with him with great severity and cruelty, without fearing thereby to have gone too far; but as you are without fault, and the times have brought us to such a pass that the worth of each one of us shall be made manifest, I am disposed to agree to what you have asked, and I grant you leave so that you can be in this battle; from which, if you emerge unharmed, be back in this island within ten days to carry out whatever by me and by those on my side you may be ordered to do."

Arquisil thanked him profusely and so promised.

Some may ask for what reason so much mention is made in this great story of a knight of such slight renown as this one is. I say that the reason for it is this: because in the past this man with much courage dealt with all the confrontations that came his way, as you shall hear subsequently, by reason of his great lineage and noble rank he became Emperor of Rome; and he always considered Amadis, who was the chief cause of his obtaining such great sovereignty, as a true brother, as will be related in more detail at the proper time.

Well, those lords having left there and retired to their tents and quarters, Arquisil armed himself, and mounting his horse took leave of Amadis and all those who were with him, and returned by the way he had come. And the story does not tell of anything that happened to him, except that he reached the place where the emperor's army was, where all were greatly pleased at his arrival. And although they asked him many questions, he was willing to tell only about the great courtesy that he had received from that very noble knight Amadis; for you may well believe that his courtesies were of such nature and so many that they would hardly be found at that time in any other knight.

And I want you to know that the reason why these knights traveled so far without finding any adventure as in times past, was because they all paid heed only to providing and making ready the things needed for the battle; for it seemed to them that in view of the magnitude of the confrontation, to engage in other quests that would interfere with this one would be degrading.

Arquisil, having arrived at the camp, spoke with the emperor in private, and told him the truth about everything: about the large body of troops of their adversaries, as well as about the famous knights who were there, giving him the names of most of them, and how Amadis of Gaul had granted him permission to be in that battle and was not much concerned about it;

and that what he had found out was that Amadis, on learning that the emperor was moving forward with his army, would move at once against him without any fear; and that he was informing him concerning everything so that he might do what best served his purpose. The emperor, when he heard this — although he was very haughty and unreasonable, as you have heard, and he certainly was in everything that he did, recognizing the integrity of this knight (on account of which he had no great love for him) and that he would say nothing but the truth — was dismayed just as all those are wont to be who expend their efforts more on words than on deeds; and he would have liked not to be engaged in that quest, for he well recognized the great difference between the one body of troops and the other, and he had never thought in view of his own great force when joined with that of King Lisuarte, that Amadis would have had the ability or equipment to leave the Firm Island, believing that there they would have surrounded him both by land and by sea, so that through starvation by siege or by some other means he would have been able to recover Oriana and redress the blemish and discredit to his honor. And from then on, exhibiting more hope and determination than he privately felt, he tried to conform to the will of King Lisuarte and those nobles.

So they remained two weeks in that camp, mustering the troops and receiving the knights, who each day were coming to join them; so that they discovered that they were, in all, the following: the emperor brought ten thousand horses; King Lisuarte six thousand five hundred; Gasquilan, King of Suesa, eight hundred; King Cildadan, two hundred.

Then everything having been made ready, the emperor and the king gave orders to break camp, and that the troops be drawn up in that great meadow over which they were to travel. And thus it was done, for all having been placed with their respective battalions, the emperor made three brigades of his body of troops. The first he gave to Floyan, brother of Prince Salustanquidio with two thousand five hundred knights. The second he gave to Arquisil with a like number, and he was left with five thousand to serve them as rear guard. And he asked King Lisuarte to approve of his leading the vanguard, and thus it was done; although the latter would have preferred to take over that function himself, because he did not rate those troops very highly, and was afraid that from their lack of discipline some great reverse might come to them; but he agreed to give him that honor, which in such cases is viewed as bad, for with all zeal laid aside, one ought to follow what reason dictates.

King Lisuarte made of his troops two brigades; in the one he put King Arban of North Wales with three thousand knights, and ordered that with him should be his own son Norandel, Don Guilan the Pensive, Don Cendil of Ganota, and Brandoyvas. And he gave from his own troops one thousand knights to King Cildadan and Gasquilan, which with the other one thousand that they had, would make another brigade. And the others he took with him, and he gave his standard to the good Don Grumedan, who with much sorrow and anguish of heart regarded that very bad exchange that King Lisuarte had made in appointing the troops he considered unfit to lead the vanguard. Then this having been done, and the brigades organized, they moved across the field behind the supply train, which was going with the billeters to set up camp. Who could describe to you the horses and the very fine, glittering armor of every description worn by the riders? Certainly it would be a very heavy task to tell it; mention will be made only of what the emperor and the kings and a few other outstanding knights wore. But this will be when on the day of the battle they arm themselves to participate in it. But we shall not speak of them until the proper time; and now there is to be related what King Perion and those lords who were with him in the camp by the Firm Island did.

CHAPTER CVII

How king perion moved the troops from the camp against his enemies, and how he distributed the brigades for the battle.

The story tells that this King Perion, as he was a very intelligent knight and of great valor, and until then Fortune had always exalted him by protecting and defending his honor, and as he saw himself in such an outstanding confrontation in which his person and sons and most of his relatives were to be involved, and as he knew King Lisuarte to be so vigorous and such an avenger of injuries done him — for knowing about the emperor's temperament, neither for him nor his troops did he have the slightest respect — was always thinking about what was needed, for he held the opinion that if Fortune were against them, that king, like a mad dog, would not satisfy his desire with the first vanquishment; rather, very diligently and harshly, not considering any amount of effort too great, he would seek them out wherever they might be, as had been his intention all the while, if he won. And besides the other things that it was necessary to provide, King Perion always kept people in strategic places from whom he might find out what his enemies were doing, and by whom he was immediately informed as to how the troops were coming against them, and in what formation.

So this having been ascertained, early the next morning he arose promptly and gave orders to summon all the captains and knights of noble lineage; and he told them about it, and that in his opinion the camp should be broken, and that the troops having been assembled in those fields, a distribution of the brigades should be made so that all would know to which captain and standard they were to rally, and that this having been done, they should move against their enemies with great force and a good expectation of overcoming them because of the just quest in which they were engaged. They all approved this, and therefore very insistently they begged him that because of his royal dignity and great valor and prudence he take charge of commanding and governing them on that expedition, and that they would all be obedient to him. He agreed to it; for he well recognized that they were asking for what was right and he could not rightly be excused from it. Then when he ordered his plans carried out, the camp was broken, and the troops, all armed and mounted on horseback were stationed on that great plain. The noble king stationed himself in the very center on a very beautiful big horse, and clad in fine armor; and ten pages on ten horses, all bearing the same device, who were to go about during the battle and with them rescue the knights who needed horses. And as he was already of such an age that most of his head and beard was white, and his face ruddy with the heat of his armor and the pride in his heart, and as all knew about his great courage, he appeared so handsome, and such encouragement did he give to the troops who were gazing at him that he caused them to lose all fear, for they really thought that, after God, that leader would be the cause of giving them the glory of the battle. While he was thus stationary, he looked at Don Cuadragante and said to him: "Brave knight, I entrust the vanguard to you; and you, my son Amadis, and Angriote de Estravaus, and Don Gavarte of the Fearful Valley, and Enil, and Balais de Carsante, and Landin, accompany him with the five hundred knights from Ireland and the fifteen hundred of those that I brought. And you, very noble nephew Agrajes, take the second brigade; and let Don Bruneo de Bonamar and Branfil, his brother, accompany you with their troops and with yours, whereby you will be sixteen hundred knights in number. And you, honorable knight Grasandor, take the third brigade. And you, my son Don Florestan and Dragonis, and Landin de Fajarque, and Elian the Brave, with the troops of Grasandor's father the king, and with Trion and the troops of Queen Briolanja, so that you will be two thousand seven hundred knights in all, accompany him."

And he said to Don Brian de Monjaste: "And you, honorable knight, my nephew, take the fourth brigade with your troops and with three thousand of the knights of the Emperor of Constantinople, so that you will have five thousand knights; and let Mancian of the Bridge of Silver, and Sadamon, and Urlandin, son of the count of Urlanda go with you."

And he ordered Don Gandales to take a thousand knights of his own and render aid in the major melees. And the king took with him Gastiles with the emperor's remaining troops, and he placed himself under his own banner; and he requested all to look for it just as if the emperor himself were there in person.

The brigades having been organized as you have heard, everyone advanced in order over that field, playing many trumpets and many other instruments used in war. Oriana and the queens, and the princesses and ladies and maidens were gazing at them, and they earnestly besought God to help them, and if it should be His will, to put them at peace.

But now the story ceases to speak about these men, who were going to mass against their enemies, as you have heard; and returns to Arcalaus the Enchanter.

CHAPTER CVIII

How, WHEN ARCALAUS THE ENCHANTER LEARNED THAT THESE TROOPS WERE PREPARING TO FIGHT, HE SENT WORD POSTHASTE TO SUMMON KING ARABIGO AND HIS COMPANIES.

Arcalaus the Enchanter, as you have heard, was keeping on the alert King Arabigo and Barsinan, Lord of Sansuenia, and the King of the Deep Island, who had escaped from the battle of the Seven Kings, and all the relatives of Dardan the Haughty; and when he found out that the troops had come to King Lisuarte and Amadis, in great haste he sent a knight, his relative, whose name was Garin, son of Grumen, whom Amadis had killed when from him and three other knights accompanying Arcalaus the Enchanter he took Oriana, as the first Book of this story relates. And he ordered him not to rest day or night until he had notified all these kings and knights, and that he should urge them to make haste in coming. And he remained in his castle, summoning his friends and those of the lineage of Dardan, and gathering as many fighting men as he could.

Then this Garin reached King Arabigo, whom he found in his great city of Arabiga, which was the metropolis of his whole kingdom, from which city all the kings of the country took the name Arabigo, and because his kingdom included a large share of the land of Arabia; and he told him all of what Arcalaus had apprised him, and all the others who were holding their troops on the alert; and that news having been learned by them, at once without further delay they summoned them; and they were all assembled together near a very good town of the kingdom of

Sansuenia, which had the name of Califan. And they set up their tents in those fields, and in all they probably numbered as many as twelve thousand knights. And there they fitted out their entire fleet, which was quite large and carrying a good personnel, with as many provisions as they could get, as people who were going to a foreign kingdom. And with much pleasure and favorable weather they went forth on their voyage, and in a week landed in Great Britain at a place which was a seaport, where Arcalaus had a very strong castle. Arcalaus already had with him six hundred very fine knights, most of whom greatly hated King Lisuarte and Amadis because they had always harassed them as malefactors and had slain many of their relatives, and they themselves were nearly all fugitives.

When that fleet made port there, I could not begin to describe the great pleasure they had with each other; and it having been ascertained by Arcalaus's spies that the troops of King Lisuarte and those of Amadis were already advancing toward each other, and the route they were taking, they moved at once with their whole company. The vanguard was led by Barsinan, who was a young and vigorous knight very eager to avenge the death of his father and his brother Gandalod, and to demonstrate the strength and ardor of his heart, with two thousand knights and some archers and crossbowmen. Arcalaus had the second division, and you may believe that he was not inferior to Barsinan in strength and great valor; rather, although he had lost half of his right hand, in many lands there would not be found a better knight at arms than he was, nor a more valiant one, except that his evil deeds and his deceits took away from him all the glory that his courage won. He brought six hundred knights, and King Arabigo gave him two thousand four hundred of his own. King Arabigo and the other king, he of the Deep Island, had the third brigade with all the other troops, and the former brought with him six relatives of Brontajar d'Anfania, whom Amadis had killed in the Battle of the Seven Kings when he wore the golden helmet, as the third Book of this story relates. And this Brontajar d'Anfania was so valiant both in body and determination, that with him those on his side hoped to win; and thus it certainly would have been, except that Amadis saw the great havoc that he was wreaking on the troops of King Lisuarte, and that if it lasted very long it would be sufficient to give the honor of the battle to those on Brontajar's side; and he went at him and with one blow he crippled him so that he fell to the ground, where he died.

These six knights that I am telling you about came from Centaur Island, where it is said that originally the centaurs dwelt, and they were as huge in body and strength as those centaurs, for they were direct descendants of the mightiest and most valiant giants that there were in the world.

Well, these knights had found out about this great battle that was imminent, and they made up their minds to be in it, both to avenge the death of that Brontajar, who was the outstanding man of their family, and to prove themselves with those knights of whom they had heard such great reports. And for this reason they came to King Arabigo, who was greatly pleased with them, and asked them to be in his battalion, and so they unwillingly agreed to it, for they would have preferred that he order them placed in the vanguard.

In the meantime there arrived there the Duke of Bristol, who, although he had been approached by Arcalaus, had not ventured to show himself, considering what he had told him to be of slight importance; but when he saw the great gathering of troops that had assembled, he decided that it would be well for him to join them, on the chance that he might be able to avenge the death of his father — whom Don Galvanes, Agrajes, and Olivas had killed, as the first Book of this story relates — and recover his land, which King Lisuarte had taken from him, saying that his father had died as a traitor; and he reflected that if things were to go badly for King Lisuarte, he would be able to be reestablished in his own possessions, and if badly for Amadis, he would be avenged on those who had done him so much harm. And when he arrived, and King Arabigo and those lords saw him and were told who he was, they took great pleasure with him, and they were greatly encouraged by his arrival, because they valued him more — since he was a native of the land and had in it some towns and castles about which he was concerned — than someone else who was a foreigner with many more. With his men and with five hundred knights that King Arabigo gave him, this duke was outstanding.

Thus with such troops as you hear and in such order, those companies left by a shortcut with the best guards that they were able to station, having decided to place themselves in a position where they would be secure and from which they might sally forth when it was time to fall upon their enemies.

CHAPTER CIX

How the Emperor of Rome and King Lisuarte went with their entire company toward the Firm Island to look for their enemies.

The story states that the Emperor of Rome and King Lisuarte, with those companies that we have told you about, left the camp they had near Windsor and decided to travel very slowly so that the troops and horses might remain fresh, and that day they only traveled about three leagues; and they set up their camp on a large plain near a forest, and they rested there that night. And next day at dawn they departed in their formation, as we told you, and thus they continued on their way until they learned from some local people that King Perion and his companies were coming toward them, and that they had left them a two days' journey from where they themselves were. And immediately King Lisuarte gave orders to make the provision that Ladasin the Fencer, as he was called, first cousin of Don Guilan, with fifty knights go reconnoitering the land, always keeping three leagues ahead of the army; and on the third day they encountered the guards of King Perion, which he likewise had provided with Enil and forty knights with him. And there both groups of scouts halted, and each one informed his own side, and they did not venture to fight, because they were under orders not to do so; and the armies came from both directions so close to each other in a great and very level field that there was only a space of half a league between them. In these armies came many knights highly experienced in warfare, so that very little advantage could be had by either side over the other; and it appeared that almost by mutual agreement of the two sides both caused their camps to be fortified with many dugouts and other defenses, in order to take refuge there if things went badly for them.

These armies being situated just as you hear, Gandalin, Amadis's squire, arrived, who with Melicia had come from Gaul to the Firm Island, and he had tried very hard to arrive before the battle began, and the reason for it was this: You already know that Gandalin was the son of that good knight Don Gandales, who reared Amadis, and he was his foster brother; and since the day that Amadis became a knight, calling himself Child of the Sea, he knew that he was not his brother, for until then they had considered themselves brothers. And from that hour on, Gandalin had always attended him as his squire; and although Amadis had been urged many times by Gandalin to dub him a knight, he did not dare to do so, because Gandalin was the greatest confidant of his love affair. He was the one who many times saved him from death, for in view of the anguish and mortal desires he experienced for his lady Oriana, which were continually tormenting and afflicting his heart, if in this Gandalin he had not invariably found comfort, he would have died a thousand times over; for, as the latter was his confidant for everything, and with no one else could he speak, if in any way he parted with him, it would be the same as parting with life. And as he knew that if he made him a knight they could not be together, because then Gandalin would have to go in search of adventures whereby he might win honor although logically Amadis was under great obligation to knight him, as this great story has set forth, both because of Gandalin's father who had brought him up after rescuing him from the sea, and on account of Gandalin himself, who had served him better than any other knight was ever served by his squire, he did not dare to part with him. And since Gandalin understood this, for he was very intelligent, because of the abundant love that he had for him, although he greatly desired to be a knight in order to show himself the son of the good knight Gandales and reared by such a man, on account of seeing Amadis in such great need of him, he had not dared to pressure him in the matter. But now, on seeing how he already had his lady Oriana in his possession, and that willingly or by force he would not part from her except in death, he decided that with much justice he could ask for knighthood, and especially in view of a thing as great and outstanding as that battle would be. And with this thought, after having delivered the greetings from the queen, Amadis's mother, and having told Amadis of the coming of his sister Melicia and of how delighted Oriana and Mabilia and all those ladies had been with her and how it was the most beautiful sight in the world to see her together with Oriana and Queen Briolanja, in which three ladies all the beauty of the world was embodied; and likewise that Don Galaor his brother was somewhat better, and the greetings he brought from him, he took him one day through that field, where no one could overhear them, and said to him: "Sir, the reason why I ceased to ask you with that insistence and volition befitting me that you dub me a knight, so that I might fulfill the honor and great debt that I owe to my father and to my lineage, you know; for that desire that I have always had to serve you, and the understanding of the need that you have always had for my service, have brought it about that, although my honor up till now may have been tarnished, I aided your interests rather than my own, which were so repressed. Now that it can be avoided — for I see in your possession that lady who used to occasion us so much anguish — neither for myself nor even less for any others would I be able to find any honest excuse for my failing to follow the order of knighthood. Wherefore I beg of you, sir, to be pleased as a favor to me to grant it to me, for you know how much dishonor, if I do not have it, henceforth will accrue to me; for however and wherever I may go, I am yours to serve you with the love and good will on my part that you have always known."

When Amadis heard this he was so disturbed that for a while he could not speak; then he said to him: "Oh my true friend and brother, how very grievous it is for me to comply with what you request! For certainly I would not suffer from it in any less degree if my heart were torn from my flesh; and if in some reasonable way I could desist from doing it, with all my strength I would so desist. But I see that your petition is so just that it can in nowise be refused; and more pursuant to my obligation than my desire, I am determined that it be done just as you request. My only regret is not having found out about it previously, so that with those arms and a horse that your honor deserves this distinction that you wish to receive might be realized."

Gandalin knelt to kiss his hands; but Amadis raised him up and held him in his embrace, tears coming to his eyes because of the great love that he had for him, for he was already imagining the great loneliness and sadness in which he would find himself when he did not have him with him; and Gandalin said to him: "Sir, don't worry about that, for Don Galaor, out of his kindness and courtesy, when I told him how I would like to be a knight, ordered that I be given his horse and all his arms, since they were of little benefit to him, with his illness. And I considered it as a boon and I told him I would take the horse, because it was very good, and the cuirass and the helmet; but that the other arms were to be white as is fitting for a novice knight. He was going to give me his sword, but I, sir, told him that you would give me one of those that Queen Menoresa had given you in Greece. And while I was there I had all the other arms made that are necessary, together with their device, and here I have everything."

"Well, since that is the way it is," said Amadis, "it will be well that the eve of the day we are to have the battle, you, clad in armor, keep vigil in the chapel of the tent of the king, my father, and the next day, mount your horse thus armed, and when we are about to charge against our enemies, the king will dub you knight; for you already know that in the whole world one could not find a better man, nor one from whom you may receive more honor in this act."

Gandalin said to him: "Sir, everything you say is true, and I would be hard put to it to find another man as chivalrous as the king, but I shall not be a knight except by your hand."

"Since you wish that," said Amadis, "so be it, and do what I tell you."

"All will be done as you command," said he, "for Lasindo, Don Bruneo's squire, told me just now, when I arrived, that already he had his lord's promise to dub him knight; and he and I shall keep vigil together. And may God through His compassion guide me so that I may carry out the things in His service and those to my honor just as the order of chivalry commands, and that in me may appear the training that I have received from you."

Amadis did not say any more, because he felt great emotion on hearing that from him, all the greater when he reflected that what Gandalin said would be carried out. So Amadis went to where the king his father was engaged in causing the camp to be fortified and preparing the things necessary for the battle, just as his enemies were doing. Thus the armies remained for two days, for they were concerned only with making ready all the troops, each one for his own duty, that they might be quite prepared for the battle. And in the afternoon of the second day the spies of King Arabigo arrived high up on the mountain that was near there, and in accordance with their orders they did not seek to show themselves; and they saw the rival camps as near each other as we have told you, and immediately they informed King Arabigo; who with all those knights decided that the sentinels should go back to where they could observe well what was going on, and that they should remain hidden as best they could and where, although those troops should join and seek to challenge them, they would not be afraid, and that by crossing the mountain ridge they might take refuge in their ships if they were in such straits as to need to do so; and that if they fought, they should come forth from there unsuspected and attack in safety whomsoever they pleased. And so they did, and they placed themselves in a very rugged location, which moreover was strong, and they commanded all the passes and approaches of the mountain, and King Arabigo fortified everything so that it was as secure as a fortress, and there they awaited the warning of their sentinels. But they were unable to conceal themselves well enough before they arrived there to prevent King Lisuarte from being informed concerning how they had landed in his country and the troops that were coming. And for this reason he gave orders to remove all the food supplies of cattle, as well as of everything else, to the vicinity of that town, and that the people of the villages and weak settlements should take refuge in the cities and towns, and watch and patrol them, and not leave there until the battle was over. And he left in them some of his knights, whom he sorely needed for the situation in which he was; but he did not ascertain any more about what the intruders had done or where they had stopped.

King Perion also found out about those troops, and distrusted them but did not know where they were located, so that they instilled fear on both sides.

Then matters being at this stage, as you hear, at the end of three days after the camps had been set up, the Emperor Patin was impatient for the battle to begin, for whether conquered or a conqueror, he longed to be back in his own land; for thus it often happens to capricious men who take hasty action, to detest as quickly what they have done, as this man was doing out of fickleness. Amadis and Agrajes and Don Cuadragante and all the other knights likewise were complaining very much to King Perion that the battle should be begun, and let God be judge of the truth. Well, the king did not wish for it any less than all the others, but he had restrained them until things were properly made ready; and then the order was proclaimed that everyone at daybreak should attend mass and arm himself, and each body of troops should report to its captain because the battle would be waged immediately. And the same thing was done by the enemy, who found out about it at once.

Then dawn having come, they sounded the trumpets, and the trumpeters on both sides heard each other as clearly as if they had been together. The troops began to arm themselves and saddle their horses, and in all the tents to hear mass, and all to mount and repair to their respective standards. Who would be of such perception and memory, assuming that he had seen this and concentrated upon it, as to be able to tell or write of the armor and horses with their devices and riders who were massed there? Certainly the man who would think that he could take upon himself that project would be quite mad and bereft of all understanding. And therefore, omitting generalities, some of the details will be told here, and we shall begin with the Emperor of Rome, who was brave physically and in spirit, and would have been a very good knight, if his great pride and slight discretion had not been a drawback.

He armed himself in armor that was sable, including his helmet as well as his shield and his device, except that on the shield he bore depicted a maiden resembling Oriana from the waist up, done in gold, very skilfully embroidered and adorned with many precious stones and pearls of great value, attached to the shield with golden nails; and over the back of his helmet's visor he wore woven chains very richly embroidered, which he took as a device and swore never to forego them until he took Amadis prisoner in chains and all those who were a party to taking Oriana away from him. And he rode a beautiful big horse with lance in hand; thus he came out of the camp and went where it had been agreed that his troops should assemble. Then behind him came Floyan, brother of Prince Salustanquidio, armed in yellow and sable quartered armor, and there was nothing else noteworthy about it, except that among his men he appeared strikingly conspicuous. Behind him came Arquisil; he wore blue and white armor of a white verging on silver, and dotted all over with golden roses, so that he was a very striking figure. King Lisuarte wore black armor with white eagles depicted on it, and an eagle on his shield, without any other adornment; but finally they certainly turned out to be of great significance, in view of what their owner accomplished in that battle. King Cildadan wore armor totally black, for after he had been defeated in the battle of the one hundred against one hundred, fought with King Lisuarte, whence he became his tributary, he never wore any other kind. As for Gasquilan, King of Suesa, nothing will be told about the armor that he wore until the proper time later on, when you shall hear about it. King Arban of North Wales, Don Guilan the Pensive and Don Grumedan chose to wear armor more utilitarian than showy, as an indication of the sadness they felt on seeing the king their lord placed in a great dangerous confrontation with those who previously had been at his court and in his service, and who had given him such honor.

Now we shall tell you about the armor worn by King Perion and Amadis and some of those great lords who were on their side. Of the armor of King Perion, the helmet and the shield were undecorated and of very good bright steel, and his device was of very bright red silk and he rode a big horse that his nephew Don Brian de Monjaste had given him, for Don Brian's father, the King of Spain, had sent his son twenty very beautiful horses, which he distributed among those knights; and thus King Perion himself came forth with the banner of the Emperor of

Constantinople. Amadis was armed in green armor — such as he wore at the time that he killed Famongomadan and Basagante, his son, who were the two strongest giants that were to be found in the world — very beautifully adorned all over with lions in gold. And he was very fond of this armor, because he had adopted it when he came from the Poor Cliff, and had worn it when he went to see his lady at the castle of Miraflores, as the second Book of this story relates. Don Cuadragante appeared wearing brown armor decorated with silver flowers, and mounted on one of the horses from Spain. Don Bruneo de Bonamar did not want to change his arms, as his shield had a maiden depicted upon it with a knight kneeling before her, who seemed to be asking mercy of her. Don Florestan, the great and good jouster, wore red armor adorned with gold flowers, and rode one of the big horses from Spain. As for Agrajes, his armor was of a fine rose color, and on his shield appeared a maiden's hand, which had a heart in its clasp. The good Angriote did not want to alter his arms of blue enamel and silver. And all the others, of whom no mention is made in order not to bore those who may read about it, wore very fine armor of the colors that they liked best; and thus they all came forth on the field in good order.

Then the troops being all assembled, each man with his own captain, as you have heard, they moved very slowly over the field at the hour that the sun was rising, which was reflected on the armor, and as it was all new and fresh and shining, it was so resplendent that it was simply marvelous to behold.

Then at this hour there arrived Gandalin and Lasindo, squire of Don Bruneo, both wearing white armor, as befitted novice knights. Gandalin went to where his lord Amadis was, and Lasindo to Don Bruneo. When Amadis saw him coming thus, he left his battalion to go to him, and he asked Don Cuadragante to detain the troops until he dubbed his squire a knight. And he took him with him, and went to where King Perion, his father, was, and on the way said to him: "My true friend, I beg you sincerely today in this battle to try to watch your step, and not to become separated from me, so that in case of need I may be able to aid you; for although you have seen many battles and great confrontations, and hold the opinion that you will know how to do what is essential, and that all that is needed for it is courage, don't believe it; for there is a very great difference between observing and execution, because each one thinks when he watches things that if he were a participant, he would achieve better results than the one who is dealing with them; and after he sees himself involved, he faces many obstacles that are irksome to him because of being unfamiliar, and great variations are encountered that had not been anticipated. And this is because everything consists in execution, although something can be learned by observation. And since your initiation is in such a great contest at arms as the one we now face, and you must protect yourself from so many, it is necessary in order to safeguard your life as well as your honor, which is more precious and must be more cherished, that with much discretion and good understanding, not giving such free rein to your courage as to inhibit your good sense, you conduct yourself and attack our enemies; and I shall take great care to watch out for you as much as I can, and you do the same for me every time you see that it is necessary.

Gandalin, when he heard this, said: "My lord, all shall be done as you command to the extent that I am able and my knowledge permits me, and may it please God that it be so; for it will be overwhelming for me to place myself in those situations where I may need your aid."

Thus they came up to where King Perion was, and Amadis said to him: "Sir, Gandalin wants to be a knight, and it would have pleased me greatly had it been by your hand; but since he would like it to be by mine, I come to beg you that he receive the sword from your hand, so that when he has need of it, he may remember this great honor that he is receiving and who gave it to him."

The king looked at Gandalin and recognized his son Galaor's horse, and the tears came to his eyes, and he said: "Friend Gandalin, how did you leave Don Galaor when you parted from him?"

And he said to him: "Sire, much improved in his illness, but with great sorrow and distress at heart, for no matter how much your departure was concealed from him, he indeed found out about it, although not the reason for it, and he entreated me to tell him the truth if I knew it, and I said to him, 'Sir, that from what I had learned about it, you were going to go to the aid of the King of Scotland, father of Agrajes, who had a dispute with some neighbors of his.' And I did not want to tell him the truth, because in such a situation and he being in such a precarious state of health, as he is, I thought that was best."

Then king sighed very deeply as for one whom he loved and to whom he was closely attached; and thought that except for Amadis there was not a better knight than he in the world, not only in courage but in all the other traits that a good knight should have, and he said: "Oh my good son! May it please our Lord that I not behold your death, and that you may see yourself honorably free from this very great fondness that you have for King Lisuarte, so that, once free, you may freely aid your brothers and your lineage."

Then Amadis took a sword brought to him by Durin, the maid of Denmark's brother, whom he had ordered to attend him, and gave it to the king; and he dubbed Gandalin a knight, kissing him and placing on him the spur for his right foot, and the king girded on him the sword; and thus his knighting was carried out by the two best knights who ever bore arms. And taking him with him he returned to Don Cuadragante; and when they came up to him, he advanced to embrace Gandalin in order to honor him, and he said: "My friend, may it please God that your knighthood be by you as well employed as up until now have been the virtue and good habits that a good squire should have; and I believe that it will be, because a good beginning usually assures a good outcome."

Gandalin bowed, deeming the honor that was being paid him a favor.

Lasindo was knighted by the hand of his lord, and Agrajes gave him the sword. And you can believe that these two novices did so well at arms in this their first battle, and in it experienced so many dangers and trials, that they won honor and great glory for all the days of their lives, as the story will relate to you in more detail later on.

With the battalions moving ahead as I say, it was not long before they saw their opponents coming toward them in the order that you have already heard about. And when they were close together, Amadis observed that the standard of the Emperor of Rome was being carried in front, and he was very pleased that the first blows were to be with those men, for although he had no love for King Lisuarte, he kept remembering that he had been at his court, and the great honors that he had received from him; and what above all he had on his mind and was perplexing him was that Lisuarte was the father of his lady, whom he so dreaded to distress. And in his heart he was resolved, if he could do so without much danger to himself, to withdraw from King Lisuarte's vicinity in order not to encounter him or afford an opportunity to molest him, although he well knew, in view of past events, that he would not expect that courtesy from the king, but that as a mortal enemy he would seek his death.

But as for Agrajes, I say to you that his thought was very far removed from that of Amadis, for his only prayer to God was that He guide him so that he might be able to bring death to King Lisuarte and destroy all his men, for he always had before his eyes the discourtesy and scant gratitude that he had shown them in the matter of the Island of Mongaza, and what he had done to his uncle Don Galvanes and those on his side; for although he had given him this island itself, he considered it more of a dishonor than an honor, since it was after they were conquered, whence all the honor remained with the king. And if he at that time had been there, he would not have consented to his uncle's taking it; rather, he would have given him one like it in his father's kingdom. And with this great rage that he had, many times he would have been lost in that battle by entering the greatest crushes in order to kill or seize King Lisuarte; but as the latter was strong and experienced in fighting, he did not greatly concern himself with him, nor did he stop fighting everywhere else where it was necessary, as will be told later.

The battalions being about to charge at each other, only waiting for the sound of the bugles, and Moorish trumpets, Amadis, who was in the vanguard, saw a squire on horseback coming as fast as he could from the enemy's side, and in a loud voice asking if Amadis of Gaul was there. Amadis motioned to him to approach. The squire did so, and when he reached him, Amadis said: "Squire, what do you want, for I am the one for whom you are asking?"

The squire looked at him, and in his opinion he had never seen a knight in his whole life so impressive when armed and mounted; and he said to him: "Noble lord, I well believe what you tell me, for your bearing affords testimony of your great fame."

"Then tell me now what you want of me," said Amadis.

The squire said to him: "Sir, my lord Gasquilan, King of Suesa, informs you that on an occasion now past, when King Lisuarte was at war with you and with Don Galvanes, together with many other knights on your side and his, over the Island of Mongaza, he joined King Lisuarte's side with the intention and desire to fight with you, not out of any enmity that he bears you, but on account of the great reports that he had heard concerning your great knightly exploits; in which war he remained until badly wounded he returned to his own land, on ascertaining that you were not where his desire could be carried out; and that now King Lisuarte has informed him of this war in which you are engaged, where in view of its cause, a great fight or battle cannot be avoided; and that he has come to it with that same desire, and he says to you: Sir, that before the battalions engage in combat, you break two or three lances with him, for he will gladly do so, because once the battalions come to grips, he will not be able to encounter you at will; for he will be hindered by many other knights."

Amadis said to him: "Good squire, tell the king your lord that all that he sent you to tell me I learned at that time when I was unable to participate, and that what he wishes, I attribute to greatness of courage rather than to any enmity or ill-will, and although my deeds are not as great as reported, I feel very happy that a man of such high rank and of such renown should hold me in such high regard and that, since this quest is more voluntary than exigent, I should like, if he pleased, for him to test my excellence or insufficiency in a way more to his honor and advantage. But if he prefers what he sends word to tell me, I shall do for him what he asks."

The squire said: "Sir, the king my lord knows well what happened to you with his father Madarque, the giant of the Sad Island, and how you overcame him in order to rescue King Cildadan and Don Galaor, your brother; and although this concerned him as an affair involving his father, to whom he is so closely related, since he knew about the great courtesy that you exercised with him, you deserve thanks rather than punishment; and that if he has a desire to test himself with you, it is only because of the considerable envy he has of your great excellence, for he realizes that if he vanquishes you it will mean praise and fame for him over and above that of all the knights in the world, and that if he be defeated it will not be for him a great disgrace or shame to meet defeat at the hands of one who has overcome so many knights, and giants and other unnatural foes."

"Since that is the way it is," said Amadis, "tell him that if, as I have said, this which he asks for satisfies him most, I am ready to do it."

CHAPTER CX

WHY THIS GASQUILAN, KING OF SUESA, SENT HIS SQUIRE TO AMADIS WITH THE REQUEST THAT YOU HAVE HEARD.

The story tells why this knight came twice to look for Amadis in order to fight with him; for it would be unreasonable that such a great prince as he was should have come with such an intention from a land so distant as his kingdom was without his desire having been ascertained and publicized. Book III has already told you that this Gasquilan was the son of Madarque, the giant of the Sad Island, and of the sister of Lancino, King of Suesa, on whose account he was accepted there as king, because Lancino died without heirs. And as Gasquilan was physically of great avail, being the son of a giant, and of great strength, in the many armed conflicts in which he engaged he acquitted himself so completely to his honor that in that whole part of the world no knightly excellence was so talked about as was his, although he was a youth. He was greatly enamored of a very lovely princess, called Pinela the Beautiful, who after the death of the king her father, succeeded him as suzerain of the Strong Island, which bordered on the kingdom of Suesa, and out of love for her he undertook great enterprises and challenges, and underwent many risks to his person in order to induce her to love him. But she, knowing him to be of the lineage of giants and very boastful and arrogant, had never been willing to give him any hope of achieving his desires. But some of the grandees of her seignory on noting that he had no remedy for his love and fearing his eminence and haughtiness, and that this great love might turn into hatred and enmity, as sometimes happens, and that their peaceful situation might be converted into cruel war, deemed it well to advise her not to spurn his proposals so harshly, and with some feigned encouragement to keep him a suitor as long as possible. So with this decision, when this lady saw herself greatly beset by him, she sent word to him that since God had made her the mistress of such a great landholding, her intention was, and so she had promised her father at the time of his death, not to marry except with the best knight that could be found in the world, even though he not be of high rank; and that she had tried hard to find out who was the best by sending her messengers to many foreign lands, and the latter had brought back to her reports concerning one named Amadis of Gaul, to the effect that he was unsurpassed among all those in the world as the most powerful and valiant knight by reason of undertaking and carrying out dangerous enterprises that others did not dare to undertake; and that if he, Gasquilan, was so valiant and courageous, he should fight with this Amadis and overcome him; whereupon she, in fulfillment of his desires and the promise that she had made to her father, would give him her love and would make him lord and master of her and her realm, for she would indeed believe that after him, no equal in excellence would be left. This beautiful princess answered this in order to free herself from his importunities, and also because from her own men who had seen Amadis and had heard of his great deeds, she found out that the excellence of Gasquilan was far from being the equal of Amadis's.

When this was told to Gasquilan, not only because of the great love he had for this princess, but also because of his presumption and pride, he was impelled to seek a way whereby what was enjoined upon him could be effected. And for this reason that you hear, he came from his kingdom on these two occasions to seek Amadis: on the first one, to the war over the Island of Mongaza, whence he returned wounded by a mighty blow that Don Florestan gave him in the battle they had with him and King Arban of North Wales; on the second, in this present dispute with King Lisuarte, because until then he had never been able to ascertain any news about Amadis, because the latter traveled incognito, calling himself the Knight of the

Green Sword, through the islands of Romania, and through Germany and Constantinople where he performed rare deeds at arms that the third Book of this story relates.

The squire of this Gasquilan returned to him with Amadis's reply just as you have heard, and when he gave it to him, he replied: "Friend, now you bring what I have greatly desired, and everything is coming out as I wish; and today I intend to win the love of my lady, if I am that Gasquilan you know."

Then he called for his arms and armor, which were decorated in this wise: the field on the device and that of the visor of the helmet brown adorned with golden griffons; the helmet and shield shone like a bright mirror; and on the middle of the shield, pegged with gold nails was a griffon adorned with many precious stones and pearls of great value, which had in its claws a heart that was completely pierced by them, giving to undertand by means of the griffon and its great ferocity, the harshness and extreme cruelty of his lady, and that just as it held that heart pierced by its claws, so his own was by the great worry and the mortal desires that continually came to him from her; and these arms he intended to bear until he had his lady; and also because, when he reflected that he bore them in remembrance of her, they gave him strength and great relief from his worries.

Then armed just as you hear, he took in his hand a heavy lance with a large bright point, and went where the emperor was, and begged him as a favor not to command the troops to charge until he had a joust that he had arranged with Amadis, and that he not consider him a real knight if at the first encounter he did not eliminate Amadis for him. The emperor, who knew Amadis better than he did, and had tested him, although he did not reveal his thought, was quite convinced that that would be more difficult to accomplish than he thought. Then Gasquilan left him and went on past the battalions. All were standing still to watch the battle of two such famous and outstanding knights. Thus Gasquilan arrived at the place where Amadis was ready to receive him, and although he knew that Gasquilan was a valiant knight, he considered him so conceited and proud that he did not greatly fear his valor, because God breaks the excessive pride of such men at the time when they expect to do the most and have the most need of Him, so that their fellowmen may learn a lesson. And when Amadis saw him coming, he faced his horse in his direction and covered himself with his shield as best he knew how, and applying his spurs he went at him as hard as he could. And Gasquilan likewise went very impetuously as fast as his horse could carry him. And they struck each other on their shields in such a way that the lances went flying through the air in pieces, and when they struck each other the shock was so severe that everybody thought that both were shattered to bits; and Gasquilan fell out of his saddle, and as he was robust of body and the blow was very heavy, he fell so forcibly to the hard ground that he was so stunned that he couldn't rise, and he had his left arm broken on which he had fallen; and so he remained on the field stretched out as if dead. Amadis's horse sustained a broken shoulder, so that it could not remain on its feet, and Amadis was somewhat dazed, but not so much as not to be able to leave his horse before it could fall with him. And so he went on foot to where Gasquilan lay, to see if he was dead. The Emperor of Rome, who was watching the combat, as he saw him dead — for so he, like all the others, thought — and Amadis on foot, shouted to Floyan, who was leading the vanguard, to render aid with his battalion, and so he did. And when Don Cuadragante saw this, he spurred his horse and said to his men: "Strike them, men, and don't leave any alive!"

Then they went after one another and joined in combat; but Gandalin, when he saw his lord Amadis on foot, and that the brigades were charging, was very fearful for his safety, and went forward a bit to rescue him. And he saw Floyan coming in front of all his men, and went toward him, and they both clashed with mighty blows; and Floyan fell from his horse, and Gandalin lost both stirrups, but did not fall. Then many Romans came up to rescue Floyan, and Don Cuadragante to do the same for Amadis; and each one placed his own man on horseback, for they were not concerned with anything else. But, as the Romans arrived in large numbers and very quickly rescued Gasquilan, who had revived somewhat more, they extricated him from the melee with great effort. When Don Cuadragante came on the scene, before losing his lance he knocked four knights to the ground, and from the first that he overthrew, the horse was taken by Angriote de Estravaus, and he brought it quickly to Amadis; and Gavarte of the Fearful Valley and Landin followed Don Cuadragante's lead and inflicted great damage on the enemy, as men versed in such an occupation.

These men about whom I am telling you came ahead of their brigade; but when both battalions joined in conflict, the noise and the shouts were so great as to be deafening. And there you would have seen horses without riders and some knights dead and others wounded, and those who were strongest trampled them. And Floyan, as he was brave and desirous of gaining honor and of avenging the death of his brother Salustanquidio, when he saw himself again on horseback, took a lance and went for Angriote, whom he saw performing rare feats at arms; and struck him in the side so hard that he almost knocked him off his horse and he broke his lance; and he grasped his sword and went and attacked Enil, whom he encountered in front of him, and he struck him on top of his helmet such a mighty blow that the sparks flew from it. And he passed so quickly by both through the battalions that neither of them was able to wound him, so that they marveled at his undaunted courage and great prowess. And before he reached his own men he happened upon a knight from Ireland, a ward of Don Cuadragante's, and gave him such a blow on his shoulder that he cut through to his flesh and bones and the Irishman was so badly wounded that it was necessary for him to leave the battle.

Amadis at this time took with him Balais de Carsante and Gandalin, and with great fury, on seeing that the Romans were defending themselves so well, entered as quickly as he could a flank of the brigade, as did those who followed him, and he delivered such great blows with his sword that there was not a man who saw them who was not terrified; and much more were those who awaited him, for he frightened them so greatly that none of them dared to wait for him; instead they took refuge among the others, as cattle do when they are attacked by wolves.

And as he was going ahead without encountering any resistance, there came forth to meet him a bastard brother of Queen Sardamira, who had the name Flamineo, a very fine knight at arms. And when he saw Amadis performing such wonders, and that no one dared to await him, he went at him, and struck him on the shield with his lance, which penetrated it, and the lance was broken to pieces; and when he passed him, Amadis thought he would strike him on the helmet, but as Flamineo passed with such impetus, he could not; and he struck his horse on the back near the saddle, and cut through most of its body and guts, and it fell to the ground with him in such a hard fall that he thought that he had split his back open. Don Cuadragante and the other knights who were fighting in another area pressed their enemies so hard that if it had not been for the fact that Arquisil came to their aid with the second brigade, all would have been cut to pieces. But when he arrived, everyone was invigorated and they plucked up their courage to a great extent. And because of his arrival more than a thousand knights from both sides were unhorsed.

This Arquisil met with Landin, nephew of Don Cuadragante, and they gave each other such mighty lance thrusts and their horses collided with such force, that both fell to the ground. Floyan, who was going about everywhere with fifty knights, had come to the aid of Flamineo, who was on foot, and they gave him a horse; for Amadis after he had unhorsed him, paid him no heed, because he saw the second brigade coming; and in order to be the first to receive them, he left him in the hands of Gandalin and Balais, who thought that he was dead, and they went and attacked Arquisil's brigade in order that their own men on arriving might not receive any injury, for they were coming on the scene quite fresh. And as Floyan saw the unhorsed Arquisil, who was fighting with Landin, he shouted saying: "Oh knights of Rome, aid your captain!"

Then he launched a violent attack, accompanied by more than fifty men; and if it had not been for Angriote and Enil and Gavarte of the Fearful Valley, who saw him and shouted to Don Cuadragante, for they were bringing aid in great haste and many of their knights were with them, Landin would have been slain or a prisoner at that hour. But when they came up, they attacked with such force that it was a marvelous sight to see. Flamineo, who, as has been said, was already on horseback, rescued as many as he could and aided his men like a good knight.

What shall I tell you? The press of battle was so great there and so many knights killed and unhorsed that the whole field where they were fighting was occupied by the dead and wounded. But the Romans, as they were numerous, rescued Arquisil in spite of his foes, and Don Cuadragante and his companions rescued Landin, and thus each one saved his own man, and they mounted each one on a horse, for there were many there without riders.

Amadis was going about in the other sector performing marvels at arms; and as they now recognized him, most of them yielded free passage to him wherever he wanted to go. But everything was in dire straits, for as the Romans greatly outnumbered their opponents, if it hadn't been for the outstanding knights on the other side, they would have dominated them. But Agrajes and Don Bruneo of Bonamar came immediately to render aid with their brigade. And they came on so hard and in such close formation that, since all the Romans were going about disorganized, they very quickly split their ranks in two, so that they would have had no recourse, if the Emperor with his battalion, in which he brought up five thousand knights, had not come to their aid. This body of troops, as it was large, gave such great encouragement to his men that they very quickly made up for what they had lost.

The emperor came up on his big horse, armed as has been told, and as he was large of body, and came at the head of his men, he seemed so fine to all those who saw him that it was a wonder, and he attracted much attention. And the first man he encountered was Balais de Carsante, and he struck him on his shield so hard that he broke his lance, and he crashed into him with his horse, which was quite fresh; and as Balais's horse was weary, it could not withstand the hard blow and fell with its rider in such a way that he was badly shaken up. The emperor, after accomplishing this feat, took great pride in himself, and he grasped his sword and began to shout: "Rome, Rome, at them, my knights; do not let any escape!"

And then he thrust himself into the melee after the manner of a good knight, meting out very great and powerful blows to all those whom he encountered in his path. And while he was thus wreaking great havoc, he met up with Don Cuadragante, who likewise was going about sword in hand striking and unhorsing all those whom he overtook. And when they saw each other, they charged one another very violently with their swords held high in their hands, and gave each other such blows on top of their helmets that sparks flew from them and from their swords; but as Don Cuadragante was the stronger, the emperor was so overwhelmed with blows that he lost his stirrups and had to clutch his horse's neck, and was left somewhat dazed. At that time Constancio, brother of Brondajel de Roca, and a good young knight, happened to be there; and as he saw the emperor his lord in such straits, spurred his horse and went at Don Cuadragante with lance held high, and struck him a mighty blow on the shield, which pierced it and wounded him slightly in the arm; and while Don Cuadragante turned to strike him with his sword, the emperor had time to betake himself to where his men were.

Constancio, when he saw that he was safe, did not stop, but rather, since he was coming on rested and riding a fresh horse, he made a very quick sally where Amadis was; and when he saw the rare deeds he was doing, and the knights he was leaving on the ground wherever he went, he was so frightened that he could only think that it was some devil who had come there to destroy them. And while he was watching him, he saw approaching him a knight who was governor of the principality of Calabria for Salustanquidio, and he attacked Amadis with his sword striking the neck of his horse. And Amadis struck him on top of his helmet such a blow that not only his helmet but his head was split in two, and immediately he fell to the ground dead; whence Constancio felt great sorrow, as he was a good knight; and then he called out to Floyan in a loud voice and said: "Have at this man, attack and kill him; for he is the one who is destroying us without any pity!"

Then both came at him together, and they gave him mighty blows with their swords. But Amadis struck Constancio, whom he encountered in front of him, such a blow on the boss of his shield that he broke it in two, and the sword did not stop there; instead it reached his helmet, and the blow was so great that Constancio was stunned and fell from his horse. When the Romans who were guarding Floyan saw him with Amadis, and saw Constancio on the ground, more than twenty knights banded together and fell upon him, but they could not unhorse him and they didn't dare tarry with him, because he needed only one blow for anyone within his range.

The battle thus being at a stage where the Romans, since they were greatly superior in numbers, had somewhat the advantage, Grasandor and mighty Don Florestan came in aid, and they arrived at a time when the Romans had Agrajes and Don Bruneo and Angriote surrounded; for they had killed their horses; and Lasindo and Gandalin, and Gavarte of the Fearful Valley and Branfil, who by chance found themselves together, had rescued them; but the horde of troops attacking them was so great that these men I mention, although they unhorsed and killed many knights, and braved much danger, could not reach them. And when Don Florestan came up, and saw there such a great melee, he indeed thought that it probably wasn't without good reason; and when he arrived he recognized those knights who were rescuing Agrajes and his companions; and when Landin saw him, he said: "Oh, Sir Don Florestan, help us here! If you don't, your friends are lost."

When he heard this, he said: "Then draw near to me and let us attack those who will not dare await us."

Then he entered the thick of the fight, unhorsing and killing everyone he overtook, until his lance broke. And he grasped his sword and struck such powerful blows with it that he infused fear in all those who were there. And those knights that I have mentioned continued to keep pace with him until they reached where Agrajes and his companions were on foot, as you have heard. Who could tell you what they experienced there in that rescue and what those who were surrounded had accomplished! Certainly it cannot be adequately recounted that so few as they were should be able to defend themselves against so many who sought to kill them. But withal, they all would have been in great danger of losing their lives, if chance had not brought Amadis there, whom Floyan and his men had left, because out of the twenty knights who I told you had helped Constancio, he had unhorsed and killed six; and when he saw that they were leaving and withdrawing from him, and heard the loud shouts that were being uttered in that melee, he hastened there. And when he arrived, he immediately recognized them from their arms, and began to call his own men, and there joined him more than four hundred knights. And as there was the greatest press that there had been in the whole day, there hastened also from the Romans' side, Floyan and Arquisil and Flamineo, with as many troops as could; and there began the fiercest and most dangerous battle ever seen. There you would have seen Amadis performing miracles the like of which accomplished by a knight never had been seen or heard of; so that he caused the enemy as well as his own men to marvel greatly, not only at those that he killed but also at those that he unhorsed. And as the shouts were many and the noise very loud, not only the emperor, but also most of those who were in the battle, hastened there. Don Cuadragante, who was going about in another area of the battlefield, was told by a mounted crossbowman how things were going, and at once in great haste gathered together more than a thousand knights of his brigade who were guarding him, and said to them: "Now, sirs, let your excellence be demonstrated and follow me, for our aid is greatly needed."

All went with him, and he ahead; and when they reached the melee, there were so many troops from both sides that they could scarcely reach their enemies. And when he saw this, with his troop in the close formation in which he was bringing it — and which was very effective, being made up of good knights — he made such a strong flank attack that at his arrival more than two hundred knights went to the ground, and I tell you truly that those whom he reached with a direct blow were beyond the help of a physician.

Amadis, when he saw what Don Cuadragante and his troop were doing, was quite astounded, and plunged so violently into the enemy's ranks, dealing so many and such heavy blows, that he left no man in his saddle. But at that hour Arquisil and Floyan and Flamineo, and many others with them, fought so fiercely that few there were who could have done better; and they tried as hard as they could to bring death to Agrajes and the companions who were with him on foot, and to Don Florestan and the others we mentioned to you who were near them to protect them; for after they went through the great press of the troops and reached them, never, by any forces that had come nor by blows that they struck, could they dislodge them from there. And as they saw what their own men were doing and such great injury to the enemy, they pressed the Romans so powerfully, both on the part of Don Cuadragante and that of Amadis and of Don Gandales, who came up with as many as eight hundred of the knights of whom he had charge, that in spite of themselves, although the emperor shouted very loudly — who after Don Cuadragante had struck him that mighty blow with his sword paid more heed to directing his troops than to fighting — they forced them to evacuate the field, so that Agrajes and Angriote and Don Bruneo, who had suffered great distress and danger, were able to acquire horses on which to mount; and at once they entered the fray against the Romans, who were losing, and thus they held them until the latter reached the battalion of King Arban of North Wales, at a time when the sun had already set. And for this reason King Arban took them with him and did not seek to charge, for such were the orders of King Lisuarte to him on account of the time of day and because of his enemies there remained many to enter into the fray, and he was afraid of receiving from them some reverse; for he really had thought that against his first opponents the emperor and his men would have sufficed. And so on this account and because night had come, which was the chief reason, they withdrew the Romans, and the enemy halted, for they did not pursue them any further, so that the battle ceased with great losses on both sides, although the Romans received the greater share.

Amadis and those on his side, as the battlefield was under their control, had all their own wounded removed and their forces despoiled all the others, and there remained on the field the wounded and dead of the Romans, whom they had not sought to kill, of whom many died from lack of succor.

Then the troops of both sides having returned to their camps, there were some men in holy orders, who were wont to come to battles to minister to the souls of those who needed it; and who, when they saw such great destruction and heard the cries that the wounded uttered in asking for pity and mercy, decided, with regard to both sides, to devote themselves to God's service in trying to bring about some truce in which the wounded might be cared for and the dead be buried. And thus they did, for these men spoke with King Lisuarte and with the emperor, and the others with King Perion, and they all considered it good that a truce be established for the following day. That night they spent with many men on guard, and they cared for the wounded, and the others rested from the great effort that they had expended. Morning having come, many went out to look for their relatives and others for their lords; and there you would have seen the very great lamenting of both sides, which when heard causes great sorrow and even more when seen. They carried all the living to the encampment of the emperor, and the dead were buried, so that the field was cleared.

So they spent that day making ready their arms and taking care of their horses. And they treated Don Cuadragante's wound in the arm and they saw that it was slight; but although any other knight would have considered it such that he would not be able to arm or exert himself, he did not seek on account of this to refrain from aiding his comrades in the ensuing battle.

Night having come, they all retired to their tents, and at daybreak they got up at the sound of the bugles and heard mass; and immediately all the troops were armed and mounted, and each captain assembled his own men. And on both sides it was decided that the battalions that had not fought should be in the vanguard, and thus it was carried out.

CHAPTER CXI

WHAT HAPPENED TO EACH SIDE IN THE SECOND BATTLE, AND FOR WHAT REASON THE BATTLE WAS HALTED.

King Lisuarte placed in the vanguard King Arban of North Wales, and Norandel and Don Guilan the Pensive, and the other knights you have heard about. And he with his battalion and King Cildadan were stationed behind them, and back of them the emperor and his men, each one in his own brigade with its captains, according to, and in, the order established.

King Perion gave over the vanguard to his nephew Don Brian de Monjaste, and he and Gastiles, with the standard of the Emperor of Constantinople, were stationed behind them, and all the other battalions in their predetermined arrangement; so that those who on the first day they fought were farthest removed from the front were now nearest.

In this order they all moved ahead, and when they were close together, the bugles sounded from all sides, and the brigades of Brian de Monjaste and King Arban of North Wales joined in battle so fiercely that from the first engagement more than five hundred knights went to the ground and their horses ran loose over the field. Don Brian found himself with King Arban, and they engaged in very great clashes, so that their lances were broken, but they did no other harm to each other. And they took their swords in hand and began to strike each other everywhere that they could do most injury, as men who had frequently carried on and experienced such activity. Norandel and Don Guilan attacked together the troops of their opponents; and as they were very valiant and courageous, they inflicted much harm;

and they would have done more had it not been for a knight named Fileno, a relative of Don Brian, who had come with the troops from Spain, and who took with him many of the Spaniards, who were good warriors, and attacked so fiercely that area where Don Guilan and Norandel were operating that not only them but all those that they caught in front of them, they thrust back for some distance on the field; but there Norandel and Don Guilan performed rare deeds in order to bring relief to their own men. King Arban and Don Brian were cut off from their battalions, both of them, on account of the great melee that there was on the other side; and each one of them began to encourage his own men by attacking and unhorsing the enemy. But as the troops from Spain were more numerous and better mounted, they had such a great advantage that if King Lisuarte and King Cildadan had not brought aid with their brigades, they would not have held the field against them, and all would have been lost; but with the arrival of these kings all was restored. King Perion, when he saw the standard of King Lisuarte, said to Gastiles: "Now, my good lord, let us move forward, and always watch for this standard, for I shall do likewise."

Then they charged headlong against their enemies. King Lisuarte received them like one who never lacked courage and strength, for certainly you can believe that in his time there never was a king who risked his life more admirably or more gratuitously in matters relating to his honor, as in this great story you can see in all the battles and attacks in which he participated.

So these troops having thus come back so augmented in numbers, who would be able to relate the deeds of chivalry that were accomplished there! It would be impossible for anyone who sought to tell the truth, for so many good knights were there killed and wounded that the horses could scarcely move forward without trampling them. Concerning King Lisuarte I tell you that as a man whose honor had been impugned and who cared not a whit whether he lived or died, he attacked his foes so fiercely that few did he encounter who dared await him. King Perion, while he was going about in another battle sector performing prodigious feats, by chance encountered King Cildadan; and when they recognized each other, they were unwilling to engage in combat; instead they passed each other by, and went on to attack those whom they encountered in their path; and they unhorsed many knights whom they left lying dead or wounded.

When the emperor saw such a great fray, and it seemed to him that those on his side were in grave danger, he gave orders to his captains that with all their brigades they should charge as boldly as possible, and that he would do likewise; which was done, for all the battalions in concert with the emperor attacked their foes. But before they came up, the brigades on the opposite side, when they saw them coming, likewise all together charged across the field; so that all were jumbled together in such wise that they could not achieve any concerted action, nor could anyone protect his captain. But they were so intermingled and at such close quarters that they could not even attack with their swords, and they were tugging at, and unhorsing, each other, and there were more who died under the horses' feet than from the wounds that they were inflicting on each other. The confusion and the noise were so great, not only from the shouting but also from the clash of arms, that it seemed as if everyone in the world had assembled there; and certainly you can believe that, not the whole world, but most of Christendom and its flower were there, where so much injury to it was received that day, that for many a long period it could not be repaired. So this may be presented as an object lesson to kings and great lords in order that before they do things, they consider them and think them over first very conscientiously, observing fully the difficulties that may result from their action, so that not through their fault and errors and zeal, those who are blameless suffer and die, as frequently happens, though it may be that the innocence of these said people will bring their souls to a good place. So, although at present they are still alive, major and much more perilous loss of lives can be charged to those causing havoc such as this which was occasioned by this King Lisuarte, although he was wont to be very discreet and knowledgeable about everything; but this catastrophe was brought about by his unwillingness to follow the advice of anyone else.

Then putting all this aside, for in view of the great haughtiness and anger with which we are dominated to the point of involving ourselves in great suffering and great tribulations, concerning which I believe that admonishments are futile, we shall return to the matter at hand, and I say to you that as the battalions were going about thus, and many people were dying, the press was so great, that neither side could prevail, for all were busy and were facing opponents with whom to fight. Agrajes was constantly preoccupied with looking for King Lisuarte, and he had not seen him because of the great melee and the multitude of troops; and while he was going about through the battalions, he saw that the king had just unhorsed Dragonis in an encounter in which he broke his lance, and that he had his sword in hand ready to strike him. And Agrajes went toward him with his sword and said to him: "Attack me, King Lisuarte, for I am the one who hates you the most."

He, when he heard him, turned his head and went for him, and Agrajes at him, and they both came at one another so hard that they could not strike each other; and Agrajes unfastened his sword from the chain on which he carried it suspended, and seized him in his arms; for, as is already stated elsewhere in this story, this Agrajes was the most aggressive and stout-hearted knight that there was in his time; and if strength as well as courage had helped him, there would have been no better knight than he in the world; and as it was, he was one of the few excellent ones to be found, were one to search far and wide.

Then, as they gripped each other with each trying as hard as he could to unhorse the other, Agrajes would have found himself in great danger because the king was the stronger of body and spirit, if it had not been for good King Perion, who intervened; and with him came Don Florestan and Landin and Enil, and many other knights. And when he saw Agrajes thus, King Perion endeavored to aid him; and from the other side, Don Guilan the Pensive hastened to the scene, and also Norandel, and Brandoyvas, and Giontes, King Lisuarte's nephew, for the latter, although they on other parts of the field were executing their assaults and performing great knightly deeds, always kept an eye on the king, because it was their responsibility to watch over him. So when they came up, they attacked with their swords — for their lances were broken — all of them striking so fiercely that it was a rare thing to see, and the knights were coming from both sides, each to rescue his own. But the king and Agrajes were gripping each other so tightly that they could not be separated, nor could either one unhorse the other because those on the side of each were holding them in the middle and supporting them so that they would not fall. As here was the greatest press of the battle and the loudest din of loud shouts, many knights from each side hastened there, among whom came Don Cuadragante. And as he came up, and saw the melee, and the king and Agrajes locked in an embrace, he plunged very ruthlessly through the crowd and seized the king so violently that he nearly unhorsed both of them; but he did not dare strike the king lest he hit Agrajes; but in spite of the fact that those who were defending the king struck him many blows, he did not ever loosen his grip on him. King Arban of North Wales, who was accompanying the Emperor of Rome and who had not seen the king for a while, arrived there; and when he saw him in such great danger, he was beside himself with excitement, and seized Don Cuadragante very tightly. Thus all four were locked in close embrace, and around them King Perion and his men, and from the other side Norandel and Don Guilan and their men, who never stopped fighting each other.

Then while the situation was so confused and dangerous, the emperor and King Cildadan intervened on behalf of King Lisuarte with more than three thousand knights, and from the other side Gastiles and Grasandor with many other companies; and they all charged into the fray with such violence and clamor that perforce they scattered those who were fighting each other, and those who were gripping each other found it well to let go; and all four remained on horseback, but so very tired that they almost fell out of their saddles. And so many were the troops of King Lisuarte's side who charged, that the affair was close to being lost, if it had not been for the great prowess of King Perion and of Don Cuadragante and Don Florestan, and others who were friends of theirs, who as vigorous knights endured so much that it was a great marvel.

While they were in this melee, just as you hear, there came up that very valiant knight Amadis, who had gone to the right sector of the battle, and had killed Constancio with a single blow and laid low most of that sector; and he bore in his hand his good sword stained with blood up to the hilt. And there came with him Count Galtines and Gandalin and Trion. And when he saw so many people attacking his father, and the emperor ahead attacking his own men and fighting as if in a battle he considered already won, he spurred his horse, which he had just taken from one of his father's pages, and which was fresh, and rode forward so hard and so boldly through the troops that it was a marvel to see. Floyan, who recognized him by his device, was afraid that if he reached the emperor all of them together would not be strong enough to defend or protect the latter against him; and as quickly as he could he put himself in front, risking his life to save the emperor's. Don Florestan, who happened to be thereabouts, charged forward along with Amadis; and when he saw Floyan, he went at him as quickly as he could, and they struck each other with their swords very mighty blows on top of their helmets. But Floyan was dazed so that he could not stay on his horse, and he fell to the ground and there was killed, not only by the great blow but also by the many riders who trampled him.

Amadis did not heed this battle; rather, since he was keeping his gaze fixed on the emperor, and even more in his heart the intention to kill him if he could, because the emperor was already among his own men, he dashed in among them with great fury to attack him; and although from all sides great blows were given him in order to defend the emperor against him, the foes were never able to prevent him from coming to grips with him. And when he reached him, he lifted his sword and struck him with all his might, and gave him such a powerful blow on top of his helmet that he robbed him of all his strength, and his sword fell from his hand. And when Amadis saw that he was going to fall from his horse, he struck him very quickly another blow on his shoulder, which cut through all the armor and flesh to his armpit, so that all that section, along with his arm, was dangling and he fell from his horse in such condition that shortly afterwards he was dead.

When the Romans who were very close to him saw it, they shouted loudly so that many came up and the battle again intensified; for very quickly Arquisil and Flamineo hastened there, and they arrived with many other knights where Amadis and Don Florestan were, and they struck them very great and hard blows from all sides. But Count Galtines and Gandalin and Trion called to Don Bruneo and Angriote to join with them to aid them. And all five in spite of everyone came to their aid, inflicting much havoc.

King Perion was with Don Cuadragante and Agrajes and many other knights in the area where King Lisuarte and King Cildadan with many others were; and they were fighting each other very vigorously; so that right there was the fiercest battle that there had been all day, and a greater mortality of troops. But at this time Don Brian de Monjaste and Don Gandales intervened, who had gathered together out of their own forces close to six hundred knights; and they attacked the enemy so fiercely in the sector where Amadis and his companions were that despite their resistance they forced them back quite a distance. At the loud shouts that were then being given, Arban, King of North Wales, turned his head and saw that the Romans were losing the field, and he said to King Lisuarte: "Sir, let us withdraw; otherwise you will lose."

When the king heard this, he looked, and well recognized that he was speaking the truth. Then he said to King Cildadan that he should help him withdraw his men so that they not be lost; and so they did, for facing their foes all the while, and exchanging very hard blows with them, they withdrew until they were even with the Romans, and there they all halted, because Norandel and Don Guilan, and Cendil of Ganota, and Landasin, and many others with them, went over to the side where the Romans were, which was weakest, in order to reinforce them; but all was in vain; for already the struggle was hopeless.

The battle being at such a stage as you hear, Amadis saw that King Lisuarte's cause was irrevocably lost and that if the affair continued, it would not be in his power to save him, nor those great friends of his own who were with the king. And above all, he remembered that this man was the father of his lady Oriana, the one whom he loved and feared more than anything in the world, and the great honors that he and his relatives in times past had received from him, which should take precedence over these harassments, and that everything that might be done in such a situation would be to his own great glory and would be accounted abundant virtue rather than scant effort. And he saw that many of the Romans were carrying their lord away while uttering great laments and that the troops were dispersing. And because night was coming on, he decided, although he might experience the ignominy of some embarrassment, to try to see whether he could serve his lady in such a publicized affair, and he took with him Count Galtines, whom he had near at hand, and went as fast as he could between both the battalions, though with great difficulty because the troops were many and the press great; for those on his side, since they were recognizing their advantage, were pressing their enemies very hard and in these others there was no longer scarcely any defense, except on the part of King Lisuarte and King Cildadan and the other outstanding knights. And he and the count came up to King Perion his father, and he said to him: "Sire, night is coming on, so that in a short time we would not be able to recognize one another; and if the conflict were to last much longer it would be very dangerous in view of the multitude of troops, for we might kill friends as well as foes, and they, us. It seems to me that it would be well to withdraw the troops, for according to the damage that our enemies have received, I certainly believe that tomorrow they will not dare to make a stand against us."

The king, who had great sorrow in his heart on seeing so many men dying without any fault of their own, said to him: "Son, let what seems best to you be done, not only on account of what you say but also so that no more people die; for that Lord who knows all things, perceives clearly that this is being stopped more out of service to Him than for any other reason; for we can bring about their total destruction since they are defeated."

Agrajes was near the king, and Amadis had not seen him, and he heard all that they had said; and he came with great fury to Amadis and said: "What, lord cousin, now that you have your enemies conquered and laid low, and you are enabled to become the most honored prince in the world, do you want to save them?"

"Lord cousin," said Amadis, "I would like to save our men so that with the coming of night they may not kill one another; for I consider our enemies conquered, because they have no resistance left."

Agrajes, as he was very intelligent, well recognized Amadis's desire, and said to him: "Since you don't want to conquer, you don't want to rule; for you will always be a knight errant, since at such a juncture compassion overcomes and subdues you; but do as you think best."

Then King Perion and Don Cuadragante — in whom this did not cause regret, on account of King Cildadan, with whom he had so close a kinship and whom he loved so much — on the one side, and Amadis and Gastiles on the other, began to withdraw the troops, and they did so with ease, for already nightfall was dispersing them.

King Lisuarte, who had no hope of being able to recoup his loss, and was determined to die rather than be conquered, when he saw that those knights were withdrawing the troops, was greatly astonished and really thought that it was being done only as some great ruse. And he stood there waiting to see what might come of it. And when King Cildadan saw what the enemies were doing, he said to the king: "It seems to me that that body of troops will not pursue us and is doing us honor; and since that is the way it is, let us gather our own and go rest, for it is high time."

Thus it was done, for King Arban of North Wales and Don Guilan the Pensive, and Arquisil and Flamineo with the Romans, withdrew all their troops. Thus this battle was brought to a close as you hear; and inasmuch as the beginning of this entire great story was based on that notable love affair that King Perion had with Queen Elisena, which was the cause of this knight Amadis their son's being engendered, from which amour and from the one that he has with his lady Oriana, has proceeded and is proceeding such a great and extensive written account, although some of it may seem to be irrelevant, it is right not only in exculpation of these people who loved so unconventionally, but also in that of others who love in the same way that there be set forth what a great force love is, over and above all others; for in an event so transcendent and so outstanding as this was throughout the world, in which so many people of high rank were involved and there were so many deaths and such very great honor accruing to the victors, putting everything aside there in the midst of the anger and fury and great pride, along with enmity of such long standing — and the least of these emotions sufficing to blind and disturb anyone, no matter how very discreet and valiant he may be — the love that this knight had for his lady exerted such force that forgetful of the greatest glory that can be attained in this world, which is to conquer, he set up an impediment whereby his enemies would receive the benefit that you have heard; for most certainly you can believe that in the hands and will of Amadis and of those on his side rested the complete destruction of King Lisuarte and his men, without their being able to defend themselves.

But there is no reason to attribute it to anyone except to that Lord who is the restorer of all things; for one can well believe that by Him it was permitted to be done in view of the peace and harmony that resulted from this very great enmity, as we shall relate to you subsequently.

Then the troops having been withdrawn and returned to their camps, a truce of two days was established because the dead were many; and it was agreed that each side might carry away in safety its own slain. The labor expended in burying them and the lamenting carried on for them it will be unnecessary to state, because the death of the emperor, in view of the mourning it occasioned, caused all else to be forgotten. But an account of both matters will be omitted, not only because it would be prolix and tedious, but also in order not to digress from the main narrative.

CHAPTER CXII

HOW KING LISUARTE HAD THE BODY OF THE EMPEROR OF ROME CARRIED TO A MONASTERY, AND HOW HE SPOKE WITH THE ROMANS ABOUT THAT SITUATION IN WHICH HE WAS, AND THE REPLY THAT THEY GAVE HIM.

King Lisuarte arrived at his tent and asked King Cildadan to dismount there and disarm in order that before they rested they might plan how the body of the emperor might be placed where it was fitting for it to be. And when they were disarmed, although they were quite bruised and weary, they went together to the tent of the emperor where he lay dead, and they found all his top-ranking knights gathered around his body mourning deeply; for although this emperor by nature was haughty and gruff, whence those with such mannerisms should be disliked, he was very free and generous in bestowing on his own men so many good benefits and favors that thereby he concealed many defects, although everyone naturally is quite content with those who receive with grace and courtesy people who come to them, they are much more content with those who, although with some harshness, carry out requests made to them, because the real effect consists in practicing virtue, and not merely in talking it.

These two kings having arrived there, they stopped those knights from mourning, and asked them to go to their tents and disarm and care for their wounds, for they would not leave there until that body was placed where such a great prince ought to be. Then all having gone, so that only the functionaries in charge of the tent remained, King Lisuarte gave orders to make ready the emperor so that they could travel with him at once and bear him to a monastery which was one day's journey from there near one of his towns, which was called Lubayna, in order that with greater ease it might be transported from there to the chapel of the emperor in Rome.

This having been thus arranged, the kings returned to the tent they had left, and there supper was being held in readiness for them; and they supped, and in the opinion of those who were there, with good countenances; but a certain man was there who inwardly was not cheerful; rather, at heart he was greatly distressed and preoccupied, and this man was King Lisuarte; because once the truce expired, he expected no remedy for his situation, for in view of the advantage that his foes had had over him in the two past battles, and the great weakness that he recognized in his troops, especially in the Romans, which was preponderant, and having a knowledge of the great strength of his adversaries, he deemed it a foregone conclusion that he was not up to sustaining the third battle, and in it he expected only to be dishonored and conquered, although the most certain thing was that he would be killed, because he did not desire life any longer than he could maintain his honor. And when King Cildadan had supped, he went to his tent, and King Lisuarte remained in his own.

Thus they spent the night, placing heavy guards around their camp; and morning having come, the king arose; and after he had heard mass, he took King Cildadan with him and went to the tent of the emperor, whom they had already taken away, and Floyan with him, to the monastery that I told you about; and he had Arquisil and Flamineo summoned, and all the other great lords who were there in their company; and they having come before him, he spoke to them in this wise: "My good friends, the great sorrow and regret I have on account of the death of the emperor and the desire and will to avenge it, only God knows. But, as these be things very common in the world, and they cannot be avoided, as each one of you will have seen and heard, there remains no recourse except that, putting aside the matter of the dead, the living who remain apply such a remedy to their honor as to show that from the literal demise of those who have died no pseudo death is resulting for those who are surviving. The past is irreparable; for the present and future, through the goodness of God so many of us remain that if with that love and good will to which good men are found and obligated we help ourselves, I trust in Him that with much glory and benefit we shall recover that which up to now has been lost. And I want you to know that as for me, if I had everyone against me, and those who are with me should leave me, I shall not leave this place except as a victor or dead. So, my good friends, consider who you are and the lineage from which you come, and act in this affair in such wise as to make known to everyone that the death of the lord does not mean the death of all his men."

King Lisuarte having finished his talk, as Arquisil outranked all the Romans both in strength and in lineage, because, as you frequently have been told, on him rightfully devolved the succession to the throne of the empire, he stood up where he was, and answered the king, saying: "Ever since Rome was founded, the great deeds and exploits that the Romans in times past have achieved to their honor have been known to everyone; of these the histories are full and in them are noted their achievements as outstanding among all those in the world as is the morning star among the stars. And since we come from such excellent stock, don't believe otherwise, good Sir King Lisuarte, than that now better than at first and with more effort and concern, leaving behind all the danger and fear that might come upon us, we shall pursue what our famous ancestors pursued, whereby they left in this world a fame so eulogized by perpetual memories of it. And since the virtuous ought to pursue it, do not let yourself falter, or become faint-hearted, because on behalf of all these lords and for the others whom they and I have been charged with governing and commanding, I promise that after the expiration of the truce, we shall take the lead in the battle, and with greater effort and courage we shall resist and press our foes just as if the emperor our lord were our leader."

What this knight said seemed very good to all those who were there, especially to King Lisuarte; and it made very clear that quite rightfully he deserved the honor and great domination that God gave him, as will be told later on. With this reply King Lisuarte went away very happy, and he said to King Cildadan: "My good lord, since we find such assurance in the Romans, and that they are helping us with such good will as I had not believed possible, and since they have so good and vigorous a knight for a leader as is this Arquisil, it is quite right and very just that we, ignoring all danger, undertake this business as reason obliges us to do. And for my part, I say to you that, once the truce has expired, there will be nothing except immediately the battle, in which if God does not give me victory, I do not want Him to give me life, for death will be for me a greater honor."

King Cildadan, as he was a very good knight and of great courage, although in his heart he always lamented that very great shame weighing on it at seeing himself a vassal of that king, heeding more that to which he was in duty bound by this promise and oath than the satisfaction of his will or desire, said to him: "My lord, I am very happy about what is discovered in the Romans, and much more in having become acquainted with the strength of your heart; for things like this that are past, and the present ones that are hoped for are the touchstone in which it is of import to reveal its virtue. And with regard to what concerns me, rest assured that where you are, whether I am alive or dead, there this body of mine will be."

When the king heard this, he thanked him profusely, and he esteemed him so highly that from that hour on, according to what was ascertained later by Cildadan, the king was resolved, however prosperous or adverse his fortunes might become, to set him free from the sovereignty which he exercised over him; which was so carried out, as later you will hear.

It is an impressive thing, one to be carefully noted by anyone who reads about it: that King Lisuarte merely by becoming cognizant of the great zeal with which this king offered to die in his service, although it did not come to this, saw fit to set him free from the vassalage in which he was holding him; from which one is given to understand that true good will, not only in spiritual matters but also in what is temporal, deserves as great a reward as if the deed itself were performed, because from it is derived the effect of what is good, and from the opposite, what is evil.

These kings having reached their tents, dined and rested, taking care of what was essential to putting an end to this very great and outstanding affront that they were sustaining to their honor and lives.

But now we shall leave both sides in their encampments, as you have heard, each hoping that in the third battle glory and conquest would be for itself, although the certainty of it for one side might have been very clearly recognized; and we shall relate to you what occurred in the meantime; whereby you will recognize that pride and great anger, and the danger so close and imminent in which these troops were from each other, could not prevent what God, powerful in all things, was pledged to bring about.

CHAPTER CXIII

How the saintly hermit Nasciano, who had reared the handsome youth Esplandian, having learned of the great rupture existing between these kings, took steps to reconcile them, and what he accomplished in the matter.

The story relates that that saintly man Nasciano, who had brought up Esplandian, as the third Book of this story records, having occupied his hermitage, in that great forest you have already heard about, for more than forty years — and since it was a very forbidding, remote place, seldom did anyone go there, whence he always maintained supplies sufficient for a long time; and it is not known whether by the grace of God or by means of reports that he was able to hear about the matter — found out that these kings and great lords were in such peril and danger, not only to their own persons but to all those who were engaged in their service; whereat he was greatly grieved and sad of heart. And because at the time he was so ailing that he could not walk or even rise, he prayed to God to grant him health and strength so that he could be an instrument for peace to those men who were of His holy faith; because, since he had heard confession from Oriana, and from her had learned the whole secret concerning Amadis and that Esplandian was their son, he clearly recognized the great danger that was being incurred in having her marry another person. And apropos of this, he thought that since Oriana was in a place where she could not fear the anger of her father, it would be well, although he was very old and weary, to set forth and go to the Firm Island, so that with her permission, for otherwise it could not be, he might set the king right concerning what he did not know, and might take such steps, by imposing peace and harmony, as to bring about marriage with Amadis.

With this thought and desire, when he felt somewhat improved in health, he took with him two men from that village where his sister lived — who was the mother of Sargil, the one who went about with Esplandian — and on his ass he took to the road although with great weakness; and with short day's journeys and great effort he traveled until he reached the Firm Island at the time that King Perion and all the troops had already left for the battle, at which he was very sad. Then having arrived there, he informed Oriana of his arrival. When she learned this, she was very happy for two reasons: the first, because this saintly hermit had reared and, after God, had given life to her son Esplandian; and the other, to take counsel with him concerning the welfare of her soul and conscience. And at once she gave orders to the maid of Denmark to go out to him and bring him to where she was, and so she did. When Oriana saw him enter the door, she went to him and knelt before him, and began to weep very grievously; and she said to him: "Oh, saintly man! Give your blessing to this unfortunate and very sinful woman, who was born into this world to her own misfortune and that of many others!"

Tears came to the eyes of the hermit out of the compassion he felt for her, and he raised his hand and blessed her, and said to her: "May that Lord who is the restorer and is all-powerful bless you, and may He be the guardian and repairer of all your affairs."

Then he took her by the hand and lifted her up and said to her: "My good lady and beloved daughter, with much fatigue and great effort I have come to speak with you; and when it pleases you, command that I be heard, because I cannot tarry, nor do my way of life and my clerical garb permit me to do so."

Oriana, still weeping, took him by the hand, without making any reply to him, for her great sobbing did not permit it; and went into her chamber with him and gave orders to leave them there alone. Thus it was done. When the hermit saw that he could say whatever he wished without fear, he said: "My good lady, while I was in that hermitage where for such a long time

I have besought God our Lord to take pity on my soul, and have been laying aside all worldly things so as not to receive any setback to my purpose, I learned that the king your father and the Emperor of Rome with many troops have come against Amadis of Gaul; and likewise he with his father and other princes and knights of high rank are going to give battle to them. What can result from this anyone will recognize; for certainly, in view of the multitude of troops and the great rigor with which they are challenging and seeking out each other, there can only result from it a great loss of life to them and a great offense to God our Lord. And because the cause, according to what I am told, is the marriage by which your father wishes to unite you with the Emperor of Rome, I, lady, undertook to make the present journey as a person who knows the secret of how your conscience is in this matter and the great danger to your person and reputation if what the king your father wishes were to be carried out. And because from you, my dear daughter, I ascertained it in confession, I have not been free to apply to it that remedy which befitted such a great wrong as that which is in prospect. Now that I see the state in which matters are, it will be more sinful to remain silent than to tell it. I come, beloved daughter, so that you may consider it better for your father to know the past, and that he cannot give you any husband except the one you have; than that, not knowing it, thinking that what he wishes can rightly be carried out, his stubbornness be such that with great destruction of his own men and of the others, he pursue his intention and at the end it be made public, just as the Gospel says that nothing can be so hidden as not to be ascertained."

Oriana, whose frame of mind was somewhat calmer, took him by the hands and kissed them many times against his will, and said to him: "Oh, very saintly man and servant of God! In your desire and will I place and leave all my trouble and anxieties for you to do that which is best for my soul; and may it please that God whom you serve, and whom I have offended so deeply, out of His holy compassion to show the way, not as I as a great sinner deserve, but as He through His infinite goodness is accustomed to do with those who have greatly sinned against Him, if wholeheartedly, as I now do, they beg Him for mercy."

The good man answered her with great pleasure: "Then, beloved daughter, in this Lord who you say fails no one in urgent need if with true sincerity and contrition He is besought, have great faith; and it is incumbent on me, as one who with most propriety can and should do so, to apply whatever remedy be in His service, to the end that your honor be protected with that security that is essential to your soul's conscience. And because from delay much harm and evil can ensue, it is fitting that by you, my good lady, I be given leave to depart at once, so that the effort of my person may obtain, if possible, some of the fruits that I desire."

Oriana said to him: "Sir Nasciano, that youth to whom after God, you have given life, I entrust to you so that you may pray to Him on his behalf; and if you return here, strive hard to bring him with you; and may you go committed to God that He may guide you on your way, so that your good desire may be fulfilled to His holy service."

Thus the saintly hermit took his leave, and with great weariness of natural forces and great hope of carrying out his good desire started on his way to where he knew the troops were on the move. But as he was so old, just as the story relates, and he could travel only on his donkey, his progress was so slow that he was unable to arrive until the two battles had already taken place as related, so that while the armies were occupied under truce in burying the dead and caring for the wounded, this very saintly man arrived at the camp of King Lisuarte; and when he saw so many people dead and many others wounded with diverse wounds, on account of which they were making loud laments everywhere, he was greatly shocked; and he lifted his hands to the heavens, weeping out of great pity, and said: "Oh, Lord of the world! may it please you out of your holy compassion and the suffering that you underwent for the sake of us sinners, that without paying heed to our very great errors and sins, you give me divine grace whereby I may be enabled to forestall such great evil and harm as is in store for these servants of yours."

Then on entering the encampment, he asked how to reach the tents of King Lisuarte, to which he went without resting anywhere. And when he arrived there, he dismounted from his donkey, and went to where the king was. When the king saw him, he recognized him at once, and was greatly surprised at his coming because in view of his great age he had the definite impression that he would not even have been able to leave his hermitage. And he at once suspected that such a man as he, so weighted down with afflictions and of such a saintly life, would not have come except for some all-important reason, and he went to him to welcome him; and when he came up to him, he knelt and said: "Father Nasciano, friend and servant of God, give me your blessing."

The hermit raised his hand and said: "May that Lord, whom I serve and whom all the world is obligated to serve, protect you, and give you such understanding that by not esteeming highly the perishable things in it, but rather by rejecting them, you may perform such good works that thereby your soul may have and attain that glory and repose for which it was created, if you do not lose it through your own fault."

Then he gave him his benediction and raised him by his hands and knelt to kiss them, but the king embraced him and did not permit it; and taking him by the hand, he had him sit beside him. And he gave orders that food should be brought to him immediately, and this was done; and after he had eaten, the king retired with him into a private room of the tent, and asked him the reason for his coming, saying to him that he was greatly surprised in view of his age and great seclusion, that he was able to have come to a locality at such a distance from his dwelling place. The hermit responded to him saying: "Sire, very logically one should believe all that you say; for certainly in view of my great age, of body as well as of will-power and condition, I am no longer in a position to do more than go from my cell to the altar. But it is incumbent on those who wish to serve our Lord Jesus Christ and desire to follow His holy teachings and in His footsteps, that at no season of their age, on account of any travail or fatigue that may come to them, should they weaken for a single moment; for remembering how God, being the true creator of all things, without anything compelling Him except only His holy compassion and mercy, made the effort to come in order to give to us Paradise, which we had closed to us in this world, where with so many insults and acts of irreverence from such dishonorable people, he received death after very cruel suffering, what can we do, however much we may serve Him, that would reach as high as his shoe latchet as that great friend and servant of His [St. John the Evangelist] said to him? And considering this, putting aside the fear and danger to my petty life, thinking that here I could function better in His service than where I was, I resolved with much hardship to my body and extreme willingness as regards desire, to make this journey, during which may it please Him to guide me, and you, my lord, to receive my message, putting aside all anger and passion and above all, wicked pride, enemy of all virtue and conscience, so that by continuing in God's service, those things be forgotten that in this world are of value in the opinion of many and in the next world, which is the more real one, are abhorred. And coming to the point, my lord, I say to you that while I was in that hermitage to which chance guided you — a hermitage hidden away in that thickly wooded, rugged mountain — where you talked with me concerning everything pertaining to that very handsome and well-reared youth Esplandian, I learned of this very great confrontation and cruel war in which I find you, and also the reason and cause of its being waged. And because I know very definitely that what you, my good lord, were seeking, which is to marry your daughter to the Emperor of Rome, on account of whom so much trouble and harm has come about, could not be done, not only on account of what many grandees and other lesser men of your kingdom many times told you, saying that this princess was your legitimate heiress and successor after the end of your days, which was and is a very legitimate reason for desisting with much reason and good conscience; but also for another reason that is concealed from you and others, and made known to me; which with more cogency, according to divine and human law, averts it, so that in nowise can it be done; and this is because your daughter is joined in matrimony with the husband that our Lord Jesus Christ considered good and it is in His service that she be married."

The king, when he heard this from him, thought, since this good man was already of very advanced age, that he was losing his mind, or that someone had coached him very well on what he had said; and he responded, saying: "Nasciano, my good friend, my daughter Oriana never has had a husband nor does she have one now, except that emperor to whom I gave her, because with him, although she was removed from my kingdom, I was affording her much greater honor and a higher status. And God is my witness that my intention never was to disinherit her in order to make my other daughter my heiress, as some say, but because I reckoned that this kingdom of mine if joined by ties of affection with the empire of Rome, His holy Catholic faith would be greatly exalted; for if I had known or imagined the enormity of the events that have resulted from all this, with very little urging my desire and will would have changed into willingness to take other advice. But, since my intention was just and good, I conclude that neither what has happened nor what is in the future can or ought to be deemed my fault."

The good man said to him: "My lord, just for that reason I said to you that what to you was concealed, to me is made known. And putting aside what you tell me of your sincere and noble intention, for in view of your great discretion and the very high honor God has conferred upon you, it should and can be believed, I want you to know from me what you could hardly find out from anyone else, and I tell you that the day I arrived by your command at the tents in the forest where the queen and her daughter Oriana were with many matrons and maidens, and you were there with many knights, when I brought with me that lucky youth Esplandian, who was conducting the lioness on a leash — Esplandian to whom the Lord has promised so much good fortune, as you, my good lord, have heard — the queen and Oriana told me all the secrets on their consciences, so that in the name of the One who created them I might impose on them the penance that was indicated for the salvation of their souls. I found out from your daughter Oriana that after the day that Amadis of Gaul took her from Arcalaus the Enchanter and the four knights who with him were carrying her off as a prisoner, at the time that you were deceived by the maiden who lured you out of London on account of the boon that you promised her, and you were seized and in great danger of losing your life and your whole dominion — from which situation Don Galaor, his brother, set you free at the great risk of his own life — not only for that great service that Amadis rendered her but also even more on account of that which his brother performed for you, as a reward she promised marriage to that noble knight, restorer of many distressed people, flower and mirror of all the knights in the world, in lineage as well as in strength and all the other good qualities that a knight ought to have; whence it followed that by the grace and will of God, there was engendered that Esplandian whom He willed to make so superlative and outstanding over and above all others living, for truthfully we can say that in many long periods of the past — and the same will be said in the future — no mortal has been known by man to have been reared so miraculously; then what concerning his deeds that great woman sage Urganda the Unknown publicly reveals, you, Sire, know much better than I; so that we can say that although that came about by chance, according to all appearances, it was naught else but a mystery of God that He was pleased to have take place as it did. And since it pleases Him so greatly, it should not trouble you, my good lord; rather, considering this to be His will, and the nobility and great value of this knight, deem it well to accept him, along with all his great lineage, as servant and son, giving the order, as it can be given, that your honor having been protected, the present danger be removed, and in the future such procedure be followed as persons of good conscience may determine to be in the service of that Lord whom we are born into this world to serve; and you, in subordination to Him, are His minister in temporal matters. And now, noble King Lisuarte, I wish to see whether that great discretion is well employed with which God has willed to adorn you, and likewise the augmented high estate in which more out of His infinite goodness than because of your own merit, He has placed you. And since He has done for you more than you deserve, do not consider it excessive to follow somewhat what His holy doctrines teach."

When this was heard by the king, he was greatly astonished and said: "Oh, Father Nasciano! Is it true that my daughter is married to Amadis?"

"Certainly it is true," said he, "for he is the husband of your daughter, and the youth Esplandian is your grandson."

"Oh, Holy Mary help us," said the king. "What a bad precaution to keep it a secret from me for so long! For if I had known or imagined it, there would not have been killed and lost so many wretched men as there have been without their deserving it. And I wish that you, my good friend, had informed me of it in time for the situation to have been remedied."

"That could not have been possible," said the good man, "because what is told in confession must not be revealed; and if now it has been, it is by permission of that princess from whom I now come, for she has been pleased to let it be told; and I trust in the Savior of the world, that if in the present situation such a remedy is given, it may be in His service, so with slight penance He will pardon what is past, since the deed, more than the intention, seems to be wicked."

The king remained in thought for quite an interval without saying anything, while he recalled the great valor of Amadis, and how he deserved to be the lord of great lands, just as he was, and to be the husband of a person who might be mistress of the world; and furthermore the great love he had for his daughter Oriana, and how he would be using virtue and good conscience in leaving her as his heiress, since by right it was coming to her, and the love that he always had had for Galaor and the services that he and his entire family had rendered him, and how many times, after God, he was helped by them at a time when he expected nothing but death and the destruction of his whole state, and especially that that very handsome youth Esplandian was his grandson, in whom he had such great expectations; for if God protected him and he became a knight, according to what Urganda wrote to him, he would have no equal in excellence in the world; and likewise how in the same letter she wrote to him that this youth would bring about peace between him and Amadis; and he also remembered that the emperor was dead, and that if through him and by becoming a relative of his was winning honor, much more he would have by being related to Amadis, as in his experience he had seen many times; and with this, besides achieving peace, not only for himself but also for his kingdom, he would so increase in honor that no one in the world would be his equal; and after he reached a conclusion regarding his concern, he said: "Father Nasciano, friend of God, although my heart and will may have been conquered by pride and not desirous of anything but to receive death or give it to many others so that my honor might be satisfied, your saintly words have had such virtue that I am determined to curb my will in such a fashion that if peace and harmony should not come into effect, you may be my witness before God that the blame and fault are not mine. Therefore do not fail to speak with Amadis, and do not reveal anything about my resolve; ascertain his opinion about what he wishes in this affair, and report it to me. And if it is such as to be in conformity with mine, there can be arranged a way whereby present and future events may be forestalled in a manner that comports with the interests and honor of both sides."

Nasciano knelt before him weeping out of the great joy he felt; and he said to him: "Oh, fortunate king! May that Lord who came to save us, reward you for what you say to me, since I cannot."

The king lifted him to his feet and said to him: "Father, what I have said to you I hold as a resolution, without any ulterior motive."

"Then," said the good man, "I must leave at once, and before the truce expires strive for a conclusion to be reached in this matter whereby our Lord will be so greatly served."

So the king and he came out to the big tent, where many knights and other people were, and as the hermit was on the point of taking leave of him, there entered the door that handsome youth, his own ward Esplandian, and Sargil his foster-brother with him, for Queen Brisena was sending them to ascertain news of the king her lord. When the saintly man saw him so grown up, already having the stature of a man, who could tell you the joy he experienced? Certainly it would be impossible. Then just as he was in company of the king, he went up to him as quickly as he could to embrace him. The youth, although it had been a very long time since he had seen him, recognized him at once, and went to kneel before him and began to kiss his hands. And the saintly man took him in his arms, and kissed him many times with such great joy that he was almost completely out of his senses; and so in this way he held him for a long interval, for he was not able to withdraw from him, in this wise speaking to him: "Oh my good son! blessed be the hour in which you were born, and blessed and praised be that Lord who through such a great miracle willed to give you life and raise you to such a high estate, the one at which my eyes now behold you!"

And while he was engaged in this, everybody was observing what the good man was doing and saying, and the great pleasure that the sight of that ward of his was affording him. And their hearts were moved to tenderness on seeing such love.

But greater than that of anyone else, although he did not show it, was the pleasure that King Lisuarte experienced; for although previously he had esteemed him highly and loved him for what he expected of him and for his very handsome appearance, it was nothing in comparison with his knowing for certain that he was his grandson, and he could not remove his gaze from him; for so great was the love that suddenly came over him that all that passion and anger that until then he had had about the past events was thereby removed and changed into the feelings he had at the time when he entertained the greatest love for Amadis. And then he recognized as a great truth what Urganda the Unknown had written to him, namely that this youth would effect peace between him and Amadis; and so he believed implicitly that everything else would come true.

After the good man held him embraced with such love, he released him from his embrace in which he had been holding him; and the youth went to kneel before the king and gave him a letter from the queen in which she begged him earnestly for peace and harmony if it could be done with honor, and many other things unnecessary to mention. The good man said to the king: "My lord, I shall receive great favor and great consolation of my spirit, if you would give Esplandian permission to accompany me while I go about here, so that I may have an opportunity to look at him and talk with him."

"So be it done," said the king, "and I order him not to leave you as long as such be your desire."

The good man thanked him profusely and said: "My good and fortunate son, come with me, since the king commands it."

The youth said to him: "My good sir and true father, I am very happy to do so because for a long time I had wanted to see you."

Then he left the tent with those two youths, Esplandian and Sargil his nephew, and he mounted his donkey, and they their palfreys; and he went on his way to where Amadis had his camp, talking with them about many things to his liking, and all the while praying God to give him divine grace so that he might be able to bring to such a conclusion the mission on which he was engaged that it might be in His holy service.

So accompanied just as you hear, that saintly man arrived at the camp and went directly to the tent of Amadis, where he found so many knights and they so well garbed that he was greatly astounded. Amadis did not recognize him, for he had never seen him and could not imagine what a man so old and feeble was seeking. And he looked at Esplandian and beheld him so handsome that he could not believe that any living being could be so to such a degree. And he didn't recognize him either; for although he had spoken with him when he asked him for the Romans that he had overcome, and he gave them to him as this story has related, that sight of him was so brief that he had forgotten how he looked. But Don Cuadragante, who was there, recognized him at once, and went toward him and said to him:

"My good friend, I want to embrace you, and do you remember that when Don Brian de Monjaste and I encountered you, you sent regards by us to the Greek Knight? I gave them to him on your behalf."

Then he said to Amadis: "My good lord, you see here the handsome youth Esplandian, from whom Don Brian de Monjaste and I delivered regards to you."

When Amadis heard Esplandian mentioned by name he recognized him at once, and that he was pleased to see him, there is no need to tell, for he was so overwhelmed by the great joy he experienced that he could hardly answer or collect his wits. And if anyone had paid attention to it, he would have seen very clearly his perturbation, but there was no suspicion of any such thing; rather, everybody had the idea that no one except Urganda knew who his father was. Then with Don Cuadragante holding him by the hand, Amadis sought to embrace him, but Esplandian said to him: "Good sir, rather do honor to the saintly man Nasciano, who is seeking you."

And when everybody heard him say that was Nasciano, concerning whose sanctity and austere life so much fame everywhere was diffused, they came up to him with deep humility, and kneeling on the ground they begged him to bless them. The hermit said: "I pray my Lord Jesus Christ that if a blessing from such a sinner as I am can be of benefit, this one of mine may diminish the great anger and pride that is in your hearts, and put you in such an understanding of His service, that forgetting the vain things of this world, you may follow the true things of the One who is true."

Then he raised his hand and blessed them. Amadis turned to Esplandian and embraced him. And Esplandian paid him respect and reverence, not as to his father, for he did not know that he was, but as to the best knight of whom he had ever heard. And for this reason he esteemed him so highly and was so happy to see him, that he could not remove his gaze from him; and since the day that he saw him vanquish the Romans, his desire always had been to travel in his company and in his service in order to observe his magnificent deeds of chivalry and to learn for the future. And now that he saw himself older and close to being a knight, he desired that much more; and if it had not been for the great quarrel that the king his lord had with Amadis, he would have already asked permission of him to join him; but this situation had inhibited him up to that time.

Amadis, who could hardly take his eyes from him, saw that the youth was gazing at him so earnestly, and he suspected that he must have been aware of something. But the good hermit, who knew the truth, was gazing at father and son; and as he saw them together and both so handsome, he was as happy as if he had been in Paradise. And inwardly he prayed to God for them and that He be pleased to afford him the opportunity to be enabled to establish between all these knights, who were the flower of the world, a great deal of love and harmony. Then while everybody was congregated around the holy man, he said to Don Cuadragante: "My lord, I must speak about some matters with Amadis; take this youth with you, since you have known and talked with him more than any of these lords."

Then he took Amadis by the hand and withdrew with him well away from them, and said: "My son, before the principal motive of my coming is made manifest to you, I wish to recall to your memory the very great responsibility, more than anyone else of those who are living today, which you have to God our

Lord; for at the hour you were born, you were cast into the sea enclosed in an ark without any protection; and that Redeemer of the world, having pity on you, miraculously brought you in sight of one who reared you so well. This Lord whom I mention to you has made you the most handsome, the strongest, and the most beloved and honored of all those known in the world. By you have been vanquished many valiant knights, and giants and many other fierce and unsightly creatures, which in this world do very great harm. You are today in the world outstanding among all those who are in it. So then since He has done so much for you, what should you rightfully do for Him? Certainly, if the Evil One were deceiving you, with more humility and patience than anyone else you ought to attend to serving Him; and if you do not do so, all the benefits and favors that you have received from God will be to the detriment and discredit of your honor, because just as His holy pity is great in those who obey and recognize Him, so his justice is more severe for those who have received the greatest benefits from Him without having any recognition of, or gratitude for them. And now, my good son, you shall know why, while exposing this tired and old body of mine to all the dangers to its well-being and seeking to pursue that purpose on account of which I willed to abandon the things of this perishable world, I have come with great effort and anxiety of mind, with the aid of that One, without whose aid nothing can be done that is good, to establish peace and love where so much rupture and misfortune exist according to present indications. And because I have spoken with King Lisuarte, and in him I find what every good king as a minister of God ought to obey, I have sought to find out from you, my good lord, whether you will have a better recognition of that One who created you than of the vainglory of this world, and in order that you may speak with me without any misgiving or fear, I inform you that before I came here, I went to the Firm Island; and with the permission of Princess Oriana, from whom I know in confession all her heart and her deep secrets, I have undertaken this negotiation in which you see me involved."

Amadis, when he heard him say this, fully believed that he was speaking the truth, because this was a saintly man and under no condition would he say anything except what was true, and he answered him in this manner: "Friend of God and holy hermit, if the recognition that I have of the benefits and favors that I have received from my Lord Jesus Christ would fulfill the services that I owe Him, I would be the most fortunate knight ever born, but by receiving from Him all and much more than you have said, and not only by not recognizing or repaying Him, but offending Him each day in many respects, I consider myself very sinful and erring against His commandments. And if now by your coming I can make amends somewhat for the past, I shall be very happy and contented that it be done. Therefore say what is in my power; for that with complete dedication shall be fulfilled."

"Oh, my fortunate son!" said the good man, "How much you have gladdened this very sinful soul of mine and comforted my grief at seeing so much evil; and may that Lord who will save you give you on my behalf the reward for it! And now I without any fear want you to know what I know after coming to this land."

Then he related to him how he had spoken with Oriana and how by her request he had come to the king her father, and all the things that he had talked about with him, and how he had told him outright that Oriana was married to Amadis and that the youth Esplandian was his grandson, and how the king had accepted it with great forbearance, and that he was brought to the verge of peace; and that since he, Nasciano, with the help of God, had put him in such a frame of mind, he, Amadis, should facilitate a way, since he was married to that princess, whereby peace might be arranged between him and the king. When Amadis heard this, his heart and flesh trembled with the great joy that he felt in knowing that by his lady's own wish the secret of their love affair was revealed, and having her in his power without any risk of danger; and he said to the hermit: "My good sir, if King Lisuarte is of this mind and wishes me for his son, I will take him for lord and father, to serve him in all that may be to his honor."

"Since that is the way it is," said the good man, "how does it seem to you that these two wills can be united completely without more trouble ensuing?"

Amadis answered: "It seems to me, father, that you ought to speak with King Perion, my father, and tell him the motive and desire of your coming, and ask him whether he will approve, if King Lisuarte agrees to what Don Cuadragante and Don Brian de Monjaste on our behalf will ask of him concerning the matter of Oriana, of making peace with the king; and I have such firm trust in his virtue that you will find all the assurance you desire. And tell him that you talked over some of it with me, but that I leave everything up to him."

The holy man considered good what he said, and proceeded accordingly; for he at once left the tent of Amadis with his young men and other companions, and went to that of King Perion, by whom, when informed who he was, he was welcomed with great affection and good will. The king gazed at Esplandian, whom he had never seen, and was greatly astounded on seeing a boy so handsome and so gracious, and he asked the holy man who he was. The saintly man told him that he was his ward, whom God had given to him very miraculously. King Perion said to him: "All the more so, father, if he is the youth who was bringing on leash the lioness with which he hunted, and whom you reared in the forest where you dwell, and of whom the great sage Urganda the Unknown has sent to tell us many extraordinary things that will come about for him, if God lets him live. And it seems to me, that when they told me about it, they said that she sent a letter to tell King Lisuarte that this youth would bring about a great deal of peace and harmony between him and my son Amadis; and if that is so, we all ought to love and honor him greatly, since as you, father, see, because of him so much that is good can come about."

The holy man, good Nasciano, said to him: "My lord, he is truly the one of whom you speak; and if now you are right in loving him, much more reason to do so will you have later on, when you learn more about him."

Then he said to Esplandian: "Son, kiss the hands of the king; for he well deserves it."

The youth knelt to kiss his hands, but the king embraced him and said: "My boy, you ought to be very grateful to God for the favor he did you in giving you such good looks and good grace, for without their becoming acquainted with you, you cause everyone to love you and esteem you. And since He has been pleased to endow you with such grace and good looks, if you are obedient to Him, He has much more in store for you."

The youth did not make any reply; rather with great embarrassment on hearing himself praised by such a prince, he blushed, which seemed very good to everyone, as they beheld him possessed of all the modesty that his age required; and they greatly marveled at a person so outstanding, who did not know the identity of his father or mother. The king asked the saintly man Nasciano whether he knew whose son he was. The good man said: "He is the son of God, who creates all things, although of mortal man and woman he was born and engendered. But in view of his beginning and the care that He took in protecting and rearing him, He appears to love him as a son; and will be pleased, out of His holy clemency and mercy for you to know more about him before long."

Then he took him by the hand and drew him to one side, and said to him: "King, fortunate in all the things of this world and in the next if you fear God and have regard for all the things that be in His service, I have come to these parts with this body of mine so weak and weary from extreme old age, with the resolve that God my Lord will give me divine grace that I may be able to serve Him by obviating all the harm that is in preparation, and my sufferings and great fatigue have not permitted me to come sooner; and I have spoken with King Lisuarte, who as a servant of God, will be willing to conclude peace if it can be made honorably for both sides. And from him I have come to your son Amadis, and by referring me to you and that I follow your orders, he excused himself from making a reply to what I said to him; so that, my lord, peace or war depends on you, since everyone knows how greatly you are obligated to avoid things contrary to the service of that very high Lord, in view of the blessings of this world, not only of a wife but also of children and a kingdom, that He has provided for you. And now it is time that He know to what extent you are grateful to Him for them and wish to do Him service in return."

The king, as he had always been inclined to peace and tranquillity, on account of the harm that could ensue from the war, as well as the fact that he had there Amadis, who was the light of his eyes, and Don Florestan and Agrajes and many other knights who were relatives, replied and said: "Father Nasciano, God is a witness of the good will that I have had in this great rupture, and that I would have avoided it if a way could be found to do so; but King Lisuarte has not given any opportunity for means to be found to that end, because much against God and his conscience he sought to disinherit his daughter Oriana, as everybody knows, who as you have found out, has been rescued. And even afterwards, he has been admonished and besought to be willing to agree to whatever is just, and told that everything would be done at his command; but he, as a powerful prince, and in this affair, more haughty than reasonable, thinking that because he had as ally the Emperor of Rome, the whole world would be subject to him, never wanted either to submit to justice or to hear of it; then from this course what has ensued and has been won for him, God knows and everyone beholds. But if he now is willing to have the insight that until the present he has not had, I trust completely these knights who are on my side to carry out and follow my counsel, which is that these bad actions be checked. And in order that you, father, may see on how little his stubbornness is based, if only in the matter of Oriana, his daughter, a solution were proposed, it would be the remedy for everything."

The good man said: "My good lord, God will grant it, and I in His place; therefore, speak with your knights and nominate persons who seek what is good; for it will be done thus by King Lisuarte; and I shall be with them, as a servant of Jesus Christ, to mend and repair what has been broken."

King Perion considered it good, and said to him: "That will be done at once; for I shall offer two knights who with all love and good will, may reach a just solution."

The holy man with this returned very happy and satisfied to the camp of King Lisuarte.

King Perion ordered all the principal knights summoned to his tent; and when they were assembled, he said to them: "Noble princes and knights, just as we are all greatly obligated in the defense of our honor and standing to expose our persons to every danger in order to defend them and maintain justice, so we are under the obligation to turn about and have recourse to reason entirely without anger and pride when it is made clear to us; because although at the beginning, with fair justice, without offense to God, matters can be dealt with; but while going ahead with the point at issue, if through presumption and poor discernment we did not reach a reasonable solution, what was just at the outset and what ultimately is unjust would cancel each other out; so that it is necessary that honor and esteem, being for the most part at their perfection, if a way to harmony be discovered, as now there seems to be by putting aside things of the past, let it be taken for the service of the most high Lord and as a remedy for our souls, for which we are so responsible. Now you shall know that this holy hermit, friend and servant of God, has come to me; and according to what he says, our foes would like peace more in conformity with good conscience than with points of honor, if we so desire. In order to put it into effect, he asks only that persons from both sides be named to decide it with good will, putting aside unjust passion. It seems to be quite fitting that you know about it and vote as seems best to you, so that your decision may be carried out."

All were silent for a long while. Angriote de Estravaus rose and said: "Since everybody is silent, I shall voice my opinion." And he said to the king: "Sire, both because of your royal dignity and great personal integrity, and even more on account of the very great love that these princes and knights have for you, they have deemed it wise on this occasion to take you as their leader, so that the matters of war and peace may be guided by your counsel, for they recognize that neither fear nor partizanship will be able to sway you. And on account of the excellence of your counsel I have faith that whatever is decided by you would not be contradicted by any one of them, so that for both matters your capability suffices; but since your Grace is pleased to hear what each one will wish to say, I want you to know my opinion; which is that since Princess Oriana is held by us along with all that was acquired with her, it would be a great injustice, since our enemies desire peace, and our honor is so greatly increased, to refuse to grant it to them, it being a request in which we risk so little. And since at the beginning Don Cuadragante and Don Brian de Monjaste were designated, so now they should be; for their discretion and virtue are so heightened that at the hour that they presently undertake the task, then and even more completely they will leave it with peace concluded or the outbreak of war."

Just as this knight suggested, it was decided by the king and by those lords that these two knights, with the agreement and counsel of the king, should determine what they were to do thereafter.

CHAPTER CXIV

How the saintly man Nasciano returned to King Lisuarte with King Perion's answer, and what was agreed upon.

The good man Nasciano returned to King Lisuarte as you have heard, and told him what he had discussed with King Perion, and that since everyone was under the latter's command, it seemed to him that he ought to pursue and further the project with the very fine words that he had used with him. As the king was already resolved and very eager not to grant any longer to the Devil any of the participation that the latter had had up to then, from which great harm had resulted, he said to him: "Father, then it will not be thwarted by me, as you shall see; stay here with your companies in this tent, and I shall go and talk with these kings, who have received such great harm and danger in order to maintain my honor."

Then he went to the tent of Gasquilan, King of Suesa, who was still in bed on account of the fight he had with Amadis, as you have already heard; and he had King Cildadan and all the principal knights summoned, both his own and the Romans; and he told them what that good man the hermit had told him, both when he first came and now the reply that he brought from King Perion, but concealing what concerned Amadis and his daughter, for he did not want it to be known then; and earnestly begged them to tell him their opinion in order that, whether the outcome of that agreement was good or the opposite, he might obtain the participation of everyone. Especially did he want to find out the opinion of the Romans, because, in view of the great loss that they had sustained in losing their lord, it greatly obligated him with disregard for his own desire to follow theirs. King Cildadan said to him: "My lord, it is quite right that the participation you mention and consider good be afforded them; and your fine courtesy obligates them finally to follow whatever your wish may be, just as I and all the others who are obedient to you will do, together with this noble King of Suesa, because in this matter his desire will not be different from ours; and now let them state what they wish."

Then that good knight Arquisil rose and said: "If the emperor, my lord, were alive, not only because of his greatness but also because this strife has been on his account, it would be incumbent on him to choose peace or make war according to his desire and will; but since he is dead, it can be said that his obligation died with him; for we who are of his blood and all his vassals, whom we have under our command and rule, are no longer an aggrieved party in the participation that you, my good lord King Lisuarte, as his equal in the same cause, may wish to have; concerning which you have already been told, and now it is reiterated to you that as long as one of us remains alive, we shall never cease to follow whatever be your will, so that, to you, as the leader and the one whom this present matter concerns more than anyone else, we relinquish the responsibility for what should be done regarding peace or war."

The king was greatly pleased with this knight as were all those who were there, because his reply was quite in keeping with complete discretion accompanied by great valor, which seldom go together; and he said to him: "Since you leave it to me, I assume it; and if any mistakes are made, let me be held mainly responsible; just as, if I am successful, I'll receive most of the honor."

Whereupon he went away to his tent; and he directed King Arban of North Wales and Don Guilan the Pensive to take charge of speaking with those persons that King Perion might name, so that with their advice arrangements might be made for the final decision. And then he said to the hermit: "Father, it seems to me, since the matter has reached such a stage, that it will be well for you to return to King Perion and tell him that I have these two knights appointed to negotiate with his men; and that it will be well — because such matters always entail delay, and while the wounded are in these camps, they cannot be given medical care nor can provisions be had for the troops and animals — that the camps be broken simultaneously and he with all of his men retire for the distance of a day's journey towards where he came from, and I likewise, which will be to my town of Luvayna, in order to arrange for the rehabilitation of these troops, who are so battered, and to have the emperor transported to his own land, and that our messengers may discuss what ought to be done — and probably he and I will come — and that he communicate his will to his men. I shall do likewise to mine, and you will be an intermediary to serve as a witness to anyone's not being reasonable; and that if it be necessary, he and I with fewer people can see you wherever you like."

The hermit was greatly pleased with this, because he saw clearly that even if agreement were not achieved, the danger would be more remote with the troops farther apart; for although this saintly man was in holy orders and leading such an austere life in so rugged a region, he had been originally a knight very good at arms at the royal court of King Lisuarte's father, and after him at that of his brother King Falangris; so that just as in divine matters he was so faultless, he did not therefore fail to have a good understanding of worldly affairs, in which he had had much experience. And he said to the king: "My good lord, what you say appears to me to be good. It only remains that on a day appointed, your messengers and theirs be here at this place, which is a half-way point; and it may be, with the help of that Lord without whom nothing can be furthered, that such arrangements will be made between them that you and King Perion may see each other as you have said, and the delays that are wont to occur between the third parties may be obviated. And I shall go back immediately and shall send word to you as to the period and hour that you may order your camp broken, so that at the same time the other may be dismantled."

So the good man returned to King Perion and told him all about the agreement, with nothing omitted. The king was pleased with it, since it was to his very great advantage that the camps be broken; and with the approval of Don Cuadragante and Don Brian de Monjaste he gave orders to proclaim that very early the next morning everybody was to be ready to strike his tent and other equipment in order to break camp there. The good man sent word of this to King Lisuarte, and that he would be with him as quickly as he could.

Then morning having come, the bugles were sounded throughout the camps, and the tents dismantled; and with great pleasure on both sides, the camps were moved, each one on its way to where it was to go. But now we shall allow them to go on their separate ways, and we shall tell you about King Arabigo, who was on the mountain, as you have already heard.

CHAPTER CXV

How king Arabigo, having learned of the departure of these troops, decided to fight with king Lisuarte.

We have already told you that King Arabigo and Barsinan, Lord of Sansuenia, and Arcalaus the Enchanter and their companies were hidden away in the wildest and most easily defended area of the mountain while awaiting word from the scouts that they continuously and very secretly were maintaining to spy on the encampments; who witnessed very completely the battles that had taken place, and likewise the fortifying of the camps, whence neither side could receive any harm by night. And as up to that time there had not been any defeat inflicted there; rather, the camps always seemed to be unharmed, King Arabigo did not venture to come forth from there since he had no means of satisfying his desire, and always his intention was to wait until the very end, for he indeed thought that although for a while each side would be held at bay by the other, in the end one side would be conquered, and he was inwardly quite pleased because from the first battle no victory was evident; for the longer the struggle continued, the more the havoc was increased; so that at the end they would be left in such shape that with but little effort and less danger he would dispatch those who remained and would be lord of the whole land without there being anyone in it to gainsay him. So with great enjoyment he repeatedly embraced Arcalaus, praising and thanking him for what he had devised, and promising him great favor, telling him that there could no longer be any mistake about their being compensated for past injuries with much more than what had been lost. Then while they were thus taking great pleasure and delight, the scouts came and told the king that the troops had broken camp, and armed were returning along the respective ways they had traversed to come there; so that they could not imagine what had happened. King Arabigo having heard this, at once thought that they might have separated under some agreement. He decided to attack King Lisuarte rather than Amadis, because if the former were killed or taken prisoner, Amadis would have little concern for the welfare of, or harm to, the kingdom, and thus he, King Arabigo, would be able to win it completely. But he said it would not be well to attack them until nightfall, because then they would catch them more unawares and more easily; and he gave orders to his nephew, who had the name of Esclavor, a man very well versed in warfare, to follow their progress very surreptitiously with ten mounted men, and note well where they set up camp; and he obeyed the order, so that he went through the most concealed part of the sierra, keeping watch over the troops who were moving along over the plain below.

King Lisuarte, who was proceeding on his way, had continued misgivings about that band, although he did not know exactly where it was; but some of those who lived in the countryside had told him that they had kept seeing people on that mountain on the side facing the sea, but that none of the observers dared to approach them; nor did the king have time to provide what was needed in the situation, for he was so occupied with what he had confronting him. And now being on his way as stated, he was warned by some people of the district that they had seen mounted men going stealthily along the hill tops of that mountain range. The king, as he was very perceptive and quick-witted, realized at once what had come about: that he would not be able to get away from those troops, if they should attack his side, without a great battle; which he feared at that time on account of seeing his own forces so battered by the past battles. But with a stout heart he did not delay in applying the necessary remedy; and summoning King Cildadan and all the captains, he told them the information he had acquired concerning those troops, and that he was asking them to have all their own troops armed and in good order so that if it were necessary they might find them with the safeguards befitting knights. They all answered that just as he commanded, his orders would be carried out by them, and that he should believe that rather than receive any discredit or harm they would lay down their lives. There were some who told him privately that he ought to inform King Perion, because those troops were many in number and fresh, and his were just the opposite, and they were afraid that he would not be able to escape from them without great danger; that it should be recognized that they were all his enemies; that if Fortune were against him, she would have no mercy on them, nor would his enemies fail to do all the harm they could. These counselors were Don Grumedan and Brandoyvas, who reckoned that if this were done, the king their lord would not have anyone to fear, and that in this way, peace between them would be accelerated and hastened.

But the king, who, as we have told you frequently, always feared more the loss of his honor than that of his life, answered that things were not in sufficiently bad shape for him to be willing to commit himself to his enemies; for it might be that what now his counselors imagined a great danger would finally turn out to be the opposite; and that they should think only about attacking the enemy with great force if the latter should come, as King Lisuarte and his men always had done in instances of dangers in which they had found themselves which were greater than that one was. And then he ordered Filispinel with twenty knights to skirt the mountain, and as prudently as could be, so that they would not lose their lives, to get some information; and he did just as he was ordered. Meanwhile he had his troops halt, for they had already traveled some four leagues, in order that they and the animals might rest, so that, if it were possible, they might reach Luvayna without any additional halt; because he was more afraid of being attacked by night than by day, and if the troops halted again, in view of their fatigue, he would not be able to prevent them from disarming and sleeping, so that a very small force would be able to put them to rout. And as soon as they had rested a bit, he ordered them to mount, and he put his whole pack train and the wounded at the head of the column, although during the days of the truce he had sent most of the latter to that town. Filispinel went directly to the mountain, and because of the great precaution that he exercised, he immediately became aware of the scouts and Esclavor's troop; and while most of those whom he had in his company remained with him, he sent a warning to the king, informing him that he had found those few knights who kept going about spying and that he believed the other troops were probably not very far away. The king's only action was to continue on his way in great haste so that the attack, if it should come, would find him near that town of his, for he realized that even if he were not completely encircled, he would be better able to protect himself in it than in the field. So in a short time he withdrew quite a distance away from the mountain.

Esclavor, nephew of King Arabigo, as he saw that they had discovered him, sent word to inform his uncle of the fact, and to tell him that in his opinion without any delay the latter should descend from the mountain to the plain; for since they were discovered, King Lisuarte would be willing to halt only where it might be to his advantage.

When this message arrived, King Arabigo and all his troops were at ease preparing for the night, without any intention of attacking their enemy by day, and they were not able to arm and ride forth quickly enough, for they were many, to avoid considerable delay — and what hampered them most were the difficult mountain passes; for just as they had chosen the roughest and rockiest area as best for defense, so they found it quite the opposite for offense.

Then, just as you hear, these troops began to follow King Lisuarte; but before they had come down from the mountain, he had already gone such a long distance that after they descended to the plain, however much they spurred ahead in his pursuit, they were not able to overtake him until quite near the town. But Arcalaus, since he was familiar with the region, kept telling King Arabigo not to hurry and weary his troops, for since they had them in view it was not possible for them to get away, and not to consider it important that they take refuge in the town, for he knew it very well, and that in view of their small force, it would be more dangerous for them in it than in the field.

Meanwhile it happened by the will of God in order that those wicked people might not be enabled to carry out their evil desire, that the good holy hermit sent Esplandian his ward and Sargil his nephew to King Lisuarte to inform him that the negotiations were going well and that as quickly as he could he should be with him in Luvayna in order to arrange the meeting of the four knights representing the two sides.

When these two youths arrived at the camp of the king, they found that it had moved on quite a while before, and they followed the route it had taken and traveled until they reached the place where the king had rested; and there they found out that he was proceeding distrustfully and in great haste, and they hastened their own pace in order to overtake him. And before they saw the king's army they beheld the troops coming down off the mountain in a great hurry, and they at once thought that they belonged to King Arabigo; for while they were with Queen Brisena, they had heard about those troops and had seen that the queen was sending forces from some towns to others in the region where those companies were said to be. And when they saw King Arabigo's army proceeding in such great force and the king their lord with such inferior strength, and his troops so fatigued that they would not be able to withstand their foes and would be in great danger, Esplandian was very sad and troubled and said to Sargil: "Brother, follow me and let us not rest until, if it be possible, the king our lord is rescued, so that that evil band of troops may not be able to harm him."

Then they drew rein on their palfreys and as fast as they could rode back along the road over which they had come during all that remained of the day and all night, for they never stopped; and next day at dawn they reached the camp of King Perion, who that day had not gone farther than four leagues and had found his camp set up on a riverbank with many trees and gardens. And he was maintaining on the side nearest the mountain his guard of many knights, because he also had a report from some shepherds about that body of troops; and as they were moving from the place where they were, he was distrustful of them and for this reason he ordered a strong guard posted. And when they arrived there, Esplandian went directly to the tent of Amadis, and found the good hermit, who was arising and about to set forth. And when he saw the youth in such a hurry, he said to him: "My good son, what hasty arrival is this?"

He said to him: "My father, it is so urgent that I cannot tell you about it until I have spoken with Amadis."

Then he dismounted and approached the bed where Amadis lay armed, for all night he had been guarding the field and at dawn had come to sleep and rest; and awakening him, Esplandian said: "Oh good sir! If at any time your noble heart has wished for great deeds, the hour has come when it can demonstrate its greatness; for although, good sir, up until now you may have experienced many and very dangerous great affronts, none could ever be so outstanding as this one. You shall know, good sir, that the troops that were said to be on the mountain with King Arabigo are going as fast as they can against my lord King Lisuarte. And I believe, sir, in view of their vast numbers and the few and ill-conditioned troops of the king, great danger to him cannot be avoided. So, besides God, the only help for him is yours."

Amadis, when he heard this, got up very quickly and said: "Good youth, wait for me here, for if I can be of avail, your labor shall not be in vain."

Then he went at once to the tent of King Perion his father, and relating to him that report, begged him earnestly to give him permission to effect that rescue, from which he could receive much honor and great prestige, and would be highly praised wherever it was known; and this Amadis begged on bended knees, for he would not rise until the king, as he was given over to every virtuous action and spent his time only on such matters as involved great fame, said to him: "Son, let it be done as you wish, and take the lead with all the troops you please, for I shall follow you; because if we are to have peace with this King Lisuarte, this will render him more firmly established; and if war, it is better that he be destroyed by us than by others, for perchance they would be more inimical to us than he is at present."

And then he gave orders to sound the bugles and the trumpets; as the troops were all armed and expecting an alarm, they immediately mounted their horses, each one with his own captain. King Perion and Amadis had Gastiles, the nephew of the Emperor of Constantinople, mount and they left the camp bearing his standard, behind which all the others sallied forth. And when all were on the field, the king told them the news he had learned, and he begged them earnestly that without heeding what was past, they be willing to show their excellence in rescuing that king who was in such dire straits with such evil people. All of them considered it good, and said that it would be dcne according to his command.

Then Amadis took with him Don Cuadragante and Don Florestan his brother, and Angriote de Estravaus and Gavarte of the Fearful Valley, and Gandalin and Enil, and four thousand knights, and the physician Elisabad; who on this day as well as in the past battles, had accomplished marvels in his profession, saving the lives of many of those who would not have been able to retain them except through God's help and his.

With this company he took to the road, and with the king his father and all the others in their respective battalions behind him.

But now the narrative ceases to speak of them, as they traveled at top speed, and returns to the relation of what the kings did in the meantime.

CHAPTER CXVI

CONCERNING THE BATTLE THAT KING LISUARTE HAD WITH KING ARABIGO AND HIS COMPANIES, AND HOW KING LISUARTE WAS OVERCOME; AND THEN WAS RESCUED BY AMADIS OF GAUL, THAT MAN WHO NEVER FAILED TO SUCCOR THOSE IN NEED.

We have related to you how King Lisuarte was warned by the knights whom he had dispatched to the mountain that they had seen already the scouts of King Arabigo's troops, and how King Lisuarte was proceeding in great haste in order to reach his town of Lubayna so that if an attack should come, he could take refuge there; for in view of the fact that he was bringing away his troops in bad shape from the past battles of which you have already heard, he had the firm belief that he would not be able to withstand the great strength of his enemies. So it was that while he was pursuing his way, the companies of King Arabigo followed him until it was night, and they kept always with them Esclavor with the ten mounted men and some forty others that the king his uncle had sent to him when he dispatched him. According to the way the troop from the mountain traveled after they came down to the plain, they might have been able to overtake King Lisuarte. But the night was becoming so dark that they could not see one another; and for this reason and also because of what Arcalaus had said about the weak defenses of the town, on which they were pinning their hopes, they did not care to fight with them, but went on right behind them and with their scouts almost in contact with those of King Lisuarte. Thus they traveled until dawn, when they beheld each other very close together, and at a short distance from the town.

Then King Lisuarte, as a courageous prince, halted with all his men and made two brigades of his forces. The first he entrusted to King Cildadan, and with him Norandel, his son, and King Arban of North Wales and Don Guilan the Pensive and Cendil de Ganota, and with them close to two thousand knights. In the second were the Romans, Arquisil and Flameneo, and Giontes, the king's nephew, and Brandoyvas, and many other knights of his household, and with them about six thousand knights; for if these two battalions had been provided with fresh arms, armor and horses, they would not have had much to fear from their enemies; but their situation was quite the opposite, for from the past battles their armor was completely rent in many places, and their horses were very weak and tired, not only from their great past efforts, but also from the present one, because during all that day and that night they had not stopped except a very short while; from all of which great harm came to them, as you will hear subsequently.

King Arabigo had Barsinan, lord of Sansuenia, in the vanguard; who, as has been said, was a strong young knight, eager to win honor and to avenge the death of his father and that of Gandalod his brother, the one whom Guilan overcame and brought as a prisoner to King Lisuarte, and the latter ordered him in London to be flung down from a tower, at the foot of which his father had been burned to death, as the first Book of this story relates; and he brought with him two thousand knights, and the other battalions at his rear as has been stated.

Then, since it was bright daylight and they saw each other close together, they went forward to attack each other stoutly, so that from the first encounters many horses were without riders; and Barsinan broke his lance and grasped his sword, and struck mighty blows with it, as one who was valiant and in a great fury.

Norandel, who was coming in front of his men, encountered an uncle of this Barsinan, brother of his mother, who had been governor of the land after his father, Barsinan the Elder, was killed until this nephew of his reached an age at which he was competent to rule; and he met him in such a mighty clash that he pierced his shield and coat of mail, and the lance penetrated through to his back and forthwith struck him dead to the ground.

King Cildadan overthrew another knight who was coming with this one and who was one of the good knights of Barsinan's company, and likewise mighty blows were delivered by Don Guilan and King Arban of North Wales and the others who were coming with them, who were all very outstanding, picked knights; so that Barsinan's brigade would have been put to rout if Arcalaus had not come to its aid. And although he had lost half of his right hand — which Amadis, when he called himself Beltenebros, had cut off at the time he killed Lindoraque, Arcalaus's nephew — with his great experience at arms, he maneuvered now with his left hand as well as with the other. And with his arrival those on his side were greatly encouraged and again recovered great intrepidity of heart, so that many of King Lisuarte's men were killed or badly wounded and unhorsed. Arcalaus plunged into their midst and was performing great feats at arms, as one who was valiant and vigorous. But at this hour you would have seen King Cildadan and Norandel accomplishing wonders, and likewise Don Guilan and Cendil de Ganota, for these were a shield and protection for all their men; but all would have been of no avail if King Lisuarte had not helped; for the enemies, since they were more numerous and fresher, were already reducing them to defeat. But King Lisuarte, who never was the slightest bit remiss in what he ought to do in the great confrontation in which he found himself, went ahead of his men, more eager to receive death than to fail to accomplish the undertaking to which he was committed; the first man whom he encountered in his path was a brother of Alumas, the one whom Don Florestan killed in a dispute over the maidens whom the dwarfs were guarding at the Fountain of the Elms, and who was a first cousin of Dardan the Proud; and he pierced all his armor, and struck him dead to the ground, and his troops attacked the others with such force that they made them yield a large share of the field.

The king grasped his sword and struck such mighty blows with it that whomever he reached with a direct blow had no further need of a physician, and at that hour he became so infuriated that, forgetting all danger, he plunged into the midst of the enemy, wounding and killing them. Arcalaus, who previously had found out what arms he was bearing, in order to recognize him and injure him in any way that he best could, for such were his methods, when he saw him thus separated from his men, went to Barsinan and said to him: "Barsinan, you see before you your enemy; for if this man dies, it is all over. Don't you see what King Lisuarte is doing?"

Barsinan picked ten knights from the men who were serving him as guards, and said to Arcalaus: "Now at him and may he die or all of us!"

Then they went for the king and attacked him from all sides, so that they unhorsed him. Filispinel was proceeding all the while accompanied by the twenty knights with whom, as you already have heard, he went to reconnoiter the sierra, and they had promised each other to stay together in that battle. So when they saw the king unhorsed, he said to them: "Oh lords! now is the time to die with the king."

Then they all moved forward and came to where the king was, and they found two knights were holding him in their embrace, for they had hurled themselves upon him before he could rise, and they had taken from him his sword. And Filispinel and his companions attacked Barsinan and Arcalaus and their men, so that they forced them against their will to withdraw. But already at the shouts that Arcalaus was uttering in summoning his men, the troops attacked so many of the enemy that if chance had not brought King Cildadan and Arquisil and Norandel and Brandoyvas there along with a few knights whom they had rescued, the king would have been lost. But these killed so many that by force of arms they recovered the king; for Norandel, as he came up, let himself drop from his horse, and struck heavy blows at those who were holding him, and recovered the king's sword and put it into his hands; and said to him: "Take my horse," and the king did so, and did not leave there until Brandoyvas gave another horse to Norandel and had him mount. And then they went to aid their men, who were fighting so hard that their foes did not dare to await them. Arcalaus said to a knight of his: "Ask King Arabigo why he is allowing us to be killed."

This knight went up to King Arabigo and asked him this, and he said to him: "For some little time I have been perceiving that rescuing them was in order, but I was refraining in order that the enemy might withdraw farther away from the town. But since such is his wish, let it so be done."

Then the bugles sounded and he went with all his troops, and with him six knights of the Island of the Centaurs. And as he found them in confusion and weary, he attacked with impunity, and wrought great havoc among them. Those six knights that I mention performed marvelous deeds in unhorsing and killing everyone they overtook; so that, on account of what they accomplished and the achievements of the large number of fresh troops coming with King Arabigo, King Lisuarte's men could not withstand them and began to give ground like defeated troops. King Lisuarte, who saw his cause lost and perceived that in no way could it be won back, took with him King Cildadan and Norandel and Don Guilan and Arquisil and others of the most select group, and placing himself at the head of his men, ordered the other troops to retreat to the town, which was nearby. What shall I say to you? That in this flight and defeat the king did so much in defending his own men that never before had his excellence and courage been so well demonstrated since he had been a knight as at that time, and likewise that of all those knights who were with him.

But at last with great loss of troops slain as well as many taken prisoner and others wounded, they went, perforce in rout, through the gates into the town. And as the troops began to crowd in, and their enemies to charge at them as at adversaries already defeated, there were many more who lost their lives there. And King Arban of North Wales, and Don Grumedan with the standard of King Lisuarte, were unhorsed and taken prisoners by their enemies. And so the king would have been, except that some of his men seized him, and by force put him inside the town, and at once the gates were closed and the troops that entered there had been very few.

Their foes drew back, because they were being shot at with bows and crossbows, and they took with them King Arban and Don Grumedan with the king's standard. Arcalaus had wanted them to be killed at once, but King Arabigo did not permit it, telling him to restrain himself, that soon they would have King Lisuarte and all the others, and that in concert with him and the other great lords who were there, justice would be meted out to them. And he gave orders to certain men of his to take and guard them very carefully.

Just as I tell you, King Lisuarte was overcome and routed, and the majority of his troops lost, as dead or imprisoned, and he and the others with him confined in that weak town where he expected nothing but death. Well, what shall we say brought it about? God and his own bad luck? Certainly not, only he himself, on account of having his ears more receptive and ready to receive defamatory words by believing what those evil men Brocadan and Gandandel had told him about Amadis, rather than what he with his own eyes saw. And he trusted more the iniquities of those men than the good deeds of Amadis and his relatives, by whom he had been elevated to a higher pinnacle of fame than any other prince in the world had reached. Then besides God our Lord, who will come to his aid? Will perchance the harm he has sustained and the danger he is in be repaired by Brocadan and Gandandel and those of their families, or by those who, like them devoid of conscience, had and still have such a function, which is to be envious of the virtuous and of the brave who place themselves in jeopardy for the sake of pursuing virtue, and not with any desire to pursue what the virtuous do, other than that of harming and defaming to the utmost the pursuit of virtue? So it seems to me that if King Lisuarte awaited the latter, quickly there would be avenged the death of Barsinan, Lord of Sansuenia, and the great loss that King Arabigo sustained in the battle of the Seven Kings, and the rage of Arcalaus. Then by whom will he be aided and rescued? Certainly by that famous and strong Amadis of Gaul, by whom he had been many other times, as this great story has set forth. Then had he much reason to do so, aside from serving his lady? Rather, I say that, in view of the great and fruitful services he had rendered him, and the poor recognition and gratitude that he had from him, with good reason and cause he ought to favor Lisuarte's complete annihilation. But, as this knight had been born into this world in order to win glory and fame from it, he only gave thought to noble deeds of great virtue, just as you will hear he did in the case of this king who was beaten, besieged, and brought to the verge of death and the loss of his kingdom.

Then returning to the subject matter, I say that after King Lisuarte had been put under siege in that town of his, King Arabigo withdrew to the countryside where he was in the company of those great lords, asking them their opinion about how to conclude that business. Among them there were many opinions, some of them in opposition to others, as is wont to occur among those to whom Fortune is favorable; for they are so well off that they don't know how to choose what is best from what is good. Some of them said that it would be well to rest a while and make preparations for the combat, and to set up strong guards so that the king might not get away. Others said that it would be well to fight them at once before they would be able to make further preparation for their defense, and that since they were defeated and faint-hearted they would be quickly penetrated and seized.

All of this having been heard by King Arabigo, all were waiting to carry out his resolve, because he was the leader and head of them all; and he said: "Good lords and honorable knights, I have always heard that men ought to follow up good fortune when it comes to them, and not seek respites or excuses to abandon it; rather, with more courage and diligence to undertake the task simultaneously so that simultaneously there may come rejoicing. And therefore I say that without any more delay Barsinan and the Duke of Bristol, with the troops that they desire, should go at once to the edge of the town; and I and Arcalaus with the King of the Deep Island and these other knights, remain on this other side. And with the equipment that we have, which is this with which we fight, let our enemies be attacked at once before nightfall, for less than two hours of daylight remain. And if by this combat we do not force an entry to them, we shall withdraw outside, and the troops will be able to refresh themselves somewhat, and at dawn let us fight again. And as for myself, I say to you, and so shall I say to all my men and to the others who may wish to follow me, that I shall not rest until either I die or I take them before I eat or drink, and as a king I promise that either my death or theirs can be counted on by dawn."

King Arabigo afforded great encouragement and rejoicing to those lords, and they all agreed to what he said and promised.

And immediately they gave orders to bring some of the ample provisions they carried, and they had all their troops eat and drink while rallying them for the combat and telling them that when it was all over they were bound to be rich and favored by Fortune if they did not lose through lack of courage. This having been done, Barsinan, lord of Sansuenia, and the Duke of Bristol, with half the troops moved on to the edge of the town; and King Arabigo and the other half remained on the other side of it. And they all immediately dismounted and made preparations to fight on hearing the sound of the bugles.

King Lisuarte, inside the town though he was, did not seek to rest, for he well envisaged his destruction; and although he recognized he was in a place where he could not defend himself for very long, he decided to put forth all his efforts until the very end of the misadventure, and to die like a knight rather than be taken prisoner by those very deadly enemies of his. And when he and his men had had something to eat that those of the town gave him, at once he distributed all the knights together with those of the town on the parts of the wall where the greatest weakness was, admonishing and telling them, that, after God, their well-being and lives consisted in defense by their own hands and hearts. But they were such that they had no need of anyone to embolden them; for each one of his own accord expected to die like the king his lord.

Then while they were deployed as you hear, their enemies came recklessly to the combat with that energy that victors are accustomed to have; and without any fear, covered by their shields and with their lances in hand if they still possessed them intact, and the others with swords and with the crossbowmen and archers at their backs they came up to the wall. Those inside received them with many stones, and arrows from crossbowmen as well as from archers; and as the wall was very low and in some places broken down, they made mutual contact as if they were in the field; but with that limited defense that those inside had, and more so with their great courage, they defended themselves so fiercely that their opponents, having lost that impetus and momentum with which they arrived, for the most part began immediately to slow down and were turning aside; and others were fighting stoutly, so that there were many dead and wounded on both sides.

King Arabigo and all the other captains, who were going about on horseback, never stopped urging the troops forward; and the captains came up to the wall fearlessly so that their men would come up to it; and from their horses they struck with their lances those on top of the wall so that King Lisuarte was very close to having them force an entrance; but God sought to protect him by the fact that night had fallen with impenetrable darkness. Then the troops withdrew because they were ordered to do so, and they took care of their wounded; and the others were distributed to encircle the town, and a very strong guard was posted. And they held the opinion that next day at the first combat the affair would be settled, as indeed it was.

But now we shall tell you what Amadis and his companions did after they departed from King Perion to rescue this King Lisuarte.

CHAPTER CXVII

How Amadis went to rescue King Lisuarte and what happened to him on the way before he reached him.

We have already related how that very handsome youth Esplandian arrived in great haste at the camp of King Perion and informed Amadis of Gaul about the great danger and peril in which his lord King Lisuarte was, and how immediately King Perion with all the troops moved forward in his support, with Amadis in the vanguard with those knights, as you have already heard. But now we shall tell you what they did. Amadis, after he left his father, strove mightily to arrive in time to be able to effect that rescue so that his lady Oriana might recognize that rightly or wrongly he always had her image in mind to the end that he might serve her. And however hard he pushed his troops — as the journey was long, for from where he started to the camp where King Lisuarte had been when the great engagements took place, it was five leagues, and from there to the town of Luvayna, eight, this making in all thirteen leagues — he was not able to go fast enough to avoid night's overtaking him more than three leagues from the town. And with the extreme darkness and because Amadis ordered the guides to keep skirting the mountain in order to prevent King Arabigo from being able to take up some strong position, he lost his way; for the guides became confused and did not know where to go nor whether they had passed the town or had left it behind; which fact they immediately reported to Amadis. And when he heard it he had such great concern that he was close to being consumed with anxiety; and although he was the most long-suffering man in the world and the one who best knew how to control his anger in any emotional matter, he was unable at that time to refrain from cursing many times himself and his luck that was so contrary; and there was no man who dared to speak to him. Don Cuadragante, who also was greatly distressed because of King Cildadan, whom he loved very much and with whom he had such close kinship, came up to him and said: "Good sir, do not become so distraught, for God knows what is best; and if He is served by our providing this aid to those kings and knights, who are such friends of ours, He will guide us; and if it is not His will, no one has the power to do anything else."

And certainly in view of what occurred afterwards, if there had not been that error, such an outcome — one so replete with honor for them — would not have come about as it did, as you will hear later.

So being thus at a standstill and they not knowing what was to be done, Amadis asked the guides whether the mountain was nearby. They told him they thought it was, as they had always kept wending their way by skirting it, as he had ordered them to do. Then he said to Gandalin: "Take one of these guides and try to find a slope and climb it; for if the troops are encamped, they will have fires, and note well whether you see anything."

Gandalin did so; for as the mountain was at his left, he had only to keep going in that direction and in a short while he found himself at its foot. And Gandalin went up as far as he could and looked down toward the plain and saw at once the fires of the troops, at which he was greatly pleased; and he called the guide and showed them to him, and he asked him whether he would know how to reach there; he said that he would. Then they returned as quickly as they could to where Amadis and the troops were, and they made their report to him, at which he was quite pleased, and said: "Since that is the way it is, lead on and let us travel as fast as possible, for already a good part of the night has passed."

So they all followed the guide in as orderly a formation as possible, for they did not know about King Perion, nor he about them. But the same distance that he went in following the troops' tracks, they covered, and they approached the town, for they saw the campfires, which were numerous. And whether they were pleased by the fact need not be told, especially that vigorous Amadis, who never before in his life had wanted so much to find himself at a given place, so that King Lisuarte might recognize that he was always his protector against all dangers and that, after God, by him the king's life and whole high estate would be rendered secure; for he indeed thought that Lisuarte could not escape from being defeated and killed in this present danger, in view of his small number of troops and the great number possessed by his foes, and that without seeing him or speaking to him, his life would be restored.

And at this hour day was beginning to break, and they were still one league from the town. Then, daylight having come, King Arabigo and all those knights made ready for the fight with great energy and pleasure. And when they were armed, they all came to the wall and to its postern gates, but King Lisuarte with his men defended them valiantly against them. But finally, as the troops were many and encouraged by their good fortune, and those of the king few and most of them wounded and in dismay, they were not able to resist nor to prevent their enemies from entering by force with very great outcry; so that the noise was very loud in the streets along which the king and his men were defending themselves stoutly, and from the windows the women and youths and others capable of no more aggression than that were aiding them. The uproar from the knife- and lance-thrusts and the stone throwing, and the noise of voices was so great that there was not a person who witnessed it who was not frightened.

When King Lisuarte and those knights who served him saw themselves lost, since now they deemed it more serious to be taken prisoners than to be killed, one would not be able to describe to you the great marvels that they performed there and the hard blows they struck, so that their foes did not dare come up to them; but with their lance thrusts they kept driving them back. Then as for King Cildadan and Arquisil, and Flamineo and Norandel, who found themselves opposite King Arabigo, you can well believe that they were not idle, and with them there was a fierce fight; for King Arabigo entered the town and Arcalaus with him, and they brought with them the six knights of Centaur Island of which you have already heard, whom the king was continually keeping at his side to protect him. And as he saw things at such a pass, he sent two of them through a short-cut street to where Barsinan and the Duke of Bristol were fighting, and the other four he stationed with himself where King Cildadan was defending; and he said to them: "Now, my friends, is the time to avenge your fury and the death of that noble knight Brontaxar de Anfania, for you see there those who killed him. Attack them, for they have no defense."

Then these four knights, when they found themselves free of the king, grasped their great strong knives and with great fury went through all of their men, thrusting them aside and knocking them down, until they came to where King Cildadan and his companions were; who when he saw them so tall and exceedingly large, was not so ardent and courageous that he did not have great fear; and he said at once to his men: "Come now, lords, with these men death is well employed, but let it be in such wise that if possible, they go ahead of us."

Then they went at each other very violently and fiercely as men who were desirous of no other outcome than to kill or be killed. One of these knights came up to King Cildadan and raised his blade to strike him on top of his helmet, for he really intended to split his head in two. And the king, when he saw the blow coming, raised his shield to receive it, and it was so powerful that the sword pierced it halfway down and cut the arc or rim of steel. When he tugged at the blade he could not withdraw it, and hauled in the shield along with it. King Cildadan, as he was very strong, and had seen himself many times in such a predicament, at that time did not lose heart or self-possession; instead he struck him with his sword on the arm, which on account of the weight of the shield he could not withdraw from him quickly enough, and he cut through the sleeve of his coat of mail and his whole arm except for a very little, so that it was left dangling, and the blade thrust through the shield fell at his feet. He withdrew as if paralyzed, and the king went to the aid of his own companions who were fighting valiantly the three, and thus both with the blow that he delivered and with his help, their opponents became dismayed; so that in that sector the street was being defended very well without much damage being received, although King Arabigo was behind them, shouting to them not to leave a man alive. The other two knights, who were in the other sector, joined the fight, and on their arrival, King Lisuarte and his men were forced back to another intersection, where some of their men were remaining inactive without fighting because there was no room for them in the street, and there they halted. But all was to no avail, for so many troops were charging at them from all directions and were taking from them their rear guard, that if God through His mercy had not come to their aid with the arrival of Amadis, in less than a half hour all would have been dead or taken prisoner, in view of the wounds they had and their shattered armor. But even if everything had been safe and sound, it would not have made any difference, for they were already conquered and killed, for as such they considered themselves; but at this moment Amadis and his companions arrived with that body of troops that you have already heard about; for after daybreak, he spurred ahead as fast as he could so that before they were noticed they might be able to take them. And when he reached the town and saw the troops inside, and some others who were going about outside, he at once went all the way around the town, and they struck down and killed as many as they could overtake. And he through one gate and Don Cuadragante through the other entered with their troops, shouting: "Gaul, Gaul; Ireland! Ireland!"

And as they found the troops leaderless and unsuspecting, they killed many, and others took refuge from them in the houses. The ones ahead who were fighting heard the shouts and great noise with which the rescuers were proceeding with their men, and their battle cries. At once they thought that King Lisuarte was rescued, and they were greatly dismayed, for they did not know what to do: whether to fight with those they had in front of them or to go in aid of the others.

King Lisuarte, when he heard that noise and saw that his opponents were weakening, plucked up his courage and began to encourage his own men; and they charged at them so fiercely that they pushed them back to where they made contact with those who came fleeing from Amadis and his men; so that they had no resource except to place themselves back to back and defend themselves. King Arabigo and Arcalaus, when they saw the struggle lost, took refuge in a house, for they did not have the courage to die in the street; but they were seized at once and taken prisoners.

Amadis delivered such hard blows that he no longer would have found any who would make a stand against him, if it had not been for those two knights of Centaur Island, who, as you have heard, were fighting in that area and who came at him. And he, although he saw them as brave as the story has already stated, was not frightened by them; instead he raised his very good sword, and struck one of them such a mighty blow on top of his helmet that although he was very strong, he did not have the strength to keep from falling on both knees to the ground. And Amadis, when he saw him thus, came up quickly and pushed him with his hands, and made him fall on his back; and he passed on over him. And he saw that Florestan, his brother, and Angriote de Estravaus had unhorsed the other one and had left him in the hands of those who came behind; and when all three passed on to where Barsinan and the Duke of Bristol were, who had been immediately vanquished, Barsinan came and embraced Amadis, and the Duke of Bristol Don Florestan, because King Lisuarte was pressing them so hard that there was no longer anything in prospect for them but death; and they asked them for mercy. Amadis looked ahead and recognized King Lisuarte; and as he saw that there was no one there with whom to fight, he turned back as much as he could over the way he had come, and took with him Barsinan and the Duke of Bristol. And he sought to go to the place where Don Cuadragante had entered, and he was told how he had already finished the business and was holding King Arabigo and Arcalaus prisoners. When he learned this news, he said to Gandalin: "Go tell Don Cuadragante that I am leaving the town, and that since this business is concluded, it will be well for us to go away without seeing King Lisuarte."

And he at once went down the street until he reached the gate of the town through which he had entered. And he had the troops who were going with him mount, and he did likewise.

King Lisuarte, when he beheld his life saved so quickly and his enemies dead and annihilated, was in such a state that he did not know what to say; and he called Don Guilan, whom he had beside him, and said to him: "Don Guilan, what is this? Who are these men who have accomplished so much good?"

"Sire," said he, "who can it be but the one it is wont to be? It is none other than Amadis of Gaul, for you certainly heard how he called out his own name as a war cry, and it will be well, sire, for you to give him the thanks he deserves."

Then the king said: "Then go ahead, and if it be he, detain him; for he will certainly stop for you, and I shall be with you immediately."

Then he went down the street; and when Don Guilan reached the gate of the town, he ascertained at once that it was Amadis, and that he had already mounted and was going away with his troops, for he did not want to wait for Don Cuadragante lest he be detained. And Don Guilan shouted for him to turn back, that the king was there. Amadis, when he heard this, was greatly embarrassed, for he well recognized the man who was calling him to be one whom he greatly esteemed and loved. And he saw the king standing beside him, and he turned back; and when he was closer he looked at the king, and the latter had all his armor shattered and covered with blood from his wounds, and he felt great pity on seeing him thus; for although their disagreement had become so great, he kept remembering that this man was the wisest, most honorable, and most courageous king there ever was in the world. And when he came closer he dismounted and went toward him, and knelt and sought to kiss his hands. But he would not yield them to him, instead he embraced him very affably and lifted him up.

Then Don Cuadragante arrived, who was coming behind Amadis, and likewise King Cildadan, and many others with them; and they were coming out to stop Amadis from going away before he saw the king. And King Cildadan and Don Florestan and Angriote came up to kiss King Lisuarte's hands. Amadis went to King Cildadan and embraced him repeatedly. Who would be able to describe to you the pleasure that they all took in seeing themselves thus together and with the destruction of their foes? King Cildadan said to Amadis: "My lord, go back to the king and I shall remain with my uncle Don Cuadragante."

And he did so. At this juncture Brandoyvas reached them with great effort for he had many wounds; and he said to the king:

"Sire, your men and those of the town are killing so many of the foe who had taken refuge in houses that all the streets are flowing streams of blood; and although their lords might deserve it, their men do not. Therefore give orders as to what is to be done in the face of such cruel destruction."

And Amadis said: "Sire, give orders to correct it; for in such attacks and vanquishments magnanimity of heart is exhibited and displayed."

The king ordered his son Norandel and Don Guilan to go there and not let them kill those they found alive, but to take them to prison and put them in good custody; and thus it was done.

Amadis gave orders to Gandalin and Enil that together with Gandales, his foster father, they set a strong guard over King Arabigo and Arcalaus and Barsinan and the Duke of Bristol, and not leave them; and so they did. King Lisuarte took Amadis by the hand and said to him: "Lord, it will be well, if you please, that we give orders to rest and relax, for we indeed need to do so; and let us enter the town and remove the dead."

And Amadis said to him: "Sire, be kind enough to excuse us so that these knights and I may be able to return in time to my lord King Perion, who is coming with all the other troops."

"I shall certainly not excuse you; for although no one can outdo you in virtue and courage, in this matter I wish that you be outdone by me, and that we await the king your father, for it is not right that we part so quickly after an event so outstanding as the one which now has occurred."

Then he said to King Cildadan: "Hold this knight, since I cannot."

King Cildadan said to him: "My lord, do what the king begs of you so insistently, and don't let such discourtesy be shown by a man as well-bred as you are."

Amadis turned to his brother Don Florestan, and to Don Cuadragante and the other knights, and said to them: "Lords, what shall we do with regard to this which the king commands?"

They said that whatever he considered good should be done. Don Cuadragante said that since they had come there in order to help and serve him, and had done what was most important, what was least important should be done.

"Then, since that is your opinion, my lord, let it be done as you command," said Amadis.

Then they ordered their troops to dismount and put their horses out in that field and to look for something to eat. At this juncture, they saw King Arban and Don Grumedan coming, for the guards who had been holding them had released them; but they still had their hands tied, and it was a wonder that they had not been killed. When the king saw them he was greatly pleased, for he had considered them dead, and that would have been the case except for the help that arrived. They came up and kissed his hands, and went at once to Amadis with that enjoyment that you can imagine that his greatest friends to be found anywhere would have. They all told the king to take those knights with him and to lodge in the monastery until the town was cleared of the dead. At this point Arquisil arrived, who had been seeing to it that care was being afforded Flamineo, who was badly wounded; and when he saw Amadis, he went to embrace him, saying to him: "My lord, you brought aid to us at a good time; for though you have killed some of us, many more you have saved."

Amadis said to him: "My lord, I am very happy to give aid to you, for you may believe and be certain of my will to love you whole-heartedly."

Then as King Lisuarte was about to go to the monastery, they saw arriving the battalions of troops that King Perion was bringing, who had come at top speed. And Don Grumedan said to the king: "Lord, that is good succor, but if the first had been delayed, our welfare would have been permanently postponed."

The king said to him laughing genially: "If anyone engaged in debate with you, Don Grumedan, on whether the exploits of Amadis are well done or not, it would be for him a very long quest, and even greater would be the danger that would come to him from it."

Amadis said: "Sire, it is quite right that all we knights should love and honor Don Grumedan, for he is our model and guide for our honor. And because he knows with what obedience I would carry out what he commands, he loves me dearly, and not because he may have received from me any good service except good will."

Thus they were enjoying themselves, although some of them with plenty of wounds; but everyone considered that of little importance since they had escaped from that very cruel death that had been facing them. King Lisuarte called for a horse, and told King Cildadan to take another so that they might go welcome King Perion. Amadis said to him: "Sire, I would deem it better, subject to your approval, that you rest and that your wounds be cared for; because my lord the king will not fail to keep on his way until he sees you."

The king said that in any event he wished to go. Then he mounted a horse, with King Cildadan and Amadis on theirs, and they went in the direction from which King Perion was coming. Amadis ordered all his troops to remain quiet until he returned, and told Durin to go ahead of them and inform his father that King Lisuarte was coming.

So they went forth just as you hear, and many of those knights with them; Durin went faster and reached the battalions; and at their forefront he was told that the king and Gastiles were leading the rear guard. Then passing by them, he came to the king and gave him Amadis's message. The king took with him Gastiles and Grasandor, and Don Brian de Monjaste and Trion, and he asked Agrajes to come with the troops. He did this because of the anger that he knew Agrajes felt for King Lisuarte, and in order not to involve him in a confrontation. Agrajes was pleased thereby; and as King Perion went ahead, he continued to hold back with the troops so as not to have any reason to talk with King Lisuarte.

King Perion reached King Lisuarte with the escort about which I tell you; and when they saw each other they both came forward to each other and embraced with right good will; and when King Perion beheld him so wounded and hurt with his armor shattered, he said to him: "It appears to me, my good lord, that you did not leave camp so badly hurt as I now see you, although there your arms and armor were not in their sheaths, nor your person in the shade of the tents."

"My lord," said King Lisuarte, "I have deemed it well that you see me thus, so that you may know how badly off I was at the hour that Amadis and these knights came to my aid."

Then he related to him almost the whole story of the perilous engagement in which he had participated. King Perion was greatly pleased to learn what his sons had accomplished with good fortune and with the very great honor that was accruing to them thereby; and he said: "I give many thanks to God that the dispute has been stopped in this way and that you, my lord, are served and aided by my sons and by others of my family; for certainly, however things may have happened between us, it always has been and is my wish that they respect and obey you as a lord and father."

King Lisuarte said: "Let us leave this now for when we have more time, for I trust in God that before we separate, we shall remain united and bound by much kinship and love for many long periods."

Then he looked around and did not see Agrajes, whom he highly esteemed not only for his excellence, but also for his close kinship with those lords; and because already his mind was made up to do what you shall hear later on, he did not wish a trace of any anger to remain, for he well knew that Agrajes more than any other was offended by him, and publicly was announcing that he wished him ill; therefore he asked for him. And King Perion told him that at his request he had remained with the battalions so that there might not be the dissension that frequently there is wont to be among soldiers in the absence of anyone to control them whom they fear.

"Then have him summoned," said the king, "for I shall not leave here until I see him."

Then Amadis said to his father: "Sir, I shall go for him."

And this he did, because he really thought that if at his request he would not come, no one else would bring him. And he did what he said, for he went at once to where the troops were, and spoke with Agrajes and told him all that they had done and how they annihilated and destroyed that whole body of troops, and the prisoners they were holding, and how when he himself had come away without speaking to King Lisuarte, the latter had started out after him, also what they had said to each other; and that since that enmity was finally about to become friendship while leaving their honor so augmented, he was begging him earnestly to go with him because King Lisuarte was unwilling to leave there without seeing him. Agrajes said to him: "My lord cousin, you already know that neither my anger nor my pleasure will endure any longer than you wish; and as for this assistance that you have rendered this king, may it be God's will it be better rewarded than those of the past, which were not few in number. But I understand that defeat and damage have come to him, for it has pleased God that this should be so because his poor discernment deserved it; and thus it will happen to him in the future if he does not change his ways. And since it pleases you that I should see him, let it be done."

And he ordered the troops to remain quiet until they had his order.

So they both left, and on coming up to the king, Agrajes sought to kiss his hands, but he did not yield them to him, instead he embraced him and held him thus a while, and said: "Which has been for you the greater affront, to be now locked in an embrace with me, or when we were locked in the battle? I understand that you consider this the greater."

They all laughed at what the king said, and Agrajes with great self-restraint said to him: "Sire, more time will be needed for me to be able to answer quite truthfully what you ask me."

"Then it will be well," said the king, "that we go immediately to rest. And you, my good lord," said he to King Perion, "shall go be my guest with these knights who come with you; and have as many of your troops enter the town as there is room for, and the others can camp in these meadows. We shall lodge in the monastery, and I shall give orders that all the pack trains of provisions that are coming from my land to the camp should come on here, so that what we may need be not lacking."

King Perion thanked him heartily, and asked him for permission to leave, since he no longer needed them. But King Lisuarte was unwilling; instead he urged him so insistently and King Cildadan with him, that he had to yield; and so together they turned back to the monastery, where they were comfortably lodged.

Then the physicians whom King Lisuarte was summoning there cared for his wounds; but they all knew nothing in comparison with Master Elisabad, for he treated and restored to health not only the king but all the others in a way wondrous to behold, and also Amadis and some of those on his side, who had a few wounds, although not serious ones. But King Lisuarte for more than ten days did not leave his bed, and each day there were there with him King Perion and all those lords in conversation on very pleasant topics without touching on anything having to do with peace or war, but only talking and laughing about how Arcalaus, being a knight of low character and not of high rank, had incited so many people to seditious revolt, as you have heard. And there it was recalled how he had enchanted Amadis, how by great deceit he had taken King Lisuarte prisoner and seized his daughter Oriana; how Barsinan, lord of Sansuenia had died because of him; how afterwards he had caused the seven kings to come to the battle against King Lisuarte; how he had held in prison King Perion and Amadis and Don Florestan, who had been deceived by his niece Dinarda; how later he had escaped from Don Galaor and Norandel by calling himself Granfiles, first cousin of Don Grumedan; and now how again he had involved King Arabigo and those knights, and would have had his objective accomplished if he had not been thwarted by the very great coincidence of that rescue's being so opportunely at hand; and many other things that they told about him in jest, but which were not far from the truth — things at which they laughed heartily. Then Don Grumedan, who as has been demonstrated to you in this great story, in all his affairs was a knight very intelligent in every respect, said: "You see here, my good lords, why many dare to be wicked, because in beholding a few examples of good fortune the Devil by his evil machinations causes them to achieve, because of that pleasure that they experience they do not heed or think about the very dishonorable and perilous calamities that therefore finally befall them; for if we were to consider what we have said about this Arcalaus that can be counted in his favor, he being now imprisoned, old with a crippled hand, at the mercy of his enemies, he alone would suffice as an object lesson for no one to deviate from the path of virtue for the sake of pursuing what brings about so much harm and misfortune. But, as virtues are hard to endure, and there are in them very rough paths, and evil deeds are just the opposite; and as all of us are naturally more attracted to evil than to what is good, we follow with utmost zeal what most pleases and satisfies us at the moment, being unmindful of what has a fortunate outcome and end, although forbidden at the outset.

And by following more the craving of our evil desire than equitable reason which is mistress and mother of the virtues, when we are most exalted we arrive at a fall, where neither body nor soul can be saved, just as Arcalaus the Necromancer, this wicked man of evil deeds, has done."

What this knight said seemed very good to King Perion, and he considered him a discreet man. And he frequently asked about him subsequently, for he well recognized that such a knight as he was worthy and deserving of being at the side of kings.

In the meantime the good and holy man Nasciano arrived, at which all were overjoyed, for just as until then because of the rupture everything had happened to both sides amid great shock and weariness of spirit, so now with everything changed to the opposite with the advent of peace, their minds, to their great pleasure, were at rest and in repose. When the good man saw them all united in such affection, when it had not yet been three days since they were killing one another with so much cruelty, he raised his hands to the heavens and said: "Oh, Lord of the world, how mighty is thy holy compassion, and how thou dost use it with those who have some understanding of thy holy service, for these kings and knights do not have the blood dried yet from the wounds that they inflicted on each other, the Evil One being the cause of their strife. And because I in thy name and with thy grace set them on the right road, they being willing to recognize the very great error into which they had fallen, thou, Lord, hast brought them to such love and good will as could never be imagined by anyone. Therefore, Lord, may it please Thee that by thy permitting the outcome and goal of this peace, I, as thy servant and a sinner, before I part from them may leave them in such tranquillity that desisting from the things contrary to thy service, they may have insight in promoting thy holy Catholic faith."

This saintly hermit kept going from one man to another, setting before them many moral lessons and doctrines so that they might follow through and provide a good outcome to the situation in which he had placed them, in such wise that their hard hearts he was completely softening and rendering amenable to reason.

Then one day while they were all in the room together, King Lisuarte asked King Perion from whom he had found out that the troops were in pursuit of him. King Perion told him that the youth Esplandian had told Amadis about it, and that that was all he knew about it. Then King Lisuarte gave orders to summon Esplandian, and he asked the latter how he had become aware of that body of troops. He told him that on coming to him in camp at the request of the good man his foster father, he had found it gone, and that when continuing on his way, he had seen the whole body of troops coming down the mountain towards where he was going, and that he thought at once, in view of their great numbers and the small, weak force that he was bringing, that he would not be able to escape from them without great danger; and that immediately he and Sargil had ridden their palfreys all night at top speed without halting and had informed Amadis of the situation. King Lisuarte said: "Esplandian, you have done me a great service, and I trust in God that you will be well rewarded by me."

The good man said: "Son, kiss the hands of the king your lord for what he says to you."

The youth came up, knelt and kissed his hands. The king clasped his head and thus drew him to him, kissed him on his face, and looked toward Amadis. And as Amadis had his gaze fixed on the youth and on what the king was doing, and saw that he was observing him at that time, his face turned crimson, for he clearly recognized that the king already knew about the whole affair between him and Oriana, and that this youth was their son. And that love that the king showed Esplandian rendered him so happy and so touched his heart that it increased his desire more than ever to serve him, and it had the same effect on the king; for the appearance and charm of that boy was so satisfying to them that as long as he was a bond between them, nothing could come about to prevent them from having love and esteem for each other.

Gasquilan, King of Suesa, had remained in the camp, battered from the battle he had with Amadis, and his men with him, those who had survived the battles. And when King Lisuarte parted from him, he had earnestly requested that he depart in a litter by another roundabout way bearing as much as possible to the right of the mountain; and he left with him persons who would guide him very well. And so he did, for he set out over a plain going downstream along the bank of a river, which he put between himself and the mountain; and he camped that night under some trees, and the next day went his way, but very slowly, so that on account of the roundabout route that he followed he was unable to reach Lubayna in five days; and without knowing anything about what had happened, he arrived at the monastery where the kings were. And when they told him about it, he was very sad not to have participated in such an outstanding action on account of being physically incapacitated; and as he was very conceited and haughty, while complaining with great arrogance he said some things that those who heard did not like.

When King Perion and King Cildadan and those lords found out about his arrival, they came out to him at the gate of the monastery where he was in his litter, and they helped him get out of it, and knights took him in their arms and placed him where King Lisuarte was lying, for the latter had sent word to ask them to do so. And there in the room where the king was they made for him another bed and placed him in it. Gasquilan, once he was there, looked at all the knights from the Firm Island and saw them so handsome, with such fine figures and so adorned with the insignia of war, that in his opinion he had never seen people of such fine appearance; and he asked which of them was Amadis, and they pointed him out to him. And as Amadis saw that he was asking about him, he came up to him, holding King Arban of North Wales by the hand, and said: "My good lord, may you be very welcome, and it would have pleased me greatly to find you in good health, rather than in your present state; for in such a good man as you are, illness is ill employed; but God will be pleased for you to get well quickly, and what disaffection there has been between you and me will be mended with kindness."

Gasquilan, when he saw him so handsome and so calm and polite, if he had not known so much about his prowess, both by hearsay and through having tested it, would not have esteemed him highly; for in his opinion he was better prepared for association with matrons and maidens than with knights and acts of war; for since Gasquilan was bold by strength and courage, so he prided himself on being so in speech, because it was his belief that he who was to be very courageous, needed to be so in everything, and if he lacked any of this quality, it would greatly damage his reputation. And for this reason he did not consider it a defect to be haughty; rather, he greatly prided himself on being so; and whether he was mistaken in this, anyone can judge. And he answered Amadis, and said to him: "My good lord Amadis, in all the world you are the knight I most wished to see, and not for your own good, or for mine, but rather to fight with you to the death; and if it had happened to you with me as it happened to me with you; and if what I received from you, you had received from me, besides considering myself the most highly honored knight in the world, I would have won thereby the love of a lady whom I love and desire very much, and at whose behest I had been seeking you until now; and it has turned out for me in such wise that I do not know how I can appear before her; so that insofar as my ills are concerned what is unseen is much greater than what is evident and obvious to all."

Amadis, when he heard this, said to him: "This matter of your ladylove must trouble you deeply. Likewise it does me, for you ought not to be greatly concerned about everything that would have been gained in overcoming me; because in view of the fact that your deeds are so great and famous throughout the whole world, and are so outstanding at arms, you would not gain much in surpassing a knight of so little renown as I."

Then King Cildadan said to King Lisuarte, laughing: "My lord, it will be well for you to interpose your royal wand between these two knights."

And the king for their benefit became jocular and incited them to more joking. Thus these kings and knights remained in the monastery, very abundantly provided with all that they needed; for as King Lisuarte was in his own land, he had many viands brought there in such abundance that it afforded everyone great contentment. King Perion asked him repeatedly to permit him to go with the troops to the Firm Island, and said that then he would have the two knights come there, as per their agreement; but King Lisuarte was never willing to do so; and he said to him that since God had brought him there, by no means would he willingly let him go until everything was settled; so that King

Perion was embarrassed to ask him any more. And so he waited to see what the outcome would be of that good will that King Lisuarte was manifesting.

Arquisil spoke with Amadis, asking him what he was ordering him to do about his imprisonment, for he was ready to carry out the promise that he had made him. Amadis told him that he would speak with him not only about that but of other things that he had in mind, and that the next morning, after hearing mass he should have his horse brought around, for he wanted to talk to him in the countryside; which was done thus, for immediately next day they mounted their horses and went riding around outside the town. And when they were far away from everyone, Amadis said to him: "My good lord, all these past days that I have been here I had wanted to speak with you, and because of being busy, as you have seen, I have not been able to do so. Now that we have time, I want to tell you what I have in mind for you. I know that, in view of the direct line of your ancestry, once the emperor of Rome is dead, as he is, there remains in the entire empire no direct successor or heir but you; and I also know that by all those who are lords there you are greatly beloved. And if you were not by some one, it was only by your relative the emperor, for his envy of your good breeding gave him cause, by reason of his bad temperament, to hate you. And since the matter has reached such a stage, it would constitute a cogent reason to take care of a thing of such great importance as this is. You have here most of the best knights of the kingdom of Rome, and I have on the Firm Island Brondajel de Roca, the Duke of Ancona and the Archbishop of Talancia, with many others who were taken prisoner at sea. I shall send for them at once; let us talk about the matter; and before they leave here, let some way be found for them to pledge their allegiance to you as their emperor. And if some oppose it, I shall support your rights to the fullest extent; therefore, my good friend, keep the matter in mind and work on it, recognizing the opportunity that God gives you, and don't let it be lost through any fault of yours."

When Arquisil heard this from him, you can readily understand the pleasure he must have had from it; for he was expecting only that he would be ordered imprisoned in some place which he could not leave for a very long while; and he said to him:

"My good lord, I do not know why everybody in the world does not solicit your affection and acquaintanceship and is not engaged in increasing your honor and status. And for my part I tell you that whether or not what you say can be accomplished now, and however Fortune may deal with it, never shall I live at a time that I do not repay, even to the point of laying down my life, this favor and great honor that I am receiving from you; and if thanks could suffice for such a great benefit, I would give them. But what can they be? Certainly nothing less than my own person, as I have said, together with all that God and my fortunes may be able to give; and from now on I leave in your hands all my welfare and honor. And since you have expressed it so well, bring it to a conclusion, for what may be won is more yours than mine."

"Then I take charge of it," said Amadis, "and with the help of God you will go forth from here an emperor or I shall not consider myself a knight."

With this they broke off their [serious] conversation, and Amadis said to him: "Before we return to the monastery, let us enter the town, and I shall show you the man who, out of the whole world, hates me most."

So they entered Lubayna and went to the lodging of Don Gandales, where he was holding as prisoners King Arabigo and Arcalaus and the other knights about whom you have already heard. And when they entered it, they went at once to the room where King Arabigo and Arcalaus were alone, and they found them dressed and seated on a bed; for ever since they had been taken prisoners they had been unwilling to undress. And Amadis recognized Arcalaus at once, and said to him: "What are you doing, Arcalaus?"

And he said: "Who are you to ask?"

"I am Amadis of Gaul, the one whom you wanted so much to see."

Then Arcalaus observed him more closely than before, and said to him: "Certainly, you speak the truth, for although it has been a long time since I saw you, my memory does not fail to recognize you to be that Amadis whom I had in my power in my castle of Valderin. And that pity that I had then for your tender youth and for your very handsome appearance — that pity for long years has plunged me into many great tribulations, to the point that finally you have brought me to such straits that I must ask mercy of you."

Amadis said to him: "If I had pity on you, would you cease to commit those very evil deeds and acts of cruelty that up until now you have committed?"

"No," said he, "for now my age, so protractedly accustomed to it, would not be able voluntarily to withdraw from what for such a long time I have deemed a pleasure; but constraint, which is a very hard and strong restraint causing every habit to change from good to bad, and from bad to good, according to the person and cause affected, would make me do in my old age what my youth and freedom did not seek, nor were of sufficient avail to accomplish."

"Well, what constraint could I impose on you," said Amadis, "if I should let you go free and released?"

"That," said Arcalaus, "which, on account of my maintaining and enlarging it, has done much harm to my conscience and reputation, namely, my castles, which I shall order given and handed over to you with all my land, and I shall not take from all that any more than what through your goodness you may wish to give me, because at present I cannot set myself at anything else. And it may be that this very great necessity and your great kindness will bring about in me that change that up until now reason has not been able in any wise to effect."

Amadis said to him: "Arcalaus, if I have some hope that your harsh nature will be improved, it is based only on the knowledge that you exhibit in considering yourself wicked and a sinner. Therefore, pluck up your courage and take comfort, for it may be that this imprisonment of the body which you now are undergoing and so greatly fear, will be the key to set free your soul, which so long you have held enchained and captive."

And when Amadis was about to leave, Arcalaus said to him: "Amadis, look at this unfortunate king, who a short while ago was very near to being one of the greatest princes in the world, and in one moment that very same Fortune, who was favoring him in the matter, has overthrown him and placed him in such cruel captivity. May he serve as a moral lesson to you and to all those who have or desire honor and high estate; and I wish to remind you that strong minds and hearts are the basis for conquest and pardon."

Amadis did not seek to answer since he held him prisoner, that indeed he entertained this argument in rebuttal against him: that although by arms and enchantments Arcalaus had overcome many, he had never learned how to pardon anyone. But on account of that he did not fail to recognize that he had made a fine plea.

So he and Arquisil left the room, mounted their horses and went on to the monastery. And at once Amadis gave orders to summon Ardian, his dwarf, and he ordered him to go to the Firm Island and tell Oriana and those ladies everything he had seen. And he gave him a letter for Isanjo to the effect that he should send to him at once under a good guard Brondajel of Roca and the Duke of Ancona and the Archbishop of Talancia, with all the other Romans who were prisoners there, as quickly as they could come. The dwarf was quite pleased to carry this news, because from it he expected great honor and much advantage. He mounted his hackney at once, and traveled day and night without much rest, until he arrived at the Firm Island, where nothing had been known about these latest events, for Oriana had had no news except concerning the two battles and about how Nasciano, the holy hermit, was holding them to a truce; and that the Emperor of Rome was dead, from which she took no little pleasure. But of the events from there on she knew nothing; instead she was in great anxiety, because she thought that that good man Nasciano would not be equal to bringing about peace in such a great rupture. And she did nothing but pray and perform many acts of devotion and pilgrimages in and to the churches of the Island, and implore God for peace and harmony between the contenders. And when the dwarf arrived, he went at once directly to the garden where Oriana was; and he told a lady-in-waiting who was guarding the gate to tell Oriana that he was there and that he was bringing news for her. The lady told her, and Oriana commanded him to enter; but while she awaited what he would say her heart was not calm, but rather it was greatly agitated because she could not hear it except to the advantage of one side and harm to the other; and as on one side was her lover Amadis and on the other her father the king, although she feared harm to Amadis to the maximum degree, at whatever might befall her father she would be greatly grieved. And as the dwarf came in, he said to Oriana: "Lady, I demand a reward for good news, not because of my identity, but because of yours and the great news I bring you."

Oriana said to him: "Ardian, my friend, according to your expression, it relates to your lord; but tell me whether my father is alive."

The dwarf said: "What do you mean, my lady, by whether he is alive? He is alive and well, and happier than he ever has been."

"Oh, Holy Mary!" said Oriana, "tell me what you know; for if God grants me something good, I shall make you very fortunate in this world."

Then the dwarf told her the whole event just as it had taken place, and how the king, her father, when he was about to lose his life, being conquered and hemmed in by his enemies without any recourse, the very handsome youth Esplandian so informed Amadis, who immediately set out with the troops, and all the things that happened to him on the way which he himself had witnessed; and how Amadis reached the town, and the situation of the king her father, and how at Amadis's arrival all their foes were annihilated, being killed or taken prisoners; and that King Arabigo and Arcalaus the Enchanter and Barsinan, lord of Sansuenia, and the Duke of Bristol were prisoners; and afterwards how the king her father went out after Amadis, who was going away without seeing him, and how King Perion arrived. In fine, he, as an eye-witness, told her everything that had happened and how they were all together in that monastery with great enjoyment. Oriana, who, on hearing it, was as if out of her senses from the great joy that she felt, knelt down on the ground, raised her hands, and said: "Oh, powerful Lord, restorer of all things! Blessed be thy holy name; and since thou, oh Lord, art a righteous judge, and knowest the great injustice being done me, I always have had hope that thy mercy, with great honor for me and for those who might be on my side, would put a stop to this business. And blessed be that very handsome youth who has been the cause of so much good and who thus has endeavored to prove true the prophecy which Urganda the Unknown wrote concerning him, whence one can and ought to believe all the rest she has said about him. And I am greatly obligated to love and cherish him more than anyone can imagine, and to reward him for the good fortune that is coming to me through him."

Everybody thought she was saying this with reference to his having been the cause of that rescue of her father the king, which he had brought about, but what was secret came from her innermost being as from a mother to a son. Then she arose and asked the dwarf whether he would be returning at once. He said that he would, that Amadis had ordered that after he had told her and those ladies who were there that news, he should give a letter to Isanjo, which he was bringing to him, in which he ordered him to send him at once the Romans whom he was holding prisoners there.

"Ardian, my friend," said Oriana, "do tell me, what are said to be the pleasurable things they will seek to accomplish there?"

"Lady," said he, "I do not know for certain, except that the king your father is detaining King Perion and my lord, and all the lords and knights who came from here, and he says that he does not want them to leave there until everything that remains between them is settled very peacefully."

"May it please God that it be so," said Oriana.

Then Queen Briolanja and Melicia, who were together, asked him to tell them how that very handsome youth Esplandian was, and how King Lisuarte regarded that great service that Esplandian had rendered him; and he said to them: "My good ladies, when I was with Amadis in the king's chamber, I saw Esplandian come up to kiss the king's hands for the favors that he was promising him, and I saw the king clasp his head and kiss his eyes. And concerning his good looks I tell you that although he is a male and you pride yourselves on being very beautiful, if you were in his presence you would hide without daring to show yourselves."

"Then it is a good thing," said they, "that we are secluded here where he won't see us."

"Don't count on that," said he, "for he is such that although you may be quite secluded, you ladies and all others who are beautiful will go forth to look for him."

They all laughed heartily because of the good news that they had heard, and at what the dwarf responded. Oriana looked at Queen Sardamira and said to her: "My lady queen, cheer up, for that Lord who has given help to those of us who are here will not want you to remain forgotten."

The queen said: "My lady, I have hope in Him and in you that you will look out for my welfare, although I do not deserve it of you."

Then she asked the dwarf how those wretched, unfortunate Romans were who were with King Lisuarte. He said: "Lady, many of them as well as many of the others are missing, and those who are alive are badly wounded. But since the death of the Emperor and Floyan and Constancio, no other Roman of consequence is missing; for I saw Arquisil in good health and engaged in much conversation with my lord Amadis; and Flamineo your brother is wounded but not badly according to hearsay."

The queen said: "May it please God that since there is no help for the dead, there may be some for the living, and may He grant them the favor that not heeding past events, they may remain friends with great affection at present and in the future."

The dwarf asked Oriana whether she had any messages, for he wanted to go carry out the command of his lord. She said that since he had not brought a letter, he should convey her regards to King Perion and Agrajes and to all those knights.

Thereupon he went to Isanjo and gave him the letter from Amadis, and when he saw in it what the latter was commanding him to do, he immediately brought out of a tower those Roman lords for whom Amadis was sending, and gave them mounts and a son of his together with other persons to escort and guide them, and he had them provided with food and everything else that they might need; and he set free all the others who were imprisoned, who in number were probably close to two hundred men, and sent them to Amadis.

Thus they went their way until they reached the monastery where King Lisuarte was, and they kissed his hands, and the king welcomed them with great pleasure — although in secret he felt otherwise — in order not to cause them more distress than they already had inwardly. But when they saw Arquisil, they could not prevent the tears from coming to their eyes, nor to his. Amadis spoke to them very courteously, greatly heartening them, and he took them to his living quarters, where from him they received great honor and consolation. Then after their arrival there, and after they had rested somewhat from their journey, Amadis withdrew with them without Arquisil and said to them: "Good lords, I have had you come here because it seemed to me in view of the fact that matters are progressing toward a good outcome, that it is quite right for you to be present at everything that will be done — for very properly one ought to take into account such honorable men — and also because I wish to inform you that I have Arquisil's promise, as I believe you have heard, that he will suffer imprisonment wherever it may be indicated by me. And recognizing the noble lineage from which he comes and his own nobility, which cause him to be deserving of very great recompense, I have agreed to speak to you — since in the empire of Rome you do not have anyone else left who ought to have it as rightfully as this knight — so that a way may be found not only by you but by all those who are here, whereby he may receive your oaths of fealty and be accepted as your overlord. And in this you will accomplish two things: the first, the fulfillment of your obligation by giving the sovereignty to the one to whom it rightfully belongs, and who is a knight so perfect in every good quality and will do you many favors; and the other, that with regard to his imprisonment and yours, I shall consider it good to set you all free, so that without any delay you may be able to go to your own estates, and I shall always be a good friend to you as long as you please, for I esteem Arquisil highly and have as much love for him as for a real brother, and thus I shall maintain it for him, if it is not lost by him, in this matter and in everything else that may concern him."

This having been heard by those Roman lords, they asked Brondajel de Roca, who among them was outstanding and very well spoken, to respond to him; he said: "We esteem very highly your gracious speech, Lord Amadis, and we must be very grateful to you; but since this matter is of such large scope, and for it the consent of many is needed, we should not be able at present to answer, until it is discussed with the knights who are here, because although many of those who come here are not being taken into account, they are very important for this matter that you, my lord, broach to us; for in our land they have many fortresses and cities and towns of the empire, and other community offices that are greatly concerned in the choice of an emperor. And therefore, if you please, you will give us an opportunity to see Flamineo, who is a very honorable knight, who we have been told is wounded; and into his presence everyone will be summoned by us, and it will be possible after deliberation to give you our reply."

Amadis considered it good and told them that they replied like prudent knights and properly, and that he asked of them that there be no delay because he believed his departure from there would be immediate. They told him that it would be done thus, for delay would be even more serious for them.

So then all mounted immediately and entered the town, which had already been cleared of the dead, for King Lisuarte had given orders for many people to come from the environs to bury them. And when they came to the dwelling where Flamineo was, they dismounted and entered his room. And they were very happy to see each other, although very sad of countenance because of the great misfortune that had come to them. And they at once told him that it was necessary to summon all the mayors and other persons of consequence who had remained alive there, because it was needful that they be informed of a speech that Amadis had made to them, on which their freedom or their imprisonment forever depended. Flamineo ordered them summoned, and those who were able to come, having arrived and assembled, Brondajel de Roca said to them: "Honorable knight Flamineo, and you, good friends, already know about the bad luck and great misfortune that have overtaken all the Romans since by command of our emperor, whom may God forgive, we came to this island of Great Britain; and because they are so well-known to you, it will be unnecessary to repeat them now. While we were prisoners on the Firm Island, Amadis of Gaul was kind enough to have us come here where you see us; and with great love and good will he has brought us and has shown us many courtesies; and he has spoken to us at great length, saying that since our Roman empire is without a ruler and by right the succession falls to Arquisil more properly than to anyone else, he will be gratified if the latter be accepted as lord and emperor by you and us; and that not only will he give us freedom from the imprisonment he exercises over us, but will be a faithful friend and helper to us in everything in which we may have need of him. And it has seemed to us — in view of that predilection he has shown for this action about which we are telling you — that he deems it a foregone conclusion that if it is done by us voluntarily, he will reward us in the way you have heard; and if not, he will exert himself to have it done by other means. Therefore, good lord, and you, good friends, that is why you have been called here. And so that your wishes may be determined by knowing ours, it is quite right that the latter be stated to you; which are: that we have discussed this matter at length among us, and we have found that what this knight Amadis asks and begs of us, is what we would beg and ask very insistently of him; because, as you know, that very great dominion of Rome cannot remain without an overlord. So who by right, by strength, by virtues, deserves this more than Arquisil? Certainly, in my opinion, no one. He is our fellow citizen, reared among us. We know his good manners and customs. From him without apprehension we can ask by right of law what, even though it were right, another who perchance might be a foreigner would deny us. Besides this, we gain this famous knight Amadis as a friend, who just as when he was an enemy has had so much power to harm us, so also, by being a friend, with that same power, can render us great honor and benefit and make amends for the past. Now say what is your pleasure; do not take into account our imprisonment or fatigue, but only that to which reason and justice may guide you."

As just and honest things have so much strength that even wicked men cannot spurn them without great embarrassment, so these knights, as discreet persons of good intelligence, on seeing that what that knight Brondajel de Roca said was quite just and for them obligatory, could not contradict it. Even if it always happens that among the desires of many people, there would be diverse kinds of dissent, there were so many there who observed and followed reason that those who had desired something else found no room for their desire, and all unanimously said that it should be done just as Amadis was asking and that they should return with their emperor to their homes without lingering any longer in those lands where they had been badly errant, and that they left them as leaders in charge of what Arquisil was to swear and promise. And with this agreement they returned to Amadis at the monastery and told him what was agreed upon, with which he was greatly pleased. So finally all the knights and great lords of the Romans and the other people of lower rank of the empire, having gathered together in the church, swore an oath of allegiance to Arquisil as their emperor, and promised him vassalage, and he swore to them to uphold all their laws and customs, and rendered and granted them all the favors for which they asked him with justification.

So because of this we can say that sometimes it is better to be subdued and constrained by good men without our liberty, than with it to serve and obey wicked ones; because from what is good, good is expected finally, without casting any doubt concerning the matter; and from what is evil, although for some time it may yield flowers, at the end they will be withered along with their roots; whence it follows that this Arquisil was reared with a man of his family who was the Emperor Patin, for whom he performed many outstanding services to the honor of his imperial crown; and instead of showing any recognition of them, the emperor brought him up as one cast aside and mistreated and almost banished from where he was, fearing that the virtue and good qualities of this knight, for which he would be loved and esteemed and done many favors, would take away his own rule from him, and later being a prisoner of his enemy in a situation where he expected no favor or honor, but rather entirely the opposite, from the latter on account of his being so different and so perfect in the virtue that was lacking to the other, there came to him that very great honor, and such high rank as to be emperor of Rome; in which fact, all should find a moral lesson and adhere to virtuous and prudent men, so that their share of what is good may overtake them; and should withdraw from scandalously wicked men who are envious, of scant virtue and of many vices, so that they be not ruined.

CHAPTER CXVIII

How king Lisuarte caused the kings and noble lords and many other knights to gather together in the monastery of Lubayna, where they were with him, and how he told them about the great services and honors that he had received from Amadis of Gaul, and the reward that he had given him for them.

Just as you have heard, this virtuous and valiant knight Arquisil was accepted as emperor of Rome because of his good friend Amadis of Gaul. Now the story relates that all these kings, leaders and knights remained quite given over to enjoyment in that monastery and in the town of Lubayna until King Lisuarte was in a better state of health and had risen from his sickbed, along with many others of his noble knights who had been wounded, he and they being under the care of that great physician Elisabad. And when King Lisuarte saw himself so improved in health, he one day had the kings and noble lords of both factions summoned; and in their company in the church of that monastery he said to them: "Honorable kings and famous knights, it seems to me very unnecessary to recall to your memory the past events, since you have seen them just as I have, in which events if they had not been forestalled, those of us who are alive would have become peers of the dead. So putting those events aside, recognizing the great injury that not only to the service of God but also to our own persons and dominions would have resulted by continuing with them, I have detained the noble King Perion of Gaul and all the princes and knights on his side so that what you are about to hear may be said in their presence and in yours."

Then turning to Amadis, he said to him: "Valiant knight Amadis of Gaul, in accordance with the goal and purpose of my speech, so foreign to my habit, which is not to speak highly of anyone in his presence, and so foreign to your desire, which is always embarrassed by such praise, it will be necessary for me before these kings and knights to recall to their memory past events of the relationship between you and me since the day you became in my court a knight of Queen Brisena my wife. And, although they be well known to all, seeing that they are known by me exactly as they took place, everyone would probably approve and consider well justified the reward of merit I wish to give to the aforesaid relationship. It is a fact that while you were at my court after you overcame Dardan the Proud and had brought me for my service your brother Don Galaor, who was the greatest gift ever made to a king, I was hoodwinked, as was my daughter Oriana, by this evil Arcalaus the Enchanter, and both she and I taken prisoner without the possibility of my being defended or rescued by all my knights, who were constrained to respect my order forbidding them to do so; whence she and I were in danger of cruel incarceration and death, and my dominion close to being lost. Then at this time, when you and Don Galaor were coming back from where the queen had sent you, on your learning of the situation I was in, by placing both your lives at the point of death in order to preserve ours, we were saved and rescued, and those enemies of mine who had taken us prisoners were killed and annihilated. And immediately through you the queen my wife was rescued, and Barsinan, father of this Lord of Sansuenia, who held her besieged in my city of London, was killed; so that just as I had been taken prisoner under circumstances involving much deception and great danger, so with much honor and security for me and my realm I was restored by you. This having taken place, after some elapse of time a battle was arranged between me and King Cildadan — who is here present — with one hundred knights fighting on each side; and before we had come to it, you relieved me of the opposition of this knight Don Cuadragante, and that of Famongomadan and Basagante, his son, the two bravest and strongest giants there were in all the islands of the sea. And you took my daughter Leonoreta away from them together with her ladies-in-waiting and maidens, and ten of the good knights of my household, who were being carried off as captives in carts — from whom with all my power I never would have been able to recover her; since in view of the forces that King Cildadan brought to the battle, not only of strong giants, but also of other very valiant knights, if it had not been for you who with one blow killed the mighty Sardaman the Lion, and with another freed me from the hand of Madanfabul, the giant of the Vermilion Tower, who by snatching me out of my saddle while I was stunned and helpless, was carrying me away under his arm to put me on board ship — and had it not been for many other famous deeds that you performed in that battle, it is well known that I would not have had the victory and great honor that I acquired there. Then in addition to this you overcame that very valiant and world-famous Ardan Canileo the Feared, whereby my court was greatly honored by there being at it what could not be found in any of the other courts which he had frequented: for neither at them nor elsewhere that he had gone had one knight, or three or four knights together been able or dared to make a stand against him in the lists. Then if we wish to declare that you were duty-bound to do all this, since you were in my service, and that the great need and the obligation that you had to your honor constrained you to do it, let there be told what you have done for me since: more through my fault for having heeded evil counsellors than through yours, you left my court more as an opponent and enemy than as a friend or servitor; for when you found out, at the time that we were most inimical, about the great battle that I had in prospect with this King Arabigo and the other six kings, and many other foreign peoples and folk who came with the purpose and expectation of subjugating my dominions, you took measures with the king your father and with Don Florestan your brother, whereby you came to the battle to aid me — whereas with more reason and just cause, in view of our rigor and anger, you should have been arrayed against me — and almost entirely by dint of the prowess of you three, although there were on my side very good and highly esteemed knights, I obtained such a great victory that by annihilating all my enemies I rendered my person and my royal states secure with much more honor and grandeur than I had before. Now in conclusion, I know that because of you, in the second battle that we had, the great danger in which I and all those on my side were, was removed and obviated, as they know — for it is my understanding that each one has the same feeling about it that I do — so that in this final rescue it will be indeed unnecessary to remind you of it, for the blood still flows from our wounds, and our souls have not had an opportunity to return to their dwelling place, in view of the way they had already been put aside and dismissed in farewell. Now, good lords, tell me what reward can be given that can repay in equal measure such great services and burdens. Certainly none save that, my person being honored and respected while living, these dominions and seignories of mine, which together with my person have been rescued and restored so many times by the hand and prowess of this knight, he have through wedlock with Oriana my daughter; and that just as of their own free will, they two are joined in matrimony without my having known it, so now that I know it and desire it, they may remain as my issue, successors and inheritors of my kingdom."

Amadis, when he heard the consent that the king was giving so publicly for him to have his lady, and in comparison with her all the other things by him recounted and told he considered as nothing, went to the king and knelt; and although the king was unwilling, he kissed his hands and said to him: "Sire, if it had pleased Your Grace, all this which has been said in praise of me might have been omitted, because, in view of the favors and honors that I and my relatives have received from you, we would be duty-bound to render much greater services. And therefore, sire, I do not wish to give you any thanks. But for the last thing you said, and I do not mean the inheritance of your great domains, but Your Grace's willingly giving me Princess Oriana, I shall serve you all the days of my life with the greatest obedience and circumspection that ever a son served a father or a vassal his lord."

King Lisuarte embraced him with very great love and said to him: "Then in me you will find that love as deep as that king who engendered you has for you."

All were greatly astonished at how the king in his speech had extinguished those great fires of enmity that had endured such a long time, without there remaining anything about which it would be necessary to come to an understanding. And whether they were pleased about it there will be no need to say, because, even if at the beginning both sides very haughtily sought each other [in combat], in view of their having beheld the deaths of their men and their own so near at hand, they were very happy to have peace. And they were asking one another whether they knew why the king had said that Amadis and Oriana were joined in wedlock, because after they took her from the sea and brought her to the Firm Island never did they perceive any such relationship in their deportment, and before that it was unthinkable. But the king, who overheard, begged the saintly man Nasciano to tell it to those lords just as he had told him about it, so that they might learn the small part that Amadis had played in having taken possession of her at sea; and also that he, the king, was without blame in giving her to the emperor because he himself did not know about that relationship; and that if his daughter without his permission and knowledge had entered into it, they might learn the cogent cause and reason which obliged her to do so. Then the good man told them all about it, just as you have already heard him tell King Lisuarte in his tent at the camp.

When the youth Esplandian, whom the good man held by the hand beside him, heard that those two kings were his grandfathers, and Amadis his father, there is no need to ask whether he was pleased. And at once the hermit knelt with him before both kings and before his father, and told him to kiss their hands, and they to give him their blessing. Amadis said to King Lisuarte: "Sire, just as from now on it is pleasing and fitting for me to serve you, so it will be necessary to ask favors of you. And may the first be, since the Emperor of Rome has no wife and is disposed to have one, that it may please you to give him Princess Leonoreta your daughter, and I beg him to accept her so that their wedding and mine be together and that together we may remain as your sons."

The king considered it good to take him as his kinsman, and immediately promised him Leonoreta as his wife, and the Emperor accepted her with great contentment.

King Lisuarte asked King Perion if he had had any news concerning Galaor his son. He told him that since his arrival

Gandalin had come, who had left him somewhat improved, and that he himself was greatly concerned about his illness and in great fear of its being critical.

"I say to you," said the king, "that although he is your son, I do not esteem him any less; and if it were not for the controversy that arose at the time, I in person would have visited him. And I earnestly beg you to send for him if he is in condition to come, because I shall depart at once for Windsor, to which I bade the queen come; and I wish, in honor of Amadis, with her and with Leonoreta my daughter to return then to you in the Firm Island, where Amadis's and the emperor's wedding will be solemnized, and we shall see the rare things that Apolidon left there; and if I find Don Galaor there, the sight of him will give me great joy, for I have desired it for a long time."

King Perion told him that it would be done just as he wished. Amadis kissed the hands of King Lisuarte for the favor and honor he was doing him. And Agrajes begged him very insistently to send for Don Galvanes his uncle and for Madasima, and to bring them with him. King Lisuarte said that he would be pleased to do so and that it would be done without fail, and that immediately the next morning he wanted to leave in order to return quickly; for already it was time for those knights and their troops to go back to their own lands to seek repose, of which they were in great need, in view of the travail that they had undergone for their sake, and that they all should have their ships brought to the port of the Firm Island, so that from there they might all embark on their journeys. The Emperor earnestly entreated King Lisuarte to order his fleet to come to the Firm Island; and since he and the queen were to return there, to grant him permission to leave, for he wished to accompany Amadis because he was to speak with him at length about his affairs; and the King acceded to it.

CHAPTER CXIX

How king Lisuarte arrived at the town of Windsor, where Queen Brisena his wife was, and how with her and his daughter he agreed to return to the Firm Island.

King Lisuarte took with him King Cildadan and Gasquilan, King of Suesa, and with all their troops returned to the town of Windsor, where he had sent word commanding Queen Brisena his wife to wait for him. Since nothing more is related of what happened to him, except that he arrived at the town in five days, exhibiting a demeanor to a greater degree joyful than he was at heart; for he well recognized that although Amadis remained as his son, and his daughter with him very honorably, and that not only of him but also of the Emperor of Rome and King Perion and all the other noble lords he remained as chief, and all of them at his orders, he was not satisfied in his desire, because all this honor and gain had come to him after being overcome and reduced to dire straits, as has been related to you; and Amadis, against whom he had been going as at a mortal enemy, was carrying off all the glory. And such great sadness had taken possession of his heart that he could in nowise be joyful. But as he was already well along in years, and was very weary and troubled to see so many deaths and great misfortunes — all of them among Christians — and to perceive that the causes from which they sprang were worldly and perishable, and that to him, as a very powerful prince it had been granted to remove them as a threat to his power — even though some of his honor, which had always pursued quite the opposite course, had been tarnished by esteeming worldly honor so highly that it had caused him to forget completely the welfare of his soul — and that with just cause God had given him such great chastisements, especially the last one about which you have already heard, he consoled himself and dissimulated as a man of great prudence so that no one might perceive that his thought was concerned with anything other than considering himself the lord and superior of everyone, and believing that with great honor he had won it.

So with this pretended joy and with a very complacent appearance he came to where the queen was with her very richly attired ladies and maidens-in-waiting, and he was leading by the hand the youth Esplandian, for the things of the past, both dangerous and pleasurable, she now knew about through Brandoyvas, who on behalf of the king had come ahead from the monastery to afford her joy. When the king came into the room, the queen came to him and kneeling sought to kiss his hands, but he withdrew them from her and lifting her up with great love, embraced her as one who loved her with all his heart. And while the ladies and maidens came up to kiss the hands of the king, the queen took into her arms the youth Esplandian, who was kneeling before her, and began to kiss him many times, and said: "Oh, my handsome and fortunate son! Blessed be that hour in which you were born, and may you have the blessing of God and my own, for so much good has come to me because of you; and may He be pleased through His holy mercy to give me the opportunity to repay in full this very great service that you have rendered the king my lord in being the cause, after God, of saving his life."

Then King Cildadan and Gasquilan, King of Suesa, came up to speak with the queen, and she received them with great courtesy, as one of the sensible and well-bred ladies of the world, and afterwards she greeted all the other knights who came up to kiss her hands. By this time it was already the supper hour, and there remained with the king those two kings and many other knights, to whom was served for supper many and diverse viands, as at the table of such a man as he was he had provided so many times, as was his wont.

After they had supped, the king had those kings stay in his palace in very luxurious apartments, and he retired to the queen's chamber. When he was in bed, he said to her: "Lady, if by chance you have been surprised at the news that you have been told about Oriana your daughter and Amadis of Gaul, I also have been; for certainly I really think that that thought was far removed from you and from me without our having any suspicion of it. I am troubled only by the fact that we did not know of it previously; for there could have been avoided so many deaths and injuries that have occurred, due to our not knowing it. Now that it has come to our attention, and no remedy can be found or given that would not be with more dishonor, let us accept as a solution that Oriana remain with the husband that she is pleased to take, for if with anger and passion put aside we recognize what is true and just, there is today in the world no emperor or prince who can equal him; and not merely equal, for also with his surpassing discretion and great courage — Fortune being more favorable to him than to any other mortal — from being in the guise of a poor knight errant, he has advanced to have today at his command the entire flower of the great and small who live in the world; and Leonoreta will be empress of Rome, for this I have authorized. Therefore, it is necessary — since I of my own free will have given my word, in order to honor Amadis that you and I and Leonoreta would be on the Firm Island, where they await us to bring everything to a conclusion — that you prepare yourself as is fitting and with your face showing such joy, while ceasing to talk about past events, as is necessary and ought to be done in such situations."

The queen kissed his hands because thus she sought to constrain his passion and strong will, and assent to what was already settled without further argument; and she told him that his commands would be carried out as given and that since two such sons subsisted for him, and all the others because of them were remaining at his service, it should be considered good, and that he should thank God because He thus had willed it to be done, although the manner thereof had not been quite in conformity with his desire.

So they took their ease that night, and next day the king arose and gave orders to King Arban of North Wales, his majordomo, to make ready very quickly all the things needed for that journey; and the queen did likewise in order that her daughter Leonoreta might go in a guise befitting the empress of such a great sovereignty.

CHAPTER CXX

How king Perion and his companies returned to the Firm Island, and what they did before King Lisuarte was there with them.

Now the story relates that King Perion and his companies, after King Lisuarte left them to go to Windsor, where Queen Brisena his wife was, all mounted with their battalions in military formation just as they had come there, and with great pleasure and joy in their hearts started on their way to the Firm Island. The Emperor of Rome regularly lodged with Amadis in his tent, and both slept in the same bed so that never for a single hour were they separated. And all the troops and tents and equipment were in the custody of Brondajel de Roca, as the emperor's chief majordomo, just as he was under the Emperor Patin, his predecessor. Their daily marches were very brief, and they always camped in very pleasant and agreable places. And when they had kept King Perion company for a while in his tent, they were all accustomed to gather together in the tents of Amadis, or sometimes in those of the emperor; and as most of them were young and of noble rank and upbringing, they were always playing and having fun at pleasurable activities, so that they were leading the best life that they had enjoyed in a long, long time.

So thus they arrived at the Firm Island, where in the garden they found Oriana and all the noble ladies who were there, so beautiful and so richly attired that they were wondrous to behold; for don't think that they seemed to be earthly or mortal persons, but that God had created them in Heaven and had sent them there.

The great joy that one and all experienced on seeing themselves thus gathered together and in good health with so much honor and such agreement upon peace, words fail to describe. King Perion went ahead, and all the ladies paid him great respect, and with much humility he was greeted by those who properly should do so, and the others kissed his hands. Amadis took the emperor by the hand and came up to Oriana and said to her: "My lady, speak to this knight and great prince, who has never seen you and greatly esteems you."

She, as she already knew he was the emperor and was to be the husband of her sister, went up to him and sought to kneel and kiss his hands, but he bent down with very great respect and lifted her up, and said: "My lady, I am the one who ought to show humility before you and before your husband, because he is the lord of my land and of my person; for you may without fail, madam, believe that with reverence to both, there will be done only what be your desire and his."

Oriana said to him: "My lord, I acquiesce as far as your good gratitude is concerned, but with regard to the respect owed your virtue and high estate, I am the one who ought to treat you with great obsequiousness."

He thanked her profusely for this.

Agrajes and Don Florestan and Don Cuadragante and Don Brian de Monjaste went over to Queen Sardamira and to Olinda and Grasinda, who were together; and Don Bruneo of Bonamar to his greatly beloved lady Melicia; and the other knights to the other princesses and other very beautiful maidens of high degree who were there, and they talked with them with much enjoyment about what was most to their liking.

Amadis took Gastiles, nephew of the Emperor of Constantinople, and Grasander, son of the King of Bohemia, and brought them to Princess Mabilia his cousin, saying to her: "My good lady, take these princes and do them honor." She took them by the hand and sat down between them. Grasandor was quite pleased at this, because, as we have told you, the first day that he had seen her, he had lost his heart to her; and knowing who she was and her great goodness and gentility, and the close kinship and great love that Amadis had for her, he was determined to ask for her hand in marriage; so he wanted very much to hear her speak and to engage her in intimate conversation, and therefore he was very pleased to see himself so near her. But as this princess was a maiden so surpassing in all goodness and modesty and grace with a large share of beauty, Grasandor was so delighted with her that he was moved to feel much greater affection that he had before.

Just as you hear, all those lords were enjoying what they most desired, except Amadis, who greatly wished to speak with his lady Oriana, and couldn't on account of the emperor. And when he saw Queen Briolanja, who was beside Don Bruneo and his sister Melicia, he went to her and brought her, leading her by the hand, to the emperor, saying to him: "Sire, speak to this lady and keep her company."

The emperor turned his gaze, for until then he had not taken his eyes from Oriana, for he was astonished to see her great beauty; and as he beheld the queen so elegant and beautiful, and the other ladies who were talking with those knights, he greatly marveled to see ladies so excelling any others he had ever seen, and he said to Amadis: "My good sir, I truly believe that these ladies are not born like other women, but that that eminent sage Apolidon through his great art created them and left them here on this island, where you have found them, and I can only imagine that they and I are enchanted; for I can say, and it is the truth, that if through the whole world one were to seek such a company as this, it could not possibly be found."

And Amadis embraced him laughing, and asked him if he had seen another such company in any other court, however large it might be. He said to him: "Certainly neither I nor anyone else could see it unless it were in that of Heaven."

While they were occupied as you hear, King Perion, who had been speaking for quite a while with the very beautiful Grasinda, came to them and took Queen Briolanja by the hand saying to the emperor: "My good lord, let us, you and I, remain with this beautiful queen, if you please, and let Amadis talk with Oriana, for I certainly think that he will take great pleasure in her company."

And so they both remained with Queen Briolanja, and Amadis went with great joy to his lady Oriana, and with deep humility sat down with her apart from the others, and said to her: "Oh, lady, with what services can I repay the favor you have done me in the fact that by your wish our love affair has been revealed."

Oriana said: "My lord, it is no longer a time for you to offer me such courtesy, nor for me to receive it; because I am the one who must serve you and do your bidding with that obedience that a wife owes her husband. And from now on in this matter I want to recognize the great love that you have for me, by being treated by you, my lord, as reason dictates and in no other manner; and about this let nothing more be said, except that I am so desirous of knowing how my father is, and how he has taken all this concerning us."

Amadis said: "Your father is very sagacious, and although in secret may have considered it otherwise, according to the way he has seemed to everyone he remains quite content, and was so when he left us. Already, my lady, you know that he is to come here as are the queen and your sister."

"I already know that," said she, "and the joy that my heart feels I cannot express. May it please our Lord that it all be carried out as arranged without there being any change in it; for you can believe, my lord, that after you, there is no one in the world I love as much as I do him, although his great cruelty very rightly ought to have caused me to feel just the opposite. And now tell me about Esplandian, how he is, and what you think of him."

"Esplandian," said Amadis, "in his appearance and habits is your son; for it is not possible to say more, and I had greatly desired the holy man Nasciano to bring him to you; Nasciano is probably here now, for he did not wish to come with the troops; but the king your father begged him to be allowed to take Esplandian to the queen so that she might see him, and said that he would conduct him to her."

They remained talking about this and other things until it was time to sup, when King Perion arose and took the emperor, and they went to Oriana, saying to her: "Lady, it is time that we go to our quarters."

She told them to do what they liked best. So they all left, and the ladies remained wondrously happy and contented.

All the men supped that night in the quarters of King Perion, for Amadis gave orders that it be made ready there; where they were very well served and supplied with everything befitting a gathering of so many and such great lords. After they had supped, jugglers came who performed many sleight of hand tricks, from which they derived great enjoyment until it was time to sleep, when they all went to their quarters except Amadis, whom the king his father ordered to remain because he wanted to talk over a few matters.

Then all the others having gone, the king retired to his room and Amadis with him; and when they were alone, he said to him: "Son Amadis, since God our Lord has been pleased that these confrontations and great battles should bring such honor to you, for although in them many very worthy princes and great knights have risked their persons and estates, to you, through the goodness of God, accrues the major glory and fame, just as on the other hand your honor and great fame ran the greatest risk, as you have known. Now nothing else remains except that, with that same concern and great diligence that at the beginning of this so greatly augmented and dangerous confrontation when you were under the compulsion of such a great necessity you brought together and encouraged all these honorable knights, now being free of it you be even more greatly concerned to show your gratitude to them, deferring to their desires as to what ought to be done, not only about these prisoners, who are such mighty princes and lords of great lands, but also since you already have a wife, that they may have wives along with you, in order that it may be apparent that just as in troubles and dangers they were your helpers, so now in benefits and pleasures they may be your companions. And therefore I defer to your wishes with respect to my daughter Melicia, so that you may give her to the man who will cherish most her virtue and great beauty; and the same you can do with Mabilia, your cousin; moreover I well understand that Queen Briolanja will do only what you deem best; also remember to include with these ladies your friend Grasinda, and even Queen Sardamira since here is the emperor, who can command her. If these ladies are pleased to marry in this land, there will not be lacking knights who are their equals in estate and lineage; and remember your brothers, who are now ready to have wives, in whom they can beget a new generation to keep their memory alive. And let this be done at once, because good deeds that are done with difficulty and delay lose most of their value."

Amadis knelt before him and kissed his hands as a token of gratitude for what he had said to him, and as assurance that it would be done just as he commanded. With this resolution Amadis went to his lodging. And in the morning he arose and had all those lords assemble in the quarters of his cousin Agrajes, and when they were all together he said to them: "My noble lords, the great hardships of the past and the honor and glory that you have gained through them very rightfully entitle you to give your weary spirits some rest and repose. And since God has willed that out of your indebtedness and love I should achieve the things that I most desired in this world, so should I like those that are desired by you, if I can be instrumental in the matter, to be restored to you. Therefore, my lords, don't hesitate to make known to me your wishes not only in what concerns your loves and desires, if you love some of these ladies and wish them as wives, but also concerning what should be done with these prisoners, whom you overcame through the great virtue and courage of your hearts; because it is very fitting, since you received many wounds amid great danger because of them, that now while they are suffering you should enjoy and find repose in those great dominions that they possessed."

All those lords expressed their thanks for what Amadis was offering them, and they were quite pleased with him. And what related to their marriages was made known there at once: first Agrajes indicated that he would take his lady love Olinda. And Don Bruneo of Bonamar told him that he certainly believed that he knew he had all his hope and good fortune concentrated on his lady Melicia. Grasandor said that his heart had never been given to any woman of all those he had seen except to Princess Mabilia, and that he loved her and was asking for her as his wife. Don Cuadragante said to Amadis: "My good lord, time and youth until now have been very averse to any repose for me, or for me to have any concern other than for my horse and arms;

but now reason and age induce me to adopt another fashion; and if it pleases Grasinda to marry in this part of the world, I will take her for my wife."

Don Florestan said to Amadis: "Sir, although my desire had been, once these matters in which we have been engaged were settled, to go at once to Germany, of which I am a native on my mother's side, not only to see her but also all my other relatives — for in view of how long it has been since I left there, I would hardly recognize them — if here the consent of Queen Sardamira can be obtained, it could change my intention."

The other knights told him that they thanked him very heartily for his good will, but that, both because for the time being their hearts were not in subjugation to any of those ladies or to any others, and also, since they were quite young and of little renown, hence their age had afforded them scant opportunity to win fame, they purposed not to involve themselves in any gain or repose, but in the quest for adventure whereby they might exercise their bodies; and both in the matter of those ladies for whom those knights were asking and in what he said to them about the prisoners, they were totally abstaining; and he should allot everything among the former, since they were pleased to lead lives of more repose and with wives, and that as for themselves he should involve them in military operations and confrontations in which he might think they could win most fame and prestige.

Amadis said to them: "My noble lords, I trust in God that what you ask will be in His service and will be accomplished with His help. And since these young knights leave it all to you, I intend to divide it according to the way I have it planned, and I say that you, Sir Don Cuadragante, who are a king's son and brother of a king, and your estate is quite far from corresponding to your lineage and great merits, may have the sovereignty of Sansuenia, for since its lord is in your power, without much effort you can possess yourself of it. And you, my good lord Don Bruneo of Bonamar, besides my bestowing on you forthwith my sister Melicia, you shall have the kingdom of King Arabigo along with her; and the seigniory that you expect from your father the marquis make over to your brother Branfil. My brother Don Florestan shall have this queen for whom he asks, and besides what she possesses, which is the Island of Sardinia, the emperor, at my request, will give him the whole seigniory of Calabria, which was Salustanquidio's. You, my lords Agrajes and Grasandor, must content yourselves for the present with the great kingdoms and dominions that you expect from your parents after they die, and I with this small nook of a Firm Island, until our Lord bring about an occasion on which we may be able to have more."

All approved and praised very highly what Amadis had decided, and they earnestly requested that it be done as he indicated. And because, if one were to relate what he went through with those ladies on the subject of these marriages, and with the emperor concerning that of Queen Sardamira, it would be too long a story, you shall know only that Amadis carried everything out as those knights had requested, and the emperor fulfilled that for which Amadis had asked for Don Florestan, and much more later on, as the story will relate. And they were then betrothed by the hand of that holy man Nasciano, the weddings being left for the day that Amadis and the emperor might set for them.

CHAPTER CXXI

How don Bruneo of Bonamar and Angriote de Estravaus and Branfil went to Gaul for Queen Elisena and Don Galaor, and the adventure they experienced as they came back.

Amadis said to King Perion, his father: "Sire, it will be well that you send for my lady the queen and for my brother Don Galaor — for whom I hold in reserve the beautiful Queen Briolanja, with whom he will always be happy — so that they be here, as was agreed upon, when King Lisuarte comes."

"So let it be done," said the king, "and I shall write to the queen, and you send whatever most you like."

Don Bruneo arose and said: "I wish to make this journey if it pleases your Grace; and I shall take with me my brother Branfil."

"Well that journey will not be made without me," said Angriote de Estravaus.

King Perion said: "To you, Angriote and Branfil I consent, for Don Bruneo is not speaking sincerely, because he who takes him away from the side of his beloved would not be his friend; and because I have always been his friend, and in order not to lose him, I shall not give him permission."

Don Bruneo replied laughing: "Sire, although this is the greatest favor of those that I have received from you, I still want to serve the queen my lady, because from there comes contentment for everything else."

"So be it," said the king, "and may God grant, my good friend, that you find Don Galaor your brother-in-law in such a state of health as to be able to come."

Isanjo, who was present, said: "Sire, he is well now; for I so ascertained from some traders who were coming from Gaul over to Great Britain, and in order to ensure their safety, they came by here, for they were afraid of the war that was going on at the time; and I asked them about Don Galaor, and they told me they saw him up and going about the city, but quite thin."

All were very pleased with that news, and the king more than anyone, for at heart he was constantly worried and troubled by the illness of that son, and he was very much afraid of losing him, in view of its long duration.

So the next day these three knights about whom you have heard gave orders to make ready immediately a ship with everything they needed for that journey; they had their arms and horses placed aboard, and with their squires and sailors to guide them, they put out to sea. And as the weather was good, in a short while they crossed over to Gaul, where they were very well received by the queen. But I tell you that when Don Galaor saw them, so great was his pleasure that emaciated as he was he went running to embrace all three of them, and thus embraced he held them for a while, and the tears came to his eyes and he said to them: "Oh my lords and great friends! When will God be willing that I travel in your company by returning to arms, which I have forsaken for such a long time because of my misfortune?"

Angriote said to him: "Sir, do not be distressed, for God will bring about everything just as you desire, and be concerned only with learning the great and very joyous news that we bring you."

Then they told the queen and him all the events that you have heard that occurred, including how they began and the favorable outcome of the whole matter. When Don Galaor heard all this, he was greatly disturbed and said: "Oh, Holy Mary! And is it true that all that has happened to my lord King Lisuarte without my being with him? Now I can say that God has done me an outstanding favor in giving me at such a time so serious an illness; for certainly, although the king my father and my brothers were on the other side, I would not have been able to avoid placing this body of mine in King Lisuarte's service until death. And certainly if I had learned of it before now, given my weakness, I would have died of anxiety."

Don Bruneo said to him: "Sir, it is better thus, for with honor for all, and with you winning for a wife that very beautiful Queen Briolanja, whom your brother Amadis designates for you, peace is made, as you will see when you arrive there."

Then they gave the letter to the queen, and told her that their coming was for the purpose of bringing her so that she might be present at the weddings of all her children and might see Queen Brisena and all those noble ladies who were there. As the queen was very noble and loved her husband and her children, and after great risk and danger saw them in such peaceful tranquillity, she gave many thanks to God and said: "My son Don Galaor, look at this letter and take courage, and go see the king your father and your brothers, for it appears to me that there you will find King Lisuarte with more honor from your family than he desired."

Angriote said to her: "Madam, that you can very well say, for your son Amadis is today the chief flower and glory of the world, and dependent on his will and desire is that of all living grandees of most importance in it; which, good lady, you will see with your own eyes, for in his house and at his command are gathered emperors and kings and other princes and noble knights who love him deeply and appreciate him to that degree that his merit deserves. And therefore it is necessary that your departure be as early as possible; for we indeed believe that King Lisuarte and Queen Brisena his wife will already be there with their daughter Leonoreta in order to bestow her as wife upon the Emperor of Rome, whom your son Amadis has placed in that great sovereignty that he now holds as his own."

She said to them with very great delight: "My good friends, it will be done at once as you say, and I shall give orders to prepare ships in which to travel."

So those knights stayed with the queen for a week, at the end of which the ships were outfitted with everything necessary for the voyage, and they forthwith embarked in them very lightheartedly and began to sail away to the Firm Island.

Then while they were journeying over the sea as I say, and with very good weather, on the third day they saw coming on their right a galley equipped with sails, and they decided to wait for it in order to find out who was coming on it, and also why it was proceeding directly on the course they were pursuing. And when it drew near, a squire of Don Galaor's went out to meet it in a skiff and asked who was coming on the ship. One of those on board told him very courteously that it was a lady who was going to the Firm Island in very great haste. The squire, when he heard this, said to him: "Then tell that lady whom you mention, that this fleet you see here is going there, and that she not be afraid to approach it, for on it are persons in whose company she will greatly enjoy traveling."

When he heard this, that man very quickly and joyfully went to tell his lady. And she gave orders to launch a skiff with a knight in it, to find out whether what the former said was true. The latter reached the ship on which the queen was, and said to those knights: "Sirs, by the faith that you owe to God tell me whether that ship yonder in which a lady of high rank is traveling en route to the Firm Island, can approach in safety, because this squire said you were pursuing the same course."

Angriote said to him: "Friend, the squire has told you the truth, and that lady you mention can come in safety, for no one is aboard here from whom you may receive any harm; rather, people from whom you will have all the help that can rightly be given against anyone who may seek to do her harm."

"Thanks be to God," said the knight, "now I ask you to be kind enough to wait for her, and I shall have her come to you at once, for since you are knights, you will have great sorrow when you are apprised of her situation."

He returned at once to the ship, and when he told her what he had discovered, they went directly to the ship on which the queen was, for that ship appeared to them to have the finest equipment. Then when they arrived there, a lady with veiled head and face emerged, and asked who was coming with those ships. Angriote said to her: "Madam, a queen of Gaul is aboard, who is going to the Firm Island."

"Then, sir knight," said the lady, "I beg of you in the name of your obligation as a knight, to arrange for me to speak with her."

Angriote said to her: "That will be done at once, and likewise your coming aboard this ship; for she is a lady who will enjoy meeting you, just as she enjoys meeting all those who seek her out."

The matron boarded the ship, and Angriote took her by the hand and brought her to the queen, saying: "Madam, this lady wishes to see you."

"May she be welcome," said the queen, "and I ask you, Angriote, to tell me who she is."

Then the lady came up to her and greeted her, and said: "Madam, that good knight will not be able to answer that, because he does not know. But from me you shall ascertain it, and there will be no little to relate, in view of the disastrous misfortune and great hardship that undeservedly have overtaken me. But I wish, my good lady, to receive assurances from you that all my company and I will be safe, if what I say perchance moves you to anger rather than to pity."

The queen answered that she could safely say whatever she wished.

Then the lady began to weep very bitterly and said: "My good lady, even if from here I obtain no relief other than that of relating my misfortunes to such a noble lady as yourself, it will afford some rest to my grieving heart. You shall know that I was married to the King of Dacia, and with him I found myself a very happy queen; and by him I had two sons and one daughter. Then this daughter, who to my misfortune was begotten of me, the king her father and I gave in marriage to the Duke of the province of Sweden, a great dominion that borders on our kingdom; their marriage, just as it was celebrated very joyously amid great festivities and rejoicing, so subsequently has brought very great weeping and sorrow; for as this duke is a young man eager to rule, no matter by what means, and the king my husband was advanced in years, the duke reckoned that by killing him and seizing those two sons of mine, who are mere boys, for the elder is fourteen, he would quickly be able through his wife to be king of the realm. And just as he planned it he carried it out; for pretending that he was coming on a pleasure trip to our kingdom, and that his coming well accompanied was in our honor, when the king my husband was coming out with great pleasure and hearty good will to welcome him, the wicked traitor killed him with his own hands. And God sought to protect the boys, for as they were coming behind on their palfreys, they took refuge in the city from which they had come, and with them most of our knights and others who afterwards at great risk likewise entered, because that traitor at once laid siege to them and thus holds them. Well, at that time I had gone on a pilgrimage that I was pledged to undertake to a very old church of Our Lady, which is situated on a rock in the ocean about half a league offshore. There I was informed of the misfortune I had unknowingly sustained; and as I saw myself alone, I had no recourse other than to take refuge in this ship on which I had gone there. For, my lady, I come with the intention of going to the Firm Island to a knight called Amadis, and many others of noble rank who they tell me are there with him; and I shall tell him of this very great treachery whence so much harm comes to me, and I shall beg him to have pity on those princes and not allow them to be killed so wrongfully; for if only a few were to go who would encourage my subjects and serve as their leaders, that wicked man would not dare to stay there very long."

Queen Elisena and those knights were astonished at such great treachery and greatly pitied that queen; and at once the queen took her by the hand and had her sit beside her, saying to her: "My good lady, if I have not paid you the respect that your royal rank deserves, pardon me, for I did not know you, nor did I know the state of your affairs as I do now. And you may believe that your loss and hardship have moved me to sincere compassion and anguish on seeing that adverse Fortune spares no rank, however high it be, and that the one who finds himself happiest and most exalted ought most to fear her mutations; because when people deem themselves most secure, then there comes to them what has come to you, my good lady. And since God has brought you here, I consider it good that you go in my company to the Firm Island; and there you will find the protection that you desire, just as all do who have had need of it."

"I know that already," said the Queen of Dacia; "for some knights who were crossing over to Greece told the king my lord the events that have occurred in connection with Amadis's seizing the daughter of King Lisuarte, who was disinheriting her in favor of another younger daughter, and was sending her to be the wife of the Emperor of Rome. And this caused me to seek this blessed knight, rescuer of the unfortunate who suffer wrongs."

When Angriote and his companions heard what Queen Elisena said, all three knelt before her and begged her earnestly to give them permission in order that that queen might be aided and avenged by them, if it were the will of God, for such great treachery; and that this could very well be done, because now they were quite near the Firm Island, where any obstacle to their arrival would not rightly be expected. The queen wanted first to arrive where the king her husband was, but they urged her so strongly, that she had to agree.

Then at once they boarded their own ships with their arms and horses and servants, and told the Queen of Dacia to give them someone to guide them, and said that she should go with Queen Elisena to the Firm Island. She answered them that she would not remain; instead she wanted to go with them, for her appearance would be worth a great deal in repairing and remedying the situation. So they went together, since they perceived her determination.

Queen Elisena and Don Galaor went on their way, and without anything happening to them, they arrived one morning at the harbor of the Firm Island. And when their arrival became known, the king her husband and their sons rode forth, along with the emperor and all the other knights, in order to welcome her. Oriana, with those ladies, had wanted to go with them, but the king sent word to beg her not to trouble to do so, for he would bring her to her immediately, and so she stayed behind.

Then the queen and Don Galaor disembarked and were received there with great pleasure. Amadis, after he kissed the hands of his mother, went and embraced Don Galaor, and the latter sought to kiss his hands, but he did not wish it; instead he remained for a while asking him about his illness. Don Galaor said that he was much improved and that he would be more so from then on, since an end had been put to the anger and rage at each other felt by King Lisuarte and by Amadis.

After the emperor and all the other lords had greeted the queen, they placed her on a palfrey and went to Oriana's apartment in the castle, where the latter and the queens and noble ladies in very rich attire were at the gate of the garden to welcome her. The emperor led her horse by the reins and would not allow her to dismount except into his arms. Then when she entered where Oriana was, the latter clasped the hands of Queens Sardamira and Briolanja, and with them came up to Queen Elisena, all three kneeling before her with that submission due a real mother. The queen embraced and kissed them, and lifted them up. Then there arrived Mabilia, and Melicia and Grasinda, and all the other ladies; and they kissed her hands, and taking her in their midst, they went with her to her apartments. At this juncture Don Galaor arrived, and one could not begin to tell you the affection that Oriana showed for him, because, excepting Amadis, there was no one in the world she loved more, both on account of her lover, for she knew how much he loved him, and because of the very great love that King Lisuarte her father so truly had for him and the desire of Don Galaor to serve him against the whole world, as evidenced many times by his deeds. All the other ladies received him very well. Amadis, taking Queen Briolanja by the hand, said to Galaor: "Lord brother, this beautiful queen I entrust to you, for already on other occasions you have seen her and have become acquainted with her."

Don Galaor took her with him without any embarrassment, as one who is not frightened or disturbed on seeing women; and he said: "Sir, I consider it a great favor on your part that you give her to me, and on hers because she takes me and wishes me for her own."

The queen said nothing; rather, she blushed, which rendered her much more beautiful. Galaor, who was gazing at her, for since he had left Sobradisa at the time he brought his brother Don Florestan there (except afterwards briefly at the court of King Lisuarte when she came seeking Amadis), he had never again seen her, and at that time she was very young; but now that she was at perfection of age and beauty, he was so taken with her and so attractive did she seem to him that although he had seen and been intimate with many women, as this story tells when it speaks of him, never out of true love had he yielded his heart to anyone but this very beautiful queen. And likewise she had given her heart to him, for knowing his great worth, both at arms and in all the other good qualities that the best knight in the world ought to have, all the great love that she had for his brother Amadis, she gave to this knight whom she already considered her husband. And just as their desires coincided at that time so completely, remaining so after they went away to their kingdom, they led a most gracious and honorable life and with greater love than could be fully described to you. And they had sons who were very handsome and very famous knights, who accomplished great and dangerous feats at arms, and won extensive lands and dominions, as we shall tell you in a continuation of this story that is called *The Exploits of Esplandian*, for this will be told there in full; and with Esplandian they maintained a close companionship before he was the emperor of Constantinople and afterwards.

So this reception of this noble Queen Elisena having been accomplished, and she now being lodged with those ladies, where no man other than King Perion entered — for it was so agreed upon until King Lisuarte and Queen Brisena and their daughter came, and the marriages of Oriana and of all the other ladies performed in their presence — all went to their own quarters to divert themselves in the many pastimes that they had in that island, especially for those who were fond of woodland hunting, because off the island on the mainland about a league away, there were the most beautiful groves and dense upland thickets, which, as the land was very well protected, were all full of deer and boar and rabbits, and other wild creatures, of which they killed many, not only with dogs and snares, but also by pursuing them in their haunts on horseback. There was also the hunting with falcons of many hares, partridges, and water-fowl; so that one can say that in that tiny nook there was a gathering together of the whole flower of chivalry of the world — that is to say, those who upheld chivalry to the highest degree — and of all the beauty and loveliness to be found in it. And afterwards there were great pleasures and delights about which we have told you, and others too numerous to relate — natural ones as well as artificial ones contrived by the enchantments of that very great sage Apolidon, who had left them there.

But now the story ceases to tell of these lords and ladies who were waiting for King Lisuarte and his retinue, in order to relate what happened to Don Bruneo and Angriote and Branfil, who were accompanying the Queen of Dacia, as you have already heard.

CHAPTER CXXII

CONCERNING WHAT HAPPENED TO DON BRUNEO OF BONAMAR AND TO ANGRIOTE DE ESTRAVAUS AND BRANFIL DURING THE RESCUE THAT THEY WENT WITH THE QUEEN OF DACIA TO EFFECT.

The story relates that Angriote de Estravaus and Don Bruneo of Bonamar and his brother Branfil, after they left Queen Elisena went ahead on their voyage, guided by those who knew the way. And the queen, because she was distraught, and also on account of her pleasure at having found those who would aid her in her extremity, had never asked them from where, or who they were. And as they sailed onwards just as I am telling you, one day she said to them: "Good lords and friends, although I have you in my company, I know no more of your estate than what I knew of you before I found you or saw you. I earnestly beg of you, if you please, to tell me, so that I may be able to address you with that degree of propriety befitting your honor and my own."

"Good lady," said Angriote, "although your ascertaining our names, in view of the slight acquaintanceship with us that you have, neither increases nor diminishes your peace of mind or your being helped, since you are pleased to obtain this information, we shall tell you. Know you that these two knights are brothers, and one is called Don Bruneo of Bonamar and the other Branfil, and Don Bruneo is through his spouse a brother-in-law of Amadis of Gaul, whose services you were going to enlist. And my name is Angriote de Estravaus."

When the queen heard them say who they were, she said: "Oh my good lords! I give many thanks to God for having found you at such a time, and to you for the relief and pleasure that you have given to my troubled mind by informing me who you were; for although I am not acquainted with you, for I had never seen you before, your great fame resounds everywhere; because those knights from Greece about whom I spoke to Queen Elisena and who had passed through my land, told and recounted to the king my husband the great battles that had taken place between King Lisuarte and Amadis. They, while relating the events they had seen, told him the names of all the leading knights who participated and many of the great deeds of chivalry acomplished by them. And I remember that you were there accounted among the best, for which I give many thanks to our Lord; for certainly I have come with great concern at seeing you so few in number, and not knowing what protection I was bringing to this great emergency. But now I shall proceed with greater hope that my sons will be aided and defended against that traitor."

Angriote said: "Lady, since this is already our responsibility, more cannot be devoted to it than all our energies together with our lives."

"May God give you thanks," said she, "and bring me to a time when my sons and I may repay you by enhancing your estates."

Thus they traveled over the sea without pausing until they reached the kingdom of Dacia. Then having arrived there, they decided that the queen should stay on her ship out at sea until she saw how they were faring. And they had their horses landed and they armed themselves, and with their squires accompanying them and with two unarmed knights to guide them, who were with the queen at the time that she embarked, they went their way straight towards the city where the princes were, which from there was probably a good day's journey. And they had ordered their squires to bring along something to eat for them and forage for the horses, because they would not enter any populated area.

Just as I am telling you, these three knights went forth and traveled all day until evening. Then they rested at the edge of a forest of dense undergrowth, where they dined and fed their horses. And then they mounted and traveled so far by night that they arrived an hour before dawn at the camp; which they approached as stealthily as they could in order to see where the greatest concentration of troops was, so that they might avoid it and go on through where there were but few until they entered the town. And so they did, for they ordered their squires and the two knights who were accompanying them to try to enter the town while they themselves remained on guard.

All three together attacked as many as ten knights whom they discovered in front of them, and from the first encounter on, each one unhorsed his man; and they broke their lances and grasped their swords and attacked them so fiercely that not only because of the powerful blows that they were dealing them, but also because the latter thought there were more people attacking, they began to flee, shouting for help. Angriote said: "It is well that we leave them and go reenforce the besieged." This was accordingly done, for with their company they arrived at the town walls, to which at the noise of their combat some one of those inside had come up. The two knights who came there with them called out and were at once recognized, and they opened a small postern gate through which they sometimes sallied forth at their enemies, and through it Angriote and his companions entered. The princes hastened there, for at the disturbance they had arisen and had ascertained that those knights were coming to their aid and that the queen their mother was well and in safety — for until then they had not known whether she was a prisoner or dead — news which greatly pleased them. All those of the town were greatly encouraged by their arrival when they found out who they were, and they had them housed with the princes in their palace, where they disarmed and rested for quite a while.

In the camp of the duke great confusion had been caused by the shouts that the knights who were fleeing had uttered, and very quickly all the troops came out, on foot as well as on horseback, for they did not know what was the matter; and before they calmed down, daylight came. The duke learned from the knights what had happened to them and how they had seen only about eight or ten mounted men — although they had thought that there might be more — and that these had entered the town. The duke said: "It is probably only some men from the countryside who have dared to enter. I will give orders to find out, and if I learn who they are, they will lose outside all that they leave here."

And then he ordered all to disarm and go to their quarters, and he did likewise.

Angriote and his companions, as soon as they had slept and rested, arose and heard mass with those youths whom they were protecting. Then they told them to order their ranking men to come there; and they did so. And from those ranking men they sought to find out what troops they had, in order to see whether there would be enough to go out and fight with their foes; and they earnestly besought them to have them all arm themselves, and they would review them in a large square that there was there; and so they did. Then all of them having turned out, and it having been definitely ascertained what troops the duke had, they perceived clearly that the situation could not be met with them except by means of some one of the artful strategems customarily sought in wars; and all three having taken counsel, they decided that night to go out and attack the enemy with great circumspection, and agreed that Don Bruneo and the younger prince, who was about twelve years old, should try to leave by another exit, and should concern themselves only with getting past their foes and going to a few nearby villages of that area — whose inhabitants, as they had seen the king killed, their lords under siege, and the queen in flight, did not dare to show themselves; instead, much against their will they were sending food to the duke's camp — and that they having arrived there, when the prince had been seen by the villagers and likewise the encouragement that Don Bruneo would give them, they would assemble a force in order to be able to help those under siege; and if such an arrangement were found possible, that by night they give them certain signals, whereupon while they would be sallying forth to attack the camp, Don Bruneo would come with the troop that he had to the other side, where they had no fear of attack, and that thus they would be able to wreak great harm on their enemies.

This seemed to them a good resolution, and they discussed it with some of those knights who were most worthy and most trusted to serve the princes in that very great confrontation and danger in which they were. All approved of its being done thus.

Then, night having come, and a good part of it over, Angriote and Branfil with all the people of the town went out to attack their foes, and Don Bruneo with the prince went out on the other side as we told you. Angriote and Branfil, who were going in front of them all, entered a street bordered by gardens that they had seen that day — a street which ended at a large field where the camp was. And there was no guard outpost there by day, but at night some twenty men were standing guard in it; these they and their company attacked so fiercely that the guards were at once routed, and they moved ahead in pursuit of them. And some were killed and others wounded; for as they were people of low degree and these knights were so elite, very quickly they were all rendered powerless and were annihilated. The shouting was very loud, as was the resounding of blows; but Angriote and Branfil kept moving forward to attack the others who were hastening there from the camp and the other guard outposts, and they left many of them in the custody of their men, for they did nothing but seize and slay until they issued forth into the field where the camp was.

At that hour the duke was already on horseback; and as he saw his men annihilated by so few of his enemies, he was full of rage. And he spurred his horse, and went to attack them — and likewise all his troops that were there with him — so fiercely, that as it was night it seemed only that the whole of that field was red-hot molten metal; hence the forces from the city were seized with great fear and all of them took refuge in the alley through which they had passed to the field; so that there remained outside only those two knights Angriote and Branfil to await the whole fury of the duke. But so many men attacked them, that however much they achieved at arms — and they dealt the leaders notable blows and unhorsed the duke — perforce they had to retreat to the street where their men had sought refuge; and there, as the place was narrow, they halted. The duke was not wounded although he fell; and at once he was very quickly rescued by his men and placed on his horse. And he saw his enemies stationed in the street; and as he came up to them, he was greatly chagrined that only two knights were defending themselves and holding that passageway against all the troops he had with him. And he said in a voice audible to all: "Oh, erring knights errant, to whom I am lending my own resources, what a disgrace it is that your strength does not suffice to overcome only two knights, for you are no longer contending with more!"

Then he attacked and many others with him, and so fast did so many come on the scene that in spite of themselves Angriote and Branfil, along with their men, were forced by them to retreat for some distance farther up the alley. The duke thought that they were already beaten and that there in the melee his forces would be able to kill many and enter together with the others into the town. And as a victor he went ahead of his men and came up sword in hand to Angriote, whom he encountered facing him, and struck him a mighty blow on top of the helmet. But he was not slow in receiving payment; for as Angriote was ever on the lookout for him after he heard him abuse his own men, he raised his sword, and with all his might he struck him on the helmet such a blow that he rendered him powerless and knocked him to the ground at his horse's feet. And when he saw him thus, he shouted to his men to seize him, that he was the duke; and Branfil and he advanced against the others and dealt them very great, heavy blows, so that they did not dare await them; for as that place where they were fighting was very narrow, they were unable to strike them except frontally. In the meantime the duke was taken and imprisoned by those of the town, but so stunned and out of his senses that he did not know whether his own men or his enemies were carrying him.

When his men saw him thus, they thought he was dead, and they retreated until out of that narrow alley. Angriote and Branfil, when they saw that, not only because the duke was dead or taken prisoner, but also because their adversaries were many and it was not prudent to attack them in such a large area, decided to turn back and be content with what they had accomplished on their first sally. And so they did, for very quietly they returned to their own men, quite content with the way the affair had turned out, although with some wounds but not serious ones, and with their armor badly battered. But their horses in a short while died from the wounds that they had received; and with their forces gathered together, they returned to the town. And they found at the gate Prince Garinto, for that was his name, who when he saw them coming safe and sound and the duke, his enemy, taken prisoner, you can well understand the pleasure he felt. Then they all took refuge inside the town, rejoicing because they thus were bringing in their mortal enemy, who, as stated, had not yet regained consciousness, nor did he in all that remained of the night nor until noon of the next day.

Don Bruneo, who had gone out of the town on the other side, did not know anything of this except the shouts and great racket that he heard. And as the majority of the troops on the outside had hastened in the direction of the noise there only remained in that area a handful of foot soldiers, a few of whom, since they were going about disorganized and had no one to lead them, he was able to kill; but he stopped in order not to lose the prince whom he had in his charge, and he passed on by them without meeting any resistance. And they traveled all that remained of the night behind a man who was guiding them, who was riding a hackney; and morning having come, they saw nearby a town to which the guide was taking them. It was of respectable size and was called Alimenta; and there were coming out of it two armed knights, whom the duke had sent to find out who the men were who had entered the main town; and so they had carried their inquiry to other localities, but had found no trace or explanation of them. And they were returning to say so. Also on behalf of the duke they had ordered those of the town, with severe penalties for non-compliance, to send as much food as they could to the camp. And Don Bruneo, who saw them, asked that man if he knew who those two knights were, and on which side.

"Sir," said the man, "they are on the side of the duke, for I have already seen them many times wearing that armor while walking around outside the town in company with others who were companions at arms.

Then Don Bruneo said: "Well, you look after this youth and don't leave him; for I wish to see what kind of knights protect such a bad overlord."

Then he advanced somewhat and went to meet them; and they were paying no heed to him, believing him to be one of those from the camp. When he came near he said: "Wicked knights, who live with that traitorous duke and are his friends, protect yourselves from me, for I defy you until death."

They replied to him: "Your great arrogance will pay you back for your madness; for thinking that you were one of our men we were willing to leave you alone; but now you will pay with that death you mention for what as a man of little sense you dare to undertake."

Then they went toward each other at the full speed of their horses, and struck each other hard on their shields, so that their lances were shattered to pieces; but the one of the knights who met Don Bruneo went to the ground without any delay, and he experienced such a great fall on the field, which was hard, that he stirred neither hand nor foot, but rather was stretched out as if he were dead. And Don Bruneo grasped his sword very stout-heartedly and went for the other one, who likewise had sword in hand, and well covered by his shield was waiting for him; so they struck very mighty and solid blows. But as Don Bruneo was the stronger, and was more versed in that profession, he belabored him with so many blows that he made him lose his sword from his hand and both stirrups, and he flung his arms around the neck of his horse and said: "Oh, sir knight, for God's sake don't kill me."

Don Bruneo desisted from striking him and said: "Acknowledge that you are defeated."

"I so acknowledge," said he, "in order not to die and lose my soul."

"Then get off your horse," said Don Bruneo, "until I make up my mind."

He did so, but was so dazed that he could not hold himself erect, and fell to the ground; and Don Bruneo forced him against his will to rise, and he said to him: "Go to that companion of yours and see whether he is dead or alive."

He did so as best he could, and went over to him and took his helmet from his head. And when he gave him air, he breathed better and to some degree recovered consciousness. At this moment, Don Bruneo looked around for the youth and saw him at some distance from him; for the man, not having much faith in his prowess, had moved away from them with him. And with his sword he beckoned to them to come to him, and so they did; and when the youth came up, he was dumfounded at what Don Bruneo had done. And as he was a child and had never seen the like, he became quite pale of countenance, and Don Bruneo said to him: "Good youth, kill these enemies of yours, although it will be small vengeance for the great treason that their lord committed against your father."

The youth said to him: "Sir, perchance these are without blame for that treason; and it will be better, if it please you, that we bring them back alive rather than kill them."

Don Bruneo considered it good and was pleased with what the prince said; thinking that he would be a good man if he lived. Then he gave orders to that man who was accompanying them to help the other knight, and to place that one who was most stunned crosswise on the saddle of his horse, and for the other to mount, so that they might go on into the town. And so it was done.

And when they arrived there, many came out to see them and marveled at how they thus brought in those two knights who had left there that morning. So they went through the street of the town to the public square, to which many people had come. And when they saw the prince, they came up to him weeping to kiss his hands, saying to him: "Sir, if our hearts dared put into execution what our will desires, and if we saw a way to do so, we would all be in your service until death; but we do not know what action to take, since there is no leader or chief among us who knows how to command us."

Don Bruneo said to them: "Oh, people of little courage! Although until now you have been honorable, don't you remember that you are vassals of the king who was father of this youth and of the prince, his brother, who will be king? How do you as native-born subjects repay them what you owe them on seeing your lord killed so treacherously and his sons confined and besieged by that traitorous duke, his enemy?"

"Sir knight," said one of the most honorable men of the town, "you speak great truth; but as we do not have anyone to guide or command us, and as we are all people who lead a life of ranching rather than by bearing arms, we do not know how to give ourselves the security befitting our loyalty. But now since this lord of ours is here, and you are in charge of him, determine what we ought and are able to do, and it will be done at once to the best of our ability."

"You speak as good men," said Don Bruneo, "and it is right that the king should grant favors to you and to all those who subscribe to this vow and opinion; and I come to lead you, and in your company to die or live."

Then he told them about the guard he had left in the town with the other prince, and how they had come with the queen their lady and where they had left her; and how as they were going to the Firm Island, they had met her at sea; and that they should not fear, for with a little help from them, their enemies would be very quickly annihilated and killed. When those people heard this, being greatly heartened and encouraged, they all became quite excited and said: "Sir knight of the Firm Island, since there never has been a knight there who was not fortunate since that famous Amadis of Gaul won it, command and direct for us all that we should do, and it will be done at once."

Don Bruneo thanked them heartily and had the prince thank them; after which he said to them: "Then give orders at once to close the gates of this town and place guards, so that by no one from here our enemy may be warned. And I shall tell you what must be done."

This was carried out immediately, and he said to them: "Then go to your homes and eat, make ready your arms, whatever they may be, and be ready to guard your town; and let there be no fear of those wicked people, for where they are they have enough to worry about in view of the protection remaining with the prince. And as soon as we dine and rest our horses a bit, the prince and I shall go on to another town which this guide whom I bring says is three leagues distant from this one. And we shall take all the people from there and come back here, and I shall conduct you in such a way that your enemies, if they are waiting, will be defeated, laid low and in your power."

They told him that they would do as he ordered, and at once they all went very willingly to do as he had commanded. And they served the prince and Don Bruneo a good meal in the palace that was the king's. And as soon as they had eaten, since it was already past mid-day, they were about to mount in order to leave, when two men on foot arrived who had come at full speed to the gate of the town and had told the guards to let them enter, for they were bringing news which would please them. The guards took them to the prince and Don Bruneo, and they asked them what they were reporting. They said: "Sirs, we have come only to those of this town, for we did not know of the prince's and your arrival, because we had never seen you. And the news that we bring is such that both you and they will be quite pleased to learn it. Now know you that last night many people came out from the town, attacked the guards, and killed and took prisoner many of the duke's men. And when the duke learned of it he hastened there and encountered two foreign knights about whom they tell marvels, for they were killing his men; and he, to rescue the latter, fought with one of them, and with a single blow he knocked the duke from his horse, and he remained in the custody of those of the town; it is not known whether he is dead or alive. None of the troops of the camp know what to do, other than to gather in groups to talk things over; and it seemed to us they were preparing to move from there out of the great fear they have of those foreign knights about whom we are telling you. And we are from a village near here, and had the provisioning of the camp; and when we saw this, we decided to tell it to the gentlemen of this town so that they might be on their guard lest troops in flight harm or rob them."

When Don Bruneo heard this, he went out on horseback, and the prince with him, to the square, and had those who had arrived on foot tell the news to all those assembled there, so that they might be encouraged and heartened; and he said to them: "My good friends, I am of the opinion that I ought not to go farther than here; for according to this news, you and I suffice for the plan I had left for you. Therefore it is necessary that you all be armed at nightfall, and that we leave here; for it would be a great injustice that those of the big town should carry off all the glory of this victory without our sharing in it."

"Everything will be done immediately as you, sir, command," said they.

Thus they were occupied all day making ready their arms with such good will that they longed to be at grips with their enemies, because they already considered them annihilated, and they wanted to avenge themselves for the harm and injuries that they had received from them.

Night having come, Don Bruneo armed himself and mounted his horse, and took all the troops out to the countryside. And he asked the prince to wait there, but he wanted only to go with him. So just as you hear, they all went on their way to the camp; and Don Bruneo, after part of the night had passed, ordered the guide who had come with him, to make the signal to those of the town from where they might see it, as had been agreed upon, and he did so. And as soon as it was seen by them, they at once thought that Don Bruneo had good reinforcements, and immediately they made preparations to sally forth before dawn to attack the camp. But those of the camp had decided on another course of action, for as they saw the duke their lord in the power of their enemies and beheld those fire signals made by night, and because they had lost hope of recovering him; — on the contrary if they stayed it would be very dangerous for them — after part of the night had passed they gathered together all the troops and their baggage train and the wounded; and very secretly, without being noticed, they broke camp and started on the way to their own land; so that before their departure was detected they had traveled a long distance.

Then the hour having come when those of the town sallied forth, and Don Bruneo reached the other side of it, they found nothing; instead, not recognizing each other, as it was night, they might have had a great fight with each other, every one thinking the others were enemies as soon as no troops were discovered between the groups. But when they recognized each other, they were greatly distressed because their adversaries had escaped from them; and immediately they followed their trail, but with great difficulty, for because of the darkness they were at a loss and proceeded gropingly until dawn came. Then they saw them very clearly, and therefore those on horseback hastened and overtook the whole baggage train and the foot soldiers and the wounded; for the rest of the forces, as they were already beaten, had not sought to do guard duty as soon as daylight came, because they were still going through the land of the enemy.

Of those overtaken they killed many, and took others prisoners, seizing a great deal of booty; and with great joy and glory they returned to the town. And then they sent knights to bring the queen; and when she came and saw her sons safe and sound, and her enemy taken prisoner, who can describe the great joy she felt?

Angriote and his companions, since they knew the arrangement of things at the Firm Island, and that those noble lords would be awaiting them, asked the queen for permission to leave, telling her that on an appointed day they were to be on the Firm Island and that since they were no longer needed, they wished to proceed on their way. The queen begged them out of regard for her to stay two days longer, because she wanted in their presence to proclaim her son Garinto king, and to mete out justice to that traitor of a very cruel duke. They said that they would be pleased to be present at the ceremony for her son, but not at the punishment of the duke; for since he was in her power, after their departure she might do with him whatever she liked. The queen gave orders to build at once in the square a large wooden platform, covered with very rich and attractive cloths of gold and silk, and ordered to come there all the leaders of her kingdom who were closest at hand; and they took up there Prince Garinto and the three knights. And they brought the duke, injured as he was, on a hackney without a saddle, and before him they sounded many trumpets hailing the prince as King of Dacia. And Angriote and Don Bruneo placed on his head a very fine crown of gold with many pearls and precious stones.

Thus they remained at those festivities a large part of the day, to the great distress and anguish of that duke who was watching, to whom the people addressed many insults and much abuse. But those knights asked the queen to order him taken away from there, or they would leave, for they did not wish to see any man who was a prisoner and vanquished receive abuse in their presence. The queen ordered him taken to the prison, since she saw his being there irked them; and she begged them to take rich jewels which she caused to be brought there to give to them. But they, however much she besought them, would not take anything except — because they knew that in that land there were very beautiful whippets and beagles — that it be her pleasure to order some given to them for use in the hunting preserves of the Firm Island. At once they brought to them there more than forty from which to choose the most handsome and most to their liking. When the queen saw that they wished to go, she said to them: "My friends and good lords, since you do not wish to take my jewels, it is required that you take one, which is the one I love most in the world, and this is the king my son, whom on my behalf you may present to Amadis, so that in his company and that of his friends he may acquire the good breeding and manners that befit a knight, for with worldly goods he is abundantly provided. And if God brings him to full maturity, he will be better able to become a knight by Amadis's hand than by any other's. And tell him that both through his fame and through your prowess, this kingdom that you have won for me, has been won for him and for you."

They agreed to it as soon as they saw she desired it with such eagerness, and because it was a great honor to have in their company a king such as he, who though of such high rank, was soliciting their company in order to be more worthy.

The queen had a ship very lavishly equipped, as befitted a king, not only with fine adornments but also with rich and precious jewels on board for him to give to the knights and other persons on whom he might wish to bestow them, and his tutor with other servants. And she went with them down to the sea, and from there she returned; and on arriving at the town, ordered the duke executed with dishonor by hanging, so that all might see the fruit that the flowers of treason bore.

They boarded their ships and sailed until they reached that great harbor of the Firm Island, where they were being awaited with keen desire. Having arrived at the port, they sent a message to tell Amadis that they were bringing with them the King of Dacia and the reason why, so that he might see to what should be done at the arrival of such a prince. Amadis mounted his horse, taking only Agrajes with him, and half way down the hill leading up to the castle they met the knights with the king, who came richly clad and on a palfrey wondrously caparisoned. Amadis went up to him and greeted him, and the boy greeted Amadis very courteously, for he had already been told who he was. Afterwards they all embraced each other laughing from the pleasure they took thereby; and thus together they went to the castle, where that king was lodged in the company of Don Bruneo until other youths should come, whom they were expecting. So those lords were on that island waiting for King Lisuarte; and in order to tell about him, we shall leave them until their time comes.

CHAPTER CXXIII

How King Lisuarte and Queen Brisena, his wife and their daughter Leonoreta came to the Firm Island, and how those lords and ladies came out to welcome them.

As has been told, King Lisuarte, after he arrived at Windsor, ordered the queen to get ready the things needed by her and her daughter Leonoreta; and King Arban of North Wales, his chief majordomo, what he himself needed. And everything having been done and made ready in accordance with his eminence, he departed with his retinue. And he was willing to take with him only King Cildadan, and Don Galvanes, and Madasima, the latter's wife — who at the time had arrived there at his command from the Island of Mongaza — and a few others, who were knights of his own and luxuriously garbed; for Gasquilan, King of Suesa, from there had returned to his kingdom.

So with great joy they pursued their journey day by day until they stopped for the night four leagues away from the Island, a fact which was ascertained at once by Amadis and by all the other princes and knights who were with him there. And they decided that all together, and with those ladies accompanying them, they would go forth to welcome them at a distance of two leagues from the Island. Thus it was done, for the next day they all sallied forth, and with all the queens headed by Queen Elisena. The garments and rich adornments that they wore and the fine trappings of their palfreys, one's memory would not suffice to enumerate, nor one's hands to describe in writing. This much I tell you: that neither before nor afterwards was there ever known to have been in the world a company of so many knights of such exalted lineage and such great courage, and so many ladies, queens, and princesses, and other high-born women of such beauty and so well adorned.

Thus together they traversed that plain until King Lisuarte was in sight; who when he saw so many people coming toward him, at once divined what it was all about; and with his whole company he went forward until he encountered King Perion and the Emperor and all the other knights who were coming ahead. All stopped there to embrace each other. Amadis was coming a little behind, talking with Don Galaor his brother, who was still so very weak that he could scarcely ride horseback, and as he arrived near the king he got off his horse. And the king shouted to him not to do so, but he did not stop on that account, and came up on foot; and although the king did not wish it, he kissed his hands. And he went over to the queen, whose mount that handsome youth Esplandian was leading by the rein; and the queen dismounted from her palfrey to embrace him; but Amadis took her hands and kissed them. Don Galaor came up to King Lisuarte; and when the king saw him so weak he went and embraced him, and tears came to the eyes of both. And thus the king held him for a while, for neither was able to speak a word for so long that some said that this emotion was from the pleasure they had in seeing each other, but others characterized it by saying that their remembering the past events, and not having participated together in them as their hearts desired, had brought those tears. This may be ascribed to whatever motive you like; but at any rate it was because they loved each other very much.

Oriana came up to the queen her mother after Queen Elisena had greeted her. And when her mother saw her, the one she most loved, she went to her and took her in her arms; and both would have fallen to the ground if it had not been for some knights who supported them; and the queen began to kiss her on the eyes and the face, saying: "Oh, my daughter, may it please God through His mercy that the hardships and anxiety that this great beauty of yours has given us, that beauty may now be the means of remedying amid great peace and happiness from now on!"

Out of joy Oriana made no reply except to weep. At this juncture Queens Briolanja and Sardamira came up and removed Oriana from her embrace; and they spoke to the queen, and afterwards all the other ladies likewise with great courtesy, for they considered this lady one of the best and most honorable queens in the world. Leonoreta came up to kiss the hands of Oriana, and she embraced her and kissed her many times; and so also did all the matrons and maidens of the queen her mother, who with heart-felt affection loved her more than themselves; for as has been told you, this princess was the most noble and most courteous lady of her time in doing honor to everyone; and for this reason she was very much beloved and cherished by all the men and women who knew her.

The reception having been described, not as it was — for it would be impossible to do so adequately — but as befits the organization of this book, they all went on together to the island. When Queen Brisena saw so many knights and so many ladies and maidens of such high rank with whom she was very well acquainted and knew how high their standing was, and that all were subject to the will and command of Amadis, she was so astonished that she did not know what to say; for until then she had really thought that there was nowhere in the world a house or court equal to that of the king her husband; but having seen what I am telling you about, she thought of her own state as that of a mere count. And as she looked about her, she saw that everybody was walking behind Amadis and that they regarded him as their lord, that the one who was closest to him considered himself the most honored, and that wherever he went, they all went. She marveled at how a knight who never had acquired anything but arms and a horse could win such an exalted status; and although she considered him the husband of her daughter and punctilious in service, she could not avoid having great envy of him, because she had wanted that high standing for her husband, and thereafter Amadis would inherit it through her daughter. Therefore as she saw the situation to be just the opposite, she could not rejoice at it. But as she was very prudent, she pretended not to see it or understand it; and with a happy face and a troubled heart she talked and laughed with all those knights and ladies whom she had surrounding her; for the king, once he had spoken with Galaor, never once left him during that whole journey until they reached the island.

While they were proceeding on their way, Oriana could not take her eyes off Esplandian, for she loved him very much, as was natural. And the queen her mother, who noticed it, said: "Daughter, take this youth to escort you."

Oriana stopped, and the boy came up with very great humility to kiss her hands. Oriana had a great desire to kiss him, but the considerable embarrassment that she felt caused her to refrain. Mabilia came up to him and said to him: "My good friend, I also wish a share of your embrace."

He turned his face with a mien so gracious as to be wonderful to observe, recognizing her at once, and he spoke to her with great courtesy. So they brought him along between them, while talking with him on subjects most pleasing to them; and they were delighted with the way he answered, for his witty conversation and his graciousness made them very happy. And Oriana and Mabilia glanced at each other and then at the youth, and Mabilia said: "Does it seem to you, my lady, that this was fine food for the lioness and her offspring?"

"Oh my lady and friend!" said Oriana, "for Heaven's sake don't remind me of that, for even now I am sick at heart when I think about it!"

"Well, I understand," said Mabilia, "that his father experienced no less danger at sea when he was just as tiny. But God preserved him for what you see here; and so He will do, if it so please Him, for this one, who will surpass him and all those in the world in excellence."

Oriana laughed very heartily and said: "My true sister, it seems to me that you wish to test me to see for which of them I shall indicate a preference. So I do not wish to say, 'may it please God for it to be so,' but that He render both such that they have no equal, just as until now each one at his own age has not had a peer."

While speaking about this and other very agreeable matters, they all arrived at the castle of the Firm Island, where King Lisuarte and the queen his wife were lodged very comfortably where Oriana dwelt, and King Perion and his wife, in Queen Sardamira's quarters. Oriana, with all the other brides-to-be, took the highest of the towers. Amadis had given orders to set the tables in those very fine arcades of the garden; and there he had that whole company dine very splendidly with such an abundance of foods and wines and fruits of all kinds, that it was very wonderful to see. Each one was seated according to protocol, and it was all done in very orderly fashion. Don Cuadragante took with him King Cildadan, whom he loved very much, and each one of all the other knights escorted one of the king's men according to his preference. And Amadis took with him Arban of North Wales, Don Grumedan and Don Guilan the Pensive. Norandel lodged with his good friend Don Galaor. Thus they spent that day with such pleasure as you can well imagine. But what Agrajes did with his uncle and with Madasima, one could in nowise relate or imagine; for he held him in as much respect and reverence as he had always held the king his father; and he had Madasima stay with Oriana and those queens and great ladies who were there, taking Don Galvanes with him to his own quarters. Esplandian at once approached the King of Dacia, who was of his own age and seemed to him a very good fellow, and such mutual affection resulted from the time that they first saw each other, that it lasted all the days of their lives; so that, for very long periods they traveled together after they were knights, and participated in mighty deeds at arms amid extreme danger to their persons, being very courageous knights. This knight was completely the confidant of Esplandian's love affair; through his good advice the latter was relieved many times of great anguish and mortal cares that came to him concerning his lady, and brought him to the point of death. This king I tell you about went to a great deal of trouble to speak to this lady and tell her what this knight was suffering out of love for her and to bid her have pity on his grievous suffering from the pangs of love. These two princes about whom I am telling you, for love of this lady, taking with them Talanque, son of Don Galaor, and Maneli the Moderate, son of King Cildadan — who procreated them with the nieces of Urganda when they were imprisoned, as the second Book of this story tells at great length — and Ambor, son of Angriote de Estravaus, all novice knights, crossed the sea in the region of Constantinople to the land of the pagans, and had there great battles, not only with strong giants but also with other foreigners of different ways; in which battles they participated to their great honor; whereby their extreme prowess and great deeds of chivalry were proclaimed through the whole world, just as at greater length we shall relate to you in that continuation which, called *Esplandian,* stems from this story and tells of the latter's great deeds and of the love affair that he had with the flower and greatest beauty of the entire world, who was that shining star, before whom all other beauty grew pale: Leonorina, daughter of the Emperor of Constantinople, the girl who was a mere child when his father Amadis took leave of her in Greece after going there and slaying the mighty Endriago, as we have already told you.

But let us now leave this until the proper time and return to the present subject-matter of our story. Then the day that they arrived having passed, and another in resting from the journey, the kings gathered together with great pleasure to arrange how the marriages should be solemnized, and for their return to their own lands, for much remained for them to do: some to go to conquer the dominions of their enemies, and others to give them aid to that end.

And while they were together under some trees beside the fountain you already have heard about, they heard loud outcries that the people were making outside the garden, and a great hubbub of voices. And it having been ascertained what this was all about, they were told that the most frightful and strangest thing they had ever seen was approaching by sea. Then the kings asked for their horses and mounted, as did all the other knights, and they went to the harbor. The queen and all the other ladies went up to the top of the tower, which commanded an extensive view of the land and the sea. And they saw a cloud of smoke, blacker and more frightful than any they had ever seen, approaching over the water. All stood still until finding out what it was. And in a short while when the smoke began to clear away, they saw in the midst of it a sea serpent, much larger than the largest galley or ship in the world, and it had such enormous wings that they extended farther than one could shoot an arrow, and it had its tail coiled upward much higher than a tall tower. Its head and mouth and teeth were so big, and its eyes so frightful that there was no one who dared gaze at it; and from time to time it spewed out through its nostrils that very black smoke, which was rising into the sky and with which it was completely covered. It was emitting raucous sounds and hisses so loud and terrifying that it seemed as if the sea was about to sink. It was ejecting from its mouth jets of water so powerful and to such a distance that no ship, however large it might be, could have approached it without being submerged.

The kings and knights, although they were very courageous, gazed at one another and did not know what to say, for they opined and believed that against a thing so frightful and appalling no resistance would suffice, but they stood their ground. The great serpent, as it now drew nearer, made three or four turns through the water, displaying its ferocity and flapping its wings so hard that the clashing of its scales resounded for more than a half league round about. When the horses which those knights were riding saw it, no one was strong enough to restrain his own mount; instead with them their steeds went running away through the countryside until their riders perforce had to dismount from them. Some said that since it was a fierce marine animal, it would not dare to come out on land; and that even if it did leave the water, there would be time for them to take refuge on the island, and that the serpent on seeing the land, was beginning already to suspend its activity.

Then while everybody was marveling at a thing the like of which they had never heard of or seen, they perceived that from the serpent's side they were lowering a small boat entirely covered with very fine cloth of gold, and with a lady in it who at each side had a very elegantly clad page, and she was holding on to their shoulders for support, and two fantastically ugly dwarfs, each rowing one oar, were bringing the boat to land. Those lords were greatly astonished on seeing such a strange sight; but King Lisuarte said: "If this lady is not Urganda the Unknown, don't believe a word I say; for you certainly ought to remember," he added, addressing Amadis, "the fear she inspired in us when we were at my town of Fenusa at the time when she came by sea with those fireworks."

"I thought so," said Amadis, "after I saw her small boat; for before that I thought only that that serpent was some devil with which we would have our hands full."

At this moment the boat reached the shore, and as it was near at hand, they recognized the lady as Urganda the Unknown;

for she was pleased to show herself in her own form, which she seldom did; instead she was wont to assume strange disguises, sometimes that of a very old woman, sometimes that of a very young girl, as has been told in many parts of this story. Thus she arrived with her very handsome and richly adorned pages, for their costumes were at many points embellished and adorned with precious stones of great value. The kings and great lords went ahead on foot just as they were, going alongside the place where she was landing. And as soon as she arrived she left the boat, holding on to the hands of her two handsome pages, and went at once to King Lisuarte to kiss his hands; but the king embraced her and did not wish to yield his hands to her, and King Perion and King Cildadan followed suit. Then she turned to the emperor and said to him: "My good lord, although you do not know me, nor have I ever seen you, I know a great deal about your affairs, not only who you are and the worth of your noble self, but also your high rank. And on this account and because of some services that before long you together with the empress will receive from me, I wish you to know me favorably and to esteem me, so that you may remember me, when you are in your own kingdom, by sending me word of anything in which I may be of service to you; for although it seems to you that this land where I dwell is very far from yours, it would not be for me any great task to travel the whole distance — all of it — in one ordinary day."

The emperor said to her: "My good lady and friend, I consider myself happier to have gained your love and good will than to have won most of my dominions. And since out of your goodness of heart you have invited me to do so, I beg you not to forget what you have promised me; for whether my heart and will are resolved to show you gratitude with all my might, you know better than I."

Urganda said to him: "My lord, I shall see you at a time when by me the first fruit of your procreation will be restored to you."

Then she looked toward Amadis, for she had not had time to be able to speak with him, and said: "Well, noble knight, one ought not to miss your embrace; although, in view of the way favorable fortune has raised you to such heights and placed you at the summit, probably you will not esteem very highly the services and pleasures of us who can be of but little avail, because these mundane things very quickly following the course of world affairs, with but little cause and even without any at all could change. Now that it seems to you that you will be able to spend your life in most carefree fashion, especially since you have in your possession what you most in the world desire and without which everything else would be for you the occasion of grievous loneliness; now it is more necessary to maintain everything with redoubled effort; for Fortune is not content when at such heights it strikes and shows its power, because it would be a much greater disgrace and discredit for your great honor to lose what has been gained, than without it to carry on before it be won."

Amadis said to her: "In view of the large benefits that I have received from you, my good lady, together with the great love that you have always had for me, although for the satisfying of my desires I may have found myself very effective, very poor would I feel on using my resources in matters concerning your honor that might be entrusted to me by you; for what I have won cannot be so great, even were it the whole world, as to render it wrong to risk it in what I am talking about."

Urganda said: "The great love that I have for you causes me to talk nonsense and to give advice where it is not needed."

Then all those knights came up and greeted her, and she said to Don Galaor: "Neither to you, my good lord, nor to King Cildadan do I say anything now, because I shall sojourn here with you for a few days and we shall have time to talk."

And turning to her dwarfs, she ordered them to return to the Great Serpent and to bring her a palfrey in a small boat, and one for each of her pages, which was done at once. The horses of the kings and lords were at some distance away from there, for the fear they had of that fierce creature did not give their riders an opportunity to approach them; and they left men there to put her on her palfrey, and they went on foot to recover theirs. She told them that she earnestly entreated them to approve of no one's escorting her except those two pages, who were devoted to her; so thus it was done, for all the others went ahead to the castle, and she behind them with her retinue; and they continued on until they reached the garden where the queens and the noble ladies were, for she did not want to lodge anywhere else. And before entering with them she said to Esplandian: "To you, very handsome youth, I entrust this treasure of mine for you to keep; for nowhere near here would there be found so fine a one."

Then she handed over to him the pages and entered the garden, where she was so well received by everyone that never was a woman anywhere so welcomed. When she saw so many queens, so many princesses, and an infinite number of other persons worthy of high esteem and who were of high rank, she gazed at them all with great pleasure and said: "Oh, my heart! What can you see from now henceforth, that will not be the cause of great nostalgia, since in one day you have seen the best, most virtuous and most courageous knights that there have ever been in the world, and the most honorable and beautiful queens and ladies ever born? Certainly I can assert that here is perfection of both; and I say even more, for just as here are gathered together all the great prowess at arms and the beauty of the world, so also is love sustained here with the greatest loyalty that it ever has been at any time."

So she went into the tower with those ladies, and she asked permission of the queens to be permitted to room with Oriana and those who were with her, who immediately took her up to Oriana's apartment. When they were in her chamber she could not remove her gaze from Oriana, and Queen Briolanja and Melicia, and Olinda, for no other woman was the equal of these in beauty, and she kept embracing them all. Thus she was with them as if beside herself with pleasure, and they honored her as highly as if she were the mistress of them all.

CHAPTER CXXIV

HOW AMADIS HAD HIS COUSIN DRAGONIS MARRY THE PRINCESS ESTRELLETA AND CAUSED HIM TO GO WIN DEEP ISLAND, OF WHICH HE WOULD BE KING.

Now the story relates that Dragonis, cousin of Amadis and of Don Galaor, was a very honorable young knight of great courage, as he had demonstrated in past events, especially in the battle that King Lisuarte had with Galvanes and his companions over the Island of Mongaza, where this knight — after Don Florestan and Don Cuadragante and many other noble knights had been incapacitated and taken prisoner by Don Galaor and King Cildadan and Norandel and by all the great body of troops on their side that attacked them, and Don Galvanes had been carried to the aforementioned island very badly wounded — stayed with the few that remained on his side, and with his father's knights whom he had there, as the defense and aid of them all; whence because of his prudence and fine efforts they were afforded relief, as the third Book of this story had related in more detail.

He was not on the Firm Island at the time that Amadis arranged the marriages of his brothers and the other knights that you have already heard about, because from the monastery of Lubayna he went off with a maiden to whom he had promised a boon. And he fought with Angrifo, lord of the valley of the Deep Pool, who was holding her father prisoner in order to seize a fortress that he had at the entrance to the valley. And Dragonis had a cruel and mighty battle with him, because that Angrifo was the most valiant knight to be found in those mountains where he dwelt; but he was finally overcome by Dragonis, since the latter was fighting for what was right, and he rescued the father of the maiden from Angrifo's custody, and he commanded Angrifo to go within twenty days to the Firm Island and submit himself to the mercy of Princess Oriana. And because Dragonis was near the Island of Mongaza he wished to see Don Galvanes and Madasima; and while he was with them, the messenger of King Lisuarte arrived with the summons to bring them to the Firm Island, just as the king had promised Agrajes. Dragonis went with them to Windsor, where they were received with much love and great honor. And from there, as you have already heard, he went with the king and queen to the Firm Island, where Dragonis discovered the marriage arrangements and the allotment of sovereignties, as has been related, at which allotment he was greatly pleased. And he highly praised what his cousin Amadis had done, and prepared himself as much as he could to participate in that conquest, for he truly had held the belief that it could not be brought to a conclusion without great deeds at arms. But Amadis, as he loved him sincerely, thought it would be a gross injustice and to his own great shame if such a knight should remain without a goodly share of what he had helped to win with so much effort; so one day taking him aside in that garden, he spoke to him thus: "My lord and good cousin, although your youth and great courage, desirous of increasing your honor in great armed encounters, take from you the wish for greater rank and repose than that which until now you have had, reason, to which all of us are obliged to have recourse as the chief source of virtue, and the opportunity which is offered you, require that your resolve be changed, and that you follow the counsel of my meager understanding and great good will, which has as much regard for you as for my own well-being. I have learned that at the time that we rescued King Lisuarte in Lubayna, with those who fled from the enemy at the outset was the King of the Deep Island, who was wounded; and now I learn from a squire of King Arabigo who has come here that on putting out to sea he at once died. So I consider it good for that island of which he was lord to be yours and I wish that you be named king of it; moreover that by your brother Palomir your father's kingdom be inherited; and that you be married to Princess Estrelleta, who, as you know, is a descendant of kings on both sides, and whom Oriana greatly loves. And all this I deem good and it would please me that it be done, because I would rather force your will to submit to reason than that I should feel such shame, my good cousin, in your not sharing in the bounty that God has given me, just as you, more than anyone else, felt shame when I was badly treated."

Dragonis — although his wish had been to go with Don Bruneo and Don Cuadragante in order to afford them personal aid until they acquired their seigniories, and if he survived that, to go to Roman lands in quest of adventures, and to stay for some length of time with the King of Sardinia, Don Florestan, in order to see him and find out whether he, being a man in a foreign land, needed him for anything; and from there to return to see Amadis at the Firm Island or wherever he might be (and he thought that on these journeys he would be able to win much honor and great fame or die like a knight) — on seeing the great love with which Amadis had said to him what he did, was too embarrassed to answer anything except that he acceded entirely to his desire, for in that matter and to all his commands he would be obedient to him. Therefore he was immediately betrothed to that princess, and the Deep Island, about which you have already heard, designated as his, of which island he was at once named king and became so with very great honor, as later on will be told. This having been done just as you hear, Amadis asked King Lisuarte for the duchy of Bristol for Don Guilan the Pensive, for he had great affection for him; and his consent for him to marry the duchess, whom he loved so much, saying that he would hand over to him the duke [successor to her deceased husband, presumably her brother-in-law], whom he held prisoner there. The king, not only because of his love for Amadis, but also because he had many and great obligations to Don Guilan, and because the duke had been a traitor to him, willingly consented to it. Amadis kissed his hands for it, and Don Guilan wished to kiss Amadis's, but the latter was not willing; instead he embraced him with great love; for in his time, out of all the knights in the world he was the most obliging and the most gentle and kind to his friends.

CHAPTER CXXV

How the kings met to arrange the weddings of those noble lords and ladies, and what was done about it.

The kings assembled again as before, and arranged that the weddings be the fourth day, and that the festivities should last two weeks, at the end of which with all matters settled, they should leave and return to their own lands. The appointed day having come, all the bridegrooms gathered in Amadis's quarters, and they garbed themselves in such rich and costly apparel as their high estate required at such a ceremony. And the brides did likewise; and the kings and great lords took the bridegrooms with them, and mounting their very richly caparisoned palfreys, they went to the garden, where they found the queens and brides likewise on their palfreys. So thus all together they sallied forth to the church, where preparations for the mass had been made by the holy man Nasciano. The solemnizing of the marriages and marriage contracts having taken place with the impressiveness that Holy Church requires, Amadis came up to King Lisuarte and said to him: "Sire, I wish to ask of you a boon that will not be difficult for you to grant."

"I grant it," said the king.

"Then, sire, tell Oriana that before the dinner hour, she submit to the test of the Enchanted Arch of faithful lovers, and the Forbidden Chamber, which until now on account of her great sadness, it has never been possible for her to undergo, however much she has been besought and entreated by us; for because of her fidelity and her exceeding beauty, I have so much confidence that she will enter with no hindrance there where in the last hundred years no woman, however much she excelled others, has been able to enter, because I saw Grimanesa there where she was modelled with great skill by her husband Apolidon as realistically as if she were alive, and her great beauty does not equal Oriana's. And in that chamber prohibited to all other women shall be celebrated our wedding feast."

The king said to him: "My good son and lord, it is easy for me to comply with what you request; but I am afraid that with it we may cause some perturbation at these festivities because frequently — in fact usually — it happens that one's great earnestness of will deceives one's eyes, which make judgments contrary to reality; and so it might happen to you with my daughter Oriana."

"Don't worry about that," said Amadis, "for my heart tells me that just as I say, it will be realized."

"Since that is your pleasure, so be it," said the king.

Then he went to his daughter, who was among the queens and the other brides, and said to her: "Daughter, your husband asks of me a boon, and it cannot be carried out except by you. I want you to make good my promise."

She knelt before him, kissed his hands, and said: "Sire, may it please God that in some fashion an opportunity may come about for me to be able to serve you; and do command whatever you like, for it will be done if it can be carried out by me."

The king raised her up and kissed her on the cheeks, saying to her: "Daughter, then it is fitting that before you dine, the Arch of faithful lovers and the Forbidden Chamber be tested by you, for this is what your husband asks of me."

When this was heard by all those people, many were pleased to see the test carried out, and it occasioned great perturbation for others; because, since it was such a difficult thing to accomplish and so many ladies of such standing had failed in it, they indeed thought that glory would be achieved by completing it, just as by failing in it, one would run the risk of being discredited and embarrassed. But since they saw that the king was commanding it and Amadis was asking for it, they did not want to say anything except that it should be done.

So just as they were, they left the church, and on horseback they came to the boundary beyond which no man or woman was permitted to penetrate, unless worthy to do so. Then having arrived there, Melicia and Olinda told their husbands that they too wanted to try that adventure; whereupon the hearts of the latter were overjoyed at seeing the great loyalty with which they exhibited such daring; but fearing some reverse might come to them, they told them that they were very happy and satisfied with their choice of wives; and as far as they were concerned, the latter should not assume that solicitude. But the ladies told them they had to try it, for if they had been elsewhere, they could reasonably have been excused from it; but there, where no reason sufficed, they did not want it thought that they had omitted it on account of their inward feelings.

"Since that is the way it is," said the husbands, "we cannot deny receiving from this the greatest favor that ever could come to us from any source."

This they said at once to King Lisuarte and the other lords: "In the name of God," they said in reply, "and may He be pleased that it be so auspiciously that the festivities in which we are engaged be very joyously augmented."

There they all dismounted and it was decided that Melicia and Olinda should enter first, and so it was done, for one after the other they passed beyond the barrier, and very shortly they were under the arch; and they entered the abode where Apolidon and Grimanesa used to stay, and the trumpets that the image above it was holding played very sweetly so that all were greatly cheered by such a tune, for never had they — with the exception of those who had already seen and made the test — ever witnessed anything like it.

Oriana reached the barrier, turned her face toward Amadis and wavered blushing deeply, then turned to enter; and on arriving at the center of the place, the image began the sweet melody. And when she came under the arch, there issued from the mouth of the trumpet so many roses and other flowers in such profusion that the ground was entirely covered with them, and the melody was so sweet and so different from the one played for the other ladies that all experienced such great delight that as long as it lasted, they thought it proper not to leave there; but when she passed through the arch, the melody ceased at once. Oriana found Olinda and Melicia looking at those figures and their names, which were inscribed on the jasper; and when they saw her they went to her very joyously and linking arms with her they returned to the image. And Oriana looked very closely at Grimanesa's image, and saw quite clearly that neither one of those ladies, nor any of those who were outside were as beautiful as she; and she greatly feared the Forbidden Chamber test, for in order to enter it she had to surpass Grimanesa in beauty; and if it had been left to her she would have given up trying it, though she had never had any misgivings about the Enchanted Arch test, for she well knew the secret of her heart: namely, that it had never been given to anyone but her lover Amadis.

Thus they tarried a while and would have stayed longer, except that the time of day was such that they were being expected back; and they decided to come out as they were, all three together, so contented and so happy, that to those who were waiting for them and watching they seemed to have enhanced their beauty a great deal; and they themselves really thought that any of them would suffice to conclude favorably the adventure of the Chamber. And this, as I say, caused the great joy that they felt; for just as with joy all beauty is enhanced, so on the other hand, with sadness it languishes and diminishes. Their three husbands, Amadis and Agrajes and Don Bruneo, who had accomplished that adventure as the second Book of this story has already told you, went toward them, which none of the others who were there could do; and as they came up to them, the trumpet began the melody and to strew flowers, which fell on their heads, and their husbands embraced and kissed them; and thus all six issued forth.

This test having been accomplished, they decided to proceed to that of the Chamber, but there were some present who had grave misgivings about their ability to accomplish it. Then when they all arrived at the appointed place, which was in the castle hall, Grasinda came up to Amadis and said to him: "My lord, even if my beauty is not such as to enable me to realize my heart's desire, I cannot constrain my folly to the point of ceasing to desire to undergo the test at this entrance point, for certainly I would never cease to regret it if this test were completed without my trying it; and whatever the result, I still want to attempt it."

Amadis, who was thinking only that all the other ladies should try it before his lady did, so that she might have a complete victory over them all — for he had no doubt of her being able to accomplish it, as he did have concerning the others — replied to her: "My good lady, I consider nothing less than nobility of heart that you should say you wish to accomplish what so many beautiful ladies have failed to do; and so let it be done."

Then he took her by the hand and led her forward saying: "Ladies, this very beautiful lady wishes to test herself here, and so, my ladies Olinda and Melicia, should you do; for it should be considered great obstinacy, since God distributed among you all such extreme beauty, if in such an outstanding event you should fail out of any fear to utilize it, and it is possible that it will be accomplished by some one of you, and you will free Oriana from the great fear that she has."

This he said in public, but it was all feigned; for he well knew, as has been said, that it could be accomplished by none of them except his lady, for never could Grimanesa in her own time nor any other lady afterwards in any degree approach her beauty.

Everybody said that thus it should be done; and then Grasinda commended herself to God and entered the prohibited place, with but slight effort reaching the pillar of copper; and she went forward, and on approaching the pillar of marble, was stopped; but she with effort and the great courage that she demonstrated there — much more than was expected of a woman — reached the pillar of marble; but there without any pity she was seized by her very beautiful hair and thrown out of the place so stunned that she was in a faint. Don Cuadragante took her with him, and although he knew for certain that she was in no danger because of her swoon, he could not avoid being disturbed about it and having great pity for her; because as regards this knight, since he was now middle-aged and his heart had never been captivated by any woman any more than he himself could have been, what previously had been forgotten, plus what was now present, suddenly had disturbed him in such wise that he would not yield superiority to any man there in desiring and loving his lady.

So then came Olinda the Moderate with Agrajes leading her by the hand, for he was encouraging her greatly, although inwardly he had very little hope, for his great love and affection for her did not keep him from recognizing that she did not match Grimanesa in beauty; but he indeed thought that she would measure up to the foremost ladies. And on arriving at the place, he released her hand, and she entered and went directly to the pillar of copper, and from there passed on to the marble one, for she perceived nothing. But when she sought to continue on, the resistance was so great that no matter how much she persisted, she could not move forward more than a step, and then she was thrown out, like the other lady.

Melicia went in with excellent self-restraint and a gallant heart, for thus she was very graceful and very beautiful. And she passed so far beyond both of the pillars, that they all thought that she would enter the chamber; and Oriana, who thought so also, was completely beside herself with anxiety. But going one step farther than Olinda, she was immediately stunned, and like the others, taken out without any pity as unconscious as if she were dead; for the farther they went in, the worse in degree was the penalty meted out to each lady; and thus it had been done to the knights before Amadis had accomplished his feat. The rage that Don Bruneo experienced on Melicia's account moved many to pity; but those who knew how slightly she was endangered thereby, laughed heartily as they watched.

This having been done, Amadis brought Oriana forward, in whom all the beauty in the world was combined, and she reached the place, walking calmly and with a very modest mien; and crossing herself and commending herself to God, she went ahead, for without feeling anything she passed the pillars; and when she came within one step of the chamber she felt many hands that were pushing her and turning her about, so forcefully that three times they turned her around before she approached the marble pillar. But she merely pushed them aside with her own very beautiful hands, and it seemed to her that she was in contact with other arms and hands. And thus with much persistence and great courage, and especially with her great beauty, which was superior to that of Grimanesa, as has been said, very weary she reached the door of the room, and grasped one of the lintels;

then there came out that arm and hand which had laid hold of Amadis, and seized her by one hand and she heard more than twenty voices chanting very sweetly: "Welcome to the noble lady, who through her own great beauty has surpassed that of Grimanesa; and she will keep the knight company who, by being more valiant and vigorous at arms than that Apolidon — who in his time had no peer — won the sovereignty of this island; and by his descendants it will be ruled for long generations together with other great seigniories that they will win with it as their base."

Then the arm and the hand gave a tug, and Oriana entered the chamber, where she found herself as happy as if she were mistress of the world, and not so much on account of her beauty as because her lover Amadis, being the lord of that island, without any hindrance could keep her company in that beautiful chamber, while dispelling the hope that thence-forth any other lady, however beautiful she might be, might come to test herself. Isanjo, the knight who was governor of that island, then said: "Ladies and gentlemen, the enchantments of this island at this moment are all dissolved without any remaining; for thus was it established by that one who left them here; for he did not intend them to last any longer than it would take to find a lord and lady who would consummate these adventures, as this lord and lady have done. And without hindrance all the ladies can enter there, just as the men have done since Amadis's accomplishment."

Then the kings and queens entered, as did the other knights and ladies and maidens who were there, and they saw the richest and most delightful dwelling place that was ever seen, and they all embraced Oriana as if they had not seen her for a long time. So great was the pleasure and joy of all that they did not think of dining or of anything else but looking at that very extraordinary chamber. Amadis gave orders at once to bring the tables into that great chamber, and this was done. Finally the brides and grooms and the monarchs and those others for whom there was room took their ease and dined in the chamber, where they were very well served with many and diverse viands, and fruits of all kinds and wines.

Then night having come, after dining, in that very beautiful section of the room that we have already told you about in the second Book, which was much more luxurious than all the rest of it and was partitioned off by a wall of glass, they made up a bed for Amadis and Oriana where they dwelt, and for the emperor and the other knights with their wives in the other rooms, of which there were many very sumptuous ones; in which, by satisfying their great and mortal desires, because of which they had suffered many dangers and great anxieties, they made matrons those ladies who were not; and those who were had no less pleasure than they with their greatly beloved husbands.

CHAPTER CXXVI

How Urganda the Unknown assembled all those kings and knights who were on the Firm Island; and the great past, present and future events about which she told them; and how she finally departed.

The story relates that after these great wedding festivities that took place on the Firm Island, Urganda the Unknown asked the kings to order all the knights and ladies and maidens to assemble because she wanted to speak to them about the cause of, and reason for her coming — a request with which they ordered compliance.

Then with all of them gathered in a great hall of the castle, Urganda took a seat apart, holding those two pages of hers by the hands; and when all became silent, awaiting what she might say, she spoke as follows: "My lords and ladies, without being told I found out about this very great festival following all the deaths and losses that have taken place because of you; and God is my witness that if any part or all of those misfortunes could have been prevented by me, on account of no personal hardship would I have failed to devote all my efforts to that end. But as it was permitted by that supreme Lord, it was through His favor given to me to know about it, but not to remedy it; because what is ordained by Him, no one except Him is powerful enough to obviate. And since the misfortune could not have been avoided by my presence, I decided by means of it to excel in what I think is good, in accordance with the great love that I have for many of you and you for me; and also to declare openly a few facts (which previously I told you in veiled terms, according to my custom) in order that you may believe that I have told you the truth, just as in other things that at times you have heard from me previously." Then she looked toward Oriana and said: "My good lady and beautiful bride, you must recall clearly that when I was with the king your father and the queen your mother, in the town of Fenusa, lying with you in your bed, you asked me to tell you what was going to happen to you, and I begged you not to try to find out; but because I recognized your desire, I told you that the lion of the Fearful Island was going to leave his den, and with his loud roars your caretakers would be frightened; so that the lion would lay hands on your flesh, with which he would give relief to his great hunger; so one ought to recognize clearly what I meant: that this husband of yours, much stronger and braver than any lion, went forth from this island, which very rightly one can call Fearful, where he has so many very secret dens, and with his forces amid great outcry the fleet of the Romans which was guarding you was overwhelmed and destroyed; so that you were left in his strong arms, and he possessed himself of your flesh as everybody saw, without which his ravenous hunger could never have been satisfied or appeased. So you will recognize in all respects that I told the truth."

Then she said to Amadis: "Then you, good sir, very clearly will perceive to be the truth everything that at that time I told you: namely, that your blood you would give for another's, when in the battle of Ardan Canileo the Feared you gave it for your friends King Arban of North Wales and Angriote de Estravaus, who were prisoners; for when in the hands of your enemy, you saw your good sword with which he was harassing your flesh and bones, you certainly would have preferred to see it out of sight in some lake; then the reward that from this accrued to you, what was it? Certainly, none other than anger and great enmity that over the Island of Mongaza, which you won at that time, came into being between King Lisuarte, here present, and yourself, as everyone very clearly has seen; for this gain I told you you would obtain from it.

"Then the things I wrote to you, very virtuous King Lisuarte, at the time when that very handsome youth Esplandian, your grandson, you found in the forest hunting with the lioness, you well remember; and what I said concerning what is now past, you will see that I knew because he was reared by three very different nurses; namely, the lioness, the ewe and the woman, who all suckled him. Also I informed you that this young man would effect peace between you and Amadis. I leave for you and him to judge how much anger, how much severity and enmity his very attractive good looks have dispelled from your desires; and how because of him and his great discretion you were rescued by Amadis at a time that you were expecting nothing but death. So whether such service as this was worthy to remove enmity and attract love, I leave to these lords to judge. Then as regards the other things that will happen in due course, just as the letter showed you, let them remain to be judged by those who are then alive; for in view of the past they can well believe the future to have been previously known to me. I made to you another prophecy, much more important than any of these, in which is contained all that happened to you in the course of your handing over your daughter Oriana to the Romans, and the great misfortunes and cruel deaths that resulted from it; which prophecy, in order not to recall to your memory at a time when one ought to be having so much enjoyment an event from which you may have distress and annoyance, I leave for those who wish to see it, in the second Book; by means of it they will see clearly that all the things that have happened are there contained and said by me beforehand. Now that I have told you of past events, I want you to know the present, of which you have no knowledge."

Then she took by their hands the handsome pages Talanque and Maneli the Moderate — for such was the latter's name — and said to Don Galaor and King Cildadan: "My good friends, if you have received from me any vital services and help, I declare myself satisfied with the reward that I have; for it will be sufficient glory for me, since I myself am sterile, to have been the cause of there having been born of other women such handsome youths as here you see that I have; for without any doubt you can believe if God permits them to reach the age of eligibility for knighthood and to obtain the same, they will perform such deeds in His service and in upholding truth and virtue that not only those who against the command of Holy Church engendered them, and I who caused it, will be pardoned, but their merits and deserts will be so augmented that, not only in this world but also afterwards in the other, they will obtain great repose and I even more; and because the deeds that will be accomplished by these youths, no matter how much I might say, I would not finish describing, I leave them for the proper time, which will not be long delayed, in view of the ages of the protagonists."

Then she said to Esplandian: "You, very handsome and fortunate young Esplandian, who were engendered in love's fierce fire by those from whom you have inherited a very large share of it — without their losing a single bit — which your tender and unsophisticated age at present holds concealed, take this youth Talanque, son of Don Galaor, and this Maneli the Moderate, son of King Cildadan, and love them both equally; for although on their account you will be involved in many dangerous confrontations, they will aid you in others, in which no one else would be capable of doing so. And this great Serpent that brought me here I leave for you, and in it you will be dubbed a knight and provided with that horse and those arms that it holds hidden and enclosed within itself, with other and strange things that at the time your knighting is accomplished will be made manifest to you. This Serpent will be a guide in the first affair in which your strong heart will give an indication of its great excellence; this Serpent amid tremendous storms and mishaps, without any danger will carry you and many others of your eminent lineage over the broad ocean, where with great dangers and travail you will repay the Lord of the world for some of the great favors that you have received from Him; and in many places you will be known only as the Knight of the Great Serpent, and thus you will travel for many long days without having repose; for, besides the dangerous encounters that will take place because of you, your spirit will be placed in complete affliction and great anxiety by that lady by whom the seven fiery red letters on your left side will be read and understood. And that great fire and ardor which will never be quenched until the large flocks of cormorants pass from the east over the rough waves of the sea, and place in such dire straits the great eagle that it does not dare to take refuge even in its narrow eyrie; and the haughty stone falcon, more precious and beautiful than all the other birds of prey, joins with many others of its lineage and other birds that are not, comes to its aid and wreaks such destruction on the cormorants that that entire countryside is covered with their plumage and many of them perish in the clutches of their very sharp claws, and others are drowned in the water, overtaken by the strong stone falcon and his cohorts. Then the great sea-eagle will draw out most of their entrails, and will put them in the sharp claws of its ally, with which the former will cause it to lose and to cease to have that ravenous hunger that has held it quite tormented for a long time; and by making it the possessor of all its forests and great mountainous regions it will be brought back to its perch in the tree of the holy garden. At this time this great Serpent, there being fulfilled for it the hour set by my extensive learning, in the presence of everyone will be swallowed up by the mighty ocean, as a notice to you that it is more fitting for you to spend the rest of your life on dry land than on the uncertain sea."

Having said this, she said to the kings and knights: "My good lords, I have to go elsewhere on an unavoidable journey, but at the time that Esplandian will be ready to receive knighthood, as will all these young squires who together with him will receive it, I know very well that at that time, by a circumstance that is hidden from you there will be here assembled many of you who are now present; and at that time I shall come, and in my presence will be held that great festival for the novice knights, and I shall tell you many of the great and marvelous things that will come about later. And I admonish you all that no one should make bold to approach the Serpent until I return; if anyone does, everyone in the world will not suffice to keep him from losing his life. And because you, my lord Amadis, hold here a prisoner that evil man of wicked deeds, Arcalaus — who is called the Enchanter, and with his evil knowledge which has always been used to harm others, might be able to injure you — take these two rings, one will be yours and the other Oriana's, for as long as you wear them on your hands, nothing that is done by him can injure you or any one else of your court, nor will his enchantments have any effect while you hold him prisoner. And I tell you not to kill him — because by dying he would not compensate in any way for the evil deeds done by him — but to place him in an iron cage, where everybody may see him, and there let him die many times over; for much more painful is the death that leaves the person alive, than the one whereby he dies and passes away completely."

Then to Amadis and Oriana she gave the rings, which were the most splendid and rarest that ever had been seen. Amadis said to her: "My lady, what can I do that might be to your liking, in payment for so many honors and favors that I am receiving from you?"

"Not anything," said she; "because for all that I have done and may do from now on, you repaid me at the time that I was not able to take advantage of my knowledge, and you restored to me that very handsome knight, who is what I love most in the world — although his feeling for me is the opposite — when by force of arms you defeated the four knights in the castle of the Causeway, where they were keeping him from me by holding him prisoner; and you defeated the lord of the castle at the time that you made your brother Don Galaor a knight. And just as with that great benefaction, this life of mine, which could not be endured without him, was restored, so will it be devoted, during all the days that the very powerful Lord leaves it in this world, to matters pertaining to your advancement."

Then she gave orders that her palfrey be brought, and all those lords escorted her to the seacoast, where she found her dwarfs and boat. Then having bade them all farewell, she got into that boat and they watched her return to the Great Serpent; and at once the smoke was so black that for more than four days nothing enveloped in it could be seen; but at the end of that time it was removed from their view, and they saw the Serpent as before. They did not find out what had become of Urganda.

This leave-taking over, those lords returned to the island to resume their games and great merrymaking attendant upon those weddings. Finally, all matters having been settled, the emperor asked Amadis for permission to leave, because, if it was acceptable to him, he wanted to return with his wife to his own land to reorganize that great sovereignty which by God's will Amadis had given him, and he asked that Don Florestan, King of Sardinia, go with him; and he said that at once he would hand over to him the entire seigniory of Calabria, as Amadis had recommended to him, and that everything else he would divide with him as with a true brother, which he did; for after this Arquisil, Emperor of Rome, arrived in his great empire, he was received by everyone very affectionately, and he always had in his company that vigorous and valiant knight Don Florestan, King of Sardinia and prince of Calabria, by whom both he himself and the whole empire were benefited and honored, as subsequently we shall relate to you.

Having bade farewell to Amadis, this emperor, after pledging himself and his realm to carry out his wishes and commands, taking with him his wife, whom he loved more than himself, and that very noble and courageous knight Florestan, whom he regarded as a brother, and the very beautiful Queen Sardamira, and bringing along the body of the Emperor Patin and that of the very brave knight Don Floyan — which were in the monastery of Lubayna, having been placed there by command of King Lisuarte — and that of Prince Salustanquidio (which at the time that Amadis and his companions had brought Oriana there to the Firm Island he had ordered placed in a chapel very honorably so that in his own land he might be given the interment befitting his high estate); and together with all the Romans who had been taken prisoner on the Firm Island, they all having embarked on the ships of the great fleet that the Emperor Patin had left in the harbor of Windsor, which he had ordered brought from there, he returned to his empire.

All the other kings and lords made preparation to depart for their own lands. But before their departure they decided to plan how those knights who were to go and conquer the domain of Sansuenia and that of King Arabigo and the Deep Island might proceed with such safeguards as to enable them without any opposition to accomplish what was essential.

Amadis spoke with King Lisuarte, telling him that he thought, in view of the length of time that he had been away from his land, that he might be experiencing some anxiety; and if so, he asked as a favor that he not delay any longer on his account. The king said to him that on the contrary he had taken his ease there with great enjoyment, though now it was time to do as he said; but that if his help were needed by those knights for what they were undertaking, he would willingly give it to them. Amadis thanked him very much and said that since the original lords were held prisoners, no more reinforcements would be needed than the troops that were remaining there with King Perion, their lord; and that in case Lisuarte's aid was necessary he would take it as from a lord whom they all were to serve, and that conquest was being undertaken to that end. The king told him that since that was his opinion, he planned to leave at once. But first, he had all those lords and ladies assembled together in the great hall, because he wanted to talk to them. Then all being assembled, King Lisuarte said to King Cildadan: "Your great loyalty, which during past events has extricated me from many dangers and has saved me much anguish — that loyalty torments and afflicts me, because I don't know how to determine a way to reward it; and if I were to give a reward commensurate with what its great merit deserves, it would be useless to search for it, since it could not be found. And coming to what is in my hands as a possibility, I say that just as your noble person for the sake of what pertained to serving me has been involved in many dangerous situations, so my own person with everything in its power will be ready with complete willingness to carry out everything that may enhance your honor, by freeing you from this day forth from the vassalage in which your contrary fortune placed you under my overlordship, so that what up to now has been done under compulsion, be from now on, if it be your pleasure, accomplished willingly as between good brothers."

King Cildadan said to him: "Whether one ought to be grateful for this or not, I leave to those to judge, who on account of some compulsion, have had reason to follow another's will rather than their own, where anxiety and sighs always accompany them. And you may, my lord, believe that the willingness that until now you commanded by force and with dislike on my part, from now on with love and more soldiers and more obedience and respect will follow you in whatever matters be most to your liking; and let this await a time when it can be demonstrated by your experiencing it."

All those great lords considered very virtuous what King Lisuarte did, and many praised him highly for it; but none so highly as did Don Cuadragante, who always had been exclusively concerned with how that shame and very great misfortune that was weighing upon that kingdom — of which he was a native, and had been formerly greatly honored and elevated above all others — might be rid of that very great and dishonorable servitude. King Lisuarte asked King Cildadan what he desired to do, because he himself planned to return to his own land. He replied that, if it was agreeable to him, he would remain there in order to make plans for his uncle Don Cuadragante's expedition to win the seigniory of Sansuenia, and even, if it were necessary, he would go with him. The king told him that his decision was well taken and that he was pleased to have him do so, and that if any of his own forces were needed, he would send them to him immediately. He thanked him heartily for the offer, and said that he really thought those that they would be able to send from there would suffice, since Barsinan was imprisoned.

Thereupon King Lisuarte and his company departed. Amadis and Oriana went with him, although he did not wish it, for nearly a day's journey; from which they returned to plan the matter about which you have heard, which was settled in this fashion: inasmuch as the kingdom of King Arabigo bordered on the seigniory of Sansuenia, that Don Cuadragante and Don Bruneo should go together and immediately at the outset should seize what might be most expugnable by reason of being weakest; and that the rest would be easier to conquer.

And Don Galaor said that he wanted to go, and that his cousin Dragonis should go with him, since in only a short while he would be able to take up arms; for he, with all the resources he might be able to muster in his own kingdom, intended to help him conquer that Deep Island. And Don Galvanes told him that he also wanted to go on that same expedition, and that he would be able to bring a good force for it from the Island of Mongaza.

With this agreement Don Galaor left with that very beautiful queen Briolanja, his wife, and Dragonis with them; and Don Galvanes and Madasima departed for their own land in order to make ready as quickly as they could for that journey.

Agrajes, although he was earnestly entreated to remain on the Firm Island with Amadis, did not wish to do so; instead he said that he would accompany Don Bruneo with the troops of the king his father, and that he would not depart from him until he left him king and his realm in peace, and so said Don Brian de Monjaste to Don Cuadragante; and all the other knights who were there made similar statements, especially the good and vigorous Angriote of Estravaus; for no matter what reasons Amadis set forth to him as to why he should go take his ease in his own land, he was never able to dissuade him from going with Don Bruneo de Bonamar.

All these, with fresh arms and armor, and valiant hearts, taking with them the troops from Spain, those from Scotland and from Ireland, and from the Marquis of Troque, father of Don Bruneo, those from Gaul, and those of the King of Bohemia, and many other companies that came there from other regions, embarked in a large fleet, all having earnestly implored Grasandor to remain with Amadis in order to keep him company, hence the former stayed behind much against his will, for he would have preferred to make that journey. But he did not stay here in vain, nor Amadis either, for frequently they sallied forth and accomplished great deeds at arms, righting many wrongs and injuries that were done to matrons and maidens and other persons who with their own hands or facilities were unable to defend themselves, and by whom they were sought out, just as the story will relate to you subsequently.

King Cildadan, as he loved Don Cuadragante very much, besought him as insistently as he could to be allowed to accompany him; but he would in nowise consent to it; instead he begged him out of regard for him to go at once to his kingdom, in order to cheer and console the queen, his wife, and all his men with the good news he was bringing which he could very well tell: namely, that if by doing punctiliously his duty, he had lost his liberty, by maintaining his honor and fulfilling that to which he was obligated under the promise he had made and the oath he had taken, he had regained it.

Gastiles, nephew of the Emperor of Constantinople, had sent all his troops with Marquis Saluder, and he remained behind to see how that whole business came out, so that he might be able to tell the emperor his lord the whole story. And when he saw what was being done, he spoke with Amadis and told him that he was very sorry not to have troops at his disposal to help those knights on such a military expedition, but that if Amadis thought it a good idea he would go in person with some of those men who had remained with him. Amadis said to him: "My lord, what has been done ought to suffice, for because of your uncle and you I am afforded all the honor you see, and may it please God through His mercy to bring me to a time when I may render services to him in payment thereof. And you, my lord, leave at once, and kiss his hands for me, and tell him that all that was won in this past affair, he won; and that it will always be at his service and at that of whomsoever he may designate. And also I enjoin you to kiss the hands for me of very beautiful Leonorina and Queen Menoresa, and tell them I shall fulfill what I promised them, and I shall send them a knight of my family, by whom they will be enabled to be very well served."

"That I well believe," said Gastiles, "for there are so many of them in it that they would suffice for the whole world."

Whereupon he took his leave and boarded his ship, whence for the present no more will be told about him until the proper time.

What you have heard having been agreed upon and made ready, the grand fleet went out to sea from the harbor with all those knights imbued with that same courage that their great hearts were accustomed to give them in other dangerous confrontations. Amadis remained on the Firm Island and Grasandor with him, as has been told; and with Oriana there remained Mabilia and Melicia, and Olinda and Grasinda, praying God to help their husbands. King Perion and Queen Elisena, his wife, returned to Gaul. Esplandian and the King of Dacia and the other youths stayed with Amadis, waiting for the time for them to become knights, and for Urganda the Unknown, who was to arrange for the ceremony, as she had promised and stated.

But now the story ceases to speak of those knights who were going to conquer those seigniories, and of all the other matters, in order to relate what happened to Amadis after he had been there for some time.

CHAPTER CXXVII

HOW AMADIS DEPARTED ALONE WITH THE MATRON WHO HAD COME BY SEA, IN ORDER TO AVENGE THE DEATH OF THE DEAD KNIGHT WHOM SHE WAS BRINGING ON THE SHIP, AND WHAT HAPPENED TO AMADIS ON THAT QUEST.

Just as you have heard, Amadis remained on the Firm Island with his lady Oriana in the greatest delight and pleasure that ever a knight enjoyed and from which he would not have wished to be separated, were he to be made lord of the world; for just as when he was absent from his lady the cares and sorrows and anxieties of his impassioned heart were wont to torment him to the maximum degree without his finding anywhere relief or respite, so everything was reversed to the maximum when he was in her presence and beholding that great beauty of hers, which had no equal; and thus all past events left his memory, for he had no thought of anything but that fortunate situation in which he found himself at the moment. But as in the perishable things of this world there can be no happy ending, since God has not sought to provide any — for when we here think we have reached the goal of our desires, immediately and forthwith we are tormented by others as great or perchance greater — after some time, Amadis, on coming to his senses and recognizing that now unopposed he had all that for his very own, began to remember his past life, how greatly to his honor and glory up to that time he had pursued a career at arms and how, if he continued for long to lead a life of domesticity, his fame could be obscured and discredited, and was thereby greatly distressed, not knowing what to do with himself. And sometimes he mentioned it very humbly to Oriana, his lady, begging her quite earnestly to give him permission to leave there and go somewhere where he believed his help would be needed; but she, since she saw herself in that island away from her father and mother and from all her kind, and not having any other consolation or company except him to satisfy her loneliness, was never willing to grant him his request; instead with many tears she always begged him to rest his body from the travail that until then he had undergone, likewise telling him to remember that those friends of his had gone at such grave danger to themselves and their troops as might befall them in order to acquire those dominions, and if they should suffer there some reverses, that by staying there he would be much better able to go to their aid than from elsewhere — with all this and with many attempts at amorous persuasion striving to detain him. But as you have been told many times in this great story that the innermost being of this knight from his childhood on had been ablaze with that great fire of love that came to him from the first day that he began to love her, and there was coupled with this the great fear of angering her in any way or of disobeying her commands, at whatever cost to himself, with very little pressure, although his desire underwent great anguish, he was kept at home.

So now determined to do his lady's bidding, he decided with Grasandor, that while they were awaiting some news of the fleet they would go forth to scour the woods and engage in hunting in order to give their bodies some exercise — a project which was organized immediately, and with their beaters and dogs they left the island; for as you have been told in this Book, there were nearby better wooded areas and river valleys full of bear and wild pigs and deer, and many other animals, and river fowl, than could be found in any other such region. And they bagged much of it all, with which at night they — both men and women — went back to the island well content, and they led this life for some length of time.

So then it happened that Amadis, being one day among beaters on a hillside near the seashore, waiting for some wild boar or beast of prey, and holding by the leash a very beautiful dog of which he was quite fond, looked toward the sea and saw from afar off a boat coming toward where he was. And when it was nearer, he saw in it a matron and a man who was rowing it; and because it seemed to him that it must be something unusual, he left the beaters where they were, and went down the hill with his dog, passing through the thick undergrowth without any of his company seeing him. And on reaching the shore, he found that that matron and that man who came with her were dragging out of the boat a dead knight, completely armor-clad; and they laid him on the ground with his shield beside him. Amadis, when he came up to them, said: "Lady, who is that knight and who killed him?"

The matron turned her head, and although she saw him in hunting clothes such as knights were accustomed to wear on such expeditions, and alone, she recognized at once that it was Amadis, and began to tear her headdress and clothes, making very great lamentations and saying: "Oh, lord Amadis of Gaul, on account of what you owe to chivalry help this sad, unfortunate woman, and because these hands of mine took you from the belly of your mother and fashioned the ark in which you were cast into the ocean; for you were born to rescue and help the distressed and persecuted of this world in such affliction as that which has overtaken me!"

Amadis felt very sorry for the matron, and when he heard those words, he looked at her more carefully than before, and immediately comprehended that it was Darioleta, the woman who was with the queen his mother at the time that he was engendered and born; whereupon his sorrow was greatly increased. And he came up to her and removing her hands from her hair, most of which was white, he asked her why it was that she was weeping and tearing her hair so violently, saying that she should tell him about it at once, and that he would not fail to risk his life in order to repair her great loss. The matron, when she heard this, knelt before him and sought to kiss his hands, but he would not give them to her; and she said to him: "Then, sir, it is emergent that without going anywhere else where you might be hindered, you enter this boat with me at once, and I shall guide you to where my distress can be remedied; and on the way I shall relate to you my misfortune."

Amadis, as he saw her so grieved and under such great stress of emotion, thought that the matron had indeed suffered some grave affront. And as he saw himself unarmed, except only for his very good sword, and realized that if he should send for his arms and armor, Oriana would prevent him from going with the matron, he decided to arm himself with the dead knight's armor. And so he did, for he gave orders to that man to disarm the corpse and arm him, which was done immediately. And taking the matron with him, and the man who was rowing, he quickly entered the boat. And as they were about to leave the shore, by chance there approached one of those beaters of his company, who was in pursuit of a wounded deer that was seeking shelter there where the underbrush was very thick. This man, when Amadis saw him, he summoned and said to him: "Tell Grasandor that I am going with this lady, who just now has landed here, and that I beg his indulgence; for her terrible loss and her emergent situation prevent me from being able to speak to him or see him; and that I beg him to have this knight buried and to persuade my lady Oriana to forgive me, for I am making this voyage without her mandate; May she believe that I have not been able to do otherwise without incurring great disgrace."

And this having been said, the boat left the shore at top speed, and they traveled all that day and night back over the route the lady had followed to come there. Meanwhile Amadis asked the lady to tell him the predicament and danger in which she found herself and on account of which his help was so badly needed. She, weeping very bitterly, said to him: "My lord, you shall know that at the time the queen your mother left Gaul to go to this island of yours to your wedding and those of your brothers, to my husband and me in Little Brittany, where we were governors by her command, she dispatched a messenger by whom she sent word in a letter that after reading it we should follow them to the Firm Island, because it was not right that she should participate in such festivities without us; and her great nobility, and the great love that she has for us, rather than our own merit were the cause of this. So having this command, at once my husband and that ill-fated son of mine whom we left back there dead, and whose armor you are wearing, and I myself, put out to sea in quite a large vessel with a goodly company of people to serve us. And after traveling with favorable weather, through our bad luck it changed to such an extent that it caused us to deviate quite a distance from the course that we were pursuing, bringing us one night after two months and many dangers that overtook us because of that terrible storm, blown by the great force of the wind, to the Island of the Vermilion Tower, of which the giant called Balan — fiercer and stronger than any giant of all the islands — is the ruler. And as we reached the harbor, not knowing where we had arrived, as soon as we had stopped for a bit to take shelter there in that port, then in that hour people of the island in other boats immediately surrounded us so that we were all taken prisoners and held there until morning, when they took us to the giant; who when he saw us, asked if any knight was among us. My husband told him that he himself was, and also the other man, his son, who was beside him."

" 'Then' said the giant, 'it is necessary that you conform to the custom of the island.'

" 'And what is the custom?' said my husband.

" 'That you are to fight with me one at a time,' said the giant, 'and if either one of you can defend yourself for one hour, you and all your company will be free; and if you are overcome within that hour, you will be my prisoners; but you will be left with some hope for your well-being if as good men you exert yourself to the utmost. However, if perchance your cowardice be so great that it does not allow you to risk involving yourself in combat, you will be put into harsh confinement in a dungeon where you will undergo great anguish in payment for having embraced the order of chivalry while valuing life more than honor or the oath you took in order to receive knighthood. Now I have explained to you completely what is upheld here; choose what is most agreeable to you.'

"My husband said: 'We wish the battle; for in vain would we be bearing arms if through fear of some danger we should fail to do with them that for which they have been instituted. But what security shall we have, if we should be victors, that the law you mention will be observed?'

" 'There is no other,' said the giant, 'except my word, which, come what may, never with my consent will be broken; rather I would permit my own body to be broken, and to this I have made a son of mine, whom I have here, swear, and likewise all my servants and vassals.'

" 'In the name of God' said my husband, 'have my arms and my horse given to me and also my son's to him; and prepare yourself for the combat.'

" 'That,' said the giant, 'will be done at once.'

"Then they and the giant were accordingly armed and placed on horseback in a great square which was situated in front of the gate to the castle — a well-fortified stronghold — and was bordered by rock formations. Then that luckless son of mine begged his father so insistently that he unwillingly granted him the first joust; in which he was charged so violently by the giant that both he and his horse were overthrown so mercilessly that both simultaneously lost their lives. My husband went at him and struck his shield, but it was just like attacking a tower. And the giant came up to him, and seized him so forcibly by an arm, that although he is possessed of plenty of strength for his size and age, he hurled him out of his saddle as if he were a child. Having done this, he gave orders to leave my dead son on the field, and he had my husband and me, and a daughter of ours, whom we were bringing along to serve as an attendant for your sister Melicia, taken up to the fortress, and he ordered our retainers put into a dungeon. When I saw this, I began like a woman out of her senses — for so I was at the time — to shout very loudly and say: " 'Oh, King Perion of Gaul! Would that you or one of your sons were here now, for with your aid or that of any one of them, I certainly think I would escape from this great tribulation!'

"When the giant heard this, he said: 'What acquaintance do you have with that king? Is he by chance the father of a man named Amadis of Gaul?'

" 'Yes, indeed,' said I, 'and if any of them were here, you would not be capable of doing me any harm; for they would help me, a woman who has spent her whole life in their service.'

" 'Well, if you have so much confidence in them,' said he, 'I shall give you the opportunity to call whichever one you like, and it would please me most if it were Amadis, who is so highly esteemed in the world, because he killed my father Mandanfabul in the battle between King Cildadan and King Lisuarte, when my father was carrying this same King Lisuarte under his arm, having pulled him out of his saddle, and was going with him to the ships. And this Amadis, who at the time was called Beltenebros, pursued him, and although in defense of his lord and of those on his side he was able to strike in safety without my father's seeing him, it ought not to be accounted a great effort or act of valor on his part or great dishonor for my father. And if of this person who is so renowned and whom you have served so well, you wish to avail yourself, take that boat with a sailor that I shall give you to guide you, and seek him; and in order that his anger and desire to avenge you may be enkindled take that knight your son armed and dead as he is; and if Amadis esteems you as you think, and is as courageous as everyone says, on seeing your great grief, he will not fail to come.'

"When I heard this, I said to him: 'If I do as you say, and bring that knight to this island of yours, how will he be certain that you will keep faith with him?'

" 'About that,' said he, 'don't worry, nor should he; for although I may have other traits that are evil and stem from pride, this I have upheld and shall uphold all the days of my life: namely, that I would rather die than go back on my word concerning anything that I promise; which word I now give you for any knight who comes with you — and much more emphatically if it be Amadis of Gaul — that he may have nothing to fear except at my pleasure from my person alone.'

"So I, sir, in view of what the giant said to me and seeing my son dead, and my husband and lord, and my daughter taken prisoners along with our entire company, have dared to come in this manner, trusting in our Lord and in your good fortune, and in the fact that the cruelty of that devil is so opposed to His service that He will give me vengeance on that traitor with great glory to you."

Amadis, when he heard this, was very sorry about the misfortune of the matron, who was greatly esteemed by his father King Perion and by the queen his mother and by all of them, and regarded as one of the good matrons of her rank to be found anywhere. And furthermore he considered that confrontation a dangerous one, not only because of the risk involved in the battle — although it would be great in view of the renown of that

Balan — but also on account of entering his island and mingling with people with whom he would have to exercise utmost tact. But putting his problems entirely into the hands of that Lord who holds authority over everyone, and having great pity for that matron and her husband, for she never stopped weeping, putting behind him all fear, with very great courage he continued to console her and to tell her that very quickly her loss would be compensated for and avenged, if God approved of its being accomplished by him.

So just as you hear, they traveled two days and one night, and on the third day they saw on their left a small island with a castle that seemed very tall. Amadis asked the sailor if he knew whose island that was. He told him that he did, that it was King Cildadan's, and that it was called Princess Island.

"Now guide us there," said Amadis, "so that we may take on some provisions, for we do not know what may happen."

Then he turned the boat about, and in a short while they reached the island. And when they were at the foot of the rocky hill they saw a knight coming down its slope; and when he came up to them, he greeted them, and they, him. Amadis said to him: "I am a knight from the Firm Island, and I come to obtain justice for this lady, if it be God's will, for a wrong and an injury that beyond here on another island she received."

"On what island was it?" said the knight.

"On the Island of the Vermilion Tower," said Amadis.

"And who did her that wrong?" said the knight.

Amadis said: "Balan the Giant, who they say is lord of that island."

"Then what amends can you render her by yourself?"

"Fighting with him," said Amadis, "and putting a stop to the injury he has done this matron and many other people who have not deserved it from him."

The knight began to laugh, as if in scorn, and said: "Sir Knight of the Firm Island, do not let such great madness enter your heart so willingly as to seek out that man from whom everyone flees; for if the lord of that island from which you come, who is Amadis of Gaul, and his two brothers, Don Galaor and Don Florestan — who today are the flower and stem of all the knights in the world — should all three come to fight with this

Balan, it would be considered great madness on their part by those who know him. Therefore I advise you to give up this journey, because I would greatly regret that any harm and injury should come to you, for I am a knight and a friend of those whom my lord King Cildadan loves and esteems so highly; for I have been told that he and King Lisuarte are now reconciled with Amadis, and I do not know just how, merely that I am assured that they have finally achieved great love and harmony. So if you pursue what you have begun, it means only that knowingly you are proceeding to your death."

Amadis said to him: "Death or life are in God's hands, and those who wish to be praised above all others have to involve themselves in, and undertake dangerous enterprises, including those that others do not dare to undertake; and this I do not say because of considering myself such as they, but because I wish to be so. And for this reason I beg you, sir knight, not to infuse more fear in me than I already have, which is no little; and if you please, out of courtesy to aid me with some food we might use to advantage, if the opportunity presents itself."

"This I will gladly do," said the knight of the island; "and I will do more; for in order to see such a rare event, I wish to keep you company until your adventure, good or bad, takes place with that fierce giant."

CHAPTER CXXVIII

How Amadis went with the matron to the island of the giant called Balan, and the knight who was governor of Princess Island accompanied him.

That knight of whom the story tells gave orders to bring as much food as he saw was needed, and unarmed as he was, he entered a boat with men to show him the way. And they departed from that harbor together for Balan's island; and while they were proceeding over the sea, the knight asked Amadis if he knew King Cildadan. Amadis said that he did, that he had seen him and his great knightly exploits many times in the battles that King Lisuarte had with Amadis, and that he could truly say of him that he was one of the valiant and good kings of the world.

"Certainly," said the knight of Princess Island, "he is, except that contrary Fortune has been more adverse to him than to any other man in the world amounting to so much, by putting him under the domination and vassalage of King Lisuarte, for such a king as Cildadan was destined more to command and be master than to be a vassal."

"Now he is free of that tribute," said Amadis, "for the great strength of his heart and the valor of his person have removed from his high estate that stigma which was not his fault."

"How do you know about that, knight?"

"Sir," said he, "I know about it because I saw it."

Then he told him what King Lisuarte had done in releasing him, just as this Book has related it. The knight, when he heard this, knelt in the boat and said: "Lord God, may thou be praised for ever and ever for having been willing to give that king what his great virtue and nobility deserved."

Amadis said to him: "Good sir, are you acquainted with this Balan?"

"Very well," said he.

"I earnestly beg of you, if you please, inasmuch as there is no need to talk about anything else, to tell me what you know, especially what one ought to know about him personally."

"I will do so," said the knight, "and perchance you would not find anyone else who can tell you about him in such full detail. Know you that this Balan is the son of the fierce Madanfabul, that giant whom Amadis of Gaul killed when he called himself Beltenebros, in the battle of one hundred against one hundred that King Cildadan had with King Lisuarte, in which there died many other giants and strong knights of his lineage who throughout this region had many islands of very great value, and who, out of the great love and affection they had for my lord King Cildadan, chose to be in his service, in which nearly all of them perished. And this Balan about whom you ask me was quite youthful when his father died, and he inherited this island which is in all respects the most productive, both in fruits of all kinds and in all the most prized and highly valued spices in the world. And for this reason there are on it many merchants and numerous other people who safely come to it, and from whom there accrue very handsome profits to the giant. And I tell you that since this man became a knight he has shown himself stronger than his father in complete valor and strength; and his nature and manner about which you wish to find out, is very different from, and contrary to, that of the other giants, who by nature are arrogant and boastful, whereas this giant is not; instead, very calm and very truthful in all his affairs — so much so that it is a wonder that a man of such lineage can be so different in nature from the others. And everybody thinks that in this he takes after his mother, who is a sister of the fierce giantess Gromadaza, widow of Famongomadan, he of the Boiling Lake — I do not know if you have heard this — and just as this giantess has surpassed Gromadaza in very great beauty, as well as many others who in their time were beautiful, so she has been very different in all other aspects of excellence; for the other giantess was very fierce and excessively ill-tempered, whereas this one is quite gentle and devoted to complete virtue and humility. And this must bring it about that just as women who are ugly, appearing more virile than feminine, usually acquire that arrogance and manly rudeness of manner which is consistent with their natures; so beautiful ones, who are endowed with natures suitable for women, are the opposite; their nature being in conformity with a delicate voice, soft, smooth skin, and great beauty of countenance — qualities which put a woman at ease and to a large degree deflect her from aggressiveness, just as is the case with this giantess, the wife of Madanfabul and mother of this Balan; from which fact derives that mildness and poise of this son of hers. Her name is Madasima, and because of her, this same name was given to a very beautiful daughter left by Famongomadan, who married a knight named Don Galvanes, a man of equally high rank, and all who know her say that she also has a very noble nature and is very gentle with everyone. Now I want to explain to you how I know about all this that I am telling, and much more, on the subject of these giants. Know you that I have been governor of that Princess Island, where you met me, since the time that King Cildadan was a prince who held it as a fief without having any other inheritance. And more because of his courage and good ways than on account of his rank, King Abies sent word across the whole kingdom of Ireland in order to unite Cildadan in marriage with his daughter, and he inherited that kingdom at the time that Amadis of Gaul killed King Abies; and he continued to leave me in this governorship that I have. And as I am here among these people, and they all have great affection for my lord the king, I have many dealings with them, and I know that the sons of those giants who died in that battle that I mentioned to you, who are now men, have a great desire to avenge the deaths of their parents and relatives, were they to see an opportunity to do so."

Amadis, who was listening to this speech, said to him: "Good sir, I have derived great pleasure from what you have told me. I am disturbed only about the very good nature of this man whom I go seeking out; for it would please me more if he were completely the opposite with great ferocity and arrogance, because God's wrath and punishment are not slow in overtaking such as he, and I do not want to deny that I am more afraid than before. But however that may be, I shall not fail to obtain amends for this matron, if I can, for the great harm and injustice that she has received undeservedly; and this much I want to find out from you: whether this Balan is married."

The knight of the island told him that he was.

"And to a daughter of a giant named Gandalac, lord of the Rock of Galtares, by whom he has a son some fifteen years of age, who if he lives, will be the heir to that seigniory."

When Amadis heard this, he was even more disturbed and regretted very much having learned it because of the great love that he had for Gandalac and the sons of the latter, who was the foster father of his brother Galaor. He considered that all Galaor's concerns were to be protected the same as his very own. And he said to the knight: "You have told me things that cause me to have more misgivings than ever."

And this was because of what he told him about Gandalac. The knight suspected that his misgivings were out of fear of the battle, but that was not so; for even if it were to be with his very own brother Don Galaor, whom he would fear more than the giant, he would in nowise leave it without obtaining justice and redress for that matron or losing his life; because it always was his custom to help anyone who rightfully asked him for aid.

So talking thus about this matter that you have heard and many other things, they traveled all that day and night. And next day at the hour of tierce they saw the Island of the Vermilion Tower, which gave them much pleasure, and they went on until they drew near it. Amadis gazed at it, and it seemed to him very beautiful — the land with its heavily wooded hills, and what he could perceive at a distance, such as the situation of the fortress with its very beautiful fortified towers, especially the one that was called the Vermilion Tower, which was the largest and made of the rarest stone to be found in the world. And in some histories one reads that at the beginning of the populating of that island the first builder of the tower and of most of the rest of that great fortress was Joseph, the son of Joseph of Arimathea, who brought the Holy Grail to Great Britain; and because at the time most of that land was in the possession of pagans, he on seeing the situation of that island, populated it with Christians, and built that great tower where he and all of his men defended themselves when they saw themselves in any predicament. Afterwards, in due course it was ruled by the giants until it came down to this Balan, but the population always remained Christian, as it was now; the Christians lived there quite put upon and oppressed by their lords, because most of the latter embraced the pagan sect. But the Christians put up with it and tolerated it because of the immense wealth of the land; and if at any period they had some relief, it was only in Balan's time, on account of the good attitude that he maintained towards them and because of love for his father; for he came closer to adhering to the precepts of Jesus Christ than any of the others; and even much more so later on, as the story will relate.

Then having arrived there, Amadis said to the knight of Princess Island: "My good lord, if you please, since you are acquainted with this Balan, as a courtesy go to him and tell him that the matron whose son he killed and whose husband he took prisoner brings with her a knight from the Firm Island to seek redress from him for the injury that he has done her, and if he does not grant it, to fight with him and force him to grant it to her satisfaction. And secure from him a pledge that the knight will be safe from everyone save him alone, however well or badly it may turn out for him."

The knight said to him: "I am very happy to do so, and you can be certain that the promise that he gives will have no other stipulation."

Then the knight with his men entered his boat and went on to the port, and Amadis remained somewhat secluded with his matron.

Then when that knight arrived, he was at once recognized by the giant's men and taken before him. He received him affably, for a good many times he had talked to him; and he said to him: "Governor, what do you seek in my land? Tell me, for you already know that I consider you a friend."

The knight said to him: "So I do, and I am very grateful to you for it; but my coming is not with regard to any matter concerning myself, but because of a strange thing that I have witnessed, and this is that a knight from the Firm Island comes of his own free will to fight with you, and I marvel greatly at his daring to do such a thing."

When the giant heard this he said: "That knight whom you mention, does he bring a matron with him?"

"Yes," said the knight, "indeed he does."

"It is my understanding," said the giant, "that it is probably that Amadis of Gaul who is lauded throughout the world with so much praise and publicity, or else one of his brothers, for in order to bring one of them she left here, and with that purpose I allowed her to go."

Then the knight said: "I do not know who he can be; but I tell you he is a very handsome knight and very well proportioned and fair spoken. I cannot understand whether simplemindedness or great courage has impelled him to this folly. I come to you to ask security for him, so that he may fear for himself only with respect to you."

The giant said to him: "You already know that my word will never willingly be broken; bring him with my assurance of safety, and by coming you will learn at first hand which one of those two motives that you have mentioned applies."

The knight returned to his boat and went back to Amadis. And when the latter heard the reply, without any distrust he came at once to the port and they immediately disembarked from their boats. And Amadis first drew aside that man who had guided the matron on the boat, and said to him: "Friend, I ask of you not to tell anyone my name, for if I have to die here, the fact will come to light; and if I have to be the victor, on that account I shall reward you handsomely."

The sailor promised him not to tell anyone. Then they went up to the castle and found the giant unarmed in that great square facing the gate. And when they arrived, the giant gazed intently at him and said to the matron: "Is this one of King Perion's sons whom you were to bring?"

The matron replied: "This is a knight who will seek satisfaction from you for the injuries that you have done me."

Then Amadis said: "Balan, it is not necessary for you to know who I am; let it suffice that I come to demand that you make amends to this matron for the very great injury you have done her without her having deserved it of you, in killing her son and seizing her husband together with another child of hers, a daughter. And if you make such amends to her, I shall refrain from having an altercation with you; and if not, prepare yourself for the combat."

The giant said to him laughing: "The greatest amends that I can give you are to release you from your obligation and free you from death; for since you have come with such good will to repair her loss, you must value your own life as highly as hers. And although I am not accustomed to doing this for anyone without his first testing the edge of this sword of mine, I shall do it for you because through ignorance you have come to seek your harm without recognizing it."

"If I feared," said Amadis, "these threats that you make to me as much as you think, it would have been futile for me to seek you out from such a distant land. Do not think, Balan, that I challenge you through ignorance, for I well know that you are one of the most renowned giants in the world. But since I see that the custom that you maintain here is so opposed to the service of the most high Lord, and the right that I support is in accordance with His holy law, I do not esteem your valor very highly, because He will supply what I may lack. And because I hold you in high regard and I esteem you on account of others who esteem you, I beg you to make such amends to this matron as may be just."

When the giant heard this, he said to him: "You make so well your request for what you say that if it were not interpreted to my shame, I would do everything possible to satisfy this lady; but first I wish to test and see what the knights of the Firm Island are like. And because it is already late, I shall send you something to eat, and two very good horses from which you may choose according to your desire, along with two lances; and prepare yourself with all your strength, for you will really need it for the combat three hours from now. And to accommodate you if you should wish other arms, I shall give you better ones; for I think I have plenty from the knights that I have overcome."

Amadis said to him: "You act like a good knight, and the more courtesy I see in you, the more I regret that you do not have any understanding of what you ought to do. I shall take a horse and a lance, but no other armaments aside from those I bring, for the blood on them from that man whom you have killed so without cause will give me more courage to avenge him."

The giant repaired to the castle without answering him further; and Amadis to his company and the knight of Princess Island, who did not wish to leave him, no matter how much the giant begged him to go with him to the castle. They remained under the arcade of a temple that was at one end of that square, and shortly thereafter food was brought to them. Thus they rested talking on subjects most to their liking while awaiting the appointed hour for the giant to sally forth. That knight repeatedly scrutinized Amadis's face to see whether it was changing color on account of that great danger, and to him he seemed to be with ever-increasing courage, at which he was greatly astonished.

Then the hour set by the giant having come, there were brought to Amadis two very big, beautiful horses with rich trappings for such an activity, and he took the one he preferred. And after looking it over, since it came saddled, he mounted it, put on his helmet and slung his shield from his neck; and having stationed himself in that great square, he ordered the man who had brought him the horses to return and tell the giant that he was waiting for him and not to let the day pass in vain. Most of the people of the island who could come were standing around the square in order to see the combat, and the wall-tops and the windows of the fortress were crowded with matrons and maidens.

And while he was waiting just as you hear, he perceived that in the great Vermilion Tower three trumpets played sweet music very harmoniously, which was the signal that the giant was coming out to do battle. And it was his custom to have this done each time that he was to fight. Amadis asked those who were there what that was. They told him the reason it was done, which seemed to him very good and the act of a great lord; and it came to his mind that when he was on the Firm Island with his lady, if he should have occasion to engage in a combat with anyone who was in quest of one with him, he would give orders for such a procedure to be followed, because in his opinion that music was calculated to increase the courage of the knight for whom it was played. Then, as the trumpets became silent, the gates of the fortress were opened, and the giant came out mounted on the other horse that he had sent to Amadis, and with lance in hand

and armed with armor of steel as bright as a mirror, both the helmet and the shield in proportion, and with armor plate that covered most of his body. And when he saw Amadis he said to him: "Knight of the Firm Island, now that you see me armed, do you dare await me?"

"Now I want you," said he, "to make amends to this matron for the evil deed that you did to her; if not, defend yourself from me."

Then the giant came toward him as fast as his horse could carry him, and he was so big that there was not a knight in the world, however valiant he might be, who would not be greatly frightened by him. And as he was charging very hard and with great eagerness to meet him, he lowered his lance so much in order not to misjudge the blow that he struck the horse of Amadis right in the middle of its forehead and thrust the lance through its head and through its neck for quite a distance; but Amadis, whom neither his size nor his valor disturbed, being a man who already knew what such giants were like, struck him on his large, strong shield such a blow that perforce he knocked the giant out of his saddle, and he fell to the ground, which was quite hard, very violently and was thereby terribly shaken up, and Amadis's horse fell dead to the ground with him. From underneath Amadis extricated himself as quickly as he could, although with great effort, because one of his legs was caught underneath, and as he rose to his feet he saw the giant getting up, who was somewhat dazed, but not so much as to be unable to grasp at once the sword of very strong steel that he was wearing, from which he thought that there was no knight in the world so strong as to dare to await two blows without being crippled or killed.

Amadis grasped his own very good sword, covered himself with his shield and went at him; and the giant likewise came at him with uplifted arm to strike him very heedlessly, not only out of great arrogance but also because the lance thrust that Amadis had given him was right at his heart, and because of having been given with such great force, it had jammed his shield against his chest so violently that his flesh was bruised and the cartilage broken, so that it was causing him great pain and greatly inhibiting his strength and breathing. Amadis, when he saw him coming in such a condition, recognized he was defeated; and he raised his shield as high as he could to receive on it the blow. And the giant struck so hard, and his sword cut through so easily that from the boss down he cut away a third of the shield, for he did not reach any more of it; so that if he had reached it more completely, in addition Amadis's arm would have gone to the ground along with its possessor. Amadis, who was very experienced in swordsmanship, and from such dangerous situations knew how to extricate himself, not missing or forgetting a thing that he should do, before the giant withdrew his arm, struck him such a blow close to his elbow that although the sleeve of his coat of mail was very strong and of very thick mesh, it could not safeguard him or prevent Amadis's very good sword from slicing through it to the extent of cutting much of the flesh of his arm and one of its bones. That blow was very painful for the giant, and he gave ground somewhat. Amadis went at him immediately, and struck him another blow on top of the helmet with all his strength, so that sparks flew as if it had been set on fire by some other means, and it twisted the helmet around on his head in such fashion that it blocked his vision.

When the knight who was the governor of Princess Island, with whom Amadis had come there, saw the blows that Amadis was striking, not only in the encounter with the lance, in which he had unhorsed a thing as strong and ponderous as that giant was, but also those that he was giving with the sword, he began to make the sign of the cross many times; and he said to the lady whom he had beside him: "Lady, where did you find that devil who performs such feats, the like of which no other living knight has accomplished?"

The matron replied: "If many such devils as this went about the world, there would not be so many people as there are afflicted and humiliated by the haughty and the wicked."

The giant very quickly raised his hands to straighten his helmet, and he sensed that he had lost a great deal of strength in his right arm, so that he could hardly hold the sword in his hand, so he withdrew farther away; but Amadis at once joined with him as before and struck him another heavy blow on the boss of his shield, intending to hit him on the head but being unable to do so; for the giant when he saw the blow coming so hard, raised his shield to receive it, and the sword pierced it so deep that when Amadis attempted to withdraw it, he couldn't; and the giant intended to strike him, but could only raise his arm very slightly, so that the blow was weak. Then Amadis pulled on the sword as hard as he could, and the giant on the shield, so that with the great strength of both of them, the leather straps that held it around his neck had to break, and Amadis took the shield along with his own sword, which could occasion and invite great danger for the giant, because in no way could he aid himself with it. The giant when he saw it thus, and saw himself without a shield, took his sword in his left hand and began to strike Amadis mighty blows with it; but the latter protected himself with great agility by covering himself with his shield, though not in such a way as to be able to prevent the blows of the giant from cutting through his coat of mail in a few places and reaching his flesh. And it is certain that if the giant had been able to strike with his right hand, Amadis would have found himself in great danger of death; but with the left hand, although the blows were mighty and delivered with great force, they were very erratic, so that most of them missed and were in vain. Amadis, as he sought to raise the sword in order to strike him, lifted with it the shield in which it was imbedded, for he was concerned only with defending himself thus. But when he saw himself encumbered and in such danger, he decided to remedy his situation as quickly as he could and withdrew a little to one side, took his shield off his neck and threw it on the ground between him and the giant. And he put one foot on the giant's shield and with both hands pulled so hard on the sword that he drew it out of the shield.

Meanwhile the giant took in his right hand Amadis's shield, and although it was quite light in weight, he could scarcely lift it or support it with his arm, for the wound was big and beside the elbow joint, and with the amount of blood that he had lost his arm was almost numb, for he could hardly lift it or grip with his hand otherwise than very weakly; and what impeded and distressed him most was the torn flesh, and the broken bones that he had pressing against his heart as a result of the lance-thrust about which you have already heard, a condition which kept him so winded that he could scarcely breathe at all. But as he was very strong as regards driving force and courage, and saw himself in danger of death, he bore up with great effort; and this was because after Amadis's sword remained thrust in the shield because of the great blow, the latter had never been able to strike or oppose him; but when he drew it out and found himself free of that impediment, he seized by its clasps the giant's shield, which he could hardly lift, because of its size and weight, and went and struck him very heavy blows with all his might, so that the giant was so harassed not only by the pressure that Amadis was putting on him, but also with the haste he made to defend himself and to strike, that he suffered a heart occlusion from the pain he was enduring, and he fell as if dead on the field.

When the men who were watching in the fortress saw this, they shouted very loudly, and the matrons and maidens uttered loud cries, saying: "Dead is our lord; death to the traitor who killed him!"

Amadis, after the giant fell, went to him at once and took off his helmet and put the tip of his sword to his face, and said to him: "Balan, you die, unless you give satisfaction to the matron for the harm that you have done her."

But he did not respond or understand what he said to him, for he was as if dead. Then the knight of Princess Island, who had come there with Amadis, arrived and said: "Sir knight, is the giant dead?"

"I don't think so," said Amadis, "but the great suffocation he suffers keeps him in the state you see, for I do not see evidence on him of any mortal blow."

And he was speaking the truth, for the blow that he had on the breast, which inhibited his breath, he had not seen or perceived.

The knight said: "Sir, I beg you out of courtesy not to kill him until he comes to his senses and has the judgment to make amends to this matron voluntarily; and also because if he should die, no one will be powerful enough to guarantee you life."

"On that account," said Amadis, "I shall not fail to do my will with him; but out of regard for you and on account of the blood relationship that he has with Gandalac, I shall forbear killing him until I find out from him whether he will be willing to agree to what I shall ask of him."

At this juncture, they saw the giant's son coming out of the castle with as many as thirty armed men, and they came saying: "Let him die, let the traitor die!"

When Amadis heard this, you can now understand what hope he would have for his life on seeing them all come brashly to kill him. But he decided not to throw himself on their mercy, and that death should come to him only after he had done everything in his power without being remiss in anything that he ought to do. And he looked all about him and saw a gaping fissure between those rocks with which the square was encircled, for that square had been made there manually by taking away rocks and crags, but all around the outside many of them remained. And he went toward it bearing the giant's shield, which was very big and strong, and he put it at the entrance of that fissure, for he could not be harmed from any direction except from the front, nor from above because an overhang was formed there. Then the people came up, some to the giant to see if he was dead, and others to Amadis. And three men who came forward threw their lances at him, but did not harm him, for as the shield was, as has been told you, very large and strong, it protected most of his torso and his legs, which fact, after God, saved his life. And one of these three came up with his sword in order to strike him; and as Amadis saw him near, he came out at him and struck him such a blow on top of the head that he split it down to his neck and knocked him over dead at his feet.

When the others saw him outside of that shelter, they all came up to kill him; but he returned there immediately, and to the first who came up, he dealt such a blow on the shoulder that his armor was of no advantage to him, for the arm fell to the ground and the man fell dead on the other side. These two blows taught them such a lesson that no one was bold enough to approach him, and they hemmed him in from the front and on the sides, as they could not do so anywhere else; and they were hurling so many lances and darts and stones that almost half of his body was out of sight, but nothing harmed him, for the shield gave him protection from everything.

Meanwhile, they carried the giant to the castle, lamenting loudly, and they placed him on his bed as though dead without any consciousness; and those who had carried him returned at once to help their companions. And when they came up they saw that no one was approaching Amadis, and that he had the two dead men beside him; and as they arrived fresh and greatly enraged, and did not know about, nor had seen, his very rude blows, they came up to attack him with their lances; but Amadis remained quiet, well protected by his shield, and the one who came ahead and struck a violent blow with his lance on his shield, he struck such a blow that he caused the fellow's head to fly to some distance away, and immediately those men turned away along with the others, for none dared to approach him.

Then while they were thus at a standstill except to hurl many darts and numerous stones at Amadis, the knight of Princess Island felt great compassion on seeing him in this situation; and he indeed thought that if they were to kill him, the best knight who ever bore arms would die; and he went at once to the giant's son, who was unarmed because of his tender age, and said to him: "Bravor, why do you do this against the word and pledge of your father, which never until today has been found to be broken? Have regard for the fact that you are his son and are to resemble him in good qualities. And take into consideration that your father assured his safety from all his men except from himself alone, and that if after this you kill him, never more will it behoove you to appear before honorable men, for always you will be vilified and held in great contempt."

The youth replied: "How can I endure seeing my father dead before me, and not take vengeance on him who did it?"

"Your father," said he, "is not dead, nor does he have a blow from which he should die, for I saw him lying on the ground, and that knight at my request, and because he told me that he esteemed him highly on account of the blood relationship that he had with Gandalac, gave up killing him, for it was in his power to do so."

"Then what shall I do?" said the youth.

"I will tell you," said the knight. "Keep him encircled just as he is all this night, without his receiving any harm; and between now and tomorrow the condition of your father will be determined, and according to how he is, you will make a decision, for in your hands and according to your will his life or death rests, because he cannot leave here unless you order it."

The youth said to him: "I thank you very much for your advice to me, for if he should die and my father remain alive, it would not be desirable for me to live anywhere in all the world where he might find out about it, because I am indeed certain that he would search for me in order to kill me."

"Since you recognize that," said he, "do what I advise you."

"Let me speak first with my grandmother and with my mother, and let it be done with the benefit of their advice."

"That I consider good," said the knight, "and meanwhile order your men not to do any more than what they have done."

The youth said: "That order will be useless, for according as that knight seems to me to be defending his life, as I see it, except by starvation, in no way can anyone kill him; but on account of what you advise me, I shall do what you tell me."

Then he ordered them to remain there, and without anyone's harming that knight to guard well lest he leave where he was, while he himself went to the castle. All those who were there carried out his order, and he went and talked with those matrons; and although their emotion and sorrow were great, on considering that the knight would not be able to go away, and on seeing that the giant was beginning to recover his breath and some consciousness, and fearing to break his word, they told him to do just as that knight of Princess Island had advised him, an action for which it was a great help when the mother of this youth learned that that knight esteemed her father Gandalac, for she had feared that he was Don Galaor, the one whom her father had reared and who had restored him in the sovereignty of the Rock of Galtares by killing Albadan, the fierce giant, who was keeping it from him by force, as in greater detail the first Book of this story relates. Galaor she knew very well and loved sincerely because they had been reared together. And if it had not been for the fact that her husband was so critically ill that she would have been guilty of great impropriety, she herself in person would have ascertained whether the knight was Don Galaor or one of his brothers, for she had seen them all in the court of King Lisuarte, where she had stayed for some time during the period in which the battle between King Lisuarte and King Cildadan took place, in which her father and his brothers participated, and they had performed rare deeds at arms in the service of King Lisuarte out of love for Don Galaor, as the second Book of this story relates at greater length.

With this agreement the youth returned at an hour when night had already closed in; and he gave orders to light a big fire in front of where Amadis was, who knew nothing of his agreement; and then he had his men keep vigil while armed, and with good precautions against the knight's coming forth and doing them harm, for he was deathly afraid of him. Amadis remained in that place where previously he had been, with the edge of the shield resting on the ground, holding one hand on its boss and his sword in the other hand, hoping to die rather than to permit himself to be captured; for he certainly thought that since despite the fact of such a pledge of security as he had from Balan, those men had attacked him in an endeavor to kill him, no other pledge that he might be given would be honored; therefore he would not consider asking for mercy even if he knew he might experience death a thousand times over; except asking God for mercy, to whom in every situation he committed himself wholeheartedly, and more than ever in that one, for which he did not have nor did he expect any other help except His.

CHAPTER CXXIX

How Darioleta grieved because of the great danger in which Amadis was.

Darioleta, the matron who had had Amadis come there, when she saw him thus encircled by all his enemies without having or expecting any help from any source, began to lament grievously and to curse her luck, which had brought her such anguish and sorrow, saying: "Oh wretched unfortunate woman that I am, what will become of me if on my account the best knight ever born should die? How shall I dare appear before his father and mother and brothers, knowing that I was the cause of his death? For if at the time of his birth I endeavored to save his life by making and contriving out of my own knowledge the ark in which he might escape, an action for which I have been rewarded abundantly — for if he had died then, it would have been a fruitless death — now not only have I forfeited past services, but moreover I deserve to die with the greatest sufferings and torments that any person ever had, because while he is the flower or glory of the world I have brought him to death. Oh wretch that I am, because I did not give him at the time that he came to me on the seashore any opportunity to be able to return to the Firm Island and bring some knights to assist him, who at least justifiably might have died in his company! But what can I say except that my heedlessness and rashness were characteristic of womankind?"

Just as you hear, Darioleta was lamenting under the arcades of that temple with very great anguish of heart, and with no other expectation than to see Amadis die very quickly, and herself and her husband put into a dungeon from which they never would come out.

Amadis was at the edge of that fissure in the rocks, as we have told you, and he saw what the matron was doing, for with the huge fire that was in front of him, the whole square was visible, although it was quite large; and he was greatly perturbed to see her weeping and raising her hands to the heavens as she begged for mercy. Hence his fury increased so greatly that it rendered him beside himself. And he thought that much more danger could befall him when day came than at night, because then most of the people of the island were at rest and he only needed to beware of those whom he had before him; and that when morning came, many more people could attack him, so that he could not escape being killed; and even assuming that they could not harm him there where he was, sleep and hunger would overcome him and he would fall into their hands. And in this frenzy he thought that he would risk everything; and grasping his shield and with sword in hand he prepared to attack his enemies. But the knight of Princess Island, who was worried lest harm come to him, because he had pledged security to him on behalf of the giant and thus had broken his promise to him, was in their midst very much concerned lest the men at arms come at him before the giant's condition was ascertained, for it was indeed his belief that when the latter was in his right mind, he would apply such a remedy and admonishment to the situation that his word would be kept. And as he saw that Amadis was starting to come out against them, he went to him as fast as he could and said to him: "Sir knight, I beg of you out of courtesy to listen to me a bit before you come out of here."

Amadis stood still and the knight told him all that he had talked over with Bravor, the giant's son, and how he had him for the time being quite pacified until morning should come, and that in that space of time the giant would be greatly improved and returned to consciousness; and that he believed that undoubtedly he would carry out with him completely all that he was duty bound to do, even if he were at death's door, and that Amadis should be willing to be patient meanwhile, for with God's help he would remedy everything, and that he would take charge of the matter. Amadis, when he saw him speak thus, was convinced that he was stating the truth, because in that little while that he had dealt with him he had come to consider him an honorable man; and he said: "Out of regard for you I shall forbear this time; but I tell you, knight, that all the effort that you may put forth in this matter will be wasted if first of all amends are not made to the lady."

The knight said to him: "That will be done and much more, or I would not consider myself a knight, nor would I so consider this giant whom I have always regarded as such; for believe me, in him resides much truth and goodness."

Amadis remained quietly where he was as before. So just as you hear, he remained among those forbidding rocks, surrounded by his enemies, waiting, just as they were, for morning.

Now the story relates that after his men had carried the giant to the castle as unconscious as if he were dead, and had put him on his bed, he remained in that condition most of the night without being able to speak, and he did nothing but put his hand directly over his heart, indicating that the pain was coming from there. And when his mother and his wife saw that, they had the physicians examine him; and they immediately found the injury that he had, on which they applied so many medical and other remedies which eased him, that before dawn he was completely conscious. And when he was able to speak, he asked where he was. The physicians told him that he was in his bed.

"But the combat that I had with the knight," said he, "how did it go?"

They told him the entire truth, which is right to tell truthful men, for they did not dare lie to him about anything, relating to him everything just as it had occurred; and how when the knight of the Firm Island had him on the ground, his son Bravor, thinking that he was dead, had come out from the castle with his men, and had held his opponent surrounded among the rocks of the square where the combat had taken place, and that they were waiting for whatever he might command. When the giant heard this, he said to them: "Is the knight alive?"

"Yes," they said.

"Then have my son come here with all the men who are with him, and have them release the knight."

This was done at once; and when the giant saw his son, he said to him: "Traitor, why have you broken my word? What honor and what benefit could accrue to you from what you have done? For if I were dead, it would be too late for you to restore me by any other means, and much more dead would your honor be, and with greater loss by my lineage in counteracting and enduring what you did than the death that I as a knight would have received without being remiss in any respect in what I should do. For if I had remained alive, don't you know that you would not have been able to escape from me anywhere without my killing you? So that you and all those who do not uphold the truth fall far short of their objective, for when they think to avenge injuries, they incur them with much more shame and dishonor than before. But I shall bring it about that as a wicked youth you suffer for it."

Then he ordered him to be seized and bound hand and foot, and be deposited in front of the knight of the Firm Island, and that the latter be told that that wicked son of his had broken his promise, and that he should exact from him whatever retribution he pleased. So he was taken before Amadis and put at his feet. The mother of that youth, when she saw this, was afraid that the knight, as an offended man, might do him some harm, and she went as a mother, without the giant's being aware of it, and as quickly as she could, to where Amadis was. At that time Amadis had his helmet in his hand — for until then and while the men at arms had him surrounded never had he removed it from his head — and his sword in its sheath, and he was untying the giant's son in order to release him. And when the matron came and saw his face, she recognized immediately that he was Amadis, and went toward him, weeping and unaccompanied by anyone else, and said to him: "My lord, do you recognize me?"

Amadis, although he saw at once that she was the daughter of Gandalac, foster father of Don Galaor, his brother, replied saying: "Madam, I do not know you."

"Well," said she, "my lord, I indeed know that you are Amadis, brother of my lord, Don Galaor. And if you consider it right that your name be concealed, I shall do so; and if you wish that it be known, do not fear the giant, since he has assured your safety. And in this action that he takes, you will see whether he is disposed to keep his word, for here he sends you his and my son who broke it, so that you may take upon him all the vengeance you like, and for him I ask your pity."

"My good lady," said Amadis, "you already know how greatly interested all of us, as brothers and friends of Don Galaor, are in what concerns your father and his children; and I should like to demonstrate that I am interested in something else that greatly concerns you, for in this matter there is no need to thank me, because without your request I was already setting him free; for I do not take vengeance except on those who with arms are willing to defend their wicked deeds. And in this matter that you mention concerning my name, as to whether I consider it good that it be told or concealed, I say rather that I am pleased that the giant know who I am, and that you tell him that I shall not leave here until the satisfaction that I demand be rendered the matron who brought me here. And if he is as truthful as everybody says, he ought to place himself on this field in the same position as when I had him defeated, in order that I may fully wreak my will upon him; and if his being unconscious when he was carried away from here excuses him somewhat, now, if he is conscious, for no honest reason can he be excused."

The matron thanked him with great humility and said to him: "My lord, do not doubt my husband, for he will place himself according as you dictate or will carry out what you ask of him. And without any fear, come with me to where he is."

"My good lady and friend," said he, "to you I would trust my life without any misgivings, but I have a fear concerning the nature of giants, who seldom are governed by, and submissive to reason, because their great fury and rage in most matters holds them enslaved."

"It is true," said the matron, "but from what I know of this one, I beg you to come with me without any misgivings."

"Since thus it pleases you," said Amadis, "I deem it all right."

Then he put his helmet on his head and took his shield, and with sword in hand he went with her, thinking that it could be safer for him than to be as he was, expecting death without having or hoping for any help; for even if he killed all those men who had him surrounded, he would not be able to save himself thereby; because before he could obtain a ship in order to be able to leave — for all were under the control of the giant's men — the people of the island would kill him themselves because although in the other regions where the giants held sway they were hated on account of their arrogant and excessive cruelties, this Balan was not hated by his subjects because he kept all of them protected and defended without taking anything of theirs from them. Therefore it was impossible to think of being able to maintain himself thus alone. And for these reasons he ventured, without any more security than that given him at first and what the lady offered him, to enter that mighty fortress armed as he was, resolving that if they attacked him out of a desire to trick him, he would perform rare exploits before being killed.

So just as the story tells you, Amadis went with the giantess wife of Balan to the castle; and when he was inside, the giant was informed that the knight who had fought with him was there and wanted to speak with him. He gave orders to bring him to where he was in bed, and thus it was done. Having entered the room, Amadis said: "Balan, I am quite dissatisfied with you, for I, on coming to seek you and to put myself in your power while trusting your word, in order to fight with you under the safe-conduct that you gave to the matron who went for me, and afterwards to the knight of Princess Island, your men, breaking your word, have sought wickedly to kill me. I indeed don't believe that it pleases you, or that you ordered it, for you were not in condition to do so; but this fact did not rid me of the danger, for I have been quite close to death; but however that may be, I declare myself content because of what you have done with your son. I beg of you, Balan, to be willing to make amends to this lady who brought me here; otherwise I cannot release you from the combat until it be concluded, although it already has had one ending, for it was in my power to kill you or save you. I respect you and value you more than you think because of the relationship that you have with Gandalac, the giant of the Rock of Galtares, for I have learned that you are married to his daughter. But although I have this good will toward you, I cannot avoid obtaining justice from you for this lady."

The giant answered him: "Knight, although the pain and sorrow that I have on seeing myself defeated by a single knight is such a great and rare event for me, for I never have been defeated until today, and although for me it is worse than death, I feel that it is nothing in comparison with what my son and my men have done to you. And if my strength afforded me the opportunity to carry it out personally, you would see the force of my word and what it embraces. But it can do no more than to surrender to you the one responsible, although he alone is the mirror in which his mother and I see ourselves; and if you wish more, ask for it, for your desire will be satisfied."

Amadis said to him: "I am contented with what you have done. Now tell me what you will do in the matter of the lady."

"Whatever you see that I can do," said the giant, "for the son of this matron is beyond help since he is dead. I beg you earnestly to ask of me what is possible."

"I shall do so," said Amadis, "for anything else would be folly."

"Then tell me what you wish," said he.

"What I wish," said Amadis, "is that you have the husband of that matron set free at once along with their daughter and their entire company, restoring to them all of their possessions and their ship; and for the son that you have killed you give them yours, to be married to that maiden; for although you are a noble lord, I tell you that in lineage and in complete excellence she owes you nothing because even in estate and rank they are not noticeably lacking, for besides their great possessions and income they are governors of one of my father's realms."

Then the giant when he heard this looked at him more intently than before and said to him: "I beg you as a courtesy to tell me who you are to set yourself so high, and who your father is."

"Know you," said Amadis, "that my father is King Perion of Gaul, and I am his son Amadis."

When the giant heard this, he immediately raised his head as best he could, and said: "What is that? Is it true that you are that Amadis who killed my father?"

"I am," said he, "the one who in order to rescue King Lisuarte, who was about to die, killed a giant, and I am told that he was your father."

"Now I say to you, Amadis," said the giant, "that I do not know to what to attribute this very great daring in coming to my land: whether to your great courage or to my promises being reputed truthful. But your great courage has brought it about, which has never feared or failed to attack and defeat all dangerous things. And since Fortune is so favorable to you, it is not right that I from now on try to oppose her might, for she has already shown me how ineffective my own strength is to harm you. And concerning what you say to me about my son, I give him to you to dispose of him at your pleasure; and not as a good son as I was hoping, but as a bad one, because he who does not keep his word has nothing left for which to be praised. And likewise I release the knight and his daughter together with their retinue, as you command; and I wish to become your friend, to do your bidding in any situation in which you may need me."

Amadis thanked him and said to him: "I consider you my friend since you were Gandalac's; and as a friend I beg of you that from now on you do not maintain this bad custom on this island; for if you do not conform in God's service by following His holy doctrine, all other things, even if they bring you some hope of honor and benefit, in the end will not be able to keep you from suffering great mishaps. And you will see this from the following : by God's will I was guided here, without my intending to come, and it was His will to give me courage to overcome and defeat you; for in view of your huge size and abundant strength of heart and valor, I would not have been of sufficient avail to do you any harm without His mercy. But now let us drop this matter, for I think that you will do what I ask of you. Pardon your son, not only because of his tender age, which was the cause of his error, but also out of regard for his mother, whom I consider as a sister. And have him and the maiden come here, and let them be betrothed at once."

"Since I am determined to be your friend," said the giant, "all that you consider good I shall do."

Then he ordered the knight who was husband of the matron to come there, and likewise his daughter and all their companions; for Darioleta was with them with as much enjoyment at seeing such a shortcut taken as if she had been made mistress of the world. And before them and before the mother and grandmother of the youth, they were betrothed and Amadis ordered them to have the marriage solemnized at once.

Now the story wants to show you the reasons for this marriage: in the first place in order to make known to you how Amadis finished that very great adventure to his honor and to the satisfaction of that matron who had brought him there, by defeating that mighty Balan, daring — although the latter was his enemy on account of the father whom he had killed — to venture into his island, where he experienced such great danger as you have heard; the other reason being that you may know that to this Bravor, son of Balan and that daughter of Darioleta's was born a son who had the name Galeote, for already this lad took after his mother and was not so large and misshapen as giants were. This Galeote was lord of that island after the death of his father Bravor, and he married a daughter of Don Galvanes and beautiful Madasima his wife. And to these was born another son who had the name Balan like his grandfather; thus they kept succeeding to the rulership one after the other, continually ruling that island such a long time until from them was descended that valiant and vigorous Don Segurades, first cousin of the old knight who came to the court of King Arthur when he was one hundred and twenty years old, and had forty descendants — for on account of his great age he had given up the use of arms — and without a lance unhorsed all the knights of great renown who were at court at the time. Well, this Segurades lived in the time of King Utherpadragon, King Arthur's father and lord of Great Britain, and he left a son and ruler of that island named Bravor the "Brun"; for since he was so belligerent they gave him that name, because in the language of that time they said "brun" for "belligerent" [a nonsensical statement; see Notes. — E. B. P.]. Tristan de Leonis killed this Bravor in combat on that same island, on whose shores the hazards of the sea had cast him and Isolda the Blonde, daughter of King Languines of Ireland, and their entire company, as he was bringing her to become the wife of his uncle King Mark of Cornwall. And from this Bravor the "Brun" came that great and very valiant prince Galeote the "Brun," lord of the Faraway Islands, and great friend of Don Lancelot of the Lake, as this way you can learn — if you have read or do read the book of Don Tristan and Lancelot, in which mention is made of these "Bruns" — from where the founding of their lineage stemmed. And because they were the successors of that giant, son of Balan, they were always called giants, although they did not conform to them in the size of their bodies because of the influence of the distaff side, just as we have told you; and also because all those of that lineage were very strong and valiant at arms, and with a large share of the haughtiness and conceit of the giants from whom they had sprung.

But now we shall leave Amadis on that island, where he rested a few days to have the wounds treated that Balan had given him in the combat, and because the giant and his wife earnestly besought him to do so; and there he received very fine service. And the story will tell you what Grasandor did after he was told by the huntsman of Amadis's command and learned that Amadis was going away by sea in a small boat.

The story has already told you how, at the time that Amadis departed from the seashore with the matron in the boat, having armed himself with the arms of the dead knight, he commanded one of his men to tell Grasandor that he was going away, and that he should have that knight buried and obtain for Amadis the pardon of his lady Oriana. So this man went at once to where Grasandor was engaged in hunting and knew nothing about the departure of Amadis — instead he thought that, like all the others, he was with his dog among the beaters in the place assigned to him — and he told him Amadis's message and command. And when Grasandor heard about it, he greatly wondered what very urgent reason had caused Amadis to leave him, and even more his lady Oriana, without seeing them first; and he left the hunt at once, ordering the beater to guide him to where the dead knight was. Having arrived there, he saw him lying on the ground, but he saw nothing more on the ocean, for the boat in which Amadis was traveling was already out of sight; and he immediately had the knight loaded on a palfrey, and the entire party having assembled, he returned to the Firm Island, while greatly pondering what he would do. And arriving at the foot of the hill, he gave orders to those men who were coming with him to bury that knight in the monastery there, which Amadis had ordered built in honor of the Virgin Mary at the time that he came from the Poor Rock, as the second Book of this story relates; and he went to where Oriana and his wife Mabilia and those ladies were.

And as they saw him alone, they asked him where Amadis was. He told them everything that had happened to him and that he knew about him, without leaving out anything, but with a cheerful countenance in order not to frighten them. When Oriana heard it, she remained a while without being able to speak, because of the great perturbation she felt, and when she had recovered, she said: "I certainly think that since Amadis went without you and without my knowing about it, it would not be except for a compelling reason."

Grasandor said to her: "My lady, I think so, but I ask your pardon for him, for he sent word by the beater who saw him go to tell me to do so."

"My good lord," said Oriana, "it is more necessary to pray God out of His mercy to protect him than to ask me to pardon him; for I well know that never at any time has he been guilty of any transgression towards me, nor will he be hereafter, for such trust I have in the great and true love that he has for me. But what do you think should be done?"

Grasandor said to her: "It seems to me, madam, that it will be well to go and look for him; and if I can find him, to undergo that good or evil that he may be experiencing, for I shall not rest day or night until I find him."

All those ladies agreed concerning this matter that Grasandor should leave at once; but Mabilia all that night never stopped weeping over him, thinking that because of that journey great dangers and affronts could not be avoided for him. But finally, desiring more the honor of her husband than the satisfaction of her own wishes, she gave approval to his plan.

Then, morning having come, Grasandor arose and heard mass; and taking leave of Oriana and Mabilia and the other matrons, he went on board a vessel; and taking with him his arms and horse and two squires with the necessary provisions, and a sailor to guide him, he put out to sea along that same route that Amadis had followed.

Grasandor traveled on over the sea ignorant of his destination, save only that it would be wherever Fortune might carry him; for the only thing he knew for certain was that Amadis had gone in that same direction. Then proceeding as you hear all that day and night and the next day, they sailed without finding anyone who could give Grasandor any information; and his ill luck brought it about that on the second night he passed very close to Princess Island, and on account of its being a very dark night they did not see it; for if he had put into port there, he could not have missed finding Amadis because he would have discovered that he had landed there and that the knight governor of that island had departed with him, and he then would have been guided to the Island of the Vermilion Tower; but it turned out otherwise for him, for that night he went far beyond it and traveled another day, and at nightfall he found himself near the seacoast and close to a great expanse of beach. There Grasandor ordered the vessel to stop until morning in order to find out what land that was. So they remained until day came, when they could get a good look at the land, and it seemed to them the mainland and very beautiful with large groves of trees. Grasandor ordered his horse taken off, and he armed himself and told the sailor not to leave that place until he returned or he had word from him, because he wanted to see where they had landed and to try to find out some news of the man they were seeking.

Then he mounted his horse and with his squires accompanying him on foot, because they had not brought palfreys in order that the boat might not be weighted down and slowed. So he traveled most of the day without encountering anyone; and he was greatly surprised, for that land seemed to him uninhabited. And he dismounted beside a spring that he found at the edge of a forest which he was skirting, and the squires fed him and his horse; and as soon as they had eaten, they said to him: "Sir, return to the boat, for this land must be uninhabited."

Grasandor said to them: "You stay here, for you cannot keep up with me; and I shall go ahead until I obtain information. And if I do not obtain any, I shall return to you at once; and if you should see that I am late, return to the boat, for if I can, I shall be there."

The squires, who, already tired out, could not go on, commended him to God and told him that they would do just as he ordered.

So Grasandor went through that forest and after a bit found a deep, very thickly wooded valley, at one end of which he saw a small monastery located where the forest was most dense, and he went there at once. On reaching its gate he found it open, and he dismounted from his horse and tying it to the gate-bar, went inside. And he went directly to the church and said his prayers the best he knew how, imploring God to guide him on that journey so that whatever he did might be to His honor, and to direct him to where he could find Amadis. While he was on his knees, he saw a Carmelite monk coming to the church; and he called out to him saying: "Father, what land is this and under what sovereignty is it?"

"This is under the sovereignty of Ireland, but it is not now very much at the king's command because near here is a knight named Galifon; and with two brothers who are very powerful knights just as he is, and as possessor of a strongly fortified castle in which he takes refuge, he has subjugated all this wooded hill area of very good land and quite prosperous villages, and does much harm to the knights errant who pass through here; for he and his brothers travel, all three of them, together, and when they encounter some knight, two of them hide and the other attacks him. And if the knight of the castle wins, the two make no move; and if it goes badly for him in the battle, they come out and easily defeat or kill the one who is alone. And yesterday it happened that two monks of this house on coming through these towns to beg alms saw all three brothers defeat and seriously wound a knight. And those two fathers asked them for him, begging them for the love of God not to kill him and to give him to them, since in him there was no longer any defense. And they urged them so insistently that they had to do so; and they brought him in on a donkey, and here we have him. And then a short while later another knight arrived who was a companion of his; and when he found out about this episode, he left here — not long before you arrived — with the intention of dying or avenging this one who is wounded. And certainly he goes forth at great risk to his person."

When Grasandor heard this, he told the monk to show him the wounded knight. And he did so, for he brought him into a cell where the wounded man was lying on a bed. And when he saw him, he recognized him, for he was Eliseo, cousin of Don Cuadragante's nephew Landin. And likewise the knight recognized him, for many times they had seen each other and had conversed during the war between King Lisuarte and Amadis. And when Eliseo saw him, he said: "Oh my good lord Grasandor! I beg you as a courtesy to aid my cousin Landin, who goes into great danger; and afterwards I shall tell you how my adventure came about, for if I detain you now in order to relate it, your aid would not assist him at all."

Grasandor said to him: "Where shall I find him?"

"After going through this valley," said Eliseo, "you will see an extensive plateau, and on it a fortified castle; and there you will find him, for he is going to challenge a knight who is lord of it and from whom I received this wound."

Grasandor saw at once that what the monk had told him was true. And commending Eliseo to God, he mounted his horse and went as fast as he could on that road leading to where the monk indicated he could best see the castle. And when he had gone through the valley, he saw it immediately on a knoll higher than the other land around it, and on going towards it, he arrived at the edge of a forest which he had been traversing, and beheld Landin, who was in front of the castle gate shouting. But he did not understand what he was saying, for he was at some distance away. And he drew rein on his horse amid the thick undergrowth, for he did not want to appear until he saw whether Landin needed help. While remaining thus, he soon saw a very large and well-armed knight come out through the gate towards where Landin was, and he spoke a little with Landin and then they withdrew a short distance from each other, and went forward to attack one another at full speed of their horses; and they collided so violently with their lance thrusts and with their horses that both perforce fell heavily to the ground. But the knight of the castle fell much harder, so that he was stunned; but he got up as quickly as he could, and grasped his sword to defend himself.

Landin arose as a man who was very agile and brave, and saw that his enemy was prepared to receive him; so he grasped his sword, covered himself with his shield, and went at him; and the other one likewise went forward at his adversary, and they dealt each other very mighty blows on top of their helmets so that sparks flew from them; and they shredded their shields and cut the mesh of their mail in many places so that their swords reached their flesh, and thus they went on for a time inflicting on each other all the injury they could. But soon Landin began to get the upperhand to such an extent that he was dominating the knight of the castle, who now was intent only on protecting himself from the blows without being able to deliver any. And when he saw himself thus, he began to motion with his sword to those of the castle to rescue him, for they were delaying a long time. Then two knights rode out at full speed, with their lances in hand, and saying: "Wicked scoundrel, don't kill him!"

When Landin saw them coming thus, he prepared to await them like a good knight, without any change of purpose, because he had already understood that if things went badly for the first knight, he would be aided by the other two; and he said to them: "You are the evil ones and traitors, for you deceitfully and without provocation kill good and loyal knights."

Grasandor, who was watching it all, when he saw them coming thus, spurred his horse as hard as he could and went toward them saying: "Let the knight alone, you wicked traitors!"

And he struck one of them on the shield with his lance such a mighty blow that without any delay he hurled him over the horse's rump and he landed on the ground, which was hard, in such a terrible fall that his left arm on which he fell, was broken, and he was so stunned that he could not get up. The other knight went forward to deliver a lance thrust at Landin with lance held high or trample him with the horse; but he was not able to do so, for Landin dodged with such agility and skill that the other one could not catch him; and he rushed past so hard on his horse that Landin could not strike him, although he tried to cut the legs of the horse. Grasandor said to him: "Stay with that one who is on foot, and leave this one on horseback to me."

When Landin saw this he was very happy, but could not conceive who the knight could be who at such a time had come to his assistance. And he returned at once to the knight with whom he had been fighting previously, and struck him with the sword many hard and devastating blows. And although the knight tried as hard as he could to defend himself, it availed him nothing, for Landin was dominating him completely.

Grasandor was exchanging blows with the one on horseback, as they were dealing each other mighty blows with their swords, for Grasandor had severed his lance and wounded him on the hand. And thus all four were doing all the damage they could; but in a little while Landin knocked his foe down at his feet. And when the other one who was still on horseback saw this, he began to flee toward the castle as fast as he could, with Grasandor after him, for he did not leave him. And as he was in a daze, on heading for the drawbridge he missed his aim and fell with his horse into the moat, which was very deep and full of water, so that with the weight of his armor, in a short while he was drowned, for those of the castle could not rescue him because Grasandor had placed himself at the end of the bridge, as did Landin, who came up immediately on another of the horses that had remained in the field.

And when they saw the contest stopped and that there was nothing to do, they both returned to where they had left the knights, in order to see whether they had died.

And Landin said: "Sir knight, who are you who at such a time have come to my aid, when I had such great need of it?"

Grasandor said to him: "My lord Landin, I am Grasandor, your friend, and I give many thanks to God that I found you at a time when you had need of me."

When Landin heard this, he greatly wondered what chance could have brought him to that land, for he well knew that he had remained on the Firm Island with Amadis at the time that the fleet had left there to go to Sansuenia and the kingdom of King Arabigo; and he said to him: "My good lord, who has brought you into this land, so far removed from where you were with Amadis?"

Grasandor told him all that you have heard, under what circumstances he had had to leave in search of Amadis, and he asked him if he knew anything about him. Landin said to him: "Know you, Lord Grasandor, that my cousin Eliseo and I come from where Cuadragante, my uncle, and Don Bruneo de Bonamar have stopped, together with those knights that you saw depart from the Firm Island; and we bear a message from my uncle for King Cildadan asking him for some troops, for back there we had a battle with a nephew of King Arabigo who had taken control of the land when he found out that his uncle the king had been overcome and taken prisoner. And although we were victors and wrought great havoc on the enemy, we received much damage, for we lost many troopers. And for this reason we come in order to bring back more, and it was about three days ago that we put into port at Princess Island, and there we found out that a knight who was bringing a matron and only one man had come in a small boat, and that they said they were going to the Island of the Vermilion Tower to fight with Balan, the giant; and they were not able to tell me why, except that the governor of that island went with the knight to observe the battle, because according to what is said, that giant is the most valiant there is in all the islands. And as you say that Amadis departed by sea with the matron, be assured that it is none other than he, for such an undertaking was appropriate for him."

"You have made me very happy," said Grasandor, "with this news: but I cannot refrain from being very sad not to have been with him in such a confrontation as that."

"Do not regret it," said Landin, "for God created that man for the express purpose of giving to him alone the honor and great glory that all others in the world put together would not be able to attain."

"Now tell me," said Grasandor, "what happened to you; for in the monastery down yonder in a deep valley I found your cousin Eliseo badly wounded; and from him I could not find out what had happened except only that you had come to fight with this knight. And the monks of that monastery told me the evil tactics he and his brothers used in overcoming dishonorably the knights who fought with them; and in order not to be detained I asked no further questions."

Landin said to him: "Know you that we went ashore yesterday to go by land where King Cildadan is, for on arriving near that monastery you saw, we met a maiden who was coming in tears. She asked us for help. I asked her the reason for her grief and told her that if it was a matter that merited a remedy, I would provide it. She told me that a knight was holding her fiancé prisoner unjustly in order to take from him a piece of very good property that he had in his land, and he held him in chains in a tower, which was a good two leagues to the right of the monastery. I sought from the maiden a pledge that she was telling me the truth, and she gave it to me at once. I told my cousin Eliseo to stay behind in that monastery because he was more seasick than I, while I went with the maiden; and that if God guided me well, I would soon return for him. But he was so insistent on going with me that I could not avoid taking him along. And going through that valley yonder amid that thick undergrowth, with the maiden guiding us, we saw an armed knight on horseback who was already ascending to the plateau. Then Eliseo said to me: " 'Cousin, you go with the maiden, and I shall go to investigate that knight.' "

"So he left me, and I went with the maiden, and reached the tower where her betrothed was imprisoned. And I called to the knight who was holding him prisoner, and he came out unarmed to talk with me. And when he saw my face he recognized me at once and asked me what I wanted. I told him everything that the maiden had told me, and that I was asking him to set free her betrothed at once and not to do him henceforth any injury unjustly. And he complied immediately out of regard for me, because by no means did he want to fight with me, and he promised me to do as I had asked. And I reprimanded him severely, saying to him that it was not proper for a man in such good circumstances to do such things. I could talk this way because this knight was my friend, and when we were novice knights, we had traveled together in search of adventure. Then having settled this affair, I returned to the monastery as per agreement and found Eliseo badly wounded, and I asked him what had happened to him. And he told me that as he was following that knight after he left me, and was shouting at him to turn back, the knight finally had returned to him and that they had had a fierce combat; and that in his opinion he had him at a disadvantage and almost defeated when two other knights came out of the forest and clashed with him so fiercely that they overthrew him and his horse, and wounded him very badly; and that if then God had not brought there to him two monks of that monastery who earnestly begged them for his life, they would have finished killing him; but out of regard for them they desisted, and those monks took him away."

"I know all that about your cousin, for the monks told me," said Grasandor, "but I did not know anything about your own adventure except that you had left the monastery to fight with these wicked, treacherous knights. But what in your opinion should we do with them if they are not dead?"

Landin said to him: "Let us find out in what condition they are, and then we shall decide."

Then they came to where Galifon, the lord of the castle, was stretched out on the ground, for he did not have the strength to get up; but he was already breathing better and more conscious than before. And in the same condition they found his brother, who was not dead but was very badly bruised. And Landin summoned two squires, who came with them, one of them his and the other his cousin's; and he had them dismount from their palfreys; and they slung those two knights across the saddles, and had the squires mount behind them. And they went toward the monastery with the intention of killing them if Eliseo was dead or dangerously wounded; but if he was better, they would take a different course of action.

Just as you hear, they reached the monastery, and they found Eliseo out of danger, for one of those monks, who knew what was needed, had treated and greatly helped him. At this time, that Galifon, lord of the castle, was entirely conscious; and when he saw Landin unarmed, he recognized him; for both he and his brothers were all King Cildadan's men. But when they saw that the king was going to help King Lisuarte in the war that the latter was having with Amadis, these three brothers stayed in the land, for he could not take them with him. And while he was occupied in that affair, they caused much damage in that region, having little respect for King Cildadan on seeing him under the suzerainty of King Lisuarte; for when Fortune changes from good to bad, not only is it contrary and adverse in the principal matter at issue, but in many other secondary matters stemming from it, which can be compared to the consequences of deadly sin. And he said to him: "Sir Landin, would I be able to obtain some courtesy from you? And if you think that my evil deeds do not deserve it, may your good deeds merit it. And do not regard my mistakes, but what you ought to do in view of your reputation and the lineage from which you spring."

Landin said to him: "Galifon, such wicked deeds were not expected from you; for a knight who is brought up in the court of such a good king and in the company of so many good men is greatly obligated to lead a completely virtuous existence. And I am surprised to see your upbringing so corrupted by your pursuit of such an evil and treacherous life."

"The desire to exercise lordship," said Galifon, "turned me aside from what virtue constrained me to follow, just as it has many others who were worth and knew more than I; but the entire remedy is in your hands and dependent on your will."

"What do you want me to do?" said Landin.

"That you obtain pardon for me from the king, my lord," said he, "and I shall throw myself upon his mercy under your sponsorship as soon as I am able to mount a horse."

"It shall be just as you say," said Landin, "for from now on you will adopt the life style befitting the order of knightood."

"So it shall be," said Galifon, "without any doubt."

"Then I set you and your brother free," said Landin, "with the proviso that three weeks from today you be before King Cildadan, my lord, and do whatever he may command; and in the meantime I shall obtain a pardon for you."

Galifon thanked him profusely and promised to do just as he ordered.

This having been done, they all remained there together that night. And the next morning early Grasandor heard mass and took leave of Landin and his cousin in order to return to the boat he had left on the seashore, and with much joy in his heart because of the news that Landin had given him; for he was sure the knight was Amadis who had put into port at Princess Island in company with the matron and had gone to fight with the giant Balan. So he went back over the route by which he had come and arrived before nightfall at the boat; where to their mutual pleasure he found his squires.

Grasandor asked the sailor if he would know how to guide them to the island that is called Princess. He said he could, for after they arrived there, he had determined where they were, which he had not known at the time of their arrival; and that he would guide him to that island.

"Then let us go there," said Grasandor.

So they left the shore and sailed all that night; and next day at the hour of vespers they reached the island. And Grasandor landed and went up to the town, where they told him everything that had happened to Amadis with the giant, which they had found out from the governor, who had arrived there. Grasandor talked with him in order to be more certain, and he told him all he had seen of Amadis, just as the story has related it. Grasandor said to him: "Good sir, you have told me news that greatly pleases me. And this I say to you not because Amadis has come out of this adventure with such honor — for in view of the great exploits and perils in which he has been involved those of us familiar with them cannot be surprised at any others, however great they may be — but because of having found him; for certainly I would not have been able to achieve any rest or enjoyment anywhere until I obtained news of him."

The knight said to him: "I indeed believe, in view of the great deeds reported of this knight in all parts of the world, that those who at some time had kept company with him would have seen many of them. But I tell you that if, as I did, they could have seen what latterly he experienced, as I saw it, they would account it among the most dangerous."

Then they ceased talking about that, and Grasandor said to him: "I beg of you, knight, out of courtesy to give me some one of your men to guide me to the island where Amadis is."

"I shall gladly do so," said he, "and if you need some provisions for the voyage, they shall be provided for you at once."

"I thank you very much," said Grasandor, "but I am bringing everything necessary."

The knight of the island said: "Here is a man who will guide you, for yesterday he came from there."

Grasandor thanked him and got into the boat with that man who was to guide him, and went on his way over the sea. And they made such good progress that without difficulty they reached the harbor of the Island of the Vermilion Tower, where Amadis was.

And immediately he was seized by the giant's men, who asked him what he wanted. He told them that he came to look for a knight named Amadis of Gaul, who, he had been told, was on that island.

"You speak the truth," said they; "come up with us to the castle, for there you will find him."

Then he came off the boat armed as he was, and went up to the castle with those men. And when he reached the gate, Amadis was informed that a knight was there who was seeking him. Amadis immediately thought that it was probably one of his friends, and came out to the gate. When he saw that it was Grasandor, he was the happiest person in the world, and embraced him with great joy, and Grasandor likewise him, as if a long time had passed since they had seen each other. Amadis asked him about his lady Oriana, how she was, and whether she was greatly disturbed by his going away. Grasandor said to him: "My good lord, she and all the other ladies are very well; and as for Oriana, I tell you that she was greatly upset and disturbed when she found out from me about your departure. But as her discretion is so surpassingly great, she decided that you had not made this trip without good reason. And don't think that she continues to feel upset or angry over anything other than the fact that she will not be able to see you as soon as she desires. And although I come to summon you, I would be very pleased to have you stay on here for four or five days on my account, because I suffer from seasickness."

"I think it is a good idea," said Amadis, "to do so, for I also need the rest, because I still feel weak on account of some wounds that I sustained, from which I have not completely recovered. And what you tell me about my lady makes me very happy, for in comparison with her anger, all the things that could happen to me from great encounters, even death itself, I consider of no consequence."

CHAPTER CXXX

HOW WHILE AMADIS WAS ON THE ISLAND OF THE VERMILION TOWER SEATED ON SOME CRAGS OVERLOOKING THE OCEAN AND TALKING WITH GRASANDOR ABOUT HIS LADY ORIANA, HE SAW A SHIP COMING; FROM WHICH HE ASCERTAINED NEWS OF THE FLEET THAT HAD GONE TO SANSUENIA AND THE ISLANDS OF LANDAS.

Just as you hear, Amadis and Grasandor were enjoying life on that Island of the Vermilion Tower; and Amadis kept asking about his lady Oriana, because all his desires and concerns were focused on her; for although he now possessed her, he was not lacking a single jot of the love that he always had had for her; on the contrary now more than ever his heart was enthralled by her, and with even more circumspection he intended to do her bidding. What caused this was the fact that this great love affair of theirs did not come about by accident, as in the case of many who no sooner love and covet than they abhor; but it was so deep seated, and with such honorable intentions in conformity with good conscience that it became greater and greater, just as do all things established and founded upon virtue. But it is the opposite course that we all generally pursue, for our desires are more for the contentment and satisfaction of our base desires and appetites than for what we are constrained to do by goodness and reason; which we ought to keep in mind and ever present, considering that if all sweet and tasty things were placed in our mouths, and if in the end a bitter taste resulted, from the sweetness not only would the sweet taste be lost, but the desire would be so altered that because of what came last, a great distaste would be felt for what came first. Hence we can indeed say that most delight and perfection comes at the end. Then if this be so, why do we fail to recognize that although illicit things, whether they be love affairs or of some other category, were at the outset wont to bring sweetness and in the end bitterness and repentance, the virtuous things of good conscience that at first appear harsh and bitter, in the long run always afford contentment and joy? But in the case of this knight and his lady we cannot separate the bad from the good, or the sad from the joyous, because from the beginning their thought was always to pursue the honest goal at which they now have arrived. And if they experienced no slight amount of care and anxiety over each other, as this great story relates, do not think that from such preoccupation they received pain or suffering; rather, much peace and joy; because the more they remembered their great love the more such memories caused each to visualize the other as if in the flesh; which fact brought such surcease and consolation to their keen anguish that in nowise would they have wished to give over that delightful memory. But let us stop talking on the subject of these faithful lovers, not only because it is unending but also because a very long time has passed and will continue to pass without other lovers like them being seen or memorialized in writing at such great length.

So Amadis was talking with Grasandor about those matters that afforded them most pleasure. And it happened to them that while both were seated on some high crags overlooking the sea, they saw a small craft coming straight to that harbor and they did not want to leave there without first finding out who was on it. The boat having arrived at the port, they gave orders to Grasandor's squire to ascertain who the people were who were arriving; he went at once to find out. And when he returned, he said: "Sirs, in it comes a majordomo of Madasima's, wife of Don Galvanes, en route to the Island of Mongaza."

"Well, where does he come from?" said Amadis.

"Sir," said the squire, "they say from where Don Galvanes and Don Galaor are. I did not find out any more about them."

When Amadis heard this, he and Grasandor came down from the crags and went to the harbor where the boat lay. And when they arrived, Amadis recognized Nalfon, for such was the name of the majordomo, and said to him: "Nalfon, my friend, I am very glad to see you because you will tell me news of my brother Don Galaor and of Don Galvanes; for since they departed from the Firm Island I have had none."

When the majordomo saw and recognized that it was Amadis, he was greatly astonished to find him in such a place, for he well knew that that island belonged to the giant Balan, the chief enemy that Amadis had, on account of his having killed Balan's father. And he at once landed and knelt before him to kiss his hands; but Amadis embraced him and would not yield his hands to him. The majordomo said to him:

"Sir, what adventure was it that has brought you here to this land so far removed from where we left you?"

Amadis said to him: "My good friend, God brought me on a matter that later you will ascertain; but tell me everything that you have seen involving my brother and Don Galvanes and Dragonis."

"Sir," said he, "God be praised, I can indeed do so, and tell you things that will please you. Know you that Don Galaor and Dragonis left Sobradisa with many well-equipped troops. And my lord Don Galvanes with all the troops that he could muster from the Island of Mongaza joined them on the high seas at a rock that they had as a landmark, which is called the Rock of the Maiden Enchantress; I do not know whether you have heard of it."

Amadis said to him: "By the faith that you owe to God, majordomo, if you know anything about the things that are on that rock, tell me about them because Don Gavarte of the Fearful Valley had told me that when he was severely ill during a sea voyage, he passed by the foot of that Rock you mention, and his illness prevented him from ascending it and seeing many of the things that are on it. And those who have seen them told him that among them there was a great adventure in which the knights have failed who have attempted to engage in it."

The majordomo said to him: "All that I could learn about this matter that has remained in men's memories I shall gladly tell you. Know you that that Rock has retained this name because there was a time when it was colonized by a maiden who was suzerain of it and who strove very hard to learn the arts of magic and necromancy, and she learned them in such wise that she accomplished everything she wished. At the time she lived there she built her dwelling, which was the most beautiful and luxurious ever seen, and frequently it happened that she had at anchor around that rock many ships that were crossing the sea from Ireland and Norway and Sobradisa to the Islands of Landas and the Deep Island. And in nowise could they depart from there unless the maiden afforded them an opportunity by dissolving those spells under which they were held and constrained; and from them she was accustomed to take whatever she pleased; and if knights came in the ships, she held them as long as she liked, and made them fight one another until they overcame and even killed each other, for they were powerless to do anything else; and from that she derived great enjoyment. She did many other things that would take too long to relate. But since it is quite certain that those who deceive, are in turn duped and roughly treated in this world and in the next by being caught in the same snares that they set for others, after some time had elapsed during which this maiden spent her days with such great wealth and delight, thinking to penetrate with her considerable knowledge the great secrets of God, with His permission she was duped and deceived by one who knew nothing of such matters. And this came about from the fact that among those knights whom she had thus brought there was one who was a native of the island of Crete, a handsome man, twenty-five years old and quite efficient at arms. The maiden was so greatly in love with him that he completely hoodwinked her, so that neither her great learning nor the strong resistance she made to her own confused and defeated impulses was able to prevent her from making this knight lord and master of what until then no one had possessed, which was her person; and with him she spent some time to the great delight of her heart; and he likewise with her, more on account of the profit that he expected from it than because of her beauty, with which she had been very scantily adorned by Nature. So while that maiden and the knight her lover were leading such a life, he, reflecting that it would be of very little benefit to him to rule the whole world in such a strange, remote place as that, began to consider what he might do in order to leave that prison. And he thought that sweet talk and a loving countenance along with the delightful acts involved in a love affair, even though feigned, had great powers to upset and confuse the judgment of every person in love; so in their love affair he began much more than before to appear enthralled and passionately enamored, not only in public but in private, and to beg her very insistently not to entertain the thought that he was motivated by the power of her spells, but only because his desire and love for her so impelled him. Then he brought so much pressure to bear on her that she in the belief that she possessed him completely, and judging from her own captivated, constrained heart that he loved her as guilelessly as she did him, left him free to do as he liked. When he saw himself thus, desiring more than ever to leave that life, one day when he was talking with the maiden as they looked out to sea, meanwhile embracing her as on many other occasions and manifesting great love for her, he threw her down over the cliff from such a height that her body was completely broken to bits. When the knight had done this, he took everything he found there and all the inhabitants, men as well as women; and leaving the island uninhabited, he went to the isle of Crete. But he left there in a room of the chief palace of the maiden a great treasure, according to what they say, which he could not take, nor could anyone else, because it was, and is to this day, under a spell. And some, who in very cold weather when the serpents are hibernating have dared to climb the cliff, say that they reached the doors of that room, but were powerless to enter, and that on one of its doors there is an inscription in blood-red letters, and on the other, another one identifying the knight who is to enter there. And he is to win that treasure by first drawing out a sword that is inserted in the doors up to its hilt, and then they will be opened. That, sir, is what I know about what you have asked me."

Amadis, as soon as he had heard this, remained for a while meditating how he could best go and accomplish what so many had failed to do. And remaining silent on the subject, he kept his thoughts about it to himself; instead he asked Nalfon about his brothers and their friends. Nalfon said to him: "Sir, after the fleets had rendezvoused at the foot of that rock that you hear about, they went on their way to the Deep Island. But it was impossible for their coming to be so secret as not to have been made known to everyone by some persons that they had stationed at sea; and the entire island was alerted by a first cousin of the dead king. So when we arrived at the port, all the people hastened there, with whom we of the ships had a great and dangerous battle. But finally Don Galaor and Don Galvanes and Dragonis leaped ashore in spite of our enemies, and in company with many others of our men who supported them, wrought such havoc among them that the troops withdrew from that end of the beach, so that we had the opportunity to disembark. Then all together we attacked them so hard that not being able to withstand us, they turned tail. But the exploits that Don Galaor performed no man would be able to describe adequately, for there he recovered everything that he had lost during such a long period because of his great illness. And among those whom he killed was that captain, cousin of the king, which enabled us more quickly to confine all his troops inside the town, surrounded on all sides by us. But since all were men of the lower class and they had no leader — for the leading men of that island had died with the king their lord in bringing aid to Lubayna, and many others had been taken prisoner; and since they saw that we were dominating the field and they were without any hope of being rescued — they at once proposed a pact whereby they would surrender if left unharmed in possession of their own property, and thus it was settled; so that in less than a week after we arrived there the whole island was won and Dragonis elevated to the throne. And because my lord Don Galvanes and Don Galaor were wounded, although not badly, it was decided to send me to my lady Madasima and to Queen Briolanja to tell them the news. And I, sire, came here to see my lady's aunt Madasima, whom she much esteems and loves because she is a very noble lady of great excellence. We had no thought of finding you in this region."

Amadis was very pleased with that news and gave many thanks to God because He had given such a victory to his brother and to those knights whom he loved so much. And he asked Nalfon if he had found out anything there about what Don Cuadragante and Don Bruneo of Bonamar and the knights who were with them had accomplished.

"Sir," said he, "after we had won the island we found on it some persons who had fled from the islands of Landas and from the city of Arabia, thinking that there they would be safer, for they knew nothing of our coming. And they said that before they had departed from there, a great battle had been fought with a nephew of King Arabigo and with the troops of the city and island; but finally those of the island were annihilated and beaten, and that they knew nothing beyond that."

With this news, all with great pleasure went up to the castle, and Amadis talked with Balan, the giant, who had not yet risen from his sickbed; and he told the giant that in any event he himself ought to leave there, and that he was asking Balan to order restored to Darioleta and her husband everything that he had taken from them, and the ship in which they came, so that they might go to the Firm Island; and also that he, Amadis, would be pleased if Balan would send with them his son Bravor and the latter's wife, so that Oriana might see them, and that Bravor might be with other youths there of high rank until it was time to dub him a knight; and that he would send him back to him with all the honor befitting a man of such high rank. The giant said to him: "Sir Amadis, just as up to now my will had been desirous of doing you all the harm that I could, so it now desires the opposite, for I love you with a true love and I consider myself honored to be your friend. Hence this which you ask will be done at once, and when I get up and am in such a state of health as to be able to exert myself, I wish to go to see your home and that island, and to be in your company all the time you please."

Amadis said: "Let it be done just as you say, and do believe that always in me you will have a brother because of your great worth and your personal qualities, and on account of your being related to Gandalac, whom my brothers and I regard as a second father. And give us permission to leave, for tomorrow we wish to go; and do not forget what you are promising."

But I want you to know that this Balan did not make that journey as soon as he thought; instead, on learning that Don Cuadragante and Don Bruneo had laid siege to the city of Arabia and were in some need of troops, he took all that he could from the island and from other islands belonging to his friends and went to the aid of Cuadragante and Bruneo with such a well-equipped force that he enabled what was begun to be brought to a conclusion with great honor. And never did he leave them until those two sovereignties of Sansuenia and of King Arabigo were won, as later on the story will relate.

Now the story tells that Amadis and Grasandor left one Monday morning from the great Island of the Vermilion Tower, of which that lusty giant Balan was ruler. And Amadis asked Nalfon, majordomo of Madasima, to give him one of his men to guide him to the Rock of the Maiden Enchantress. Nalfon told him that he was pleased to do so and that if he should want to climb up the cliff he would have good weather for it at that time, since it was in the dead of winter, and that if he were to order him to go with him, he would gladly do so. Amadis thanked him and told him it was not necessary for him to abandon what he had already directed him to do, for he needed only one guide.

"In the name of God," said the majordomo, "may He guide you and direct you in this and in everything else that you undertake, just as He has done until now."

Then they took leave of each other, and the majordomo went on his way to Anteyna, and Amadis and Grasandor set sail out over the sea with the guide whom they were bringing along. And they traveled a good five days without sighting the Rock, although they were having very good weather; and on the morning of the sixth day they saw it so lofty that it seemed to be touching the clouds. Then they went on until they were at the foot of it, and they found there a boat on the shore without any person to guard it, at which they were astonished; but they readily believed that someone who had climbed up the cliff had left it there. Amadis said to Grasandor: "My good sir, I want to climb up this cliff and see if what the majordomo told us is true as he related it; and I earnestly beg you, although you may feel some anxiety, to wait for me here until tomorrow night, when I shall be able to come or to signal you from above as to how it goes with me. And if during this interval or on the third day I do not return, you can believe that my undertaking is not going well, and you will take whatever course of action you please."

Grasandor said to him: "I am very sorry, sir, that you do not consider me capable of enduring to the point of death whatever danger may be in store for us, especially if I am in your company;

for what vigor you have in excess can well compensate for what I lack, and I want my share of the good or ill fortune resulting."

Amadis embraced him laughing and said: "My lord, do not take in that way what I said, for you already know very well that I am a witness to how self-sufficient your courage is. And since such is your pleasure, let it be done as you say."

Then they ordered themselves given something to eat, which was done; and after they had eaten what would suffice them for such a steep climb on foot, for on horseback it would be impossible they took all their arms except their lances and set out on their way, which was entirely hewn to the top of the cliff, but very rugged to climb. And thus they climbed a good part of the day, sometimes walking and at other times frequently resting, for with the weight of their armor they experienced great difficulty. And halfway up the cliff they found a house resembling a hermitage and built of stone, and inside it an idollike image of metal with a great metallic crown on its head, and which had against its breasts a great square, gilded tablet of that same metal, which the image was holding with both hands as if embracing it. And on the tablet were inscribed some very large, well-formed Greek letters, that were quite legible, although they dated from the time that the Maiden Enchantress had been there more than two hundred years before; for this maiden had been the daughter of a native of the city of Argos in Greece named Finetor, a great sage in all the arts, and particularly in those of magic and necromancy. And the daughter turned out to be of such fine talent that she gave herself over to learning those arts and she mastered them to such an extent that she knew them very much better than her father or anyone else of that time. And as has been stated, she came to establish a settlement on that rock. The way she did this, because its narration would necessitate a lengthy and tedious digression, is omitted from our story.

Amadis and Grasandor entered the hermitage, sat down to rest on a rock bench that they found in it, and after a bit, got up and went to look at the image, which seemed to them very beautiful. And they gazed at it a long while and saw the letters, which Amadis began to read; for at the time he traveled through Greece he had acquired some knowledge of the Greek alphabet and language, much of which the physician Elisabad had taught him when they were traveling by sea, and he had also taught him the German language and those of other lands, of which he acquired a good knowledge, as a man who was learned in all the arts and had traveled through many provinces. And the inscription read as follows: "In the time that the great island will flourish and be ruled by the powerful king, and will be dominant over many other kingdoms and knights famous throughout the world, supremacy at arms and the flower of beauty, peerless in their own time, will be united. And from them will issue the one who will draw out the sword, whereby the destiny of his having been knighted will be fulfilled, and the mighty stone doors which guard the great treasure will be opened."

When Amadis had read the inscription, he said to Grasandor: "Sir, have you read this inscription?"

"No," said he, "for I do not understand the language in which it is written."

Amadis told him everything that it said. It seemed to him to be an ancient prophecy, and it was his opinion that that adventure would not be accomplished by either of them; although he certainly thought that he and his lady Oriana could well be those two by whom there was to be engendered that knight who would fulfill it. But he did not say anything about this to Grasandor. And Grasandor said to him: "If it is not fulfilled by you who are the son of the best knight in the world — the one who in his own time has held and maintained the exercise of arms at the highest level — and of the queen who according to what I have learned, was one of the most beautiful women of her time, a long period will ensue before it has fulfillment. Therefore let us go ahead up the rock and not fail to see and to test everything; for just as for others it is a rare thing to carry out a great adventure, so it will be much more rare for you to fail to accomplish it. And if such a thing happens, I shall see what no one in your time has been able to see until today."

Amadis laughed heartily and made no answer; but he well saw that Grasandor's remark was worth little, because neither the excellence of his father at arms nor the beauty of his mother equaled in any degree the corresponding attributes of himself and Oriana. And he said to him: "Now let us go up and if possible let us reach the top before nightfall."

Then they left the hermitage and with great difficulty began to climb, for the cliff was very high and steep. They progressed so slowly that before they reached the summit, night overtook them, so that they had to remain under a cliff, where they stayed all night, talking about past events, and mostly about their beloved wives, to whom they had lost their hearts, and about the other ladies who were with them. Amadis told Grasandor that if he were not afraid of the anger and fury of his lady, after coming down from the cliff they would go where Don Cuadragante, Don Bruneo, Agrajes and their other friends were in order to help Don Cuadragante. Grasandor said to him: "I should like to do so; but it would not be proper at such a time as this, because in view of the fact that you left the Firm Island in such a hurry and I with equal haste came to seek you, if we delay here, it would cause your beloved to suffer great sadness and grief, especially since she doesn't know that I have found you; so I would deem it a good idea that we go see her before taking any avoidable trip elsewhere. Meanwhile we shall ascertain more news of those knights you mention and then make the best decision possible. And if our help is needed, let us provide it accompanied by more people."

"So be it," said Amadis, "and let our journey be by way of Princess Island, and there we shall obtain a boat for one of these squires of yours in which he may bear to Balan the giant my letter in which I shall beg him to send from his island a message to where they are fighting, so that on the Firm Island, where we shall wait for him, we may quickly be advised of their progress."

"That will be a very good idea," said Grasandor.

Thus they remained under the cliff, at times talking and at others sleeping, until day came, when they began to accomplish what little remained of the ascent. And when they were at the summit, they looked all about and saw a very large plain and many ruins of houses, and in the center of the plain were some very large edifices, for the most part in ruins. They went at once to see them and entered beneath a stone arch, on top of which was a stone image of a maiden carved with great perfection. And she was gripping in her right hand a pen of the same kind of stone, held as if she intended to write; and in the left hand a placard bearing in Greek letters the inscription: "Certain knowledge is of more avail with the gods than with men, and all else is vanity."

Amadis read the writing in Greek and told Grasandor what it meant. And furthermore he said: "If wise men took cognizance of the mercy that they receive from God through His gift of so much of His grace so that many others may be ruled, counseled and governed by them, and if they would be willing to utilize their wisdom by taking care to rid their souls of those things that can inhibit them from proceeding with that same enlightenment and purity as that very high Lord of theirs caused to be brought into the world, how fruitful and helpful their knowledge would be! But when the opposite situation obtains, as generally happens to us through our wicked inclinations and natures, that knowledge that was given us for our salvation we use on things that by promising us the mundane and perishable favors, delights and advantages of this world cause us to lose the other, eternal world without end, just as this unfortunate maiden did, who in those few letters sets forth such great maxims and teachings. And although her judgment was so fully endowed and provided with all the most subtle arts, she took so little cognizance of her great learning and was so unable to profit from it. But let us now cease to talk further about this matter, since by making mistakes as did our predecessors, we shall pursue what they pursued; and let us go ahead and see what happens to us."

So they passed through that archway and entered a large yard in which there were fountains of water beside which there appeared to have been large structures that now were in ruins, and of the houses that formerly had been erected round about them, nothing was in evidence except their stone walls, which the water had not been able to wear away. And furthermore they found among those ruins many dens of serpents that were wont to take refuge there; and they really thought that they would not be able to see what they were looking for without incurring some great danger. But it was not so, for none of the serpents or anything else could they see to hinder them.

Thus they went forward through the houses, clasping their shields, helmeted with their unsheathed swords in their hands;

and passing through that yard they entered a large hall that was arched, in which the strength of the cement and stone had been able to preserve the arches so that after so many years a great part of their fine workmanship was still visible. At the end of this hall they saw more closed doors of stone so closely joined that nothing on the inside could be seen, and where they were joined a sword was thrust through to the hilt. Then they realized that was the enchanted chamber where the treasure was. They examined closely the sword guard, but could not determine the material of which it was made, so rare was its handiwork, especially in the case of the pommel and the crossbar; for the hand grips seemed to them of bone as transparent as crystal and as flaming red as a fine ruby. And likewise they saw on the right side of one door seven letters very well carved and as red as fresh blood; and on the other side were other letters much whiter than the stone, that were in Latin and read thus: "In vain will toil the knight who may seek to draw out this sword from here by dint of his own valor and strength, unless he be the one who exhibits the letters that the image bears depicted on the tablet it holds against its breast, and who will match with these the seven fiery red letters on his own chest. For this man the sword has been reserved by that woman who out of her great knowledge succeeded in learning that neither in her time nor for many years thereafter would there come any other who would be his equal."

When Amadis saw this and looked very closely at the red letters, he immediately recalled that such were those that his son Esplandian had on his left side; and he was convinced that for Esplandian, as a better knight than all others, even surpassing himself in excellence, that adventure was reserved. And he said to Grasandor: "What do you think of these letters?"

"I think," said he, "that I understand well what the white letters say, but I don't succeed in deciphering the red ones."

"Nor do I," said Amadis, "although I think I have already seen elsewhere other letters similar to these, and I believe that you have seen them."

Then Grasandor looked at them again more closely than before and said: "Holy Mary save us! These are the same ones that your son has, and to him this adventure is promised. Now I tell you that you will go from here without accomplishing it;

and blame yourself for having engendered another who is a better man than you are."

Amadis said to him: "My good friend, do believe that when we read the letters on the tablet held by the image in the hermitage through which we passed, I had this same thought that you are expressing. And because I do not consider myself as good as it says there that the one will be who engenders that knight, I dared not say so to you. But these letters cause me to believe what you have said."

Grasandor said to him, laughing good-humoredly: "Let us descend from here and return to our companions, for it seems to me that from here we shall carry off the honors and the victory in the self-same way. And let us leave all this for that young man who is beginning to ascend to where you are descending from."

Thus they both departed, much pleased with each other. And when they were outside of the great palace, Amadis said: "Let us see whether that enchanted chamber has any other place through which one could enter it by exercising cleverness."

Then they circled the buildings where the chamber was, and they found that it was entirely of solid masonry without any seams.

"Well protected," said Grasandor, "is this fortune. It will be well that we leave it for its owner, and that in hope of winning this sword that you have come to obtain, you do not leave that sword of yours that you have won with so many sighs and anxieties and such great earnestness of heart."

Grasandor said this because Amadis had won it as the most exalted and faithful lover of his time; for it could not have been achieved without his heart's having been subjected to many periods of intense anxiety, just as the second Book of this story relates.

Then they went across that plain, at the place where it seemed to them there had been the greatest density of population, and they found some ruined baths and very well-made small huts with some images of metal and others of stone, and likewise many other antique objects.

Then while they were occupied in the way you hear, they saw approaching them a knight armed completely in white armor with sword in hand, who had come up along the same path as they had, for there was no other way to ascend. As he approached them, he greeted them and they him; and the knight said to them: "Knights, are you from the Firm Island?"

"Yes," said they, "why do you ask?"

"Because I found down there at the foot of this cliff some men in a boat, who told me that two knights from the Firm Island were up here, and I could not ascertain from them their names. And because I likewise am from there, I would not like to have any dispute with anyone else from there unless it was peaceful, for I come in quest of a wicked knight and I bring the information that he has taken refuge here with a maiden whom he is abducting."

Amadis, when he heard this, said: "Knight, for the sake of courtesy, I ask you to tell us your name, or that you take off your helmet."

"If you," said he, "tell and assure me on your word of honor that you are from the Firm Island, I will tell you my name; otherwise it will be futile to ask it of me."

"I tell you," said Grasandor, "on our word of honor that we are from where you were told."

Then the knight took off his helmet and said: "Now you will be able to recognize me if it is as you have said."

When they saw him thus they recognized that it was Gandalin. Amadis went toward him with open arms and said to him: "O my good friend and brother! How lucky I have been to find you!"

Gandalin was greatly astonished, for he still did not recognize him: and Grasandor said to him: "Gandalin, Amadis holds you embraced."

When he heard this, he knelt and took his hands and kissed them many times. But Amadis lifted him up and embraced him again as one whom he loved with all his heart. Then Amadis and Grasandor took off their helmets, and they asked him what adventure had brought him there. He said to them: "Good sirs, that same thing I might ask you, in view of where I left you and the remote and rugged spot where I now find you. But I intend to answer what you ask me. Know you that while I was with Agrajes and the other knights accompanying him on those conquests that you know about, after our having won a great battle in which many troops suffered — a battle that we had with a nephew of King Arabigo, thereby putting his forces under siege within the great city of Arabia — one day there entered Agrajes' tent a matron from the kingdom of Norway, dressed entirely in black, who threw herself at the feet of Agrajes asking very humbly that he be willing to help her in her great distress. Agrajes had her get up and seated her beside him, asking her to tell him what her trouble was, and saying that he would afford her help if it could be done with just cause. The matron replied: 'Sir Agrajes, I am from the kingdom of Norway, of which my mistress Olinda, your wife, is a native. And I, being a native and vassal of the king her father, come to you in the name of the kinship and ties of love that you have with that lord and that lady to ask from you the aid of some good knight in forcing the return to me of a maiden, my daughter, who has been taken from me by force by a wicked knight, lord of the Great Tower by the Sea, because I did not wish to give her to him for his wife, for he is not in lineage and blood the equal of my daughter; rather, he is of low estate, except that he succeeded in becoming the owner of that tower, whereby he subjugates much of that region in which he lives. And my husband was a first cousin of Don Grumedan, the foster father of Queen Brisena of Great Britain. And never for anything that I have done has the knight been willing to return my daughter to me. And he says that only by force of arms may I hope to see her again in my company.'

"Agrajes said to her: 'Lady, how is it that the king your lord does not render justice to you?'

" 'Sir,' said she, 'the king is now very old and ailing, so that he cannot govern himself or anyone else.'

" 'Well, is it far from here,' said Agrajes, 'to where that knight is?'

" 'No,' said she, 'for in one day and one night with favorable weather it can be reached by sea.'

"When I heard this, I earnestly entreated Agrajes to give me permission to go with the matron, saying that if God should give me victory, I would return with the knight at once. Agrajes gave me permission, and commanded me not to involve myself in any adventure other than this one. I so promised him. Then I took my arms and my horse and embarked with the matron on a ship on which she had come there, and we traveled all the rest of that day. And the next day at noon we landed, and the matron came with me and guided me to the region where the knight's tower was. When we reached it, I knocked at the gate, and a man answered me from a window, asking what I wanted. I told him to tell the knight who was the lord of that tower to give up at once a maiden that he had taken from the lady whom I was bringing with me, or to give reasons why he could and ought to hold her; and I added that if he did not do so, it was certain that no person would come out of that tower whom I would not kill or seize. The man answered me saying: 'What you can do is of very little concern to us here; but wait, for very quickly you will have what you are asking for.'

"Then I withdrew from the tower and a little while later they opened the gates, and a very tall knight came out, armed with bright yellow armor and riding a big horse, and he said to me: 'Knight, you who make senseless threats, what is your complaint and what is it that you want?'

"I said to him: 'I do not threaten or challenge you until I know the reason that you have for holding by force a maiden, the daughter of this matron, who tells me that you abducted her.'

" 'Well, even if the matron speaks the truth,' said he, 'what can you do about it?'

" 'Exact amends from you,' said I, 'if it be the will of God.'

"The knight said: 'Then at this lance point I am willing to yield her.'

"And at once he brashly came at me, and I at him. And we had our combat, which lasted a good part of the day. But finally, as I was sustaining the truth and that knight was defending the opposite, God willed to give me the victory, so that I had him stretched out at my feet in order to cut off his head. And he begged me for mercy's sake not to kill him, saying that he would do my bidding completely. I ordered him to give the maiden to her mother and to swear never to take any woman against her will, which he agreed to do. Then this having been agreed upon, I set him free, and he asked my permission to enter the tower, stating that he himself would bring me the maiden. I trusted him and let him go; but a short while after he entered the tower, he went out through another door that faced the sea, and still armorclad he got into a boat with the maiden and said to me: 'Knight, do not wonder that I do not keep my word, for the great power of love motivates me; because without this maiden I would not live a single hour. And since I cannot control or rule myself, do not blame me, I implore you, for any action of mine that you may perceive; and so that you may lose hope of ever having her, and her mother likewise, you see that I am going away with her over this sea to where it will be a long time before anyone locates me or her.'

"And as he said this, with an oar that he was gripping he shoved off from shore at full speed and went ahead over the sea with the maiden weeping very piteously. When I saw this, I was so very sad and regretful that I would have preferred death to life, because in my presence the lady who had brought me there rent her head-dress and clothing, making the saddest lamentation in the world, very grievous to behold, saying that she had received more harm from me than from the knight; because while her daughter was in that tower she always had the hope of recovering her, which now had completely come to an end, since she had seen her go where her eyes would never again be able to see her, for which I had been the cause; for although I had been enabled to defeat the knight, my discretion was not adequate to obtain from him the justice that she was expecting; and that not only was she ungrateful to me for what I had done, but that she would complain to everybody about me. I consoled her the best I could and said to her: 'Lady, do not hold me greatly at fault for not having been able to carry out that for which you brought me; because I ought to have realized that a knight who was so perfidiously holding your daughter by force would naturally be of little integrity in all other respects. But since that is the way it is I promise you that I shall never rest or have repose until, either on land or sea, I find him and bring you the maiden, or die in this endeavor. I ask of you only, since you are remaining in your land, that you aid me by letting me have the boat in which we came, together with one of your men to steer it.'

"The matron, comforted somewhat by this statement, told me to take it; and she ordered one of her men to go with me and to note well what I had promised her and what I would be doing about it. With this I took leave of her and went back over the route I had pursued in coming there. And when I reached the boat, it was already pitch-dark, so that I had to wait until morning. When it came, I took the route that I had seen the knight take with the maiden. I traveled that entire day without finding any trace of him, and then I journeyed for five days more, sailing at random. And this morning I met some men who were going fishing; and they told me that they had seen an armed knight coming in a boat, that he was bringing a maiden with him, and that they were going in the direction of this rock that is called the Rock of the Maiden Enchantress. When I ascertained this, I ordered the man who was guiding me to bring me here; and when I was at the base of the cliff, I found those who had accompanied you, and an empty boat at some distance from them, and I asked them for information about the knight and the maiden. They told me that they had not seen him, only that empty boat that was there, and for this reason I climbed up here to the summit, for I thought that undoubtedly this faithless knight had taken refuge here, and also that I might attempt an adventure of an enchanted chamber that those fishermen told me was on this rock, to see whether I could accomplish it; and if not, to be able to give information about it to those unaware of it."

Grasandor said to him laughing: "My good friend Gandalin, let the matter of the knight and the maiden be given your attention; for this adventure of which you speak will be left for later, because it is not so easy to accomplish."

Then they told him all that had happened to them, at which Gandalin was greatly astonished. Amadis said to him: "We have gone over most of this plain and through most of these houses, but we have not seen any person. Since that is the case, let us investigate everything to satisfy your desire."

Then all three began to search all of those ruined houses. And in a short while they found the knight with the maiden in a bathhouse. He, when he saw them, came out at once, leading her by the hand and said: "Sir knights, for whom are you searching?"

"For you, master scoundrel," said Gandalin, "for now your lies and deceits will no longer be able to help you to avoid paying me for the trick you played on me and the trouble that I have taken to find you."

Then the knight recognized from his white armor that he was the one who had defeated him, and he said to him: "Knight, I have already told you that the great love I have for this maiden causes me not to be my own master. And if you or any other of these knights knows what true love is, you will not blame me for anything that I may do. Do with me what you will, provided that nothing short of death separates me from this woman."

Amadis, when he heard him speak, well recognized from the state of his own heart and because of the great love he had always had for his lady that the knight was blameless, since he no longer had the strength to control himself. And he said: "Knight, although what you say excuses somewhat your great guilt, not on that account ought this knight who comes in quest of you to forego exacting satisfaction from you on behalf of this maiden's mother, for if he did not do so, he would very rightly be adjudged culpable by honorable men."

The knight said to him: "Good sir, I recognize that to be so, and if it is agreeable to him I place myself in his custody in order that he may conduct me to the matron you mention, at whose request he fought with me, so that she may do with me whatever she wishes. And may he help me, since the daughter is content with me, to have the mother also be satisfied and give her to me for my wife."

Amadis asked the maiden if he was speaking the truth. She said he was, that although until then she had been in his power against her will, when she saw the great love that he had for her and in what on her account he had involved himself, her heart was now given over to loving and esteeming him, and having him for her husband. Amadis said to Gandalin: "Take them both and put them in the custody of that matron; and in whatever way you can, contrive that he may have her for his wife, since that is pleasing to her."

Whereupon they all came down the cliff and slept that night in the hermitage with the metal image, and there they supped on what the knight and the maiden had for themselves. Next day they went down to where they had their boats, and Gandalin took leave of them and went away with the knight and the maiden. But first Amadis and Grasandor talked with him, and told him to give their regards to Agrajes and those friends of theirs, and to say that if they needed troops, to let them know at the Firm Island; for they would go personally or would send troops at once.

So they parted. And Gandalin on arriving at the matron's home, put the knight and her daughter into her custody; and just as with the love that that knight demonstrated for that maiden she had changed her mind, as women are accustomed to do, so the mother, fortunately having the same nature as her daughter, changed hers on account of what she had been told by Gandalin and by some others who had sought to straighten out the matter, so that to the pleasure and contentment of all they were married.

This done, Gandalin returned to where Agrajes was; who was very pleased with him on account of the news that he told him concerning Amadis; and he found that everybody was quite happy because of the good fortune that had come to them at that siege; because after they had surrounded their enemies in that city, as you have already heard, they had had great fights, in which most of the best knights who were inside were killed or crippled; and also on account of the arrival of Don Galaor and of Don Galvanes, who, when they had left Dragonis on the Deep Island as its king, without any delay very quickly had boarded their fleet and had come to help them; for just as it happens that the ailing, when they leave their beds after a severe illness and continue convalescing, think only of the things that conform to their desire and will, and thereby believe they dispel entirely the vestiges of their illness; so this king of Sobradisa, Don Galaor, when he beheld himself over that severe illness in which he had seen himself many times at the point of death, thought only of satisfying his desires or of mending his health with those affairs that his valiant and courageous heart demanded of him; for in this consisted all his enjoyment and great pleasure, as one who from the day that his brother Amadis dubbed him knight in front of the castle of the Causeway in the presence of Urganda the Unknown, never had put out of his mind the desire to know and practice everything that pertained to the order of chivalry — as this great story relates everywhere that it makes mention of him — he being now heedless of the fact that he was a powerful king as husband of that very beautiful Queen Briolanja; and that in view of the feats at arms already performed by him, with much reason and cause he could have rested and enjoyed peace of mind for a long period. But considering that honor has no conclusion and is so delicate that with very little neglect it can be tarnished, especially in those whom Fortune has placed at its pinnacle, putting everything aside, this vigorous king sought to undertake the enterprise of helping Dragonis, his cousin, as you have heard; and not being content with the outcome of that confrontation and travail, to go immediately as fast as he could to help those knights who were his great friends.

Oh, how much consideration those born into this world to practice knighthood ought to give to all this, and to the fact that although for some time they may give a good account of their honor, by allowing that great obligation they have to be forgotten, not only do their arms become rusty, but their fame becomes so tarnished that for a long time they cannot rid themselves of the stigma! For just as craftsmen in any craft by following it with diligence are established honorably and free of need according to their status, whereas by becoming forgetful of it because of their heedlessness and carelessness they lose what they have won, coming to poverty and misery; so by the same token knights by failing to heed what they ought to do, have their honor, their fame and virtue attacked and demolished amid great need and misery.

And this noble king Galaor in order not to fall into this error, keeping always in mind as models his father King Perion and his brothers, who were what you have heard, the moment that the affair of the Deep Island was settled departed just as you have been told, with Don Galvanes to help him, to bring to a conclusion the winning of the other project. And their arrival infused such great vigor in those on their side and such fear in their opponents that from the day that they arrived there, never again did their enemies make bold to go outside the walls, so that in a short time they expected to win that whole kingdom.

But now we shall leave them in their camps laying plans to fight their enemies, who did not dare come out to them; and the story will tell you of Amadis and Grasandor, who left Gandalin by the Rock of the Maiden Enchantress and went on to the Firm Island. The story says that after Amadis and Grasandor left Gandalin at the foot of the Rock of the Maiden Enchantress, they sailed so far over the sea that without any difficulty or hindrance they arrived one morning at the great harbor of the Firm Island; and on disembarking, armed just as they were, they mounted their horses. And before climbing up to the castle they went to say their prayers in the monastery at the foot of the cliff, which Amadis had ordered built at the time that he came from the Poor Rock, and in fulfillment of his promise before the image of the Virgin Mary, which was at that time in the hermitage. And on reaching the gate, they found there a matron dressed in black, accompanied by two squires, and their palfreys were nearby. They greeted her, and she likewise greeted them. And while Amadis and Grasandor were kneeling before the altar, the matron found out from some people of the monastery that that was Amadis, and she waited for him at the door of the church. Then when she saw him coming, she went to him weeping, knelt down and said to him: "My lord Amadis, are you not that knight who brings aid to the afflicted and wretched, especially to matrons and maidens? Certainly if it were not so, your great fame would not be publicized with such honor everywhere in the world. Hence I, as one of the saddest and most unfortunate of women, ask of you mercy and pity."

Then she seized him so firmly with both hands by the skirt of his coat of mail that she did not let him take a single step forward. Amadis sought to lift her up, but could not, and said to her: "Good friend, tell me who you are and why you wish my help, for in view of your great sadness, even if I were to fail all other matrons, for you alone I would expose my person to every danger and risk that might come to me."

The matron said to him: "Who I am you will not know until from you I have assurance that you will accede to my petition; but what I ask is as follows: I am married to a knight whom I greatly love, and his and my great misfortune has caused him to be imprisoned by the greatest enemy that he has in this world, and he cannot leave prison and be restored to me except through your kind offices; so be assured that these knees of mine never will be lifted from this floor or my hands taken away from this coat of mail — provided that with great violence and discourtesy you don't force me to remove them — until you grant what I ask."

When Amadis saw her behave thus and heard what she was saying, he did not know what to answer, for he was afraid to pledge his word to something that might turn out later to be very embarrassing to him. But because he saw her weeping so violently, and holding so firmly to his coat of mail while kneeling, he was moved to such great compassion that forgetting to obtain assurance that his aid to her would be in a just cause, he said to her: "Lady, tell me who you are, and I promise you to take your husband out from where he is imprisoned and deliver him to you if it can be accomplished by me."

Then the matron seized his hands and forcibly kissed them, and said to Grasandor: "Sir knight, observe what Amadis promises me." And then she said, "Know you, my lord Amadis, that I am the wife of Arcalaus the Enchanter, whom you have imprisoned. I demand of you that you give him to me and place him for me where this time I need not fear losing him; for you are the greatest enemy that he has, and I ask for him, as it were, from a mortal enemy, in order to make him a friend if I can."

When Amadis heard this, he was very much disturbed to see himself so cleverly deceived by that matron; and if he had found an honorable way not to comply, he would gladly have adopted it, for he feared more the danger and the harm that from that wicked knight could come to many who did not deserve it, than what might come to him from Arcalaus. But perceiving the strong motive that that matron had and that since she was under such an obligation to save her husband, she could not rightfully be blamed; and above all desiring that his word and veracity not be in any way impugned, he agreed to do what she asked, and said to her: "Madam, you have asked a great deal of me, for you can be very certain that I regard the forcing of my will to consent to what you ask of me as a greater confrontation than to constrain my heart to rescue your husband by force of arms from anywhere he might be, however much danger might be risked in the effort. And I can indeed say that from the time I became a knight, never has any service or help that I have rendered to matron or maiden been so against my will as this one."

Then he and Grasandor mounted their horses, and Amadis told the matron to follow them, and they went up to the castle.

When Oriana and Mabilia learned of their arrival, the great pleasure and joy that they experienced was indescribable. And at once she and all those ladies who were there came out to welcome them at the entrance to the garden where they were. It will be unnecessary to describe the embraces and other signs of affection with which Amadis and his lady greeted each other, because although up to the present time mention has been made of them as lovers, now since they are already married, their relationship should be a private matter, although they continue with the same true love as ever.

Olinda the Prudent and Grasinda embraced Amadis and Grasandor, and all those present repaired to their apartments; which, as you have already heard, they had in the great tower which was in that garden, where they disported themselves with great delight, as persons who loved each other with all their hearts.

Amadis ordered the matron lodged and given everything she needed. And the next morning they all heard mass with Grasinda in her apartment. As soon as it was celebrated, the wife of Arcalaus asked Amadis to fulfill his promise. He told her that he was willing. Then all those present went together to the castle where Arcalaus was imprisoned in the iron cage. And since Amadis had spoken with him in the town of Lubayna when they had taken him prisoner, he had never made an effort to see him; nor had those ladies seen him, because except when they went forth to welcome King Lisuarte and on the day of the weddings, they had never gone out of the garden.

And when they arrived they found him wearing a jubbah lined with very valuable fur from animals captured on that island — a garment which Don Gandales, Amadis's foster father, had given him because it was winter — and he was reading a book of very good apothegms and teachings on the adversities of

Fortune, likewise sent by Gandales. He wore a very long grey beard; and as he was very large of body and ugly of countenance and always looked quite enraged, and much more so at that time when he saw them coming toward him, those ladies were quite frightened on seeing him, and especially Oriana, who remembered when she was being carried away by force, and Amadis had taken her away from him and four other knights, as the first Book of this story relates. When they arrived, he stopped reading and stood up; and he saw his wife but did not say anything. Amadis said to him: "Arcalaus, do you know this matron?"

"Yes, I know her."

"Are you pleased with her coming?"

"If it is to my benefit," said he, "you can decide; but if it bears no other fruit than what is apparent, it is not a pleasure; for as I am resolved to endure all the harm that can come to me, and already have my heart under control to that end, other than that the sight of her might bring me hope of some relief, it is the cause of greater suffering for me."

Amadis said to him: "If with her coming you are free of this imprisonment, will you be grateful to me for it and will you recognize it in advance?"

"If of your own free will," said he, "you sent for her in order to do as you say, I shall always greatly appreciate it. But if she came without your approval or knowledge and you have promised her something, I cannot thank you, because good deeds that are motivated more by necessity than out of charity are not worthy of being deemed of much merit. And therefore I earnestly beg you to tell me, if you think it proper, what has caused her and you to come to see me with these ladies."

Amadis said to him: "I shall tell you the truth about everything exactly as it took place, and I entreat you to be just as truthful in answering me."

Then he told him how his wife by deceitful means had asked a favor of him, and how she had begged him to set him free, and everything that he had said to her in reply, omitting nothing. Arcalaus said to Amadis: "However it may affect my fortunes, I shall tell you the complete truth concerning my attitude, since you wish to know it. If, in Lubayna when I asked you for pity and mercy, you had taken pity on me by setting me free, rest assured that all the rest of my life I would have been under obligation to you and you always would have found me behaving as a true friend. But by setting me free now when you are constrained to do so against your will, just as you do me wickedly this good turn so do I thus receive it and rate it as it deserves; for you still would have a low opinion of me and would have deemed me lacking in courage if I had thanked you for what I ought to hate you for."

"I have enjoyed," said Amadis, "what you have said, and you speak the truth, for on account of my releasing you from here you ought not to be indebted to me; because certainly I was determined to hold you for a long time, believing that it was more proper to give you the punishment you deserved than for you to have given it to many who did not deserve it. But because of the promise that I made to this matron I shall order you taken out of this prison and released. One thing I ask of you: namely, — even if in intent and deed you not forgive me, and even if you treat me as evilly as you always have in the past — that you spare the others who have never done you any harm. And do this for that Lord who, when you least expected release and I least expected to grant it to you, was pleased to remedy your misfortunes; for out of His boundless mercy he does so for wicked men after he has tested them, so that on account of such scourgings and trials they may put an end to the deeds that are contrary to His service. And when they recognize this, He renders good their remaining life in this world and in the next, bestowing on them blessed joy which is without end. And if they do the opposite, He gives them the opposite by executing justice with the punishment that they deserve without any hope remaining to them or any remedy for their souls after those souls have departed from their bodies."

Arcalaus said to him: "As for you, it is obvious that in nowise would I wish you well, nor shall I cease to do you all the harm I can. About the other people of whom you speak I do not know what I shall do, because in view of my very ingrained habit of doing so much evil I have little hope left that that Lord you mention will give me His grace without my deserving it; and without it my nature would not be able to resist or oppose a thing so difficult and so foreign to its desires. And even assuming that it were able to do so, I would resist doing it on your advice in order that through me you would not win the glory that you have won through everyone else. And if I have received some mercy from God, it consists only in my not having made any concession or opened my heart to you; for when I with so much humility asked you to set me free, instead God willed that it should be done in spite of you and so much against your will as to leave nothing for which I could be in your debt."

Those ladies were very frightened to hear what Arcalaus said to him, and they earnestly entreated Amadis not to set him free, because he would be erring more against God by permitting that evil man, once he was released, to carry out freely his wicked desires, than he would if he broke his promise by holding him prisoner.

Amadis said to them: "My ladies, just as it frequently happens that people in great adversity are reformed and improved by keeping their hearts quite strong and steadfast in their hope for the mercy of God, so for those lacking in this respect, that hope and that mercy (which they lack) are the cause of their despair, whereby without any recourse, they are damned. And so it could happen to this Arcalaus if I held him here any longer, since I recognize that in this way it is not possible for him to be reformed or corrected. I shall keep my word and maintain my veracity, leaving the rest to that Lord who in an instant is capable of bringing him into His holy service, just as He has done in the case of many other worse sinners."

Whereupon they broke off their conversation, and the matron by order of Amadis was put into the iron cage with her husband to keep him company that night; and Amadis returned with those ladies to the garden tower. And the next morning Amadis gave orders to call Ysanjo, governor of the island; and he asked him to take Arcalaus and his wife out of the prison and give him a horse and arms, and to have his sons with ten knights escort him to where he would be contented and his wife satisfied concerning what she had asked for. This was carried out, for the sons of Ysanjo went with him as far as his castle of Valderin, where they left him. And as they were about to take their leave, Arcalaus said to them: "Knights, tell Amadis that fierce beasts and dumb animals are accustomed to being put in cages, but not such knights as I; that he should beware of me, for I intend to avenge myself quickly on him, even if that wicked whore Urganda the Unknown comes to his assistance."

They said to him: "By this road you will quickly return to the place you left."

And thereupon they returned home.

One can well believe that since this matron, wife of this Arcalaus, was very pious and God-fearing, and at all the slayings and cruelties that her husband perpetrated, she was very sorrowful and heartsick, excusing all of them that she could, by her own worthiness she obtained this divine favor of extricating her husband from where all those in the world would not have been able to release him. So a good matron and devout wife ought to be highly appreciated and greatly esteemed because through her, many times our Lord permits possessions, children and husband to be protected from great danger.

Just as you hear, Amadis and Grasandor were in heartfelt enjoyment with their wives on the Firm Island; where in a short time Darioleta arrived with her husband and daughter and the latter's husband Bravor, all of whom added greatly to their joy.

But now the story will cease to speak of them and will tell of what was done by Balan, the giant of the Island of the Vermilion Tower. The story relates that two weeks after Amadis and Grasandor departed from the Island of the Vermilion Tower where they had left Balan, the giant, the worse for wear, the giant arose from his bed and gave orders to give to Darioleta, her husband and their daughter, many precious jewels and a very good ship in which to depart. And he sent his son Bravor with them, just as he had promised Amadis; and as soon as they had left there he had quite a large fleet made ready, not only of his own ships, of which he had many, but also of others that he had taken from those who traveled thereabouts; and he fitted out this fleet with arms and men, and with as many provisions as it could carry, and in very good weather put out to sea.

And so far did he travel without any setback that in ten days he arrived at the harbor of a small town that had the name Licrea and was under the sovereignty of King Arabigo. And there he found out that those lords had the great city of Arabia surrounded, and were besieging it vigorously, especially after

Don Galaor, King of Sobradisa, and Don Galvanes arrived there. And at once he had all his troops disembarked, and their horses and arms taken ashore along with crossbowmen and archers and all the camp equipment. Then, leaving on board the guards necessary to assure the fleet's safety, he went directly to the place where he knew King Galaor and Don Galvanes were dwelling. When they learned of his arrival from messengers of the giant, they mounted with a large retinue and sallied forth to welcome him. The giant came up with his own very good company, he himself wearing very fine armor and mounted on a very beautiful big horse, so that there could have been few of his size to appear so fine and so gallant. They already knew what had happened to him with Amadis, for Gandalin had told them about it exactly as it had happened. And Don Galaor put Don Galvanes out in front, for although in dominions he was not his equal, in age he was much his senior. For this reason, and also because of the great lineage from which he was descended, and on account of his fine personal qualities, Amadis, his brothers, and Agrajes always accorded him much courtesy. The giant did not recognize him, for he had never seen him, although he knew about him in great detail because Madasima, the wife of this Don Galvanes, was a niece of Madasima, mother of this Balan, as has already been told you. And when he came up, the giant said to him: "My good lord, are you Don Galaor?"

"No," said he, "I am Don Galvanes, and I've been looking forward to meeting you."

Then the giant embraced him and said to him: "My lord Don Galvanes, in view of our relationship so much time should not have passed without your seeing me; but the enmity that I had with one who is your very close friend has caused the delay. But this is already dispelled by the hand of that man, who in discretion and courage has no equal."

King Galaor came up laughing to embrace him affably and said: "My good friend and lord, I am the one for whom you ask."

Balan looked at him and said: "Truly your appearance is a good proof of it, in view of its resemblance to that of the man because of whom I wanted to know you."

The giant said this because Amadis and Don Galaor resembled each other very much, so much so that in many places one was taken for the other, except that Don Galaor was somewhat taller and Amadis heavier.

This done, they took King Galaor between them and went to their encampment; and while Balan's lodging was being made ready, Don Galvanes conducted him to his own tent, where he was served as was requisite and obligatory in the case of both of them.

CHAPTER CXXXI

HOW AGRAJES AND DON CUADRAGANTE AND DON BRUNEO DE BONAMAR WITH MANY OTHER KNIGHTS CAME TO SEE THE GIANT BALAN, AND WHAT THEY EXPERIENCED IN HIS COMPANY.

Agrajes and Don Cuadragante and Don Bruneo de Bonamar, when they learned of the arrival of that giant, took with them Angriote de Estravaus, Don Gavarte of the Fearful Valley, Palomir, Don Brian de Monjaste and many other knights of great renown who were there with them to help them win those dominions that you have heard about, and they all went to the camp of King Galaor and Don Galvanes, where the giant was lodged; and they found him in Don Galvanes' tent, which was the finest and best made that any emperor or king could have; and which he had acquired through his wife Madasima, it having been left to her by Famongomadan, her father.

In this tent, each year, after he had it set up in a meadow that was in front of the castle of the Boiling Lake, Famongomadan used to have his son Basagante sit on a luxurious dais together with all his relatives, who were many and who obeyed him as a master because of his great strength and wealth. And his vassals and many other people that he held in subjugation by force of arms, were wont to do homage to him as King of Great Britain. And with this in mind he sent to ask King Lisuarte for Oriana as a wife for Basagante, that son of his; and because the king did not wish to give her to him, he was waging a very cruel war against him at the time that Amadis killed both of them and released Leonoreta, sister of Oriana, together with ten knights whom they had taken prisoners with her, as the second Book of this story relates in greater detail.

Then at the time that these knights arrived, the giant Balan was unarmed and clothed in a cape of yellow silk with some roses on it beautifully broidered in gold. As he was tall and handsome and in the flower of manhood, everyone was well impressed with him, and much more so after they had talked with him; because, in view of the fact that they knew the very overbearing ways of giants, and how by nature they were all very disagreeable, haughty and utterly unreasonable, they had no idea that any of them possessed qualities so diametrically opposite, as was the case with this Balan. And for this reason they appreciated him much more than for his extreme valor — although many of them knew about great feats at arms that he had accomplished — because in their view great strength without a good nature and good discretion is frequently abhorred.

So while they were all together in that great tent, the giant looked at them, and liked them so much that he could not believe that anywhere else there were so many and such excellent knights. And as he saw that they had quieted down, he said to them: "If you are surprised at my unexpected coming to your aid, as something of which you had very little expectation or thought, so am I; because certainly I could not have believed that in any way I could be deterred from being a lifelong deadly enemy against you. But as the execution of intentions is more in the hand of God than in that of those who with great severity were seeking to carry them out, among many mighty and harsh battles that to my honor I have fought, there occurred one which constrained my intention at the outset and in the end changed it entirely; so that of my own volition I considered an honor what I had thought that I would deem a dishonor all the days of my life, until I had obtained vengeance for it. And when the thing that I most desired in this world was fulfilled in accordance with my desire, then my great rage and harshness were over and done, not in the way that I expected, but through means most pleasing to my adverse fortunes. You have already learned that I am the son of that valiant and vigorous giant, Madanfabul of the Island of the Vermilion Tower, whom Amadis of Gaul under the name of Beltenebros slew in the battle that King Lisuarte and King Cildadan had. And I, as the son of such an honorable father, being so duty bound to avenge his death, never forgot how this great desire should be carried out: by taking the life of the man who took my father's life. And when I was most without hope of doing so, Fortune together with the great courage of that knight brought him into my hands within my own dominions, he being alone without a single person to help him; and by him with his great valor I was defeated and treated with even greater courtesy, since he is the one who possesses both valor and courtesy to a greater degree than any other living man; from which fact it has come about that that great mortal enmity I had for him has been changed into a greater amount of friendship and true love; a fact which has caused my coming, as you see; since I had learned that this army was in some need of reinforcements, and I believed that most of your honor and advantage reverts to him."

Then he told them from the beginning all that had happened to him with Amadis, and the combat that they had together, and all the other things that took place, omitting nothing, just as the story has related it to you. Finally he told them that until that war was over he would not leave their company; and that when it was ended he wished to go away at once to the Firm Island, as he had promised Amadis.

All those lords were very happy to hear from him what he told them, because although they had found out from Gandalin that Amadis had fought with this giant and had overcome him, they did not know the reason for it as he had told it. And they were very pleased with his coming, not only because of his personal worth, but also on account of the great and very good body of fighting men that he brought with him, for which they had a need in view of their losses in past engagements. And they gave him many thanks for his good will as manifested by the help that was being offered to them out of his affection for Amadis.

CHAPTER CXXXII

Which tells of the reply that Agrajes made to the giant Balan's speech.

Agrajes answered him, and said: "My good lord Balan, I wish to reply to you on what concerns the enmity of my lord cousin Amadis, since these lords and I with them have expressed to you our thanks for what is promised us by you; and if my reply is not in conformity with your desire, take it as a knight; for although at arms I may not be your equal, perhaps on account of the fact that I am older, and have used them more, I shall know more completely than you what is required in order to be punctilious in their use. And I say that knights who with just cause engage in combats and in them perform their duty without being remiss in anything rightly enjoined upon them, although in it they are fulfilling what they took an oath to do, are to be greatly praised, since the will and the deed have been left free of debt. But those who out of fantasy seek to exceed the bounds of reason are adjudged haughty and flighty, rather than strong and courageous, by those who achieve the height of honor. The manner of your father's death is very well-known to all, and you, sir, must not be unaware of it; for if Fortune had permitted a happy ending to his boldness in carrying off King Lisuarte as he was doing, he would have been exalted to the heavens, and by the same token the dishonor and discredit of those who served and helped this king would have been limitless. And therefore you ought not to be surprised that Amadis, having great envy of the glory that your father expected to obtain, would want it for himself, as all good men do or ought to do. And such a slaying as this one, in view of the fact that each one sought to accomplish it, thinking thereby to achieve great fame, ought not to be the cause of vengeance being sought by anyone as in the case of those slayings foully committed, where very much honor is risked in condoning them. So, my lord, in what concerns your father, and in what befell you with Amadis, no just cause could be found for complaint, since you and he carried out very completely all that knights ought to accomplish. And if any complaint is to be made, it is to Fortune, who was pleased to bestow more help and favor on him than on you and your father. So, my good friend, consider it good that with your honor remaining intact and without blemish, you have won as allies that very noble knight and all these lords and brave knights whom you behold here, together with many others that you would see, if you were to have need of them."

When the giant Balan had heard this he said to him: "My lord Agrajes, although for the satisfaction of my desire no admonition was necessary, I thank you very much for what you have said to me, because although in this case it might have been unnecessary, that is no reason for considering it unnecessary for future situations. And dismissing this matter as over and forgotten, we shall do well to come to an understanding on how to conclude this confrontation with that courage and care that those ought to have who, leaving in security their own lands, seek to conquer those of others."

Don Galvanes said to him: "Good sir, let these knights go to their lodgings, for it is supper time; and you will rest tonight and tomorrow, and meanwhile your tents will be set up and your troops lodged. Then with your advice a plan will be devised concerning what ought to be done."

So those lords went away to their camps, and Don Galvanes and King Galaor remained with the giant, who with great enjoyment supped with them that night in that large, magnificent tent that you have already heard about. And when supper was over, the king went off to his tents and they remained and slept in their luxurious beds.

And morning having come, the giant said to Don Galvanes that he wanted to mount and circle the city to see the lie of the land, and where one could best fight. Don Galvanes informed King Galaor, and both went with him. And they circled around that great city, which, since it had a large population, was fortified by many great towers and walls; for since this city was the capital of that whole great kingdom and of the islands of Landas, which were a part of it just as it was the principal place of residence of its kings, as they ruled one after another, so did they strive to augment its population and to fortify it as much as they could, so that in size and in strength of its fortifications it was quite outstanding. As soon as they had seen it, Balan said to them: "My lords, what do you think could be done against a thing as big as this is?"

Don Galaor said to him: "There is not in the world anything stronger or better than the courage of man; and if those who are within have courage, I very much doubt that it could be taken by force. But in the many there is always great discord, especially if Fortune is adverse to them; and if with discord they are overtaken by weakness, I do not doubt that just as other impregnable things have been lost for this reason, so may this be lost."

While talking about this and other matters, all three of them went together to the camps of Don Cuadragante and Don Bruneo and other companions of theirs; for in that area which they were traversing they were observing where best the fight could be waged. And when they arrived near the tents where Agrajes was housed, the good and vigorous Enil came to meet them, saying: "My lord Balan, Agrajes asks you to see King Arabigo, whom I hold imprisoned in my tent, because he wants to speak with you; for when he was told of your coming, he sent word with much affection and great love to beg Agrajes to give him such permission and to beg you to see him."

The giant said to him: "Good knight, I am happy to do so; and it is possible that this interview may be more fruitful than other great encounters from which more was expected."

So they all continued on their way as far as Enil's tent. King Galaor and Don Galvanes went on to see Don Bruneo; and the giant dismounted from his horse and went into the quarters where King Arabigo was, which were adorned with fine rugs and hangings, and he himself was dressed in splendid garb, for here by order of Agrajes he was receiving royal service. But he was wearing such strong, heavy fetters that they prevented him from taking a single step. As the giant saw him thus, he knelt before him and sought to kiss his hands; but the king drew him to him and embraced him, weeping, and said to him: "My friend Balan, what do you think of me? Am I that great king whom your father and you have seen many times, or do you find me in that court accompanied by such noble princes and knights, and other kings, who were my friends, as many times you have found me while I was expecting to conquer and rule a very large part of the world? Certainly, instead, I think that you will adjudge me a lowly man, imprisoned, wretched, dishonored, placed in the power of my enemies as you well see. And what causes more pain to my sad heart is that those from whom I most expected help, such as you and other very strong giants whom I considered my friends, I behold coming to conclude my total destruction."

Having said this, he was unable to continue speaking on account of the paroxysm of tears with which he was seized.

Balan said to him: "It is clear to me, since my eyes have beheld it, that what you, good King Arabigo, have said, is true; for I have seen you well attended and honored with great preparations for, and hopes of, conquering great domains. And if now I see you so changed and transformed, do not think that I am greatly shocked, because although my rank is not to be compared with yours, on that account I do not fail to feel the cruel, hard blows of Fortune; for you already know, good king, how that very courageous Amadis of Gaul killed my father Madanfabul. And when I was most hopeful of avenging his death, my adverse and contrary Fortune willed that by this same Amadis I should be defeated and laid low by force of arms, he being privileged to give me death or life. And because your anguish and great sorrow overcome you to such a degree that you could not bear to hear so long a story as I could tell you about this, let it suffice you to know that as a man overcome by that knight whom I so greatly desired to conquer and to slay with my own hands if possible, I have come here, where with legitimate reason I could repay you with as many tears as, or perchance more than, my presence has given you cause to shed, so that no less than you, I would need consolation. But knowing the great and diverse ups and downs of the world, and how discretion is given in order to follow reason, I have adopted the course of becoming a friend of that very mortal enemy of mine; for I could not be otherwise, since with just cause, nothing remaining because of weakness, without my leaving unfulfilled a single bit of my obligation, I could do so. And if you, noble king, take my advice, you too will do so because I consider it obvious that it will be well for you to take it. And I, as one who, if there is harshness and discord, has to be your enemy, will be a faithful friend to you if it could be under an agreement."

He, when he heard this, said to him: "What agreement can I make if I am losing my kingdom?"

"To be content," said the giant, "with what you can obtain with ease."

"Isn't it better," said he, "to die than to see myself abased and dishonored?"

"Since death," said Balan, "takes away all hope, and many times with life and a long lapse of time, desires are satisfied and great losses are restored for those who can make out with greater loss of profit than of dishonor, that is a much better course of action than to seek death."

"Balan, my friend," said the king, "I am willing to be guided by your advice, and in your hands I leave all that you see I ought to do. And I beg of you earnestly that, even if out yonder, you may appear inimical to my interests while absent from me, on seeing me in this prison you counsel me in my presence as a friend."

"I shall do so," said the giant, "without fail."

Then bidding him goodby and taking Enil with him, he went to the tent of Don Bruneo de Bonamar; where he found King Galaor, Agrajes, Don Galvanes and many other knights of high standing, who received and welcomed him to their midst with great pleasure. And he told them that inasmuch as he had talked over with King Arabigo some matters that they should know about, they should consider whether it was necessary that a few others be present there. Agrajes told him that it would be well to summon Don Cuadragante, Don Brian de Monjaste and Angriote de Estravaus, and so it was done; they came, and with them other knights of great renown. Then the giant told them everything that had taken place during his interview with King Arabigo, for nothing was omitted, and that his opinion was, laying aside the fact that he would follow and aid them through thick and thin, that if King Arabigo were to be satisfied with some very remote one of those islands of Landas, and would hand everything else over to them without further loss of troops, an agreement and settlement would be good, especially so since there remained to be won the seigniory of Sansuenia, which not only because of its troops but also in view of its fortresses would be very difficult to take. Those lords thanked the giant very heartily for what he had said to them, and they considered him very wise, for they could not have thought or believed that a man of that lineage would have so much discretion. And it was reasonable for them to have had that opinion because formerly his great overweening pride did not leave any room for discretion and reason. But the difference between this Balan and the other giants was that, since his mother Madasima was possessed of such very noble qualities — as the story has related — and having had by her husband Madanfabul only this one son, she had tried very hard, although against the wish of her husband, who was wicked and haughty, to bring him up under the tutelage of a great scholar whom she had brought from Greece; from whose rearing and that which he received from his mother, who was very admirable in all respects, he emerged so gentle and so discreet that there were few men more judicious and sincere than he.

And those lords having come to an agreement, it was their decision that if what the giant had told them could be put into effect, it would be for them very advantageous and a great relief, even if some part of that kingdom remained in King Arabigo's hands. And they answered him that recognizing the love and good will with which he had come there and after discussing their situation, for him in preference to anyone else they would be willing to come to terms with that king.

From which it can here be noted that if in great disputes there are lacking persons who are moved by good intentions to provide a remedy, murders, imprisonments, and other things entailing infinite evil ensue and multiply.

Then this having been heard by the giant, he spoke with King Arabigo; and after many meetings and conversations that should be passed over in silence, not only because of their prolixity, but also in order not to deviate from what is pertinent to our account, it was agreed that King Arabigo should hand over that great city with all of the adjoining territory that was under his rule; and of the three islands of Landas he was to take for himself the most remote one called Liconia, which was exposed to the cold north wind, and to call himself king of it; and the other islands should be surrendered along with the rest, and Don Bruneo should be named King of Arabia. This having been approved and agreed upon by King Arabigo's nephew, who was defending the kingdom as you have heard, and by all the leading men of the city, everything was surrendered as stipulated and King Arabigo was set free. And he very wearily and sick at heart went by sea to the island of Liconia. Don Bruneo was crowned king with much pleasure and great rejoicing, not only on the part of his supporters but also on that of his opponents, because knowing his excellence and great courage, they hoped with him to be very highly honored and protected.

This having been concluded just as the story has set forth, shortly after they had rested and relaxed there in company with King Bruneo, they assembled their battalions and everything necessary for their journey, and from there went on their way to the town of Califan, which was the closest to where they had had their camp.

But those of Sansuenia, when they found out that the city of Arabia was taken, and that King Arabigo had come to terms with those forces, fearing what it meant, all gathered together, both knights and peasants, forming a very great army, for that dominion was large and its people numerous, well armed and experienced in warfare, because they had always had very haughty and turbulent overlords who had involved them in many confrontations. And when they saw themselves assembled in such numbers, out of great pride and boldness, their courage increased. With their battalions drawn up in formation, headed by captains who were the leading men of the realm, they came out to confront their enemies before the latter reached the town of Califan; whence they met in combat and had a very cruel and fierce battle, which was quite distressing for both sides and in which took place many extraordinary feats at arms, and the deaths of many knights and other men. But what the outstanding knights and that brave and valiant giant accomplished there could in nowise be told adequately. All one can do is to state that by dint of their great deeds and the courage of their militant hearts, the men of Sansuenia were so completely defeated and annihilated that most of them remained dead or wounded on the battlefield and the others so crushed that even in their strongholds they did not dare defend themselves; so that Don Cuadragante with all those lords and the troops they had left after the battle, although they suffered casualties in dead and wounded, dominated the field without encountering any defense or resistance. And if the story does not relate to you in greater detail the great knightly exploits and the mighty and courageous deeds that took place in all these conquests and in the battles over winning these seigniories, the cause of it is that this story is about Amadis, and if it does not bear on his own great deeds, there is no reason why those of the others be told except almost in summary, because otherwise not only their narration, because of its prolixity would cause readers annoyance and vexation, but also one's judgment would not be adequate to do justice to both sides; so with greater reason one ought to deal adequately with the principal subject, which is this vigorous and valiant knight Amadis, than with the other themes of which one has had to make mention on account of their connection with the story. And for this reason nothing more will be said, except that this great and dangerous battle having been won, in a short space of time that huge seigniory of Sansuenia was conquered, so that the weak towns of their own will, because they had no hope of help, and the fortified ones constrained by great battles, had all to take Don Cuadragante for their lord.

But now we shall leave them very contented and pleased with the victories that they had achieved, and there will be told you the story of King Lisuarte, who has not been mentioned for quite a while.

CHAPTER CXXXIII

HOW AFTER KING LISUARTE RETURNED FROM THE FIRM ISLAND TO HIS LAND, HE WAS TAKEN PRISONER BY ENCHANTMENT, AND WHAT HAPPENED AS A RESULT.

The story relates that after King Lisuarte with Queen Brisena, his wife, departed from the Firm Island shortly after he had left wedded his daughters and the other ladies who were married at the same time, as you have heard, he went directly to his town of Fenusa, because it was a seaport and very abundant in forests in which much game was to be found, and it was a very healthful, happy place where he was accustomed to enjoy himself very much. And as soon as he reached there, in order to afford his heart some repose and rest from his past travail, he immediately devoted himself to the chase and to things that could give him most pleasure, and thus he spent quite a period of time. But as this now bored him, just as everything in the world does that men pursue for long, he began to think about times past and about eminent knights with whom his court formerly had been well supplied, and the great adventures that these knights used to experience, from which there had come to him much honor and such great fame that through all parts of the world his praises were sung and he was lauded to the skies. And although now his age required repose and tranquillity for him, his will being nourished on, and accustomed to, the opposite, having been inured to it for so long, would not consent; so that recalling the sweetness of past glory and the bitterness of not having it or being able to obtain it at present, his thoughts were rendered so tortured that many times he was as if out of his mind, not being able to be cheered or to take comfort with anything he saw. And what aggrieved him most was to remember how in the battles and past contentions with Amadis, his honor had been so impaired, and that in the opinion of everyone, he had put an end to that great strife more out of necessity than benevolence.

So with such thoughts as these, melancholy had the opportunity to obsess him in such a way that this man who was formerly such a powerful king, so gracious, so humane and so feared by all, had turned sad, pensive, misanthropic without wishing to see anyone, as usually happens to those who with good fortune spend their time without receiving any greatly vexing setbacks or opposition; and once their strength is thus weakened, cannot bear or be able to resist the harsh and cruel blows of adverse fortune.

This king had the custom each morning after hearing mass of taking with him a crossbowman, and on his horse, armed only with his very good and valued sword, of going a long distance through the forest absorbed in very bitter thought, and at times shooting with the crossbow. In this way be believed that he received some comfort. So one day it happened that having gone some distance from the town through the dense growth of the forest, he saw a maiden coming on a palfrey at full speed through the underbrush, shouting and asking God for help. And when he saw her, he went toward her and said to her: "Maiden, what is the matter with you?"

"Ah, sire," said she, "for God's and mercy's sake help my sister whom I left over there with a wicked man who is trying to rape her!"

The king felt sorry for her and said to her: "Maiden, guide me, for I will follow you."

Then she went back over the way she had come, as fast as she could spur her palfrey. And they went on until the king saw among some undergrowth that an unarmed man was holding the maiden by the hair and was jerking her hard in order to throw her down, and the maiden was uttering loud cries. The king came up on his horse, calling out to let the maiden go. And when the man saw him near him he released her and fled through the densest thickets. The king followed him on horseback, but was not able to make much progress on account of being obstructed by branches; and when he perceived this, he dismounted as quickly as he could with a great desire to seize him in order to give him the punishment that such an outrage deserved, for he indeed thought he was probably from his land. And he ran behind him as fast as he could, calling to him from very near at hand, and the denseness of that heavy undergrowth having been passed, he found a meadow in a clearing, and on it he saw a tent pitched, and a matron, and the man who was fleeing behind her as if he intended to take refuge there. The king said to her: "Matron, is this man of your company?"

"Why do you ask?" said she.

"Because I want you to hand him over to me so that I may administer punishment to him, for if it had not been for me, he would have raped a maiden near here, where I found him."

The matron said: "Sir knight, come in and I shall hear what you may say. And if it is as you say, I shall give him to you; for since I have been a maiden and have held my own honor in high esteem, I would not allow any other woman to be dishonored."

The king went immediately toward where the matron was, and at the first step that he took, he fell on the ground as completely insensible as if he were dead.

Then the maidens who were coming behind him, approached, and the matron with them; and with the man whom she had there, they took the king, unconscious as he was, in their arms. And two other men came out from among the trees, who took down the tent; and they all went away to the seashore, which was quite near, where they had a boat hidden with boughs on it and so covered that hardly any of it was visible, and they got into it, and placing the king on a bed, they began to sail away. This was so quickly done and so secretly and in such a place, that no other person could have seen or heard it.

The king's crossbowman, as he was traveling on foot, could not pursue him, because the king had been in such a hurry to rescue the maiden, and when he arrived where the horse had been left, he was greatly surprised to find it alone. Then he plunged as fast as he could through the dense undergrowth looking everywhere, but did not discover anything. And in a short while he found himself in the meadow where the tent had been, and from there he returned to the horse and mounted it, and for a long while went back and forth through the forest and along the seashore searching. And as he found nothing, he decided to return to the city; and when he arrived near it and some people who were going about there saw him, they thought that the king was sending him for something. But he said nothing, and went on to where the queen was. Then he dismounted from the horse and entered the palace in great haste. And when he saw her, he told her everything that he had observed concerning the king and how he had searched for him very diligently without being able to find him. When the queen heard this, she was quite disturbed and said: "Oh, Holy Mary! What will become of the king my lord, if I have lost him through some misadventure?"

Then she summoned her nephew King Arban and Cendil de Ganota and told them that news. They displayed cheerful countenances, giving her hope, so that she would not be fearful, by saying that it was not a question of the king's being in danger, because very quickly he could have lost his way in that forest out of his desire to avenge the maiden; and that since he knew that land through which he had gone hunting many times, it would not be long before he returned; that if he left his horse, it would have been only that on account of the density of the trees he could not use it to advantage. But in truth considering it more serious than they revealed, they went at once to arm themselves and mount their horses; and they had all the people in the town come out, and as quickly as possible they plunged into the forest, taking with them the crossbowman to guide them; and the other people, who were many, scattered, searching in all directions. But neither they nor the knights, despite all the zeal they showed in looking for him, found any trace of him.

The queen remained all that day awaiting news with great perturbation and agitation of mind. But none was bold enough to return with such slight results as they found; instead not only those who came out from there, but also all those of the region who heard the news, never stopped searching with great diligence. Night having come, the queen decided to send messengers at full speed with letters to as many places as she could. And in this manner she spent the night without sleeping even a short while. At dawn Don Grumedan and Giontes arrived; and when the queen saw them she asked them if they had found out anything about the king her lord. Don Grumedan said to her: "We know no more than what they told Giontes and me at the house from which we were going hunting; namely, that many people were looking for him. Thinking to find here some news, we decided not to go anywhere else first; but since we find no news, we shall set out at once in quest of him."

"Don Grumedan," said the queen, "I cannot calm myself or find repose or relief, nor can I imagine what has happened. And if I remained here, I would die of great anxiety; therefore I have resolved to go with you; because if good news should come there, I will learn of it more quickly than here; and if the opposite, not until death shall I desist in making the effort that I rightly ought to make."

Then she gave orders to bring her a palfrey. And taking with her Don Grumedan, Don Giontes, and a matron, wife of Brandoyvas, she went off to the forest as fast as she could, and scoured it for three days, for she always lodged in towns; in which if it had not been for Grumedan, she would not have eaten a single mouthful; but he with great effort made her eat something. Every night she slept fully clothed under the trees, for although they found some small villages, she did not want to enter them, saying that her great anguish did not permit her to do so. [Tranlators' note: *The foregoing statements concerning the queen's entrance into towns are obviously confused and confusing.*] Then after these three days it happened that among the many people that they met in the forest, she encountered King Arban of North Wales, who arrived very sad and fatigued, and with his horse so weary and exhausted that it could no longer carry him. When the queen saw him she said to him: "Good nephew, what news do you bring of the king my lord?"

Tears came to his eyes and he said: "Madam, only what I knew when I left your presence. And believe me, madam, there are so many of us searching for him, and we have looked for him so hard and so persistently that it would have been impossible not to find him if he were on this side of the sea. But I believe that if he has been duped, it was not with the intention of leaving him within his kingdom; and certainly, madam, I have always been worried about this misanthropy of his with so much aloofness and poor security of his person, because princes and great lords who are to govern and command many people cannot exercise such functions so equitably and benevolently as not to be feared by most of them; and if this fear is unaccompanied by affection, hatred follows immediately. And for this reason they ought to take precautions against commoners attacking their royal persons; for often such attacks cause others to be put in mind of what they previously had not thought of doing, and may it please God through His mercy to enable me to see him and tell him this and many other things; and I hope to God that He will do so. And you, madam, likewise have hope."

When the queen heard this, she completely lost consciousness, and having swooned fell off her palfrey. Don Grumedan dismounted as quickly as he could and took her in his arms. He held her thus for quite a while, for she was thought to be more dead than alive. When she recovered consciousness, she said very sadly, shedding a great abundance of tears: "False and terrifying Fortune, hope of the wretched, cruel enemy of the prosperous, subverter of worldly affairs, for what can I praise you? For if in times past you caused me to be made mistress of many realms, obeyed and revered by many people, and above all joined in matrimony with such a powerful and virtuous king, in one single moment by taking him away from me you have taken away and stolen everything; for if while I lose him you leave me the worldly possessions, that does not give me hope of recovering any peace or pleasure, but will occasion me much greater pain and bitterness; because if those possessions were valued and esteemed by me, it was only on account of the man who ruled and defended them. For certainly with much more cause would I have been able to thank you if you had left me as one of these plain women devoid of fame and pomp; so that I, like her, forgetting my own petty trivial ills, might shed my tears over the harsh, cruel misfortunes of others. But why shall I complain of you? For your deceits and great fickleness are so well known to all that they ought not to complain of you, but of themselves for trusting you."

Thus was this noble queen lamenting while seated on the ground, and her foster father, Don Grumedan, was on bended knee, holding her hands, consoling her with very gentle words

—as one in whom all virtue and discretion dwelt—with that same pity and love that he had shown her as a baby in the cradle. But consolation was not necessary, for she fainted so many times that she was without any feeling and almost dead; which was the cause of great sorrow to those who saw her. And when her mind to some extent had been recovering its faculties, she said to Don Grumedan: "Oh, my loyal and true friend, I beg you that just as these hands of yours in my first days were the cause of prolonging them, so now in my last days, may they receive my death!"

Don Grumedan, perceiving that any reply to her would be unnecessary in view of her condition, remained silent without saying a word; instead, he decided that it would be well to transport her to some town where help might be procured. This was done, for he and those other knights who were there placed her on her palfrey, and with Don Grumedan seated behind her holding her in his arms she was brought to a group of dwellings occupied by the king's huntsmen, who lived in the forest in order to protect it. And they immediately sent for beds and other conveniences whereby she might rest. But she would not occupy any bed except the poorest to be found there. Thus she remained for a few days without knowing where to go or what to do with herself. And when Don Grumedan saw her more composed, he said to her: "Noble and powerful queen, at the time that you have most need of your great discretion, what has become of it, that so ill-advisedly you seek and solicit death without remembering that with it all worldly things perish? And what help will it be to that very dearly beloved husband of yours if your soul has departed from the flesh? Are you perchance buying with it his well-being or remedying his misfortune? Rather, that is certainly quite the opposite of what sensible people ought to do, for courage and discretion for meeting such challenges were instituted by that most high Lord, and the fortunes of loved ones are to be aided with great effort and diligence rather than with excessive tears. Thus if a means to this end that I mention is afforded you, I wish you to know it just as I recognize it. You well know, madam, that besides the knights and many vassals who live in your realms, who with great devotion and love will carry out and fulfill your commands, on the blood of your royal house almost all Christendom depends today, on account of its strength and its great empires and dominions overshadowing all, just as the sky does the earth; so who doubts that these above-mentioned dominions, when they learn of this very frustrating search, will wish like yourself to be helpful in it? And if the king your husband is hereabouts, we who are his vassals will provide the assistance; and if perchance the ocean has been crossed in what land however forbidding, or by what people however fierce, will resistance to his recovery be possible? Therefore, my good lady, laying aside the things that produce more harm than benefit, taking renewed comfort and new advice, let us pursue those things that can be of benefit to the furtherance and solution of this business."

Then this which Don Grumedan said having been heard by the queen, in a manner of speaking it brought her back from death to life. And recognizing that he was stating the entire truth, ceasing to weep and complain bitterly, she decided to send a message to Amadis, who was nearest at hand, trusting that out of his good fortune, just as in other matters, he would bring aid to this one; and at once she gave orders to Brandoyvas to seek out Amadis as quickly as he could, and give him a letter from her, which read as follows:

Letter from Queen Brisena to Amadis

If in times past, fortunate knight, this royal house was defended and protected by your great courage, at this juncture, being beset more than it ever has been, it appeals to you very urgently and in great affliction. And if the many benefits received from you have not been acknowledged to the extent that your great virtue deserves, be content, since that just Judge, powerful in all things, has sought to compensate for our dereliction by exalting you to the heavens and grinding us under foot. Know you, my very beloved son and true friend, that just as a flash of lightning on a dark night doubles the vision of the beholder, and by suddenly disappearing leaves that vision in greater darkness and obscurity than before; so when I had before my eyes the royal person of my husband and lord, King Lisuarte, who was light and illumination for them and for all my senses, he, having been suddenly snatched from me, has left them in such bitterness and such an abundance of tears that they expect to perish very quickly in death. And because my situation is so grievous that neither my fortitude nor my judgment could endure writing it, trusting to my messenger, I bring this letter to an end, and my sad life likewise unless I quickly see a remedy for the situation."

The letter having been finished, she gave orders to Brandoyvas to relate that distressing news in more detail; and he set out at once with that good will that a very faithful servant, such as he was, ought to exhibit.

So this having been done, she started out immediately with those knights on the road to London, because that city was the capital of the whole realm, and if some uprising were to take place, there rather than anywhere else it would be found. But that did not happen; instead, after the news had spread to all regions, the reaction of the people was such that the great and petty, men and women alike, left their towns, and as if they were out of their senses went about shouting through the countryside in such numbers, while weeping and invoking the king their lord, that the forests and mountains were full of them; and many of the matrons and maidens of high rank with disheveled hair were uttering tearful laments for that man whom they always had found at hand to defend and assist them.

Oh, how fortunate ought kings to consider themselves if their vassals with such love and such great grief were to bemoan their loss or their hardships, and when furthermore their subjects would be the kind who with good reason could and should do so, because their kings had treated them as well as this noble king had treated his own people! But what a pity! The times now are much different from what they were, judging from the scant affection and less veracity that are found in people's attitudes toward their kings. And this ought to cause the climate of the world to deteriorate, for once the major share of virtue is lost, it cannot bear the fruit that it should, just as is the case with exhausted soil; for neither much plowing nor selected seed can prevent the growth of thistles and thorns, together with other weeds of little benefit that spring up. So let us implore that mighty

Lord to apply a remedy and if because of our unworthiness he is not pleased to listen to us, may He heed those whose lives are still to be forged, they not having been born yet, so that He may cause them to be born with charity and love as enkindled as was the case in those past times, and cause the birth of kings who, devoid of anger and passion, may treat them and sustain them with a just and understanding hand.

Returning to the subject at hand, the story relates that this news was disseminated very quickly to all regions by those who had in Great Britain a great deal of business, on account of which most of the time they were sailing the seas, so that very soon it was known in those lands where Don Cuadragante, Lord of Sansuenia, and Don Bruneo, King of Arabia, and the other lords, their friends, were; who on considering the heavy responsibility that on this account Amadis would have in remedying the loss of the king, or of his kingdom, if in it any revolts broke out, decided — since there was no longer anything remaining to be done in those conquests and everything was under control — to go together just as they were to the Firm Island to be with Amadis and carry out whatever he might order. So with this agreement, Don Bruneo leaving his brother Branfil in his realm, and Don Cuadragante his nephew Landin — who had arrived a little while before in his realm of Sansuenia, with the troops of King Cildadan — and taking as many troops as they could, and leaving with the others what they deemed necessary to protect those lands, they set sail in their ships together with the giant Balan, who was loved and esteemed by all.

So far did they travel and with such favorable winds that twelve days after they departed from there they arrived at the harbor of the Firm Island. When Balan saw the huge Serpent that Urganda had left there, just as the story has told you, he was greatly astonished at such an extraordinary thing, and much more would he have been if those who came with him had told him the reason for it. At the time that these lords arrived there, Amadis was with his lady Oriana, for he dared not part from her; because when Brandoyvas had arrived on behalf of Queen Brisena with the letter that you have already heard, and Oriana had learned about her father, her grief and sadness were so extreme that she was close to losing her life. And when they told her of the arrival of that fleet on which those lords were coming, she begged Grasandor to welcome them and to tell them the reason why she could not come out. Grasandor did so, for he arrived at the port on horseback and found that there had already landed, Don Galaor, King of Sobradisa; Don Bruneo, King of Arabia; Don Cuadragante, Lord of Sansuenia, the giant Balan, Don Galvanes, Angriote de Estravaus, Gavarte of the Fearful Valley, Agrajes, Palomir, and so many other knights of great renown at arms that it would be boring to enumerate them. Grasandor told them the situation in which Amadis found himself, and that they should lodge and rest that night, for the next day Amadis would come out to bring them up to date on that matter, which was probably already clear to them. Everybody considered that a good arrangement, and at once they went up to the castle and lodged in their own quarters. And Agrajes and his uncle Don Galvanes took Balan with them in order to do him all honor possible.

Then when the night was over, having heard mass they all went to the garden where Amadis was. And when he learned of it, leaving his lady somewhat calmer, and his cousin Mabilia, his sister Melicia and Grasinda with her, he left the tower and came out to them.

When he saw them thus gathered, having become kings and great lords, and having escaped so safe and sound from all the dangers and confrontations they had experienced, although in his face he showed sadness on account of King Lisuarte, he sincerely felt very great joy — much more joy than if all that had been won by him alone — and he went and embraced them and they all embraced him. But the one to whom he showed the greatest affection was Balan, the giant, for he embraced him many times, honoring him with great courtesy.

Then, while they were thus all together, King Galaor, as one who regretted the loss of King Lisuarte as much as if it had been that of King Perion his father, told them that without delaying any time at all, what they ought to do in the matter of King Lisuarte should be decided because he, if Amadis agreed, would like to start out at once in quest of him without resting or having repose either day or night until either losing his own life or saving the king's, if the latter were alive. Amadis said to him: "Good sir brother, it would be a great injustice if that king who was so good and honorable, and such a rescuer of good men, in such an extreme emergency were not rescued by them; for aside from the close kinship that I have with him, which obliges all of us to do what you say, for his virtue and great nobility alone, he deserved to be served and helped in his perilous situations by all those in whom there is virtue and good understanding."

Then they ordered Brandoyvas to come before them, in order to find out what had been done in searching for the king, and to tell them with what the queen would be most aided and content. He told them all that he had seen, and about the multitude of people who at the time that the king was lost immediately went to look for him, and said they should believe that if somewhere in that forest or anywhere in his whole kingdom he were held prisoner, it was not a thing that could be concealed; but that the thought of the queen and of all the others was that he had been taken overseas and in the sea had been drowned; for in view of the fact that help had been available so quickly, there would not have been time to bury him; and that their opinion was, since all that realm had felt so much sorrow — and with so much love and good will all had remained at the queen's service, not expecting the opposite from any other quarter — that in that great fleet they had there they ought to fan out into many regions; for in view of the fact that in all the things begun by them, Fortune had been very favorable to them, in this one on which so much effort and zeal was being expended, she would not wish in anywise to change her ways.

The advice that Brandoyvas gave them seemed very good to all those lords, and they decided to act on it; and they asked Amadis to take charge of pointing out to them the areas of land and sea to search so that no part of either might be overlooked, and to take them before Oriana at once for to her they wanted to swear and promise never to halt their quest until they had brought her news of the king her father, either alive or dead; for in this way they thought to comfort her in her grief. So they all went to enter the tower. A man arrived who said to them: "Lords, a matron is leaving the Great Serpent, and it is thought that she is Urganda the Unknown, for no other woman would be powerful enough to enter and leave there."

When Amadis heard this, he said: "If it is she, may she be very welcome, for at this time we ought to be more pleased to see her than anyone else."

Immediately they sent for their horses in order to welcome her, but it could not be done quickly enough to forestall Urganda's disembarkation and arrival at the garden gates, mounted on her palfrey and escorted by her two dwarfs. When those lords saw her there, they went to her, with King Galaor in the lead, and he taking her in his arms, helped her to dismount. Everyone greeted and honored her with much courtesy; and she said to them: "You may well believe, my good lords, that I shall not consider it strange to find you thus assembled, because when I departed from here I told you that you would be thus gathered together about a matter at that time unknown to you. But let us now speak of it, and before I say any more to you, I wish to see and comfort Oriana, because I am more sensitive to her anguish and grief than to my own."

Then they all went with her to Oriana's apartment. When Oriana saw her enter the door, she began to weep very bitterly and to say: "Oh my lady and good friend! Why, knowing all things before they happen, did you not avert this very great misfortune that has overtaken that king who loved you so much? Now I know that since you have failed him, everyone else will do the same."

And putting her hands to her face, she let herself fall on her dais. Urganda came up to her, and kneeling took her by the hands and said: "My beloved lady and daughter, do not complain or grieve so much, for the power and high rank with which you are so adorned and provided always entails such tribulations; and without this circumstance, no one can possess them; for if it were otherwise, those of us to whom that powerful Lord has given but little could very rightfully complain; so all of us having the same disposition and nature, addicted to vices and passions and finally equal in death, He has made us so different with regard to worldly goods; some of us lords, others, vassals so oppressed and humble that rightly or wrongly we have to endure imprisonment, death, banishment, and innumerable other trials, according as the wills and desires of those in power command. And if these people who are thus put upon and oppressed experience any consolation for their great distress, it is only in beholding these workings of Fortune that bring about these dangerous downfalls; and just as this is ordained and permitted by his royal Majesty, so are all the other situations that have their ups and downs throughout the world, without anyone's being given the power, through any discretion or wisdom that he may possess, to change the situation a single bit by removing them. Therefore, very beloved lady, by compensating for what is bad with what is good, and for sorrow with joy, you will greatly relieve your distress. And in regard to what you tell me of the king your father, it is true that it was manifest to me beforehand, as in veiled terms I told you at the time that I departed from here. But it was not in my aforementioned power to be able to avert what was predestined. However, what is granted to me will be carried out on the occasion of this present visit of mine; which with the help of the all-highest Lord will be the cause of bringing the remedy that is needed for this very great sorrow in which I find you."

Then she left her and returned to the knights, who were gathered together to plan the journeys that each one was to undertake; and she said to them: "My good lords, you will probably remember well that at the time of my departure from this island, when you were together, I told you that at the time that the youth Esplandian was to receive his knighthood, because of an event hidden from you, most of you would be back here. So your presence gives testimony as to whether that prediction has been fulfilled. Now I have come as I promised, not only for that ceremony, but also to relieve you of the confrontations and great travail that can come to you from this quest on which you all are engaged, without my obtaining for you any help of the sort you desire; for if all those who are already born into the world, together with those who are about to be born, were they all alive, should try with complete diligence to find King Lisuarte, it would be impossible for them to accomplish it, in view of the region to which he has been taken. Therefore, since you have been forewarned by me, my lords, do not let such great folly enter your hearts as to seek so imprudently to learn what the will of the all-powerful Lord forbids being ascertained; and leave it to the one to whom by His special grace it is permitted. And because from delay, great harm could be caused, it is necessary for the accomplishment of what is needed that just as you are, taking with you the handsome youth Esplandian, Talanque, Maneli the Moderate, the King of Dacia, and Ambor, son of Angriote de Estravaus, you be my guests tonight and part of the following day on that great ship that looks like a serpent."

When those lords heard what Urganda had said to them, they all kept silent, for no one knew what to answer; because in view of the fact that the things said by her in the past had turned out to be so true, they really believed that her present statement likewise would be; and for this reason without saying more, they decided to comply with what she ordered, considering it best. And immediately mounting their horses, and she on her palfrey, taking with her Esplandian and the other youths, they went to the docks where Urganda told them to go out with her to the Great Serpent in one of those vessels of the fleet, which was done accordingly.

They then having arrived and boarded that great ship, Urganda entered with them a splendid, large dining hall, where she had had tables set for dinner. And she with the youths went into a chapel that was at one end of the room, and was decorated in gold and with very precious stones; and there she dined with them to the accompaniment of many instruments that some maidens of hers played very sweetly. When the meal was over, Urganda, leaving the youths in the chapel, came out to the great hall where those lords were, and asked them to go to the chapel and keep the novices company. After some time, Urganda reappeared in the chapel carrying a coat of mail, and behind her came her niece Solisa with a helmet, and Julianda, the sister of this Solisa, with a shield. And these arms were not in conformity with those of other novices, who were accustomed at the beginning of their knighthood to wear white ones, but they were the blackest ever seen. Urganda went to Esplandian and said to him: "Youth, more fortunate than any other of your time, don these arms, which in color are consistent with the compassion and melancholy of your stout, brave heart that you inherit from the king your grandfather; for just as the men of the past who established the order of chivalry considered it good that for the new joy, new, white arms be given, so I consider that for such great sorrow, melancholy sable ones be bestowed, so that on seeing them you may remember to remedy the cause of their sad color."

Then she put on him the coat of mail, which was very strong and well crafted. Solisa placed the helmet on his head, and Julianda slung the shield about his neck. Then Urganda looked at Amadis and said to him: "With good cause these knights could ask the reason why these arms lack a sword. But not you, my good lord, for you well know where you found it and how long it has been reserved for him by that woman who in her own time was unsurpassed in knowledge of all the arts, except only in that of deceitful love, by the man she loved more than herself, and at whose hand her life came to a disastrous and grievous end. So with his very strong arm and hand gripping that enchanted sword, which is capable of ending and dissolving all other spells, Esplandian will perform exploits such as to overshadow and render petty those which until now have shone resplendently."

Esplandian having been armed just as you hear, four maidens entered the chapel, each one with a set of knight's armor and arms as white and as bright as the moon, bordered and decorated with many precious stones and some black crosses. And each one of the maidens armed one of those youths; and the latter with Esplandian in the middle position knelt before the altar of the Virgin Mary and kept vigil over their arms. Just as was the custom at that time, they all had their hands and heads bare of armament. And Esplandian appeared so handsome in their midst that his face shone like the rays of the sun, to such a degree that it caused to marvel greatly all those who saw him kneeling with much devotion and great humility, begging the Virgin Mary to intercede with her glorious Son so that He might so aid and direct him that he by serving Him might be enabled to measure up to that great honor that he was receiving, and that He might give him grace out of His infinite goodness in order that by him, rather than by anyone else, King Lisuarte, if alive, might be restored in his honor and realm. Thus he remained all night without saying anything, except these aforementioned prayers and many others, reflecting that no strength or valor, however great it might be, would be more efficacious than that which was granted to him there.

Thus all the knights and ladies spent that night, as you have heard, keeping vigil over those novices. And morning having come, there appeared on top of that great Serpent a very ugly and emaciated dwarf with a great trumpet in his hand, and he sounded it so lustily that its loud sound was heard over most of that island; so that it roused most of the inhabitants and caused people to come out on top of the walls and towers of the castle, and impelled many others to post themselves on the crags and heights where they might command a better view. And the matrons and maidens who were in the great tower of the garden went up as hastily as they could to see what that could be which had made such a loud sound.

When Urganda saw them thus, she bade those lords who were there ascend to where her dwarf was, and immediately she placed the four novices in front of her and took Esplandian by the hand, and climbed up behind them, and behind her went six maidens attired in black with six golden trumpets. And when they were all topside, Urganda said to the giant Balan: "Friend Balan, just as nature has sought to set you apart from all others of your lineage in rendering you so alien to their ways by causing you to recognize reason and virtue — which until now has not been discernible in any of your forebears, whence it can be said that this gift or grace has come to you from a divine entity — so because of that deep seated affection which I recognize that you have in your heart for Amadis, I wish another distinction to be awarded to you, rather than to any other one of these very outstanding knights — a distinction which in the past, present, or future has been, is, and will be unattainable for everyone else — and it is that this youth be knighted by your hand so that his mighty deeds may testify to the truth of my words and render everlasting the glory that you attain by conferring this order of knighthood on one who will be so outstanding and so superior to so many good knights."

The giant, when he heard this, gazed at Amadis without answering anything, as if he feared to comply with what that matron had said to him. Amadis, who saw him thus, recognized immediately that his consent was necessary, and he said to him with great humility: "My good lord, do what Urganda tells you, for we all must obey her commands without their being contravened in any respect."

Then the giant took Esplandian by the hand and said to him: "Handsome youth, do you wish to be a knight?"

"I do so wish," said he.

Then he kissed him and placed the spur on his right foot, saying: "May that powerful Lord who implanted in you so much of His image and grace — to a greater extent than in anyone else ever seen — make you such a good knight that very rightly from now on I may keep the fourth promise that I make: namely never to perform this ceremony for anyone else."

Once this was over, Urganda said: "Amadis, my lord, if perchance you recall anything that you wish to communicate to this novice knight, let it be at once because he must leave your presence shortly."

Amadis, knowing the ways of Urganda, and that her admonition had not been made without good reason, said: "Esplandian, my son, at the time that I passed through the islands of Romania and arrived in Greece, I received from that great emperor many honors and favors — and after I left his presence many more, for my own needs and those of these lords who will bear witness to the fact — whereby I am obligated to serve him as long as I live; for among those great honors that I received there was one which I ought to esteem highly. And this was the fact that the very beautiful Leonorina, daughter of that emperor, and more gracious and beautiful than any other maiden to be found in the whole world, and Queen Menoresa, with other matrons and maidens of very high rank entertained me in their apartments in an atmosphere of as much delight and joy, and taking care to honor me as greatly as if I had been the son of the emperor of the whole world, although at that time they knew me only as a poor knight. And these ladies at the time of my departure demanded of me a boon: that if it were possible to do so, I return to see them; and that if it were not possible, that I send to them a knight of my lineage by whom they could be served. I promised to do so. And because I am not in a position to carry out my promise in person I entrust this commitment to you, so that if God through His mercy permits you to accomplish this quest for the king as all of us desire, you may remember to redeem my pledge made to, and held by, such a noble lady. And so that you may be believed to be the one who comes on my behalf, take this beautiful ring, which was taken by her from her own hand in order to place it in mine."

Then he gave him the ring set with the precious stone which matched the one in the fine coronet — the one given him by that princess as the third Book of this story relates. Esplandian knelt before him and kissed his hands saying that what he commanded he would carry out if God approved. But this was not carried out as speedily as they both thought it would be; rather, this knight experienced many dangers out of his love for this beautiful princess — a love occasioned merely by the widespread reports that he had heard concerning her, as will be told you later on.

This having been done, Urganda said to Esplandian: "Fair son, dub these youths knights, for very quickly they will repay you for this honor that they receive from your hand."

Esplandian did as she commanded, so at that time all five received that order of knighthood. Then the six maidens that you have already heard about played on their trumpets a tune so sweet and so delightful to hear that all those lords who were there, and the five novice knights, fell asleep without retaining any vestige of consciousness. And the Great Serpent spewed forth from its nostrils a smoke so black and so thick that no one of these who were watching could see anything save that intense darkness.

But in a little while, not knowing by what means or in what manner, all those lords found themselves back under the trees in the garden where Urganda had met with them at the time that she arrived there. And that dense smoke having been dispelled, that Great Serpent was no longer to be seen, nor did they know what had become of Esplandian or the other novice knights; hence they all were greatly frightened.

When those lords saw themselves thus, they looked at one another and it seemed to them that what had taken place was like a dream. But Amadis discovered in his right hand a manuscript that read as follows: "You, oh kings and knights, here present, return to your own lands; find diversion for your minds and rest for your hearts; leave distinction at arms and fame from honors to those who are beginning to ascend on fickle Fortune's towering wheel; be happy with what you have already obtained from her, because for you, more than for any others of your time, she has been pleased to still the revolution of her dangerous wheel. And you, Amadis of Gaul — who, since the day your father King Perion at the request of your wife Oriana, made you a knight, have overcome many knights and strong fierce giants, living dangerously all the while until today, causing great fear with the valor of your doughty heart — from now on let your zealous limbs rest; for that Fortune so favorable to you, by turning its wheel for this knight, Esplandian, and leaving all the others beneath, authorizes him to be placed at the top. Begin now to taste the bitter potions that the reigns and seigniories attract, for soon you will attain them; because just as with only your person, arms and horse, while leading the life of a poor knight, you gave help to many and many had need of you; so now with great estates, which falsely promise a life of ease, you will have to be helped, aided, and protected by many others. And you — who until now have been concerned only with winning glory by your own efforts, believing in that way that the debt for which you were obligated would be paid — will now have to distribute your thoughts and concerns among so many and such diverse problems that many times you would like to be back in your former way of life, with only your dwarf to receive your commands. Take up now the new life with more concern to govern than to fight the way you have until now. Abandon your arms to that knight to whom great victories are promised by that high Judge who has no superior to revoke his decisions, for your great feats at arms so renowned throughout the world will become extinct in the face of his, so that by many who know no better, it will be said that the son killed the father. But I don't mean that natural death obligatory for us all, but that death resulting from the fact that one, in addition to suffering greater dangers, endures greater anguish and wins so much glory that that of the past is forgotten; or if some share of it remains it can't be called glory or fame, but its shadow."

Having finished reading that manuscript, they talked a great deal together concerning what they should or could do, so that opinions varied, although they amounted in the end to one and the same thing. But Amadis said to them: "Good sirs, although it is forbidden to give any credence to necromancers and those familiar with such acts as these, the past successful predictions of this matron which have been witnessed by us ought to provide us with genuine hope for coming events, though not to such an extent that power over everything ceases to belong to that Lord who knows all and is all-powerful and by whom it can be permitted that what we could with such great difficulty find out in other ways be made previously clear and manifest by this Urganda, just as she has demonstrated up to now with regard to so many other things. And therefore, good sirs, I consider it desirable for us to do exactly what she advises and commands: you returning to your newly won seigniories, and my brother King Galaor and Don Galvanes, my uncle, taking Brandoyvas with them, go to Queen Brisena, so that from them she may learn with what good will we desired to carry out her commands, and the reason why that has ceased to be done. And from her they will learn what further action she will be pleased for us to take. And I shall remain here with my cousin Agrajes until such time as some news comes to us; and if in such an event our aid and succor be needed, we shall learn of it much better separated than together, and wherever the news may come, let those who are there be responsible for hastening to the scene after notifying the others."

To all those lords and knights this which Amadis said to them seemed to be good advice, and so they put it into execution, for King Don Bruneo and Don Cuadragante, Lord of Sansuenia, returned to their seigniories, taking with them those very beautiful wives of theirs, Melicia and Grasinda. King Galaor and Don Galvanes went with Brandoyvas to London, where Queen Brisena was. And Amadis and Agrajes and Grasandor remained on the Firm Island, and with them that strong Balan, Lord of the Island of the Vermilion Tower, who was determined not to part from Amadis until some news of King Lisuarte was ascertained; and if it were such as to require the aid of troops, to enter upon whatever adventure and task they might wish to assign him.

Brought to a close are the four Books concerning the valiant and very virtuous knight Amadis of Gaul, in which are found in full detail the great adventures and terrible battles that in his time were accomplished and won by him, and by many other knights, not only by those of his lineage but by friends of his. They have been printed in the very noble and very loyal city of Saragossa by Georg Koch, a German. Their printing was completed the 30th day of the month of October, of the year of the birth of our Savior Jesus Christ 1508.

NOTES

Chapter CXXIX

In discussing the descendants of Bravor, son of the giant Balan, mention is made of one called Bravor the "Brun," *brun* being defined as "belligerent." This is sheer nonsense, as every French-speaking person will recognize: the meaning of *brun* when applied to persons is "dark-complexioned," or "swarthy." Obviously, Montalvo knew no French and was relying on Peninsular translations of Arthurian romances composed in Old French. (Of course, *bravo* in Spanish may mean "belligerent.")

Chapter CXXXIII

Near the end of Urganda's letter to Amadis, the statement is made that Esplandian's exploits will so eclipse those of his parent that "by many who know no better, it will be said that the son killed the father." This is a veiled reference to an event of the primitive *Amadis*, Book III. On this, see Place's Preface to Book I.

PRINCIPAL CHARACTERS OF *AMADIS OF GAUL*

Abies: King of Ireland.

Agrajes: Cousin of Amadis; son of King Languines; brother of Mabilia.

Amadis of Gaul: (also known as Beltenebros, Knight of the Green Sword, Youth of the Sea, Knight with a Dwarf, Greek Knight).

Andalod: Hermit of the Poor Rock.

Apolidon: Lord of the Firm Island; son of the Emperor of Greece.

Arcalaus: The Enchanter.

Ardian: Dwarf of Amadis.

Beltenebros: Amadis.

Brian de Monjaste: Son of King Ladasan of Spain.

Briolanja: Daughter of the King of Sobradisa; later queen of same and wife of Galaor.

Brisena: Queen of England and wife of King Lisuarte.

Bruneo de Bonamar: Son of the Duke of Troque.

Cildadan: King of Ireland.

Corisanda: Lady of Gravisanda Island, enamored of Florestan.

Darioleta: Maid of Elisena.

Durin: Brother of the maid from Denmark, sent by Oriana with a letter for Amadis.

Elisabad: The Master Surgeon of Grasinda.

Elisena: Mother of Amadis; wife of King Perion.

Enil: Nephew of Gandales.

Esplandian: Son of Amadis and Oriana.

Falangriz: King of Great Britain, brother and predecessor of King Lisuarte.

Famongomadan: Giant of the Boiling Lake.

Florestan: Son of King Perion and the Countess of Selandia; half-brother of Amadis and Galaor.

Galaor: Brother of Amadis.

Galvanes Lackland: Uncle of Agrajes, brother of King Languines.

Gandalas: Giant who kidnapped and reared the child Galaor.

Gandales: Scottish knight, the one who found Amadis in the ocean and who reared him.

Gandalin: Son of Gandales and squire of Amadis.

Gandandel: The Troublemaker.

Garinter: King of Brittany, father of Elisena.

Grasinda: Niece of King Tafinor of Bohemia.

Grimanesa: Wife of Apolidon.

Grindalaya: Beloved of King Arban of Norway.

Grumedan of Norway: Tutor of Queen Elisena; knight of King Lisuarte.

Guilan the Pensive: Knight of King Lisuarte.

Isanjo: Governor of the Firm Island.

Ladasan: King of Spain.

Landin: Nephew of Don Quadragante.

Languines: King of Scotland, father of Agrajes and Mabilia.

Lasindo: Squire of Don Bruneo.

Leonoreta: Younger sister of Oriana.

Leonorina: Beloved of Esplandian and daughter of the Emperor of Constantinople.

Lisuarte: King of Great Britain, father of Oriana.

Mabilia: Cousin of Amadis; daughter of King Languines; sister of Agrajes; confidante of Oriana.

Madasima: Daughter of the Giant Famongomadan; wife of Galvanes; (two other Madasimas are minor characters).

Melicia: Sister of Amadis; daughter of King Perion and Queen Elisena.

Nasciano: Hermit.

Norandel: Illegitimate son of King Lisuarte.

Olinda: Daughter of King of Norway; beloved of Agrajes.

Oriana: Daughter of King Lisuarte; beloved of Amadis.

Palomir: Cousin of Amadis.

Patin: Emperor of Rome.

Perion: King of Gaul; Father of Amadis.

Quadragante: Brother of King Abies of Ireland; overcome by Amadis and later his good friend.
Salustanquidio: Cousin of the Emperor of Rome.
Sardamira: Queen of Sardinia.
Talanque: Son of Galaor.
Trion: Cousin of Briolanja.
Urganda the Unknown: Sorceress.
Ysanjo: Governor of the Firm Island.